"Russo has an excellent eye for the urban landscape [and] the crime writer's well-tuned ear for vernacular . . . from street punks right up to the high-level officials." —*Asimov's Science Fiction Magazine*

"Truly gripping . . . A lot more realistic than most near-future SF, as well as being just plain better written than most of it."
—*Science Fiction Chronicle*

"Lean, mean, and compelling." —*Deseret News*

"The characters are well-crafted, the setting interesting and vivid, and the pacing is brisk." —*Uncle Hugo's Newsletter*

"A tough, down and dirty story that will appeal to fans of police novels as well as science fiction fans . . . An excellent piece of writing."
—*Dead Trees Review*

"Russo skillfully blends high-tech concepts and hard-boiled prose in a novel that will keep you turning pages late into the night. Carlucci is a Chandleresque hero . . . This is classic crime fiction as well as classic speculative fiction, and a thorough pleasure to read." —*Contra Costa Times*

Ship of Fools

"[Russo] is not afraid to take on the question of evil in a divinely ordered universe . . . This is an ambitious novel of ideas that generates considerable suspense while respecting its sources, its characters, and most important, the reader." —*The New York Times*

"A tale of high adventure and personal drama in the far future."
—*Library Journal*

"Relentlessly suspenseful . . . full of mystery . . . very exciting."
—*Science Fiction Chronicle*

carlucci

richard paul russo

ACE BOOKS, NEW YORK

CARLUCCI

An Ace Book / published by arrangement with the author

PRINTING HISTORY
Ace trade paperback edition / September 2003

Library of Congress Cataloging-in-Publication Data

Russo, Richard Paul.
Carlucci / Richard Paul Russo.
p. cm
Contents: Destroying angel—Carlucci's edge—Carlucci's heart.
ISBN 0-441-01054-7 (alk. paper)
1. Carlucci, Frank (Fictitious character)—Fiction.   2. Police—California—San Francisco—Fiction.   3. Detective and mystery stories, American.   4. San Francisco (Calif.)—Fiction.
5. Science fiction, American.   I. Russo, Richard Paul. Destroying angel.   II. Russo, Richard Paul. Carlucci's edge.   III. Russo, Richard Paul. Carlucci's heart.   IV. Title.

PS3568.U8122C37 2003
813'.54—dc21   2003051952

ACE®
Ace Books are published by The Berkley Publishing Group,
a division of Penguin Group (USA) Inc., 375 Hudson Street,
New York, New York 10014.
ACE and the "A" design are trademarks
belonging to Penguin Group (USA) Inc.

PRINTED IN THE UNITED STATES OF AMERICA

10 9 8 7 6 5 4 3 2 1

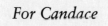

For Candace

ACKNOWLEDGMENTS

There are two people who have worked with me over the course of more than ten years and four novels (and hopefully many more to come), and I take this opportunity to express my appreciation to them.

My thanks to Susan Allison, my editor, for her support over the years, for her critical input (which has always helped improve my books), and for her faith in me as a writer.

My thanks, also, to Martha Millard, my agent, for her support, her advocacy on my behalf, and for her counsel.

Destroying Angel

1

TANNER WATCHED THE children playing among the methane fires of the neighborhood dump. Overhead, a sick green and orange haze muted the late-afternoon sun, the green curdling through the orange. It was hot, and Tanner was sweating.

The children chased one another, stumbling through the garbage, weaving in and out of the fires. Soot stained their faces, their tattered clothes. One of the girls periodically barked a patterned sequence of noises; each time she did, all the children abruptly changed direction.

Tanner walked on, away from the children. He skirted the dump and headed down a crowded, narrow street. Stone buildings rose on either side, radiating the damp heat of the day, echoing the sounds of car engines, shouts and laughter, bicycle bells, hammering, and the distant wail of a Black Rhino.

Half a block further on, Tanner entered the Carousel Club, which was hot and smoky, and dark except for several globes of emerald light that drifted randomly near the ceiling. He walked to the back of the main room, along a narrow corridor, then up a flight of stairs to the second floor.

There were a dozen tables in the second-floor room, most of them occupied, and another three outside on the small balcony overlooking a slough that fingered in from the bay. Paul sat at one of the balcony tables, gazing down at the slough, and Tanner walked over to the table. Paul looked up, his face gaunt and sallow, dark crescents under his eyes.

"You look like shit," Tanner said, sitting across from him. There was no breeze, so it wasn't any cooler than inside, and a faint stench drifted up from the stagnant water.

Paul smiled. "Thanks." He shook his head. "Just got off twelve hours in ER."

That was where Tanner had met Paul several years before—in the emergency room of S.F. General, back when Tanner had still been an undercover cop, bringing in the casualties of drug and gang wars for Paul and other doctors to patch up. Tanner wasn't any kind of cop anymore.

Tanner looked out from the balcony. Directly across the slough was a junkyard with several hundred wrecks piled four and five high. Atop one of the highest piles, a young girl sat cross-legged on the caved-in roof of a rusted blue sedan, smoking. Tanner had the impression she was looking at him.

A waitress wearing a bird mask came to their table, took their order, and left. Paul took a pack of cigarettes from his pocket, pulled one out, and lit it.

"I thought you quit," Tanner said.

"I've unquit."

"And you're a doctor."

Paul shrugged. "Hell, I figure it can't be much worse than breathing this air."

Tanner looked up at the orange and green sky, decided Paul was probably right. He turned back to Paul, but he was gazing down at the dark, still water of the slough. Long shadows lay across its surface, with a few small, bright patches where the sun broke through between the buildings and reflected off the water.

"So what's wrong?" Tanner asked.

Paul shrugged. "I'm thinking about giving it up."

"What?"

"The clinic, the ER work, all of it." He paused, shook his head. "I'm burning out."

Yeah, no shit, Tanner thought. And I'm not far behind you. Quitting the force had only given him a temporary postponement. "What will you do?" he asked.

Paul smiled. "Hang out my shingle. Do nose jobs and liposuctions and neuro-genital enhancements. Make myself a goddamn fortune."

Tanner laughed.

Drinks came. Tanner sipped at his, gazing across the slough at the girl in the junkyard. A pang went through him. There was something painfully familiar about the girl. He did not think he knew her, but she reminded him of someone. Who? He did not know. Her cigarette was gone, and now she was moving her hands and arms through the air in slow, complex patterns. Tanner still thought she was looking at him, and wondered if she was trying to send him a message. A cosmic bulletin. A spiritual communiqué snaking through the wrecked automobiles and the stinking water. Whatever it was, he wasn't getting it.

The girl stopped moving. She remained completely motionless for a few moments, then turned her head, looking toward the bay. The girl glanced back at Tanner, then scrambled down from the pile and disappeared into the heart of the junkyard.

Tanner leaned over the balcony rail, looked toward the bay, but didn't see anything unusual.

"What is it?" Paul asked.

"Don't know."

Then he heard the sound of a boat motor, and a few moments later a Bay Security boat appeared, headed slowly up the slough. Its lights were not flashing, but several Bay Soldiers stood on deck.

On the opposite bank, several men and women emerged one at a time through a gap in the chain-link fence just down from the junkyard. The first two were uniformed cops, the others in street clothes. Tanner recognized the fifth one through—Carlucci, from Homicide. Tanner had always respected him, though they had hardly ever worked together and never got along well enough to become friends. Carlucci was sharp, and you could depend on him. Tanner wondered if he'd made lieutenant yet.

One of the uniforms stopped, turned back, and said something. Carlucci shrugged, shook his head. Then all six spread out along the bank and began searching the water's edge.

Tanner felt sick. He knew, suddenly, what they were looking for, and what they would find.

The Bay Security cutter had dropped anchor in the middle of the slough, and all the soldiers were watching the cops search. Bay Security didn't have any authority here, but they wanted in on it. It was their territory, if not jurisdiction, and if bodies had been planted in the water, it affected their reputation. Tanner didn't feel any sympathy for them. They were parasites.

One of the plainclothes cops called out. He squatted at the edge of the water, looking down. The others came over, all looking down now, then the plainclothes cops moved away to make room for the two uniforms. The uniforms got the shit work as usual, Tanner thought.

The two men bent over, reached into the water, and pulled up a section of rope attached at one end to something just underwater—probably a metal stake embedded in the bank—and at the other end to something heavy and deep in the slough. They began to pull in the rope.

It was slow going. Twice, whatever was at the other end of the rope caught rocks or debris on the bottom, and the cops had to work it free. Then, as it neared shore, flashes of white skin broke the surface of the water.

Soon they had the bodies laid out on the muddy graveled bank. The cops surrounded them, trying to block them from the view of the Bay Soldiers. Tanner, though, had already seen enough.

There were two bodies, a man and a woman, both naked, back to back and chained together at the wrists and ankles.

"Jesus Christ," Paul said. "I thought that was all over with."

Tanner did not reply. He watched Carlucci and the others shifting their feet, smoking cigarettes, trying not to look at the bodies as they waited for the coroner's assistants to arrive. They should have had the coroner's men with them, Tanner thought, they should have known what they were going to find. Probably they hadn't wanted to believe it.

It had been two and a half years since the last set of chained bodies had been pulled out of water somewhere in the city. Working Narcotics, Tanner had never been directly involved with any of the investigations, but he'd pulled up a pair of bodies himself—two women he'd dragged out of Stowe Lake in Golden Gate Park—and he was glad that now he wouldn't have anything to do with it. Now it was someone else's nightmare. Wasn't it?

He looked away from the cops, finished off his drink.

"I could use another," he said.

Paul nodded. Tanner looked for the woman in the bird mask, signaled to her for two more drinks. She bobbed her feathered head and moved out of sight, deeper into the club.

Tanner looked back at the cops standing on the opposite bank. One of them tossed his cigarette into the water, where it sizzled for a second and sent up a tiny puff of smoke. No, Tanner thought, he didn't miss that work one bit.

2

SOOKIE WATCHED FROM the front seat of a two-door Sony, the middle wreck in a pile of five. She had a view of the water, the men, the naked bodies they had pulled from the slough. Drive-in movie, she thought. Sound turned low. She wished she had popcorn.

I'm thirteen, she thought. I'm not old enough to see this. She smiled, squirmed in the seat. Sit still, she told herself. She wanted a cigarette, but the smoke would give her away. Or they'd think the junkyard was on fire. She imagined sirens, giant streams of water, a helicopter dropping water bombs.

The men weren't doing anything. Talking, but she couldn't really hear it. Sookie looked at the bodies. Their skin was gray; no, white; no, gray-white. A strange color. She wondered if they were real bodies. Maybe it *was* a movie. But she didn't see any cameras. Didn't you need cameras to make a movie? Sookie wasn't sure.

The chains on the wrists and ankles were beautiful. Bright silver, shining brighter than the sun now. She couldn't see the sun, it was hidden by the buildings. Sookie closed her eyes, tried to imagine what the chains would look like on her own wrists and ankles. Pretty.

She opened her eyes, looked across the water and up at the people on the balcony. The man who had been looking at her. What a strange place! A giant bird wearing a short skirt served them drinks.

Some other men came through the fence, and then she couldn't see the bodies anymore. Flashes of light, someone was taking pictures, but they weren't movie cameras.

Sookie felt dizzy and sick to her stomach. She was thinking about being dead and naked and people taking pictures of her like that. She closed her eyes, sighed, and lay back in the seat. She didn't want to watch anymore.

3

A FEW MINUTES after Tanner left the Carousel Club, a hot rain began. He ducked into a bakery to wait it out, knowing it wouldn't last more than half an hour. The bakery was hot and crowded and noisy. Tanner felt quite comfortable in the midst of it all, lulled by the heat, the smells of baked goods and strong coffee, and the rush of Spanish voices surrounding him. In the back of the bakery, a parrot squawked incessantly, producing an occasional word or phrase in Spanish.

He bought a cup of coffee and sat by the window, watching the rain spatter against the glass. Middle of July, highs regularly in the upper nineties, and rain every morning and afternoon—it was going to be one hell of a summer. Most of the country in extreme drought, and San Francisco was turning into a goddamn tropical rain forest. He missed the fog, the *real* fog, which he hadn't seen in ten years.

Eyes half-closed, Tanner sipped at the coffee and gazed out the window. Across the way, the narrow alley between two buildings was choked with green ferns streaked with brown and rust, the leaves shaking violently as a girl chased a dog through them. Bromeliads filled the air above the ferns, dangling in colorful clusters from windows and makeshift trellises crafted from scrap metal and plastic pipe.

He thought about the two chained bodies that had been pulled from the slough. Chained bodies in water. How many had there been? Thirty-seven over a two-year period. But none in two and a half years. And now . . . had it begun again? He did not want to think about what that meant for him.

Lights came on up and down the street as night fell. Tanner finished his coffee when the rain stopped, and went back out onto the street. Time to go home.

He caught a bus and rode it to Market Street, getting off at one of the border checkpoints for the Financial District. The bus, with no access authority, turned around and headed back south.

Tanner stood at the edge of the checkpoint, looking at the bright glow of the Financial District. An enclave of towering structures of gleaming metal, bleached stone, and mirrored glass, the Financial District was the only part of the city that looked like it belonged in its own time. The rest of the city was still back in the twentieth century, or worse.

The shortest and safest route back to his apartment was through the District, but Tanner was in no mood for the ID checks and body searches. Instead, he took a more circuitous route that was almost as safe, and a lot more alive.

He walked a few blocks west along Market, then turned right into one of the city's three Cuban corridors. The street was crowded and noisy, brightly lit and filled with the smells of curry, black bean soup, bacon, and Cuban bread. Street soldiers wearing green and red scarves and armbands stood on the corners or walked casually through the crowds.

Several blocks from Market, the Cuban Corridor linked with the Chinese Corridor. Here, Tanner had a choice of streets, the Corridor encompassing nearly all of Chinatown. He cut over to Stockton, and the smells changed, shifted to seafood and incense. The street was even more crowded than the Cuban Corridor, pedestrians, cars, scooters, and bicycles moving in chaotic, halting patterns.

On the other side of Columbus, as Tanner neared the edges of the Corridor and Chinatown proper, the crowds thinned. The noise level dropped; fewer street soldiers were visible. And then the Corridor ended.

Tanner lived just a block and a half off the Corridor, but that block and a half was nearly silent, and much darker, without a single street soldier in sight. He walked quickly, but without fear, and he thought of what his father used to tell him: Don't look like a victim. He sometimes wondered if his father had forgotten his own advice.

He unlocked the outer gate to the grounds of the six-story apartment building, made sure it was securely latched, then walked through the overgrown garden to the building entrance. The plants were out of control again, damp leaves and branches crowding the walkway, streaking his clothes with moisture. Tiny insects whirled silently through the misty halo of the porch light.

Tanner keyed in the building code, his personal code, then unlocked the door bolts with his key. He stepped into the lobby, door and alarm locking automatically behind him.

The lobby was dimly lit, the air still and warm. Tanner stood motionless for a minute, listening to the building sounds filter to him from above—a faint, low hum; whispers of deeply pitched voices; a muffled rattle of glass; the whistle of a teakettle.

He opened his mailbox, but it was empty. Third day in a row. He wondered if it meant anything.

Tired, he climbed the stairs to the fourth floor, seeing no one in either the stairwell or hall. His apartment was at the far end of the hall, on the right; the door had a dozen boarded window frames without a single bit of glass. Occasionally he thought about replacing the glass, but not often enough to actually do anything about it.

The apartment was fairly good-sized for one person—front room, den, hall, bedroom, and kitchen—but more and more often recently it felt *too* large, and half-empty. He wandered from room to room, the empty feeling washing over him again, leaving a dull throb in its wake. It had always seemed the right size, warm and comfortable, whenever Valerie and Connie had spent time here. But that was long over, and they had not been here in more than a year. Well, hell, that had been his own choice, hadn't it?

He stopped at the den window, looked down at the street. Cones of light from the street lamps cast blurred shadows of trees and old cars. Apartment lights glowed dim and orange, dull rectangular eyes in the night. Oscar, the blind neighborhood cat, incredibly still alive after two years without sight, stumbled along the opposite sidewalk, head weaving stiffly from side to side. He bumped into a garbage can, hesitated for a moment, then turned into a narrow alley.

Bodies.

Another rain began.

After he ate, Tanner climbed to the roof, carrying an aluminum lawn chair. He hoped Alexandria would be there, but the roof was empty. The rain had stopped and the moon, three-quarters full, shone through the night haze with an amber cast.

Tanner set the chair at the roof's edge and sat. The night was unusually quiet. Traffic sounds were light, and he could hear the breeze rustle through the dense foliage that grew between the buildings and in the yards of the neighborhood. A damp earth smell, laced through with the odor of rotting fruit, rose to the roof, drifted across him.

Tanner gazed toward the south and the Hunter's Point launch fields, though he could not see even the tops of the rocket gantries from here. There was a freighter scheduled to go up tonight, and a part of its cargo was a contraband load of gourmet foods—primarily swiftlet nests—for one of the big investment firms in the New Hong Kong orbital. Tanner had brokered the deal, with most of his commission going to small packets of cash pressed into half a dozen different hands to make sure the shipment got through. In return, he was getting a shipment of prime, zero-gee pharmaceuticals. After a small sell-down—he had to make a living—the rest of the pharmaceuticals would be going to free clinics like Paul's.

The bright orange flame of the rocket launch appeared in the southern sky, followed a few seconds later by a barely audible rumble as the ship, carrying his load of contraband, rose into the night. Tanner watched the flame rise, growing small and faint, until it disappeared far above him.

He remained on the roof another hour, motionless, watching the night sky, thinking, trying not to think. Then he picked up his chair and returned to his apartment.

Tanner dreamed:

He climbs the hot, dark stairwell, Freeman just in front of him. His heart beats hard, and he sweats, smells mildew from rotting hall carpets. He feels for the knife in his boot, but isn't reassured by its touch. He wishes they could have risked carrying guns, but these assholes will surely search them before running the deal. Tanner feels like his ass is hanging out a window. Even knowing they have backup out on the street below isn't much help. Backup in the Tenderloin? A joke.

At the top of the stairs, Freeman stops, looking at Tanner through dreadlocks hanging over his eyes. The building's too damn quiet, Tanner thinks. Too damn hot. And too damn dark. A single bare bulb glows at the other end of the hall.

"You ready?" Freeman whispers.

Tanner nods. His throat is dry.

"Let's nail these fuckers," Freeman says.

They walk down the hall, stop in front of a cracked wooden door with a huge black number nine painted across it. Freeman knocks once, once again, then quickly three times.

The door opens, and a big bearded guy looks out at them from a room almost as dark as the hall. He doesn't let them in. Tanner smells tuna, and something thick and sweet.

"Money?" the guy says.

Freeman takes a wad of bills from his jacket pocket, holds it up long enough for the guy to get a good look, then puts it back. The bearded guy nods, opens the door a little wider, then brings up a gun and sticks it against Freeman's forehead.

Jesus.

"Eat this, nigger." He pulls the trigger and blows away Freeman's face, spraying blood and flesh and bone all over Tanner.

Jesus fucking Christ.

Tanner runs.

He nearly reaches the stairwell when another explosion sounds. Something hard and compact slams into him, knocks him off balance, still running, he doesn't know what it is. Then he *does* know, and hot pain erupts in his side, sends him flying blindly around the corner and crashing down the stairs. . . .

And Tanner wakes:

He sat up with a sharp intake of breath. Sweat rolled down his sides, the base of his spine. The adrenaline rush left a tingling in its wake.

It was not the first time. The dream, the nightmare, had repeated over the years—not regularly, not often, but often enough. A nearly exact replay of what had happened two and a half years ago, of a drug bust gone completely to shit. A replay of the way Freeman had been killed.

Tanner got out of bed, went to the open window, and looked out, rubbing at the thick scar on his side. He could see the flicker of flames a few blocks away—dump fires or burning cars. Not a neighborhood cookout.

He hadn't had the dream in several months, and he knew why he had tonight—those fucking bodies. And Tanner knew he wasn't going to be the only one with nightmares.

A few cops would, at first. Then, as the news spread through the city, and especially when other bodies were found—and Tanner knew there would be other bodies—the nightmares, too, would spread. And what would make the situation worse was the unknown. Years ago, the cops never had a clue. Never an idea who was doing the killing, or why. When the killings had stopped, the hope had been that the killer himself had bought it. Now, though, it didn't seem that way. There was the possibility of a copycat, but Tanner doubted it. Carlucci would know. Maybe Tanner should track him down, ask.

Christ, he thought, just forget it. It wasn't his problem. Except for the damn two-and-a-half-year-old message. He did not want to think about it, but unless this was just a fluke, it *was* going to be his problem. And he knew he wasn't going to forget it.

Tanner looked at the clock—12:53. He wondered if he could stay awake until dawn. Better than dreaming again. He stood at the window and watched the flickering glow of flames in the night.

4

TANNER PUT IT off for three days. Then, all it took was a phone call to Lucy Chen, who told him where Carlucci held his morning coffee-hashes.

It was a place called Spade's, a spice and espresso bar in the Tundra run by Jamie Kingston, a black ex-cop who'd had half his left leg blown off by his partner during a race riot outside City Hall. Tanner walked in just after six in the morning, and the place was packed. A dozen sparking ion poles stood among the small tables, adding a clean burn odor to the heavy smell of espresso. A deep, thumping bass line pounded beneath the babble of voices.

Tanner worked his way through the tables and ion poles, then spotted Carlucci in a booth against the back wall. Two women uniforms sat across from him, drinking green-tinted iced tea from clear glasses. Carlucci had a coffee cup in his hand and several stacks of paper laid out on the table.

Carlucci saw Tanner approach, stared at him for a few moments, then nodded toward an empty stool at the end of the main bar. Tanner sat on the stool, ordered a double espresso, and waited.

He was half through the espresso, and already regretting it—a burning pain had begun in his stomach—when Kingston emerged from the steaming kitchen and headed along the bar, smiling at Tanner. It had been more than a year since Tanner had last seen him, but Kingston still wore black leather knickers that revealed the scarred flesh of his right leg, and the gleaming metal of his cyborged left. On his feet, both the real and the artificial, were leather sandals.

Kingston took a pastry bar from under the counter and set it in front of Tanner.

"On the house." Kingston leaned against the counter. "Been a long time, Tanner."

Tanner nodded. "How's the leg?"

Kingston's smile broadened into a grin. "Same as always. Better than the real thing."

Kingston's leg was a legend in the Tundra. Rumor was he could disconnect the leg and convert it into a scattergun in less than ten seconds.

But Kingston's grin vanished, and he leaned forward, his face just a few inches from Tanner's.

"You're waiting to see Carlucci."

More statement than question. Tanner nodded again.

"What the hell for?" Kingston was angry now, and Tanner had no idea why. "You aren't a cop anymore."

Tanner wondered what he was missing, but he didn't say anything. He didn't have to justify himself to Kingston.

"Tanner." Carlucci's voice.

Tanner turned, looked at him. The two uniforms were gone. Tanner looked back at Kingston. "Go," Kingston whispered. Tanner picked up his espresso, brought it to Carlucci's booth, and sat. Carlucci was looking through one of the stacks of paper.

"What's eating Kingston?" Tanner asked.

"None of your business. Got nothing to do with you." He looked up. "Tanner the civilian. How's life out in the hive?"

"Buzzing."

Carlucci snorted. "Yeah. I hear stories about you. Most of them good, I guess." He sighed, shaking his head. "Your leaking heart is the reason you couldn't ice it as a cop."

Tanner didn't respond. Probably there was some truth to what Carlucci said. But only some. Besides, Carlucci wasn't exactly a cold-hearted bastard himself, and he was still a cop.

"All right," Carlucci said, "so why are you here?"

"I was on the Carousel Club balcony Thursday. I saw you pull them out of the slough."

Carlucci suddenly looked more tired, worn down, and he didn't say anything for a while. He finished his coffee, waved at the barman for another. He rubbed his eyes, then looked back at Tanner.

"Yeah, and so? You here to give me some lunatic theory?"

Tanner shook his head. "Been getting theories again?"

"Up the fucking ass. Mannon thinks it's more than one guy. Fuentes is convinced the guy's a Roller gone over the edge. Tinka believes it's a woman. And Harker still thinks the killer's a fucking alien. And those are cop theories. You should hear the shit we're picking up on the street. The newshawkers are having a fucking feast." His pager beeped beside him; he glanced at the readout, then reached down and touched something to silence it. "No theory, then why?"

"I pulled two of them out of Stowe Lake myself, remember? I just want to know if it's the same guy."

Carlucci slowly nodded. "Oh yeah, it's the same guy, it's the same motherfucker. Strangled. Chained together with the bands fused to the skin. A benign virus injected into Homicide's computers that froze the system and then gave the location of the bodies." He paused. "And the angel wings."

Tanner nodded to himself, picturing the tiny, silver-blue angel wings tattooed inside the nostrils of the victims. "Any progress?" Tanner wasn't sure why he asked the question. He knew the answer.

Carlucci gave a bitter laugh. "Progress, shit. There wasn't any progress for two years, you expect something in three days?" He shook his head. "They've got two of the slugs upstairs working on it full time, but that's not going to do any good."

Tanner shuddered, thinking of the slugs, imagining them in their cubicles above the station, hardly human anymore, their bodies distended and distorted by the constant injections of reason enhancers. They were supposed to be able to solve almost any problem, but they'd been useless with this one.

"That's all you want? To know if it's the same guy?"

Tanner shrugged.

"You want to come in on this from the outside?"

Tanner firmly shook his head, knowing he should be nodding, that almost certainly he *was* going to have to come in at some point. "No. But do you mind if I stay in touch on it?"

Carlucci sighed. "All right. Just let me know if you pick up anything substantial on the street, and don't bug me every other day about it. It's not going to move any faster than it did before, even if the mayor doesn't want to hear that." He glanced at the main bar. "I've got more people to talk to, so if there isn't anything else . . ."

Tanner looked at the bar, saw Deke the Geek on a stool, staring at him. Deke flipped him off, grabbing his crotch with his other hand.

"Old friends?" Carlucci said.

"Yeah." He turned back to Carlucci, slid out of the booth, and stood. "Thanks. See you around."

Carlucci nodded, then said, "Hey, Tanner."

"Yeah?"

"Do you have to use a police van to make your shipments?"

So, Carlucci knew. "Makes things a lot easier," Tanner said.

"I'm sure it does. It's a damn good thing you're discreet." Carlucci shrugged. "All right. See you."

Without looking back at Deke, Tanner left.

Outside, it was already hot, though it was still early. The sky, however, was clear, and almost blue. Tanner crossed the street to the Tundra's open space park. There were no trees in the park, only stunted clumps of mutated plants that had managed to emerge after the defoliants had been dropped onto the Tundra two years before.

Tanner sat on a stone bench that was still slightly damp from an early-morning rain. He didn't feel like moving, didn't want to do anything but sit in the growing heat and let it work through him. His shipment from the orbitals wasn't coming down until the next day, and he had nothing else going until then. He closed his eyes and tilted his head back, directly facing the sun.

A burst of shouts and the roar of board motors brought Tanner upright, eyes open. From the other end of the park, a girl was racing toward him on a motorized board, hand working the rear control line, weaving along the concrete path. Fifty feet behind her was a pack of thrashers in pursuit. The girl was grinning.

As she got closer, Tanner recognized her—it was the girl from the junk-yard. Once again a pang of familiarity went through him, then faded when he could not lock it down. People moved out of the girl's path, and she swung wide around him, throttle full open, then shot out of the park and into the street, moving skillfully among the cars.

The thrasher pack went past, following her into the street. Two of them crashed into cars, tumbling to the ground, the boards spinning their wheels. Brakes squealed, people yelled, the thrashers yelled back. The girl, two blocks past the park, turned a corner and was gone from sight. Those thrashers still on their boards, seven or eight of them, followed her around the corner, and they, too, were gone.

Tanner watched and listened, but nothing happened. He tilted his head back, and closed his eyes once more.

5

SOOKIE WAS FLYING. Chase scene. The stolen board hummed along slick and smooth. She'd picked a good one. She laughed, thinking of the thrasher she'd tumbled to get the board.

The other thrashers. She didn't look around, but she knew they were behind her, she could hear the motors. The shouts. The swearing. Wind lifted her hair, flapped her shirt. Sookie took another corner, wheels skidding across the pavement, fishtailing. She leaned, throttled up and straightened, then jumped the curb and shot along the sidewalk. Clattering wheels. Zoom!

People on the sidewalk scattered, some yelling at her, arms waving. *They* didn't know. Zap. Sookie swerved, went off the curb, hit the street. She angled across, wheels caught for a moment in a drain grate, then jarred loose as she tumbled from the board. She rolled back onto her feet, righted the board, and jumped back onto it. Sookie throttled up, flying again.

She shot down an alley. Holes and rocks. Broken windows, splintered wood. The thrashers were closer now, at least a couple of them. Sookie weaved in and out of piles of trash, emerged from the alley and turned onto the street, bouncing between a parked car and one in motion. Halfway down the block, she heard one of the thrashers go down, screaming.

Underground. She had to get underground. She looked ahead. Two more blocks, a few more turns. Sure.

She wanted a cigarette. She laughed. What a crazy idea! She flew. One block. Then two. She turned hard right, swung an arcing left through traffic and into another alley. She twisted the throttle, hoping to get just a little more speed. She felt terrific, terrific! Yow. The alley was clear, the ground almost smooth. She ducked under a loading platform, veered to the left.

At the mouth of the alley, Sookie cut back right, grazing the brick corner as she jumped the curb, shot down the sidewalk. Almost immediately she cut hard right again, into a narrow gap between buildings, toward concrete stairs going down. Sookie cut the engine, squatted, and grabbed the board as she flew off the top step and dropped. She hung on as she hit the lower steps and rolled, tumbling, sprawling across the bottom. Ignoring the pain, Sookie scrambled to her feet and pushed through the broken vent screen, into the darkness of the building.

The basement was quiet and black. She couldn't see a thing, but she knew where she was. She coiled the control line and attached it to the board, tucked the board by feel onto a shelf above the screen, then set off

across the basement. On the far side of the basement floor was a hatch leading to underground rail tunnels. As she approached the far wall, still unable
to see anything, Sookie dropped to hands and knees, moved forward until
she felt the hatch.

It wouldn't open. She adjusted her grip, pulled harder. Nothing. What
was going on? Once more, on her haunches, pushing with her legs. Still
nothing.

Sookie released the handle, stood. She wondered if something was happening down in the tunnels. Belly races? Subterranean barbecue? It made
her hungry, thinking about food. Why hadn't anyone told her?

There had to be another way out. She didn't want to go back through
the screen; not yet, anyway. Thrashers. She got out matches, used one for a
light.

The basement was nearly empty. A few shelves on the walls, the floor
hatch, a cabinet, a pile of broken glass. And a wooden door in the corner.
Was it there before? She couldn't remember. Another match, and Sookie approached the door, pulling at it. Solid but unlocked. A cracking sound, and
the door jerked loose, swung open. Behind the door was a short, narrow
passage, another door. Sookie smiled, thinking of secret passages, hidden
treasures. Electric ghosts and wailing mutants. She proceeded along the passage, lit a third match, pushed open the far door, stepped through.

She stood in a much larger room, ceiling above ground level, grimy
windows high above her letting in just enough light for her to see. Strange,
old, tall machines filled the room. Cables snaked along the floor between the
machines, huge pipes hung from the upper walls and ceiling. And then she
saw them, glinting in the feeble light—silver chains.

Hanging from hooks driven into the concrete walls were dozens of sets
of silver chains attached to wide silver bands. Sookie stepped toward a set,
reached out and touched the cold, smooth metal. Just like on the naked bodies. Beautiful. And again she wondered what they would look like on her
own wrists and ankles.

A thrum, a rumble, a high, oscillating whine. Sookie turned, stared at
machines coming to life. All of them? She couldn't tell. She saw wheels spinning, belts rolling, rods moving up and down. The floor vibrated beneath
her feet, the pipes above her shook and hissed. The vibration increased,
joined by a steady pounding.

Then, in the back of the chamber, obscured by all the machines, a deep
blue glow appeared. It grew, spread across the back wall, cast wavering
shadows among the machines. The glow brightened and moved forward.

Sookie went stiff, unable to move. She wanted to run, toward it or away
from it, she wasn't quite sure.

The glow moved through the machines, like gliding on air, and as it approached, Sookie could make out a huge, vague form within it. She caught

a glimpse of a hairless scalp half metal and light. Other flashes of metal. And, she thought, feathers. The edge of a wing. A voice emerged.

"You, girl." Man or woman? She couldn't tell. It was smooth, sounded like it came from a machine. "Girl."

Sookie turned and ran. Through the door, along the short passage, into the basement. She tripped over the hatch, sprawled on the floor, scrambled to her feet. She pushed her way through the screen and into daylight, started up the steps. The board. She came back down, started to push through the screen when she felt a breath of hot air wash across her from within, heard the scraping of metal on stone. She pulled back out and ran up the steps to street level.

On the sidewalk, Sookie stopped to catch her breath. She scanned the street, searching for the thrashers, but didn't see any—only cars, bikes, pedestrians. She looked down at the broken vent screen and watched, waiting for something to appear. Nothing did. She lit a cigarette, turned away, and started down the street.

6

TANNER'S FOOTSTEPS ECHOED off concrete in the police garage, then were drowned out by the roar of an engine, tires squealing, and finally the crash of metal against cement and the shattering of glass.

"God damnit!" someone shouted from inside the office in the far corner. "Is Walliser drunk again?" Tanner recognized Lucy Chen's voice. Somebody else inside the lighted room laughed—Vince Patricks, probably. On the other side of the garage, a car door opened, slammed shut.

Tanner approached the small office, and soon the awful stink of Lucy Chen's boiling tea overwhelmed the smells of gasoline and smoke. He stopped in the doorway and looked inside.

Lucy was sitting at her desk, head bent over a pot, breathing in the fumes of the boiling tea. Behind her, at the other desk, Vince Patricks leaned back in his chair, feet propped on the drawer handles. Wall space not filled with locked key cabinets was covered with magazine and newspaper photos taped over one another like a collage—Vince's perpetual project. The photos were all of old men and women wearing idiotic expressions. Vince taped up his photos, Lucy brewed her tea. They both figured it was a fair arrangement.

Tanner said hello, and Vince nodded, smiling. Lucy looked up.

"Want some tea?"

Vince laughed and Tanner shook his head. Lucy scowled at them, then poured herself a cup of the vile stuff; bits of slimy black herbs slopped into the cup along with the thick, dark liquid. She put the pot back on the burner and adjusted the heat.

"Hey, Tanner," Vince said. "Want in on the body pool? Only ten bucks a shot. Day the next bodies are found, which shift, how many, and which body of water. Sex of the victims as a tiebreaker."

"You're a fucking pervert," Lucy said.

Vince grinned at her, then raised an eyebrow at Tanner.

"No, thanks," Tanner said. "I never win."

"You talk to Carlucci?" Lucy asked.

Tanner nodded. "Yesterday."

"Get what you want from him?"

Tanner shrugged, didn't say anything.

"Lucy gets what she wants from him," Vince said.

Ignoring him, Lucy got up, unlocked one of the key cabinets, and removed a set of keys. She tossed it to Tanner. "Seventeen-A," she said. "And Tanner?"

"Yeah?" He knew what was coming, part of Lucy's ritual.

"Bring it back with a full tank."

"Sure, Lucy. Thanks." He pocketed the keys and headed toward the back of the garage.

Inside the office, Vince said something Tanner couldn't make out, and started laughing again. "Fuck you," Lucy said, followed by more of Vince's laughter. Tanner smiled to himself. A team. Some things really didn't ever seem to change.

Tanner drove the police van through the pelting rain. Paul sat beside him with his head against the window, eyes half-closed. The van bounced over the cracked highway, swerved around potholes. Tanner kept the speed down, unwilling to risk going more than forty. They were halfway between San Francisco and San Jose on U.S. 101, the back of the van loaded with pharmaceuticals.

Tanner turned on the radio and tuned in to a talk show.

". . . *should put more slugs to work on it, you know, cart in a few from other cities or someplace. We've got to stop this maniac and fry him before he kills more people.*"

"*You really think that would make a difference, William? They've had slugs on this since the killings began.*"

"*Yeah, what, two or three of them? I say get a whole bunch, fifteen or twenty, stick 'em together in a big room, and pump 'em full of that brain juice. It's worth a shot.*"

"And how about you, William? Do you have any ideas about who the killer is or why he's doing it?"

"Sure, I've got ideas, and I'm working on them. When I have them worked out better I'll go to the police, but I need to keep them to myself for now."

"Okay, William, I understand, and thanks for the call. We're going to take a short break here, but when we come back we want to hear what you think about the return of the Chain Killer, especially if you have any ideas about who it is."

Bouncy music came on, then crashing sounds, and a voice-over talking about Charm Magnets. Paul turned down the volume so it was barely audible, and said, "How can you stand to listen to that?"

"The radio?"

"Talk shows."

"I learn some things from them. About people."

"They depress me."

"Most of what I learn about people is depressing."

Paul nodded, but didn't say any more. He sighed and turned the volume back up.

". . . name's Silo."

"All right, Silo, what's on your mind?"

"The cops are just giving us bull SCREEE! about these killings."

"All right, Silo, you're going to have to watch your language there. This is radio. We're in modern times here, but not that modern. So, what, you think the police are witholding information?"

"They're not telling us everything the killer does to 'em, to the bodies. I know. After he kills 'em he SCREE!s 'em in the SCREE! and then he . . ."

"O-kay, so much for Mr. Silo. Remember, folks, keep it clean or I'll have to cut you off, too. All right, Milpitas, you're on the air."

"Hello? Hello?"

"Hello, this is Mike on the mike, you're on the air, Milpitas. What's your name?"

"Meronia."

"All right, Meronia, what's on your mind?"

Paul reached forward and switched off the radio. "Listen to it some other time," he said. He put his head back against the glass and closed his eyes.

The rain had stopped by the time they pulled into the Emergency entrance of Valley Medical Center. Tanner hit the horn, and a minute later Valerie, in her hospital whites, came through the double doors. Paul opened his door and Valerie squeezed in behind his seat, then crouched on the floor between them. Tanner pulled out of the drive and swung around toward the rear of the hospital.

"It's been a long time since you've had anything for us," Valerie said.

"I get what I can when I can."

"I realize that. I was just saying."

He drove along a narrow, looping roadway and stopped beside the laundry annex. He turned on the van's overhead interior light, rolled back the wire barrier, then he and Valerie crawled into the small open space between the seats and the stacks of cartons.

Valerie whistled, gazing over the boxes and crates. "You got some shipment this time. How much is ours?"

Tanner touched a stack. All the cartons in the van were labeled AGRICULTURAL IMPLEMENTS. "Here's a list." He handed her a folded sheet of paper.

Valerie spread the paper and read it by the overhead light. She whistled again. "Beta-endoscane. Nobody but the richest of the private hospitals are even getting a crack at this stuff." She continued reading, nodding once in a while, then refolded the paper and tucked it into the upper pocket of her hospital coat. From a larger, lower pocket, she removed a roll of bills and handed it to Tanner.

Twenties. He unclipped the roll and started counting.

"I know it's not even close to black market, but it's all we can come up with for now."

Tanner finished counting, then, trying to keep the disappointment out of his voice, said, "That doesn't matter. This is fine." A week ago it *would* have been fine—enough to pay the rent, buy food, and work on the next shipment. Now, though, he had a feeling he was going to have extra expenses. A lot of them. He was going to have to sell more of what remained in the van.

Paul stayed with the van as Valerie and Tanner unloaded through the side door. They carried the cartons into the annex, through storage rooms filled with linens, the warm and damp laundry room, and along a connecting corridor that led down into the hospital basement, where they stacked the cartons in an unmarked closet. Tanner knew the procedure by now: Valerie and the other doctors would work out a distribution plan later that day, trying to keep the shipment itself quiet.

Valerie made sure the closet was securely locked and bolted, then they swung by the doctors' lounge, picked up three cups of coffee, and returned to the van. Tanner gave a cup to Paul, then he and Valerie sat together on folding chairs just inside the annex.

"So how have you been?" Tanner asked.

"Oh, I've been fine. Still spending too much time at the hospital, but that's nothing new."

"No." He smiled. "And Connie?"

Valerie smiled back, shaking her head. "She's sixteen, and she's a pain in the ass sometimes. But she's a good kid at heart."

"Yes, she is."

"She asks about you," Valerie said. "How you're doing, if I've seen you. She really cares about you, Louis. She never asks about her father." She put a hand on his knee. "She'd love it if you were to come by and see her sometime, take her to a movie or something." She paused. "She doesn't understand why you and I aren't still together."

Who did? Tanner thought. But he didn't say anything. Neither of them did for several minutes, sipping at their coffee. The sun came in through the window, lighting up dust particles in the air, fluttering motes of bright silver. Someone had once told him that dust was primarily made up of the skeletons or shells of microscopic creatures. Dust mites.

"So," Valerie finally said, "it's starting again in the city."

Tanner looked at her, confused for a moment. Then he realized what she was talking about, and nodded. "Looks that way."

"How are the nightmares?"

Tanner shrugged. "They'd stopped."

He thought she would say more about it, ask something else, but she didn't. He finished the coffee and stood.

"I need to go."

She walked back to the van with him, kissed him lightly before he got in. "Take care of yourself, Louis."

"You, too."

"Good-bye, Paul." She waved.

"Bye, Valerie."

"Thanks again," she said to Tanner.

Tanner nodded and started the engine, then slowly pulled away.

"You made a serious mistake," Paul said, "when you stopped seeing Valerie."

"Christ, don't start."

Paul shrugged, then said, "Back to the city?"

"No. Make some phone calls, another couple of stops, sell some more of this stuff."

"You're going to sell more?"

"Yeah. I'm getting greedy. Just call me Uriah from now on. And help me find a pay phone that works." He drove on without saying any more.

7

THEIR LAST STOP before Paul's clinic was the free clinic in the Golden Gate Park squatter zone. The police markings on the van served as an unofficial pass, getting barriers moved and chains retracted so they could access restricted roads. Tanner drove slowly along the road fronting the Academy of Sciences, the stone walls of the buildings glistening from a recent bleaching. Schoolchildren in uniforms walked in tight formation, or clustered in well-defined groups on the steps in front of the building. Across the concourse of leafless trees, next to the manicured grounds of the Japanese Tea Gardens, the remains of the De Young Museum were covered with flowering vines.

They had to go through one more barrier, then Tanner swung the van around and behind the De Young ruins and stopped at the edge of the squatter zone—drab tents patched with faded swatches of colored fabric, shanties built of warped plywood and irregular sheets of metal or plastic, lean-tos erected over slabs of concrete. The zone filled a large meadow and sent out dozens of tentacles into the least dense sections of the surrounding woods, the trees and brush cut down to make more space for tents and shanties and to provide firewood. Mud-slick paths wound among the dwellings, the paths crowded with adults and children and animals.

The medical clinic was housed in an abandoned park maintenance building. A long line of people stretched from the clinic, snaking past the van. Seeing the police van, the people shifted and turned to one another, whispering and gesturing, though they didn't leave.

"They must have something special going on," Paul said. "Line that long. Inoculations, maybe."

"Maybe I should stay with the van," Tanner said.

Paul gave a short, hard laugh. "*One* of us better."

Paul got out of the van and walked toward the clinic. The people in line tensed, staring at him as he walked toward the building. Tanner sat behind the wheel, the heat building up inside the van despite the open windows. But he did not feel like moving. The people in line stopped staring at the van, but they did not seem to relax much. They looked like they had been in line a long time, and many of them tried to get off their feet without sitting in the mud, which wasn't easy. Most of them looked ill as well as exhausted.

Tanner glanced over the treetops and could just see the top of the hill rising from the island in the middle of Stowe Lake. It had been a long time since he had been on that hill, and he wondered if he was going to have to do something similar again. He hoped to Christ he wouldn't, but he did not have a good feeling about it.

A few minutes later Paul returned to the van with Patricia Miranda, one of the clinic's volunteer med techs. Tanner had met her two or three times before, and she shook his hand with a smile.

"This van." She shook her head, then turned to the people in line. "They are not police," she said, loud but calm. "They have medical supplies for the clinic." Then she repeated it in Spanish. The people in line visibly relaxed, though their wariness did not disappear altogether.

"What's going on?" Tanner asked. "Fever inoculations?"

"No," Patricia said. "Wish it was, though it's probably too late for most of them. No, we managed to get several thousand sets of nose filters. A lot of the people here had enough money once to get plugs implanted, but most haven't had a filter change in years, so we're trying to do them all."

Tanner sniffed, twitching his nose at the thought. He was due soon himself. He looked up at the hazy sky, thinking about the crap that got into his lungs even with the filters.

"Tanner, Patricia wants me to help out here for a while," Paul said. "You want to just go on without me? I'll give you the keys to the clinic and you can just drop the stuff."

"How long you think you'll be?"

"An hour, hour and a half tops. I've got my own shift at the hospital tonight."

"I'll wait. There's something I want to do, if it'll be all right to leave the van awhile."

Patricia nodded. "It'd probably be fine, but I'll get a couple of people to watch it."

They unloaded cartons, leaving only Paul's share in the back of the van. Then Tanner locked the van, and Paul and Patricia went into the clinic.

Tanner walked through the heart of the squatter zone, along the slick, muddy paths. Most of the tents were makeshift, heavily patched, the walls sacrificed for the roofs; the shanties were not much more solid than the tents, providing shelter from the rain but little privacy. Clothes on people were as patched and torn as the tents, often revealing unhealed wounds and large streaks of fever rash. As he walked along, half-naked kids came up to him and begged, hands held out. But they were listless and halfhearted, as if they recognized that anyone walking among them would have little or nothing to give away.

Smelling smoke and roasting meat, Tanner came to a large open area between two groups of shacks. A fire pit had been dug in the center of the clearing, and a wide, blazing fire burned within it. Above the fire, on crudely made roasting spits, were several small, unrecognizable animals (raccoons? dogs?), and one much larger, headless beast that Tanner was pretty sure was

a horse. Fifteen or twenty men and women stood around the roasting animals, talking and drinking from unlabeled bottles.

He worked his way through the shanties and tents, feeling more and
more closed in by them as he went. Eventually the zone ended and he
reached the denser foliage of the woods. Tanner pressed on, the way slightly
uphill now, and a few minutes later emerged from the trees. He crossed a
narrow strip of broken pavement and stopped on the bank of Stowe Lake.

Tanner stood at the water's edge and looked across to the island that
filled so much of the lake. The island was a heavily wooded hill, its peak the
highest point in the park. At the top, there were views of the entire park and
close to half the city. Also at the top was a small, muck-filled reservoir that
had once held two naked, chained bodies.

Tanner looked up at the top of the hill, remembering. He had been alone
that day, too, and it was alone in the muggy afternoon heat that he had
pulled the two dead women from the water, naked but covered with green
and brown muck. Chained together at the wrists and ankles, face to face, as
if embraced like lovers.

He walked along the edge of the lake for a few minutes, then crossed
one of the bridges to the island. He stopped at the foot of the long trail that
curved around the island and up to the top of the hill. Tanner did not know
why he was doing this, but he knew he would not go back until he did. He
started up the trail.

It had been hot and muggy that day, just the way it was now. There had
been a crazy run of other murders in the city, and Tanner and Freeman were
on loan to Homicide to help out with the casework overload. But Freeman had
called in sick that morning, and Tanner was working alone out in the avenues along the park when the virus came through the system giving the location of the bodies. He was given the option of waiting until one of the
regular Homicide teams was freed up, but he couldn't stand the thought of
the bodies staying in water any longer than necessary. It was irrational, but
there it was. And so he had made this climb alone, knowing what he would
find at the top.

He knew there would be no bodies this time, but that did not help his
mood much. It was, he feared, only a matter of time. A slight breeze took
the edge off the heat, whispering through the ragged eucalyptus trees that
still survived. His view of the park and the city expanded as he climbed
higher. He stopped at one point, almost at the top, and looked down at the
sprawling squatter zone. Separated from the zone by only a narrow strip of
trees were the Japanese Tea Gardens. He could see the wealthy tourists
walking along the tended paths, sitting in the tea pavilion.

Next to the tea gardens was the De Young, and as he looked at it Tanner thought he glimpsed movement within the wreckage of crumbled stone
and thick vines. He stared a long time, watching, but did not see anything
more. Animals? Or people living in the ruins? It would not be surprising.

He resumed the climb. A few minutes later the trail widened to an open area at the top of the hill. The concrete reservoir was still there, still filled with more muck than water. A heavy, warm stench rose from it, worse than the stink of the slough the other day.

Tanner sat on the concrete rim and stared down at the muck-covered water. He wondered what else was at the bottom of the reservoir. Probably it would never be drained and cleaned out because no one wanted to know. Just like everything else. He picked up a stone, tossed it into the water. The stone hit the green muck without a splash and slowly sank. It was going to be one hell of a summer.

8

NIGHT. SMOKE IN the air. Sookie sat in the open window of her room on the upper floor of the De Young. She could see the glow from burning lamps, the flicker of the tent-city fires. Smelled the smoke, the cooking meat, the shit from the portable toilets. Heard the murmur of voices, singing.

She didn't need anyone, she could take of herself. She sniffed once. Crazy people, living in the tents. All jammed in together, crawling over each other. They had nothing. Sookie had lots of things.

Sookie lit a cigarette, then climbed down from the window ledge. She lit the set of five squat candles arranged on the plastic crate in the center of the room. The candlelight, quivering, cast shadows at the edges of the room.

The room was small, but the walls were intact. In the corner nearest the window was her bed—a sleeping bag on top of two thick layers of foam rubber. The walls were covered with yellowed newspapers. And along the walls were the makeshift shelves and boxes that held her things.

Sookie moved along the walls, taking inventory. She liked doing it, taking stock, checking things. Looking, picking up a few. Touching. The things she found in empty houses and apartments. She was good at finding things other people couldn't see. Finding good things other people thought were worthless. Her things.

Two plastic mushrooms. A light bulb with a tiny hole and blue swirls of color around the hole. A set of shattered headphones. Neatly wrapped bundles of computer cable. An L-shaped length of shiny copper pipe.

She stopped and picked up the large wood woman. The top half of the woman came off, and inside was a slightly smaller wood woman. It, too, came apart, another smaller woman inside. They went on like that, ten of them until, at last, Sookie would find a tiny wood woman that did not open. She loved opening the women, one after another, but she was always disappointed when she reached the last. She expected something more.

Sookie put down the woman, moved on. An energy band that blinked dim red light, slower and fainter each day. Three neuro-tubes. A jar filled with pieces of green broken glass. Six wooden chopsticks. A clear glass ashtray.

She knelt and pulled out the box of her own private things—the few items she had not found, that she had owned ever since she was a child, that she had taken with her when she had left the place she herself had never called home. Looking at them, touching them, always made her feel both sad and special. Now she just looked at them without touching. The silver metal bracelet with her other name engraved on the band: Celeste. A string of tiny red beads. A clear glass figurine of a cat. And a drawing she had made once of an angel. She had never hung the picture because it frightened her. It pulled her, held tightly onto her, but it also scared her. *My* angel, she thought.

Sookie shivered, put away the box. She moved around the rest of the room, faster now, hardly looking anymore. She finished at the bookcase next to the bed, filled with books and magazines. On the floor was the pocket dictionary she used to help her with words she didn't know. Sometimes, when she was in the mood, she was quite a reader.

But not now. She returned to the window, looked at the lamps, the glow of fires. Look what I have, she thought. She clambered onto the ledge, one leg dangling outside. Look. Sookie slowly, repeatedly banged her fist against the windowsill, and closed her eyes tight.

9

TWO MORE BODIES were found. Two men, this time, pulled out of Balboa Reservoir. The newspaper made much of the fact that it was the first repeat use of a given body of water. Tanner, reading the paper in a cafe on Columbus, doubted it meant anything. What the two new bodies did mean, though, was that now he *had* to go back to Carlucci.

He set down the paper and looked out the window at the early-morning streets. Here, close to the border of the Financial District, the streets were busy, filled with people and cars, delivery trucks and flashers, scooters and runners—an economy that thrived on the edges of the District, living off the workers who ventured a block or two out of the District during daylight hours. When darkness fell, the area narrowed, became a blazing finger of the Chinese Corridor stretching all the way to the Wharf.

Once, Tanner's father had told him years before, this area of the city had not been part of Chinatown. It had been called North Beach, and had been heavily Italian—which explained the two or three Italian restaurants and the few cafes like this one. But Tanner's father had never explained what had happened to the Italians.

Tanner drank slowly from his coffee, putting off what he knew he had to do. He had been afraid of this on the Carousel Club balcony, watching the two bodies being pulled from the slough, but he had hoped it was a fluke, an isolated blip, and not a resumption of the killings. So much for hope. Tanner wondered if he would still be alive at the end of the summer.

He glanced back at the newspaper. This time there was a lurid photo of the bodies. The newshawkers, taken by surprise when the first two had been pulled from the slough, were now on fire alert, shadowing the police.

Tanner flipped over the newspaper, hiding the picture, then finished his coffee. It was time to see Carlucci.

Spade's was half-empty when Tanner arrived. Between mealtimes. The ion poles were turned up, sparks flying, as if Kingston wanted to scare away potential customers.

Carlucci was alone in his booth, staring at the empty seat across from him, tapping at the table with a pen. Kingston was nowhere to be seen. Tanner slid into the booth, and Carlucci blinked several times, as if coming out of a trance.

"My day is fucking complete," he said.

"I need to talk to you."

"So talk."

"Not here," Tanner said.

"Terrific. Melodrama."

"I'm not screwing around."

Carlucci waited, staring at him. "Is it about . . . ?" He left it unfinished. Tanner nodded. "All right," Carlucci said. "Should've known." He wrote something on a piece of paper, folded it several times, then handed it to Tanner.

"Thanks," Tanner said. He put the paper in his pocket without looking at it, then got up and left.

At three-thirty that afternoon, Tanner stood beside a massive concrete pier support, the freeway overpass above him casting a wide shadow. Traffic above rumbled, but was muted, a muffled echo. Two supports down from him, several teenagers in whiteface and pulse-jackets gathered, huddled around a black cylinder. A sudden explosion of sound rocked the air, music blaring from the cylinder, and the crisscrossing bands on the jackets began pulsing colors with the beat.

Tanner saw Carlucci come around a corner, then cross the street carrying a paper bag. When he reached Tanner, he opened the bag, took out two cups of coffee, and handed one to him. They popped the lids and stood without speaking for a few minutes, sipping at the hot coffee and watching the kids down the way. Already a steady procession of customers had begun, mostly teenagers with a few adults to change the pace. As Tanner and Carlucci watched, they could see the exchanges—money for packets. The kids weren't even trying to hide it.

"Not my jurisdiction," Carlucci said.

Tanner understood. Carlucci was Homicide. If he followed up everything he saw happening on the streets, he'd never get to his own job. Unless it turned to murder, Carlucci would let the kids be, though Tanner knew he didn't like it.

"Would have been yours," Carlucci added.

Tanner nodded. They didn't say anything else for a while, then Carlucci finally asked, "So what is it?"

"You're not going to like this."

Carlucci snorted. "Figured that one out all on my own, Tanner."

"Three years ago," Tanner began. "One day, a message gets delivered to me and Freeman. Inside a sealed envelope, a single sheet of paper with just two words. 'Angel wings.' Then two figures. Ten thousand slash one million. And then the name of the man who sent the message. That was all."

"And who was that?"

"Someone who claimed to know who the killer was. Those two numbers. Ten thousand dollars was admission price for a meeting, and one million for the info."

"All right, cut the phony suspense. Who sent the message?"

"Rattan."

"Christ!"

"I told you you weren't going to like it."

Carlucci looked down at his coffee, grimaced at it. "So what did you do?"

"Nothing. We talked about it, tried to figure how to run it. If we went upstairs with it, we were pretty sure it would be killed. Pay ten thousand dollars to a scumbag who'd jumped bail and disappeared with a couple dozen felony drug charges outstanding? They'd argue that he couldn't know anything, that some cop had leaked the info to him about the angel wings."

Carlucci nodded. He stopped grimacing, now just sipped his coffee and watched Tanner, listening.

"So we thought about going after it on our own. We thought we could come up with the ten thousand from slush funds, and if it turned out Rattan's information was good, they'd have to buy it upstairs."

Tanner paused, looking at the kids. Business was complete—it didn't take long—and they turned off the cylinder, packed it away, and moved on. In a few minutes they'd probably be setting up shop elsewhere.

"We hadn't decided for sure. It would have been a hell of a job because we'd have to track down Rattan ourselves. He was offering to sell, but he wasn't going to come to us." Tanner paused again. "Then Freeman got killed. I had other things to deal with for a while." The scar on his back began to itch just thinking about it. "By the time I got back to it, I realized it had been a long time since any new bodies had turned up. So I held off, hoping the killings had stopped. After a few more months, it looked like they had. I left it alone."

"And then you quit the force."

Tanner nodded.

"But now the killings have started again."

Tanner nodded once more. Carlucci finished his coffee, dropped the cup and crushed it into the dirt with his shoe.

"Christ," Carlucci whispered. He looked at Tanner. "Why did Rattan go to you and Freeman?"

"Probably because he thought he could trust us."

"Was he right?"

Tanner shrugged. "Sure. We'd dealt with him before, you know how it goes down sometimes. And we wouldn't have screwed him over."

"Could you trust *him*?"

"In the right situation. We would have trusted him with this deal. It was worth the risk."

"You think his offer was legit?"

Tanner hesitated before answering. He and Freeman had talked a lot about that. The key issue.

"He might have been wrong," Tanner said. "But I think he *believed* he knew who was doing the killing."

"But he wasn't going to give that information to us for nothing," Carlucci said. "And never has." He looked away, slowly shaking his head. "Jesus Christ. Trying to find that fucker now is going to be a lot harder than it would have been three years ago."

No shit, Tanner thought. Three years ago it was felony drug charges. Now Rattan was also wanted for killing two cops. For more than a year he'd managed to stay hidden despite one hell of a hunt-down. He had to be so deep inside the Tenderloin he probably never saw the sun.

They both remained silent for a long time. Carlucci, gazing off into the distance, was probably doing a lot of the same thinking Tanner had done over the last few days. Tanner didn't think he was going to like Carlucci's conclusions any better than his own.

"I'm going to have to get back to you," Carlucci finally said. He was still gazing into the distance, along the line of shrinking highway piers. "I want to talk to a couple of people, but it'll stay tight, believe me."

"You're not going upstairs with this, are you?"

Carlucci turned to look at him. "Not a chance." He paused. "Rattan came to you and Freeman. Freeman's dead. And you're out." Paused again. "You'll come in and work this?"

"I'm going to have to, aren't I?"

Carlucci stared at Tanner for a minute, then said, "I'll call you." Without another word he turned and crossed the street, leaving Tanner alone under the freeway.

Tanner sipped at the coffee. It was cold. He drank the rest of it anyway, crushed the cup in his hand, then dropped it next to Carlucci's.

10

WHEN TANNER CAME out onto the roof, Alexandra was already there, seated near the far edge, cider machine hissing beside her, surrounded by half a dozen cats. Tanner carried his chair across the roof, watching the cats get up and move aside to make room for him. The moonlight glinted off paws and legs—all of Alexandra's cats had at least one metal prosthetic limb. Kubo had all four, and his paws clicked loudly on the rooftop gravel until he settled under Alexandra's chair.

She stood and bowed gracefully, folding her long, thin body nearly in half, her pale hair touching the ground. "Good evening, Mr. Tanner." She laughed, straightened, and sat back down.

"Hello, Alexandra." Tanner set up his chair beside her.

Alexandra poured two steaming mugs of cider and handed one to him. "How's the smuggling trade?" she asked.

"You should know," Tanner said. "Don't you have the stats for it?" Alexandra did statistical research and analysis for a corporate law firm in the Financial District. She spent half her time at the company doing research for radical underground organizations and her own personal interests.

"Black-market pharmaceutical trade is up eleven percent over last year," she said. "But I haven't been able to find a thing on black-market gourmet foods. Care to provide me with some figures so I can start a database?"

Tanner smiled and shook his head. He sipped at the cider, which was hot and strong, with a deep kick. The sky was nearly clear, only a slight haze muting the stars and moon. A regular, almost explosive pounding sounded from the north, maybe near the water. Two green flares shot across the peak of Telegraph Hill, illuminating the jagged ruins of Coit Tower, followed by a short burst of gunfire. Then the quiet and the dark returned.

"People are funny," Alexandra said. It was her standard beginning when she wanted to talk about something she'd been researching.

"What now?" Tanner asked.

"These murders. The 'Chain Killer.' A lot of people in this city are scared out of their minds by this guy."

"Shouldn't they be?"

Alexandra shook her head. "Not the way they are. The numbers aren't right. Last year in this city, seven hundred ninety-three people were killed in race riots. About fifteen hundred were killed in the so-called drug wars. Three hundred seventeen died from tainted prescription pharmaceuticals. Eighty-nine died in the explosion in Macy's, one hundred fifty in the Unicorn Theater bombing. Ninety-three in the Shaklee Building fire, seventy-five in the Market Street gas leaks. And sixty-nine students mowed down at the USF anti-draft rally." She waved her hand. "I could go on. I didn't even bother digging up the numbers for other murders, or car-accident fatalities, anything like that." She paused, looking at Tanner. "Let's face it, sometimes life in this city is a horror show." She paused again. "So how many people did this 'Chain Killer' murder the first time? Thirty-seven over a two-year period. Add four new ones, and that's a total of forty-one in the last four and a half years. I'm not saying the killings aren't awful. They are. And I'm certainly glad I'm not one of those forty-one. But it's a relatively small number, compared to the others I just gave you. If this guy scares them so badly, they should be crapping their pants on a daily basis just at the thought of living in this city."

Tanner smiled. "Some people do," he said. He drank from the cup, looking at Alexandra over the rim. She seemed genuinely puzzled. "I know what you're saying, but you should know it's never that simple. It's more than the numbers. People don't understand these killings. Everything else you mentioned, people can understand why they happen. They don't like it, but it makes sense. Race riots? Awful, but comprehensible. The Macy's fire? Terrible, but only an isolated incident, and the cause was known. And people know you're asking for trouble if you walk in certain parts of the city after dark, or some parts any time of day. They *understand* that." He paused. "But people can't make sense of the Chain Killer. Nobody has any idea who it is, why he kills, no pattern to when or where. Which means that it could happen to anyone, at any time, so there's nothing, absolutely nothing they can do to protect themselves."

Three more flares went off on Telegraph Hill, but this time there was no gunfire. They watched as the glow of the flares burned brightly for a minute, then faded. One of the cats jumped onto Tanner's lap, metal claws digging through his pants.

"You could be right," Alexandra said. "I suppose it makes a kind of sense." She reached under the chair, scratched Kubo, then looked at Tanner. "You glad you're not a cop anymore? You won't have to deal with this."

Tanner gave a short, chopped laugh.

"What's that supposed to mean?" she asked.

"I'm not a cop, but I'm involved. I'm stuck in this damn thing."

"Why?"

Tanner just shook his head.

"You don't know who did it?"

"No."

"But you know something."

"Sort of. Really, Alexandra, I don't want to go into it." He held out his cup for a refill. "I just want to sit up here with you, have some cider, talk about other things, and enjoy the night."

Alexandra nodded. She poured fresh cider for them both, and they remained silent, drinking.

A series of multicolored flares filled the sky, this time to the south, sending up a brilliant, shifting glow. Several loud explosions sounded, then a column of flame rose into the air, fanned out, and showered back to earth.

"Wonderful," Alexandra said. "Probably the Purists at work again."

" 'Purity with flame, sanctify His Name,' " Tanner quoted. With the buildings of the Financial District blocking the view, he could no longer see flames, but Tanner knew that buildings were burning somewhere south of Market.

"Enjoy the night," Alexandra said.

11

THE FIRE BLAZED just a few blocks from the drive-in. The flickering glow interfered slightly with the picture on the screen that had been erected at the boundary of the junkyard. Sookie sat in the front seat of a big four-door Buick, watching the movie through the glassless windshield. Sound came from a dozen speakers scattered throughout the junkyard. Most of the top-level cars around her were occupied. Nearly a full house.

The movie on the screen was called *The Courier's Revenge,* and starred Sylvia Romilar as a corporate gene courier. It was a comedy, and Sookie had been laughing since the movie had begun. Everyone in the junkyard was laughing.

A knock came on the driver's door. Sookie leaned over, looked out the window—it was Dex, the food man, on his stilts. Racks hung from his neck, filled with boxed candy, popcorn, and canned drinks. Sookie bought a large carton of popcorn and a can of Twist, and Dex moved on.

On the screen, Sylvia Romilar, naked, was winding herself up in Saran Wrap. Empty boxes and rolls lay all over the floor of the tiny bullet train cabin. She flopped onto the bench seat, trying to wrap her arms. Sookie had no idea why Sylvia, whose name was Natasha in the movie, was doing this. That's what Sookie liked about Sylvia Romilar's movies—most of them never made any sense.

There was a dull thud on the roof of the car, then footsteps, the car rocking, and another thud. A man's head appeared upside down in the windshield.

"Hey, chickie," the guy said.

"Move it, asshole, you're blocking the picture." She shifted across the seat, trying to see the screen.

"Want some company, chickie?" He slid along the roof, blocking her view again.

Sookie slapped at him, he pulled up and away, and she slid back across the seat. "Go away!" She tried to pick up what was happening in the movie. Sylvia/Natasha was now crawling along the roof of the bullet train, still wearing only the Saran Wrap, her hair blowing wildly in the wind and shooting bright blue sparks.

The guy's head reappeared, then his body as he pulled himself through the windshield and into the car. Sookie shoved him and he lost his grip, landing half on the seat, half on the floor. He pulled himself onto the seat, next to Sookie, and she punched him in the ribs, swung at his face.

"Get out!"

The guy laughed, blocking her punches. "Hey, hey, *hey*, chickie! I just want some company, don't you?"

"No." She pulled back against the door, watching him. Slowly, she reached down next to the seat, felt for the gravy knife. She wasn't scared—the guy was a jerk, but harmless—but she'd had enough of him.

The guy was still grinning, and now he slid closer to her until his thighs were pressed against her knees. "Hey, chickie, we're at the drive-in, let's have some fun."

He leaned forward, moving slowly, then his hand darted out and up under her T-shirt, fingers grabbing at her tiny breasts. Sookie hit the charge, then brought the knife up and into the guy's arm.

The guy screamed, jerked his arm back. Sookie held tight onto the knife and it came free. The guy, still screaming, kicked wildly as he scrambled out through the windshield. His boot caught Sookie across the side of the head, knocking her into the steering wheel. The guy crawled across the hood of the car and dropped over the edge, landing heavily on the ground below. He stopped screaming, and Sookie could hear him stumble away through the junkyard.

Sookie cut the knife's charge and wiped the blade clean on her T-shirt. She put it back beside the seat. Then she groaned when she saw the popcorn scattered all over the floor of the car.

Another knock on the car door. "Sookie, you all right?" It was Dex.

Sookie leaned out the window and nodded. "Yeah."

"That your blood?"

"No. But I need more popcorn. Asshole ruined all mine."

Dex gave her a carton. "On the house."

"Thanks."

Dex moved on, and Sookie sank back against the door, looking out the far side of the car, gazing at the fire instead of the screen. What a week. Bodies in the water. Machines and a winged monster in that Tundra basement. Now this. Maybe it was time to go see Mixer again.

Sookie returned her gaze to the movie screen, settled back in the seat with her fresh popcorn, and tried to pick up the story line. On the screen, the bullet train was gone. Sylvia/Natasha, still in the Saran Wrap, sat inside a tiny shack, warming herself in front of a fire and smoking a cigarette. The fire popped loudly, and several large embers burst out, landing on her. The Saran Wrap ignited, began to melt and flame. Sookie laughed. She knew Sylvia would be just fine.

12

THE MEETING PLACE, on the outer edge of the old Civic Center, was appropriate, Tanner thought. From the concrete bench where he waited for Carlucci, he could see, a few blocks away, the upper reaches of the Tenderloin—razor wire on the roof boundaries, jagged television antennas and tiny satellite dishes, reflecting glass windows and armored balconies, vast networks of flowering vines, seeded catch-traps, and columns of steam rising through mist clouds that hovered above the enclave.

Across the plaza, a group of True Millennialists swayed and stomped in chaotic, circular patterns around a pile of broken concrete blocks and twisted metal pipe. Occasionally one of the group would leap away from the others and scream into the face of a passerby, then rejoin the circle. The True Millennialists claimed that during the years of changeover from the Julian to the Gregorian calendar a great fraud had been perpetrated, skipping

a number of years of reckoning so that the True Millennium had *not* occurred at the official turn of the century. Instead, they claimed, the True Millennium was only now approaching, due in less than two years and destined
to bring about the destruction of all civilization.

My kind of people, Tanner thought. A woman broke from the group,
ran across the plaza, and stopped in front of him, staring with widened eyes.

"Don't bother repenting!" she shouted. "It's too fucking late for that!
Too much sin and not enough time. Hah!" She leaned forward, grinning at
him. "The Chain Killer is one of the harbingers. He is the Angel of Death."
The woman was trembling. Christ, Tanner thought, that's exactly what the
media would call the guy if they ever found out about the angel wings. The
woman whirled and sprinted back to the group.

"I'd heard you had a way with women." It was Carlucci, who stood a
few feet away, watching the True Millennialists. He looked at Tanner without smiling, then approached the bench and sat.

Tanner didn't say anything. He didn't even want to ask Carlucci what he
had come up with because he knew it wasn't going to be good. So he waited
in silence, looking up at the hazy, discolored sun.

"Forecast is for two days without rain," Carlucci said.

"Is that supposed to be good or bad?"

Carlucci shrugged. A man without legs, hip stumps surgically attached
to a motorized dolly, wheeled past them, beating at his bare chest, mouth
open in a silent scream.

"I talked to a couple people," Carlucci said. "They both agreed this is
worth pursuing." He paused, shrugging again. "They also agree that you
have the only real chance of getting to Rattan."

"I wonder how much of a chance that is," Tanner said.

"That's a bad attitude."

"Yeah, well."

"We'll work together on this. Partners."

"You going into the Tenderloin with me?"

"No. You know I can't do that. I'll do everything I can from out here."

"Logistical support."

"Something like that."

Tanner looked up at the rooftop boundaries of the Tenderloin. The
steam columns, almost pure white and coherent when they first emerged
above the buildings, rose quickly toward the sun, coming apart and breaking into a scatter of dirty colors. What kind of real help could Carlucci give
him from out here?

"So I go into the Tenderloin and find Rattan," Tanner said. It wouldn't
be the Tenderloin itself that would be dangerous; it would be what he had
to do to track Rattan. He smiled. "Sounds so simple."

"Okay, so it's not simple, but yeah, that's what you do. Find him, and if
he's got the real stuff, make a deal."

"How high can I go?"

"Christ, as high as you have to. If it's for real, they'll come up with the money. The police and the city have a real public relations problem with this guy." Carlucci grinned. "The mayor says this guy's generating a very high 'hysteria quotient.'"

"Hysteria quotient? What bullshit."

"You got it. They're choking out a lot of that nonsense right now, running scared. We've got an election coming up in four months, though why anyone would want to be involved in running this city is way the hell beyond me. But that's also why they'll come up with as much money as they have to." Carlucci's grin transformed into a frown. "But one thing won't go. No way the murder charges can be dropped, not for killing cops. Never happen."

"Rattan won't ask for that," Tanner said. "He'll know."

"You give the guy a lot of credit for a cop killer and drug dealer."

"He's smart, Carlucci. How long you guys been trying to find him?"

Carlucci grimaced. "Fair enough." He looked over at the True Millennialists, who were now huddled around the mound of rubble, hardly moving, chanting in low voices. "Goddamn freaks." He turned back to Tanner. "You're going to need money just to get to him."

Tanner nodded. "I've got a little."

"Enough?"

Tanner shook his head. "Not even close."

"Day after tomorrow, go by the garage and see Lucy. She'll have whatever I can dig out of slush."

Tanner thought about asking Carlucci if he was giving Lucy anything else, but decided it wasn't worth it. Carlucci had a strong sense of family, and would probably resent any suggestion he was cheating on his wife, even as a joke.

The sun blazed down through the haze, enervating him. But it's a dry heat, he told himself. "Do we still have people inside?"

"A couple," Carlucci answered.

"Wilson?"

Carlucci shook his head. "She pulled out last year. Got blown and barely got out alive."

"Menendez?"

"He *didn't* get out alive."

"Koto?"

Carlucci smiled and nodded. "Yeah, Koto's still inside. He'll never come out. Loves it in there. Told me he wants his ashes scattered over the streets at midnight." The smile faded. "I'll tell you how to reach him, but don't go anywhere near him except as a last resort. Too many years invested to risk blowing him. You can go to Francie Miller. You know her?"

"No."

"She's good, she'll take care of you. Everything you'll need on her will be with the money."

They sat a while longer in silence. Across the plaza, a trio of Rollers, headwheels spinning and flashing green lights, had faced off with the True Millennialists, and the two groups shouted back and forth, an exchange that to Tanner seemed almost ritualistic in its tone and cadence.

"You don't have to do it, Tanner. It's not your job anymore." He paused. "You don't have to do it."

Tanner gave him a half smile. "Sure I do. I have enough trouble sleeping as it is."

"Guilty conscience?"

"No. But I don't need one." He stood. "I'll see you, Carlucci."

"Stay in touch."

"Sure." He glanced over the True Millennialists. The Rollers were gone, and the Millennialists were now settling down on their pile of rubble, as if they were going to sleep. They seemed to be at peace. Then Tanner looked one more time at the armored upper reaches of the Tenderloin, sun glinting off metal and glass, and started for home.

13

TANNER BEGAN THE night in the Financial District. With the blaze of light from all directions it was nearly as bright as day, though the light was cleaner, white and sterile as it reflected from shining alloys, polished stone, darkglass, and bleached ferroplast. Streets and sidewalks were fairly busy even at this hour—between foreign market hours and the security of the checkpoints, the District never closed down anymore; it only slowed its pace a little at night.

Tanner was still uncomfortable from the checkpoint run. He had never become accustomed to the body searches, and without a permanent pass there was no way to avoid them. He'd had to put up with the searches even as a cop—only those stationed within the District got the passes. On the other hand, Tanner thought, he didn't really *want* a permanent pass to the place. He did not like the Financial District and did not like most of the people who worked here.

Tanner pulled his raincoat tight, though there was no rain yet—an attempt at regaining some comfort. The raincoat was a marvel, coated with some kind of semi-permeable membrane that kept the water out, but actively breathed, kept him almost cool even in the damp heat.

As Tanner moved through the crowds, he noticed the glint of metal on flesh all around him. A lot of men and women appeared to have metal prosthetic limbs or facials, but Tanner knew that most, if not all, were fakes. It had become a fad, a fashion trend. *Faux Prosthétique,* Alexandra called it. Money people had taken to wearing the metal add-ons and coveralls like jewelry or makeup—put them on in the morning, take them off at night. Very expensive—they had to be custom fitted to allow full limb function—but not permanent. Like rub-on tattoos, Tanner thought.

He climbed the steps leading to the massive glass doors of the Mishima building. Workers streamed in through the doors, the evening shift coming on for the opening of the Tokyo and New Hong Kong exchanges. Tanner noticed that none of them wore metal—Mishima Investments strictly forbade any fakes.

Tanner stepped through the high doors and approached the security desk. A visitor's pass complete with his photo was already prepared for him, and after a quick and polite identity check he was passed through to the elevators.

When he emerged into the open fifty-eighth-floor reception area, Tanner was enclosed by a solid hush of quiet. A wide expanse of pale carpet, sand walls, and low furnishings surrounded him. At the matte black reception desk on the opposite wall sat a tall, dark-haired woman with a silver metal face. Tanner had never seen her before, and the shining metal disturbed him. It was not a mask; the polished metal contoured to the woman's skull *was* her face. He wondered if it had been elective.

"Mr. Tanner." The woman's voice, emerging from between metal, segmented lips, was soft and cool. "Mr. Teshigahara will see you now."

The wall to her left swung open. Tanner walked toward the opening, and as he passed the woman he thought he heard a long, low hiss. He turned to look at her, but she was facing the elevator, silent and unmoving. He turned away and went through, the wall closing behind him.

Two of Teshigahara's office walls were all glass: through them was an expansive view of the bay and the Golden Gate. The wall through which he'd entered was fronted by a series of cherry-wood cabinets; behind their closed doors, Tanner knew, was a bank of television and computer monitors. In front of the last wall was Hiroshi Teshigahara's desk. Teshigahara sat behind it, immaculately dressed in black except for a white shirt. His thin, black tie was tastefully streaked with silver, nearly matching the streaks in his hair.

"Mr. Tanner," he said.

"Mr. Teshigahara." Always so damn formal, Tanner thought.

Teshigahara stood and walked to the largest of the windows, facing north. Tanner joined him, gazing out through the glass. Almost directly ahead, out in the bay, the bright lights of the casinos on Alcatraz pulsed in the night, their reflections flashing off the choppy waters around the island. The Golden Gate Bridge, intact once again, was a beautiful lattice of amber and crimson lights spanning the entrance of the bay.

"My friends in New Hong Kong would like me to express their appreciation for the shipment of swiftlet nests." He turned to look at Tanner. "They believe the vital qualities of bird's-nest soup are of even more value in the orbitals than on Earth."

"What do *you* believe?" Tanner asked.

Teshigahara smiled, shrugged, then said, "They are Chinese." He turned back to the view. "The nights are quite beautiful from here," he said. "The worst of the city is hidden by darkness and distance, or given a false sheen by the lights." He paused. "You have something for me?"

Tanner took a sealed manila envelope from inside his jacket and handed it to Teshigahara. TO BE OPENED IN THE EVENT OF THE DEATH OF LOUIS JOSHUA TANNER, the label read. A hint of smile flickered across Teshigahara's lips.

"It sounds so ominous." He looked at Tanner. "Are you going to die soon?"

"I hope not."

"A precautionary measure."

"Yes."

"Some items you wish attended to if you are . . . incapacitated."

"Yes."

"Are you going somewhere?"

"Not far," Tanner said. "Into the Tenderloin."

Teshigahara moved his head slightly, a gesture of dismissal. "Its dangers are greatly exaggerated," he said. "Outsiders are not killed in the Tenderloin, at least no more frequently than in any other part of the city."

"I know," Tanner replied. "It's not the Tenderloin. I am looking for someone."

"Ah." Teshigahara nodded.

Tanner half expected an offer of help, but Teshigahara made none. Instead, the small man crossed the room and laid the envelope on the desk before turning back to Tanner.

"When you have completed your task," Teshigahara said, "my friends in New Hong Kong will want to resume making use of your services."

"I'll let you know."

Teshigahara nodded once more, than said, "Good-bye, Mr. Tanner."

No offer of help, no wishes of good luck.

"Good-bye."

The wall swung open. Tanner walked through, glanced at the metal-faced woman, then headed for the elevator. Once again he thought he heard hissing come from the woman, but this time he did not pause, he did not look around. The elevator doors were open. Tanner entered, the doors closed, and he descended.

Chinatown. It was a long trip to the other end of the Corridor, where it abutted the east wall of the Tenderloin, and Tanner hired a scooter. The driver was a skinny old man around seventy or eighty, with long white hair braided down to his waist. He wore black leather jacket and pants, and black leather boots with clear thermoplast heels that sparked a bright blue and crimson pattern in the night.

As he rode through the Corridor, bouncing roughly on the back of the scooter, Tanner thought of Teshigahara's observation on the view from his office. Down in the streets a lot less was hidden. Flashing neon and sputtering amber lights lit the teeming crowds and street soldiers, illuminated the scarred edges of skin and fabric, cast pulsing and shifting shadows into the alcoves and gutters. They passed a string of stunner arcades, jerking bodies visible through tinted glass; hovering outside the doors were packs of street-medicos waiting to pick up some business. A thrasher pack was walking their boards through the Corridor, blood leaking from a gash across the leader's forehead. The high-pitched singsong of Chinese music battled with explosive pockets of neo-industrial metal, an occasional blast of slash-and-burn, and the general clamor of human voices.

The scooter dropped him at the door of Joyce Wah's restaurant at the far end of the Corridor. Alexandra stood in the doorway, watching him. She wore an ankle-length raincoat of black swirled with opalescent red.

"I know, I'm late," Tanner said.

Alexandra smiled. "I knew you would be. I just got here a few minutes ago myself."

Inside, they were met by Tommy Lee, Joyce's partner. He scowled at Tanner, said, "I wish I could kick you out, you son of a bitch."

"Is Joyce in tonight?"

"No. Home sick. So why you don't just leave?"

"We'll eat upstairs."

Tommy turned and stalked off.

"He doesn't like you much," Alexandra observed.

Tanner smiled. "We had a disagreement a couple of years ago. If it wasn't for Joyce, he'd probably poison me."

They climbed the narrow, tilted stairs and sat at a window table with a view of the Tenderloin's eastern wall directly across the street. A young woman brought cups and a pot of tea to the table. Alexandra spent a few minutes looking through the menu while Tanner gazed across the street at the wall of buildings that formed one boundary of the Tenderloin.

There were no longer any regular street entrances into the Tenderloin. Buildings had been erected across the streets along the outer boundaries, filling the gaps so a nearly solid wall of buildings—broken only by narrow alleys—formed a rectangular perimeter, ten blocks long and eight blocks wide. The streets opened up again inside the boundaries, but you would never know that from the outside.

Lights were on in nearly all the windows, and would stay on through the night. Like the Financial District, the Tenderloin never closed down. In fact, the Tenderloin ran faster at night, like a colony organism on speed. Which was why Tanner was going in at night.

The young woman returned, took their order, and left. Tommy Lee came through the room, glared at Tanner, then headed up to the third floor.

Alexandra laughed. "My grandfather told me once about a restaurant in Chinatown where one of the major attractions was a terribly rude waiter. People actually went in order to be insulted by him."

"Poor Tommy. Born out of his time."

Tanner looked back out the window. Across the street and down a block, two large freight trucks were unloading into one of the Tenderloin's underground docks. The trucks blocked traffic, and men and women worked furiously with the stacks of crates. Horns blared, lights flashed.

"So you're going into the Tenderloin," Alexandra said.

"Yes."

"That should be fun."

Tanner smiled, still watching the trucks being unloaded across the street. "You going to stay inside, or go in and out?"

"I'll stay, at least for a few days. I'll be looking for someone."

"I know a place," Alexandra said. She waited a moment, then said, "My sister lives inside."

Tanner turned to look at her. Alexandra had a pained, distressed expression on her face. "You've never mentioned a sister," he said.

Alexandra nodded, turning away from him. She did not say anything for a minute, then finally spoke again, her voice hardly more than a whisper. "Identical twin."

Tanner did not respond. He watched the muscles in Alexandra's face and neck tighten. She sighed and nodded again.

"I don't talk about her because she doesn't want me to." Another pause. "You'll have no trouble telling us apart. Her growth hormones went skizzy on her when she was about ten. She's a foot and a half shorter than I am, and her bones have been rotting away since she was fifteen." She paused, pressed her face against the window. Rain had begun to fall, spattering the glass. "But her face is just like mine." She picked at loose slivers of wood on the windowsill.

The waitress brought their food: shrimp chow fun, war won ton soup, rice, and pot stickers. She checked the tea and quietly left.

"I've talked to her," Alexandra said. "She has an extra room, and she'll be expecting you. Here's her address." She slid a card across the table. Tanner slipped it into his shirt pocket.

"Thanks." He hesitated, reluctant to press her, but he felt he needed to know more. "So tell me," he finally said. "What's she like?"

Alexandra slowly shook her head. "Hell, that all depends on your timing, I guess."

"What do you mean?"

"She's got a lot of weird stuff going on inside her. The hormone stuff. And drugs—painkillers, mostly. And an occasional bout of depression. Most of the time she's all right, but when you get the downside of all those things hitting her at the same time, well, she can be just a miserable bitch." She paused, looking at Tanner. "But basically she's a good person, Louis. Remember that, even if she's in a foul mood."

Tanner nodded. "I will."

They ate without talking much. Water from the rain washed down the windows in sheets, distorting the lights and images on the street. The food, as always, was delicious, though relatively mild. Tanner had given up spicy food, as much as he liked it, back when he had been a cop. His digestive system had become too sensitive, easily irritated, and he had wanted to make damn sure he never developed ulcers. He had watched his mother suffer for years with them; whenever he thought of her he always pictured her mouth, lips ringed with chalky white from antacids. It had seemed strange when lung cancer killed her in the end, especially since she'd never been a smoker.

When the food was gone, they stayed and drank more tea. Tanner chewed on the fortune cookie, smiling to himself. Stale. Every time he had eaten there the last fifteen years the fortune cookies were stale. His fortune read: "Monkeys will guide your life. Feed them well." As always, it meant nothing to him. Alexandra would not read her fortune. Instead, she made a great show of chewing and then swallowing the narrow strip of paper, washing it down with tea.

"It will transubstantiate within me," she said. "Become a mutated neurotransmitter that will fire my brain to Nirvana. She smiled. "Or fry it into slag."

"You probably won't be able to tell the difference."

"Probably not." She stopped smiling and gazed at him silently for a long time. The restaurant was quiet, and the rain was loud against the window, slapping at the glass. "It's like watching myself decay," she finally said.

"Your sister?"

Alexandra nodded. He thought she was going to say more about it, but she just shrugged, shook her head. She gestured across the street, then said, "It's a funny place." Tanner nodded. "Watch yourself in there." She paused, gave him a half smile. "And say hi to my sister."

"I will."

Tanner stood on the sidewalk in the rain, gazing across the street at the light-filled wall of buildings. The dark, narrow alleys, misted with rain and shadows, appeared to be the only way through, but Tanner knew better. Trying to get in through the alleys wouldn't get you killed, but you would end up back outside in less than ten minutes, without a nickel, without half your clothes, and completely dazed and confused.

He glanced back and up at the second-floor window. Alexandra was still there, watching him. She did not wave, and neither did Tanner. He turned away, pulled his coat tighter against the rain, and started across the street.

14

SOOKIE STOOD IN front of the basement door, breathing heavily. Wasn't the same basement, but she was scared anyway. No machines here. No machines, no winged freak with metal skull and metal voice. An empty basement. Maybe.

She stepped back, leaned against cool concrete, lit a cigarette. Fingers shook. Save it, she told herself.

The ground rumbled and she turned, looked up at the street to see a Black Rhino thundering down the road. Chunks of pavement kicked loose, people scattered, and a string of Chikky Birds on roller skates moved along in its wake, dodging the new potholes and chunks of street. Smoke and streaks of sparkling blue electricity shot out from under the vehicle.

Sookie shook her head and turned back to the basement door. Just go. You want to see Mixer. Then go. Go. GO.

She crushed her cigarette, grabbed the doorknob, pulled. Dark and dust. Sookie slipped inside but didn't shut the door. Light, where was it? She fumbled along the wall, found the switch, flipped it. Nothing.

Oh, man. It's okay, you know this basement. She had known the other basement, too. Sookie stood against the wall, let her eyes adjust. There was dim light from outside, too. Eventually it was enough.

She could see the rows of empty metal shelving, the rolls of dirt and dust. And the hatch. She went back to the door, got her bearings, then closed it. Sookie moved quickly now, feeling her way along the rickety metal shelves, then dropped to her knees next to the hatch.

The hatch came up easily. A soft glow of light rose from below. Sookie dropped through, landing on the wooden platform, and let the hatch slam shut. She sat on the platform and breathed deeply. Completely underground, out of the basement, she felt safe again.

The tracks beside the platform hummed quietly, not quite silent. Picking light was green. Sookie grabbed a luge cart from the rack, checked the neutrality, then set it on the tracks. She stretched out onto it, feetfirst and belly up. Shoes into stirrups, head into the support, propped up so she could see ahead. Hands on brakes and controls. She cut the neutrality, and the cart shot forward.

Light, shadow, light, shadow—she moved quickly along the low, narrow tunnel. The tracks dipped steeply, diving deep to go below a flooded tunnel. Power downs cut her speed, stop and go, then rising as she approached the Tenderloin. A hard left, and the tracks headed away, curving back around toward Market Street.

Alone on the tracks. Alone again. Mixer. Time, all right. She needed something.

Sookie was counting the light/dark shifts after the hard left. At twenty-three she braked, coasted through another, and came to a stop exactly halfway between two lights. She neutralized the cart, scrambled to her feet, pulled the cart off the tracks.

The door was just a few feet away, small but heavy. Sookie pushed it open, squeezed through with the luge cart, and closed it tightly behind her.

Total darkness now. Warm and fresh, comforting. She wanted to just sit, smoke a cigarette, go to sleep. She moved along the passage, cut left at the first opening she felt in the wall, then quickly right. Ten more steps and she dropped to hands and knees. She found the tracks by sound, listening for the quiet hum. Cart onto the tracks, hook in, cut the neutrality. Once again she shot forward.

No lights at all this time. Speed kicked up, the tracks dipped, banked left then right then left again. No brakes. Wild ride. The tracks straightened. More speed. A circle of light ahead. Sookie closed her eyes, kept them tight as explosions of light went off, nearly blinding her even through eyelids. Then a gentle dip and she was through the gauntlet, under the barriers, and tracking smoothly into the Tenderloin.

15

HUDDLED AGAINST THE rain, Tanner crossed the street and entered Li Peng's Imperial Imports. "Herb Heaven," Freeman had always called it: racks of dried seaweed; jars of roots and seeds; packets of dried flowers and leaves; a wall of wooden drawers; shelves stocked with boxes, tins, bottles;

and a long glass display case filled with vessels of colored liquids in which swam bulbous, indefinable creatures. It was the kind of place where Lucy Chen would buy the ingredients for her horrible teas.

Li Peng, a small, wiry, gray-haired man, sat in a padded chair behind the counter, drinking tea and watching three silent, small-screen television sets. The televisions were propped on wooden crates at various heights; only one was in color, and all three were showing different broadcasts. He looked up at Tanner, but did not say anything.

Tanner approached the display case, and the swimming creatures appeared to orient themselves toward him, hovering in the colored liquids of their vessels, eyes staring. He pushed two fifties into a jar with a crude, handwritten label. The characters were all Chinese ideographs except for two words: HELP POOR.

Li Peng pushed something at the back of the case, and Tanner heard a loud click. He went to the door beside a rack of dried seaweed, opened it, and stepped through.

He stood at the foot of a long, steep staircase lit by strings of phosphor dangling from the ceiling. A steady thumping shook the right wall, punctuating a stream of muted shouts. Tanner started up.

There were no landings, no doorways at any of the floors, just numerals and geometric symbols painted in red on the concrete wall. Above the third floor the thumping and shouts faded away, and the rest of the climb was silent except for a single, loud crack somewhere between five and six.

On eight, the stairs ended at a metal door that opened into a bare corridor. Tanner walked the length of the corridor, then through another door and into a room. A tall, thin Chinese sat at a metal desk, surrounded by monitors, terminals, and keypads. He wore a bowling shirt with the name "Al" stitched onto the pocket.

"How much?" Al asked.

"Seventeen thousand, five hundred," Tanner said. He pulled the rolls of cash from his pockets and set them in front of the man. He was keeping several hundred for the street.

Al counted the money, put it away in a floor safe, then worked at one of the computers for a minute. He had Tanner look into a lighted tube for a retinal scan, then slid a keypad across the desk; Tanner keyed in an access code he had ready. Al finished things off, and another minute later reached under the desk to get Tanner's credit chip.

"Seventeen thousand five hundred," he said. "Two percent transaction fee for every withdrawal. You know where you can access it?"

Tanner nodded, took the chip, and secured it inside his shirt. Al nodded back, and Tanner crossed to the other door and went through. Another short passage, then Tanner stepped out on a large balcony overlooking the swarming, brightly lit street below. He was inside.

The Tenderloin was alive. A fine, warm mist fell, adding a lacy sheen to the lights and the snakelike movement of people, animals, and vehicles. Red, orange, and green streamers of light—the colors of the Asian Quarter—drifted through the mist, swimming in the air from one building to another, and the noise was louder even than the peak of the Chinese Corridor. Tanner could feel the energy of the Tenderloin rise from the streets, could smell the adrenaline rush of the crowds below.

He walked to the other end of the balcony and a second door leading back into the building. He opened the door, stepped through, and entered a world of shimmering lights and colored smoke, dizzying stairways and precarious balconies, steaming tables and glass reflections, and an incessant babble of voices that nearly washed out the underlying sounds of clacking cards and tiles, rattling glasses, and strains of music.

Tanner walked between two sets of jinking tables to the nearest interior balcony and looked over the railing. The swirling smoke was so thick he could not see more than two floors down. A man approached Tanner and asked if he wanted into any of the games or intimacy booths. Tanner shook his head, and the man bowed and left. Tanner located the nearest staircase—a constantly reversing double helix that shook with each of his footsteps—and descended.

He descended through warm, billowing smoke and dancing electric lights. The restaurant floor smelled thickly of curry and peanut oil. The floor below that smelled of musk and incense, and throbbed with a deep, steady bass line more felt than heard. More gaming floors followed, wild and raucous except the last, the second floor, which was quiet and hushed, the sounds from above and below silenced by huge arrays of acoustical baffles mounted on the balconies. Tanner paused, watching the serious-looking players seated at the tables, most of them wearing mirrorshades and subdued suits, most of them smoking, most of them drinking. It was all show, Tanner knew. The real players, the real games, with irrevocable stakes, were deep in the Tenderloin buildings and out of public view—high above ground level in the heart of interior mazes, or buried in below-ground bunkers.

Tanner continued to the ground floor, an open concourse ringed by trash arcades, electronics boutiques, video parlors, bars, and tea shops. He worked his way through the crowd, out open doors, and onto the streets.

The mist had ceased falling, but the warm night air was still thick with moisture. The sidewalks teemed with people, and the streets were filled with the chaotic motion of scooters, mini delivery vans, pedal carts, and jitneys. The light streamers danced in the air above him, periodically coalescing to form advertisements: JUNEBUG MICROBIOTICS—JACK INTO LIFE!; TESTOSTERONE DAYS, PREMIERING TONIGHT, CHANNEL 37B, 2:00 A.M.; CHUNG'S NIGHT SKY SECURITY—A NEW CAREER ON THE EDGE.

Tanner walked down the street, feeling the energy rush rise within him, the pump of excitement. He understood why people lived here by choice—life played out at higher levels of intensity than anywhere else in the city, and that intensity never let up, night or day. He knew how addictive that could be. Almost anything could be addictive, and Tanner often thought that everybody alive was addicted to something.

He stopped at a sheltered sidewalk cafe and sat at a table with a view of the street, just under the awning. When the waiter came he ordered coffee, wishing he could handle an espresso, but his stomach was strung tight and sensitive. He sat back to watch the people on the street.

A young woman came up to Tanner, took his hand warmly in hers, and kissed him deeply on the mouth. She sat across from him, setting her handbag on the table. She was Southeast Asian, and wore a short black dress over skintight metallic black leggings. A band of pulsing energy beads circled her neck. Three glistening blue tears were tattooed to her left cheek. Tanner had never seen her before.

"I don't know you," he said.

The woman smiled, shaking her head. "No."

"Do you know me?"

"No," she said, still smiling. "Will you buy me coffee?"

Tanner hesitated, not wanting to get into anything unexpected. It had been too long since he had spent any real time in the Tenderloin, and it would take a while to get back into the rhythm of its ways, relearn the codes and patterns of its streets. "All right," he eventually said. "But I'm not interested in buying anything else."

The woman nodded once. "Fine with me. I just want to get off my feet for a few minutes."

The waiter brought Tanner's coffee, and when the woman ordered a double espresso, Tanner smiled to himself. She did not tell him her name, nor ask him his. In fact, she did not seem to be at all interested in talking to him. She sat facing the street and Tanner watched her as she watched the people moving past. He did not think she was looking for anyone in particular, her gaze seemed too passive and relaxed. He drank his coffee slowly, his attention shifting back and forth from the woman to the street.

Rat packs in metal-strip rags sauntered past, each member with a pack color bead tied to the end of hair-loop earrings. Head tuners strolled along the sidewalk, hawking their plugs and bands. Street musicians played their instruments, sale discs dangling from their clothes. Small-time drug dealers moved among the crowds, offering what Tanner and almost everyone else on the street knew was shit so stepped on there was nearly nothing left for a buzz; but they had customers anyway, those who couldn't afford anything else, or who no longer cared. The sidewalk was so thick with people Tanner only caught occasional glimpses of the various carts and vans moving along the roadway itself.

When her espresso came, the woman took a jimsonweed stick from her purse and chewed on it between sips of her espresso. Tanner guessed the stick was also laced with ameline. She was going to get one hell of a kick soon.

She finished off the espresso, popped the rest of the stick in her mouth, and chewed on it as if it were gum. Then she grabbed her purse, stood, leaned over, and kissed him again, this time on the cheek. "Thanks, honey."

"What are the tears for?" he asked on impulse.

She gave him a sad smile. "One for every month he's been away."

He had the feeling she was quoting something—a song, perhaps. The woman turned quickly and walked off, sliding easily into the crowd.

Tanner's coffee was nearly gone, and he signaled the waiter for a refill, then returned his attention to the street. Things happen, he thought, and most of them don't mean a damn thing. He wondered if the woman meant anything.

As he drank his coffee and watched the people move past him, Tanner thought about finding Rattan. He had no real plan yet, no step-by-step procedure to follow; there *was* no rigorous procedure he could follow in this case. He just had to work his way back into the flow of the Tenderloin, reestablish some contacts, send out a few feelers, and hope.

The one thing he did know was that he would start in the Euro Quarter. Despite being half-Mongolian, Rattan would go nowhere near the Asian Quarter, and would probably stay away from the Latin, Arab, and Afram Quarters as well. Once he had gone to ground, the cops would have looked in the Euro Quarter first, but Rattan would have expected that; and it was in the Euro Quarter that he would have the best protection, the most loyalty, the best sense of security. He had been *somewhere* the last year, and Tanner felt certain it was the Euro. He sure as hell hoped Rattan was not holed up in the Core.

Tanner looked at the card Alexandra had given him. Rachel, her sister, lived in the Euro Quarter, near the edge of the Latin. That's where he should be now. But he wasn't ready just yet. He remained at the table, drinking his coffee, watching, and letting the Tenderloin wash over him.

Tanner ended the night on the outer edges of the Euro Quarter. It was nearly dawn, the coolest part of the day, when he arrived at the building where Alexandra's sister lived. Not cool, exactly, but no longer hot, and that was something. The building was a twelve-story monstrosity of scarred brick, splintered wood, and dangling, disconnected sections of a metal fire escape—anyone above the second floor would have to jump if there was a fire.

A pack of teenagers blocked the building doors, ten or twelve boys and girls wearing pressed brown shirts and red arm bands emblazoned with black swastikas. That shit never dies, Tanner thought. It was one of the few things that still surprised him whenever he saw it, though he should have known better.

He pushed his way through the pack, and they grudgingly gave way to him. He guessed he was white enough for them. Tanner wondered if it was an all-white building; and what, if anything, that said about Alexandra's sister. Rachel. Some kind of biblical name, he thought.

The lobby was dark and smelled of mold. Rotting gold foil wallpaper peeled away from dark red walls, and large sections of the carpet were worn through to the flooring. Tanner walked past a huge bank of metal mailboxes and stopped in front of the elevators. One was closed, marked with an OUT OF ORDER sign. The other was open, and a dim light burned inside, illuminating a sign that had been taped to the back wall: USE THIS ELEVATOR AND YOU'RE DEAD, MOTHERFUCKER. Rachel lived on the eleventh floor, but Tanner decided he could use the exercise.

Fifteen minutes later, breathing heavily, Tanner reached the eleventh floor and leaned against the stairwell doorframe, gazing down the long hall. He had to smile at the possibility that Rachel would not even be here. He could not imagine why he had not thought to call first. Once again he looked at the card Alexandra had given him. Yes, there was a phone number.

He walked along the hall, glancing at the room numbers, metal figures tacked to the doors. He could hear faint music, barking voices, clattering, a yowl, running water. Rachel's apartment was at the far end of the hall, and he stopped in front of the door, reading the several handwritten quotations pinned to the dark wood. "Deep in the hearts of all men is a black core that needs purification." "White, white, everywhere it was white, and all was good." "Trust not in yourself, until you know you are pure." "And then the angels rose up and destroyed them all." Tanner did not have a good feeling about Rachel.

He knocked on the door and waited. A few moments later a voice called out from within. "Who is it?"

"Louis Tanner. Alexandra said she talked to you about me."

Rachel did not answer, but Tanner heard a bolt being thrown. He expected to hear several more locks being released, so he was surprised when the door opened after the first.

Alexandra was right. Rachel's face was just like hers, except for her hair, which was shorter; but the body was not even close. Rachel stood less than five feet tall, supporting herself with a cane in her right hand. She wore a pale brown dress that reached her calves, and heavy black shoes, the right built up six or seven inches.

Rachel stared at him a moment, her eyes with a hard glitter, then backed away, swinging the door wide. "Come on in," she said, her voice a harsh growl. "I just got back from work, getting ready for sleep." Tanner stepped inside and Rachel shut the door, locking it. The front room was sparsely furnished, but immaculate and well lighted.

"Nice bunch of kids at the street entrance," he said.

Rachel shrugged. "They help keep out the impure."

Was she serious? Christ, he thought, a Purist? Did Alexandra know? Why hadn't she told him?

"You look tired," Rachel said.

"I've been up all night."

"That's pretty standard around here," she responded. "But I guess I know what you mean. You've been up all day, too, right? Out there?"

Tanner nodded.

"Come on, then, I'll show you where you'll sleep. Like I said, I'm going to bed myself."

She limped across the room, digging at the floor with her cane, and Tanner followed her to the hallway, then into the first room on the right. She flipped on the light, revealing a small room with a desk and chair and a futon. On the futon was a neat stack of folded sheets and blankets, and a pillow. "Your bed. I'll show you the rest of the place."

In the hall, she pushed open a door on the left with her cane. "Bathroom." Then, farther down, she swung her cane and banged on a closed door. "My bedroom. You stay out of it."

Tanner didn't say a thing. Rachel led the way into the last room, the kitchen, which had large windows that looked out at more buildings across the way. The gray light of the coming dawn came in through the windows, casting soft shadows across the floor.

"You can help yourself to any of the food here," Rachel said. "But don't bother looking for booze, I don't have any." With that she turned away and limped back down the hall. She opened her bedroom door, went inside without turning on a light, then slammed the door shut. This time he did hear several locks and bolts—one, two, three, four.

Tanner walked back down the hall and into his room. He sat on the futon and leaned back against the wall. He had expected to like Rachel because she was Alexandra's sister, because Alexandra had arranged this for him. Now, finding that he did not like her at all made him uncomfortable. Alexandra had warned him, but still, this was worse than he had expected, especially if she was a Purist. He wondered if he could stay here very long while he looked for Rattan. For tonight, yes, or this morning, whatever it was, get a few hours' sleep. But how much longer? Maybe he could stay out of her way, not see her much.

Not a good start, he said to himself. But at least he could sleep; he was exhausted. He undressed, turned out the light, and lay on the futon, not bothering to set up the sheets or blankets. Tanner closed his eyes and slept.

16

TANNER WOKE TO the strong aroma of coffee. He looked at his
watch, saw that it was just after noon. Through the open door he could hear
trickling water, footsteps creaking wood, and generalized city sounds filter-
ing in through open windows. He had slept deeply, without any dreams that
he could remember, and he felt rested.

Tanner showered, finishing off with cold water to cut through the heat
of the day. He dressed, the sweat already dripping under his arms, then
walked down to the end of the hall.

The kitchen was empty. It had a different feel now, light and open. All
the windows were open wide, letting in the damp heat and the city sounds.
The kitchen table was set for two, including a filter-pitcher of clear water.
On the counter was a coffee maker, the pot full and steaming. Next to the
coffee, laid out on a cutting board, were eggs, chopped onions and tomatoes, and a pile of grated cheese.

"Good morning," Rachel's head appeared outside the window above
the sink. She was smiling. "Come on out," she said. She gestured to his left.
"Around the corner's a door."

Tanner skirted the table, squeezed past the bulky fridge and around the
corner to an open door leading out to a wooden platform built onto the
walls of the building. An awning of clear plastic sheltered the platform, letting through light but, presumably, keeping off the rain. The platform was
covered with potted plants, most blossoming with large, colorful flowers.
Rachel, barefoot and dressed in a loose sarong, moved among the plants
with a pink watering can, poking at the dirt with her fingers. Tanner was
stunned by the bright, lush, unbroken green of the leaves—no brown
streaks or spots, no holes eaten away by the rain.

Rachel set down the watering can and sat on a bench against the wall.
Her arms and face glistened with sweat. "Have a seat," she said.

Tanner sat beside her. She bent forward to massage her right leg, moving from thigh to calf and back.

"You like eggs?" she asked. "Cheese, onions, tomatoes?" She turned to
him and smiled. "A shot or two of Tabasco?"

"Sure. If you'll hold the Tabasco."

"Great, I'll make us an omelet. Coffee's already done, or I could find
some tea if you prefer."

"No, coffee's fine, thanks."

She released her leg, stretched her back. "Come on, then."

They went back inside, Rachel's limp more pronounced without the built-up shoes. Now Tanner noticed the six-inch blocks fixed to the floor in front of the stove, counter, and sink. Rachel gathered up the food on the counter and carried it to the stove. With her right foot on the block, she started the omelet.

"Anything I can do?" Tanner asked.

"How about pouring us some coffee?"

There were two glass mugs next to the coffee maker, and Tanner filled them, brought one to Rachel at the stove, then sat at the table with his.

The coffee was hot and strong, and he drank it slowly as he watched her cook. Soon the smell of frying butter joined the coffee aroma, and then she was pouring eggs into the pan with a loud sizzle. Tanner felt relaxed and almost peaceful. It seemed like such a traditional domestic scene. He thought of mornings like this spent with Valerie and Connie, either in his place or at their apartment in San Jose; usually he had done the cooking. Sour cream French toast and bacon had been his specialty and Connie's favorite. The last time had been more than a year ago, but it seemed much longer—another century, another goddamn life. Most of the time he doubted he would ever experience anything like that again. This world stinks, Tanner thought.

Rachel turned off the gas, cut the omelet in half, then brought the pan to the table and slid a half onto each plate.

"Thanks," Tanner said.

She set the pan on the table and sat across from him with a shrug. "Least I could do." She poured two glasses of water from the pitcher. "Sorry about this morning. You showed up at a bad time."

He expected her to go on, explain further, but she didn't. Instead, she opened a plastic bottle next to the pitcher, shook out three white tablets. She popped all three into her mouth and swallowed them with half a glass of water.

Tanner looked at the bottle, then at Rachel, but did not ask the question. He knew they were not vitamins, and it was none of his business.

Rachel shrugged, then gave a short laugh. "Dilaudid," she said. "Only way I can keep the edge off the pain.

Dilaudid. It reminded Tanner of McMurphy, who had been Freeman's prime snitch. McMurphy used to take Dilaudid for "headaches." Last time Tanner had seen him, the crazy son of a bitch was getting headaches three or four times a day, popping those things and dry-swallowing them. McMurphy hated needles.

They did not talk while they ate, which was fine with Tanner. The omelet was good, and he was enjoying it. He was even, for some reason, enjoying the heat. The water, too, was good, tasted clean but not sterile. He pulled the pitcher close and looked at the filter. Braun.

"It was expensive," Rachel said. "But it's worth it. I've got a large one for the plant water, too."

That explained the lush green color, the absence of dead brown streaks on the leaves. Some of the plants were visible in the windows, the deep green and bright reds, yellows, and blues taking some of the harshness out of the heat. Maybe that was why he was enjoying it.

When they were done eating, Rachel cleared off the table, poured fresh coffee, then took a set of keys from under the upper cabinets and handed it to Tanner. "How long will you be staying?" she asked.

Staying. Yes, he guessed he was. It seemed all right now. "I don't know," he said. "A few days at least. Maybe longer, if that's all right."

"However long, it doesn't matter." She paused. "You weren't too sure about it this morning, were you?"

"No." He still wasn't sure, but he felt better about it now. Again he thought she was going to explain, but again she said nothing. "That stuff taped onto your door," he said. "The quotes."

Rachel smiled, shaking her head. "I'm not a Purist, if that's what you're asking. But there are some in this building, the people who run the place. Putting that stuff on the door makes life a lot easier. And safer. They leave me alone." She shrugged. "And we all need to live somewhere, right?"

Tanner nodded. They took their coffee out onto the back platform and sat on the bench seat. Although the sun was high, the building gave them a narrow strip of shade so that only their legs and feet were exposed.

"Why are you here?" Rachel asked. "Alexandra didn't say."

"I'm looking for someone."

"Someone who's trying not to be found, I assume?" When Tanner shrugged she said, "Then you may be staying here a long time." After another pause, she asked, "You know the Tenderloin at all?"

"When I was a cop, I worked the Tenderloin."

Rachel snorted, a half laugh. "Cops don't work the Tenderloin. The Tenderloin works them."

Tanner nodded. "True enough. We did what we could."

"That's reassuring," she said, grinning. Then, "I'm sorry, I suppose that wasn't nice."

"That's all right. I understand."

"What part of the Tenderloin?"

"I started working the Asian Quarter." He could not keep the smile off his face, thinking of Nguyen Pham, his partner at the time. The guy was certifiable, the grandson of some old-timer Vietcong hotshot who had been a hero during the war. Pham was big on practical jokes that often nearly got them killed, and the one time Pham did get shot up he laughed all the way to the hospital. But Pham's sister and her husband were killed in some gang power struggle, and Pham took his two nieces back to Vietnam. Tanner had never heard from him again. Which was how he ended up with Freeman as his partner. Tanner stopped smiling.

"Then I switched to the Afram and Euro Quarters."

"Black partner?" Rachel asked.

Tanner nodded, then shrugged. "Those days are over. I'm not a cop anymore." He did not want to talk about anything else, and Rachel seemed to sense that because she did not ask him another question, did not say a word. He shifted positions and leaned his head against the windowsill, a heavy yellow blossom brushing his cheek. Tanner closed his eyes and breathed in deeply the cool, clear scent. He was in no hurry to move from this spot. He was relaxed, and it was probably going to be a long time before he felt this way again.

The teenage Nazis were still crowded around the building entrance when he left. Once again they opened a path for him, though he thought it was a different group this time. Across the street, strung out on second-floor balconies and wearing their trademark khaki jumpsuits and black headbands, half a dozen Daughters of Zion kept vigil.

Tanner spent several hours wandering through the Euro Quarter, checking out old haunts, getting the feel of the streets. He did not really feel at home—he had never felt "at home" in the Tenderloin, even after working in it for several years—but he felt comfortable. The streets were that way, which was a funny thing. People who did not know the Tenderloin thought the streets were dangerous, wild and uncontrolled, where you would get mugged or killed or mauled because they were always so crowded, jammed with people, loud, bright with flashing lights and chaos. But the streets were the safest part of the Tenderloin. Inside was the real danger—in the warrenlike mazes of rooms and corridors that wormed through so many of the buildings; in the fortified below-ground basements and tunnels; in the vast, open attics run by the gangs and co-ops. Inside, things could get bad. People disappeared. Killed, certainly. You just didn't see the bodies most of the time; except for the occasional window fliers, they didn't show up in the streets or anywhere else. There were organ runners and crematoriums here in the Tenderloin to take care of that. For now, Tanner would stay in the streets, but he knew that eventually, if he was going to find Rattan, he would have to go inside.

He had a beer at Stinky's, but Stinky had died or moved, no one was sure, and Tanner did not know the new owner—a loud, obnoxious man called Rooter who smelled a lot worse than Stinky ever had. No one in the place looked familiar, and he left.

He stopped by the Turk Street Fascination Parlor and watched the old Russian women roll pale pink rubber balls up into the machines, numbers lighting silently on the vertical displays. But Lyuda was not in, and Tanner returned to the street.

A couple of bars, hotel lobbies, Tin Tin's Video Arcade, a transformer shop, two music clubs, and Mistress Wendy's House of Pain and Shame. Nothing, nobody he knew other than several people he wanted to avoid.

Just as the early-evening rain began, Tanner caught the last seat at a sheltered snack counter. He had a plate of curried bratwurst and french fries, and a tall glass of warm lemon soda that was too sweet. He sat sideways on the stool, watching the street as he ate, but still saw no one he recognized. When he was finished, he resumed walking the streets.

He bought a couple of changes of clothes, shaving gear, vitamins, and a few other things, and a small duffel bag to carry everything, then took it back to Rachel's. He had hoped to talk to her some more, but she was gone, so he went back out into the Quarter.

Darkness was falling when Tanner passed a window display that caught his eye outside a nightclub called The Open Gate. In large blue letters was:

RED GIANT AND WHITE DWARF
Beat Poets of the Twenty-First Century
TONIGHT 10:00

There was no picture of the beat poets. White Dwarf. Max? It seemed probable, if White Dwarf was an accurate physical description. Max was a poet of sorts. And if it *was* Max, Tanner had lucked out far sooner and closer to Rattan than he had hoped. He entered the club.

It was nearly full, the stage empty and dark. The floor consisted of table-covered platforms set at various heights. Spider lights hung from the ceiling in sheets, fluttering gently with the air currents. Cocktail jazz played softly from speakers mounted in the corners.

Tanner found an empty table near the back, on one of the higher platforms, five or six feet above the stage. A waiter dressed in a deep blue floor-length coat and wearing an eye patch over the center of his forehead approached the table.

"Here for the show?" the waiter asked.

Tanner nodded.

"Two-drink minimum before they start, two drinks at the break."

"How soon does the show start?"

The waiter grinned. "Five minutes."

Tanner ordered two scotches. Then, as the waiter turned to go, Tanner asked, "What's with the patch?"

The waiter swung around, still grinning. "My third eye went blind last week." He turned back, and left.

Tanner scanned the club, searching for familiar faces. It was a strange crowd, ranging from people in their twenties to some quite old, dressed in everything from SoCal casual to metallic Asteroid Gear. But he did notice that there were no metal add-ons, no fake prosthetics. No *Faux Prosthétique* here, and probably very little anywhere in the Tenderloin.

Just behind him, against the wall and only partially hidden by shadows, a woman was on her hands and knees under a table, her face buried in a man's lap. There was no pleasure on the man's face, only a grimace of pain.

The waiter brought Tanner's drinks and took his money without a word. A minute later all the lights went out, plunging the club into darkness. The jazz cut off; the audience went silent. Spots came up, lighting the stage and revealing Red Giant and White Dwarf. Red Giant was just that, a hulking man around seven feet tall with flaming red hair and beard. Rimless mirrorshades were grafted over his eyes, and he wore a black beret. White Dwarf was indeed Max—an albino dwarf also wearing grafted mirrorshades. He sat on a stool with a set of bongo drums in his lap.

A minute or two of silence followed, then Max tapped out a brief, loud intro on the bongos, followed by more silence. A smooth, woman's voice came over the speakers.

"Red Giant and White Dwarf," the woman's voice announced. "Stars at the end of their life cycles. Beat poets of the twenty-first century, of the future and the past."

More silence. Then Max resumed on the bongos, a slow syncopated rhythm, and Red Giant began to recite. His voice boomed, resonating throughout the club. The first piece was called "White Fountains and the Death of Angels." Tanner did not understand most of it—something about the arrogance of man's ventures into space, he thought, with a lot of vague references to relativity, the space-time continuum, and various astronomical objects like black holes and white fountains. When they finished, the applause was loud, but not extreme. Red Giant and White Dwarf followed with "Dancing With a Black Hole," "The Blue Light," "You Burn Me Up, Baby, I'm a Cigarette," and several others. Red Giant did all the speaking, and Max kept the beat. After they finished "Party in My Head," they announced a break, and the lights went out again. When the spider lights came back up, the stage was empty.

Tanner took out one of his business cards—LOUIS TANNER, IMPORTS AND EXPORTS—and wrote on the back: *Max. Let's talk. Tanner.* When the waiter came by, Tanner handed the card to him.

"Will you give this to Max? I'm a friend of his."

"Max? Max who?"

"White Dwarf."

The waiter hesitated, said, "You're a friend of Max's?"

"Sort of."

The waiter grinned. "That's the only kind of friend Max has. So what'll you have?"

"Two drinks?"

"That's right."

"Make it two coffees this time."

The waiter shook his head. "No courage." He pocketed the card and moved on to the table behind Tanner. The woman was no longer on her hands and knees; now she sat next to the man, apparently asleep with her head on the table.

Tanner searched out the men's room and joined the line for the urinals. He could hear moaning and grunting from one of the stalls, and the click of vein injectors from another. A graying man all in black leather stood at the mirror carefully applying mascara. Another man, in a powder blue leisure suit, stood in the corner with his huge cock drooping out of an open zipper, but he wasn't getting any takers.

Tanner had just stepped up to one of the urinals when he felt a hand on his shoulder. He turned and look into Dobler's broken face. Most of the muscles in Dobler's face did not work anymore, so Tanner couldn't be sure, but he thought Dobler was grinning.

"Dobler," he said.

"It's been too long," Dobler said.

Not nearly long enough, Tanner thought.

"You just finish things here, Tanner. I'll be waiting for you outside." He released Tanner's shoulder and turned to the man in the leisure suit. "You goddamn faggot, you're lucky I don't go over there and bite that fucking monster off."

The man smiled, and Tanner realized the guy had no idea Dobler was capable of doing just that. Dobler growled, then turned and walked out.

When Tanner came out of the men's room, Dobler was waiting in the hall, his face worked into something resembling intense concentration.

"I heard you ain't a cop no more," Dobler said.

"That's right."

"Your partner gets it, and you gets out."

Tanner didn't reply. He considered just walking away, but he knew Dobler wouldn't let it go like that.

"I'm sorry Freeman got killed before I had a chance to do his face the way he done mine," Dobler said. He leaned forward, bringing his face to within an inch or two of Tanner's. His breath was warm and foul. "If I'd got to that damn nigger, it would've looked a lot worse than this." He pulled back a little. "Maybe I'll do *your* face since I can't do his." Something close to a smile worked its way onto his lips. "You think about that, Tanner. Think about *your* face." The smile twisted, then Dobler marched down the hall and out the rear exit.

Tanner returned to his table. The waiter was sitting in the second chair, sipping one of the coffees.

"You on a break or what?" Tanner asked.

"Max says he'll meet you after the show. Wait for him at this table." The waiter finished off the coffee and stood. "You let me know if you need a refill." He held out his hand, palm up. Tanner paid him, and he left.

Tanner sat and looked at the remaining coffee, thinking about Dobler. Just what he needed, something else to worry about. Dobler probably wouldn't do anything, but you never knew with that lunatic. Tanner drank from the coffee, grimacing as it hit his stomach. He didn't need the coffee, either. The lights went out, the spots came up, and the second act began.

17

MIXER WASN'T HOME. Sookie climbed into his place through the bathroom window, almost falling headfirst into the toilet. Her arm went in to the elbow, and she bumped her head on the rim of the bowl. After drying off, she wandered around the rooms for a while, checking for signs of new girlfriends, but she didn't see any. Looked like Mixer was alone again.

She left, out the way she came in, and caught a ride with a transplant man. She unhooked around the corner from The Open Gate, the nightclub Mixer ran. But he wasn't at the club, either.

Sookie sat in Mixer's office, face pressed against the one-way glass. She shivered, seeing the stage below her. Max and Uwe were performing. She didn't like either one of them, Max especially. She'd seen them do some things. Torch a pair of mating dogs. Torch each other. Do four-way foamers for a private audience of mondo pervs. And she'd heard a lot worse.

She looked around at the audience. Faces were hard to see except the ones close to the stage. Winnie and Rice were here, but it looked like they were mad at each other again—Rice was wearing ear cones focused on the stage so he could hear the show while blocking out Winnie's voice; and Winnie was wearing polarized blinders. So what's new, Sookie thought, smiling to herself.

Near the back, alone at a table—something familiar about that guy. Sookie shifted her position, cutting out some of the reflective glare. It looked like the man on the balcony that day, when the bodies were dragged out of the water. He'd been watching her. She'd waved goof signals at him. Was it the same guy? She couldn't be sure.

Sookie slid open the one-way glass and carefully crawled out onto the strings of dark spider lights. The webbed strings sagged under her weight, and she froze a moment. If she got any bigger she wasn't going to be able to do this.

The swaying stopped, she started forward. The sag and sway resumed immediately, but there was nothing she could do about it. Hope. Move slow and careful. She smiled, imagining the strings breaking, herself swinging down and crashing into the tables and people below. It wasn't that far, she wouldn't get hurt. Or not much. Scare the noodles out of some people. Get Max and Uwe mad at her. Oh, maybe not such a good idea.

It was slow going, but Sookie was having fun. The spider light strings were like a circus safety net, but with bigger holes. She could slip through if she wasn't careful. That was part of the fun.

She was two-thirds of the way across the club when she spotted Froggle directly beneath her. Sookie almost burst out laughing at the crazy head mask he was wearing. Then, looking more closely, she realized it wasn't a mask. A square patch of his hair and skull was gone, replaced by a metal panel with knobs and sockets, glowing lights. Over the sounds of Max and Uwe she could just hear an electronic buzz coming from the panel; Froggle's head twitched, tiny vibrations going through him. Feeling queasy, Sookie looked away and moved on.

A few minutes later she was almost directly above the man, in front enough to see his face. It *was* the man on the balcony. She wondered if he remembered her.

Sookie felt among the strings until she found the links, then unhooked several so a section of the lights swung down, dangling like a rope ladder. Halfway to the table. She clambered down. Legs dangling free, down a few more strings to the end of the section, hanging by her hands. Shoes only two or three feet above the table. Looking down between her arms, she could see the man looking up at her. Sookie let go the lights, and dropped.

18

THE GIRL CRASHED to the table from above and the coffee cups went flying. Tanner put out his hands to keep her from sprawling to the floor. Red Giant and White Dwarf continued without pause. The girl smiled at him, and scrambled off the table. She picked up the two coffee cups, both amazingly unbroken, set them on the table, then sat in the other chair and stared at Tanner.

It was the girl from the junkyard across the slough. A pang went through him, that sense of painful familiarity again. This time it did not fade. Instead, the pain grew, and he felt close to recognizing the source, but it still eluded him. He felt flush, and a sweat broke out under his arms. What *was* this?

"Do you remember me?" the girl asked, voice barely above a whisper.

More than you know, Tanner thought. More than *I* know yet. He nodded.

"It wasn't a movie, was it?" the girl asked.

"What?"

"That day. They weren't making a movie, were they? Those bodies, they were real."

The brief images came back to him, the two dead white bodies being pulled from the slough. "The bodies were real," he said.

The girl nodded. She glanced at the stage, then turned back to Tanner, but did not say any more.

"What's your name?" Tanner asked.

She started to say something, stopped, then started again. "Sookie," she said. "What's yours?"

"Tanner."

She glanced at the stage again, then grimaced at Tanner. "You like this kind of stuff?"

"It's all right."

"They're sleazebugs."

"Red Giant and White Dwarf?"

"Max and Uwe, yeah."

"You know them?"

"I know who they are." She turned her chair so she could watch the show, and that did it.

Carla.

The pain blossomed again, expanding in his chest. It was Sookie's profile that made the final connection. She looked just like a thirteen- or fourteen-year-old Carla. Jesus.

He had not known Carla at that age, but she had given him pictures—photos of her as a baby, a young kid, a teenager. He still had them, along with dozens of pictures of her taken during their few years together. He had not looked at any of them in a long time. Christ, she had been dead almost fifteen years now.

Tanner turned away from Sookie; he just could not keep looking at her. Carla. Jesus. Twenty-six and dead. He picked up one of the empty coffee cups, wishing he had a double scotch right now. Twenty-six and . . .

He tried to concentrate on the stage. Max was frantically pounding at the bongos, and Red Giant was grunting explosively between unintelligible words. The pounding and grunting crescendoed, then ceased abruptly. Red Giant raised his arms, shouted, "Devolution of the species!" and the lights went out.

Applause filled the club. It faded gradually as the spider lights slowly came back up, revealing an empty stage. Cocktail jazz began playing once again over the speakers.

"That's their closer," Sookie said. "Show's over." She turned the chair around to face him. "So where you going now?"

It took Tanner a few moments to realize she had asked a question. "Nowhere," he said.

Sookie grinned. "*Everybody's* going nowhere. That's what Mixer says, and I think he's right."

Carla.

"Who's Mixer?" he asked.

"A friend. So where?"

Where the hell *was* he going? Staring at her, he had to force himself to concentrate on the reasons he was here. Rattan, the Chain Killer. Max. "I'm staying right here," he finally said. "Waiting to talk to Max."

"Max? He's coming here?" She sprang to her feet, looking around the club. Max wasn't in sight. "He's not a good person."

"I know that."

"He's the worst, you should stay away from him." She kept looking around the club. Max came out from the back of the stage and headed for Tanner's table. "Oh no, here he comes." Sookie grabbed her chair, lifted it onto the table, and clambered up beside it.

"What are you doing?" Tanner asked.

"I'm getting *out* of here." She climbed onto the chair and stood, crouching slightly, hands stretched upward.

"Wait, why don't you just . . . ?"

Sookie jumped, caught the hanging panel of lights. Tanner heard something tear, and thought the whole thing was going to come down. But the lights held, Sookie swinging back and forth. Tanner thought of Carla again, the ache rising in his chest. "Bye," Sookie called down. She hooked a leg onto the panel, pulled herself up, and climbed. When she reached the main web of lights, she started crawling along them. He soon lost sight of her behind the glare, but he could follow her progress by the sag and sway of the lights. She was halfway across the club when Max reached the table.

"Who the hell was that?" Max asked.

"I don't know."

Max watched the movement of the lights for another minute, then turned his gaze toward Tanner. Tanner could not see Max's eyes through the grafted mirrorshades; all he could see was his own reduced and distorted reflection duplicated, one in each lens. Max took the chair down from the table, brushed off the seat, and sat in it. Sookie was right, of course. Max was *not* a good person. One hell of an understatement. But he was the way to Rattan.

Neither of them said anything. The club slowly emptied, and a crew came out on stage, setting up electrical equipment: microphones, floor lights, wrack boxes, and other things Tanner did not recognize. The waiter appeared with a large scotch for Tanner and a stein of beer for Max. The waiter's eye patch was gone, revealing a metal and glass eye embedded in his forehead. The glass was clouded, and *did* look blind.

"On the house," the waiter said, and immediately left.

Max drank half his beer, belched long and loud, then drained the other half and belched twice more. He sat back in the chair and stared at Tanner without a word, waiting.

"I need to talk to Rattan," Tanner finally said.

Another long silence followed. Tanner did not like being unable to see Max's eyes.

"I'm not a cop anymore," Tanner said.

Max snorted. "I know that."

"I don't expect you to take me to him. Just let him know I'm looking for him. It's an old matter, and all I want to do is talk. He *will* want to talk to me, Max." He paused. "Tell him it concerns angel wings."

Max did not respond. Tanner sipped at his scotch, resisting the urge to down it all at once. Max wasn't a hell of a lot more predictable or stable than Dobler. And he was far more dangerous.

Max turned away from him and watched the crew at work on the stage. "You're fucking crazy, Tanner, you know that?"

"Will you talk to him?"

Max turned back. "Got a pen?"

Tanner gave him his pen, and Max wrote on the back of the beer coaster. He slid the pen and coaster across the table.

"Tomorrow night, at exactly the time and place written there, you show up. Follow the damn instructions. You won't be talking to Rattan, but I'll be there to let you know if it's possible."

Tanner pocketed the pen and coaster. "Fair enough."

Max shook his head and stood. "Tomorrow, then." He walked down to the stage, around it, and through the back door.

Carla. He could not stop thinking about her now. Tanner finished his drink, then got up to leave. A bar, he thought, a real bar. That's what he needed now. He headed for the street.

Tanner was drunk, and it wasn't helping. Why am I doing this? he asked himself. It wasn't making him feel any better, and it wasn't making him forget. Hell, he wasn't really sure he *wanted* to forget.

He was in a drinker's bar—no glowing ferns, no doo-wop neon, no lounge show entertainment. The place was dark and quiet except for the occasional clink of glass and vague muttering. The television set above the counter was on without sound, showing an old black-and-white sports movie. Taped to the corner juke was a sign: PLAY THIS ON PENALTY OF DEATH. A recurring theme, he thought. And the place was full. Every seat at the bar was taken, and most of the tables and booths were occupied. Tanner was sitting at the bar between a bald old man who stank and a middle-aged woman wearing lederhosen. He had not spoken to either one.

The bartender came by and looked into Tanner's eyes. "Another," he said. Statement, not question. Tanner nodded, and the bartender refilled his glass.

Tanner looked down at the scotch, but wasn't sure if he could drink any more. Carla. Carla never drank, but she had no problem putting anything else into her body: pills, needles, smoke, inhalers, injectors. Whenever he was with her, Tanner had felt helpless, unable to do anything except watch her, try to keep her from lurching in front of cars, crashing through plate glass, or taking a header down a flight of stairs.

And then the day came when she pumped too much of the shit into herself and stopped her own heart. Dead. Twenty-six and dead. Accident or deliberate, he never knew. It was, he came to believe, an irrelevant distinction. She was fucked up, and she was dead.

That was why he had become a cop, and why he had gone into Narcotics. A personal crusade, save the world, save people like Carla from themselves. What a dumbfuck. It had not taken long for him to realize the absurdity and hopelessness of it. But it had taken years of swimming in the shit, and Freeman's death, to finally give it up.

But Carla. Late morning, early afternoon, that had been the best time. After she worked through her hangover but before she started in again. Her eyes clear and smile bright, her laughter clean and real. Her skin warm and firm, with color. Her tongue and lips delicious. Her body wrapped around him, her arms and hands and thighs and breasts . . .

Christ.

The bartender came by again, looked at Tanner, and said, "Another?" This time there was some question.

Tanner looked down, saw he'd emptied his glass without realizing it, then looked back at the bartender. "I'm not unconscious yet, am I?"

The bartender refilled his glass.

Tanner woke with cotton-mouth and a clouded head. He lay on the futon in Rachel's extra room, fully clothed, with no clear memory of getting here from the bar. He thought he remembered some kind of bouncing ride, sprawled out on the back of a cart, something like that. Surprisingly, he had no headache.

He got up and wandered through the apartment. It was one in the afternoon, and the place was empty. Rachel was either gone or locked in her bedroom.

Tanner shaved and showered and put on clean clothes. In the kitchen he ate two pieces of dry toast while making coffee. The heat was oppressive, the humidity so high there was a sheen of moisture on his arms and face. Breathing was like being in a sauna.

When the coffee was done he poured a cup and took it out onto the platform and sat on the bench. The narrow strip of shade wasn't any comfort. He drank the coffee steadily, not really thinking about anything. In the window across the way he could see two naked women dancing together, holding each other tightly. Street sounds, floating down from over the building, were muted.

He finished the coffee, went back inside for another cup, then returned to the bench. The women were still dancing. His head felt clearer now and he let himself think about the night before. Stupid, he told himself. Get completely drunk like that in the Tenderloin. And for what? It didn't change anything. All that was over, years ago. Fifteen years. She was dead. She was dead yesterday, and she would still be dead tomorrow. Nothing new.

Tanner set down the coffee, put his head in his hands, and quietly wept.

19

TANNER DID NOT like the feel of the place. He stood at the end of a long, windowless corridor of concrete. Pale blue fluorescents hummed and flickered overhead. The door behind him, solid metal, had locked automatically when he closed it, so there was no way back.

Just after midnight, as instructed, Tanner had entered the Dutch East India Company, a store specializing in exotic electronic imports: head juicers, spastic vibrators, mind tuners, orgone generators, spitzers, spinal frequencers, bone boomers. The sales clerk, wearing electronic wrist and neck collars, led Tanner through the back rooms, then pointed him to the door, which was now locked behind him. Nothing else to do, he thought. He moved forward.

His footsteps echoed off the concrete walls. There were no doors, nothing to break the surface of the walls except an occasional featureless panel of shiny metal. No one appeared, and he could hear nothing but the hum of the lights and the echoes of his own footsteps.

At the end of the corridor was a narrow opening in the left wall. Tanner stepped through it into a tiny cubicle as featureless as the corridor. A metal panel slid across the opening, slamming tightly shut. He tried pushing and pulling at it, though he knew it would not open. Nothing. Tanner stood and waited.

The he heard the quiet hiss of gas. He looked down and saw the faint signs of air movement—eddying dust—near tiny vents, though the gas itself was invisible. He did not move. His lungs quit working for a few moments, connections broken. He wanted to shout at Max that he was being absurd and melodramatic. He also wanted to bang and kick at the door. He fought down both urges. Breath came finally, halting, then regular, taking the odorless gas into his lungs. There was nothing he could do, except hope that the gas was meant to put him to sleep, not death.

A few more deep breaths, struggling for calm. Tanner sat on the floor and waited, wanting nothing more now than to awaken from sleep one more time.

And he did awaken. Tied to a chair. The glare and heat of the sun in his face. Max seated in another chair a few feet away, mirrorshades brightly reflecting the light.

"Good morning," Max said.

Tanner turned his head from the glare, blinking rapidly. They had him next to the window, directly in the sunlight. Eyes turned away from it, his vision adjusted and he could see the rest of his surroundings. The room was small and unfurnished; Red Giant stood in the middle of the room, head and upper body in shadow, mirrorshades directed at Tanner. He did not say a word. Tanner had the feeling the duo's roles were now reversed—here, Red Giant would remain silent, and Max would do all the talking.

Tanner looked back at Max. He had to keep his eyes partly closed against the glare. "Why are you doing this?" he asked. He tried to keep his voice calm and even.

"Questions," Max said. "And then I may kill you."

"Did you talk to Rattan? He'll want to talk to me, Max, he'll want to hear this."

Max nodded slowly. "I imagine he would."

"Did you *talk* to him, for Christ's sake?"

Max snorted. "If I ever do talk to him again, one of us will be dead by the end of the conversation."

Jesus Christ, Tanner thought, have I ever fucked up.

Max cocked his head. "You really didn't know, did you?"

Tanner shook his head. "I still don't."

Max grinned. "We had a parting of the ways. A difference of opinion. A contretemps." He paused, leaning forward. "I tried to kill the motherfucker, and I missed, and he knows." Max leaned back. "Now, what I want to know is what you, and the cops, and Rattan have going."

"Christ, Max. I told you I wasn't a cop anymore. You said you knew."

"And I still know, but that doesn't mean shit. You and Rattan and the cops are running something, and I want to know what it is."

"I don't know what you're talking about, Max, believe me." He *didn't*, but he began to wonder about it. "What I need to talk to Rattan about, it's old business. It's personal, it's got nothing to do with cops."

Max slowly shook his head. "You don't get it, do you, Tanner?" Max leaned forward again. "I *will* kill you. I got no problem with that."

Tanner breathed in deeply, and slowly let it out. "I get it, Max. But I don't know a thing about it. Christ, Rattan killed two cops, they aren't going to have anything to do with him."

Max erupted from the chair and lunged forward, but stopped with his face just a few inches from Tanner's. "I don't want to hear that kind of shit, motherfucker!" He straightened and turned to Red Giant. "Bring her in."

Red Giant left the room. Christ, now what? Tanner thought. He was having trouble breathing again, and it wasn't because of the ropes. He wished he *did* have something to tell Max. "Not a good person," Sookie had said. No shit. How the hell was he going to convince Max he didn't know anything?

Max paced the room, not talking. Tanner wanted to say something, try to get Max to understand, but he could not think of a thing to say that wasn't just as likely to make things worse. Try telling him about the Chain Killer, Rattan's three-year-old message? Shit. He closed his eyes and waited.

The door opened and closed. Tanner opened his eyes and turned to see Red Giant leading a woman across the room. Tanner did not know who she was. She was gagged, her hands bound behind her back. Strands of her blond hair were plastered to the sweat on her face. She looked strong, but she hung limply in Red Giant's grip, and her eyes were dead with despair. She had given up, and seeing Tanner did not, apparently, give her renewed hope.

Red Giant pushed her into the chair Max had been using and tied her to it. Max turned his gaze to Tanner.

"*She's* looking for Rattan, too," Max said. "And not for the killings. She's a cop, the two of you are both looking for Rattan, and you tell me there's nothing going on."

There probably *was* something going on, Tanner thought, but he had no idea what it was.

"For Christ's sake," Tanner said, "I don't even know her."

Max went crazy again, stomping across the floor, shoving his face into Tanner's. "What *is* this shit from you?" He dug a wad of paper from his back pocket. "And what is *this*?" He unwadded the paper and held it in front of Tanner's face. It was the note Lucy Chen had given him with Francie Miller's name and address. "You don't fucking know her?"

Jesus, this was Francie Miller? Man, they were both in deep, deep shit. He looked at the woman, who gazed emptily back at him. "No," Tanner said. "I don't know her. I've never seen her before. It was just a name someone gave me, said she could help out if I got into trouble."

Max slowly shook his head, crumpling the paper and dropping it to the floor. "Well, Tanner, you're in trouble, but I don't think she's going to be much help." He backed away and looked at Red Giant. "Hand it."

Red Giant withdrew a knife from a sheath strapped to his belt and handed it to Max. Max took the knife, approached Francie Miller, and put the tip of the blade against her throat. She blinked once, and her eyes widened, coming back to life. But with fear. Max looked back at Tanner. "I am not fucking around here, Tanner. And I want some answers."

Before Tanner could say a thing, Max jammed the knife deep into Francie Miller's throat. Blood gushed, Francie lurched violently backward as Max let go and retreated, leaving the knife in her throat. She hit the ground, her legs kicked, her body jerked spasmodically for several moments, and Tanner could see the blood running and spattering across the floor, the knife flipping free.

Jesus.

He was a dead man.

He didn't have much time. A minute, maybe two. He opened up and shut down, letting pictures and thoughts click through his mind. Knife on the floor. No. Legs and feet. Blood. The window. How high above the street? Didn't matter. Max standing over the woman, watching the final spasms. Lower legs free enough? Only a foot from the window, it was low, wouldn't take much. Try not to land headfirst on the street. Now or die, man. Go.

Tanner leaned forward, lifting the chair from the floor. He dropped slightly, then lunged sideways at the window, closing his eyes. Glass shattered, hip hit the sill, he fell outward, through the glass, glass slicing skin, then out the window. He hit metal immediately, twisted, bumped, started down, then jolted to a stop. He opened his eyes.

Tanner was three floors above the street, upside down. A leg of the chair was caught in the tangled remnants of a fire escape. He glanced at the shattered window just a few feet above him, waiting to see Max's face. Jesus.

He shook himself, rocked and jolted, side to side, up and down. Harder. The chair leg cracked, then finally broke, and he dropped.

Tanner tried to twist himself as he fell, legs kicking. He hit the street hard on his side, a wall of pain jolting through him. A burst of silver glitter, then he couldn't see anything at all for a few moments. The darkness cleared away, and he saw people standing over him. He wanted to pass out, but he was afraid to. If he passed out now, he would probably die; Max would find him and he would die. He didn't know if he could even free himself from the rope and chair. The pain was a pounding vibration jamming through him, like bone boomers strapped all over his body. He wanted Rachel's Dilaudid.

Then Sookie's face appeared above him, and she dropped to her knees. There was a man with her, a gaunt spikehead with clear, bright wide eyes. The spikes of twisted skin seemed to move across his forehead.

"I told you to stay away from him," Sookie said.

Tanner tried to speak, but couldn't get anything out.

"We've got to get him the hell out of here *now*," the spikehead said.

"We'll take care of you," Sookie told him. "Don't worry."

For some reason Tanner found her voice completely reassuring. When he felt their hands on him, he closed his eyes and let himself slip away.

20

SOOKIE LOOKED UP, saw Max's face in the shattered window. Mirrorshades. Who knew what he was seeing?

"Come on!" Mixer said.

Sookie and Mixer grabbed Tanner's arms and shoulders and lifted.

"Don't move him," someone in the crowd said. "You know, in case of spinal—"

"Shut the fuck up!" Mixer said. Then, to Sookie, "Let's move it."

They half carried, half dragged Tanner, pieces of rope and broken chair still hanging from him. Sookie watched his face, his closed eyes. It had to hurt.

They pushed through the crowd, around a corner. Mixer let go, and Sookie fell with all the weight. Mixer jumped a pedal cart going by, jamming it to a stop, almost knocking the driver off.

Sookie was back on her feet by the time Mixer got the cart backed up, and they loaded Tanner into the storage well. Sookie stayed with him while Mixer hung on behind the driver. "Go!" he yelled.

The driver swore and pumped, and the cart moved slowly forward. Too slow, Sookie thought, looking back. She didn't see Max or Uwe, but she was sure they were coming. Anyone else following? Hard to tell.

The cart picked up speed. Mixer yelled in the driver's ear, and the driver whacked Mixer on the side of the head. The driver was a stocky woman with short hair and a necklace tattooed around her neck. She kept calling Mixer names, and he kept shouting directions at her. Sookie couldn't keep up with it all, but it seemed that the driver was following Mixer's instructions, zigzagging from one street to another.

They turned a corner, and Mixer had the driver stop. Mixer and Sookie pulled Tanner off the cart, dragging him against the wall. Mixer glared at the driver and pointed down the street. "Keep going, bitch!"

The woman nodded. "You owe me for this, you goddamn spikehead. I know your face." She pushed off, gaining speed more quickly now.

Mixer unlocked a metal door, pushed it open, and they dragged Tanner through. Mixer jammed the door shut, cutting off all light.

"All right," Mixer said. "We're safe for now. No way they'll find us here."

"Where we going to take him?" Sookie asked. She couldn't see Mixer in the dark, but she could smell him—something like sweat and sawdust. Tanner smelled like pain. She held on to one of his hands. "It's a good thing we followed him," she said.

"I know a place." Mixer laughed. "I know a lot of places." He lit a cigarette, and the match light showed a small passage empty except for the three of them. Mixer blew out the match; his cigarette glowed. "Let me think a minute." The glow moved back and forth in the darkness, as if he were shaking his head. "Every time you show up, Sookie, something like this happens."

"My life is too weird," she said.

Mixer laughed again. "Yeah, no shit. But wait'll you grow up. It's only going to get weirder."

"Great." She sat on the floor beside Tanner and waited for Mixer to make a decision.

21

TANNER CAME TO in a narrow, windowless room. He lay on a cot, surrounded by concrete walls, a lamp at his head, a tiny fan whirring in the far corner. The door was closed, the air stifling despite the fan.

He remembered waking several times, disoriented from dull pain and drugs. He remembered fluids trickled into his mouth; he remembered being walked down a hall to a toilet. Someone had been keeping him sedated. He didn't know if that was good or bad.

Tanner sat up slowly, a little woozy but otherwise feeling all right. He was wearing a pair of light cotton pants, but nothing else. His left wrist was heavily taped and in the dim light from the lamp he could see dark, yellowing bruises on his arms and chest, particularly on his left side; also a number of cuts that seemed to be healing. Overall, though, he did not appear to be too badly hurt. Everything except his wrist moved freely and without much pain.

There was a plastic pitcher of water next to the lamp, and Tanner, looking at it, realized how thirsty he was; his mouth was dry, yet gummy. He drank deeply from the pitcher, and the water went to his head, almost like alcohol. He had to lean back against the wall to keep from losing his balance. He drank some more, then set down the pitcher.

He rose to his feet, took the five steps to the door, and tried the handle. Locked. Had Max got hold of him? Tanner did not think so. He thought he remembered seeing Sookie during his brief conscious periods, and the spikehead who had been with her. Also some other guy, a thin unshaven man, gaunt face bent over him. Who the hell was that?

Tanner looked around the tiny room. Nothing but the cot, the lamp, the water, the fan. No clothes. No money, no credit chip. And no way out. He banged on the door a few times, but got no response. He would have to just sit and wait. That was all right. Waiting was bearable, it was something he had learned to do—wait without going crazy. He could do it again.

He spent some time pacing the room, then did some stretching, working through the pain in his muscles. He sat on the cot, breathing heavily. The pacing had tired him, but the muscle pain felt good. He sat with his back against the cool concrete wall, waiting and thinking. He thought a lot about Francie Miller. He tried not to, but the images kept returning—Max driving the knife into her throat; blood; Francie arching violently, chair driven back and over; Francie jerking spasmodically on the floor; blood again; the knife flipping free; Max's shaded eyes.

When no one appeared after an hour or so, Tanner lay out on the cot and slept.

He dreamed of Freeman again: the hot, dark hallway; the fat man with the smell of tuna; the gun at Freeman's face, the explosion of blood and flesh and bone. This time, though, as Tanner ran down the hall, before the second gunshot, he tripped over Francie Miller's body. He tumbled to the floor, somehow twisting around so his face was looking into hers, staring at the knife still embedded in her throat. Her eyes stared back at him.

Then he awakened.

A junkie stood over him, staring into Tanner's face. Tanner could see needle marks in the guy's neck. A gaunt, unshaven face, glittering eyes. The face he had seen before.

"I'm your doctor," the junkie said. He grinned, retreating a couple of steps.

Tanner lay without moving for a minute, watching the junkie, who continued to grin. Tanner slowly sat up, saw a medical kit on the floor beside the cot, and realized the junkie was serious.

"I'm a hell of a doctor when I'm not strung out or just shot," the junkie said. He shrugged. "I fixed you up, and you're going to be fine." Another shrug, then he put out his hand. "My name's Leo."

Tanner did not shake Leo's hand. "Why have you been sedating me?" he asked.

Leo dropped his hand. "To keep you quiet. This room's safe enough, but . . ." He shrugged again. "Didn't want you crying out."

"Why would I cry out?"

"Pain." Still another shrug. "Nightmares."

Tanner did not respond. He didn't remember any nightmares other than the one he'd just had, but then he didn't really remember much of anything after hitting the street.

"You have a small fracture in your left wrist," Leo said. "It doesn't need to be casted, just taped like that to keep down excess movement. Couple weeks should do it. Other than that, nothing serious. Bruises and abrasions, minor lacerations."

"I want my clothes," Tanner said.

"Mixer has them," Leo said.

"Get them."

"He's not here." Another shrug. The shrugging, Tanner thought, was like a facial tic with this guy. "He'll be back soon, half hour, something."

Tanner nodded, more to himself than to the junkie. He stood. "I've got to piss."

Leo looked at the door, then back at Tanner, but didn't say anything.

"You holding me prisoner?" Tanner asked.

"Of course not. It's just . . . I think Mixer wants to talk to you."

"The spikehead?"

Leo nodded.

"I'm coming back. Where the hell am I going to go without clothes?"

Leo laughed. "In this part of town, you could go far." He shrugged once more, then gestured at the door. "Take a right, second door on the left."

Tanner crossed the room, opened the door, and stepped out into the corridor. Sputtering fluorescent lights, spaced irregularly along the ceiling, cast a shifting, fragmented illumination. The corridor stretched into darkness in both directions as the lights gave out. Tanner was fairly certain he was underground. He went right, following the junkie's directions. The cement floor was warm under his bare feet, but the flickering lights hurt his eyes. Second door on the left. Tanner stopped, pulled open the door.

A woman sat on the toilet inside the small bathroom, trousers bunched on the floor. She looked up at him, her expression even and unalarmed.

"Sorry," Tanner said. He backed out and closed the door. She had not seemed at all embarrassed. Tanner stood against the opposite wall and waited, listening to the sounds of the corridor. A nearly inaudible hum emanated from the walls, and now that he wasn't moving he could feel a slight vibration in the floor. The hum and vibration ceased for a moment, then resumed. Tanner notice now that there was graffiti on the walls—the lettering was tiny, and not inked but etched into the concrete with acid pens. ABOVE GROUND RADIO. LOVE IS NOTHING MORE THAN BIO-HYDRAULICS. BE RIGHT BACK—GODOT.

The bathroom door opened and the woman came out. Her blouse was transparent, and Tanner found himself staring at her breasts—one was only half the size of the other, but they seemed—somehow, to match. A design job, he figured. He looked up at her face.

The woman was staring at his crotch. Only fair, he decided. She stared at it, he thought, as if she could see through the pants. Then she tipped her head up to meet his gaze.

"It's not augmented, is it?" she asked.

"No."

She shook her head slowly. "You're missing out. And so is she, whoever she is." Then she smiled, said, "Bye, Slick," and headed down the hall. Soon she was no more than a shadow moving in and out of the sputtering lights, footsteps growing faint. Then she was beyond the lights and gone.

Tanner opened the bathroom door and stepped inside. The room was brightly lit with silver-gray fluorescents, and was far cleaner than he had expected. The porcelain was white and almost shiny, the metal fixtures polished and bright. A large mirror above the sink reflected his image from the waist up. In the fluorescent light the bruises around his ribs looked worse, and he could see more of them now. A cut on his neck had opened, and a thread of dark red blood oozed slowly from it. His face didn't look too bad, though he needed a shave. Three days, he guessed.

Tanner moved to the toilet, raised the seat, and stood there, waiting. Nothing happened. He could feel the pressure of his bladder, but nothing came. Then there was a brief, sharp pain, and the stream burst forth. After the initial jolt, the pain eased, until it was nearly gone. When he was finished he felt empty, and a little dizzy. He flushed the toilet, then went to the sink and splashed cool water across his face. He stared at his reflection for a few moments, watching the water drip from his skin, then left and walked back.

Sookie and the spikehead were in the room with Leo when Tanner walked in. Sookie sat on the cot next to Tanner's clothes, his shoes on the floor at her feet. Tanner gazed at her, pain and memories of Carla surfacing once again.

He turned away and looked at the spikehead. Over his eyes, the spikehead was wearing a contraption of bamboo, something like glasses. A weave of bamboo formed eye shutters that slid back and forth on tracks across his eyes like moving cages. His forehead was studded with twenty-five or thirty crust-tipped spikes of twisted skin.

Leo approached Tanner, looked him over. "That cut'll be all right," he said, pointing at Tanner's neck. "Any blood in the urine?"

"Not that I noticed."

Leo nodded. "Good. There was a little at first. Fall like that's hard on the kidneys."

"I'm going to get dressed and leave," Tanner said.

Leo shrugged, glanced at the spikehead.

"We risked a lot saving your ass," the spikehead said. "I want to know why."

"Your name Mixer?" Tanner asked. The spikehead nodded, then Tanner said, "You risked it because you're a nice guy."

Mixer tipped his head forward, looking at Tanner through flicking shutters of bamboo. "No, I'm not. So what are you doing that's got Max after you? Got a right to know why I'm taking chances."

Tanner shook his head. "No, you don't. I didn't ask for your help."

The shutters flicked sideways; a twist formed on Mixer's lips. A smile? "You'd be dead if we hadn't."

"Maybe so. I appreciate what you did. But it's my business, and it's going to stay that way."

Sookie stood, stepped to Mixer's side. "Maybe we can help," she said. "Mixer knows the Tenderloin. He knows the runners and the grounders, and he knows . . ."

Mixer reached out and put his hand gently but firmly over Sookie's mouth. She tried to bite him and he pulled his hand away, but she did not say any more.

Tanner walked to the cot and dressed. His clothes, though torn or frayed in spots, were clean. His I.D. packet was, surprisingly, intact, but there was no money, and the credit chip was gone.

"There wasn't any money when we found you," Sookie said. "Really. We wouldn't take anything."

Tanner glanced at Leo, then turned to Mixer. "And no credit chip?"

Mixer shook his head, and they both looked at Leo. The junkie shrugged once more. "What the hell am I going to do with your credit chip? I don't have your eyes, do I?"

Mixer's bamboo shutters clicked several times. "Sell it back to the originating streetbank for two cents on the dollar."

No shrugging this time, just a set expression on the junkie's face. "I wouldn't do that."

Mixer turned to Tanner. "I believe him."

Tanner nodded. "I'm leaving."

"All right," Mixer said. "We'll show you a way out."

"I'll find my own way."

"I know a way'll bring you up outside the Tenderloin."

"What if I want to stay inside?"

"Do you?"

Tanner shook his head. "Not right now. But just get me up to the street, I can get out just fine."

"Not a good idea," Mixer responded. "You've got Max after you. Remember?"

"I have to face that sooner or later."

"Why? You coming back in?"

Now it was Tanner's turn to shrug. "I don't know. Probably."

"Fine. Then face it later. For now let's do it my way."

Tanner hesitated. There was something to be said for Mixer's thinking, and he was getting tired of arguing with the guy. "All right," he said.

Mixer started toward the door, then stopped, looking at Tanner. "Maybe Sookie's right. Maybe we *can* help you."

Tanner was going to shake his head, but stopped himself, thinking about the offer. Mixer did seem to know his way around the Tenderloin, and he and Sookie had pulled Tanner out of some deep shit. Tanner did not have to reveal much, nothing about the Chain Killer, nothing about *why* he was looking for Rattan. And, Tanner had to admit to himself, he didn't have much else at this point. In fact, he didn't have shit. But he hesitated, looking at Leo.

Leo shook his head. "I don't want anything to do with it. I'm gone." He retrieved his medical kit and left.

"I'm looking for Rattan," Tanner said.

Mixer rolled his head to the left, gaze swinging toward the ceiling. "Je*sus,* I don't even want to *know* you." He looked back at Tanner, the bamboo shutters clicking rapidly. How the *hell* did he do that? Tanner wondered. "Forget I asked you anything," Mixer said.

Tanner nodded. "Forgotten."

Mixer shook his head, dug his hand into his pocket, and pulled out several bills, then handed them to Tanner. "You'll need a few bucks to get you wherever."

Tanner took the money, pocketed it.

Mixer led the way, with Tanner next and Sookie following. The corridor was empty, and they headed left, gradually moving into a gray darkness as they moved beyond the lights. The corridor curved sharply, grew still darker. Tanner could barely make out Mixer in front of him.

Mixer stopped, slipped a plastic card into a slot, then punched a sequence of numbers into a glowing, recessed keypad. Metal slid aside, revealing a narrow, brightly lit passage, one wall metal, the other concrete. Tanner and Sookie went through, then Mixer followed, sealing the doorway behind them. Mixer took the lead again.

As they moved along the passage, Tanner thought about Mixer's question—"You coming back in?" He had to, didn't he? There was no other way to find Rattan, he knew that. But it wouldn't do anyone any good if he got killed while looking.

And he thought about Carla. Whenever they stopped or changed from one passage to another, he would turn around and look at Sookie. Every time he did, the pain twisted in his chest, building steadily. One time, as he silently stared at her, Sookie held her hands out in exasperation and blurted, "What?" He did not have an answer for her.

They shifted to a metal-walled passage with dim, sputtering lights and a ceiling so low they were forced to proceed on all fours. Tanner was wearing down, and finally he called out to Mixer and stopped. He felt dizzy, queasy, short of breath. He sat with his back against the warm metal wall and breathed deeply. Mixer squatted a few feet ahead while Sookie sat in a lotus position at Tanner's side. Mixer lit a cigarette.

"Don't," Tanner said. "Unless you want me puking all over you."

"*Jeez!*" Sookie waved at Mixer. "Put it out, *I'm* the one closest to him."

Mixer crushed the cigarette against the floor. He rocked on his haunches, the bamboo shutters gliding slowly, smoothly from side to side. "It's not much farther," he said.

They sat awhile in silence, and with each minute's rest Tanner felt stronger, though he knew it would not last long once they resumed.

"Something I want to ask," Mixer said.

Tanner looked at him.

"You're looking for Rattan, and you go to Max?"

Tanner nodded. "I didn't know. I haven't been here in a while." He paused. "It was a mistake."

Mixer snorted. "No shit. Mistakes like that find you dead."

Tanner did not reply. There was nothing to say to that.

They resumed moving, still on all fours. The sputtering lights gave the passage a surreal cast, tiny but silent explosions of light and shadow. Several minutes later the passage began to rise, angled off to one side, then ended in a wide, circular chamber. Metal rungs were bolted into the wall leading up to the ceiling a few feet above their heads.

Mixer put his plastic card into another slot, and the metal ceiling slid back, revealing more rungs leading upward. "This'll take you right up to street level," Mixer said. "There's a grille, and to the right on the wall will be a switch that'll open it."

Tanner was breathing heavily again, and sharp pain jabbed his ribs, but he figured he could make it the rest of the way. "Where do I come out?" he asked.

"Tornado Alley"

"Terrific. What time of day is it?"

"About two in the morning. Want to wait for daylight?"

Tanner shook his head. "Night's not much worse than day, really. Better, maybe. Most of them are asleep."

Mixer smiled. "The smell's worse."

Tanner nodded. The pain in his ribs had eased a bit, and he put a hand on one of the rungs. "Thanks for the help."

"Sure thing," Mixer said. "But I'd forget about looking for Rattan if I were you."

Tanner sighed, then looked at Sookie. The ache swelled in his chest again, worse in some ways than the physical pain of his bruised ribs. "Good-bye, Sookie. Thanks."

She remained silent a few moments, then looked away and said, "Bye."

Tanner turned back to the rungs and started climbing.

By the time he was a few feet above the chamber, the smell reached him. Unwashed bodies, mainly, mixed with the ammonia odor of piss and traces of alcohol and Sterno. People who hadn't bathed in weeks, or months, even years. Tornado Alley.

The stench increased as he climbed, making him queasy in the close confines of the vertical shaft. The shaft opened in front of him, elbowing horizontally for a few feet to the metal grille. Tanner crawled forward and looked out through the bars.

Tornado Alley wasn't really an alley. It was a block-long strip of empty lots on both sides of a barricaded street, lit at night by half a dozen cords of phosphor strung between surrounding buildings, and now occupied by several thousand sleeping forms. It had acquired its name a few years before when a city politician, vowing to clean it out along with other street-people havens, had said it looked as though a tornado had swept through the city, sucked up all the derelicts and homeless, then dumped them all in one place—Tornado Alley. The politician hadn't cleaned up anything, of course, and the city pretty much left Tornado Alley alone. There was no other place to put these people anyway. The city certainly was not going to find housing for them.

Tanner felt for the grille switch, pressed it, and the grille clicked ajar. He pushed it open, crawled through, and stepped down onto a tiny space of cement between two sleeping, stinking bodies, one of them snoring heavily. Tanner pushed back the grille, pressing until it clicked shut.

The stench was almost overwhelming in the heat, and he stood motionless for a minute, trying to get his bearings. During the winter Tornado Alley would be ablaze with trash-can fires, but at the peak of summer only a few small flames flickered—Sterno cooking fires. There was nothing else but body after body, most keeping a little space between themselves and the bodies around him.

Tanner worked his way through the Alley, carving out a wandering path among the sleeping bodies. The Alley was fairly quiet, silence broken only by snores, mutterings, and occasional stifled cries. Once someone clutched at his ankle, but he freed it easily—the person's grip was weak, sickly—and resumed his progress.

When he reached the boundary of the Alley, Tanner looked up and down the street, trying to decide where to go next. Finding a cab in this part of the city, this time of night, would be impossible. Walking back to his apartment was too far and too dangerous. Besides, he wasn't so sure going back to his place was a good idea—Max almost certainly could learn where he lived.

A transient hotel? Not a great idea, either. Who lived around here? The only people he could think of were Hannah and Rossi. Tanner sighed heavily. He knew they would take him in, no matter what time of night it was. But the idea depressed him. Still. It was his best option; he did not want to stay out on the streets any longer than was necessary, and it was better than sleeping in Tornado Alley.

It was a short walk, a total of three blocks to a five-story building on Larkin. Tanner pushed Hannah and Rossi's doorbell, waited a minute, then pressed again. He pressed it a third time, and Hannah's sleepy, gravelly voice came over the intercom.

"Who is it?"

"It's Tanner."

"Tanner who?"

"Hannah, it's Louis."

A pause, then, "It's three in the fucking morning."

"I need a place to drop for the night."

Another pause, then the door buzzed several times, locks and bolts thunking back. Tanner pushed the door open and stepped into the building. He climbed the stairs to the third floor, walked down the hall, and knocked on Hannah and Rossi's door.

The door opened and Hannah, wearing only a long T-shirt, stepped back to let him in. She was in her early forties, but looked older, worn out and worn down. Living with Rossi had done that to her.

"So nice to fucking see you," she said, closing the door. "You look like shit."

The front room was lit by a floor lamp. Rossi was passed out on the sofa, one leg drooped over the edge, surrounded by piles of cracker crumbs. He reeked of gin. Rossi had been a cop once, too. He hadn't quit, though. He'd been shit-canned. The force put up with a lot of drinking these days, but Rossi had gone above and beyond the call too many times. He had fucked up too many times. Tanner knew he still did.

"You can sleep with me," Hannah said. "You'll never move him off the couch."

They went into the bedroom, and Hannah immediately got into bed, her back to Tanner. In the light from the front room, Tanner undressed, then climbed into bed with his own back to Hannah's. They both shifted positions until their backs were firmly pressed together. Neither said a word. Tanner closed his eyes and fell immediately asleep.

22

TANNER WOKE TO the sounds of vomiting. Bright orange light slashed through the window blinds, ragged strips across the bed. He was alone in the room, the bed rumpled but empty beside him. He felt better than the night before, but not really rested. He lay in the late-morning heat without moving, listening to Rossi.

The vomiting sounds ceased; they were followed by the toilet flushing, then water running in the sink. A minute later Rossi stumbled out of the bathroom, came around the corner, and stopped in the bedroom doorway, grinning sickly at Tanner. He was barefoot, wearing jeans and no shirt, belly drooping over his belt, holding cigarettes and matches in his left hand. He looked even older than Hannah.

"Hey, Tanner. You haven't been screwing my wife, have you?"

Tanner did not answer. He was fairly sure Rossi wasn't serious. He sat up, wincing at the stab of pain in his ribs. "Good morning, Rossi."

Rossi coughed several times, then lit a cigarette. "You haven't been by in a while," he said.

"No."

"Maybe you should be," Rossi said.

"What?"

"Screwing my wife." He shrugged, looked out the window. "You might as well. I mean, *somebody* should be."

Jesus, Tanner thought, I don't need this now. "Is Hannah still here?"

Rossi shook his head, still looking out the window. "She went to work." He turned back to Tanner. "I'm going to take a shower."

"Can I use your phone?"

"Sure. I think Hannah's paid the bill." He turned, staggered back into the bathroom. Tanner heard a spluttering hiss of water, then a steady spray.

Tanner got up and dressed, then went out to the front room. Gin smell still hung in the air along with stale cigarette smoke. He stepped into the kitchen, hoping to see some coffee already made, but all he saw were stacks of dishes in the sink, glasses all over the counter, and half a dozen open cracker boxes. Tanner returned to the front room, sat in the stuffed chair next to the phone, and picked up the receiver.

His first call was to Carlucci. The dispatcher patched him through to Carlucci's comm unit, and he keyed in his old priority code and Rossi's phone number. He hung up and waited. Two minutes later, Carlucci called.

"Tanner?"

"Yeah."

"Figured it was you. The priority code came up blank. I'll set up a new one for you."

"We need to meet," Tanner said.

"We sure as hell do. I was hoping to hear from you sooner. Some shit's gone down in the Tenderloin you should know about."

"I probably already do, but yeah. I've been off-line for a couple of days."

"Where are you now? Inside or out?"

"Out. Rossi's place."

There was a pause, then, "How's Hannah doing?"

"All right, I guess. Surviving." Tanner looked toward the bathroom, listening to the shower sounds. Carlucci wouldn't ask about Rossi. Carlucci had no tolerance for drunks, especially if they were cops. Especially when it was Rossi.

"You know where Widgie's is?" Carlucci asked. "It's not far from you."

"Yeah, just a few blocks. Meet there?"

"Yes. An hour okay?"

"Make it two. I've got a few things to do, and I've got to get something to eat."

"Two hours, then. I'll see you."

"Right."

Tanner hung up. The shower was still going. He should call Rachel, make sure she was okay. Max must have the card with her name and address. Tanner called information, but there was no listing for Rachel, so he called Alexandra.

"This is Tanner," he said when she answered.

"About time you called."

"Why?"

"Rachel called me. Said she hadn't seen you for three days, and that an albino dwarf and a redheaded giant had come to see her, asking about you."

"Jesus. She all right?"

"Oh yeah, what were they going to do, beat up a cripple? She told them the truth, that you'd stayed a couple of days, then disappeared without a word. They took your stuff and left her alone. But I don't think it'd be a good idea to go back to her place.

"No." Images of Francie Miller surfaced, then sputtered away. At least Rachel was all right. "I'm not even going back to my own place for a while."

"You've got another problem," Alexandra said.

"What's that?"

"Connie."

"Connie?"

"Yes. She showed up in the building courtyard two days ago, waiting for you. I told her you weren't around, but she wouldn't leave. I've put her up in my place, but she won't go home until she's had a chance to talk to you."

"Christ." Tanner rubbed at his face, at the rough stubble on his cheeks.

"She's a good kid, Louis. I've spent a lot of time with her the last two days, and I really like her."

Tanner sighed. "Yeah, she is, but right now she's being a goddamn pain in the ass."

"Louis . . ."

"I know, I know." He paused, closing his eyes. "Is she there now?"

"Yes. Will you talk to her?"

"Sure."

Tanner sank back in the overstuffed chair, gazing up at the ceiling. The plaster was heavily cracked, the paint peeling away; someone had painted the cracks blue so they looked like rivers on a map.

"Hi, Louis."

"Hello, Connie." He wanted to ask her what the hell she thought she was doing, but he didn't think that would be very constructive. Instead, he waited for her to take the initiative.

"I need to talk to you, Louis." Her tone was even and self-assured, without a hint of pleading.

"Now is not a good time," Tanner said. Jesus, he thought, what an idiotic thing to say. "What I mean is, I'm in the middle of some things, I've got too much going on. Give me a couple of weeks, until I can finish things here, then I'll come down to San Jose and talk to you. Take a day, spend all the time we need together."

"Don't patronize me, Louis."

"I'm *not*, Connie. I'm in the middle of some complicated shit, and I just can't pull away from it. It's important."

"So is this. And I'm not going back until I see you. I just won't."

Tanner did not say anything, unsure of how to respond.

"Do you understand me, Louis?"

"Yes." He understood how damn stubborn she could be.

"Do you believe me?"

"Yes, Connie. I know you, *testa dura*." Hard head. What his Italian grandmother had called him when he was a kid. He heard her laugh; it was a term of affection he'd had for Connie for years. "All right. But listen, it's not a good idea for me to go back to my apartment right now, so how about we meet for dinner? Alexandra can bring you."

"Okay."

"And will you go home after we talk?"

"Yes."

"Have you talked to your mom, let her know you haven't been kidnapped or anything?"

"Of course, Louis. She doesn't know where I am, but she knows I'm okay."

"All right, why don't you put Alexandra back on, and I'll see you tonight for dinner."

"Okay. Bye."

A moment later Alexandra came back on.

"So what is it?"

"Dinner at Joyce Wah's tonight. Make it seven o'clock. I'd like you to come with her, then bring her back. It's not a good idea for her to be . . ."

"I know, Louis. We'll be there."

"All right, see you then."

"*Ciao.*"

He hung up the phone and looked back up at the ceiling. Rivers in the plaster. The shower was still going. What the hell was Rossi doing?

Tanner got up and hurried into the bathroom, afraid something had happened to Rossi. The shower curtains were wrapped completely around the big old clawfoot bathtub, and the water hissed steadily behind them. Tanner pulled open the curtain. Rossi was curled up in the bottom of the tub, fast asleep and snoring under the steady shower of lukewarm water.

Tanner reached in, turned off the water. He thought about waking Rossi, but decided it wasn't worth it. Let the bastard sleep. He folded a towel, put it under Rossi's head for a pillow, then walked out.

Widgie's was something like an open-air cafe, a vast network of interconnected fire-escapes between two red brick buildings; swaying catwalks linked the fire-escape platforms across the alley, along with a seemingly random system of dumbwaiters that moved up and down among the dozen or so levels. Another network of pneumatic tubes for orders ran among the ladders and catwalks. A clear plastic dome covered the entire alley, shelter from the daily rains.

Tanner entered the alley, searched the platforms, and spotted Carlucci at one of the most isolated tables, up on the sixth or seventh level. Shit. It was going to be a climb.

A host approached Tanner to seat him, but Tanner said he was meeting someone. The host frowned, bowed, then retreated, and Tanner started up the nearest ladder.

After leaving Rossi's place, Tanner had gone to a cafe down the street for breakfast, a tiny run-down place called Maria's Kitchen, where he had an enormous, and delicious, plate of black beans, rice, eggs, and salsa. He had eaten every bit of it, including two warm tortillas, surprised at his appetite. He decided it had something to do with being alive. It was only now sinking in just how lucky he was.

Tanner stopped twice to rest on the way up, and felt exhausted by the time he reached Carlucci's table, sweating heavily in the damp heat. But the exertion and sweat felt good, almost cleansing. He dropped into the seat across from Carlucci. There was a thermal pot of coffee on the table, along with two cups. Carlucci poured a cup for Tanner, pushed it to him. Tanner was ready for coffee, something to help get his head going again.

"You look like shit," Carlucci said.

"Thanks. That's what Hannah said, too." He drank from the coffee, which was hot, but not too strong. It would help, and his stomach would survive it.

"Well, she was right. What the hell happened to you?"

"Long, painful story," Tanner said. "You won't like it."

Carlucci grimaced. "I don't guess I will." He shook his head. "You know that name I gave you? For help in the Tenderloin. Francie Miller." He breathed deeply once. "She's dead."

Tanner drank from his coffee, sipping slowly, not looking at Carlucci. "I know," he finally said, turning to face him. "I watched her die."

Carlucci didn't say anything for a long time, staring back at Tanner. When he finally spoke, his voice was quiet, almost without inflection. "Jesus . . . Christ." Another long pause, a shake of his head, then, "So tell me about it."

Tanner did. Everything from the time he entered the Tenderloin until he emerged into Tornado Alley. Carlucci listened without interruption, occasionally grimacing or shaking his head or pressing his temples, but not saying anything. When Tanner was finished, neither one of them said anything for a long time. Tanner looked around Widgie's, listening to the mix of voices, clattering dishes, dumbwaiter squeals, muffled thumps of pneumatic tubes, echoing footsteps.

"Well, shit," Carlucci eventually said. "This is real fucking progress." He leaned back and patted at his shirt pocket. "God damn it, times like this I wish I hadn't quit smoking." He set both hands on the table, stared at them for several moments, then looked up at Tanner again. "And we've got more bodies."

"How many?"

"Four. One triple, and a single."

"A single?"

"Yeah, that's a new one. Kind of strange, guy chained to himself. We pulled him out of a cistern back of a condemned warehouse." He rubbed his face with his hands. "Not typical, but it's definitely our old friend, the same mother fucker. Maybe he's just 'expanding his horizons.'" Carlucci made a harsh growling sound in his throat. "Wonderful thought."

"Are they coming faster than last time?"

"So far, looks that way. Making up for lost time, that's what Rollo says. He may have something."

Carlucci poured another cup of coffee for himself. Tanner held his own cup with both hands, tipping it from side to side, watching the dark brown liquid swirl. High above them, rain started on the plastic dome, a high, echoing clatter; at the far end of the alley, Tanner could see it coming down in sheets, a real downpour. He did not like the way any of this was going.

"What about what Max said?" Tanner asked. "Rattan and some cops working something together."

Carlucci breathed in deeply, slowly let it out. "May be true. I've heard some things the last few months. Didn't pay much attention, really, none of it seemed too likely." He paused. "No idea what it's all about, but I guess I'll have to check it out now."

"Yeah, do that. I don't like feeling like I don't know shit about what's going on. It's my ass out there, and I've already come damn close to losing it."

Carlucci nodded once. "Maybe it's not a good idea to go back in there looking for him."

Tanner gave him a brief, chopped laugh. "It's a *terrible* idea. But have you got a better one?"

Carlucci shook his head. "I tried. I even set up a crash session with one of the slugs, fed him the info about you and Freeman and Rattan, anything I had."

"So what did he come up with?"

"A lot of useless bullshit, and one concrete course of action."

"Which was?"

"Find Rattan."

Tanner tried laughing. "That's fucking great. The slug boosted all that brain juice to come up with that?"

Carlucci shrugged. "You want to reconsider?"

"I'm constantly reconsidering," Tanner said. "But I'll go back in. I'll find the son of a bitch." Tanner wished he actually felt that confident.

"Where you going to stay now?" Carlucci asked.

"Probably not inside. I'll be better off now going in and out. And with Max running loose, I'll have to stay away from my apartment."

"I know it probably won't do much good, but we'll put out a warrant for Max's arrest, try to pick up the little fucker. Another goddamn cop killing." He paused, looking steadily at Tanner. "I wonder what the hell Francie was up to, trying to find Rattan."

Tanner nodded. He had asked himself the same question. One more thing he didn't know. "Trying to nail him for the cop killings?" Tanner suggested. "A boost for her career?"

Carlucci shook his head. "No, not the way it played out, something not right about the whole thing. So where *are* you going to stay?" Carlucci asked again. "I want to be able to reach you."

"With Hannah and Rossi, probably. I'm sure they'll put me up."

Carlucci nodded. He sipped at his coffee, made a face, then poured it back into the thermal pot. He swirled the pot, poured himself a fresh cup, then poured some for Tanner. "You don't carry a gun, do you?"

Tanner shook his head.

"You should. Now, anyway."

Tanner shook his head again. "A gun wouldn't have done me a damn bit of good with Max. What I could use, though, is some cash. I'll be able to get most of the money back from the streetbank, but I'm broke until then."

Carlucci took several bills from his wallet, handed them to Tanner, who stuck them into his pocket. "I'm also trying to work up a few more grand," Carlucci said. "In case you need it."

"I hope I get the chance."

They drank their coffee in silence. Tanner listened closely to the sounds of the rain, letting it wash out all the other sounds in Widgie's. He was tired and depressed, yet somehow invigorated as well. A part of him wanted to just collapse and sleep for a few days. But another was anxious to get back into the Tenderloin, anxious to resume his search for Rattan, anxious to *talk* to Rattan. Tanner wanted to know what the hell was going on, and what, if anything, it had to do with the Chain Killer.

"I want to meet every two or three days," Carlucci said. "We've got to stay in touch. We have *got* to keep together on this, or we'll both end up in deep shit, and you deeper than me."

Tanner nodded. "I'll call you," he said.

"You going to rest up a couple days?" Carlucci asked.

"No, I'm okay. I want to get back at it. I'm tired of hearing about more and more dead bodies."

"Yeah, well just make sure yours isn't one of them."

Tanner smiled. "Good thinking. I'll keep it in mind."

23

SOOKIE FOLLOWED HIM all night and day. Behind him up the rungs and out into Tornado Alley. Creeping along a few feet back, silent and on all fours, crabbing among the bodies. What a stink!

Worse, though, was waiting all night across from the apartment building. He went in and didn't come out, so she had to wait. She wedged herself onto a second-floor ledge directly across the street, jammed between a window frame and a sewage pipe. It rained once. Noises from the pipe all night; wood jammed into her side. She didn't sleep much.

Morning, and nothing. Lots of other people came out of the apartment, but not Tanner. Maybe she'd missed him? She crawled down from the ledge, her ribs and knees aching, walked around, working it out. She had to keep moving to stay away from the pervs who kept after her.

Then, close to noon, he came out, and she followed him to Maria's Kitchen. Hung out while he sat inside and ate. Crouched behind a trash bin, she could see him in the window. Her stomach twisted in on itself, a few sharp pains. A long time since she'd eaten, but she was afraid of losing him.

On to Widgie's, more than an hour in there, then back to the apartment for a couple more hours. What was he doing in there, taking a sleep? Maybe. And what was *she* doing out here, waiting for him? Goofball.

Finally, early evening, he came back out again. She followed him over to Chinatown and a restaurant on the edge of the Tenderloin. Joyce Wah's. He met two people in front. A very tall, long-haired woman, beautiful in a dark shimmer coat. And a girl wearing white jeans, brown jacket, and blinking sneakers. Fifteen or sixteen years old, Sookie thought. Tanner hugged the girl, and that made Sookie feel funny. Then they all went inside.

She waited a few minutes, then went in and ordered some food to go. Three small cartons and a pair of chopsticks. She liked eating with chopsticks, they were like funny long fingers. Sookie took the food and crossed the street. When she looked back, first at the ground floor, then up, and up again, she saw Tanner and the woman and the girl in one of the third-floor windows. The girl was sitting across from him, and they were talking to each other. Arguing, maybe. The woman didn't seem to be talking at all, sitting back a little.

Sookie squatted down against the brick wall, opened one of the cartons, and dug in with her chopsticks. Ate and watched. She didn't really know why she was following him. She wanted to talk to him again. The way he had kept looking at her. What was that? She wanted to ask him.

But there was something else, too. Something she wanted. She just couldn't figure out what it was.

Sookie sat and ate and watched . . . and waited.

24

"WHY DID YOU stop seeing Mom?" Connie asked.

There it was, Tanner thought, the point of all this. He drank from his tea without taking his eyes off Connie, trying to decide how to answer her. Alexandra was silent, sitting back and away from them. She had offered to go somewhere else, or eat at a different table, whatever, but Connie had insisted she stay. Moral support?

Dinner itself had been relatively quiet, no one talking much. No one ate much, either. A lot of picking at the food, picking at conversation, both Connie and Tanner biding time. Then the meal was finished, the plates taken away, fresh tea brought to the table. And Connie asked the question.

There was not, of course, a simple answer to it. He had learned that a little over a year ago when he had tried to explain things to Valerie. Tanner wondered why Connie had waited so long to come to him with the question.

"I was afraid of hurting her," he finally said. The statement was so broad and general that it was true to a certain extent. Tanner felt almost embarrassed at giving it as an answer.

"What do you mean?" Connie asked.

"You remember the time I broke your mother's nose?" He felt a little sick now just thinking about it.

"You said it was an accident."

"It was. I'd had a nightmare, and I'd come out of it swinging my fists. It wasn't the first time I'd hurt her like that, but it was the worst." He paused. "I didn't want to risk doing that again to her."

"Nightmares that bad?" Connie said.

Tanner nodded, glancing at Alexandra. She was not looking at him.

"Do you have them a lot?" Connie asked.

Tanner breathed in slowly, deeply, then gradually let it out as he shook his head. He did not like talking about this. "Not really," he said. "Now and then. More than I'd like, though."

Connie didn't say anything for a minute or two. She sipped at her tea, and Tanner could see she was thinking about what he had said. She frowned, shaking her head, and set her teacup carefully on the table.

"You know, Louis," she said, "that's just bullshit. If that was the real problem, it's so easy to take care of." She stopped; hesitating, Tanner thought, to actually mention sleeping arrangements. She finally went on. "If you really loved each other, you could live with that. And you did love her, didn't you? I know she loved you." She paused, looked down at the table, then back up at him, defiant. "She still does. Do you?"

Jesus, Tanner thought, how was he supposed to answer that? He looked at Alexandra, who was holding her teacup without drinking from it, gazing out the window. She glanced at him, then looked away without expression. Alexandra had asked him the same questions a year ago, trying to pull answers out of him with patience and persistence. He resisted now, as he had then, and said nothing.

"Why did you stop seeing Mom?" Connie asked again. "Did you stop loving her?"

"No," Tanner answered. He tried to leave it at that.

"Then *why?*"

Stalling—he *knew* she would not be satisfied with anything less than a full explanation—he asked, "Why did you wait so long to ask me?"

Connie sighed. "I was afraid. But I'm older now, and I'm not afraid anymore, and I think I have a right to know."

Tanner nodded. He guessed she did have that right. Except he did not know if he could explain it to her. He did not think he had been very successful at explaining it to either Valerie or Alexandra. Or to himself.

"Things were always real hard between your mom and me," he began. "It wasn't that we didn't get along. We didn't fight, it wasn't that kind of thing, but it was hard, it took a lot of work. Which is all right, to a point. But it just got harder and harder, kind of wore us down. Wore *me* down." He paused, still struggling to put things into words after all this time.

"It had a lot to do with being a cop," he continued. "The people I saw, the things I watched people do, the things *I* had to do, it all depressed the hell out of me. The bad thing was, I brought a lot of it home. I tried to keep it from you and your mom, but I really wasn't able to." He smiled. "You remember, when you were younger, you used to come up to me and scream 'Lighten up!' right in my face?"

Connie smiled and nodded. "Yeah, I remember. It worked, too."

Tanner shrugged. "Yes, but never for very long. I thought that when I quit the force things would be easier for me, for us. I thought I'd 'lighten up.'" He paused. "But I didn't. I don't know, in some ways things just got worse, I felt like I was bringing clouds into the room every time I walked in. I just . . ." He shook his head. "I don't know, I tried real hard, Connie, I tried a long time, but I just couldn't do it anymore, I . . ." But that was it, he couldn't get out another word.

Connie did not say anything at first. She was not making a sound, but he thought she was shaking slightly. Her hands were out of sight beneath the table.

"Do you still love her?" she finally asked.

Jesus, Tanner thought, why won't she let me be? He rubbed at his face with his hand, but did not answer.

"*Do* you? Do you still love *me?*"

Tanner looked down at the table for a moment, then back at Connie, a terrible ache in his chest. "Yes," he finally said. "I still love you both."

"Isn't that enough?"

How could he answer that? He slowly shook his head. "No. It's just not that simple."

"Why not?"

Tanner did not know what to say. He *wanted* to give her an answer, he wanted to be able to say something that would make things all right with her.

"I don't know, Connie," he finally said. "I just don't know."

Connie was shaking her head slowly from side to side as if she could not believe what he was saying. She was crying now, quietly, steadily, and she put her head in her hands.

Tanner reached across the table, put his hand on her arm, and said, "I'm sorry, Connie."

She pulled her arm away from him, not quickly, but sadly, he thought. She raised her head and looked at him, dark makeup streaking her face. He thought of the woman with the tattooed tears.

"You're such an idiot sometimes, Louis. You probably think I'm crying for myself, don't you? Well I'm not, I'm crying for you." Connie breathed in deeply, held it for a minute, then let it out. She stopped crying, and wiped her face, smearing the streaked makeup. She slowly shook her head, looking at him, then stood up and said, "Excuse me, I'll be back in a minute." She turned and walked to the back of the restaurant and into the hall leading to the rest rooms.

Tanner looked at Alexandra, who gazed steadily back at him. He could not read her expression.

"Don't look at me like that, for Christ's sake," he said. "I'm doing my best."

Alexandra blinked twice, but otherwise did not change her expression. "And it's not good enough, is it?" she said. "She's young, Louis. But she's probably right about a lot of it."

He turned away and looked out the window. Night had fallen, and he wished a rain would start, fall long and hard, wash things away. Across the street a small figure huddled against the building, partially hidden by shadows, eating with chopsticks from a white carton. He could not be sure, but he thought it was Sookie. Was she following him? Why else would she be here?

Connie returned to the table, but did not sit. Her face was clean, but her eyes were puffy. She looked at Alexandra.

"I'm ready to go now," Connie said. "I asked my questions, and I'm ready to go home." She turned to Tanner. "Good-bye, Louis."

"Connie . . ." But that was as far as he got. He still had no idea what to say. "Good-bye, Connie. Take care of yourself."

Connie nodded. "Sure, Louis."

Alexandra stood. "I'll make sure she gets off okay tomorrow," she said to Tanner. "Keep in touch, will you? And if you have a problem, go ahead and get to Rachel, she'll find a way to help."

"Thanks for everything," Tanner said.

Alexandra nodded, then she and Connie walked away. He watched them cross the room and start down the stairs. Then he was alone.

Tanner stood on the sidewalk and gazed across the street at Sookie, who was standing now, her back against the building, watching him. Though it was not raining, the air was heavy and tense with the damp heat. At a break in the traffic, he hurried across the street and joined her.

"You've been following me," he said. When she did not deny it, he asked, "Why?"

"Why did you keep looking at me that way?" Sookie asked.

Tanner did not immediately reply, the pain returning once more. Her voice was nothing like Carla's, but her face was just too damn similar. "You remind me of someone," he finally said. "A woman I knew. You look a lot like she did when she was your age."

Sookie's eyes widened, and she gnawed at her lower lip. "Who is she?" Sookie asked, her voice hushed and tentative. "Maybe . . . maybe she's my mother." A brief pause, then, "I never knew her."

Tanner shook his head. "She died before you were born." He had wondered briefly about that himself when he had first made the connection; but if Carla had had a child before he had known her, the child would be close to twenty years old now.

Sookie kicked at the empty Chinese food cartons at her feet.

"So why were you following me?" Tanner asked again.

Sookie shrugged. "I don't know." She looked up at him. "To ask you that, I guess." She gestured with her head at the building. "You going back into the Tenderloin?"

"Yes."

"Even with Max after you?"

Tanner nodded. "Which is why you shouldn't be following me. You should stay away."

"You *need* someone following you," Sookie said.

Tanner shook his head. "Don't, Sookie. I'll be fine, and I don't want to be worrying about you. I mean it."

"I know a safe way in," she said.

"Don't you understand?" Tanner wanted to grab her by the shoulders and shake her. "You *know* what Max is like."

Sookie nodded. "I understand." She looked down at the food cartons, crushed one slowly with her foot. Then she looked back at him. "Was she your daughter?" she asked.

Tanner did not reply at first, confused. Was she talking about Carla? "Who do you mean?"

Sookie glanced across the street, pointed at the windows of Joyce Wah's. "The girl. You met her there."

"No," Tanner said. "She's the daughter of a friend."

Sookie nodded once, still gazing across the street. "You don't want me to show you a way in."

"I have my own ways."

"And you want me to stay away from you."

Tanner hesitated. He had the feeling something more was going on with her questions than he understood. "Because of Max, yes."

Sookie kicked at the food cartons again, smiled softly, and looked at Tanner. "Good-bye, then." She turned and walked quickly down the street.

"Sookie . . . wait."

She kept on without slowing, without looking back.

"Sookie . . ."

Tanner started forward, then stopped, letting it go, and wondering why he felt as if he had screwed up. What could he have said different? What *should* he have said? Christ. He watched her until, a block away, she slipped out of sight—into the crowd or into a building, he couldn't tell. Tanner turned around and headed the other way.

25

TANNER RETURNED TO the Euro Quarter, walking the hot night streets. He wore nightshades, which looked like mirrored sunglasses from the outside but did not actually cut down on the light that reached his eyes. And he had decided not to shave. He did not really expect the nightshades and a few days' growth of beard to be much disguise, but he hoped it would at least make things more difficult for Max.

He had most of the money back on a new credit chip—replacing the chip had cost him five percent—and several hundred in cash. Having less money did not bother him, though; he suspected it would be more than enough. Tanner had the feeling that money was no longer a key issue in any of this.

But he felt a greater sense of urgency now. Part of that was Max—Tanner had to find Rattan before Max found *him*. But he also had the feeling that other things were coming to a head, all this stuff with Rattan and the cops. If they did, he might lose Rattan, one way or another, and he would be back where he had begun—nowhere. He had to find Rattan, and he had to find him soon.

It was just after midnight, street life peaking, when Tanner stopped by the Turk Street Fascination Parlor. The place was jammed, every single Fascination machine being played, almost all of them worked by old Russian women in their sixties or seventies, a few even older. They rolled the pink rubber balls into their machines, hoping to eventually win enough game tickets to cash in for a Tenderloin Flight Coupon, good for a month in a Life-Sim Spa.

This time Lyuda, who owned and ran the parlor, was in. Tanner spotted her behind the bar in back, pouring comp Stolis for the old women. Two waiters, skinny old guys older than the Russian women, carted the tiny glasses of vodka from the bar to the machines. Tanner slowly worked his way to the bar, careful not to bump any of the players.

Lyuda, a small blond woman in her forties, was the only junkie Tanner had ever known who had managed to quit the stuff by slowly tapering off. She hadn't any other choice. She had started shooting up in her teens and, defying the odds, had survived into her mid-thirties, when she decided she had to quit—or die. Twice she tried it cold, and both attempts nearly killed her—twenty years of doing junk had changed her body too much; she needed heroin to live.

But she was still determined. So she began slowly, patiently, cutting back. She set up a strict regimen, tapering off minutely and infrequently, sticking to it for more than three years until she thought she had cut back enough. Then she quit completely . . . and lived. Now she ran the Fascination Parlor, and generously kept the old Russian women tanked on imported Stolichnaya vodka.

As Tanner approached the bar, he watched Lyuda's expression change from puzzlement to a smile and then to a tight frown. Tanner leaned against the counter, the two waiters left with full loads, and Lyuda shook her head.

"Didn't recognize you at first," she said. "Is that supposed to be some kind of disguise?" When Tanner shrugged, she said, "I gotta say I'm surprised to see you here, with that lunatic after you."

Max? It was difficult for Tanner to believe that Max would go that route, taking it public. He thought Max would want to come after him as privately as possible. "What lunatic?" he asked.

"Dobler."

"Dobler?"

"Yeah, Dobler, *that* lunatic, that amateur. You didn't know?"

Tanner shook his head.

"Sure, he's put the word out on the street. Wants you alive, if that's any consolation."

"What's the price on my head?"

"Negotiable upon delivery."

"What kind of nonsense is that?"

"I told you he was an amateur. Want a Stoli?" She held up a bottle, and when Tanner shook his head she poured one for herself and went on. "Anybody with any brains'll just ignore the whole thing, but he'll have other lunatics and amateurs shooting for you. And because they're amateurs they won't have too much control over the keeping-you-alive part of the deal."

"Terrific." Tanner scanned the Fascination Parlor, half expecting some psychotic moron to leap out from under one of the machines and take a potshot at him.

"So why you here?" Lyuda asked.

Tanner turned back to her. "I'm hoping you can help me out with something. I need to talk to you."

Lyuda pressed a button, and a buzzer sounded faintly through the walls. "We'll go to my office. Beyat can watch things."

"How clear is your office?"

Lyuda raised one eyebrow. "Like that, is it?"

Tanner nodded.

"All right."

A tall black woman in a shiny silver aviator jumpsuit appeared from the back hall, and Lyuda came around the bar.

"I'll be gone, I don't know how long," Lyuda said to Beyat. "Watch things, all right?"

Beyat nodded, adjusting the Stolichnaya bottles. "Keep the old dames juiced."

"Just keep them happy," Lyuda said.

Beyat grinned. "That means keeping them juiced."

Lyuda finally smiled and nodded. "All right." She glanced at Tanner, then led the way to a bolted door between the two rest rooms. She unlocked it, and they walked down a narrow passage, then into a small room filled with cases of Stolichnaya. They went through another door at the back, then up a flight of stairs to a covered porch looking out over an alley filled with garbage cans, packing crates, loading docks. In the mist-filled cones of light, people moved about the alley, either on foot or narrow transport carts. There were three chairs in the room and Lyuda sat in one, gesturing at the other two. Tanner chose the one farther from the window. He wondered if he was becoming paranoid.

"So what is it?" Lyuda asked.

"I should tell you, someone else is looking for me. Other than Dobler." He waited for her to ask him who, but she didn't. She sat silently, waiting for him to continue. "Max," he said.

She did not respond immediately. Her gaze was steady, penetrating. Almost accusing. "You've got no business being in the Tenderloin," she said. "You get out right now, quickest way you can."

"I can't," Tanner said. "I'm looking for someone. Here. I have to find him."

Lyuda shook her head. "Everybody's looking for somebody. What the hell is all this?" She breathed in, expelled it slowly. "All right, who you looking for?"

"Rattan."

Again there was a silence before she replied. He could not read her expression.

"You are not a good insurance risk," Lyuda finally said.

"Can you help me find him?"

Lyuda slowly shook her head from side to side. "Shit, Tanner. I shouldn't even try."

"Will you?"

Lyuda did not answer.

Tanner and Lyuda walked the crowded streets, headed deeper into the Tenderloin. Two Red Dragons had flown in from the Asian Quarter and now hovered thirty or forty feet above the street, engaged in mock combat while video ads for Red Dragon sake shimmered along the length of their bodies. Green sparks flashed from their eyes while smoke poured from the dragons' nostrils and drifted down to street level. Tanner breathed in the smoke, which smelled faintly of incense and opium.

Lyuda had spent nearly three hours making phone calls and going out to talk to people, while Tanner waited on the porch. He had sat on the floor with his back against the wall, dozing, slipping in and out of a dreamlike state. At one point he thought he was involved in an intense, incomprehensible conversation with Carla, who was quite young, and who gradually transformed into Sookie. He only halfheartedly fought the exhaustion and the fragmented dream images, and several times nearly slipped into a deep sleep. Finally, close to four in the morning, Lyuda had returned and told him they would go to meet someone who *might* know something. Now they were on their way as night came to a close, though there were not yet any traces of light in the sky.

By the time Lyuda turned into a busy alley lined with street-level shops, cafes, and taverns, they were very close to the Core. Tanner wondered again if that was where Rattan had gone to ground. But he could not believe it, could not believe that Rattan was that desperate.

They entered a crowded espresso bar and Lyuda led the way through it to the opposite entrance, which opened into a large lobby. Three people stood in the lobby, talking and sipping from paper cups. All the lobby windows were boarded over, but the lobby itself was brightly lit. This was, or had once been, an office building.

Lyuda nodded at the boarded windows. "Faces the Core," she said. "Every window on the first seven floors of that side is boarded over, steel plating on the outside."

"We're that close?" Tanner said.

"Just across the street."

One of the elevators was open and waiting. Inside, Lyuda pushed the ninth-floor button, the doors closed, and the elevator rose with a jolt. Tanner had been up and down a lot of floors in the last few days, but this was his first elevator ride since he had seen Teshigahara.

The elevator stopped at five, and three short, fat men got on. They wore business suits, but they smelled bad. Milky green fluid oozed from an open sore on one man's forehead. They did not push any of the floor buttons.

At nine, Tanner and Lyuda got off. The elevator doors remained open for a minute, the three men standing silent and motionless. Then the doors closed, and the lighted arrow showed the elevator descending. Odd, Tanner thought.

The hall floor was beige linoleum, edged with ragged strips of rotten carpet that had once covered the floor. Offices on the Core side of the building were dark and silent. On the other side were lighted door windows of frosted glass, muffled voices, the clatter of machinery, music, and the whine of a dentist's drill. At the end of the hall was a staircase, which they climbed to the tenth floor. Here, all the offices were dark and silent.

Lyuda unlocked a door on the Core side of the building, and they entered a dark room. She took Tanner's hand and led him through the darkness, along a corridor, then into another room with two large windows. They stepped up to the windows, and looked out onto the Core.

The Core was four square blocks of hell. Some people thought the hell was literal, and believed supernatural demons and ghosts haunted the place. Most of the buildings were in ruins, and those that were not looked as if they soon would be. Unlike the rest of the Tenderloin, the streets and buildings of the Core were not brightly lit, though a few dim lights were visible in the ruins—wavering lights of candles or fires, pulsing blue glows, drifting clouds of pale phosphorescence. The streets were deserted except for the shadowy movement of animals.

Tanner had heard the stories, though no one really knew for sure what went on inside. The Core was populated by those who could not, or would not, cut it in either the city or the Tenderloin. For all that the Tenderloin functioned outside the laws of the city, state, and country, it *did* function quite well with a structure and order of its own. The Core, so the stories went, had no order, no structure, no laws or rules or morals. Nothing. Tanner suspected it was not quite the chaos-driven place it was said to be, but certainly the rules were different. The Core itself existed, but that was all that could be said of it.

Lyuda raised the window, and Tanner half expected to hear wild screams and wailing, but there was relative quiet. Several floors up in the building across the way, something resembling a large cat stuck its head out a window and growled. A huge, furred hand grabbed it and pulled it back inside.

"You don't think Rattan's in there, do you?" Tanner asked.

Lyuda shook her head. "He's not insane." She looked at her watch. "Quiet, now. Listen. It's almost time." She gestured at the Core.

For what? But Tanner kept quiet, and listened.

The Core, already quiet, grew quieter still, almost completely silent. Even the surrounding areas of the Tenderloin became quiet. An acoustic guitar began playing somewhere inside one of the buildings across the street. The sound, loud and clearly defined, echoed among the ruins, and Tanner could not pinpoint its origin. The music was classical and delicate, with a Latin feel. Then a woman's voice joined it.

Her voice was strong and beautiful, a clean, high soprano. She sang something from an opera, Tanner thought, though he did not recognize it. The words were Spanish or Italian, he couldn't be sure. Clearly, she'd had professional training. There was no way anyone could sing like that without years of training and practice. And here she was, singing from within the Core.

Tanner stood and listened, amazed at what he was hearing, amazed at where it came from. Spanish, he finally decided. A love song of some kind, filled with yearning, tempered with anxiety. He searched the ruins, looking for a light or something that would tell him where she was. He saw nothing.

The song ended. There was a brief silence, then the guitar started in on another song, playing a few measures before the woman joined it again. This song was sadder than the first, melancholy and quite moving, though again Tanner had no idea what any of the words meant. Her voice had great power, and Tanner felt a dull ache develop in his chest. During the most intense section of the piece, the woman hit a series of incredibly high notes with such painful perfection that a shiver ran through Tanner from his neck to the base of his spine, leaving a strange chill in its wake.

By the time the second song was finished, the sky had noticeably brightened, and morning was fully upon them. There was another extended silence, then the natural city sounds gradually resumed, filling the morning air. There was no more guitar, no more singing. Lyuda closed the window.

"She sings every Saturday at dawn," Lyuda said. "Started about three and a half months ago."

"Who is she?"

"No one really knows. I've heard of people who say they recognize her voice, who say it's Elisabetta Machiotti."

"Name sounds familiar," Tanner said. "But . . ." He shrugged.

"A highly acclaimed soprano with the Berlin Opera who disappeared a year ago. But like I said, no one really knows. Whoever she is, though, she's really quite good." She looked at her watch again. "Arkady should be here any minute now."

They waited without speaking for several minutes, watching the morning sky brighten. Tanner could see the first reflections of the rising sun glint off glass and metal on building roofs in the Core.

The office door opened, closed, and a moment later a tall, young blond man walked into the room. Lyuda shook the man's hand.

"Arkady . . . Tanner," she said. "Tanner . . . Arkady."

Tanner nodded at Arkady and they shook hands. Arkady nodded back, then turned to Lyuda and began speaking in Russian. She replied, also in Russian, and Tanner realized their entire conversation was going to proceed in a language he did not understand. At first he watched them, watched their faces and listened to their voices, hoping to get some sense of the conversation. But their expressions told him nothing, nor did their voices, and soon he stopped even trying to understand.

Tanner turned back to the window and looked out onto the Core. Although he could not see anyone in or around any of the buildings, did not directly detect any motion, he was struck by a vague sense of movement from within the ruins, a shifting of atmospheric patterns. Something. An alien place. Though the heat of the day was growing, the sweat already filming across his skin, he could somehow imagine a light dusting of snow laid over the Core, cold and silent.

Elisabetta Machiotti. In a way it did not matter *who* the woman was. What mattered was that she was in the Core, and that she sang. Tanner was certain that most people would be dumbfounded at the idea of a world-famous opera singer living in the Core; but, amazed and awed as he was by the woman's performance in that hellhole, Tanner was not any more surprised at her presence in the Core than he was at the presence of *anyone* in that place. Given that the Core existed, why *not* a world-famous opera singer?

The conversation stopped, and Tanner turned away from the window. Arkady nodded once at him, shook hands with Lyuda again, then walked out of the room. A few moments later Tanner heard the outer door open and close. He looked at Lyuda, who shook her head.

"I don't have a damn thing for you," she said.

"Nothing?"

"Nothing. No one has any idea where he is, and no one *wants* to know. Something's in the air with Rattan, but nobody knows what. Something more than Max, though Max doesn't make the situation any easier. People don't want to deal with Max, and people don't even want to talk about Rattan." She shook her head. "You're going up against thick walls, Tanner. You want, I can keep asking around, put out a few sensors, but Arkady was my best shot, and to be honest I'm not wild about the idea of pushing it any further. I've got myself to watch for."

"No," Tanner said. "It's not worth the risk. I have some other lines to try. I appreciate what you did, and let's leave it there." He turned to the window once more, looking out at the Core as if it somehow had the answers he was searching for. He knew it did not have the answers to *anything*, but he gazed at it all the same.

Lyuda joined him at the window. "You know what she is?" Lyuda asked.

"The woman who sang?"

Lyuda nodded. "You'll think I'm crazy, but . . ." There was a long pause, and Tanner waited silently for her to continue. "Hope," Lyuda said. "That's what I think of when I hear her sing."

Tanner stared at the Core. Hope. Not even close to what he now felt. Standing at the edge of the Core, with no leads to Rattan, no leads to a psycho who was going to keep on killing again and again and again, all Tanner felt was despair.

26

SOOKIE KNEW THAT voice. Hearing those songs made her want to cry. She didn't understand any of the words, but the tears came anyway. It was the third time she'd heard the woman sing. Who was she? Sookie thought the woman must be trapped in the Core, chained to a wall, unable to do anything but sing.

Two songs, then the woman stopped. Sookie closed her eyes, still crying a little, listening, hoping for another song. But there wasn't any more.

She wiped away the tears, looked into the Core. It was filled with long shadows from the rising sun. Sookie sat on top of one of the street barricades at the edge of the Core. Mixer would think she was crazy, but she wasn't afraid, as long as she was outside.

She'd been inside the Core once, by accident. Not far inside. A couple of years ago, when she'd been younger and kind of stupid. She'd been running away from someone, middle of the night, she didn't remember who or why. She'd climbed one of the barricades to get away, dropped down to the other side, then run across the street and into the closest wrecked building. She hadn't really known what the Core was, not then. She didn't really know what it was now, either, but now she knew enough to stay out.

No one had followed her over the barrier or across the street. Sookie had figured she was safe. She was inside a dark and dusty room, with a couple windows looking out on the street. Silver light from across the road came in through the windows, lighting up the dust. Something brushed her foot and she jumped away. A huge rat as big as a small dog scampered through one of the light beams and Sookie squealed. Rats didn't bother her too much, but she'd never seen one that big.

Then she heard a moaning laugh from the corner of the room. A click, then a pale light came on overhead. Sookie saw a young woman dressed in a white body suit crouched at the edge of a pit in the floor. The woman, head shaved, held a metal pipe in one hand and a hammer in the other. Her mouth was open, making the moaning laugh. Then the laughter stopped.

The woman leaped across the pit and ran at Sookie, pipe and hammer held high. Sookie turned and ran, stumbled, fell. The woman couldn't stop, tripped over Sookie, yowling. Sookie scrambled to her feet, headed for the door. Something hit her arm—the hammer. She made it to the door, out, onto the street, and dashed for the barricade. The woman did not follow her out of the building. Her arm hurt, but she clambered up the barricade. Someone grabbed her, helped her up and over and back into the Tenderloin. It was a spikehead who had helped her up. That was how she had met Mixer, escaping from the Core.

Sookie shivered, remembering. Sometimes she dreamed about the woman. In her dreams, the woman sometimes shouted "Dinner!" just before leaping across the pit at Sookie. In her dreams, the woman always caught her.

Clouds started to fill the sky. It was going to rain soon. Sookie climbed down from the barricade and returned to the head of the alley. She stood and watched the store entrances, waiting for Tanner to reappear.

27

TANNER WAS SOAKED by the time he reached Hannah and Rossi's, drenched by a second and unexpected cloudburst. He dripped water on the carpets as he climbed the stairs, walked down the hall, then entered the apartment. The place was quiet. There was no sign of Hannah, and Rossi was asleep in the bedroom, lying faceup on the bed. In the bathroom, Tanner undressed, hung everything on hooks and racks. He took a short, cool shower, then put on clean, dry clothes.

He stretched out on the couch and tried to sleep. He was hot, exhausted, and depressed, and sleep would not come. A clock ticked weakly in the bedroom. Someone in the building was playing loud music, and Tanner could feel the beat gently thumping up from the floor and through the sofa. He looked up at the blue-painted cracks in the ceiling and imagined water dripping from them, splashing across his face, cooling him. Sweat trickled under his arms, down his neck.

He was nowhere. Things were slipping away from him. He and Carlucci knew no more now than they had several days before, which meant they were losing ground. And tonight he would head back into the Tenderloin and go through it all again. Flying blind, that's what it felt like. How long could he keep it going without making a mistake? It did not matter how careful he was, eventually there would come a night when he would ask the wrong person the wrong question, like he had with Max, or simply be in the wrong place. Tanner wondered again if he would survive the summer.

Unable to sleep, he got up from the couch and walked into the kitchen. It was still a mess of food and filthy plates and stained glasses. Hannah, too, had given up on a lot. Well, it gave him something to do.

Tanner spent the next hour washing dishes and glasses and silverware, cleaning counters, putting some of the food away while dumping most of it into the garbage. He swept the floors and washed the table. Then he dug through the cupboards looking for something to drink. There was plenty of gin, but he couldn't stand the stuff. In the back of a cupboard, behind some jars of Hungarian preserves, he found a dusty pint of cheap scotch.

He fixed himself a drink, drank it slowly, then fixed another. It had been a long time since he had needed alcohol to sleep. His thoughts were scattered, but they kept moving through his head at wild speeds, and he needed something to slow them down, ease them back, put them away for a little while. So he sat at the table and drank.

When he finished his third drink he returned to the front room. A pleasant warmth had settled in his limbs, and his thoughts had slowed and fuzzed over. He lay out on the couch, staring at the blue cracks once more, then closed his eyes. Heat of the day, warmth of the scotch. It was enough. Tanner slid slowly and softly into sleep.

Tanner woke to the sensation of being watched. He lay facing the back of the sofa, and he slowly turned over to see Hannah in the overstuffed chair, gazing at him. The room was stuffy and hot, late-afternoon sun slashing in through the window. Hannah's face was in shadow from her nose up, her mouth and chin brightly lit.

"How long have you been there?" he asked.

"About a half hour," Hannah said. "Couldn't think of anything better to do." She looked beat, as usual.

Tanner sat up, stretched cramped muscles, popping neck and shoulder bones. He felt as tired as Hannah looked.

"Where's Rossi?"

"Down at the Lucky Nines having a few beers with the guys. It's a daily ritual." She ran her hand slowly through her hair watching him. "Make love to me, Louis."

Tanner stared at her a few moments without answering, then said quietly, "No, Hannah."

"Louis . . ."

"No, Hannah."

She looked away from him. The sun was dropping quickly now, and the stream of light had worked up to the bridge of her nose, just below her eyes.

"You did a hell of a job in the kitchen," she said. "You'd make someone a good wife." She turned back to him. "I just don't care about much anymore."

Tanner did not know what to say. He did not want to be sucked down into the pit of Hannah and Rossi's life; he had enough problems of his own. But he had known them both a long time, Hannah for more than twenty years. Hannah had known Carla, had been there to help him through all the shit when Carla had died.

"I know," Hannah said. "You want to know why I don't leave him."

"I'm not going to ask that anymore," Tanner said. "I know it's not that simple."

Hannah sank back slowly into the chair. Now her entire face was bathed in the deep red glow of the setting sun, and she squinted against the glare.

"Look at us," Hannah said. "I should leave Rossi, and you should never have left Valerie. You and Valerie are both still paying for Carla's death."

"She died fifteen years ago," Tanner said. "They don't have anything to do with each other."

"You don't think so?"

Tanner shook his head. "No."

Hannah slowly shook her head in return, a sad smile working its way onto her face, but she did not say anything. She closed her eyes for a few moments, then opened them slightly, still squinting in the sun. Tanner waited for her to speak, but she remained silent.

"I'll buy you dinner," he finally said.

Hannah sighed and nodded. "All right." She stood up from the chair and went to the front door. Tanner got to his feet, joined her, and they left.

When they got back from dinner, Tanner called Carlucci. He suggested meeting at the apartment, but Carlucci refused; he did not want to take the chance of seeing Rossi. Instead, they agreed to meet at a coffee shop down the street.

Tanner arrived first and sat at a booth by the front window. He ordered coffee from the sour-looking waitress, and while he waited for it he looked around the restaurant. The place was dirty and run down, which matched most of the customers at the tables and counter. A pall of despair hung over the place, cut through with the smells of charred toast and frying food. A thin layer of grease on the window blurred his view of the street.

When the coffee arrived, Tanner looked at it with concern. It was too dark, and a burnt smell drifted up from the cup. He sipped it tentatively and burned the tip of his tongue; the coffee was so hot he could not really taste it, which was probably just as well.

He could not stop thinking about what Hannah had said about Valerie and Carla. Carla had died fifteen years ago, he *must* have let that go by now. Right? But Hannah's words stuck hard somewhere inside him, almost painful, and he could not shake them loose. Which made him think there was something to them. He did not want to think about it, though, he could not afford to right now. There were too many other, more immediate, concerns. Like the Chain Killer. So why *couldn't* he stop thinking about it?

He pushed the coffee cup from him in disgust. The coffee was just too much; he had managed less than half a cup. He signaled the waitress, told her to take the coffee away, and asked for tea. She glared sullenly at him, but took away the cup.

Carlucci slid into the booth, across from him, just as the waitress brought Tanner's tea.

"Stay away from the coffee," Tanner said.

Carlucci grunted, ordered coffee anyway, and the waitress smirked at Tanner. It was the closest thing to a smile he had seen from her. She was probably in her thirties, and in a few more years, Tanner thought, she was going to look like Hannah. Or worse.

"I hope you're not going to tell me more bodies have been found," he said to Carlucci.

Carlucci shook his head. "No new bodies, not a damn thing new on this son of a bitch. What about you, any luck?"

"No," Tanner said. "Nobody wants to even talk about Rattan. Lot of people seem to think something's on the move with him, but no one knows what. And they don't *want* to know. The more people I ask, the greater the chance that someone's going to end up dead. I don't like it at all." Tanner sighed. "But what the hell else are we going to do?" He gave Carlucci a half smile. "Tell you, though, I'm going to be real pissed if I find Rattan and it turns out he doesn't know shit. A three-year-old message. Christ."

"I've been looking into things, digging around trying to find out if something's going down between Rattan and some of our 'fellow officers.'"

"*Your* fellow officers."

"Fine, whatever. I haven't got a whole lot, and I doubt I'm ever going to get much more. Any cop actually dealing with Rattan in *any* way is going to keep it real tight, or find himself either out of a job or dumped dead in an alley somewhere. Hardly anyone liked the two cops he killed, they were bad cops, but they were still *cops*. Hell, it's the same thing you're running into. A lot of cops have heard about something shaking out with Rattan, but they don't know what it is, and they don't *want* to know."

Tanner nodded. "We're both hitting walls." He shook his head. "I've been on this for a week, but it feels like a fucking month."

"'Fucking'? I don't usually hear you use that word," Carlucci said, smiling.

"Yeah, well, this is the fucking time for it."

Someone on the street banged at the window. It was Rossi. He pointed at Tanner and Carlucci, then at himself, then hurried away. A few moments later he came through the front door and walked up to the booth. He did not sit down, and neither Tanner nor Carlucci asked him to.

"Hey, Carlucci," Rossi said. He stuck out his hand. "It's been a long time, yeah?"

Carlucci would not shake Rossi's hand. Tanner could smell the alcohol on Rossi, mixed with the heavy odor of sweat. Rossi continued to hold out his hand, which shook slightly. Tanner watched Rossi's smile fade, his expression tighten. Carlucci stared back at Rossi, his face blank. Finally, Rossi pulled his hand back, made a fist, and pounded the table.

"What's the matter with you?" Rossi said. "Can't you ever forget? Can't you ever forgive?"

"Not you," Carlucci said. His face remained expressionless, his voice quiet.

The two men stared at each other for a minute, and Rossi finally pushed back from the table. He turned to Tanner, arms shaking, lips quivering. Tanner felt he could actually see Rossi breaking apart inside.

"I'll see you later," he said, voice cracked and hoarse. He turned and walked out, crashing loudly through the front entrance. Tanner watched him run awkwardly across the street and into the apartment building.

"You're awfully hard on him," he said to Carlucci.

"Shouldn't I be? He cost my best friend an arm."

"That was six years ago."

"Six years, ten years, what difference? Brendan still doesn't have an arm. When it grows back, I'll ease up on Rossi."

Which meant never, of course. Tanner had heard about experimental work on full limb regeneration being done up in New Hong Kong, yet as far as he knew there had been no successes. But he nodded to Carlucci. He *did* understand. Brendan had never adjusted to the loss of his arm; he would not even consider a prosthesis. His marriage had disintegrated, and he had lost most of his friends. Carlucci blamed Rossi for more than the loss of Brendan's arm; he blamed him for the loss of Brendan's life.

The waitress stopped by, refilled Carlucci's cup, and poured more hot water for Tanner's tea. Tanner bobbed the tea bag in the water, swirled it, watched the water grow slowly, slowly darker.

"The coffee's not that bad," Carlucci said.

Tanner looked at Carlucci's cup; the coffee did not look any better than what he had tried, and he just shook his head.

"You going back in tonight?" Carlucci asked.

"Sure. What else?" He lifted the tea bag, watched it drip. "There are some other people I might be able to talk to, if I can find them." He dropped the tea bag back into the water. "I don't expect too much, to be honest. In fact, if you want to know the truth, I'm hoping to stumble onto something by accident more than anything else."

"I wish I had something better to offer."

"What about Koto?" Tanner asked.

"What about him?"

"Can't we go to him, see if he can't find a way to get to Rattan? He's been in the Tenderloin all these years. I mean, now that I'm thinking about it, what the hell is he being saved for? Isn't this important enough to use him?"

Carlucci did not answer. He leaned back in the booth and looked out the window. A light mist was falling, swirled by gusting winds. Tanner waited patiently, watching Carlucci, drinking his tea. Carlucci turned away from the window, finished his coffee, carefully set the cup in the saucer, and finally looked at Tanner.

"It's not that simple," he said.

Phrase of the day, Tanner thought. "I don't doubt that," he said, "but you want to explain why?"

"No. I can't. But it is something worth considering. Let's give it a few more days, and if we still aren't getting anywhere we can talk about it again."

Tanner nodded, looking outside at the swirling mist. "All right. Who knows? Maybe I'll get lucky tonight and we won't need him."

Tanner did not get lucky. In fact, the night was a complete washout. An hour after he entered the Tenderloin, a freak monsoonlike storm struck, with heavy rains and gale-force winds, effectively clearing the streets. Tanner spent a couple of hours in a video parlor watching a program of five-minute riot videos intercut with a series of one-minute animations about a scrawny, ugly dog named Fifi.

When the program ended, the storm still raged. Water ran in streams down the sidewalks and gutters, flooding at the intersections. Tanner left the video parlor, pushed through the wind and rain, down half a block and into a building, then up two flights of stairs to a music lounge. He took a seat at the window counter and ordered a beer. A slash-and-burn band was playing somewhere inside the building, the music blaring from speakers scattered throughout the lounge. The music was harsh and loud, frenetic, with only a hint of melody. It suited him, providing a wall of sound that gave him a sense of privacy as he sat at the window, watching the rain sweep through the streets. He nursed a couple of beers through the next two hours, enclosed by walls of music, glass, and driving rain.

Around two in the morning, the storm ceased almost as abruptly as it had begun. Tanner left the lounge and joined the throngs of people returning to the streets. The air smelled fresher, clear and crisp even in the heat. Windows, vehicles, pavement, lights, buildings, *everything* seemed sharper and cleaner, as if purified by the storm. Tanner wandered the streets, moving back and forth between the Euro and Asian Quarters, not really looking for anyone, just taking in the refreshed and invigorating feel of the streets.

But then, around four, he got caught in a ground skirmish. Within seconds, barriers went up at either end of the block he was on, and there was no way out. Everyone in the street knew what the barriers meant, and they all got off the street as best they could.

Tanner managed to get inside a noodle shop just before the doors were locked. The shop was jammed, and most people crowded around the front window to get a view of the action on the street. Tanner had no desire to watch people mauling each other. He moved to the back of the shop and sat on a stool at the bar.

He spent the next hour drinking tea, eating a bowl of noodles, and talking occasionally with the cook, who had no more interest in the fighting than he did. The window spectators made noises throughout the skirmish, but Tanner paid no attention to them, paid no attention to the other sounds of the street that penetrated the glass and walls. Instead, he concentrated on the bubbling hiss when the cook dropped fresh noodles into a pot of boiling stock; on the fragrant sizzle of frying pork; on the tick-tick-tick of cooling metal when the cook turned off the flame under the teakettle.

At dawn, the skirmish ended, and people returned to the streets. Tanner stayed in the noodle shop for a few minutes, finishing his tea. Then he got up, thanked the cook, and left.

When he stepped outside the shop, the air had a different feel. It no longer smelled clean and fresh; now it carried the faint stench of blood, smoke, and charged sweat.

Tanner stood on the sidewalk, watching the sky slowly brighten with the morning. He could see, in the gutter across the street, a splash of thick, darkening blood, flies already gathering above it. He did not want to move. It was time to go back to Hannah and Rossi's, try to get some sleep before coming back here tonight for another run. Time. What did it matter where he went? Tanner remained motionless, hands at his side, waiting for the first appearance of the sun.

28

THE NEXT NIGHT did not start out any better. He walked the streets almost in a stupor, without direction or purpose. He was hoping to see someone or something that would give him an idea; hoping for a flash of inspiration, a bit of luck.

He spent half an hour wandering through the maze of The Bomb Shelter, glancing into the rooms and cubicles, turning down a wide variety of propositions. He did not know who or what he was looking for in the place, and he felt like an apathetic voyeur, observing people engaged in intimate acts but with no real interest in what they were doing.

After The Bomb Shelter, Tanner checked half a dozen fang fights, thinking he might find the Barber at one of them, betting on his favorite wolverine or leopard. He saw lots of blood and flying fur and feathers, but no Barber.

At the edge of the Asian Quarter he stood gazing at the building that housed the Gang of Four tong. It was very likely that they knew where Rattan was, or at least how to reach him, but there was no asking them. He would not be able to get an audience, let alone ask any of them a question. And of course even if by some fluke he *could,* no one would answer him.

Tanner felt a tugging at his shirt and turned to see a young girl looking up at him. She was a Screamer, her lips smoothly, surgically fused together, with two trache tubes in her throat—one for eating, one for breathing. She was about ten or eleven years old. He wondered if, when she was old enough, she would want to undo what her parents had done to her. Probably not; most of them didn't.

The girl held up a clenched fist, rotated it, then uncurled her fingers, revealing a folded sheet of paper in her palm. Tanner took the message and the girl ran off, disappearing into the crowd. Tanner unfolded the message and read it—an address, followed by the words "Watch the sky."

He looked up and down the street, searching for a familiar face, for someone who might be watching him. He didn't see anything unusual, no one he recognized. Who had sent the message? The answer to that was pretty damn important. Max? Dobler? Either one was bad news. Sookie or the spikehead? Probably not; they would have signed it. Someone who knew he was looking for Rattan? Someone after Dobler's bounty? Most of the possibilities were trouble, but Tanner knew—he *knew,* damn it all—that he could not afford to ignore the message. For a moment he wished he had followed Carlucci's advice and carried a gun.

Tanner stood motionless, rereading the message as a new, hard-edged energy worked through him. Here it was, he tried telling himself, the break he was waiting for. But he knew that probably wasn't true, this was more likely to get him worked over and killed.

The address was three blocks away. Once again he scanned the street around him, but still did not see anyone he knew. He refolded the note, stuffed it into his shirt pocket, and started off down the street.

His stupor was long gone now, replaced by heightened sensations and blazing nerves. Everything around him had an extra shot of clarity around the edges, a shimmer of light. It was like being on speed. He even felt a little jumpy. Adrenaline rush. Tanner wished he could tone it down a bit. He felt just slightly out of control.

When Tanner reached the address, he stood in front of a tattoo parlor that was locked shut, bars over the windows and door. He checked the note to make sure he had the correct address and street; he did. He banged on the bars, rapped at the glass, but got no response. He searched the window and bars for another message, some sign, and found nothing. There was a donut shop on one side of the tattoo parlor, and a juicer studio on the other, but nothing seemed out of place. The crowds and traffic around him were normal for the Tenderloin.

Maybe it made sense. "Watch the sky," the note said. Perhaps the address was just an observation point, a place for Tanner to be when something happened in the skies above. As long as it wasn't death falling on him. He looked up, saw a sick green haze blocking out the stars, but again nothing unusual.

A sound blasted the air, like an air-raid siren. Tanner's chest tightened. He knew what was coming. Someone would soon be flying out a window. People in the street looked up, searching the upper reaches of the buildings on both sides of the street. Most of them, too, knew what was coming.

The signal finally appeared—a black flag telescoped out from the roof of the building directly across the street from Tanner; it flapped gently in the breeze. People quickly cleared the sidewalk below the flag; even the street traffic adjusted, halting and clearing out that part of the road. People took up positions in doorways, on ledges, in windows, watching and waiting; a few people dragged cafe tables and chairs out onto the sidewalk and settled in for the show.

This time, though he would have preferred not to, Tanner watched and waited as well. Whatever was coming, he knew, was meant for him to see.

A window on the tenth floor opened. The street noise swelled for just a moment, then dropped quickly to near silence. Nothing happened for a minute or two. The air grew heavy and tense, as if the heat had jacked up a bit, almost pulsing through the night.

A muffled roar emerged from the window, growing louder, then a large figure shot out headfirst. As the figure plummeted, still roaring, hands bound behind its back, Tanner saw that it was Red Giant. The roar continued all the way down, then ceased with a sickening crunch as Red Giant hit the edge of the street. His body shuddered once, then was still. Tanner could see blood already pooling around the man's head, trickling into the gutter.

No one in the street moved; the tension did not break. Tanner looked back up at the window. It remained open, and the flag continued to fly, which meant someone else would be coming. Tanner had a pretty good idea who was next.

No cry, no roar this time. Max hurtled out the window, hands bound, back arched. There was no sound at all as he fell until, at the last second, his mouth opened and an explosive scream burst forth, only to be abruptly cut off by impact as he struck the ground next to Red Giant.

No shudder, just a motionless, crumpled and broken form. Tanner felt sick as he stared at the two bodies just twenty feet away. Max's face was crushed, his grafted mirrorshades shattered. He still could not see Max's eyes, only a mess of flesh, blood, plastic, and bone.

Tanner glanced up at the top of the building, saw the window close and the flag pulled in. He returned his gaze to the two crushed figures, but his view was soon blocked by crowds as people returned to their business and the street traffic resumed.

Tanner felt a hand on his shoulder. He turned to see the Asian woman with the tattooed tears. A new tear had been added to her cheek.

"That's taken care of," the woman said. She took his hand in hers. "Rattan is ready to see you now."

29

SOOKIE FLINCHED AND shuddered when Uwe hit the ground. A couple of minutes later she jerked again when Max hit, and she had to turn away. She thought maybe she was going to be sick. She hated them both, and she wasn't sorry they were dead, but . . . She breathed deeply, leaned her head against the brick.

When she looked up again, she saw a woman talking to Tanner. The woman took hold of Tanner's hand. Sookie was too far away to hear the woman, but Tanner didn't look happy to see her. He didn't give her a kiss or hug or anything. But he didn't pull his hand away. Maybe she wouldn't let him.

The woman pulled Tanner back a few feet, then let go of his hand. She unlocked the door of the tattoo parlor and waved Tanner inside. The woman followed him and pulled the door shut. Sookie hurried down the street, stopped in front of the tattoo parlor, looked inside. She didn't see anyone in the tiny front room. She tried the door, but it was locked. Sookie wrenched at the door handle, kicked at the door, but it just wouldn't budge.

Rats. She had the feeling he was going to be inside a long time. She also was pretty sure that when he *did* come back out, it wouldn't be here. Somewhere else, who knew? Maybe not even the same building.

If he came back out. That scared her, thinking about it. He needed someone watching out for him. Well, maybe not so much anymore, with Max and Uwe dead. But maybe still, looking for Rattan. She didn't know who

Rattan was, but Mixer said he was pretty bad. She just didn't know about Tanner. She hoped he would be okay.

A young Screamer grabbed hold of Sookie's arm, pulled at her. Sookie resisted, and the girl yanked harder, dragging Sookie away from the tattoo parlor.

"What?" Sookie said.

The Screamer just shook her head. She let go Sookie's hand, pointed at the tattoo parlor, and shook her head again.

"All right," Sookie said. She backed away from the tattoo parlor, then turned and worked her way through traffic across the street. A transplant crew was already set up, loading the bodies into their van. Lots of money was changing hands, and she didn't see a single cop anywhere. Cold smoke rolled out of the van. The crew got the bodies lashed down inside and slammed the doors shut. They climbed into the cab, and the van pulled away.

Sookie stared at the street and gutter, watching the blood. Some of the deeper pools rippled from traffic vibrations. Pieces of Max's mirrorshades were scattered across the pavement, and she could almost see herself in one of them.

"You still following him?"

Sookie looked up, saw Mixer crouched against the building, watching her. She shrugged, walked over to him.

"Who?"

"Hah." Like a dog bark. "You know, Sookie. You're still following him."

"I guess." She sat down next to Mixer. He took out a couple of cigarettes and gave one to her. Flicked open a lighter, lit them. "I'm worried about him," she said.

"You should be," Mixer said. "He's going to get himself killed. Which is why you shouldn't be following him. You can't help him, Sookie, but you're liable to get yourself offed along with him."

"I can take care of myself."

Mixer sighed heavily. "I know," he said. "But I know you, Sookie. Weird shit happens around you, you know that. And anyone can get into it around here. Just leave it alone, Sookie. Leave *him* alone."

Sookie nodded, looking at the tattoo parlor. She wondered how long it would take her to pick up Tanner again. She sucked in on her cigarette and settled in to wait.

30

TANNER STOOD ALONE in the corridor, waiting to be admitted to Rattan's "sanctum." That was what the woman had called it, though she *had* been smiling. He felt as if he were waiting for an audience with a king. Maybe that was how Rattan thought of himself.

The corridor was short but wide, the walls dark gray cinder block. There were only two ways out—the door at the far end of the corridor, through which the woman had brought him, and the door he now faced, which led to Rattan. The woman, whose name was Britta, had ordered him to wait in the corridor, then had gone through the door. He had been waiting fifteen or twenty minutes now.

He could not be sure, but he thought he was underground again. The way in had been relatively simple, though extremely secure: multicoded door seals, body searches, radiation scans, and two elevator rides so smooth he had not been able to gauge distance or direction for either one. He and Britta had encountered only two other people; both were silent and thorough guards.

The door opened and Britta appeared. "You can come in now," she said.

Tanner entered a large room filled with a cool, swirling fog of odorless smoke. The ceiling was high, close to twenty feet above the floor, and there was too much smoke to see how far back the room went. Through the mist, Tanner made out stretches of bamboo along the windowless walls, and the flickering light of torches. This was Rattan, all right. Theatrics. Absurd, Tanner thought. A machine was probably producing the smoke, swirling it about the room.

Rattan was nowhere to be seen. Hidden in the mists? Tanner walked farther into the room and nearly stepped into a narrow stream of water that flowed silently through a curved channel in the floor. The channel was no more than a foot and a half across, maybe two feet deep.

"Wait," Britta said.

Tanner stood at the edge of the channel and gazed about the room, searching through the mist for Rattan. On the right wall, set against a stand of bamboo, was a wooden bench flanked by two flaming torches. Toward the left, along the channel where it entered another stand of bamboo, was a second bench. He still could not make out the rear wall because of the smoke.

"All right now," Britta said. "Cross the water, go to the right, and sit on the bench."

Tanner stepped across the channel and walked to the right, listening for Britta's footsteps. She did not follow him. He reached the bench, glanced at the two flaming torches, then looked into the dense stand of bamboo, wondering if it hid anyone or anything. He could see nothing inside the bamboo, could only hear a slight hiss and creak of the plants rubbing against one another.

"Sit," Britta said.

He turned around and looked at her. Partially hidden by the shifting mists, she remained at the door. Tanner sat.

There was silence for several minutes. No, not complete silence. The torches, burning atop wooden poles, made an occasional light whipping sound, and there was the irregular hiss and creak of the bamboo, as if its own height and weight were too much to maintain without great effort.

Then new sounds, almost inaudible—a faint whir, a sliding sound, a tiny squeal. Tanner looked at the rear wall. The smoke had parted enough to reveal an opening like the mouth of a tunnel. A large, complex wheeled contraption appeared at the opening, then moved into the room. Rattan.

The contraption was a fantastic wheelchair mounted with a framework of scaffolding and hooks from which hung clear plastic sacks filled with variously colored fluids and a complex network of tubes and modular units, all feeding into Rattan's limbs. Or what remained of his limbs. Rattan sat in the midst of it all, manipulating the controls with his right hand—the only whole limb remaining. His left arm was cut off at the elbow, his left leg halfway up his thigh, his right leg at the knee. Strange sacks and webs enveloped the cut-off limbs, with several fluid tubes emerging from each. Rattan's face was still recognizable, intact except for a long, ragged scar on his left cheek.

Rattan maneuvered himself to a spot a few feet in front of Tanner, then locked the chair into place.

"Hello, Tanner." He gestured at the various fluid bags dangling above him. "Can I offer you something to drink?" He laughed, closing his eyes, then shook his head as the laughter faded. He opened his eyes. "Seriously, Tanner. Britta can get you whatever I haven't got."

"Nothing," Tanner said. He did not want to be affected in any way during the coming encounter with Rattan—not by alcohol, not even caffeine. And he did not want to be affected by pity. Much of Rattan's presence and power appeared to be gone now. Entrapped in the fantastic wheelchair, Rattan seemed very much a different person. But Tanner knew that could also be deceptive.

Rattan reached back and opened a small cabinet mounted on the right side of the wheelchair, withdrew a glass, then a bottle. He poured himself a drink—scotch or bourbon, Tanner thought—then set the bottle in one of the holders on the chair arm. He held out the glass toward Tanner, nodded, then drank from it.

"I hear you're looking for me," Rattan said.

"Yes."

Rattan nodded, smiling slightly. "You wouldn't have found me."

Tanner did not doubt that. He had no illusions about that now, nor did he have any illusions about this meeting. Rattan had not set this up out of generosity. Rattan wanted something from Tanner. The biggest question, though, was whether or not Tanner had any chance of getting what *he* wanted from Rattan.

Rattan adjusted himself in the wheelchair, then took another drink. Tanner glanced toward the door, but Britta was gone. He searched through the mists, but did not see her anywhere. He had not noticed her go out the door, nor had he noticed her leave through the tunnel. He wondered if she was still in the room somewhere, hidden.

"You sure you don't want something to drink?" Rattan asked.

Tanner returned his attention to Rattan. "I'm sure."

Rattan nodded, finished off his drink, then poured himself another. "I drink a lot these days," Rattan said. "Takes the edge off the pain." He shook his head. "Never liked pharmaceuticals. They're a great business, but I've never trusted them for myself." He frowned, set down his drink, then manipulated the controls, unlocking the wheels and moving the chair slightly before relocking them.

"You know who did this to me, don't you?" Rattan asked.

"Max."

"Yeah, Max. And he almost killed *you*. I screwed up on that one. But Max is taken care of now, permanently, and you're here." He paused. "Three weeks ago, I didn't give a rat's ass where you were or what you were doing. I want something, I'm sure you realize that, but three weeks ago I had no way to get to you. I've been pushing some other lines, without much luck. But something changed."

"The Chain Killer."

"Yeah, the Chain Killer. You all thought he was dead, didn't you? Well. You were wrong."

Rattan lapsed into silence, gazing into his half-empty drink. Tanner needed patience now. He wanted to press Rattan, ask him questions, but he knew that would only work against him. Rattan was in control of the situation, and they both knew it. He would get around to things in his own way, at his own speed. Tanner just had to be patient and wait: everything would come out.

"I knew you'd come looking for me," Rattan said. "I know you, Tanner. I knew you'd remember my message, and I knew, I know you're not a cop anymore, but I knew you'd come looking for me. I knew you wouldn't be able to let it go." He swirled his drink, but did not bring it to his mouth. "I was waiting for you. With Britta. I wasn't in any hurry, I mean, I had some other things playing out, I wanted to kind of check in on you, let you flop around a couple of days. Pump up the pressure a little." He shook his head. "But I screwed up, and I didn't count on Max, that bastard's been more fucking trouble. Well, not anymore, not where he is. I let you go, and I didn't know you'd made contact with him. I would never have let it go any further, I'd have brought you in, but by the time I picked you up again, you were on your way to meet him, which I didn't even know, and I lost you. Nearly lost you for good."

He stopped and took a few sips from his drink. He punched several buttons on the chair console, studied some figures flashing across the display, flickering green lights reflecting from his eyes.

"It's what I get for being an honorable man," he resumed. "Max and I had an arrangement. After he tried to kill me. We were both out to kill the other, someone was going to get it sometime, but it might take months, or longer, for one of us to pull it off. Max, he's an artist. *Was* an artist. I didn't care much for his crap poetry or his performances with the Red Giant, but that was beside the point. I understood and appreciated his . . . what? Dedication. So we worked out an arrangement. We had a way, he'd notify me in advance when and where he would be performing. I'd stay away, pull all my people back during his performance, an hour before and after, too, so he could come and go without giving away where he was bunkered in. We could trust each other. He knew I'd honor the agreement and stay away, and I knew he wouldn't pull any shit, like maybe set up a phony performance to put me off guard so he could come at me again. With this, we *could* trust each other. Might seem kind of weird, but there it was." Rattan sighed heavily, melodramatically. "Which was how I missed you meeting him."

Patience, Tanner reminded himself. Rattan was liable to ramble on for hours, but Tanner had to go with it. Patience. He'll get there eventually. *We'll* get there.

"How's the smuggling business?" Rattan asked.

Tanner hesitated a moment, surprised by the change in direction. "It's all right."

Rattan nodded slowly. "Think you could smuggle a body up to New Hong Kong? A *live* body?"

Again Tanner hesitated. A live body. Who? Rattan? Yes, he thought—Rattan. He was starting to put it together. "I don't know," he said. "Never thought about it before. Not as a passenger, you mean."

"Not as a passenger."

"I suppose it would be possible. It would be expensive as hell, but I imagine it could be done. Who do you want smuggled up?"

Rattan shook his head and waved his glass in dismissal. He put the glass in another of the holders, then grasped the wheelchair armrest, fingers tightening over it.

"I *do* know who the Chain Killer is," Rattan said. "And I know *where* he is."

Tanner watched Rattan and waited.

Rattan smiled. "You know what he calls himself?" Rattan said.

"What?"

"Destroying Angel." He nodded. "I may be the only person alive who knows that. And now you know it."

Destroying Angel. Christ. It fit with everything the bastard did. Destroying Angel, angel of death. Jesus Christ, Tanner thought, the hard bite of certainty digging at his chest. Rattan *does* know who it is.

Tanner breathed deeply and slowly, trying to calm himself. *Who is it?* he wanted to ask, but he knew he couldn't. He had to wait.

"I want my legs back," Rattan said. "I want my arm back." He tossed off the rest of his drink, poured another. He stared hard at Tanner. "I want them back."

So did Brendan, Tanner thought. So did Spade. Well, maybe not Spade, he probably *liked* having a leg that converted into a scattergun. And Rattan wanted his legs and arm back. Here it comes, he thought.

Rattan looked at his left arm, what was left of it, and moved it slowly, raising arm and sacks and tubes. What *was* all that stuff? Tanner wondered. He had never seen anything like it.

"I don't like being confined to this damn thing," Rattan said. "I want to walk again. I *will* walk again."

There was something going on here that Tanner did not understand. The kind of money Rattan had, he could buy the best cyborged prosthetics available, be walking around as well as he ever had with his real legs.

"I know what you're thinking," Rattan said. "And if you knew . . . well, if you knew some things, maybe you wouldn't be wondering. Prosthetics, right? That's what you're thinking. State-of-the-art cyborged prosthetics. Look and move like the real thing, if you want. Better." Rattan finished off his drink, shook his head, then leaned forward, staring at Tanner. "Never. Never. I want to remain human."

Rattan glared at Tanner for another minute, silent and tight. Then the intensity left his eyes and he sank back in the wheelchair, apparently exhausted. He closed his eyes. The only movement Tanner could detect was the labored rise and fall of his chest with each breath. Rattan opened his eyes.

"You don't know what all this is for, do you?" Rattan gestured with his hand and head at the sacks and tubes.

"No," Tanner said.

"To keep the stumps from healing over," Rattan said. "An artificial circulatory system to keep the wounds open but alive." He paused. "I've been like this for three months, ever since that motherfucking dwarf got at me." Another pause. "It gives me the best shot at full regeneration."

There, finally, confirmation; he had been right about what Rattan wanted. With the realization came a rush of elation, which he tried to control, because he knew he probably *could* give Rattan what he wanted, and get in return what *he* wanted.

"It was a mistake to kill those two cops," Rattan said. "I didn't think I had any choice at the time, but I guess I should have found, I don't know, another way. It's been causing me grief for two years. They were scumbags, Tanner. The worst, most corrupt cops I've ever known. They wanted a percentage of the profits, which was bad enough. But when I refused, they threatened the lives of my sister and her family. Not *my* life, my sister's. So I killed the fuckers. No choice, I thought. But it's been nothing but trouble ever since."

Rattan stopped, picked up the bottle, started to pour another drink, then changed his mind. He recapped the bottle, then put it and the glass back inside the cabinet.

"I've had too much," he said. "It's not enough, but it's too much." He looked up at Tanner. "You see where we're going?" he asked.

"I think so."

"From the beginning I figured you could help me, but I knew you wouldn't. You might be doing a bit of smuggling, but it's too well intentioned, and you're basically too damn honest, and what the hell did I have to offer you? Money. You wouldn't have done it for money, would you?"

Tanner shook his head. "No."

"You know what I want, don't you?"

"You want to get up to New Hong Kong."

"Yes." He was leaning forward again, straining the limits of the tubes running from his left arm.

"Have they been having successes I haven't heard about?"

Rattan sagged back into the chair, slowly shook his head. "No. Some partial successes, with a very few. I know my chances aren't good. But they get better with each one, and they're the best damn chances I've got." He smiled. "But I can't get up there. The doctors doing the regen work are expecting me. We've made arrangements, I've even done the funds transfers. One hell of a lot of money. But I can't get up there, and they can't get me up there, either."

Tanner understood. You couldn't just book a flight on a shuttle as if it were an airplane or a train. Trying to use a false name would be completely useless because the security checks on every passenger involved fingerprint and retinal scan confirmations. No matter what name Rattan used, or how he made arrangements, there was no way to bribe his way through the security clearances. A few crates of cargo was one thing, if the loaders knew who you were. But passengers? Not a chance. And Rattan would be arrested on the spot when his name came up on the monitors.

"I've been trying to buy a way into police records," Rattan said. "Get everything in the fucking computers changed. Prints, retinals, everything, so my prints and scans will match a nice, clean profile with a different name.

But I'm not getting shit. That's where killing those two cops has fucked things up for me. The only cops I've been able to buy into are scumbags so low they can't do shit for me. Security on records is too damn tight."

So *that's* what's been going on between Rattan and some of the cops. Things were starting to make sense.

"You're another way up," Rattan continued. "But like I said, I had nothing but money, and I knew that wouldn't buy you. Then a stroke of luck. A few weeks ago I start hearing things about . . . well, some things, and then *three* weeks ago, it starts up again. A stroke of luck for me, not for the poor bastards being killed by this guy. And suddenly, I have something to offer you."

"Who is it?" Tanner finally asked. He just could not keep it back any longer. Rattan was capable of stretching this out for hours.

"Will you find me a way up to New Hong Kong?"

Tanner did not have to think about it, not after everything he had gone through to get here. "If I can, yes. And you tell me who the Chain Killer is, this Destroying Angel."

"When it's set," Rattan said. "When I'm about to get loaded up onto a shuttle headed for New Hong Kong." He paused, as if waiting for Tanner to object, but Tanner remained silent. "I told you," Rattan went on, "I'm an honorable man. I *will* tell you who it is, and where to find him. You can trust me. Just as I'll have to trust *you*, trust you won't fuck me over, have things set up to haul me off as soon as I've told you. We both have to trust each other. And we can, can't we?" Rattan paused, his expression serious and intent. "Do we have a deal?"

Again there was no hesitation, no need to consider. Rattan was right, they had to trust each other. He nodded. "Yes, Rattan, we have a deal."

31

THE FIRST CALL he made was to Alexandra. It was early morning, and he was back at Hannah and Rossi's. He was exhausted from his encounter with Rattan, which had continued until dawn—working out details, putting up with Rattan's rambling. Tanner wanted to sleep, but he needed to talk to people first, get things going.

There were two real options for getting Rattan up to New Hong Kong. The first, which was what Rattan expected from Tanner, was to actually crate up Rattan like cargo and smuggle him aboard the cargo holds. A doctor would have to be crated with him; he was going to need medical attention just to survive the trip, and going this way would be riskier from that perspective than going as a passenger. Which was the second option. As a passenger. Rattan was convinced that going as a passenger was impossible, but Tanner was not. It was by far the better way to go, so it was worth exploring fully. Which was why he called Alexandra.

When he got her on the phone, he explained what he needed, and asked her if she could do it. "You're the hotshot computer demon, right?" he said.

"Right," Alexandra said. "First time you ever ask me to do something, and you ask the near impossible."

"But you did just say *near* impossible."

"Yes. Very little in this business is truly impossible, but that doesn't mean I can do it. I *do* know that I can't do it on my own. I'll need to talk to one or two other people, maybe even bring somebody in to actually make the run. That a problem?"

"Yeah, but acceptable, if you can trust the person."

"I won't use anybody I can't."

"All right. How long will it take you to find out if it can be done?"

"I should know by tonight. You at the same number?"

"I am now, but I may go home today, so you could try me there."

"I'll call you, then, one place or another. Or drop by."

"Thanks, Alexandra. I appreciate it."

"Sure. *Ciao*."

"Bye."

He broke the connection, then punched up Paul's number. There was no answer—Paul refused to get an answering machine—so Tanner tried the hospital. The receptionist told him that Paul was with a patient, so Tanner left his name and both phone numbers.

He hung up the phone and sank back in the overstuffed chair, thinking. He was not sure what to do about Carlucci. He did not know how far Carlucci would be willing to go. Carlucci would do almost anything to find the Chain Killer, Tanner knew that, but would he let a cop killer escape to New Hong Kong where he would be free and untouchable? Tanner could imagine Carlucci promising Rattan anything, and then, as soon as Rattan told them what he knew, coming down on him and hauling him in.

Tanner could not allow that to happen. He understood Carlucci, but he had given his word to Rattan. He could not take the chance. No, he could not tell Carlucci what he was going to do.

Hannah appeared at the doorway in her T-shirt, hair mussed, eyes half-closed.

"Good morning," she said. Her voice was harsh and gravelly.

"Morning, Hannah."

She remained in the doorway without saying any more, looking at him. Tanner did not know what to say, either, so they stared at each other in silence until Hannah finally turned away and went into the bathroom. He listened to her morning noises—toilet seat dropping, streaming liquid, the toilet flushing, then the spitting of the shower.

There was no reason to stay here any longer. With Max and Red Giant dead, there should be no problem going back home. He missed his apartment, the quiet warm comfort of familiarity. He missed his own bed. It struck him as absurd, but it was true.

The phone rang and Tanner picked it up. It was Paul. Again Tanner explained the situation, as briefly as he could. He emphasized Rattan's physical condition, why he was going to New Hong Kong.

"He's going to need a doctor with him either way," Paul said. "Even as a passenger. He'll be lucky to survive liftoff."

"*Can* he survive it?"

"Oh, yeah. If he's got a good doctor with him who knows what he's doing and watches him every second."

"You willing to be that doctor?" Tanner asked.

"Figured you were getting to that," Paul said. He did not say anything else for a while, and Tanner listened to his regular breathing over the phone. In the background he could hear the faint sound of someone screaming, then a crash, and then laughter.

"Yes or no," Tanner said. What were his options if Paul said no? Leo, the junkie doctor?

"Let me think about it. How soon you need an answer?"

"Soon. Today."

"Give me an hour or so. You be there?"

"I hope I'll be home."

"Okay. I'll let you know. Talk to you then."

"Good-bye."

He set the phone down but did not move. He remained motionless, listening to the shower until it stopped. A couple of minutes later Hannah emerged from the bathroom wearing a thin robe, her hair half-wrapped in a towel. She sat on the sofa, facing him.

"Can I fix you some breakfast?"

Tanner shook his head. "I'm leaving. I'm going back to my apartment."

"I thought it wasn't safe."

"It should be all right now."

"You get what you were looking for?"

"I think so."

Hannah nodded. She rubbed at her hair with the towel, then pulled it away from her head and let it drop into her lap. "We're a lot better at figuring out other people's lives than we are at figuring out our own." When Tanner did not say anything in response, Hannah said, "I hope you think about it, Louis, what I said about Valerie." Tanner still did not respond, and Hannah shook her head. "Fine." She got up, wrapping the towel around her shoulders. "Good-bye, Louis." She walked into the bedroom and closed the door.

Tanner got up from the chair and began packing.

Tanner splurged and took a cab. He still had most of the money from Carlucci, and he figured he had earned it. Inside the cab, he punched up the intercom, gave the driver his address, then told her to take a longer route, up and through the Marina along Marina Drive. The driver, an Arab woman wearing a black flash suit, confirmed, and turned up the radio. Ether jazz rolled smoothly through the cab.

Tanner could hardly stay awake during the trip. It was not just exhaustion. Tense situations and nervous anticipation tended to make him sleepy. When he had been a cop he had often fallen asleep during the tensest moments of waiting before some action was to begin. Once things started, the adrenaline kicked in and he was fine, but until then he could hardly keep his eyes open. Freeman had spent a lot of energy kicking Tanner in the shins trying to keep him awake.

The cab came over the top of a hill and dropped down toward the Marina and the bay. The water was steel gray, overlaid with bits of color: streaks of dark orange, splotches of yellow foam, patches of red, all bobbing in the waves whipped up by a stiff breeze. Two Bay Security cutters were anchored close to shore, almost touching each other, and the Bay Soldiers, jumping back and forth between the boats, seemed to be having a party.

At the bottom of the hill, the driver swung the cab along Marina Drive, between the abandoned art colony at Fort Mason and the cyclone fence surrounding the twenty-four-hour Safeway. Tanner punched up the intercom again, said, "Stop here a minute." The driver pulled over and parked, engine and meter still running.

Tanner gazed at the Safeway parking lot, which was filled with cars, carriages, shopping carts, and people moving between the vehicles and the store, many of them with armed escorts. It was here his father had been killed, seven years ago. Two in the morning, decided he had to have some ice cream, drove to the Safeway. He had gotten the ice cream. When Tanner had arrived, called in by someone he knew in Homicide, the melted ice cream had formed a puddle beside his father's body, leaking out of the carton, mixing with the blood from a torch wound in his father's belly. Häagen-Dazs. Vanilla fudge ripple. His father should have know better.

"Go on," he told the driver. The driver pulled back out into traffic; Tanner laid his head back against the seat and closed his eyes, listening to the ether jazz, drifting again toward sleep.

The cab stopped abruptly, jolting him awake. The driver's voice rattled through the intercom. "We're here."

Tanner put money in the metal box, told the driver to keep the change. The driver slotted the money through, counted it, then released the door locks, tapping at the partition with her knuckles. Tanner got out, closed the door, and the cab pulled away.

A woman who lived on the second floor was in the front courtyard cutting back the overgrown foliage. She and Tanner nodded their greetings as he walked along the path and entered the building. His mailbox was full, jammed with crushed and mangled envelopes—the carrier had managed to cram a week's worth of mail into the narrow box. Tanner sorted through it, but there wasn't anything of interest. He climbed the stairs to the fourth floor.

His apartment was quiet and stuffy. There was a strange, abandoned feel to the place, and he felt as if he had been away for several weeks. He walked through the apartment and opened all the windows. It was hot outside, but a slight breath of wind came in, which helped a little.

Tanner went into the kitchen and opened the refrigerator. There wasn't much inside, and half of it had gone bad since he had left. He knew he should clean it out, but he was too tired. He opened a half-empty bottle of apple juice, smelled it, then drank deeply from the bottle. The cold, sweet liquid hit him hard; it made him a little dizzy, and the cold sent a shot of pain through his sinuses, right behind his left eye. But the pain and dizziness passed, and he felt much better, even refreshed.

The phone rang. He put the juice away and went into the hall to answer it. It was Paul.

"I'll do it," Paul said. "But I'd like to see if you can set something up for me."

"What's that?"

"I'd like to stay up in New Hong Kong for a few months and work with the regeneration teams up there. I told you I've been getting burned out, and this sounds like the kind of thing I need. Something positive, for a change. Beats the hell out of the ER night after night."

Tanner could actually hear the renewed interest in Paul's voice. He had not felt that from Paul in years.

"I'll see what I can do. My guess is I'll be able to work something out."

"Thanks. I appreciate it."

"No problem. You're helping me a lot with this. I'll let you know."

When he hung up, he dialed the number Rattan had given him. Britta answered the phone. Tanner told her he needed to talk to Rattan, and Britta said she would pass on the message. Rattan would return the call sometime later in the day.

Tanner could not decide whether or not to go to sleep. He was tired, but it was only noon, and now that he was out of the Tenderloin he wanted to go back to something like a normal schedule. He was afraid that if he slept now he would be unable to get to sleep tonight. But he did not know if he could stay awake.

He went into the front room and turned on the television. He could not remember the last time he had watched it. Three, four weeks, maybe longer. He flipped through the channels until he came to a video call-in show; only callers with videophones and willing to appear on-screen were allowed. The host was the only participant *not* on camera. The topic was universal health insurance, which was up in Congress again this session. A man on the screen was ranting about the poor getting better health care than they deserved, punctuating each statement with a thrust of his fist. He had just launched into an incomprehensible analysis of the connection between economic status and the desire to be diseased, when Tanner fell asleep.

Tanner woke to the ringing of the telephone. The TV was still on, now showing a soaper. Still half-asleep, he staggered into the hall and picked up the receiver, expecting either Alexander or Rattan. It was Carlucci.

"You're back home," Carlucci said.

"Yes."

"You sound awful."

"I was asleep."

"I talked to Hannah. She said you told her you thought it was safe now."

"Yes."

"Why?"

Tanner hesitated, trying to decide what to tell Carlucci. Lying was no good. "Max is dead."

There was a slight pause, then, "Did you kill him?"

"No."

"Who did?"

"I don't know," Tanner said. Technically that was true. He did not know who had thrown Max and Red Giant out the window. He did know that Rattan himself could not have done it.

"How do you know? You see this one happen, too?"

"Yes. A kind of show was arranged for me."

"Yeah?"

"I was told to go to a place, and then Max was thrown out of a tenth-floor window." He paused. "I think Rattan is responsible."

"What, did you find him?"

"No." He found *me*, Tanner thought. "But I'll be talking to him soon. I'm close, Carlucci. He knows I've been looking for him."

"Then he's contacted you."

"Yes. And I'll be talking to him."

"When?"

"I don't know. Soon."

There was another silence, longer this time. "What aren't you telling me?" Carlucci finally asked.

"Nothing."

"Bull*shit*, Tanner. What is it?"

Tanner started to say "nothing" again, but held back. There was no point saying it when Carlucci knew it wasn't true. But he didn't know what to say instead of that, so he did not answer Carlucci's question at all. "Don't worry about it," he eventually said. "There's no problem. When I get anything, I'll let you know."

"We'd better meet somewhere and talk. Now."

"No," Tanner said. "I've got too much to do, and I've got to get some sleep. There just isn't time."

"God damn you, Tanner, don't go solo on me now. I don't want to be calling in the coroner for you."

"It's okay, Carlucci, it's nothing like that."

"Shit, Tanner." But he did not say anything else.

"I'll call you when I've got something," Tanner said again.

After a short silence, Carlucci said, "Yeah, all right." Resigned and pissed. "Shit, just don't do anything stupid."

"I won't." Tanner smiled to himself. "I'll talk to you." He hung up the phone before Carlucci could start in again.

He walked back into the front room. On the soaper, a man with a cyborged leg, an eye patch, and several days' growth of beard, held a gun and was threatening a woman with it. They were on the balcony of a resort hotel, a swimming pool visible far below them.

Tanner turned off the TV. He felt more tired now than before he had fallen asleep. Maybe he should just give in, crawl into bed, and sleep. Maybe he would sleep all the way through to morning.

Except he had two calls coming in. Rattan and Alexandra. He had to stay awake. Tanner walked into the kitchen and put the teakettle on to boil. Coffee might help. Probably not. He had noticed that, as he got older, drinking coffee when he was tired often would just about put him under. So why was he making coffee now? Something to do. And maybe it *would* help.

He was halfway through his second cup, his stomach souring, when the phone rang again. He answered it, and a harsh voice said, "Tanner, it's me." Rattan.

"I've got a doctor to go with you," Tanner said. "But there's a condition."

"What is it?"

"He wants to stay in New Hong Kong for a while and work with the regen teams up there. Can you set that up?"

"Fuck, I'm paying those bastards enough, I sure as hell hope so. Anything else?"

"Yes. Don't know for sure yet, but I think you'll be going as a passenger. It'll be a lot less dangerous for you, a lot easier for the doctor."

"And the security checks?"

"I'm working on that right now. Tonight or tomorrow I should know if we can pull it off."

"There's a shuttle leaving in two days," Rattan said. "I want to be on it."

"We'll see," Tanner replied.

"I want to be on it," Rattan said again.

"I'll talk to you." Tanner hung up. He stood by the phone, half expecting it to ring again, Rattan calling him back. But the telephone remained silent.

Tanner was half-asleep, listening to Taj Larsen, a wild trumpet player from the late nineties, when he realized someone was pounding on his front door. Not buzzing from the street, but banging at the door. He got up from his easy chair, turned down the stereo, and went to the door. "Who is it?" he called.

"Me."

Alexandra. He opened the door and let her in.

"I think we've got a way to do it," she said. Then she cocked her head at him. "You growing a beard?"

"Only until I find the energy to shave it off."

They went into the kitchen. Alexandra took a couple of beers from the refrigerator, opened them, handed one to Tanner, then they walked into the front room. Alexandra sat on the small sofa, Tanner in the easy chair.

"So there's a way," Tanner said.

Alexandra nodded. "Getting into those kinds of records is a bitch," she said. "So many walls, so many alarms, and traps ready to suck you right in and bury you." She shook her head, smiling. "But we got in."

"Who's 'we'?"

"Me and Kaufman. You wouldn't believe this guy, looks nothing like a computer demon, but man is he good. Mid-forties, bit of a potbelly, wears nice tailored suits, runs a very conservative business distributing toilet-seat liners to office buildings downtown. But sit him down at a keyboard and he just goes nuts. Sometimes I think maybe he's a little schizoid. A functional schizoid."

"So you and Kaufman got in."

"We got in, but getting in's not the same as doing anything. And there's no way to change anything in there without blowing off a dozen alarms and leaving traces. But . . ." She shrugged, drank from her beer. "Kaufman thinks there's a way to take care of your problem. It's only good for one shot, but it should cover you. You only need one clearance and confirmation, right?"

"Far as I know. Just the boarding."

"Well, here it is. What Kaufman does is create a mimic. Kind of a program overlay right at the access point of Rattan's ID data. It'll only work once, and it'll only work with Rattan once he sets it up. Rattan will have to make arrangements for the shuttle trip, and get basic document ID for someone else who's already in the data base. It's got to be someone clean, of course, who will get approval for all the initial arrangements. But it's also got to be someone no one at Hunter's Point will know. You don't want some freak co-incidence of pulling a name at random and it turns out to be the upstairs neighbor of the guy running the confirmation check. Rattan's got to choose the name, he's going to be in the best position to know what's safe.

"So what happens is this, without getting too damn technical. Actually, I can't *be* too technical, because I don't really understand it all myself, but Kaufman says it'll go, and I trust him. So. Rattan goes through security at the launch field, they check the documents, then hook him up. All his fin-gerprint and retinal data go into the system and search for the matchup, right? Finds the match, and Rattan's name and status come off and head back out. This is where the mimic kicks in. It rides piggyback on the confir-mation all the way out to the Hunter's Point field terminals. Just after it en-ters the system, before it comes up on the screens, it does a dump of Rattan's name and status and substitutes this other guy's info, which then comes up on their screens. Identity and status confirmed. Then it all does a self-destruct, program and data, and there's not a trace anywhere. No traps, no alarms go off, Kaufman says, because nothing in the data base or programming is changed, nothing even touched, really. All basically passive until the final step." She paused, drank the rest of the beer, and breathed deeply. "Anyway, Kaufman says it'll work."

"Can it be set up in two days?"

"Probably. Kaufman's working on the mimic right now. He'll just need a name from Rattan to complete it."

Tanner slowly nodded, more to himself than to Alexandra. That's what *he* needed from Rattan as well. A name.

"Why are you doing this for him?" Alexandra asked. "You must be get-ting something from Rattan."

"Yes, I am."

"What, then?"

Tell her or not? He knew she would do it without an answer, but that was not really the point. Tell her. "The name and whereabouts of the Chain Killer."

"Jesus. Rattan knows?"

"If he doesn't, I'm going to follow him up to New Hong Kong myself and cut off the one intact limb he's still got."

It was well after dark, nearly ten o'clock, by the time Tanner was finally done for the day, but he felt good. Things were falling into place, and in two days he should have what he wanted from Rattan.

Rattan had called back just a few minutes earlier. He had been in touch with the New Hong Kong doctors, and arrangements were set for Paul. Tanner had told him what he needed for Alexandra, and Rattan had said he would have it for Tanner by the next day. It was all moving forward. Tanner had done everything he could, and now he just had to wait.

He went into the bedroom and stood at the window, looking down at the street. Oscar, the blind cat, sat on the sidewalk, licking himself. The night was quiet. Tanner was back home, and things were done, and he could sleep now. He would need the sleep. Once he got the name from Rattan, he and Carlucci would probably get very little sleep until they had tracked down the Chain Killer and taken him in. *If* they could find him. There was no guarantee, no matter how good Rattan's info was.

Then what? Once they had the guy, then what? What would it mean, anything?

Don't think about it now, he told himself. He undressed, got into bed, and closed his eyes. He slept.

32

SOOKIE WAS FEELING pretty proud of herself. She'd been the one who spotted the ambulance. She could hardly sit still, she was so excited. Mixer sat beside her, and they were both smoking. Mixer seemed a lot more relaxed than she was. They were sitting outside a crasher shop, watching the ambulance.

She had lost Tanner for two or three days. Mixer had stuck with her a lot of the time. Worried about her, she guessed. She tried to tell him not to bother, she was fine, but he just grumbled a lot and stuck with her anyway. Sookie really liked Mixer. He was a good person.

They had wandered around the Tenderloin, but they'd hung out a lot near the tattoo parlor, since that was the last place they'd seen him. And it paid off.

Tanner had shown up with another man. Sookie thought maybe it was the man Tanner had been sitting with that day by the water, when she'd seen the bodies. They had met the woman again, in front of the tattoo parlor. Then they'd all gone inside. The tattoo parlor was still closed and locked.

Sookie and Mixer had waited around a while, and then they'd decided to check out the other streets, the back of the buildings, the alleys. That's when she'd spotted the ambulance and pointed it out to Mixer. Mixer had grinned and said, "Good girl, Sookie. Good eyes." And they'd set up outside the crasher shop to watch.

A real city ambulance was a rare sight inside the Tenderloin, and it meant money. Money to get in, money to get out. It might have nothing to do with Tanner, but Sookie had a good feeling about it. So did Mixer.

Hah! Sookie said to herself. She'd been right. Tanner came out of the building nearest the ambulance, waved at the attendants and guards. Ambulance doors were opened. Then the other man and the woman came out of the building, pushing a crazy-looking wheelchair with a chopped-up man in it. There was all kinds of stuff hanging all over the wheelchair.

"Man," Mixer said, "will you scope out that thing. That guy's a fuckin' mess."

Sookie was holding on to her legs to keep them from wiggling too much. "Who is he?"

Mixer shook his head. "No idea."

The woman and the attendants were working with the wheelchair, loading it into the back of the ambulance. The man swore at them once. Tanner and his friend and the woman all got in the back with the wheelchair, along with an attendant. Guards closed up the doors, then got into the front with the driver.

"Let's go," Mixer said. He jumped up and pulled Sookie to her feet. "Follow me."

They hurried along the streets, running hard whenever there was room. Sookie didn't know where they were going, but she was sure Mixer knew what he was doing. They hitched a ride with an organ runner for a few blocks, to the edge of the Tenderloin, then hopped off and hurried through a bunch of shops to an exit leading out of the Tenderloin. Once outside, they ran a couple of blocks to the end of an alley leading back into the Tenderloin.

"There's only two places you can get in and out with something as big as an ambulance," Mixer said. "This is the closest one, so I figure this is where they'll show up. Man, it must have cost a lot to buy passage in and out."

Mixer started moving around the street, looking into cars and trucks and carts, trying doors.

"What are you looking for?" Sookie asked.

"A free ride. How else we going to follow them when they come out?"

Sookie tried to keep an eye on the alley and stay with Mixer while he bounced around. All the doors were locked, he couldn't get into anything. Somebody yelled at Mixer, told him to get the hell away from his cart. Mixer ran across the street, Sookie right behind him

Suddenly Mixer stopped, and Sookie almost ran into him. "Hey," he said.

"Hey what?"

Mixer was staring across the street at a parked brown car with a man sitting behind the wheel, drinking something out of a paper cup. The man in the car looked familiar. Sookie *knew* she'd seen him before. But where?

"That's the same guy," Mixer said.

"What same guy?" She still couldn't remember where she'd seen him.

"That guy Tanner kept meeting outside the Tenderloin. I told you I'd check him out, see who he is." He turned to Sookie and grinned. "He's a cop."

"A cop?"

"Yeah. His name's Carlucci. Tanner *used* to be a cop. I checked him out, too. He quit a couple years ago after his partner got killed. He got shot pretty bad himself."

Sookie was about to ask him more when the ambulance appeared, creeping out of the alley. There wasn't more than a couple of inches of space on either side, and it couldn't even turn, it had to come straight all the way out.

"Damn," Mixer said, hitting the roof of the locked car beside him. "We're going to lose them."

The ambulance cleared the alley, turned south, and picked up speed. The brown car with Carlucci started up and pulled out into the street, following the ambulance.

"I'll be damned," Mixer said. "Wonder what the hell is going on here?" Within a minute both the ambulance and the brown car were out of sight. Mixer sat on the hood of the car, and Sookie hopped up beside him. "Carlucci's Homicide."

"What's that mean?" Sookie asked.

"He investigates murders. He's the top guy on the Chain Killer case."

"Chain Killer?"

"Yeah, that guy who kills people and chains them together and dumps them in the water."

Sookie got a funny feeling in her stomach, like something bouncing around inside.

"I've seen him," she said.

"Who?"

"The Chain Killer."

Mixer turned and stared at her, grabbed her shoulder. "You serious, Sookie? You're not screwing around?"

"I saw him," she repeated.

"Where?"

"In the Tundra."

She told him about trying to get away from the thrasher pack, going down into the basement. How the hatch was locked. Seeing the door, going down the passage, into the room. All the machines, and the chains hanging on the wall, then the man with the metal skull and machine voice and something like wings coming after her.

"Shit," Mixer said. "Sookie, you gotta show me where this is. You remember it? You can find it again?"

Sookie nodded, the funny feeling changing to fear inside her.

Mixer jumped off the hood. "Let's find a car and go," he said.

33

THEY ARRIVED AT the Hunter's Point launch field more than four hours before liftoff. Night was falling quickly, the sky a strange deep purple headed toward black. Paul, Britta, and Tanner helped unload Rattan from the ambulance, and wheeled him into the processing station. Through the station's huge view windows Tanner could see the shuttle, its form outlined by lights, cradled in the brightly lit gantry.

The processing teams were prepared for Rattan, though they thought he was someone else, of course. They informed him that he would be boarded first, a half hour early, so all the special physical arrangements could be made; formal processing and security checks would start in about forty minutes.

Rattan had dyed his hair, shaved his mustache, patched one eye and shimmered the other, and added a few ritual strips to his cheeks. Tanner would never have recognized him.

"It's time to talk now," Tanner said. "Or you don't go any further."

Rattan nodded. "We'll go back outside. Britta, stay here with Dr. Robertson. Mr. Tanner and I have some things to discuss."

Tanner and Rattan went back out the front entrance, Rattan expertly guiding the wheelchair out the doors and down the concrete ramp to the tarmac. Tanner followed as Rattan turned the corner of the building and wheeled to within a foot of the charged fencing. He positioned himself for a direct view of the lighted shuttle, and locked the wheels. Tanner stood beside him.

"Am I really going?" Rattan asked. He turned and looked at Tanner.

Tanner nodded. "You'll get through. You'll get aboard, and you'll still be aboard at liftoff." He paused. "I gave you my word."

"I wonder if I'd be able to tell if you were lying."

"I'm not."

Rattan stared at him, then grunted. "What about Carlucci? You're working with him on this."

Tanner was not surprised that Rattan knew. "Carlucci doesn't know. He knows I'm looking for you, he knows about your old message, but he doesn't know I've talked to you. He doesn't know we're here."

Rattan slowly nodded, but did not say anything.

"So who is it?" Tanner asked.

"The name won't mean a damn thing. You won't find him with it. But it's Cromwell. Albert Cromwell. What a name. Least his parents didn't name him Oliver." Rattan emitted something like a chuckle. But it quickly faded, and he wiped sweat from his forehead with his hand.

"If I get my arm and legs back," Rattan said, "I'm going to give up this business." He sighed. "Hell, even if I don't. I'm getting too old for it. I *feel* too old." He shook his head. "You know how old I am?"

"No."

"Thirty-nine. Forty next month. I know, it's not really that old, but . . . I've been doing this a long time. What is that, younger than you, right?"

"A little," Tanner said.

"Do you feel old?"

"Not really. I don't think about it much."

"*I* do. Getting your legs blown off'll make you feel old, tell you that. I don't know, I've been dealing drugs too many years now, and I like the odds less and less. *My* odds. I keep thinking they're going to catch up with me, I've had it my way too long." He wiggled his left arm stump, jiggling the overhead sacks. "I guess they did. And I don't want to push it any further."

He remained silent a long time, staring at the shuttle, and Tanner had the feeling Rattan was not going to say any more unless he prodded him. But, just as he was preparing to ask him for more about Albert Cromwell, Rattan began talking again.

"It cost me a fucking fortune to get onto this flight," he said. "Damn thing was full, and I had to buy four people off of it, and they didn't come cheap. Not much is cheap anymore. Shit, not much of any value ever *was*." He shook his head, gazing out at the shuttle. "You ever been in love, Tanner? You must have been, sometime in your life."

Tanner could not figure where Rattan was headed, but he could not think of anything to do except answer.

"Yes."

Rattan nodded. "I never was, up until a year ago. Always thought it was too much a pain in the ass, too much trouble. I *still* feel the same, but I fell in love anyway. Another sign of getting old, maybe. But of course I can't do it right, I've gotta fuck it up, I've gotta fall in love with guess who?"

"Not me, I hope."

Rattan laughed, so hard the chair shook. "Very good, Tanner. Don't want to be getting too . . . what's the word? Not *morbid*."

"Maudlin?"

"Yeah, maudlin." He shook his head, sighing heavily. "No, not you. Britta. Fucking crazy, yeah?"

"Why crazy?" Tanner asked.

"Because she's young and she's in love with a carnival stud who's got an augmented cock and, according to Britta, the strongest, longest tongue in the city. Me, I say who gives a shit, you can get a fucking machine to do all of that, if you want. But see, that's just it. We've got different priorities. Different interests. Different everything."

"She's going with you to New Hong Kong," Tanner said.

"Purely business. Purely temporary." He shrugged, then violently shook his head. "Why the *fuck* am I telling you all this? I must be going fucking senile." He turned and grimaced at Tanner. "You don't really care, either, do you? All you really want to hear about is Mr. Albert Cromwell, yes?"

Tanner shrugged. "That's what all this is about."

Rattan nodded, but did not resume speaking immediately. He spent a minute with the chair's controls, making minute adjustments to his position. When he was finished, nothing looked any different to Tanner.

"He was a customer," Rattan said. "A damn good customer. I mean, I didn't know he was the Chain Killer. He was just some guy who bought a lot of expensive shit. Well, not just some guy. See, he's fucking half machine. Maybe more than half." He turned to look at Tanner. "Yeah, he's the closest thing to a real cyborg *I've* ever seen. I mean, I don't know what the technical definition of a cyborg is, but I got a feeling this guy is it. *One* human arm and hand is all the guy had. The other arm's metal, and both legs. No flesh look-alikes. Fuckin' high-tech state-of-the-art cyborged. For all I know, the guy's got a metal dick, too. Metal plating up one side of his neck, and half his skull's been removed and replaced with all kinds of hot-shit microcircuitry. And who knows what else? And here's the fuckin' kicker. This guy *chose* to have all this stuff done to him. He *volunteered* to have them cut off his arm and legs and turn him into a fucking machine."

"Volunteered to have *who* do this?"

Rattan nodded and grinned. "Yeah, that's a question, isn't it? He's a fucking military project." He snorted. "Yeah, those bastards. Trying to see what kind of killing machines they can make out of human beings."

"How do you know all this?"

"I had a long conversation with the guy. A couple, actually. He liked to talk." Rattan shrugged. "I don't make a habit of seeing all my customers personal, but this guy, he was buying quantity. He was a good customer, I want to give a little personal service, right? Besides, I want to see what's going on with him. I mean, he's buying a *lot* of expensive shit, hard to believe he's doing it all himself. He's paying my prices, why should I care, right? Except I like to know what he's doing with it all, if anything weird's going on. Good business. So I go see him."

"What was he doing with the stuff?" Tanner asked.

"Shit, the guy's using it all himself. I mean, here I go see this guy, turns out he's half machine, and it turns out he's pumping all this stiff into himself. He's living in a flat in the Euro Quarter, which is where I go see him. First time, he won't let me into the back rooms, and the front room and kitchen are practically empty. Front room's got a couple chairs, and a bunch of electronic shit, which he tells me he hooks up to his cyborged parts.

"I get the feeling right off he doesn't have any friends, and he wants to talk, but he's got no one to talk to, and maybe it makes him crazy, I don't

know, but he wants to talk to me. Doesn't hardly shut up, which is when he
tells me about volunteering to be cyborged, how he's a big military project
trying to see about making killing machines. Could be a load of shit, but he
looks the part, right? So I ask him where are they now, the military, why
isn't he on some army base somewhere, in some lab or whatever. He says he
changed his mind, he didn't want to be a killing machine for the army, he
didn't want to work for anyone. He was special now, he said. He said a lot
of stuff like that, being special and powerful, and he wasn't going to take orders from anyone, he wasn't going to do anything he didn't want to do himself. So he escaped from wherever it was they had him. He didn't say where."

Rattan paused, adjusted his position in the chair. Tanner asked if he
could do anything, but Rattan shook his head. He popped open the chair
cabinet, took out a container of water, and drank deeply from it.

"Like I said," he continued, "could be a lot of crap, but I believe him.
He says he hooks up a lot of this electronic stuff to himself, it does all kind
of weird things to his body and his head, and then he pumps in the drugs,
and he's like in another universe. I don't know, I hear that, it makes a lot of
sense to me. I don't want to try it myself, but I can see it could be the ultimate rush.

"Still, something's off with this guy, I'm not sure what it is. I believe him
about being a military project, and that he's using all the drugs himself, but
there's something else, I have this gut feeling. So I ask can I come see him
again, next time he needs a delivery, and he says sure. I think he likes the
company, someone to talk to. So I go see him again, and this time I bring a
few tick-ears, you know?"

"Listening bugs."

"Right. This time he trusts me some more, I guess, he takes me into one
of the back rooms and shows me his special things. Now I know there's
something weird about this guy. The room's full of angels and wings. Pictures of angels, some sculpture things. Lots of paintings and drawings, even
a couple of things that look like photographs. And on the back wall is an actual set of wings, damned if they don't look like real angel wings. Made of
something like feathers, but not real feathers, something else. I don't know
if I can describe them, except they really looked like angel wings. As unreal as
angel wings must be. I mean, I've never actually seen an angel, right, but . . .

"Now, here's where it gets good. He's showing me all this stuff, and then
he takes off his shirt. His body's all crisscrossed with bands of metal, and he
turns around so I can see his back. His back's *all* metal, from his neck down
to his waist, real flexible and segmented or whatever, and up around his
shoulder blades is some special device, all the way across his shoulders, with
all kinds of slots and flanges and things I don't know. What he does then, he
goes to the back wall where the angel wings are. I see now they have something that looks like it might hook up with what's on his back. He backs up
to them, and I hear these clicking sounds, and then he steps away from the

wall. The angel wings come with him, they're attached now. Somehow he's able to control the wings, they spread out, I don't know, maybe nine or ten feet across. Big fuckin' wings. He stands in the middle of the room, holding out his hands and arms, one metal, one human, remember, with the wings spread out behind him, rising a little. And then he says, 'When I'm wearing my wings, I am an angel. Destroying Angel.'

"So he's standing there, and he's smiling. He says the wings were his price for letting the military turn him into a cyborg. They had to give him wings." Rattan paused, shook his head. "That point, I'm glad I brought the tick-ears and dropped them around the place. This guy seems pretty fucking psycho to me now, and I'd like to know what's going on in his head."

Rattan stopped again, shook his head. "The next few days I listen to the tick-ears whenever I can. I mean, turns out I'm right about he has no friends or anything, no one comes to see him. But the guy likes to talk, right? So he talks to himself a lot. Most of the time he doesn't make any sense, I can't understand *what* the fuck he's talking about. But it's all pretty weird, and enough of it *does* make sense that after a few days I'm getting a pretty good idea that this guy's the fucking Chain Killer. I keep at it, I spend a lot of time listening, and when I'm pretty sure, I send you the message. I figure this is going to make me a lot of money."

"How did you know about the angel wings on the victims?"

Rattan smiled. "I didn't, really. It was a guess. He kept saying so much weird shit about angel wings, after a while I had the feeling he was doing something with angel wings to the bodies. So I was right?"

Tanner nodded. "He tattoos angel wings inside the nostrils of the victims."

"The nostrils? Why the hell does he do that?"

Tanner shook his head. "No idea." He paused. "So then what?"

"Then nothing. After a few days, I don't hear anything more. I think maybe he's found the tick-ears, so I send someone around to check on the building, see if she can pick up the guy and follow him around, see what he does, where he goes. Nothing. Do some more checking, the guy's gone. The flat's empty, and I mean stripped and cleaned out, not a damn thing left. I sort of bide my time, put out some feelers, see if this guy's showing up anywhere else, buying from my competitors, maybe. Nothing. After a while I realize the killings have stopped. I'm wondering what the hell's going on, the guy's gone, the killings stopped, I haven't heard a word from you or Freeman. I wonder has he been caught, but no, there's no way you guys wouldn't make a big deal catching that guy. Then I heard about Freeman being killed and you in the hospital, I realize why I haven't heard from you. Time goes on, the guy never shows, the killings never start again. I wonder if he's moved to some other city, but the killings don't start up anywhere else, near as I can figure. He's just gone."

"What do you think happened?"

"He didn't die, right, we know that now." Rattan nodded slowly to himself. "I think the military found him. They figured out he was the Chain Killer, and they found him and his angel shit, and they hauled him off and locked him up, and covered up everything." He turned to look at Tanner. "You don't think they were going to let anyone know that one of their pet projects had been running around killing people?"

Tanner shook his head. "No, I guess not. So what's happened now? He escape again?"

Rattan nodded. "Escaped, and picked up right where he left off two and a half years ago."

"And you know where he is."

Rattan nodded again, but did not say anything.

"Where?" Tanner said. "That's part of the deal."

"Yeah. Just remember, when there's bad news there's no use killing the messenger."

Great, Tanner thought. "All right, so what's the bad news?"

"He's in the Core."

The Core. Jesus. "You've seen him?"

"Oh no," Rattan said. "I don't go in there. Besides, I've been in this damn chair since he showed up again. But I've got a business, right, and I've got a few customers in the Core. I hear things from inside. Most things I don't care about, and most of what comes out of there you can't believe anyway. But when I started hearing that some half-metal freak with wings had shown up in the Core, I knew. I *knew*."

"Jesus," Tanner said. "Why the Core?"

"Hey, his kind of place, way I see it. Besides, he got found in the Tenderloin. He's trying to stay hidden from the military guys. How much deeper can you go than the Core? And who knows what the hell he's been doing in there? I heard about him several weeks before the first bodies showed up. Setting up shop, maybe. Who the fuck knows?"

Tanner did not say anything for a long time. The Core. Christ. They were going to have to go into the Core to find the bastard.

Rattan *had* come through. Tanner did not doubt his story at all, did not doubt that this man, Albert Cromwell, *was* the Chain Killer. The Destroying Angel.

"Now do you understand?" Rattan asked.

"Understand what?"

He wiggled his left arm stump. "Why I won't get cyborged prosthetics. I want to stay human. Look at that bastard, he's half-machine and look what he's doing, killing all these people."

"There have been serial killers before," Tanner said, "and they've all been completely human."

Rattan shook his head. "I don't care, I've seen this guy, and getting cyborged, shit, that's *done* something to him. Destroying Angel, complete with the fuckin' wings. I mean, just look at what he does to them, fusing metal chains to their bodies, to their skin. I mean, what *is* that?"

"You think it's connected to him being cyborged."

"Shit, don't you?"

"How? Why do you think he's doing it?"

"How the fuck should *I* know?"

"You've talked to him."

"He didn't tell me he was killing people. He didn't tell me why. But I tell you, I've been dealing drugs for a lot of years, and as far as I can see, wanting to turn yourself into a machine is a lot worse than taking drugs. At least when you're doing drugs you're still human. Bad shit, this cyborg crap. And it's not just this bastard. It's the fucking future, Tanner, and I don't like it at all."

There was another silence, Tanner trying to decide what else he should ask Rattan. He could not think of anything. He knew who it was, and where he was.

"I gave you what you wanted, didn't I?" Rattan asked.

Tanner nodded. Neither spoke for a long time. Tanner gazed at the lights of the shuttle and the gantry, the moving lights of vehicles snaking across the tarmac. Rattan would soon be going into space, leaving all this behind. Leaving it for Tanner.

Was Rattan right, that being cyborged had turned Albert Cromwell into the Destroying Angel? A madman, a monster, a killer? He could not believe it was that simple, but that did not mean there was nothing to it. And what about Rattan's other comment, that a transition from human to machine was the future? What the hell did *that* mean, if there was any truth in it?

"What would you have done?" Rattan asked. "If I hadn't actually known who it was? If I hadn't known a damn thing?"

Tanner looked down at Rattan's unrecognizable face, at the strange sacks over unhealed stumps. "I probably would have let you go anyway." He paused, thinking about it a minute, then smiled and shook his head. "No, actually, I wouldn't have. I probably would have ripped every goddamn tube out of your miserable body."

Rattan laughed. "What I like about you, Tanner. You're an honest man. Could use a few more like you in the drug trade."

"Which you're getting out of."

Rattan laughed again, and nodded. "And which you're already into in your own way. Smuggling from the rich and giving to the poor." He shook his head. "Let's go back inside. It's time."

Tanner followed him back around the corner of the building, up the ramp and through the automatic doors and back into the station. The processing teams had already run Paul and Britta through the system and were waiting for Rattan. Tanner kept back and watched as they put him through.

First was the most important—identity confirmation. Rattan laid his right hand over the reading plate and put his head into the retinal scanner. The security man punched it through, Rattan pulled out of the scanner, and they all waited. A minute later the confirm came up on the screens, and they moved Rattan down the line.

The security inspection took the longest as the teams worked over Rattan's wheelchair, running scanners over and through it, opening accesses, taking sections of it apart. No one really thought he was smuggling anything aboard, no one thought he was bringing weapons or explosives, but they were thorough nonetheless.

When they were done, the teams escorted Rattan, Britta, and Paul out of the station and onto a loading van, which then headed out toward the shuttle.

There was still a long time until liftoff, so Tanner went to the viewing lounge in the upper floor and sat at a table beside the dome window. He drank a beer and watched the activity on the field. He tried not to think about much, tried to empty his mind. The final stage, he hoped, was about to begin. With the information from Rattan, they finally had a direction to go, a place to look. He thought he should feel happy and excited, but instead he only felt vaguely depressed. He did not know why.

Sirens blasted, announcing imminent launch. Tanner turned his attention to the shuttle. Wisps of smoke, strangely illuminated by the gantry lights, curled away from the ship, disappearing into the night. The countdown began, broadcast throughout the station.

First came the rush of smoke pouring out and away from the shuttle, along with silent explosions of flame, quickly followed by the muted roar and the vibrations rumbling through the station. The shuttle began to rise, quite slowly at first, then picking up speed, rising above the gantry, trailing smoke and flame, climbing into the night. Tanner watched it rise, fading into the darkness so that only the flame itself was visible, and he continued to watch the flame as it rose and grew smaller and smaller until it was only a star moving slowly across the night sky. Rattan was gone.

Footsteps approached the table, and Tanner turned to see Carlucci. Carlucci hesitated a moment, then sat across from him. Tanner did not know what to say.

"Didn't expect to see me here, did you?" Carlucci said.

"No." He was half-tempted to ask Carlucci if this was just a coincidence, but he knew Carlucci had been following him. How much did he know? Did it matter?

"Who was that guy in the wheelchair?" Carlucci asked.

There was no point avoiding it now, Tanner decided. It was too late for Carlucci to do anything. "Rattan," he said.

Carlucci nodded. "I was afraid of that. But I didn't know," he said, staring at Tanner. "It could have been anybody."

He had deliberately waited until it was too late, Tanner realized. Carlucci must have been here since Tanner and the others had arrived.

Carlucci looked out the window and up at the night sky as if he could still see the shuttle carrying Rattan up to New Hong Kong. "This the price for the info?"

"Yes," Tanner said.

"Was it worth it?"

"Yes."

Carlucci nodded, then stood. "Then let's go get the motherfucker."

It was not going to be that easy, Tanner thought. But telling Carlucci could wait. He nodded, stood, and they headed out of the station.

34

THEY DROVE BACK into the heart of the city in Carlucci's car, headed for the Tenderloin. On the way, Tanner related everything Rattan had told him. Carlucci asked only a few minor questions for clarification, and did not ask Tanner why he had not told him about any of the arrangements with Rattan. Neither of them even mentioned it.

When Tanner was finished, Carlucci pulled off to the side of the road and parked. He called into the department, got patched through to Info-Services, and a woman's voice came over the speaker.

"Diane?" Carlucci said.

"Yes. That you, Frank?"

"Yeah, it's me. I need two things. First, get someone to make a formal request to the Defense Department for information on Albert Cromwell. My guess is that'll draw zeroes, so get one of the freelance demons to make 'informal inquiries.'"

"You want to wait for a response from DOD before sending out the demon?"

"No, get the demon started right away."

"Sure thing. Frank, this have anything to do with . . ."

"Not a word, Diane. Not a word."

"I'll get right on it."

"Thanks."

Carlucci replaced the comm unit and stared out the windshield for a minute, silent. The car's headlights lit up a metal drum lying on its side, liquid leaking through two holes onto the concrete. Tanner waited, also silent. He had nothing more to say at the moment.

"Do we go in now, or wait until morning?" Carlucci eventually said. It did not really sound like a question he expected Tanner to answer.

"Into the Core?" Tanner asked.

Carlucci nodded. "That's something we ask Koto." He looked at Tanner. "*Now* we use him."

"Yeah?"

"Yeah. That's why he's in there. He knows the Tenderloin, better than most, but the real reason we've got him in there is the Core."

"He doesn't live in it, does he?"

"No. But he knows it. He knows the ways in and out, he knows some of the people. He's *our* way in. Without him, we wouldn't have much of a chance. With him . . . With him maybe we find this fucker."

"So we go see Koto."

Carlucci nodded. "We go see Koto." He put the car in gear and pulled out into the street.

Koto lived in the Asian Quarter, in a building just two blocks from the Core. It was close to two in the morning when Tanner and Carlucci arrived at the building. They had left Carlucci's car in Chinatown, entered the Tenderloin through Li Peng's Imperial Imports, and walked in from there.

They stepped into the small lobby of Koto's building, looked around for a minute, then approached the security desk. The guard was a big, beefy man wearing a T-shirt that said KOREAN AND DAMN PROUD. He also had a palm gun in his right hand.

"Don't like the looks of you two," the guard said, glaring at them. He gestured at the front door with the palm gun. "Good-bye."

"We're here to see Ricky Toy," Carlucci said.

The guard did not respond. He kept the gun pointed at the door.

"Just buzz Toy," Carlucci said.

The guard hesitated, scowling, then said, "Names and IDs."

Tanner and Carlucci laid their driver's licenses and city residential IDs on the counter. The guard scrutinized them, then punched some buttons on his console. A voice came through the console speaker.

"Yes, Bernie."

"Frank Carlucci and Louis Tanner to see you, Mr. Toy."

"Punch up the video."

Bernie punched more buttons and said, "Look into the cameras," nodding at the two small swiveling cameras mounted on the wall behind him.

There was a long pause, then, "All right, Bernie, let them up. I'll buzz you if I need to kick them out on their asses."

Bernie grunted, then gestured toward the elevator. "Fourth floor, number four oh one."

They had to wait several minutes for the elevator, and when it did arrive, three short older women dressed in identical purple body suits got off. Only their leather headbands varied in color—one white, one black, one gray. Tanner and Carlucci got on and rode to the fourth floor without a stop. Apartment 401 was the first door on the right.

Carlucci knocked, and the door opened. Though Tanner had heard about Koto over the years, he had never met him, never even seen a picture of the man, and he was surprised to see a tall, very handsome, and well-built man answer the door. For some reason he had always imagined Koto as a small, skinny guy who shunned the light. Koto was nothing like that, and even his stance, the way he held himself, exuded a sense of strength and confidence.

Carlucci took care of introductions, then Koto led them into a room with two huge windows looking out onto the Tenderloin night. The room was furnished with several comfortable chairs, a couple of small tables, and a huge, complex audio and video system. The walls were lined with cabinets holding hundreds of disks and tapes, even two racks of old vinyl recordings.

Koto offered food and drink, both of which Carlucci and Tanner declined, then they sat in chairs near the two picture windows. Tanner remained silent while Carlucci laid things out for Koto, condensing the information Tanner had received from Rattan, adding any other background info he thought would be helpful. When he was done, he turned to Tanner.

"I leave anything out?"

Tanner shook his head.

"You don't doubt that Rattan's information is accurate?" Koto asked.

Tanner shrugged. "There are always doubts, but in this case, not really. I'm convinced. This guy is the Chain Killer, and he's living in the Core."

Koto nodded. "And you think that's the best way to find him, go into the Core."

"Far as I can tell," Carlucci said, "it's the *only* way."

"I don't suppose we could set up posts on all the ways in or out of the Core?" Tanner asked. "Then just wait for him?"

Koto smiled and shook his head. "No one knows all the ways in and out. I only know a few. And even if you did, everyone in the Core and anywhere around it would know what was happening within hours. He wouldn't come near you."

"Then what do you think?" Carlucci said.

"How many to go in?"

"Just the three of us."

Koto nodded. "That's a max. Any more causes real logistical problems. Also, you shouldn't tell anyone what we're doing. Not even Boicelli." Boicelli was a deputy chief, Carlucci's immediate superior, and his longtime friend.

"Fine with me."

Koto looked away from them, out the window. Some kind of flashing lights were going off in the distance, bursts of white and blue.

"I'm willing to do it," Koto said. "But you should both understand, it's a real risk. The Core is a funny place. It's not really quite as bad as most people think, but it can be a disaster. You don't watch it, it's easy to get killed or worse. I don't go inside much myself, and only when I'm convinced everything's right for it. Call it superstition, whatever you want, but different ways apply in there. I'm willing to push it a bit for this, but not much, which means maybe we don't even go in right away. Or maybe not far. Once inside, we go by my gut feelings. If I have the slightest doubts, we get back out fast, no matter where we are. You have to be willing to be patient, move at my pace. Maybe it'll take several trips in to find this guy, maybe more. I know you want to find him before he kills anyone else, but you can't push it or you're likely to end up dead. You have to accept those conditions, or I won't go."

Carlucci shrugged. "Hey, whatever, let's just do it. So when's the best time to go?"

"Dawn or dusk," Koto said. "It's a transition time, day and night people shifting, starting up or running down."

"Can we go at dawn, then? Today?"

Koto smiled. "I love your patience, Carlucci." Then he nodded. "We can try, feel things out. I won't promise any more than that."

"Good enough." Carlucci turned to Tanner. "This time, I want no arguments. You'll carry a gun."

"I'll insist on something," Koto added. "Even if it's only a blade or handjet."

Tanner nodded. "I'll carry a gun."

An hour before dawn, they left Koto's apartment. Koto had come up with several weapons for Tanner to choose from, and he had selected a nine-millimeter Browning. The gun felt cold and hard against his side.

Koto led them out of the building and onto the street. He carried a small knapsack over his shoulder. The sky was still dark, and the street was noisy and crowded and brightly lit. They walked one block closer to the Core, then Koto led them into a restaurant called Mama Choy's. The restaurant was packed, noisy and hot and smoky; the aroma of Chinese food hung thickly in the air. Koto spoke a few words in Chinese to the head waiter, then headed toward the back of the restaurant. Tanner and Carlucci followed him, working their way in a zigzagging path through the tables.

In the rear of the restaurant was a narrow extension with a single row of half a dozen booths, the seats covered in bright red vinyl. Most of the booths were empty. Koto continued on to the last booth, right up against the back wall. An old woman sat in the booth. She was small and thin, and looked quite dignified, Tanner thought, until she grinned at Koto with a mouth empty of teeth. Koto made introductions. The woman was Mama Choy, and she invited them all to sit with her. Koto sat beside her, while Tanner and Carlucci sat on the opposite bench.

After the initial introductions, Koto and Mama Choy pretty much ignored Tanner and Carlucci. They spoke to each other in Chinese, laughing and nodding, Mama Choy occasionally slapping Koto's hand with a loud smack. Tea was brought—a pot and four cups—and then a few minutes later four small bowls of egg flower soup. The laughter and talk between Koto and Mama Choy continued as all four drank tea and soup.

Tanner tried to relax, tried to block out the sounds around him. The soup was good, and he tried concentrating on that, on the heat and flavor. He could sense Carlucci's impatience. He did not know what they were doing here with Mama Choy, but he did not care. He trusted Koto, even though he didn't know him.

When the tea and soup were gone, the laughing and talk ceased, and Mama Choy got very serious. She pulled the teapot close to her, and a waitress took away the cups and bowls. Mama Choy and Koto spoke a few more words, softly now, without laughter. Then Mama Choy removed the lid from the teapot and, grinning widely, looked inside. She studied the bottom of the pot, tapping at the sides a few times with her silver fingernails.

The grin faded and she pushed the pot away with a gesture of dismissal. Then she took Koto's hands in hers and closed her eyes. She and Koto remained silent and unmoving for a minute. Tanner looked at Carlucci, who just shrugged. Then Mama Choy smiled, released Koto's hands, and opened her eyes. She and Koto talked a little more, then Koto nodded. He said something, Mama Choy laughed, then he leaned forward and kissed her on the cheek. She slapped his hand again, and Koto, smiling broadly, slid out of the booth and stood.

Koto nodded to Tanner and Carlucci, and they got up from the booth, thanking Mama Choy, who smiled and nodded, clicking her silver nails on the table. Koto said a few more words, then headed toward the front. Tanner and Carlucci followed him out of the restaurant and onto the street.

"I never go without Mama Choy's blessing," Koto told them when they were outside. "If she says I shouldn't go, then I don't go." He shrugged, smiled. "She says we will have good fortune this morning."

"What?" Carlucci said. "She reads tea leaves?"

"No, she doesn't believe in that nonsense. She just does that with the teapot as a kind of personal joke."

"Then what does she do?"

Koto shook his head, but would not say any more.

Just down the street from Mama Choy's, Koto went into a store and bought three large packages of cheese and put them in his pack. He did not explain that, either, but no one asked him about it. Tanner was content now to just follow and wait. Patience, Koto had said. Wise counsel, Tanner decided.

They continued down the block, went left at the corner, then entered an alley halfway down the next block. The alley was narrower than most, the air filled with fire escapes and metal balconies jammed together, the ground filled with trash cans, wooden platforms, and deep potholes. A few people wandered through the alley, most with faces turned to the ground.

Not far along the alley was a flight of concrete steps descending to a basement door. They went down the steps and Koto opened the door, which was not locked. They entered and closed the door behind them. The basement was dark. A bright, narrow beam from a flashlight in Koto's hand appeared. He had the pack open, and took out two other flashlights, handing one each to Tanner and Carlucci.

The basement was empty. Koto led the way to the far corner and another door, also unlocked. "The Core doesn't exactly need any security," Koto said. Behind the door was another flight of steps, descending one more level. At the bottom of the steps, a long corridor—walls of stone, floor of dirt—stretched out before them. A metal sign hung from the ceiling a few feet away, big letters etched into it with color acid pens.

ABANDON ALL HOPE

ABANDON EVERYTHING

WE ARE ALL SUCH SORRY MOTHERFUCKERS

"Someone's a philosopher," Carlucci said.

Koto turned to face them. Their lights crisscrossed one another, shining in three directions, creating a strange web of light and shadow on their faces.

Carlucci nodded. Koto nodded back, then said, "Let's go."

They started forward.

35

SOOKIE LOST THEM almost immediately. She blundered around in the darkness for a while, no idea where she was, where she was going. Then she stopped, tried to figure out what to do. She was kind of scared.

She'd had no trouble following them to Mama Choy's, then around the corner and down the alley. She'd seen them go down the stairs. Through a small, grimy window she'd seen flashlight beams and shadowy figures moving around the basement, going through another door.

She'd almost backed off going into the basement, it was so dark, too much like that other basement. But she'd gone in, felt around and found the door in the back, and gone down more stairs in darkness. Up ahead in the corridor she could see the thin, moving lights and the dark forms walking along. Easy to follow, she'd thought. But somehow, after making a few turns, taking a couple of side passages, the lights disappeared, and she'd lost them.

It was dark. Silent. Sookie lit a cigarette, used the match to look around. Nothing except stone walls. She kept the match going until the flame burned her fingertips, then dropped it to the floor. Dark again. She had to work hard to keep herself from breathing too fast. Where was she? She had the bad feeling she was under the Core. Or was that the same as being *in* the Core?

Think, think, *think*. Light another match? What was the point? She pressed herself back against the cold stone wall. Dragged in deep on the cigarette. Which direction? Forward or back? Back, but would that really get her out? She was lost, turned around. Now she just wanted to find the basement again, get out of here. Mixer was right. Following Tanner was a bad idea.

Sookie crushed out the butt and breathed in slowly, deeply. She had to do *something*. She didn't know where she was, so any way was as good as any other. Staying put was pointless. Just *move*.

Sookie started walking, keeping her right hand on the wall for guidance. Whenever she came to a break in the wall she lit a match to see the choices. She gave herself just until the match went out to make a decision, then went with it.

An hour passed. She was running out of matches. She was tired. Sometimes she felt real calm about everything, but sometimes she got real scared. She went up and down like that, and didn't have much control over it. If she didn't find a way out soon, she thought, she was going to be a mess. She kept on.

Gray light ahead. She hurried forward, came to a low, slanting passage leading up toward dim light. Sookie squeezed into the passage and started up the slope on her hands and knees. Strange noises grew louder as she climbed: slapping sounds, choked cries, gurgling.

Sookie slowed down as she got close to the end of the passage. She crept forward real slow, listening to the sounds. Then she was at the end. It came out about six feet above the floor of a room with half a dozen windows letting in the morning light. But what she saw made her sick. Sick, and scared again.

A man and a woman, both naked, circled each other, each holding leather whips, which they periodically swung at one another. Their bodies

were covered with huge red marks and streaks of blood. On the floor nearby
was a small, crushed form, so mashed Sookie could not tell if it was human
or not. From the smell, though, she knew it had been dead a long time.

Sookie could see only one way out of the room, a doorway on the opposite side. She'd have to go past the man and woman, around the crushed
body. The windows were too high. No, she decided. She was not going into
the room with those two people. She flinched as the woman struck the man
hard and loud across the face, knocking him to the ground. The woman
stopped moving, waited until the man got back to his feet, then they began
circling each other again. Sookie, feeling dizzy and sick, started crawling
backward down the passage.

Back into the dark. Sookie staggered along for a while, no longer using
matches, just bumping from wall to wall, down one passage or another. She
felt kind of numb, hardly even scared anymore.

She came to a passage lit by coils of fuzzy green light. The walls were
covered with graffiti, but the passage was a dead end. She didn't read the
graffiti, she didn't want to know what any of it said. She just pushed on,
leaving it behind.

She thought she heard footsteps behind her. She stopped, listened hard,
but didn't hear anything. It might be anything, it might be nothing, she was
so tired. When she resumed walking, though, she thought she could hear
them again. Sookie stopped again, and this time they kept on, getting closer.
Someone was following her.

The numbness left her, and she was getting scared again. She kept thinking about the woman in white who had tried to get her before. Someone was
after her, somebody was trying to catch her.

Sookie ran. She was blind in the dark, and she crashed into walls, but
she kept running. She tripped over stones and chunks of wood, scraping her
skin, bashing her elbows and knees. She splashed through water, slipped on
mud, fell over a ditch, got to her feet, ran on.

She ran headlong into a wall and crashed backward to the ground,
stunned. She didn't move for a minute, unsure of what had happened. Then
she scrambled awkwardly to her feet, and a metal hand grabbed her shoulder.

Sookie tried to scream, but another hand, flesh, clamped over her
mouth. She struggled, kicked and squirmed as the hands and arms pulled
her back, crushed her against the hard chest and legs of her pursuer.

"I know you, girl."

No! It was that voice, the thing from the basement with all the machines.
Sookie went crazy, flailing legs and arms, but the thing was too strong, it
kept wrapping her tighter, cutting off her movement. She tried to bite the
hand over her mouth, but its grip was too strong, she couldn't move her jaw.

"Don't struggle, girl. It changes nothing."

The metal hand let go of her shoulder, then the fingers dug into her neck.
A funny pain went up into her head, sharp and cold and hard, and she

started to feel very strange. She stopped moving, just hung there. Things were getting even darker, but spotted with glittering lights, and she suddenly wondered if she was going to die.

"Sleep now," the machine said.

Sleep or die, Sookie wondered. Sleep or . . .

Then nothing.

36

"UNDERGROUND TO GET into the Core," Koto said, "and to move between blocks. But it's not a good idea to stay down here any longer than necessary."

They were still underground, though they had switched passages several times through nearly invisible doors and light baffles. So far they had encountered few people: a group of three men wearing shocker suits and carrying flaming torches, the men sweating profusely, their bodies giving off electric blue sparks; a woman with two parrots on her shoulder and two cats on leashes; a man who charged them with a pair of handjets until he got close enough to recognize Koto, then gave Koto a tremendous hug and ran off screaming.

Soon after they encountered the man with the handjets they passed a lighted alcove dug out of the rock. Inside, seated on a folding chair and working a laptop, was a man wearing a tattered business suit, including a striped tie; thick-rimmed glasses reflected the flashlight beams as he glanced up at them. But he did not say anything, and he turned his attention back to his laptop. The man's fingers frantically worked the keyboard, but there was nothing at all on the screen, no power hook-up, and Tanner wondered how long ago the batteries had gone dead. Days? Weeks?

Just past the alcove, Koto led the way up a metal ladder mounted in the stone. Several feet above the passage ceiling, Koto leaned away from the ladder and stepped across the gap, as if into the stone itself, to the door of another passage that Tanner figured must be near ground level. He and Carlucci followed, flashlight beams showing the way. The passage curled to the right, slanting steeply upward, then opened into a concrete stairwell.

They continued upward, climbing one flight of stairs after another. There were no windows, no illumination except for their flashlights, and the doors at each floor appeared to be welded shut.

Tanner had not counted, but he thought they were seven or eight floors up when the stairwell ended at a small platform with a door. Koto took out the cheese packages, unwrapped them, and handed one each to Tanner and Carlucci.

"When the rats appear, just feed them. You'll be fine."

Koto turned off his flashlight, and Tanner and Carlucci did the same. Then Koto pushed open the door, letting in light from the room on the other side. Tanner heard scurrying sounds, glimpsed large dark shapes moving across the floor. Koto broke off several chunks of cheese and tossed them far into the room. More scurrying, and hisses. Tanner did not realize rats could hiss.

Koto moved into the room, followed by Carlucci, and finally by Tanner. Tanner blinked at the harsh light, but he could see several dozen rats swarming over the floor, sticking close to shadow whenever possible. Tanner and Carlucci broke their cheese into chunks and tossed them into the room, and watched the rats scramble.

The room was empty except for the rats. Light came in through several large windows in one wall and from an opening in the ceiling. A makeshift ladder of wood and plastic and metal led up to the opening.

"Hey! Sunrat!" Koto called. "It's Ricky Toy."

Scuffling noises came though the opening in the ceiling, then a few moments later a long, thin face appeared, eyes covered by tiny plastic goggle-shades. The man's skin was deeply tanned, his black hair short but wild and streaked with gray.

"Hey, Sunrat," Koto said.

"Who's that with you?" Sunrat asked.

"Two friends. We want to talk to you."

Sunrat squinted, looking back and forth between Tanner and Carlucci. "You two look like cops," he said.

"*I* am," Carlucci said. He pointed at Tanner. "He's not."

Sunrat turned his face toward Tanner, cocking his head. "You *look* like a cop."

"I'm not," Tanner said.

"You sure?"

Tanner smiled and nodded. "I ought to be sure."

Sunrat sniffed. "I guess. Maybe you *should* be a cop."

"And maybe not."

Sunrat grinned, then turned his gaze to Koto. "You sure these two are okay? Even the cop?"

Koto nodded.

Sunrat nodded in return, said, "Give me a minute to power down the grid." The face pulled back, and there were more scuffling sounds, then some clicks and loud knocks.

"You'd do a complete fry in about five seconds if you tried to climb the ladder with the grid up," Koto said. "He doesn't like surprise visitors."

"All right, come on up!"

Koto went first. As Tanner climbed, he looked back and watched the rats. All the cheese was gone and now they were settling down, hissing and nipping at each other, fighting for spots in the shade.

Tanner came up inside a room with no ceiling and the walls in ruins. Sunrat lay in a lounge chair, directly in line with the blazing sun. He wore only a tiny racing swimsuit, and his skin, except for his face, was incredibly pale. A shining, oily substance covered his skin, thick and clear. Twenty or twenty-five plastic bottles surrounded him, most of them filled with colored liquids, but a few already empty.

"Have a seat, anywhere," Sunrat said. He reached for one of the bottles, drank deeply from it, and set it back down. "Help yourself to a cooler."

Koto looked at Tanner and Carlucci and subtly shook his head. There were no chairs, so they all sat on the floor. Tanner could not figure out how, lying exposed like that, Sunrat could manage to get only his face tan and keep the rest of his skin so white. Maybe the oil, some kind of sun block. Why would he want to do that? Then it occurred to him that it might not be by choice, that it might be a result of some very strange genetic mutation; but when he thought about it further, that seemed pretty unlikely.

"So what is it?" Sunrat asked.

"We're looking for someone," Koto said.

Sunrat shrugged and snorted. He wasn't looking at any of them. He kept his face directed at the sun. "Don't know why you're here, I don't know anyone. I'm a social outcast." He grinned.

"He's being modest," Koto said. "Sunrat knows a lot of people, don't you, Sunrat?"

Still grinning, Sunrat said, "Nah. I don't know no one. And yeah, I know that's a double negative, I'm an educated man. So sue me." He took another long drink from one of the bottles.

"Do you know the woman who sings at dawn on Saturdays?" Tanner asked.

Sunrat's grin vanished, and he sat up, frowning. He pointed at Tanner, his hand shaking. "You looking for *her?* Then you just get the hell out of here right now. I mean *now,* before I throw you over the wall and . . ."

Tanner put up a hand and shook his head. "No, no, you don't understand. We're not looking for her. I was just asking. I heard her sing a few days ago, I was just curious."

Sunrat kept his hand pointed at Tanner, and said, "You're sure you're not looking for her?" He looked at Koto. "Toy?"

"He's telling the truth," Koto said. "We're not looking for her. You know me, Sunrat. I wouldn't run anything over you. He didn't know, that's all. He's an outsider."

Sunrat turned back to Tanner. "You heard her sing?"

Tanner nodded.

"What did you think?"

"She has a beautiful voice. It was something, listening to her sing."

Sunrat lowered his hand, and his expression softened somewhat. "All right," he said. "But I don't want to hear you mention her again. Not a single word. Got it?"

"Got it."

Sunrat lay back down, shook himself, and directed his face at the sun once again. "So then, who you looking for?"

"A freak," Koto said.

Sunrat laughed. "Hey, wrong place, Toy. No freaks here. Not a single freak in the Core. All normal people."

"A real freak," Koto said. "He's something like three-quarters cyborged. Showed up a couple months ago, maybe?"

Sunrat turned toward Koto. "Cyborged. Anything else about this guy?"

"Well. Maybe he's got wings."

Sunrat's expression hardened, and he stared at Koto for a few moments, then turned his gaze to Carlucci, then to Tanner. He reminded Tanner of Max, since Tanner couldn't see his eyes behind the goggle-shades.

"Wings," Sunrat said.

"Wings."

Sunrat grinned, shrugged, then lay back down. "Nope. Never heard of any freak like that."

He finished off a bottle of blue liquid, then threw the empty bottle hard at Tanner's head. Tanner ducked, and the bottle clattered across the floor behind him. Tanner and Carlucci both looked at Koto, who just shook his head again.

"Sun's rising," Sunrat said, "but we'll get rain soon. You should think about getting an umbrella. Before you get *drenched*."

"That sounds like a good idea," Koto said. He stood, nodded at Tanner and Carlucci. "We'd better go now."

"Yes," Sunrat said. "You'd better."

Tanner and Carlucci stood.

"See you, Sunrat," Koto said.

"Not too soon, I hope."

Koto turned, walked over to the floor opening, and started down the ladder, with Carlucci and Tanner behind him. When they got to the bottom of the ladder, they moved toward the door, and the rats shifted positions to open a path for them.

"Later," Koto whispered, before Tanner or Carlucci could ask him a question. "Let's get out of here now while we can."

He reached the door, opened it, held it for Tanner and Carlucci, then closed it tightly. "Down, quickly now."

They turned on the flashlights and hurried down the stairs. From above, screeching laughter sounded, punctuated by a series of popping explosions.

"Just keep going," Koto said.

They hurried on.

At the top of the ladder leading back down to the underground passage, Koto stopped. "Wait here a minute," he said. "I want to check something. What Sunrat said, about getting drenched. Probably means someone's planning to flood the tunnels." He shrugged, smiling slightly. "Happens."

Koto climbed down the ladder, stood in the passage, and played the flashlight beam back and forth, checking both directions. Then he closed his eyes and cocked his head from one side to the other. He opened his eyes and looked up.

"Come on down," he said. "We get the hell out of here now." He nodded. "Everything's just fine."

37

SOOKIE WOKE IN pain. Her eyes ached, and her arms and legs burned. Burned like they were on fire. She choked out some sounds, opened painful eyes to see if she was burning up.

Chains. Silver chains were burned onto her, melted to her skin. Her *skin* was melted. Metal bands on her wrists, bands on her ankles. Bracelets. Chains between them.

No.

"No," she said.

"Yes." The machine voice.

Sookie blinked her eyes, looked around. She was in that basement room again, lying on the floor, surrounded by machines. Chains and bands on the walls. Windows and gray light. Everything hurt. And there was something strange on her eyelids, she thought, dark smudges when she closed them. Something. She didn't know what.

Where was he?

She didn't see him. All she saw were the machines. The machines were silent, unmoving. Sookie worked herself up into a sitting position, her back against the stone wall. Every motion was painful. Every movement burned her. But the rock was cool, almost soothing. Where *was* he? The Chain Killer. No.

A rumble, and the machines came to life. All at once—spinning, whining, rumbling, groaning. The ground shook, the stone behind her shook.

A blue, glowing light appeared in the midst of the machines. It hovered motionless for a minute, then slowly moved forward. Sookie could not move—the chains held down her arms and legs with their weight and the burning pain. She thought her skin was tearing free from her bones. She had to get away, but she couldn't move. The blue light kept moving forward.

The figure took form in flashes appearing between the machines. Sookie saw bits of feathers first, then reflecting strips of metal. A head half-metal, half-flesh, no hair. Face half-metal, too. Then the figure and the glow disappeared. Sookie couldn't see or hear anything except the machines. She stared hard into them, but still didn't see anything, not even a glimpse.

Light again, and he stepped out from behind a machine, now in full view just a few feet away. Wings of shining feathers lifted and spread out behind him. He wore no clothes, and as far as Sookie could see he didn't need any. Both legs were metal, up to his waist, and there was nothing between them. Sexless. His body was a crisscross of metal and flesh. One arm and shoulder was normal, but the other was metal, steel fingers flexing. Metallic bands went up the side of his neck. More metal covered half his face, but she thought both eyes were real.

"I know you," the angel said.

Sookie shook her head. "No," she whispered.

The angel nodded, said, "I know you," again. "You were here before. You ran away."

No, Sookie thought, but she couldn't even manage a whisper this time.

"I am . . . Destroying Angel," he said. The wings flexed, moved slowly forward, then back.

"Leave me alone," Sookie whispered.

The angel took two steps forward, looking down at her. He reached toward her with the metal arm, curled and uncurled the metal fingers.

"This is the future," the angel said. "Man's future. The fusion of metal to flesh, flesh to metal. The organic with the inorganic. Man with machine."

Sookie was so scared now she didn't think she could take any more. She thought her chest was going to explode, her heart was going to come apart on her. He's going to kill me, she thought, and she closed her eyes.

"What do you *see?*" The angel's voice boomed, shaking inside her head. A bright light came on just in front of her closed eyes. "What do you see?"

"Nothing," she said. There was bright orange from the light, and dark smudges in her eyelids.

The light brightened, hot and painful, and then the angel's fingers gently touched her eyelids, the metal cool and soothing. "What do you see here?"

"Nothing," Sookie said again. "Orange light and dark shadows."

"Wings," the angel said. He took his fingers away. "Wings," he repeated. "The wings of death. *My* wings. *Your* wings." He paused. "And you can't see them."

The light faded, and Sookie slowly opened her eyes. The angel was only a foot away, gazing down at her.

"Angels . . . angels are the breath of God," he said. He breathed deeply, slowly shook his head. "The future is here," the angel said. "Those who refuse to join it must be destroyed. *I* must destroy them."

And then Sookie knew, way deep inside, that she was going to die. The fear went away, replaced by a terrible numbness that went completely through her. She suddenly felt so tired she knew she couldn't have moved an inch even without the chains. She *knew*.

The angel knelt before her, his two real eyes staring hard into her own. Maybe they weren't real, she now thought. How could they be? How could *he* be a human being? She didn't know, and now it didn't matter. She was all cold and numb inside, even her brain seemed cold and numb, and so it didn't matter. She thought maybe she was already dying.

The angel reached forward with his human hand and gripped her throat, pressing hard and tight. It surprised her, the feel of warm flesh. She thought it would have been the metal hand.

The fingers dug deep into either side of her throat, and the awful fear rose up again inside her, shooting through the numbness. She tried to struggle now, reaching up with her hands, trying to push him away. But she had no strength. It was hopeless, and the fingers dug in still harder.

Pain drove up into her head, and silver glitter fell in front of her eyes, blocking out the angel's face. She tried digging her fingers into his arm, but the pain drove the last of her strength away, and she stopped struggling. I'm dying, she thought. I'm dying.

The glitter rushed across her sight, a storm of it now, then exploded into a ball of dark, hot red, blinding her to everything. There was nothing but the flaming red now, and the pain driving up into her head and behind her eyes. The red brightened, blending into orange, then yellow, then finally a blazing white. The pain exploded, shooting all through her, bursting with the white light, and the light and pain grew brighter . . . and brighter . . . and brighter . . . and . . .

38

TANNER AND CARLUCCI were sitting in the Carrie Nation Cafe, drinking coffee, when the spikehead found them. It was the day after their trip into the Core, and it was noon—the day was extraordinarily hot and muggy, suffusing the Tenderloin with stagnation and lethargy. The streets were nearly empty, and many of those few people who *were* on the streets looked half-asleep or half-zoned.

The two of them were talking about when to take another shot at the Core. Koto had admitted that Sunrat probably knew something about the Chain Killer, but it was obvious that Sunrat was not going to tell them a thing about it. He had said he might go back to see Sunrat alone; maybe in a couple of days he would go see Mama Choy again, see what she had to say.

Carlucci had wanted Koto to go see her again right away, at least to ask her, but Koto had refused, insisting it didn't work that way. The two of them had gone back and forth awhile, Koto digging in, Carlucci getting more and more pissed.

Tanner had the feeling Carlucci was arguing more for form's sake than anything; despite their concerns about time, and the possibility of another killing, Carlucci knew better than to really push Koto. Carlucci was just frustrated. The DOD request was being stonewalled, and the demon hadn't gotten anywhere yet, and they all felt that even though they now knew who the killer was, and *where* he was, they hadn't made any real progress.

So Koto had gone off to think about things, and Tanner and Carlucci had gone to the Carrie Nation. They were drinking coffee and trying to sort things out when the spikehead came in through the door and walked up to their booth. The spikehead put his hands on the table, stared at Tanner, and said, "I've been looking for you."

"Mixer, right?" Tanner said.

The spikehead nodded.

"Okay, you've found me."

Mixer gestured toward Carlucci, said, "You're Carlucci. Homicide."

"Shit," Carlucci said. "You want to just shout it?"

Mixer shrugged. "Your problem, not mine."

"What *is* your problem, then?" Tanner asked.

Mixer did not seem too sure he wanted to say anything. "It's about the Chain Killer," he eventually said.

They were silent a few moments, looking at Mixer, then Tanner finally said, "So tell us."

Mixer shrugged, shifted from one foot to the other, then slid onto the bench next to Tanner. "I think I know where he does the shit with the chains. You know? Melting them to the bodies?"

"Yeah?" Carlucci said. He sounded skeptical.

"Yeah."

"Where is it?" Carlucci asked.

"In the Tundra."

"Not in the Core?" Tanner said.

Mixer shook his head. "You gotta be out of your fucking head you think I'd go in there. No, it's in the Tundra. A big basement room under a building."

"How do you know that's what it is?" Carlucci asked.

"It's full of a whole bunch of strange old machines, which means I don't know what, really. Maybe just that it's weird. But there are silver chains hanging all over the walls. The same fucking chains, I'm telling you."

No one said anything for a few moments, then Tanner asked, "How did you find it?"

Mixer shrugged, looked directly at Tanner. "I didn't. Sookie did."

"Who the hell is Sookie?" Carlucci asked.

"A girl," Tanner replied. Then, to Mixer, "*Sookie* found it?"

Mixer nodded. "She showed me where it was, couple days ago. I've been trying to find you two ever since." He looked at Carlucci. "I knew you were head guy on this thing, figured you two were working together on it. Thought you guys would want to know."

"Where's Sookie now?" Tanner asked. "She didn't stay there, did she?"

Mixer snorted. "Not a chance. I don't know where she is, but I know she's not there. I had to drag her just to get her to show me where it was. She's too damned scared of the place." He paused. "She said she saw the guy there that time, when she found it."

"She *saw* the Chain Killer?"

"She thinks that's who it was. He scared the hell out of her. She said he was some weird guy with a metal skull." He paused, cocking his head. "And get this. She thinks the guy had wings."

"Jesus Christ," Carlucci said. "That's him."

They got into Carlucci's car—Carlucci and Tanner in front, Mixer in back. Carlucci called in, made arrangements; several other Homicide detectives would be waiting for them on the street.

The late-afternoon rain began soon after Carlucci pulled onto the road. It burst upon them, obscuring their vision until Carlucci managed to get the wipers going.

"Shit," Carlucci said. He rolled up the windows and turned on the air conditioning, which hissed and sputtered at them, dripping fluids to the car floor. The heat had not dissipated much from its early-afternoon peak.

Tanner turned and looked back at Mixer. "How long ago did Sookie find this place?" he asked.

"Two weeks ago, something like that."

"And she didn't say anything to you, anyone else?"

Mixer shrugged. "You know Sookie. I don't think she really thought about it." He tapped the side of his head with one finger. "She's all right, you know, but she doesn't think the same way as most people. I doubt it ever occurred to her that telling someone about it might help get this guy."

Tanner nodded. That sounded right. He wondered where she was now. Holed up somewhere, still afraid?

They hadn't gone more than a few blocks when Carlucci got a call on the radio. Another location had come up on Homicide's computers—the lagoon by the Palace of Fine Arts—which meant more bodies. Carlucci said he was on his way, then pulled over to the side of the road. He looked at Tanner.

"You want to go with me?" he asked.

Tanner nodded, feeling a little sick. "Time, I think."

Carlucci nodded his head at Mixer. "What about him?"

"We still need him to show us the basement. We've got to see it."

Carlucci shrugged. "All right." He turned to Mixer. "Just stay the hell out of our way."

"Hey," said Mixer.

Carlucci turned back, pounded once on the air conditioner, which only spat out more fluids. "Fuck this thing." He pulled away from the curb and shot out into traffic.

The lagoon was on their left, large and expensive houses on their right. Tanner could see several cops standing in the rain at the water's edge, down at the far end of the lagoon. Two of them were uniforms—called in to do the shit work, Tanner imagined. He wondered what the residents here were going to think of the Chain Killer's victims being dumped in their exclusive neighborhood.

When they were even with the group of cops, Carlucci pulled over and parked. He and Tanner got out and started across the grass, the rain drenching them. Mixer followed just behind them, and when Carlucci told him to stay in the car he just shook his head. Carlucci grimaced, said, "Then stay back, out of the way. Got it?" Mixer nodded, and they continued toward the water.

Incredibly, when they were halfway to the lagoon, the rain stopped. But they were still wet, hot and sticky, and even the rain had not cooled down the air. The sun was a dim, orange glow in the west, barely visible through the dissipating cloud cover.

The grass ended several feet from the water's edge, and Tanner and Carlucci had to carefully work their way through the strip of mud that circled the lagoon. When they reached the group of cops, there was no round of hand shaking, no chorus of hellos and greetings. One of the uniforms, a big blond woman, pointed at the water and said, "There it is."

Tanner could see the top of the spike a few inches above the water, and the rope tied to it. Carlucci looked around the empty streets.

"Coroner's men should be here soon," he said. He turned back to the uniform. "Go ahead and pull them in."

The woman nodded, glanced at her partner, a tall skinny guy with a mustache; he frowned, then nodded back. They got down on their knees in the mud and shallow water, took hold of the rope, and started pulling.

It looked too easy, Tanner thought; the two uniforms were hardly straining. The woman confirmed that when she said, "Mother, this must be a solo. There's hardly any weight."

Another solo? Tanner wondered for a few moments if it might be a phony, a sack or something, not a body at all. But that hope quickly faded as chained wrists appeared, tied to the end of the rope, and a mass of swirling, dirty blond hair.

It *was* a solo, a small, naked body facedown. The two uniforms backed up and pulled the body the rest of the way out of the water, onto the mud slope.

"Aw, shit," the woman said. "It's just a kid. That fucking son of a bitch."

A terrible, sick feeling went through Tanner as he looked down at the body still lying facedown in the mud, bound at the wrists and ankles by silver bands and chains. A kid, yes, a girl. He did not want them to turn her over.

He took a few steps back, so he was just behind and to the side of Carlucci, but he still could see the body. The two uniforms slowly turned her over, and even though her face was mostly covered by wet hair and mud, Tanner recognized her.

Sookie.

Tanner felt dizzy, and his vision went funny on him, twisting slightly. The two uniforms carefully pulled the hair away from her face, then gently washed away the mud with lagoon water. Christ. Angel wings had been tattooed onto her eyelids. Tanner thought he was going to lose his balance and he reached out, grabbed Carlucci's shoulder to keep from falling.

Carlucci turned, said, "What is it?" Then he stared into Tanner's eyes for a few moments. "What, Tanner, do you know her?"

Tanner nodded, still staring at the body. He could not quite accept that he was seeing her. "It's Sookie," he said.

"Sookie? The girl who found the basement?"

Tanner nodded again. He thought he should stop looking at her, but he couldn't. He wasn't sure he was breathing. The cops were moving around, but he didn't really hear anything, little more than a background hum. He felt Mixer push past him, heard the spikehead say her name, saw him kneel down at Sookie's side until one of the cops pulled him back to keep him from touching the body. And then, as Tanner took in a deep breath, as he thought he was starting to pull everything back together, as he was about to let go of Carlucci's shoulder, the vertigo got worse, and a paralyzing ache went through him.

It was like seeing Carla dead all over again. As if she had been reincarnated, and now had died again, and he had to see her dead body once more. It was like seeing two dead people, both of whom meant something to him, both of whom he cared for in different ways—Sookie and Carla, he was seeing both of them. And then a third, as Connie's face superimposed itself over

Sookie's. They weren't that different in age, just two or three years. It occurred to him that it could have been Connie lying there, dead and chained. It could have been both of them, Sookie and Connie, dead, face to face in chains.

"You all right?" Carlucci asked.

Tanner shook his head and finally pulled his gaze away. He released Carlucci's shoulder and took a few steps back, almost losing his footing on the slick mud. He looked around for a place to sit—a bench, a stump, a rock, anything—but there was nothing except mud and grass and water nearby.

He stood motionless, feeling somehow stupid and lost. A phrase came into his mind, from a movie or a book, he couldn't remember. "Catch the killer, and save the girl." Something like that. They had definitely failed at the second part of that, and it was still uncertain whether or not they could even manage the first.

He saw the coroner's van pull up, the men getting out and starting across the grass toward the lagoon and Sookie's body. Tanner finally moved, making his way through the mud and onto the grass, then walking slowly, unsteadily toward Carlucci's car. He could not really figure out what was happening to him. As he walked he kept sensing the ground coming up at him as if he were pitching forward, crashing face first into the grass; but he was moving along just fine, maintaining his balance, walking upright.

He reached Carlucci's car, opened the passenger door, and dropped onto the seat. He glanced toward the lagoon, saw Carlucci talking to the coroner's men, then looked away. He leaned his head back against the seat and closed his eyes.

Tanner breathed slowly and deeply. He tried to concentrate exclusively on his breathing, blocking out all other thoughts. In, long and deep . . . then slowly out. In . . . hold . . . out . . . in . . . hold . . . out. . . . He managed to induce a kind of trance; he focused on his breathing, the way it eased the pressure in his head, his chest.

Carlucci's voice intruded, breaking the trance. Tanner opened his eyes. Carlucci stood a few feet away, looking at him.

"What did you say?" Tanner asked.

"You going to be all right?"

Tanner nodded. He sat up, swung his legs outside the car. "I'll be fine."

"Have you known her a long time?"

"No. But it's not just her." He shrugged. "It's complicated."

Carlucci nodded, and did not say anything. They both were silent for a minute, and Carlucci looked back toward the lagoon. He ran his hand through his hair twice, then jammed it into his pocket.

"Why do you think the angel wings were on her eyelids?" Carlucci finally asked.

Tanner shook his head. "I don't know. Maybe because she had seen him before? It could be that simple, I suppose. I don't know. Right now I feel like I don't understand this guy at all."

"Did you ever?"

Tanner shrugged, then shook his head once more.

Tanner looked back toward the lagoon. The coroner's men were strapping Sookie's body to the stretcher. Mixer stood nearby, watching them. They cinched the straps, checked them, then lifted her and started back toward the van. One of the men slipped and fell, dropping his end of the stretcher into the mud. Tanner half expected Sookie's body to slide off the stretcher, but it remained secure. The man got to his feet, picked up his end, and they started again. They moved more slowly, carefully, until they reached the firmer footing of the grass. Mixer watched them for a minute, then headed back for the car. He seemed to be having as much difficulty walking back as Tanner had.

When Mixer reached the car, he did not say a word. He and Tanner looked at each other, but neither spoke.

"You feel up to going into the Tundra?" Carlucci said to Tanner. "I assume you want to be part of this."

Tanner turned to look at Carlucci. "Christ, yes, let's just get this over with."

Carlucci nodded, then walked around the car and got in behind the wheel. Tanner got back into the car and closed the door. Mixer climbed into the back, still silent. Carlucci started the engine.

"Wait a minute," Tanner said.

The coroner's men had reached the van. They loaded Sookie's body into the back, secured the stretcher inside, then backed out and shut the doors.

"All right," Tanner said. "Let's go."

Carlucci put the car into gear and swung out into the street.

39

THEY CAME AROUND a corner, and Tanner saw four people standing on the sidewalk, talking to each other. He recognized the woman—Fuentes—and one of the men—Harker. The other two were probably Homicide detectives as well. Carlucci pulled the car up onto the sidewalk and cut the engine. He dug two flashlights from under the seat, handed one to Tanner, and then they got out.

Mixer led the way into a narrow gap between two buildings. Fuentes and Harker joined them while the other two detectives remained out in the street. About twenty feet into the alley, Mixer headed down a flight of concrete steps to a basement. It was a lot like the way they'd gone into the Core, Tanner thought. He and Carlucci followed him down; Fuentes and Harker remained in the alley at the top of the steps.

"Used to be this vent screen was open," Mixer said. "How Sookie got in the first time. But the other day when she brought me here, it was boarded over. Solid. I had to bust my way in through the door."

He opened the door, and they went inside, Tanner and Carlucci switching on the flashlights. The room was nearly empty. A few rickety shelves hung from one wall, a steel cabinet was propped against another, and broken glass lay in two piles next to the cabinet. There was a hatch in the floor, and in the far right corner was a wooden door.

"Through there," Mixer said, pointing at the door. "She only found it by accident. She'd wanted to get to the underground lines, but the hatch was stuck or sealed or something, so she'd gone through the door."

"All right," Carlucci said. "Fuck this room, let's get right to it."

Carlucci led the way, and Mixer joined them. There were no locks on the door, and they entered a short, narrow passage, the room at the other end dimly lit but partially visible through an open door.

One at a time they emerged from the passage and into a huge room filled with machines. The ceiling was high, and windows near the top, though grimy, let in light from outside. On the walls hung sets of silver bands and chains.

Carlucci approached the wall and closely examined the chains without touching them. "Jesus," he said. "This is the place."

Tanner stood and looked around the room. The machines were old, but clean and dust free. There were some he did not recognize, but most he did. A drill press, a grinder, two band saws, a router, a polisher. Toward the back he thought he saw a mold press and a die cutter. Sookie had been here. The Chain Killer had brought her here. He sniffed the air, smelling something odd, and wondered if it had anything to do with the machines. A kind of burnt odor.

"Anyone else smell that?" he asked. He watched the others draw in sharp, deep breaths.

"Yeah," said Mixer. "Stinks, but what?"

"Burned flesh," Carlucci said. "I know that smell. Jesus," he said again. "I wonder how recently that bastard's been here."

No one answered him. Tanner wondered if any of them really wanted to know.

"I'll get Porkpie to come in and go over this place," Carlucci said. Porkpie was one of the senior crime-lab techs. "Don't know if he'll be able to get anything that'll help us, but I guess you can't ever tell." He shook his head and looked at Tanner. "He's still in the Core, that motherfucker. But maybe, just maybe . . ." He shrugged. "Think about this, will you? Do we keep taking runs at the Core, or do we wait here instead and hope he shows up before he does the next one? I suppose it's possible this isn't the only place he's got."

Tanner shook his head. "I don't know. How likely is it, though, that he's got another setup like this? Posting teams here around the clock just might catch something."

"Why not just bust your way through the hatch?" Mixer said. "That's gotta be the way he comes and goes. Follow the way back, maybe to where he lives."

They looked at Mixer. What he said made sense, Tanner thought. "Might be something to that," he said. "He's probably got any alternate ways in sealed off, to keep people out of here, so maybe there's only one place to end up. Like working a maze backward, from the finish to the start."

Carlucci grunted, said, "Worth thinking about, I guess."

Tanner and Carlucci wandered among the machines, working their way through them toward the back of the large room. Tanner wondered what the Chain Killer did with all these machines. Anything? He could not see a connection with most of them. Maybe they were just for effect. But then for whose benefit?

In the rear of the room, the machines gave way to a large open area occupied primarily by an operating table. Beside the table were smaller machines and tools, including gas canisters, welding torches, and other tools he did not recognize. This was where he did it, Tanner realized, noticing the restraints attached to the table. This was where he fused the chains to his victims.

Sookie had been on this table. Sookie had . . .

He turned away from the table. "Carlucci," he said. Then, "Something you should see."

He waited for Carlucci to work his way through the machines, scanning the area for anything else that might be significant. He felt numb again, slightly sick.

"Jesus," Carlucci said when he reached Tanner's side. He stared at the table and tools, then said, "Jesus Christ, look at that." He pointed to the floor, at something Tanner had not noticed—small pieces of what appeared to be melted or burned skin. "Something for Porkpie to sink into." He sighed heavily and turned to face Tanner. "The spikehead's right," Carlucci said. "No more fucking around. We bust through the hatch, we get this fucker now, whatever it takes."

Tanner nodded, silent and still numb. There was nothing else to say, there was nothing else to do.

•   •   •

Tanner stood in the Tundra basement and watched the two techs working on the floor-hatch locks; he did not much care about this anymore. Sookie was dead. Yet it was Sookie, however unintentionally, who had made this possible; it was Sookie who had led them here.

Four people would be going through the hatch: Tanner, Carlucci, Fuentes, and Harker. More than that in the close, underground confines would make for too many potential problems. Mixer was *not* going, if only because Carlucci had proved to be more stubborn than the spikehead.

Tanner himself was ambivalent. His part of this was over, it seemed to him. He had made his contribution. He had found, or been found by, Rattan, and had learned who and where the Chain Killer was. It no longer mattered if Tanner was along. Carlucci and the other cops would either find the Chain Killer or not, it made no difference whether or not Tanner was with them.

He wondered if Sookie's death should have enraged him, made him eager for revenge and justice, eager to be part of the Chain Killer's capture. But it had always seemed to him that revenge was vastly overrated, and justice was far more complicated and far less easily attained than most people wanted to admit.

Seeing Sookie's dead, mutilated body had depressed him more than anything else. She had very likely saved his life after he'd gone out that window, saved him from Max, but he had not come close to saving hers. He had not even known she had needed saving. What the hell did that mean? Anything?

Still, here he was, waiting with Carlucci for the techs to do their work. Why? If nothing else, he felt a need to see it through.

He felt for the trank pistol jammed into his back pocket. They were all armed with tranquilizer weapons in addition to their guns. The other weapons were to be a last resort. They wanted the Chain Killer alive. The mayor and the chief of police, in particular, wanted to see him tried, convicted, and publicly executed. One more thing Tanner did not really care much about.

"Got it," said one of the techs. Lights were trained on the hatch as the techs raised it, swinging it open on its hinges. "It's all yours."

Tanner and Carlucci crouched at the edge of the opening, aimed their lights through it. A metal ladder led down to a platform beside a set of rail tracks. The platform was empty, and the tunnel in both directions was silent. "Let's go," Carlucci said.

Carlucci went first, then Tanner, and the other two followed. There was barely enough room on the platform for all four of them, and the ceiling was only a few inches above their heads. Tanner had the urge to duck as he moved, though it was not actually necessary. The walls were part stone, part concrete, part solidly packed dirt. The ground along the tracks was a mix of dirt, gravel, and rock.

The tunnel leading to the right, away from the Tenderloin and the Core, was sealed just a hundred feet or so beyond the platform—a brick and concrete wall filled the tunnel, blocking the tracks. Not even a rat could have found a way through it.

Carlucci led the way in the other direction, stepping off the platform and walking along the side of the tracks. Tanner and the others followed, single file, flashlights casting wide, shaky beams through the dark.

They spent the next hour slowly following the tracks. It was a relatively straightforward path, necessitating little discussion and no decisions of significance. During that hour they came across several passages branching away from the main tunnel and the tracks, and they investigated each one; but in every case, as expected, they found the branching passages sealed, usually quite close to the main tunnel.

Graffiti covered the walls in some stretches of the tunnel, and they even came across several large and beautiful paintings done on the stone walls, preserved by clear fixatives: an abstract done in yellows and black, framed in white; a machine with a man-shaped head and dozens of mechanical arms, hovering above a deserted city square; a portrait of a dark-haired woman.

Tanner trudged on, just behind Carlucci, still quite numb. The air in the tunnel was not as cool and fresh as it should have been, as most underground tunnels were in the city. Too many passages blocked off, too much natural venting and circulation eliminated. Stagnant and tepid, like death.

The tracks ended.

The ceiling rose, and the tunnel widened into a closed chamber. Two large carts that apparently ran on the tracks were mounted against one wall. A large door was the only other way out.

They spent a couple of minutes checking the room, but did not find anything. No one spoke, and they moved with hardly a sound. Carlucci stepped up to the door, tried the handle. Unlocked. At his signal, all lights were extinguished. The darkness was complete; Tanner could not see a thing.

A slight cracking sound as Carlucci open the door. A faint slash of light appeared, slowly widened, cut across the room. A wide passage lay beyond the door, dimly lit from an unidentifiable source. The passage appeared to be empty.

Carlucci swung the door completely open and Tanner joined him in the doorway, gazing down the passage. There was nothing to be seen except blank walls. The passage extended nearly fifty feet, then ended at another door. There were no sounds except a faint, humming vibration that seemed to roll smoothly through the air around them.

Carlucci and Tanner started down the passage, and the others followed at ten-foot intervals. When they reached the door, Tanner and Carlucci drew the trank guns. Carlucci gripped the door handle, slowly pushed it down.

This door, too, was unlocked. He turned, checked to make sure everyone was ready; the others all had their trank guns out. He pressed down on the door handle, there was a quiet click, then he pushed open the door.

The door opened into a huge room fifty feet across with a thirty-foot-high ceiling. Standing in the center of the room, illuminated by blue, shimmering light from a dozen spirals of phosphor strings hung about the room, was the Chain Killer. Destroying Angel.

He appeared much as Tanner had expected—both legs and one arm cyborged, no clothes, part human, part machine, with large, beautiful wings of glistening silver spread high above and behind him. Fifteen or twenty cables ran from his artificial limbs and across the floor, where they were plugged into electronic consoles that lay against the walls. The floor around him was littered with drug vials and injectors. The man's eyes were rolled back into his skull, and his body and wings quivered as he stood in the middle of the room.

The hum was loud in here. Tanner and Carlucci entered the room, Tanner moving right, Carlucci moving left, and the others came in behind them.

"Mother . . . fuck." It was Harker.

The man's eyes rolled back down so he was looking at Harker, who still stood in the doorway. Fuentes had joined Tanner on the right and they continued moving farther in along the wall, Carlucci doing the same on the other side of the room. Everyone had their trank guns aimed at the man.

Wings flexed, swinging forward then back. Tanner imagined the movements as preparation for takeoff, though he knew the man couldn't fly. The wings flexed again, but otherwise the man did not move.

"Albert Cromwell," Carlucci said.

The man's head turned, slowly, stiffly, until he was facing Carlucci.

"We've found you," Carlucci said. "Why don't you just make things easier for everyone, get down on the floor, arms and legs spread."

The man—machine, Destroying Angel—still did not move except to slowly shake his head.

"We don't want to kill you," Carlucci said. "So get down on the floor. And disconnect the wings."

The man opened his mouth, and a harsh, stuttering sound emerged. But no words. The wings flexed one more time, then the man staggered toward Carlucci, trailing cables, his motions stilted and slow. Why? Tanner wondered. He was outnumbered four to one, he had to know he didn't stand a chance, cyborg or not.

"Watch the crossfire," Carlucci shouted. "But shoot. Take this fucker down."

Suddenly the man began to move toward Carlucci with great speed. Tanner aimed and fired, heard the muffled bursts of the other guns, then heard the clanking sounds of pellets striking metal. He wondered if any of the shots were hits. He saw Carlucci fire twice and run to his left. The man turned and tried to follow, hampered by the wings and the cables. Tanner and the others fired again, Tanner aiming more carefully for flesh—the arm, upper chest, neck, face.

This time he was sure there were hits, the man jerked twice, though he kept after Carlucci. Carlucci dashed across the center of the room, avoiding the cables, leading the man toward Tanner and Fuentes. More shots from the trank guns, more hits.

The man staggered, dropped to his knees, got to his feet, then fell again, wings folding up around him, crumpling in a heap. He tried once more to get up, the wings spasmed, then he finally collapsed. He did not move.

Carlucci approached him first, then Fuentes, and Harker. Tanner kept back, watching from a few feet away, watching the three cops standing silently over Albert Cromwell. No one seemed to know what to say, what to do. Finally, Carlucci knelt beside the man, checked his pulse and breathing.

"All right," he said. "We've got him. Now let's get him out of here alive."

Tanner and Carlucci watched the paramedics load Albert Cromwell into the ambulance. It was difficult to think of him as Destroying Angel now. Night had fallen, and half the lights around them were flashing. There probably hadn't been this many cop cars inside the Tenderloin in years.

The senior paramedic walked over to them. "Can't guarantee anything," she said, "but all his vitals are strong. We'll be running toxics on the way over, and we're already countering the tranks. He looks a lot worse than he actually is. He should be fine."

"Thanks," Carlucci said.

She nodded, walked back to the ambulance, and got in the back with Cromwell. Doors were pulled shut, sirens and lights came on, and the ambulance pulled away, police escort in front and back as it headed out of the Tenderloin. There were still several other police cars nearby, one of which would be taking Carlucci to the hospital so he could stay on top of things.

They had found a quick, simple way out of the Chain Killer's place. The room *was* in the Core, but right at the edge. They had managed to get out and into the Tenderloin proper—the four of them carrying Cromwell between them—where Carlucci called in extra forces and the paramedics. The paramedics had arrived in less than five minutes.

"You want to go to the hospital with me?" Carlucci asked.

Tanner shook his head. "I can't think of one good reason I should," he said.

"Neither can I." Carlucci breathed in deeply, then slowly let it out. "It's over, I guess."

"I guess."

Neither spoke for a minute. Tanner watched the police cars loading up, pulling away.

"You'd better go," he said.

Carlucci nodded. "You going home?"

"Yes," Tanner said. "I could use a good night's sleep."

"Me too." Carlucci shrugged. "But I'm going to have to finish things up at the hospital. Who knows what time I'll get home. I'll be happy if it's still dark." He grunted, shrugged again. "I'll talk to you."

"Sure. Go on."

They shook hands, then Carlucci walked over to the last waiting car and got in. The siren kicked on, and the car pulled away.

Tanner stood and watched it move down the street, lights flashing, until it turned a corner three blocks up. People on the streets hardly paid it any attention. Within a couple of minutes all the sirens were barely audible, nearly drowned out by the normal sounds of the Tenderloin at night. Everything back to normal, Tanner thought.

Time to go home. He had been ready to do just that for a long time. He glanced back at the Core, then turned away and started walking down the street.

40

THAT NIGHT TANNER slept long and deep, and did not awaken until almost noon. Over twelve hours. If he dreamed, he did not remember anything.

He lay in bed awhile without moving, listening to the sounds of the city coming in through the open window. There was a slight breeze, and although the air was hot it was not stifling. He did not know what day it was. Whatever day, he was in no hurry to start it.

Tanner finally got up, and wandered aimlessly about the apartment for a few minutes before finally going into the bathroom. He relieved himself, then stood and looked at his reflection in the mirror above the sink. About two weeks' growth of beard. He decided he did not like it.

He spent fifteen minutes carefully shaving off the beard, bringing his face back to normal. Afterward, he took a long shower, using all the hot water, then standing under a stream of cold for several minutes until he finally felt like moving again.

He dressed and ate a single piece of toast. He was not hungry, but he thought he should put something in his stomach. Then he left the apartment for coffee and the newspaper.

On Columbus Street he stopped in front of a newsrack, struck by the morning headline: CHAIN KILLER CAUGHT, KILLED. Killed? The paramedic had said he was going to be fine. What the hell was going on?

He bought a newspaper, but did not immediately read it. He went into a cafe, ordered coffee, then sat at a table with the coffee and the newspaper.

Tanner avoided the article on the Chain Killer. He drank his coffee and went through the rest of the paper, section by section. Only when he had read everything he would normally have read, and was halfway through a second cup of coffee, did he read the headline story.

According to the article, a man named Albert Cromwell, whom the police had finally identified as the Chain Killer, had been captured and arrested deep inside the Core after a long investigation and search. Although the police had used tranquilizer weapons in an attempt to capture the Chain Killer alive, the Chain Killer's metabolism had reacted adversely to the huge doses that had been used to subdue him, and he had died en route to the hospital. There were no pictures of Albert Cromwell, and no mention that he had been a cyborg.

Tanner left the cafe and searched out a phone booth. He tried calling Homicide, but was told that Carlucci was on vacation. No one would give him Carlucci's home number, and he finally had to get it from Lucy Chen.

Tina, Carlucci's daughter, answered the phone. At first she said Carlucci wasn't around, but when Tanner identified himself she said that her father had been waiting for his call. A few moments later Carlucci came on the line.

"I expected to hear from you a lot sooner," he said.

"I just saw the newspaper," Tanner replied.

"You sleep in?"

"Yes, as a matter of fact. What the hell is going on?"

"Let's meet somewhere," Carlucci said.

So, Tanner thought, nothing over the phone. "All right."

"Any preference?"

Tanner did not answer right away, but it didn't take him long to decide where he wanted to talk to Carlucci. "Yes," he said. "You know the Carousel Club?"

"South of Market somewhere, isn't it?"

"Yes, near the slough."

"I'll find it. Half an hour?"

"Make it an hour," Tanner said.

"Fine. See you then."

"Right." Tanner hung up the phone.

Tanner arrived at the Carousel Club a half hour early and went up to the second floor. All three balcony tables were occupied, so he had to take one just inside, near the wide doors. He ordered a bottle of lime-flavored glacier water—just for the hell of it—and kept an eye on the balcony. A few min-

utes after the waitress brought the glacier water, the two women at one of
the balcony tables left, and Tanner moved out to it.

There must have been a slight breeze blowing away from the club because he could not smell the stench of the slough. The breeze, if it indeed existed, did not help much with the heat, however. Though there were no
clouds visible, the humidity was high and Tanner was already sticky with
sweat.

He drank the glacier water and gazed across the slough at the junkyard.
This was where it had all started, he thought. At least for him. He pictured
Sookie sitting cross-legged on a wrecked car, waving strange hand signals at
him. It was still difficult to believe she was dead, and Tanner could not
shake the feeling that he was at least partially responsible for her death.

When the glacier water was gone, he switched to regular mineral water.
The glacier water had not tasted any better, but it had cost three times as
much.

As he sat and sipped at the water, the other two tables emptied, and
soon he was alone on the balcony, gazing across the slough, watching the
light reflect off the water. He was still looking at the junkyard and thinking
about Sookie when Carlucci arrived. He sat across from Tanner, ordered a
beer, and looked down at the slough.

"This where you were?" Carlucci asked. "When we pulled the bodies
out?"

Tanner nodded. "That day was the first time I saw Sookie," he said.
"She was sitting on top of a car in the junkyard. By the time you showed up
she was hidden—in one of the cars, I guess. She told me she watched you
pull the bodies out of the water." He paused, a sharp ache driving through
his chest. "Three weeks later she ends up being pulled out of the water herself." He turned to look at Carlucci. "So tell me what the hell is going on?"

"Let me explain something first," Carlucci said. "I've been officially ordered not to say anything about this to anyone, period. Anyone asks me
about it, newshawkers, official investigators, whoever, I say nothing. I don't
lie, I don't confirm or deny anything, it's just 'no comment' and refer all
questions to my superiors. Which means Boicelli. I say anything, I lose my
job, my pension, and my shot at working in this city again. Okay? I told
them I would talk to you, tell you the same thing, but without any explanations. Just tell you that it's in your best interest not to say a thing. Nothing
else." He sat back in the chair, shrugged. "So what I'm going to tell you
now, well, I'm going to be way out of line. Thing is, you risked your life in
all this, damn near lost it, and I figure I owe you. You deserve to know. But
I want you to understand the situation."

"I understand," Tanner said. "And I appreciate the risk you're taking.
So tell me how the hell he died."

Carlucci shook his head. "He didn't. The bastard's still alive." He continued to shake his head. "The military's got him back."

"What's with the newspapers then?"

"Official story. The company line. Given to us by the feds. I don't know how those bastards got onto it so fast, but they were at the hospital, waiting, when the ambulance arrived. Cromwell never actually got into the building. The military guys kept him in the ambulance, kept things hung up until they got their own transport on the scene. Lots of shouting and arguing, believe me. We tried to hold on to him, get him inside the hospital, but they wouldn't budge. They had their own doctor go in and work on him. *They* didn't want him dead, either." Carlucci shook his head, drank from his beer. "Pretty much a standoff, until McCuller, Vaughn, and Boicelli arrived. They told us to hand him over. I don't know about the other two, but I know Boicelli wasn't too happy about it. No choice, he said. Said word had come down 'from so high up it'd give you nosebleeds.' So they took him away. Everybody who knew anything was given orders: none of us knows a damn thing. I got a mandatory, fully paid two-week vacation, effective immediately. And that's supposed to be the end of it. Case closed."

"Why?" Tanner asked, though he had a few ideas already floating around in his head.

"*Their* official word," Carlucci said, "is that they want him in custody so they can examine and study him, figure out what went wrong so it won't happen again." Carlucci snorted. "I'd guess there's *some* truth to that, they probably *do* want to figure out what the hell this guy's all about, why he went over the edge."

"But what they're really worried about," Tanner said, "is bad publicity. They don't want any of this public."

Carlucci nodded. "You got it. They can't afford to have him go to trial. *Everything* would come to light, any half-assed attorney would make sure of that. And if this went public, kiss off the program, whatever the hell it is they've got going. So he's dead. He's not, and they've got him locked away somewhere, but officially he's dead. Albert Cromwell, deceased."

"So everything we did was for nothing," Tanner said. He slowly shook his head, returning his gaze to the slough and the junkyard on the other side of the water. "It's all so goddamn futile."

"No," Carlucci said. "We caught him. He would have killed again if we hadn't, who knows how many more?"

"He still could if he escapes again."

"That's pretty unlikely," Carlucci said. "They can't afford that happening, so they'll pretty much make it impossible. If it ever happened again, they know the shit would fly. All agreements would be void, and we'd blow them out of the fucking water over it."

Tanner just shook his head. "You may be right, but it's still shit." He looked at Carlucci. "You know, this is one fucked-up world we live in."

Carlucci gave him a short, hard laugh. "Big surprise, Tanner. Look, I won't argue that. But there's something you ought to keep in mind."

"Yeah? What's that?"

"This is the only world we've got."

Tanner did not reply. They sat in silence for a few minutes, both of them gazing out over the slough, the junkyard, the other ramshackle buildings and overgrown lots lining the water. The waitress came by for reorders, but Carlucci shook his head, saying, "I need to go soon." Tanner ordered another mineral water. He wanted to stay awhile and think some more.

After the waitress came back with the mineral water, Carlucci got up from the table.

"I'm on vacation," he said. "I'm going to spend it with my family. I don't know, maybe we'll take a trip somewhere. Where it doesn't rain so damn much."

He put out his hand, and Tanner gripped it with his own. "Thanks for talking to me," Tanner said.

Carlucci nodded, then said, "Sure thing." He released Tanner's hand and stepped back.

"Enjoy the vacation," Tanner said.

"I will. You might want to take one yourself."

"I may do that."

"I'll see you, Tanner."

"Yeah."

Carlucci turned and walked inside, made his way through the tables, then headed down the stairs and out of sight.

Tanner remained on the balcony a long time, thinking and watching the shadows lengthen across the surface of the water. People's faces shifted around in his thoughts, making appearances, then shifting away to reappear again later: Sookie, Carla, Valerie and Connie. Carlucci. Albert Cromwell. Destroying Angel. Sookie and Carla were dead, but they were still there with him. Maybe Carla too much so. Was that what Hannah had tried to tell him? Maybe Hannah was right. Could it be that he still had not let her go? And what about Valerie? Was Hannah right about her, too? He had not known what else to do.

And there was Albert Cromwell, Destroying Angel. Back with the military, who knew what was happening with him? Gone, missing again. But Carlucci's words came back to him: 'This is the only world we've got.' It seemed to Tanner now, sitting here thinking and gazing out over the slough, that Carlucci was absolutely right.

It was late afternoon when Tanner finally left the Carousel Club. He had to walk three blocks before he could find a working telephone. He picked up the receiver, then put it back down and walked off. Two blocks farther on he stopped at another phone booth and again picked up the receiver. This time he ran his card through and punched up Valerie's home number.

As he listened to the ringing, he thought about Connie and hoped she wouldn't answer. He still wasn't sure what to say to her; he still had not worked all that out. He wasn't sure he even wanted Valerie to answer, so when the phone kept ringing, he felt relieved. Finally, he hung up.

He hesitated before trying the hospital, almost walked away from the phone, then finally punched up the number. When his call was answered, and he asked for Valerie, he was switched up to ICU, and the nurse who answered said Valerie was busy. Tanner left the phone booth number and hung up.

He was unsure about this, wondering if it was a mistake, wondering if it was worth trying. But it seemed like something he had to do. Something he needed.

The phone rang.

Tanner stared at it, again nearly turned and walked away. His heart was beating hard. The phone kept ringing. Then, something inside him released, and he let out a breath he had not realized he'd been holding in. He knew what he wanted to do. He knew. Tanner breathed in deeply once again, put out his hand, and picked up the phone.

Carlucci's
Edge

Prologue

SMOKE AND SWEAT and hot lights and the smell of beer filled the club, all cut through with the ripping wail and thunder of the slash-and-burn band on stage. Three women—drummer in tank top and blue jeans, bleached hair whipping up and down with the beat; guitarist in dark emerald-green shimmer pants and silver rag vest, black on black hair falling across her face; and Paula, in black jeans and boots and white T-shirt, tearing at the bass and shouting and howling out the vocals. Black Angels.

Paula sang and rocked in a kind of cocoon, earplugs protecting her from the worst of the sound. But she felt the bass pounding through her, driving into her bones, moving her. She was soaked with sweat, filled with fire. She was flying.

The Palms was jammed. It was a tiny club, more of a bar, really, but there must have been seventy or eighty people squeezed inside to see the Black Angels. Beer seemed to be the drink of choice, bottles and glasses everywhere; the smoke was a mix of cigarettes, pot, and fireweed. A few people up near the stage were trying to dance, jumping up and down in place. If she reached out, Paula could touch them.

She backed away from the mike and Bonita ripped into her solo, fingers clawing at the strings. Sheela lost a drumstick; it flew forward, bounced off the back of Bonita's head, but she didn't notice. This was their last song, they were too deep into it. Paula kicked the stick out of the way, pounding at her bass.

Too old for this? That's what Pietro had told her. Because she was pushing forty. Shit. The fucker didn't have a clue.

The screech of Bonita's solo cut through the earplugs, not painful, just enough to pump her up even more. The crowd was into it, too; Paula could see it in their faces—eyes clamped shut or wide open, necks, cheeks, and lips clenched tight. Bonita was burning tonight, and Paula hoped someone was getting it on-line. Damn, she wished Chick could have been here.

Bonita took it longer and further than usual, but eventually swung it back around and down, turning to Paula and Sheela, and then it was time for Paula to come back with the final rep of the chorus. She moved up to the mike, waited for it, then sang:

> Yes, the night will drown us
> And the stars will burn us
> If we step out on the ledge.

Oh, the fear will take us
And it just might break us
When we live out on the edge.

Then back from the mike, Paula and Sheela and Bonita all facing each
other, closing it down with the final strokes, all of them smiling. They knew
they'd been burning tonight, they *knew*. A crash of drums and guitars, then
another. Two beats of silence. One final crash. Lights out.

Paula felt good. Wrung out, but good. They were playing The Palms the
next night as well, and they had all their equipment packed away and
locked up in back. Bonita and Sheela were already gone. Time to go home,
wind down, get some sleep. Or maybe go see Chick. It was only two-thirty,
he was probably still up.

The Palms was nearly empty now. Recorded music played softly in the
background. A few stragglers sat at tables and the bar, nursing their last-call
drinks. Randy and Carmela and the new kid (what was her name, Laurel?)
were cleaning up, trying to close. A guy at the bar tried to wheedle another
drink out of Carmela, but she just ignored him.

Jacket over her shoulder, Paula headed for the front door, waving good
night to Carmela and Randy.

"Hey, babe, need a lift?" It was a guy she didn't know, at the table closest to the door, so drunk he could hardly keep his head up. He wasn't going
to be any trouble.

"No, thanks, Ace. You'd better get a ride of your own." The guy didn't
look like he could drive five blocks without crashing.

The drunk gave her a sloppy grin, then pointed his finger at her like a
gun, made a kind of shooting noise. Asshole.

Paula stepped through the front door and out onto Polk Street. The air
was warm, muggy. San Francisco nights. She put on her jacket anyway, left
it unzipped. There were still people out, wandering, or lost, and a few street
soldiers were in sight. She smiled, shaking her head. The Polk was such a
half-assed Corridor. The street soldiers always had their hands out, and a lot
of them were as likely to try to nail you on your doorstep as give you safe
conduct. Still, they kept the street itself relatively safe, and Paula could take
care of herself.

So, home or Chick's place. Shit, she was too wound up to sleep. It had
been a great set. Chick's place, then. It was closer, anyway.

She started up the street, headed uphill and west. There wasn't much
traffic—a few cars, pedalcarts, and scooters. An electric bus heaved down
the street, flashes of blue sparking off the overhead wires; it was almost half
full. On the opposite sidewalk, a street medico was working on someone lying half in the gutter, two street soldiers standing over them. Paula watched,

trying to figure if something shifty was going down, but she couldn't tell. She let it go.

She passed a stunner arcade that was still open, but it was mostly dark inside, and she could see only a single jerking figure within. A scooter cab swung to the curb alongside her, the old, long-haired driver lifting an eyebrow. Paula smiled and shook her head, and the cabby pulled away. Two men, hardly more than boys, staggered in tandem along the sidewalk, and Paula had to step into the street to avoid them. She could see it in their eyes and their twitching—net zombies. Poor bastards.

Most places were closed, but a couple of eateries were still open, and Margo's Spice and Espresso Bar, a video parlor, Sherry's Shock Shop. Paula stopped in front of Tiny's, a twenty-four-hour donut house, seriously thought about going in. She had a real weakness for the damn things; all that fat and sugar, she knew they were bad for her, but she loved them. But the Mulavey twins were inside, the two women pouring coffee all over their donuts and the table, burning the cups with their cigarettes; coffee and ash and melted plastic dripped onto the floor. No, she didn't want to deal with that shit tonight.

She walked up two more blocks, still energized. She was starting to sweat under her jacket. Two street soldiers offered to escort her home, but she declined. Neither followed her.

She turned a corner and headed away from Polk. Chick's place was just two blocks down, but it was a creepy two blocks at night, not really a part of the Corridor. The street lights seemed to cast more shadows than light and the building windows were mostly dark. Paula didn't see anyone on either sidewalk, which was just as bad as seeing someone coming toward her. She put her hands in her jacket pockets and gripped the charged gravity knife with her right hand. She wasn't scared, but she wasn't completely comfortable either.

Nothing happened, no one jumped out from behind a parked car or out of a doorway. When she reached Chick's apartment building—a seven-story brick monstrosity called The Monarch—she unlocked the porch gate, went through, then climbed the half dozen steps and unlocked the building door. The lobby was well-lit for a change, but the elevator was still out of order.

She started up the stairs. Five flights. Good thing she was in shape. The building was quiet, though she did hear the faint sounds of a television as she passed the third floor, and saw the two Stortren kids sleeping in the hall on the fourth. Who knew what their parents were doing inside their apartment? Paula figured she probably didn't want to know.

The sixth floor was just as quiet. Only ragged strips of the carpet remained intact, huge sections worn through to the wooden floor. Her footsteps were a mixture of soft and hard sounds. Chick's apartment was at the far end of the hall, on the right. Nightclub notices for Pilate Error, the band Paula and Chick played in together, were tacked all over the door.

Paula knocked. No answer. She didn't hear any sounds, which meant he

was asleep or had his headphones jacked in. Before she dug out her keys
again, she tried the door. Unlocked, as usual. Dumbshit. The couple next
door had been cleaned out just last week.

She pushed open the door and stepped into the tiny entryway. All three
rooms led off from it, and lights were on in all of them. Jesus, the place
smelled worse than usual. She pictured rotting food leaking out of his fridge.

"Chick?"

She stuck her head in the kitchen first. The usual piles of dishes and crap
on the table and counters, but otherwise empty.

"Chick?"

She checked the front room, which, as always, was a mess, books and
discs and tapes scattered everywhere, half a dozen overflowing ashtrays. Chick
was a chain-smoker and a slob: two of the reasons they didn't live together.

She said his name once more, then walked into the bedroom.

Oh, Jesus Christ, no.

Paula stood just inside the room, looking down at Chick. He was
sprawled face-up on the floor, headphones plugged into his ears, and three
holes in his head—one under each eye and one in the middle of his forehead.
She couldn't move, just stared at him, at the blood and the bits of flesh and
bone and hair sprayed out on the floor around his head.

No, Chick, no . . .

She closed her eyes, nearly lost her balance, opened them and reached
back for the doorjamb to steady herself. Her heart was beating hard and
fast, pounding up her neck, pulsing her vision.

"Jesus, Chick, I told you," she whispered. "I told you, one day . . ."

She took a couple of steps toward him, then stopped, shaking her head.
She looked around the room, still dazed, not quite remembering it. The
overstuffed chair, she could reach that without getting too close to him,
without stepping in the blood.

She worked her way through the piles of clothes and books and scattered pieces of music, then dropped into the chair. Perfect spot, she could
stare at Chick without moving her head. Jesus.

It occurred to her then that whoever had killed him might still be in the
apartment. A shot of adrenaline arced through her and her heartbeat
jumped up again. No, she told herself, she'd been in all the rooms; she
couldn't believe someone was hiding in a closet or somewhere. Besides.
Paula looked at the blood around Chick's head, the pieces of bone and flesh
and, yes, Chick's brain, that were stuck in it. She wasn't an expert, but too
much had dried; she could tell it must be hours old.

She tilted her head back and stared up at the ceiling so she wouldn't
have to look at Chick. Flyers and posters covered the cracked plaster, yellowed and wrinkled notices for Pilate Error, Black Angels, his old band Tab
Rasa, and even a couple for Sister's Machine, the first band they'd played in
together, more than fifteen years ago.

She wasn't going to cry now, she knew that. She thought she should, and she knew she would later, but right now she just didn't have it in her. She was too damn numb, too wiped out.

She looked back at Chick, his skinny arms with all those fucking tracks, none of them fresh, but still . . . His blue eyes, cool and pale, now wide and staring. The tiny green snake tattooed on his neck. And those goddamn headphones socketed into his ears, cord trailing in the blood, along the floor, then up to the sound system, which was still on, the bright green peak meters spiking back and forth. Paula wondered what his destroyed dead brain was listening to.

"Oh, Chick," she whispered. She pushed herself off the chair, onto her knees, then moved across the floor and sat next to him, taking his cold hand in hers. "You stupid shit. What am I going to do now?"

Call the police, the practical side of her said. Yeah, yeah, in a minute. What's the hurry? No one's going anywhere.

Paula sat motionless on the floor, holding Chick's hand, and waited for the energy and will to move again.

PART ONE

1

CHRIST, DAYS LIKE this, Carlucci wanted to resign. And why not? He had more than his twenty-five years in, and at lieutenant he wasn't going any higher, he knew that—he'd pissed off too many of the wrong people over the years. Sometimes he was amazed he'd ever made lieutenant; the only reason he had was the capture of the Chain Killer three years earlier, and the fact that the higher-ups wanted him to keep his mouth shut.

He pushed his chair back from his desk, rolled it sideways until his face was directly in the wash of the fan. Sweat streamed down his sides, ran from his forehead and neck. Carlucci closed his eyes, letting the fan blow across his face and hair, and tried to imagine he was somewhere else, somewhere cool and breezy.

Carlucci was a stocky man, just over six feet, maybe fifteen pounds overweight, not much fat, really; he carried it well. His hair was short and black, heavily streaked with gray, and though he'd shaved this morning, he looked like he needed another. His shirt was soaked with sweat, and it itched, stuck to his skin. Carlucci opened his eyes, dismayed. No miracles. He was still here.

He pulled himself back to his desk and stared at the dead computer screen. He picked up his coffee cup, looked down into it, saw a miniature oil slick on top of the coffee, and drank it anyway. Cold and bitter, just the way he liked it.

The day had started off badly, and then had just gone to shit. First thing, five minutes after he'd arrived, Harker and Fuentes came in, demanding to be split up. Carlucci knew immediately that it was serious, not just the typical bitching that cropped up with regularity around here. Neither would say what the problem was, but both insisted they couldn't partner together anymore. Which probably meant that Harker had gone back hard and heavy to the booze, and Fuentes didn't want a drunk as a partner. Carlucci couldn't blame her; he'd feel the same way. He had told them he would work something out as soon as he could. It was going to be a pain in the ass trying to figure new partners, shift things around again. God damn.

Later in the morning the air conditioning had crapped out, the sixth or seventh time this summer. Summer, shit, it was late September, it was supposed to be fall. Once again they'd hauled out the fans, but the building's ventilation wasn't worth a damn, so the fans could only do so much—mostly they just stirred around the hot, sticky air, kept it from being completely intolerable.

Then the mayor's nephew was found dead in his penthouse apartment, throat cut, belly slit open. What a fuckin' mess. The mayor's nephew had been an asshole—a lot like the mayor, actually—and word was already on the street that he had tried to scam some black-market data sharks, and paid for it. But the mayor, ignorant bastard, was jumping all over the Chief, and the Chief was jumping all over Carlucci, and would keep on jumping until something broke. The mayor wanted justice. Sure thing, Your Honor. Carlucci was going to be wasting an awful lot of time on this bullshit, and it probably wouldn't go anywhere.

And finally this, Carlucci thought, still staring at the dead screen. The system had crashed. Again. He looked out the glass wall of his small office, watching the other men and women sitting around, sweating and swearing, talking on phones or to each other, everyone miserable. He glanced at the clock on his desk. Almost three-thirty. Fuck it, he wasn't going to get anything else done today. Go home. He nodded to himself, and prepared to leave.

•   •   •

Carlucci walked out of headquarters and stood in front of the building, trying to decide whether to take the bus or the streetcar. It didn't make much difference, he just liked to switch around a lot, try to keep the commute from being routine. The sky was a rust-brown haze hanging over the city. It hadn't rained at all for five or six days, and Carlucci wasn't sure whether that was good or bad. Probably bad. He thought he could feel the hot, filthy air turning his sweat into some putrid, oily substance.

He had just decided on the streetcar and started down the block, when a woman approached and stood directly in his path, forcing him to stop. She was wearing boots and jeans and a black T-shirt. There was a hard look to her, a sharp and dark edge.

"Frank Carlucci?" she said.

"Yes."

"Homicide, right?"

Carlucci nodded, wondering where this one was headed.

"My name's Paula Asgard. I need to talk to you."

"What about?"

"A murder."

Carlucci smiled. "Hey, there's a surprise. Look, I'm off-duty. Why don't you go inside the station"—he waved back at the building—"talk to someone who's on." He had a feeling she wasn't going to go for that, but he had to try. "I'm sure they can help you."

The woman shook her head. "I need to talk to *you*. And privately, not in your office. Why do you think I waited out here for you?"

"Look," Carlucci tried again, laying it on thick. "I'm a homicide detective, a lieutenant, we've got procedures. . . ."

"Mixer said you were the one I should talk to," Paula Asgard said.

"Mixer."

"He's a friend of mine."

Terrific, Carlucci thought. He started to shake his head, then turned it into a nod. "All right, I'll let you buy me a cup of coffee, and we'll talk. I know a place nearby."

"I appreciate it," the woman said.

Carlucci shrugged. "Don't thank me yet."

They sat at a small window table on the second floor of a place called The Bright Spot, a cafe just a few blocks from police headquarters. It was too late for afternoon coffee breaks, too early for dinner, so while the first floor was half full, the second-floor section was nearly empty—exactly what Carlucci had expected.

Neither said anything while they waited for their coffee. Carlucci's attention alternated between the street below and the woman across from him.

Paula Asgard. He liked the name. She was attractive, he thought, in a real earthy way. Somewhere in her thirties, about five-seven, five-eight, a few strands of gray in her dark hair. Almost but not quite slender. She looked strong, like she worked out.

Not much was happening on the street. A man with only one arm and one eye walked a string of three pit bulls leashed together with wire muzzles. Two thrashers on motorized boards ran the gutter directly below the cafe. A woman stood in front of an electronics store across the street, hawking her products and wearing a set of bone boomers; Carlucci got a headache just watching her. Then three teenage girls strolled past wearing rag vests, no bras, budding breasts appearing and disappearing among the strips. Christ, Carlucci thought. He watched until they were gone from sight, but nothing happened to them.

Margitta brought their coffees—iced for Paula Asgard, hot for Carlucci—and asked Carlucci how his wife was.

"Fine," Carlucci said, smiling. He knew what Margitta's game was: trying to guilt him just in case he was even *thinking* something funny about the woman across the table from him. Margitta and Andrea were good friends. "It's just business," he told Margitta. She shrugged and left.

Carlucci turned back to Paula Asgard. "So tell me."

"Mixer says you can be trusted." She turned her glass mug around and around, but didn't drink. "He said you're a cop who does what a cop is *supposed* to do."

"As opposed to all the cops who *don't* do what cops are supposed to do?"

A hint of a smile appeared on Paula's mouth. "You said it."

"Mixer." Carlucci shook his head and frowned. "That guy."

Paula's mouth moved into a full smile. "Yeah, that guy." She drank from her iced coffee, cubes rattling against glass. "He said you don't like spikeheads."

"I don't. I think they're fucking nuts. Self-mutilation doesn't do it for me." He shook his head again, picturing Mixer with the crusted, twisted spikes of skin all over his forehead. "But Mixer, well, we have an understanding of sorts. We get along all right."

"He told me you caught the Chain Killer."

"Not really," Carlucci said. "I was there, I was 'in charge,' but it was other people who were really responsible." He remembered sitting with Tanner at the Carousel Club three years earlier, telling him about the Chain Killer's faked death, "justice" taking it in the ass again—almost no one knew the Chain Killer was still alive, locked away in some military compound. And he thought of a poor thirteen-year-old girl they had pulled out of a lagoon: Sookie. "One of them got killed," he said.

"A friend of *mine's* been killed," Paula said.

Carlucci looked at her, bringing himself back to the present, then slowly nodded. "Who was it?"

"A friend," she repeated, more quietly.

Carlucci watched her, wanting to look away, not wanting to see what he saw in her eyes. She might be a hardass on the outside, but he could see hints of what was happening inside her, the way she was fighting to *keep* it inside. Someone she loved had died, been killed. He knew that look, because he had seen it too many times.

And then he thought of his older daughter, Caroline, and he wondered if he would have that look in *his* eyes when she died. One day he would be grieving over her death, a day that would be way too soon in coming.

"His name was Chick Roberts," Paula finally managed. She looked out the window, swirling the ice cubes and coffee.

"A friend," Carlucci prompted. The name wasn't familiar. Should he have come across it? Maybe not. He wanted to get straight to it—when was he killed, how, why, whatever—but he knew he'd have to take it slow, at her pace, ease into it.

"Yeah, a friend. More than a friend. I don't know, boyfriend?" Paula turned back to him and shook her head. "Doesn't seem the right word." She drank from her coffee. "Lover?" Then she tried to smile. "Never liked that word either, but I guess that's as close as I'm going to come. We'd known each other a long time. Sixteen, seventeen years."

"Did you live together?"

"No," she said, almost laughing. "Tried once. Didn't last a year." She didn't offer any explanation, and Carlucci wasn't going to ask her for one.

"When was he killed?"

"A week and a half ago. I stopped by his place after a gig, found him dead. Shot three times in the head."

She didn't go on, and Carlucci let the silence hang between them for a bit. He was tempted to ask her for more details, but this wasn't his investigation, probably never would be. But there was one question he had to ask if she wasn't going to get to it herself.

"Why me?" Carlucci asked. "Why are we here?"

Something in her expression changed, hardened. The grief was gone, replaced by anger.

"I want to know what the hell is going on."

Yeah, Carlucci thought, we all do.

"What do you mean?" he asked.

"I've been trying to keep on top of it, the investigation, the case, whatever it's called." Paula finished off her iced coffee, set the mug down, shook the ice cubes. "I want to know who killed him, and why. I want to see whoever did it pay." She pushed her mug to the side, and Carlucci could see the anger burning inside her. "His parents don't give a damn, but *I* do."

"So what's the problem?"

"I call the cop who's supposed to be in charge, see what's going on, and he gives me the biggest crock of shit I've ever heard. First, he tells me the investigation has been a dead end, no leads, nothing. Fine, I can sort of accept that, though I don't really buy it." Paula grabbed her mug again, tried to drink coffee that wasn't there, then put it back down. She looked hard at Carlucci. "But then the guy tells me the case is closed. Now, you tell me how the case can be closed if the cops have no idea who killed him?"

"Well," Carlucci said, "there's closed and there's closed."

"What the fuck is *that* supposed to mean?"

"*Technically* the case won't be closed. What he meant is that they think they've gotten as far as they can, which apparently is nowhere. They don't think they'll be able to solve it, and they probably won't be putting much more time into it."

"They haven't put jack into it yet."

"You don't know that," Carlucci started. "I'm sure . . ."

"Bullshit!" Paula was getting angrier; her neck muscles had tightened and her fists were clenched. "As far as I can tell, they haven't talked to any of Chick's friends about it, they haven't asked anyone anything. That's why I can't buy this dead-end crap." She leaned forward. "They haven't even asked *me* a damn thing, and I found him."

Carlucci was starting to get a bad feeling about this. He was beginning to wish he had never agreed to talk to her. "What do you mean by that?" he asked. "One of the investigating officers interviewed you, right?"

"Wrong." Paula shook her head. "They asked me about five questions when they first showed up that night, sent me home, and told me they'd get back to me. No one did."

"No one?"

"That's what I said. I found out who was in charge of the case, talked to him, but all I got was the runaround. Said he didn't need to talk to me, that they had all the information they needed. I even volunteered to come in and talk to him, but he said no. That's when I started checking with people Chick knew. Cops didn't interview *any* of them. Now, you tell me what that's all about."

He had no answer for her. He signaled to Margitta for more coffee. She came over, refilled his cup, then poured some over what remained of the ice cubes in Paula's mug. Carlucci could see the ice cubes melting from the hot coffee. "Want some more ice, hon?" Margitta asked. Paula shook her head, not looking at the waitress, holding her stare on Carlucci. Margitta took the hint and left without another word.

"Who was the investigating officer?" He had to ask. He didn't want to hear her answer, but he had to ask.

"Ruben Santos."

Not a name Carlucci expected to hear. Two or three other names, sure, he wouldn't have been surprised. But Ruben?

"Ruben Santos," he said. "Are you sure?"

"Yes, I'm sure. How do you think I came up with the name? Picked one at random?"

Christ, the whole thing was turning on him. He had been prepared to take Paula Asgard pretty much at her word—he'd seen this kind of thing often enough—but now he began to doubt her. Ruben was about as straight a player as cops came. Carlucci really didn't know what to think.

"It gets better," Paula said.

"How?"

"Last time I talked to this guy Santos, he said they were looking into the possibility that it was suicide."

Sure, Carlucci thought, a kind of backdoor way out, even if it was bullshit. "Could it have been?"

Paula let out a chopped laugh. "Right. Three bullet holes in the face, half the back of his head blown off, and no gun in the apartment. The most amazing goddamn suicide in history."

Yeah, but Carlucci could see how they'd play it. The girlfriend, wanting to avoid the stigma of suicide, pops him a couple extra shots in the face to make it look like murder, then dumps the gun. All bullshit, but the cops just might make that case to close it up, and the coroner could be depended on not to shut the door completely on it.

"Why would the cops want to let this case go?" Carlucci asked. "Laziness? Maybe they just think it's unimportant?"

Her eyes got real hard again. "Unimportant to who?"

Great. That hadn't been the most sensitive thing he'd ever said. "Point taken," Carlucci said.

"Besides," Paula went on, "they're not just letting it go, they're trying to bury it."

"Maybe so." *Probably* so, he thought. But Ruben? He couldn't shake his doubts. "But why? Do you have any idea why they'd want to cover it up, or not find out who killed him? There must be some reason; they wouldn't do something like this just to be assholes."

"You tell *me*. That's why I'm here." Paula sighed, looked away from him. She picked up her coffee mug, drank absently from it. There was no ice left. She turned back to him.

"Chick—" she began. She gave him a half smile. "Chick made a living his own way, and most of the time his own way wasn't exactly legal. Low-end stuff, really. Deal a little bit, run a scam on a jack lawyer, middle-man something hot, things like that. Nothing too big, nothing that would catch the attention of the sharks. You know what I mean?"

"Sure," Carlucci said. A bottom feeder, picking up the crumbs and the crap.

"That was the biggest reason we didn't live together. I couldn't tell him how to run his life, but I didn't want to be a part of that shit, not even on the edges."

"I understand."

Paula looked away, out the window. "Theory is one thing, the real world is another. Trying to stay small-time, out of the way of the sharks, well, impossible to do all the time." She turned back to Carlucci. "Every so often he'd get himself in over his head, riding on the edge, but he always managed to slip out of it. My guess is he got in over his head again, and this time he couldn't get out. In with the sharks, chewed up and spit out." She paused. "And the cops don't want to touch it. I don't know, you tell me why."

Carlucci looked down at his coffee cup, didn't drink, then looked back at Paula. "What do you expect me to do? I can't go in and take over the case. I can't interfere in the investigation without damn good cause."

"What investigation?"

"You know what I mean."

Paula nodded. The anger was gone from her expression, replaced by exhaustion and a return of the grief. "I don't know. *Something* should be done. Mixer said you could help. Do *you* like it when your fellow cops try to bury something? Don't you want to know why?" She shook her head slowly. "Somebody should be trying to find out who killed him." She paused, and Carlucci thought he saw tears welling in her eyes, but she managed to keep them back. "Chick deserves better than this. Anybody does. He wasn't a saint, but he never hurt anyone if he could help it. This may sound weird, but for all his fuckups, Chick was a good person. Do you have any idea what I mean?"

"I think so."

"And he deserves better. He deserves *something*."

Carlucci didn't say anything for a while. Not everyone gets what they deserve, he wanted to tell her, good or bad. But he realized she already knew that. Still.

"All right," he finally said. "I'll look into it. No promises, though. Understand? I'll have to be careful, and I don't know how much I can push it."

Paula nodded. Her expression didn't hold out much hope. She wasn't naive.

"I may not be able to do much at all," he said.

Paula nodded again, but didn't say anything.

"Where can I reach you tomorrow? Afternoon or evening?"

She blinked, as if she'd been thinking of something else. "Um, at Chick's place, actually. His parents don't want any of his things, so I'm going to go through his stuff, clean out his apartment." She smiled sadly. "He was such a fucking slob." She shook her head. "You have something to write with?"

Carlucci took two of his cards and handed them to her along with a pen. "Keep one for yourself. Write Chick's number and your number on the other."

She wrote the numbers on the card and handed it back to him.

"I'll call you tomorrow, or the next day. And when you go through Chick's things tomorrow?"

"Yes?"

"Make a note of anything you think is missing."

"And if there is, who will have taken it?" Paula asked. "His killer, or the cops?"

Carlucci didn't answer. "No promises, remember?" he said again.

Paula nodded. "I understand."

Carlucci got up from the table. "You coming?"

"No. I think I'll stay here for a while."

Carlucci wanted to say something to her, something that would be comforting, or reassuring. But there wasn't anything. He stood for a few moments, watching her, then turned away and left.

2

LONG AFTER DARK, Paula and Sheela were still out on the fire escape outside Sheela's apartment, drinking beer. A hot, muggy night, no rain in the air. Sheela was smoking the longest, skinniest cigarettes Paula had ever seen—Silver Needles. Paula was sitting on a crate, her back against the building; Sheela sat on the metal grating, legs and arms and head dangling through the railing and over the edge. A block and a half away, a vacant lot served as the neighborhood dump, and a methane fire burned on the street-side slope of the huge mound of garbage.

"Pilate Error was supposed to play at The Black Hole tonight," Paula said. She'd gone through seven or eight beers, and she was fairly drunk, but it didn't seem to do much to blunt the pain inside her.

"Chick was a pretty good guitar player," Sheela said. "Not as good as Bonita, but pretty good." Sheela had dropped three melters about fifteen minutes ago, but they hadn't kicked in yet, so she was still coherent. Still, Paula knew she would lose her soon.

"Bonita never liked Chick much," Paula said.

Sheela giggled. "She hated his guts."

Paula smiled, brought her beer up to her mouth, and drank. Cold and bitter and smooth, biting her throat. "Yeah, I guess she did."

"*I* liked him okay," Sheela said. "Even if he did try to prong me that one time." She turned and looked at Paula, her blonde hair covering one eye. "He didn't know I don't go for guys."

Oh, God, Paula thought, let's not go through this again, not tonight. When Sheela got drunk . . .

"You want to stay here tonight?" Sheela asked.

"No. I want to be in my own place, sleep in my own bed." She also had to meet Mixer at midnight, but she wasn't going to tell Sheela that. Sheela would misunderstand. "But thanks."

"I could always . . ." Sheela started. Then she turned away and stuck her head back between the railing bars, looking down at the street. "Sorry."

"It's all right," Paula said. And it was. They'd been close friends for too many years.

A corporate recruiter van appeared on the street a few blocks away and headed toward them. The van, lights flashing and rolling, moved slowly, at little more than a crawl. White text and images flowed along the side of the van, but it was too far away and the angle was wrong, so Paula couldn't make out the words or the pictures.

"I wonder what they're trolling for tonight," Sheela said. She drank from her bottle, shook it, then set it down. She coughed violently, whacking her head against the metal railing. She'd had a terrible, hacking cough for years, and never seemed able to shake it. When the coughing let up, she said, "Have you ever thought about going for one of those deals?"

"No," Paula said. "You?"

Sheela nodded. "Once, a few years ago. I was broke, I was living in the cab of an old truck, and I was sicker than shit. Thought I had brain fever, even though I didn't have the rash. Turned out to be some bad flu, but I didn't know it then." She held her beer bottle up to the light from the street lamp across the way. "I need another." She set the bottle on the grate beside her. "A recruiter for the New Hong Kong orbital rolled down the street one night while I was out trying to scrounge up some food cash. I watched it roll past, all those pictures of outer space, gleaming apartments, clean air and healthy plants, glittering lights and fancy restaurants, tables filled with food." She shook her head. "I almost went for it. I knew what it would really be like for someone like me—scut work, a tiny hole to live in, institutional food. But I almost went for it. Actually got the van to pull over for me. But as soon as it stopped, and the side doors opened, I freaked. Ran like hell. I thought they were going to come after me and force me to go." She paused, gripped the railing bars tightly and pressed her head against them. "I told a friend of mine about it the next day, and that night she went out looking for the van herself."

Paula thought she knew how this story ended. She drank the rest of her beer, then said, "And she found it?"

Sheela nodded. "She found it. Signed up and went off to New Hong Kong."

"What happened to her?"

"I don't know. Never heard from her again. Never tried to find out for myself." She turned to Paula. "You know, I hear the medicos up in New Hong Kong are working on immortality."

Paula shook her head. "Not immortality. Life extension."

"Same thing."

"Not really." Paula shrugged. "Those stories have been drifting around for years. *Everyone's* searching for longer life."

"Yeah," Sheela said, "but I hear they're getting close."

"I've been hearing *that* for years, too. I doubt it. Doesn't really matter if they are. You think *we'd* get a shot at it? They sure as hell won't want people like us living forever with them."

"Yeah, I guess." Sheela looked down at the beer bottle once more. "Want another?" she asked.

"Sure."

Sheela grabbed her empty bottle, pulled herself to her feet, then reached out for Paula's empty. Paula handed it to her, and Sheela said, "I'll be . . ." then stopped. She dropped the bottles, her head jerked twice, a kind of smile forming, and she slowly, slowly crumpled to the metal grating. The melters had kicked in.

Paula sighed, looking down at Sheela, some of the lyrics for "Again," a Black Angels song, going through her head:

> *I'm never . . .*
> *I'm never . . .*
> *I'm never gonna get*
> *Fucked up*
> *Like this*
> *Again!*

In fact, Sheela had written those lyrics. Sheela, who now lay in a crumpled heap on the fire escape, eyelids fluttering, fingers twitching occasionally. Live forever? Right. Why in hell would you want to be doing this any longer than you had to?

Paula moved the bottles out of the way, then knelt beside Sheela and grabbed hold of her under her arms. She pushed herself slowly to her feet, leaned back, and pulled Sheela to the open bedroom window.

After that it was a struggle—propping Sheela against the building, going in through the window, reaching back out to take hold of Sheela again, heaving her up and onto the windowsill, dragging her over the sill and into the apartment. Once she had her inside, it was a little easier. She dragged Sheela across the floor, then pulled and pushed her onto the bed. It was plenty warm, so there was no need for a blanket. Besides, the melters would be heating her just fine.

Paula sat on the edge of the bed for a few minutes, recovering her breath, and watched her friend. Sheela didn't move much, other than the fluttering eyelids and the mild twitching of her hands and feet. One day, Paula thought, Sheela's nervous system was going to do a hard crash if she didn't stop this. She was one hell of a drummer, but she put way too much shit into her body.

Paula looked at the glowing digital clock in the wall next to the bed. Eleven fifteen. She should be leaving soon to meet Mixer. She got up from the bed and crawled back out onto the fire escape to get the empties. The recruiting van was almost directly below her now, and she could read it.

ATLANTIS II, the huge, lighted letters spelled out as they flowed across the panels attached to the van roof. So it *wasn't* for New Hong Kong. On the side of the van itself, three video panels showed a running series of images—color shots of the first undersea dome being built on the floor of the Caribbean, along with computer-generated conceptions of how it would look when completed. The images were probably even more appealing than the ones Sheela had seen of New Hong Kong. Crystalline blue water, lush aquatic plants; a dome filled with spectacular buildings and gardens; incredible views of the water through the dome itself, with schools of brilliant tropical fish.

Then more text scrolled across the roof panels: WORKERS NEEDED ** SKILLED OR UNSKILLED ** EXPERIMENTAL SUBJECTS ** GOOD PAY, FINE HOUSING, EXCELLENT BENEFITS. The pictures and images and text repeated as the van rolled slowly past and continued down the street.

Atlantis II, the undersea dome. It all sounded so peaceful and inviting, Paula thought. Paradise on Earth. And New Hong Kong was Paradise in Orbit. It might almost be tempting if she didn't know what was really being offered. Still, this recruiter might do all right. It was probably a better contract than most, and there were always people desperate enough to go for it, even if they knew the reality.

Paula picked up the empties and crawled back inside. It was time to go meet Mixer.

Paula stood on the roof of her apartment building, waiting for Mixer. Midnight meetings on rooftops. Mixer was a romantic at heart—mystery, melodrama, suspense, atmosphere. From here she could see the upper reaches of a corner of the Tenderloin: elliptical strings of blinking lights marking the rooftop mini-satellite dishes; spinning reflections of seeded catch traps; irregular outlines of razor wire; a couple of small fires, shadowed figures moving among the flames. The Tenderloin. Mixer's home.

Gravel crunched, and Paula turned to see Mixer walking toward her. He was wearing jeans and a long-sleeved shirt, and as he approached, she could see lines of metal—narrow tubing, wire, complex joints—surrounding his right hand and fingers and extending up his arm beneath his shirt. Exoskeleton. She wondered how far it went, and why he had it.

"Hey, Paula," Mixer said, grinning and saluting her with his right hand, metal brushing the twisted spikes of crusted skin on his forehead. She could just barely hear the soft whir of the exoskeleton's motors. She could also see now that it extended all the way along each finger, past the last knuckle, with special finger pad attachments so he could grip normally, hold onto things. "What do you think?" he asked. "It's an exoskeleton."

"I know what it is," Paula said. "You do something to your arm?"

Mixer shook his head. "No, it's just an augmentation." He stripped off his shirt, revealing the entire thing. The exo ran up his arm to the shoulder, where it connected to a metal, plastic, and leather harness that fit across his upper back and chest. "Rabid, isn't it?"

"How did you manage it?" A true exoskeleton was incredibly expensive, and had to be custom-designed, built, and calibrated.

"I did someone a favor." He put his shirt back on. "It took six months and a dozen fittings before it was finished." He stretched out his right arm and looked at it with admiration, though only the hand section of the exo was now visible. "Final fitting just an hour ago." He flexed the fingers, then wiggled them at a fantastic speed, metal flickering like a strobe.

"Must have been some favor."

Mixer shrugged. Paula knew he wouldn't tell her about it, which was fine. She didn't want to know.

"So you saw Carlucci today?" Mixer said.

"Yes."

"What did you think?"

"What's to think? I talked to him for maybe half an hour." She put her hands in her jacket pockets. "You're probably right about the man. I got a good hit off him."

Mixer nodded. "He's a good cop. An honest cop."

"Maybe so. But I don't know if he'll be able to do anything," Paula said. "He kept telling me, 'No promises.' "

"He's got to be careful," Mixer said, nodding slowly. "If the cops are trying to sink this thing, he'll have to go real easy." He shrugged.

"Sounds to me like he might not be able to go after it at all."

"He'll go after it," Mixer said. "I know him. And if he doesn't go on his own, I'll give him a nudge."

Paula looked at him. "You know something about Chick's death?"

"Maybe." He shrugged again.

"Jesus, Mix, how much *do* you know?"

"Nothing, really," Mixer said, "and that's the truth, babe. I've heard some things, been hearing some things for weeks. I tried to warn Chick, told him he might be getting in up to his neck again. Looks like he got in a hell of a lot deeper than that." Mixer shook his head. "I don't know who killed him, Paula. I don't really know *why* he got himself killed, but I have an idea or two."

"Like *what*?"

Mixer shook his head; he wasn't going to say any more.

"Jesus, Mixer, I hope you're not in this enough to get yourself killed, too."

"Not me, babe."

"Mixer." Paula sighed heavily. "Don't call me 'babe.' We've been through that before."

"Yeah, yeah, you're right. Sorry."

They stood together at the edge of the roof, looking out at the night. Paula hadn't heard a siren in a long time, which gave the night an eerie, quiet feel, though of course it wasn't all *that* quiet. On the street below, an all-female thrasher pack cruised past, motorized boards growling at low idle. A trio of rollers wandered in and out of the street, chanting, their head-wheels spinning. And from somewhere nearby came the distorted racket of metal-bang rock.

"I miss the skinny bastard," Mixer said.

"Yeah."

Mixer turned to look at Paula. "How are you doing?"

The ache jammed up against her chest again. When was it going to stop? "Got a hole in my heart," she said.

Mixer nodded and put his arm around her shoulder, pulling her close to him. The ridges of the exoskeleton felt strange to Paula, yet comforting.

"Need anything?" Mixer asked.

Paula shook her head.

Mixer leaned into her, kissed her on the cheek. "Let me know." Paula nodded. "And let me know what you hear from Carlucci." Paula nodded again, and he let her go. "I'll talk to you." He turned and walked toward the roof ladder, gravel crunching under his shoes.

Paula gazed down at the street below and listened to Mixer's footsteps until he'd crossed the roof, descended the ladder, and was gone. Gone. Just like Chick, except she'd never see Chick again. "Aw, shit," she whispered to herself. "Chick . . ." But she didn't know what else to say except his name. "Chick . . ." she said again, then nothing more.

Paula remained on the roof a long time, fighting the tears until she just didn't have the energy to hold them back any longer. She sat on the roof ledge, legs dangling, arms pressed into her sides, and cried.

3

MIXER WAS BACK on home turf, surrounded by light and sound, crowds and moving vehicles, color and the crash of city music. Walking the streets of the Tenderloin at night. One in the morning, the Tenderloin was still peaking, humming all around him. Message streamers shimmered above the street, swimming in and out of existence, hawking goods, announcing special events, calling for job applicants, crying for help or love.

Mixer didn't pay much attention to the activity around him. He was feeling out of sorts. It was his talk with Paula about Chick, about Carlucci. He liked Carlucci all right, but thinking about the homicide cop always made him think about Sookie, which brought up the old aches inside him. No, he didn't just feel out of sorts, he felt damn shitty.

Sookie. Thirteen years old, the final victim of the Chain Killer. Tanner and Carlucci had caught the bastard, and the guy had ended up dead, but not before he had killed Sookie, tattooed angel wings onto her eyelids, and grafted metal bands and chains to her wrists and ankles. Mixer had been at the lagoon with Tanner and Carlucci when she'd been pulled out of the water. Shit, he wished he hadn't seen that. Three years later it still made him sick when he thought about it, still gave him nightmares once or twice a month. He had seen a few dead people in his life, and some things a lot worse, but nothing had ever bothered him like that. Sookie had been special to him, and he figured it must be like losing a sister or daughter, though he'd never had either.

Mixer stopped in front of a crasher shop and lit a cigarette. He had a little trouble flicking the lighter with the exoskeleton, but he managed it. He still hadn't decided whether to keep the exo on around the clock, or just put it on for special occasions. For now he'd leave it on, see how awkward it was. Might be worth any hassles, it was pretty fucking rabid.

Mixer checked his watch. Ten minutes to his meet with Chandler. Better move it. He started down the street, thinking how Chandler would be impressed with the exo. But, impressed enough to tell him something about Chick?

Two blocks, walking fast, he tossed the cigarette, then shot across the street, darting through traffic. He bumped into a patchwork beggar who was stumbling along the sidewalk with eyeblinds and a fingerless stub for a hand. The beggar cried out, swung his good fist blindly toward Mixer, but Mixer blocked it with his right arm, and the beggar's fist banged into the exoskeleton. The beggar yowled and staggered away. The exo *was* good for something, Mixer thought.

He pulled open the lobby door of the Caterwaul Building, twelve stories of ugly, and stepped inside. Gunther, the beefy security guard with a hole in his face where his nose should have been, looked up from his chess game, recognized Mixer, and waved him through to the elevator. The chessboard spat a bishop at Gunther's face, but he caught it inches away from his forehead, grinned at Mixer, and put the bishop back on the board.

The elevator doors were already open and waiting, and Mixer entered. He hesitated, breathed deeply, and pushed the twelfth-floor button. As the doors closed, his chest tightened. There was a click, then the elevator lurched upward. Mixer started to sweat.

Mixer hated elevators. Something like claustrophobia, he guessed. He had an irrational fear that the elevator would get stuck between floors and he would be hopelessly trapped for hours. But to meet Chandler he didn't have a choice; Chandler had blocked off the stairs at the tenth floor, making the elevator the only access.

Mixer stood in the middle of the elevator as it slowly rose, listening to the double *ca-click ca-click* at each floor, counting silently . . . five . . . six . . . He realized he had stopped breathing, and forced himself to start again, slowly in and out . . . ten . . . eleven . . . The elevator ground to a halt with a terrible groan. The doors slid open. Mixer stepped out.

Chandler had gutted the entire twelfth floor several years back, turning it into a single, enormous room. Chandler traded in almost anything, and usually there were crates and cartons and foam-pack bundles stacked against the walls, several tables and chairs scattered throughout the room with computers, printers, and various kinds of analyzers and measurement devices, a dozen or more people, half of them security, and the whole place lit with lamps strung from the ceiling. Now, though, the room was nearly empty, silent, and dimly lit by a single overhead light. A few boxes against the right wall, under a window. A single folding chair in the middle of the room. Two wadded pieces of paper on the floor. Dust rolls.

No Chandler. Nobody at all.

Something was very wrong.

The elevator doors started to close behind him. Mixer turned, watching them close and seal. He could have reached them in time, kept them open, but his gut said to let them go. Might not be a good idea to be in the elevator when it reached the ground floor. A groan sounded, and the elevator began its descent.

On the other hand, if someone—Chandler?—wanted him, why hadn't they been waiting when he stepped out of the elevator? Mixer scanned the shadows of the vast, empty room, half expecting someone to appear, lights to go on, or some explosion to go off. Nothing happened.

Mixer felt calm and unafraid. There was no way to know what was going on here, no way to know if it even had anything to do with him. Chandler was into all kinds of shit, with all kinds of people, even New Hong Kong. The body-bags were only a sideline for him. This could be anything.

Mixer walked around a little, listening to his own echoing footsteps. He could search the place, maybe find something. A clue. Right. What he should do is get out. Now. Stupid to take chances.

But how? He still didn't like the elevator. And the fire escape was out. Chandler had ripped it off the side of the building years ago. Elevator shaft, maybe. Force open the door, climb down the shaft to the tenth floor, force that door open, and he'd be able to reach the stairs, maybe find a way out on one of the other floors.

He went back to the elevator, tried to force open the outer door. There was nothing to grip; the edge of the door went too far into the wall, and the door didn't budge. The exo would give him extra strength, but it wasn't any help if he couldn't get a grip on anything.

He gave up on the elevator shaft, and stood gazing around the huge, empty room, thinking. He still wasn't much worried, but he didn't want to stay here any longer than he had to. Shadows, pillars, barred windows. Ventilation shafts way too small.

Stairs. The stairwell was in the corner, now deep in shadow. They were blocked at the tenth floor, but there might be a window in the stairwell, or . . . something. Mixer walked to the corner, slowing as the darkness increased, letting his eyes adjust. He hesitated at the top of the stairs, looking down, unable to clearly see more than a few steps in front of him. No sign of a window. Hell, just go. What else was there? He started down.

Halfway to the next floor the stairs cornered and switched back, actually got a little bit brighter, light coming in from the door opening onto the eleventh floor. He stopped on the landing and stuck his head into the hallway. There was a window at the far end of the corridor, and open doors on both sides, light emerging in angled bands from most of them. He didn't see or hear anything, but there was a mild stench coming from somewhere. He'd never been allowed on this floor, never known what Chandler used it for.

Mixer looked down the stairwell. It got darker again. No window, and access to the tenth floor was blocked by brick and concrete; he'd seen the barrier the one time he'd tried using the stairs in defiance of Chandler's instructions. No choice, then. He had to see if there was a way out on this floor.

The window at the end of the hall was probably his best shot. He took a few steps into the hall, then stopped, listening for voices or other sounds. Nothing. He continued slowly along the hall, trying to keep his footsteps silent.

The door to the first room on his left was open, and light emerged through it. No sounds. Mixer stopped, then leaned forward and looked inside. Empty. The stench was worse; he could almost feel it wafting out of the room, but he couldn't see anything that would cause it. What the fuck had Chandler been doing in here? Bare walls, bare floor, boarded windows, an overhead fluorescent light. Nothing else.

Mixer moved on. The next room was on his right; it, too, was open. When he looked inside, he again saw bare walls, bare floor, a fluorescent light. Once more he felt and smelled the stench, heavy and warm and cloying.

Bad, bad, bad. He hadn't been afraid on the floor above, standing in that vast, empty room. But here? Something was wrong, seriously wrong, and Mixer was damn sure he didn't want to be here.

He moved quickly now, not quite jogging, a fast walk, still trying to stay quiet. No more looking into the rooms as he passed them; he hoped there wasn't anyone or anything inside. Just get to the window, he told himself, and get out.

Mixer reached the end of the hall and looked out the window. Good and bad luck. The next building was no more than eight feet away, but the roof was at least a full floor below, maybe more. The gap would be easy, the drop a bitch. At the far end of the roof was a rat-pack hut with a few soldiers moving in and out of the lights. Mixer knew the building, knew the head rat. He wouldn't get free passage, but he'd be able to buy his way down.

The window was old, counterweight and pulley. Mixer grabbed the bottom handle and pulled up. The window rose smoothly, surprising the hell out of him. He opened it all the way, put his head through and looked down. A cement ledge ran along the wall about two feet below the window. Narrow, but wide enough to use as a launch pad.

Mixer pulled his head back in and was just about to put his leg through the open window when he sensed something approaching from behind. He spun and crouched, preparing himself, but the hall was empty. The sensation remained, however, the feel of some presence there in the hall with him. There were no sounds, no signs of movement, just the steadily increasing stench and the eerie, prickly feeling that flowed over him. *Fuck me,* Mixer thought. *I've got to get the hell out of here.*

He worked his way backward through the window, feeling his way with his shoes to the ledge below, never taking his eyes off the hallway. When his footing was secure, he eased his chest and head through, keeping hold of the sill, watching the hall. Still nothing.

He didn't want to turn his back to the hall, not for more than a few seconds, anyway, so he geared himself up to turn and jump at the same time. He ran through it in his head, glancing back and forth from the hall to the roof below. He'd jump, land feet first, buckling his legs and doing a tuck and roll to absorb the impact. Okay. One last look down the hall, and go.

Mixer turned, let go of the windowsill, and pushed off the ledge, leaping across the gap and down. Almost immediately he hit the roof hard, pain flaring in his ankles as he pitched forward and sprawled across the rough surface, scraping his arms and hands and face. Shit, so much for the tuck and roll theory.

He pushed himself up to hands and knees, then slowly to his feet. Both ankles hurt, the left worse than the right, but he'd be able to walk. The exo had protected his right hand and arm, but the other was badly scraped and bleeding in several places.

Mixer turned around and looked up at the eleventh-floor window. Nothing. He was about to turn away, when he thought he saw something, a shadow, a shimmer of movement. He stared hard, but didn't see anything else. A minute passed. Nothing. Then the window slowly, steadily, slid down and closed.

Fuck me, Mixer said to himself again.

He kept watching the window, listening to the rat-pack soldiers coming toward him, but he saw nothing more. One hard, long shiver rolled through his body. Mixer turned away and limped across the roof to the rat-pack soldiers waiting for him.

4

CARLUCCI WAS ALREADY exhausted by the time he got to his office and dropped into his chair. His morning coffee-hash at Spade's had gone almost three hours, most of that time spent trying to organize the murder investigation of the mayor's nephew with LaPlace and Hong, who were in charge of the case. They were getting almost as much heat as he was, and so far they were getting nowhere. They'd arranged to meet later that afternoon at the nephew's penthouse for another look-through. Then, after dropping him off at the station, LaPlace and Hong had gone off to talk to people they knew weren't going to tell them a damn thing.

The air conditioning was still out, but the fans had been left on all night, and it was early, so the air wasn't too bad yet. Carlucci cleared a spot on his desk, piling files and notepads on top of other piles, then turned on his computer terminal. To his surprise, the system was back up and running. He logged on, then called up his file on the nephew—William Kashen. There wasn't much in it, and there wasn't much to add—the official report would be done by LaPlace and Hong, since it was their case—but with all the political pressure on this thing he had to keep a kind of management file to show he was staying on top of it.

Carlucci spent a half hour working on the file, most of that time staring at the screen and doing nothing, not even thinking about the case. When he thought he'd done enough, he printed out a hard copy, grabbed the sheets from the printer on the side of his desk, and stuffed them in the blue case folder. Then he sat staring at the monitor for a while longer, thinking about Paula Asgard and Chick Roberts.

Gotta start sometime, he thought. Carlucci called up the case file for Chick Roberts. The cover sheet came up on the screen, which gave the most basic information: case number, date, first officers on the scene, investigating officers (Santos and Weathers, Santos senior-in-charge), and status (open, pending). When Carlucci tried to call up the rest of the case file, he got "the message."

FILE ACCESS RESTRICTED
CAPTAIN MCCULLER/CHIEF VAUGHN FOR AUTHORIZATION

Pretty much what he had expected. A temporary dead end. There was no way he could go to McCuller or Vaughn for authorization. At this point he didn't want either of them to know he was at all interested in the case.

Carlucci exited the case file and logged off, then picked up the phone and punched in Ruben Santos's number. There was no answer, and after three rings Carlucci heard the click as he was transferred through to the front desk.

"I'm looking for Ruben Santos," he told the clerk.

"Ah, let's see . . . he's out with Weathers, interviews, probably back this afternoon. Page or message?"

"No." Carlucci hung up.

One step at a time, no hurry, Carlucci told himself. Chick Roberts wasn't going anywhere, and he had to be careful. But it nagged at him, and he had a crappy feeling about the whole thing. He wanted to move on it, or forget about it completely. Forgetting about it, though, wasn't something he could do. So . . . patience. There was nothing more he could do until he talked to Santos. For now, just muck around at the desk, grab a bite to eat, then go out to the nephew's. Chick Roberts would have to wait.

The nephew's apartment was still a mess. The only thing missing was the body. Even the stink of death remained, if only a trace. Blood was spattered everywhere in the front room, dark and dry now. Deep, solid patches on the white carpet radiated from the vague outline of a body, interspersed with wide, fanning streaks. Everything in the room was white—carpet, walls, furniture, lampshades, even the entertainment system and picture phone—and in the bright lights the blood stood out like phosphor. There were even a few splatters on the white textured ceiling.

"We should rip up the carpet," LaPlace said. "Frame it, and put it up in a gallery. Post-neo-industrial-modern-slasher art, or something like that."

Peter LaPlace, a heavy, balding man, removed his glasses, rubbed the bridge of his nose, then replaced them. Joseph Hong, who was taller and much thinner than LaPlace, also wore glasses, and a lot of the homicide cops called them the Spec Twins.

LaPlace turned slowly, gazing around the room and through the doorways into the rest of the apartment. "Fuckin' weird place to live," he said.

"Weird guy," Hong said, shrugging.

Carlucci just nodded. They'd been through the apartment pretty thoroughly the day before while the coroner's men worked on the body. Most of the rooms were monochrome, like this one, furnishings matching the wall paint and carpeting. The two enormous bedrooms were all black, an office room was blue, the bathrooms bright red, the kitchen white. The dining room was the exception, a combination of white and black and chrome.

None of them were quite sure what they were looking for. The crime scene techs had already gone through it with all their sophisticated detection equipment, slicking up prints, hairs, fibers, skin flakes, and various other particles which they were now analyzing with a fortune in lab machinery. With the mayor on their asses, no expense would be spared. And plenty would be wasted. Additionally, the three detectives had already tagged and bagged several boxes of articles from the apartment, which were now back at the station and which they would go through again and again later on, along with the dozens of photographs that had been taken. They were here now hoping to see something they'd missed, or think of something, or get kicked off into a line of thought that none of them had come up with before. They were searching for intangibles and gut feelings. Anything.

And Carlucci wanted to talk to Hong and LaPlace alone, where they wouldn't be overheard by department squeakers, the way they might have been at Spade's this morning. Carlucci hadn't seen anybody suspicious, but he hardly trusted anyone these days.

"Pete, Joseph," Carlucci said. The two men looked at him. "I've got something I want to say. Didn't want to talk about it at Spade's."

"Squeakers?" LaPlace said.

"Yeah, Pete, you just never know."

Hong slid a cigarette from his shirt pocket, stuck it in his mouth, dug out a lighter from his pants, and lit the cigarette, all his motions slow and deliberate. Hong thought they were about to get ragged on, Carlucci realized.

"Look, this is your case," Carlucci said. "You two are in charge, you make all the decisions, handle it the way you think best. The only reason I'm here is because of all the heat from the mayor and the chief. I'm not trying to butt in on the case, I've just got to do this for appearances. It's all bullshit, but I've got no choice. As much as possible, we do this like we would any other case—it's yours, and you report to me. I'll be around more, I'll be on the streets with you once in a while, but I'll try to stay out of your way." Carlucci shrugged. "I don't like this arrangement any more than you do."

Hong and LaPlace looked at each other, Hong nodded, then LaPlace turned back to Carlucci. "Joseph and I have already talked about it," LaPlace said. He half smiled. "We can see what's going on. We just didn't know how you were going to be about it. Hell, Frank, you might have decided to jump all over our asses. We didn't think you would, but who the fuck knows? We figured if you did, we were going to be assholes about it. But hell, since you're not, we'd just as soon you actually worked with us as much as you can. This is going to be a bitch investigation, for a lot of reasons."

"Yeah, it is." Carlucci sighed and nodded. "All right, then. Everything's clear between us?" Hong and LaPlace both nodded. "Good. Then let's get to work, see if we can find *anything* in this freaking place."

They split up. Each man would go through the entire apartment separately, hoping somebody would spot something the others missed. Wasn't much of a hope, Carlucci thought, but it was worth a shot.

As he worked his way through the apartment, Carlucci had to struggle to keep from being distracted by all the extravagance and luxury, the fortune in high-tech gadgets and the incredible views, even though he'd seen it all the day before. Picture phones and internal video systems were built into the walls of every room, including the bathroom, along with control panels for the Bang and Olufsen entertainment system, which also had speakers and monitors in each room. The larger of the black bedrooms had a set of neural head-nets, and hanging in the closet was an assortment of exotic sexual electronics, some of which Carlucci didn't even recognize. The other bedroom, aside from the friction bed, had a set of bunked bubble tubes, one of which was still half filled with a pink, gelatinous fluid.

The blue room was filled with computers, data-scanners, and more electronic equipment that was only vaguely familiar to Carlucci. Most of the equipment had been damaged or destroyed, presumably by the nephew's killer. The department's electronic salvage crews had been in and removed what few disks and chips and bubbles were left behind, and were working to recover any data that remained. Carlucci didn't hold out much hope for that line of investigation, either.

Saunas and whirlpools and automated massagers in the bathrooms, auto-chef and espresso machine and ionizers in the kitchen. A heat scanner in the dining room, digitizing paintings on the hallway walls. And the entire penthouse wired with the most sophisticated alarm and shield system Carlucci had ever seen, which hadn't prevented the mayor's nephew from being gutted in his own living room.

The nephew. He had a name, Carlucci reminded himself. William Kashen. Except no one referred to him by name. He was the mayor's nephew, which was his most significant feature as far as the investigation was concerned.

Carlucci didn't spot anything in any of the rooms that seemed worthwhile, and an hour after they had begun, they met back in the living room, where they stood looking down at the largest of the bloodstains on the carpet. Hong was on his fourth or fifth cigarette, which actually helped cut the leftover stink in the apartment. Nobody had found a thing.

"Bet we get the autopsy report pretty damn quick," LaPlace said.

Carlucci nodded. "Prelim's due on my desk this afternoon. Maybe we can go over it later today, or first thing tomorrow."

"Tomorrow," Hong said. "My grandmother-in-law is one hundred today. We're having a dinner celebration in our flat tonight. Twenty people, and I'm the cook."

Carlucci smiled. "Tomorrow, then."

"Bet the report says he was still alive through most of the gutting," LaPlace said.

"I wouldn't be surprised." Carlucci ran his gaze over the wide scattering of blood once again.

"I suppose they're going to put the slugs on it, aren't they?" Hong asked.

"Yeah," Carlucci said. "They've got one on it now, and they'll put all of them on it once the autopsy report comes in and a good chunk of the lab work is done. Everything's got a goddamn rush on it. Info-Services is already putting together the Prime Level Feed for them, and a few people are working on the sublevel feeds. They might start the rest of the slugs tomorrow or the next day." Carlucci didn't look forward to it. It had been years since he'd had a session with the slugs, and the thought of doing another made him queasy. The slugs were repulsive—bodies, limbs, and faces twisted and distended by the frequent injections of reason enhancers and metabolic boosters. He had a hard time even thinking of them as human.

Hong put out his cigarette in an immaculate white porcelain ashtray atop a quartz table; then, as if reading Carlucci's thoughts, he frowned and said, "The slugs aren't people, not anymore. We don't need them."

No one was going to argue with him. Most cops hated the slugs and felt they got a lot more credit than they deserved, felt they got in the way more than they helped. Carlucci knew they *had* been responsible for real breakthroughs in several major cases that had dead-ended before the slugs were put on them, but if he had a choice he would as soon do without.

"Anything else?" he asked.

Hong and LaPlace both shook their heads, then LaPlace said, "I'd like to keep the apartment sealed off another couple days or so. I'd like to be able to come back and look around."

"Sure." Carlucci understood. They were all afraid they had missed something important, and probably all three of them would come by here at least one more time, alone, most likely in the middle of the night. "We done here for now?" Both men nodded. "All right, then, let's get out of here."

Back in his office, there was no preliminary autopsy report, which was just fine with Carlucci; it would shift some of the heat from him to the coroner, at least for today. He punched up Santos's number on the phone, and a woman answered.

"Weathers."

"Toni, this is Frank. Ruben around?"

"Yeah, somewhere. I'll go see if I can find him."

"Thanks."

"By the way," Weathers said, "how's progress on that paragon of virtue, the mayor's nephew?"

Carlucci snorted. "We're pursuing several potentially fruitful lines of inquiry," he said, imitating the PR hack who'd been on television the night before.

Toni Weathers laughed. "You haven't got jack shit."

"That's about right."

"I'll go see if I can find Ruben."

He heard the clunk of the receiver being dropped to the table, then a scattering of background noises as he waited, including what sounded like an incredibly long and loud belch.

Toni Weathers, like Ruben, was a good homicide cop, and as straight as Ruben. They'd been partners for more than ten years. Carlucci wondered what *she* thought of the Chick Roberts case.

More clunking sounds, then, "Frank?" Santos's voice.

"Yeah, Ruben."

"What's up?"

"Got a half hour? Buy you a cup of coffee."

Santos didn't answer at first. Carlucci could hear his deep, raspy breath over the phone.

"There's something you need to talk to me about?" Santos asked.

"Oh, just this and that, get your thoughts on the mayor's nephew."

Another hesitation, then, "You want to come by here and talk to me while I write up these interviews?"

"I thought we'd take a walk. Get out of this damn hot box. Get some fresh air."

This time the pause was even longer. Santos probably had a good idea what Carlucci really wanted to talk about, and didn't want to touch it. But he would also know he couldn't avoid it for long.

"Sure, Frank," Santos finally answered. "I'm suffocating in here anyway. Meet you downstairs in, say, fifteen minutes."

"Fine," Carlucci said. He hung up.

They met in the station lobby, and immediately left the building. Santos was thin and wiry, with curly hair the color of rust, and was growing a beard again. Carlucci figured it was about two weeks along, and there was more gray in it than there had been the last time around.

It was late afternoon, and hot. It looked like it might finally rain for the first time in days, orange-brown clouds moving across the hazy sun, the air heavy and charged and damp. Carlucci stopped at the Cuban bakery on the corner and bought two large cups of coffee, then he and Santos continued down the street, sipping at it through openings torn in the lids. The coffee was strong, and so hot it burned Carlucci's tongue and lips.

"Chick Roberts," Carlucci said when they were several blocks from the station.

"Fuck you and fuck me," Santos said. "I *knew* you were going to ask me about that goddamn case. Mayor's nephew, my ass. God damn!" He turned to glare at Carlucci. "I'm not saying a fucking word about it."

"Come on, Ruben. This isn't like you. What the hell's going on?"

"Frank, I'm not screwing around. I've got nothing to say."

"Ruben, shit, it's *me* you're talking to. Why are you burying this thing?"

Santos didn't answer. He led the way across the street and down half a block to a vacant lot that had only recently started filling up with garbage. Five kids around nine or ten years old sat in a shallow cave dug out of the side of the garbage mound, playing some kind of game with a batch of dead green neurotubes.

"Hey!" Santos called to the kids. "Why aren't you in school?" They looked up at him but didn't respond. Santos repeated his question in Spanish. Still no response. Santos shrugged. "Hell, they probably don't even know what school is."

"Why, Ruben?" Carlucci asked again.

Santos drank some more of his coffee, then suddenly threw the cup at the mound of trash. The lip flipped off and coffee sprayed in twisting arcs through the air. Santos turned to Carlucci, eyes glaring.

"How the hell do *I* know why I'm burying it? Jesus Christ, Frank, you think they tell me why? You know better than that. 'Bury it, Ruben.' That's all they said. So I'm fucking burying it."

"Ruben . . . Christ, Ruben, why not demand reassignment?" Automatic reassignment was an option that had always been available, to allow any cop to stay as straight as he wanted. The vast majority of investigations proceeded on regular tracks, but there were always a few that the top hogs, for whatever political or financial reasons, wanted buried, or fouled up, or just ghosted, and anyone involved in one of those cases had the option of being reassigned so they wouldn't have to be a part of it. It was an informal arrangement that had worked well over the years. Any cop could get off a dirty case, and in return they agreed not to raise a stink—they let it go. A clean cop could *stay* a clean cop.

Santos seemed to sag, and he slowly shook his head. "You think I didn't ask, Frank?"

"They turned you down?" Carlucci could hardly believe it. The reassignment option was one of the few things cops counted on.

"They fucked me, Frank. That shit McCuller, he'd bend over for anyone above him who said 'asshole' in his hearing. Called me before I even got to the scene, asked me if I wanted my job and my pension and my health benefits. I asked for reassignment right then, before he had a chance to tell me what he wanted done. I didn't even want to know." He stopped, gazing at the mound of garbage and the kids playing in their cave. "McCuller said there would be no reassignment on this case, unless I wanted to resign and forfeit all my pension and benefits." Santos turned to Carlucci. "I've got twenty-three years in, Frank. I'd never get another job as a cop, you know that. What the hell am I supposed to do, start all over again someplace? Doing what? At my age? With Consuela and the kids?" He paused, breathing deeply, shaking his head. "Jesus Christ, Frank, they're not supposed to be able to do this to us." He stopped again, ran his hand through his hair, then rubbed at his neck. "I had about thirty seconds to make my decision. I thought about fighting it, bringing it to the Association, threaten to go public, whatever, but I didn't think about it long." He looked at Carlucci. "I couldn't afford to lose that one, Frank. So I made the decision, and I'm stuck with it."

They started walking again, slowly, neither speaking. When they came to a liquor store, Santos went in, then came back out with a pack of cigarettes. He opened it, shook one out and lit it.

"I've been trying to quit," he said. "I'd been doing all right until you called. God damn you, Frank." He dragged in deep on the cigarette, and they continued along the street.

"How's Toni feel about it?" Carlucci asked.

"The same. She hasn't said anything, but I think she's going along with it mostly for me. She's younger, she's got no kids. I think she'd have been willing to fight it, try to blow these fuckers out of the water, if it wasn't for me. Which only makes me feel worse about the whole fucking mess."

"But why wouldn't they let you and Toni off the case?"

Santos shook his head. "I've been thinking about that. Two possibilities. One, they want clean cops on the file so it looks like nothing funny's going on. Or two, they just don't want more people to know about the case." He shook his head again. "I don't know, Frank. I think someone panicked on this thing."

"Why?"

"You know anything about this Chick Roberts? A part-time rocker, part-time two-bit petty thief, ex-junkie who probably still popped too much shit. If nobody says anything to us, how much time and effort were we going to put into the case? Not a hell of a lot. We'd have written it off to a drug deal gone to shit, something like that. Probably would have just faded away all on its own. Now? Who knows, it might stay buried. But it just might blow up in somebody's goddamn face."

A shimmering flash of light appeared in the clouds, followed a few moments later by a roll of thunder. The first drops fell on the two men. They hurried around the corner and under the shelter of an abandoned bus stop just as the rain poured full force from above. Santos dropped his cigarette to the ground, crushed it with his shoe, then turned to Carlucci.

"This isn't some kind of official inquiry, is it, Frank?"

"Ruben. You know me better than that."

Santos shrugged. "I had to ask." He lit another cigarette, dragged on it. "How the hell did you find out about this thing? The files and reports were supposed to bypass you completely."

"They did," Carlucci replied, but he didn't say any more.

"Then . . . ?" Santos cocked his head, then nodded to himself. "The girlfriend, right?" Carlucci didn't answer. "Yeah, has to be; she'd been dogging me about it. I thought she'd finally gotten the message and dropped it." He shook his head. "You talk to anyone else about this, Frank?"

"Of course not. I came to you first, Ruben."

"Then leave it that way, for Christ's sake. And tell the girlfriend the same thing. I don't know why they want this thing buried, and I don't want to know. You don't either, Frank. Go find out who killed the mayor's nephew, get a citation, and leave this case the fuck alone."

"You really don't know why it's being buried, Ruben? Not even a hint?"

"Shit, Frank, if I did I wouldn't tell you. Forget this goddamn case. *I'm* trying to. And forget we even talked about it."

They stood under the shelter, the rain pouring down all around them. Another flash, then rolling thunder. It pissed Carlucci off, what McCuller and Vaughn had done to Santos. It just wasn't fair. Well, shit, he told himself, not much *was* fair. Santos knew that, and Paula Asgard probably knew that as well. He was going to have to talk to her soon, and what the hell was he going to say?

Carlucci turned to Santos and nodded. "You're right, Ruben. We haven't talked about this."

Santos nodded back, but didn't say anything. They remained in the shelter, silent, waiting for the rain to stop.

5

WHAT A FUCKED day. Paula lay back on Chick's bed and closed her eyes, incredibly tired. Her arms and legs felt heavy, and the heat seemed to drain all the energy from her; the air was so still and quiet, and she didn't want to move. So don't move, she told herself. Why bother?

First there had been the horrible stench of the place after being closed up for almost two weeks. Then, seeing the bloodstains all over the rug. She'd almost walked away and left everything, but in the end she just couldn't do that. So she'd stayed, and spent the day going through all Chick's stuff, trying to decide what to keep, what to get rid of.

There were surprises. Like tens and twenties stashed all over the apartment, in books, wedged onto shelves; she must have found over three hundred dollars so far. A collection of twentieth-century Hungarian postage stamps. A complete set of Torelli's fifteen vortex novels. And finally, she'd found a box of all the letters she'd ever written to Chick over the years.

She'd had no idea he'd saved them, no idea that they would be important to him, and that had made her even more tired and depressed.

Paula was nodding off, almost asleep, when someone pounded on the front door. Before she could get up and out of the bedroom, the pounding repeated, louder this time.

"I'm coming!" she called as she came into the entryway. At the door, she looked through the peephole. It was Graumann, the building manager. Paula unlocked the door and opened it.

Graumann was huge; not much taller than she, but at least three hundred and fifty pounds, large arms and legs and an enormous gut. His puffy face glistened with sweat and he was breathing heavily.

"You've got to get out of here," he said. "I gotta rent this place."

Good afternoon to you, too, asshole, Paula thought. "I'm going through Chick's things now," she said. "I need some time to sort through it all, pack it up, and move it."

"You haven't got time," Graumann said. "You want me to call the cops? The owner's on my butt. You've gotta get out, unless you wanna make up all the back rent. Chick was behind again."

Of course he was. Chick was always getting behind on his rent, and then he'd pop something, catch up, maybe even pay a little ahead, and slip Graumann three or four hundred dollars for letting it go so long. It had worked out fine for both of them.

"Give me a fucking break," Paula said. "I've got a lot of shit to go through."

"No one's paying rent," Graumann said.

"Chick's dead, for Christ's sake!"

Graumann looked down at the floor for a moment, but then returned his gaze to her. A bead of sweat hung from his chin. He shrugged, knocking the bead free, but didn't say anything.

The telephone rang. Oh, terrific. Graumann looked over her shoulder. What did he expect to see, Chick appearing to answer the phone? It rang again. Okay, okay. Paula dug her hand into her pocket and pulled out the wad of bills she'd collected. She shoved it all into Graumann's hand and said, "I need three or four days." A third ring. Fuck.

Graumann shrugged again. "Okay," he said and Paula slammed the door in his face. The phone rang once more and Chick's answering machine clicked on. Shit, she'd forgotten about that. Chick's voice spoke from the machine, and she felt like crying again. Or laughing.

"This is Chick, and you can suck my dick. Or leave a message. Your choice." A high beep sounded, followed by another click.

"Ah . . . this is Lieutenant Frank Carlucci, calling for Paula Asgard. I'll try to . . ."

Paula hurried into the bedroom and looked around for the phone.

". . . this message you can . . ."

She spotted it under the edge of the overstuffed chair, crossed the room, dropped to the floor and picked it up, interrupting Carlucci's message.

"Hi, this is Paula."

"What? Oh, yes, this is Lieutenant Carlucci. I just wanted to let you know that I've checked into the case."

Jesus, he sounded so damn formal. "And?"

"And, well, I'm afraid there's nothing I can tell you. Everything possible has been done, but unfortunately without much success. Despite a thorough investigation, there have been no leads. Although the case is not technically closed, for all practical purposes it is pretty much over."

Paula was speechless. It was Carlucci's voice, she was sure she recognized it, but it hardly sounded like him, spouting all this crap.

"I'm sorry, Ms. Asgard," Carlucci went on, "that I couldn't have been more help."

God damn, the bastard was caving with the rest of them. "That's all you've got to say?" she asked him.

"No, there is one more thing, Ms. Asgard. I know this has been difficult for you, and that it's especially frustrating when the person or persons responsible for the death of your friend have not been apprehended, or even identified. But I think it would be best if you put this whole thing behind you." He paused. "Let this go, Ms. Asgard."

"Just like that, huh?"

"I know it won't be easy, but yes. Forget about it, Ms. Asgard. Believe me, it will be better if you do."

All right, I've got the message. "Fine," she said to Carlucci. "I get the picture. Thanks a lot for nothing."

"I'm sorry, Ms. Asgard." There was another long pause, and when Paula didn't reply, Carlucci said, "Goodbye, Ms. Asgard," then hung up.

"Yeah, goodbye, asshole." Paula sat on the floor for a minute, holding the receiver, listening to the dial tone. Terrific. Carlucci, the wonder cop. Mixer didn't know his ass from a gravity well. She hung up the phone, then pulled herself up off the floor and into the overstuffed chair.

She'd been right here that night, sitting in this chair and staring at Chick's body on the floor, what was left of his head surrounded by thick, dark blood. All that remained now were the stains in the rug. She shouldn't have bothered going to Carlucci in the first place. What did it matter in the end? Chick was dead, and he was going to stay dead no matter what happened.

But she had thought it was important, important that somebody at least *try* to find out who had killed him and why. It still was important, she decided, but it obviously wasn't going to happen. And since it wasn't, Carlucci was right. She should just forget about it. Mixer said he could "nudge" Carlucci into it, but she would tell him not to bother. If Carlucci wouldn't do it on his own, then fuck him. Just fuck 'em all.

●   ●   ●

Half an hour later, Paula decided to pack it in for the day. She was hungry and tired and depressed. She'd had enough. She would take the box of letters and a few other things with her, and leave the rest for later; tomorrow or the next day she would call Nikky and see if she could borrow her van.

Before she could pull everything together, she heard knocking at the door. Oh, God, not Graumann again. What the hell would he want this time? Paula went to the front door, looked through the peephole, and was surprised to see Carlucci.

She didn't know whether to be pissed, or just more depressed; whether to open the door, or scream at him to leave. When Carlucci knocked again, Paula threw back the bolts and pulled the door open.

"Hello, Ms. Asgard." He looked uncomfortable, which was fine with her.

"Why are you here, Lieutenant Carlucci?"

"I want to apologize for what I said on the phone."

"Yeah?"

"Yes. Look, I need to talk to you. You can forget everything I said on the phone, all that . . . well, that was just to cover my ass, and yours." He scratched behind his ear. "This case is making me paranoid, and I'm trying not to take any chances."

Paula's anger and depression lifted a little, but she remained wary. "Are you saying you *are* going to look into Chick's death?"

Carlucci scratched again, frowning, then nodded. "I think so. That's why I want to talk to you."

"But the phone call. You think your own phone is bugged?"

Carlucci shrugged. "I'd be surprised if it wasn't. Look, have you had dinner yet?" When Paula shook her head, Carlucci said, "Why don't we go get something to eat, then, and talk about this?"

Did she really want to? Did she really want to get worked up again, maybe get shot down one more time? Or should she just let it go? Paula finally nodded. "Sure. I was just getting ready to lock up here. I've had it for today. Let me get my jacket."

Carlucci waited in the hall while she walked back to the bedroom, got her jacket, checked to make sure her wallet was secured inside, then rejoined him. She closed the door, locked the dead-bolts.

"You know a good place around here?" Carlucci said. "I'll buy."

Paula nodded, throwing her jacket over her shoulder. She should give him a choice. "Thai, or Mex?" Hoping he would say Mex; she had a real yen for chile rellenos and black beans.

"Mexican," Carlucci said.

Paula smiled. Maybe things were picking up. "Great," she said. "I know just the place."

●   ●   ●

Christiano's was small and colorful, noisy and crowded, with brightly painted dolls and masks and pictures hanging on the walls and from the ceiling. Traditional cantina played through tinny speakers mounted in the corners. Isabel met them as they came in, and Paula spoke with her in Spanish. They exchanged hellos, and Isabel hugged her, offered condolences for Chick. Carlucci surprised her when he introduced himself to Isabel, also in Spanish. Isabel said they would have a table cleared in a few minutes, and left.

Christiano's was one of Paula's favorite places, with good food and good people, a real neighborhood place. As they waited just inside the front door, she looked around for familiar faces. In the back, at a small table next to the kitchen door, was Pascal, the neighborhood scrounger, sitting alone and drinking coffee with his see-through arm. Three years ago Pascal had replaced his perfectly healthy right arm with an artificial limb sheathed in some kind of clear material so that all the inner workings were visible. Word on the street was that he'd done the same thing with his cock, but Paula wasn't about to check it out for herself.

Jeff and Robert were at a table by the front window, holding hands, Robert batting neon lashes at any man who walked by. Paula liked them both a lot, and waved when she caught Jeff's eye. Jeff and Robert waved back, smiling. Deena sat with three men Paula had never seen before, which worried her a little, but Deena seemed all right; Deena could usually take care of herself.

Isabel returned with menus and led them to a booth against the left wall. Carlucci sat facing the front of the restaurant, which left Paula with a terrific view of Pascal and the kitchen door. Carlucci glanced through the menu, then looked at her. "Any recommendations?"

"Everything's good," Paula said. "I go for the chile rellenos myself. But whatever you get, have an order of the black beans. They're great."

When Isabel came by again, Paula ordered three chile rellenos and black beans; Carlucci ordered *pollo con arroz,* a side of the beans, and a bottle of Diablo Negro beer.

Paula made a face at him after Isabel left. "God, you can drink that stuff?"

Carlucci smiled. "Sure. Why not?"

Paula just shivered. It was foul-tasting beer, very high alcohol. She had gotten tanked on Diablo Negro once, and she'd been sick for days. She'd never touched it since. Isabel came by with the beer, poured half the bottle into a glass, and left. Carlucci picked up the glass and raised an eyebrow at Paula. She gave him a sick smile, and said, "Go right ahead." Carlucci drank deeply; he seemed to actually enjoy it. Paula shook her head.

She picked up a tortilla chip and nibbled at it. "You wanted to talk," she said. "So let's talk."

Carlucci scanned the restaurant, checking the people around them, and

Paula wondered if he thought coming here was a mistake. But there was so much noise between the music, conversations, and the shouting and cooking sounds from the kitchen, she didn't think he had to worry. She couldn't make out the conversations of *anyone* nearby; it was all just babble. Carlucci apparently came to the same conclusion, because he shrugged and looked back at her.

"I told you," he said, his voice just loud enough for her to make out. "This case is making me paranoid. We both have to be careful of what we say, and where. I just don't like any of this." He paused, turning his beer glass around and around on the table. "Look, I want you to think damn hard about whether or not you really want me looking into this. If I go ahead, I'll be sticking my neck out, but it's going to put you at risk as well. I'm sure of it. Believe me, I'll be damn careful, but I can't guarantee anything, for either of us. I've got no idea how dangerous it could be, but we should assume the worst." He picked up his glass, stared at it, put it down without drinking, and looked back at Paula. "If you want me to just forget about the whole thing, I'll drop it right now. Let the case close, let them bury it."

"So they *are* trying to bury it," Paula said. She hated it, but it felt good to hear Carlucci say it, to know she'd been right.

"Yes," Carlucci said, nodding. "And that might be the smartest thing to do, let them." Then he shook his head. "No, it *would* be the smartest thing. Certainly the safest."

Paula scooped salsa onto a chip, put it into her mouth, and chewed on it as she watched Carlucci. She was trying to figure what his real feelings were on all this. Was he simply trying to warn her of real dangers and risks, or was he trying to scare her off?

"What about you?" she asked. "Do *you* want to look into it? Forget about me for a minute. If you were on your own, would you be trying to find out what happened?"

"How am I supposed to forget about you?" Carlucci said, smiling. "If it wasn't for you, I wouldn't even know about the damn thing. There'd be no decision to make."

"You know what I mean," Paula said.

Carlucci nodded. "Yeah, I do." He drank more of his beer, then poured the rest of the bottle into the glass. "Probably," he said. "I'd be digging into it, yes. Friends of mine are being screwed over by this case. I'm not going to go into details, or tell you any names. You don't need to know any of that, and we're both better off if you *don't* know."

"I think I can guess one name," Paula said. "Besides, you don't really know how much you can trust me, right?"

"There is that," Carlucci said. "It's not personal."

"I understand," Paula replied. "You don't know anything about me."

"I don't. I have your phone number, but I don't know where you live. I don't even know what you do for a living. You at least know that about me."

Paula smiled. "Most of the time *I* don't even know what I do for a living." She shrugged. "Mostly, I manage the Lumiere Theater, which gives me very irregular paychecks. And I play bass in slash-and-burn bands, which makes me pretty much no money at all."

"Slash and burn?" Carlucci raised an eyebrow. "Like Chick."

"Yeah, like Chick. We played in the same band, Pilate Error. As in Pontius Pilate. We played together off and on for a lot of years. And I play in an all-woman band called Black Angels."

"How old are you?" Carlucci asked.

"Thirty nine." She watched him, waiting for the question, but Carlucci didn't say anything. He made a grumbling sound and drank from his glass. "You aren't going to ask me if I don't think I'm too old for slash-and-burn, rock and roll," Paula asked.

Carlucci smiled and shook his head. "Not me. I'm not touching that one."

Paula smiled back at him. She was beginning to like Carlucci, no doubt about that. Maybe Mixer wasn't so crazy after all. She let the smile fade.

"So, are you going to look into it?" she asked him.

"Do you want me to? I was serious about the risks. Someone with heat wants this thing buried, and we both could get scorched but good."

She'd thought a lot about it before she'd even gone to Carlucci; she'd known from the beginning that it wouldn't be easy. "I'm willing to risk it if you are," Paula said. "I trust your judgment. I think."

Carlucci frowned. "Yeah, you think. Well, like I said before, no promises. I'm willing to dig around a bit, stick my neck out a little, but I'm going to be damn careful, and if it looks like I'll get my head chopped off, I'll pull the plug. I'm not willing to sacrifice everything I've got for this. Understood?"

"Understood." She nodded. "I wouldn't expect anything else."

"Good enough."

"So," Paula said. "What's next?"

"I want to get together with you for a couple of hours so we can talk about Chick, the people he knew, anything you know about what he was doing, that kind of thing."

"All right. When?"

"I've got another case I'm working on, but I'm off this weekend. Either Saturday or Sunday, any time."

As Paula was thinking about it, their food arrived. Isabel warned them about the hot plates, asked Carlucci if he wanted another beer. He said no, and she left them alone.

"Sunday would be best," Paula said. "If we can do it early, say eight or nine in the morning. We've got a Final Films Festival this weekend at the Lumiere, and I've got to be there and make sure the thing doesn't completely fall apart."

"Final films?"

"Yeah. Final films of the great directors. The last films of Malle, Maxwell, Scorsese, Godard, Herzog, Blanchot, Fassbinder."

Carlucci nodded. "I know Malle. *Elevator to the Gallows.*"

"Sure, one of his early films. You've seen it?"

"No. I just know the soundtrack. Miles Davis. Great music." He smiled. "I'm a jazz and blues man myself."

"Really? Do you play?"

"A little. Trumpet."

Yes, Paula thought, she was going to like Carlucci just fine. "So is Sunday morning all right?" she asked.

"Yeah, probably. I'll call you in a couple of days, confirm it, and we can decide where." He looked down at his plate, then back at her. "Right now, how about we eat while it's still hot?"

"Absolutely." Paula dug her fork into one of the chile rellenos, brought it to her mouth. The egg coating was light and fluffy, the chile had a sharp bite, and the cheese inside was hot and smooth. Wonderful. She looked up at Carlucci, who seemed to be enjoying his own food. She thought about the letters Chick had kept, and Carlucci showing up at the apartment, saying he would look into Chick's murder, and now delicious food in a place like this. The day had turned out all right after all.

6

CARLUCCI SAT IN the dark basement of his home in the Inner Sunset, trumpet in hand, one of his old Big Eddie Washington discs playing on the sound system. Eddie Washington—a great blues guitarist with a harsh, haunting voice. Washington finished singing a verse of "Devil Woman Blues," and Carlucci brought the trumpet to his lips. As Washington began his solo, Carlucci broke in, counterpointing Washington's guitar with his own solo trumpet.

After his family, this was Carlucci's love—jazz, yes, but most of all the blues. Listening to it, and playing it. It took him away, not in escape, but into a world that seemed to mesh with his gut and with his heart; it brought up sadness and pain, but in ways that were somehow beautiful, and affirming.

He had been in the basement for over an hour, listening and playing. Christina, their younger daughter (not so young anymore, seventeen), had been the only one home when he came in after taking Paula to her apartment. Christina said that Andrea had called from the office and wouldn't be home until nine or ten; then she had taken off to meet Marx, her boyfriend, for a night of bone-slotting down in the Marina. Which had left Carlucci the house to himself.

The song ended and Carlucci sat back in the old sofa, resting the trumpet on his thigh, thinking about Caroline, his other daughter. Caroline, who had just turned twenty and wouldn't live to see thirty. Right after the Gould's Syndrome had been diagnosed, Caroline had moved out of the house, and they hardly saw her anymore. Carlucci thought he understood, and he didn't hold it against her, but knowing she didn't have that many years left, he wanted to see her as much as possible. Instead, they only saw her once or twice a month, and couldn't even talk to her much more than that.

The next song's solo began, and Carlucci played a few notes, then stopped, returning the trumpet to his thigh, thoughts moving for some reason from Caroline to his old blues band. Death on his mind, he guessed. When he was younger, a lot younger, he had been part of a quartet with three other cops. Right after Caroline had been born. They'd called themselves the Po-Leece Blues Band, and they'd been good enough to play in some of the clubs around the city; not regularly, but often enough to stay fresh and tight. Then Becker, the bass player, and Johnson, the drummer, had both been killed in a race riot in front of City Hall, and that had been the end of the band. Carlucci had never tried to put together another, and he had contented himself over the years with playing alone in his basement, playing along with the old greats and the new.

There were three more songs on the disc, but Carlucci just listened to them, eyes closed, silently pumping the valves with his fingers. Then the disc ended, and Carlucci remained motionless in the dark, listening to the near silence.

Sometime later he heard the muted sounds of the front door, then footsteps overhead. Andrea was home.

By the time he got upstairs, she was already in the shower. Carlucci knocked on the door, stepped into the bathroom. "It's me," he said. He watched her moving behind the shower door, her image distorted by the wedge-cut glass.

"I hope it's you," Andrea said. "Were you in the basement? I didn't hear any music."

"Yes." Carlucci closed the toilet lid and sat on it, leaning back against the tank. "I was listening to music earlier. Then I was just thinking."

"Sitting alone in the dark again," she said. "Brooding, I'd bet."

Carlucci didn't reply. He listened to the way the water sounds changed as she moved beneath the shower head. "How was your day?" he asked. She was an attorney at a firm that specialized in environmental law. She only worked three days a week, but they tended to be long days.

"Terrible and way too long."

"Why?"

"I don't want to talk about it," she said. It was her standard answer. Andrea never wanted to talk about work when she got home. The next morning would be different, and she would tell him all about it over breakfast. But he always asked.

Andrea turned off the shower. "You want to hand me a towel?" she said. "Please?"

Carlucci stood, got a dry towel from the rack, then brought it to the shower. Andrea opened the door, stuck her head and arm out and took the towel from him. "Thank you." Before she had a chance to retreat, Carlucci leaned forward and kissed her, getting his mouth, cheek, and nose wet. Andrea dried his face with the towel. "How was *your* day?" she asked as she pulled the door shut and began drying herself.

"About like yours, I imagine. Terrible."

"The mayor's nephew, or that other matter?" The "other matter" was Paula Asgard and Chick Roberts. Carlucci had told her the night before about his talk with Paula at The Bright Spot.

"Both," he said. "And they're both getting worse, in their own ways." He stood in front of the sink, watching the water drip from the faucet. He still hadn't gotten around to replacing the damn washer.

Andrea stepped out of the shower with the towel wrapped around her head, and Carlucci gazed affectionately at her nude body. She was about five foot six, and no longer as slender as she once had been. In recent years she had put a little weight on her hips, a small pot had formed on her belly, and her breasts had begun to sag a bit. She was absolutely beautiful.

"You're beautiful," he said.

Andrea smiled, then waved at him to leave. "Go on, let me do my things."

Carlucci walked out of the bathroom, leaving the door partway open, and lay on the bed, listening to the sounds Andrea made at the sink.

"How bad is it?" she asked.

"Which one?"

"The one the woman came to you about."

"Worse than I'd thought it would be." He turned onto his side, facing the bathroom door, and watched her shadow move across its surface. "Ruben's being forced by McCuller and Vaughn to stay on the case and bury it."

"Frank, I thought they couldn't do that."

"So did I," he said. "This is the first time I've heard of it." He sighed heavily. "He probably could have fought it and won, but he's afraid. He's got too much to lose."

Andrea's face appeared in the doorway. "Does this mean they could do it to you, Frank?"

"I don't know." It was the only answer he had for her. That was another reason he was willing to take risks and dive into this thing. If the honchos got away with it this time, they would be more likely to try it again, maybe even with him.

Andrea slowly shook her head, then returned to the sink. "What are you going to do?"

"A little digging. I hate what they're doing to Ruben. And to Toni Weathers. But also for self-preservation. I don't want them even *trying* something like this with me."

She didn't ask any more, and Carlucci lay on the bed in silence, listening to her, watching the shadows, and thinking. After a while he closed his eyes, not trying to sleep, just to stop the burning.

"Frank?"

He opened his eyes, and she stood in the doorway, the towel now draped over her shoulder, her wet hair falling free. "Yes?"

"Why don't you get undressed and get into bed?"

"It's too early."

"No it's not," she said.

He knew that tone in her voice. "Ah," he said, smiling. "Aren't you tired?"

"Not even close." She smiled back at him. "I'll be out in a couple of minutes."

Carlucci sat up on the bed and began to undress. He could hear the hair dryer going now. When he was completely undressed he pulled back the covers and lay naked on the bed. It was too warm to cover himself with even a single sheet.

The dryer stopped, and Andrea came out of the bathroom without the towel. She got onto the bed down near his feet, and he lay there motionless, waiting for her. She kissed her way up his legs until she came to his cock, which she gently took into her warm, wet mouth. He was hard within seconds.

A minute or two later Andrea resumed her movement upward, along his belly and chest, then lay fully across him, her face just inches from his.

"Hi, there," she said, smiling.

Carlucci wrapped both arms around her and squeezed. "Hi." They kissed deeply, then Carlucci moved his hands up across her shoulders, her neck, then to the sides of her face, holding her head gently in his fingers. "I love you," he said.

"I love *you*, Frank."

Carlucci wrapped his arms around her once more and pulled her tight against him, wanting to never, ever let go.

Near midnight Paula sat on the recliner in her bedroom and watched one of Chick's homemade music videos on her TV. The track was a Pilate Error song Paula had written, "Love at Ground Zero," a rare slow piece, slow and melancholy, a kind of slash-and-burn blues song. She wondered if Carlucci would like it.

Intercut with a distorted, digitized image of Chick singing the lyrics was footage of two naked people making love in slow motion on a sagging mattress. The faces were hidden in shadow, but Paula knew who the people were: herself and Chick. Sweat glistened on skin, on breasts and arms and thighs, reflecting orange and yellow light. She hadn't known he was filming them at the time. He hadn't asked, because he knew she would have refused. But once it was done, and mixed into the video, what could she say? No one would know who it was, and the footage was effective. Damn effective.

She was crying again. Soft and quiet now. God damn, she missed him.

The song ended, and then there was a close-up of Chick's face, looking directly at her. Paula knew what was coming, and so the ache drove into her chest again. Chick silently mouthed the words, "I love you," and then his digitized image began to slowly, slowly come apart.

"I'll find out who killed you," she said to his disintegrating image. "I will, Chick."

And then what? No idea. Paula was sure that justice was not going to be easy to come by. It might even be impossible. *No promises,* Carlucci had said to her. Was she trying to make promises to a dead man?

The last bits of Chick's face disappeared, leaving behind a random scattering of light and shadow. Paula stopped the player, turned off the TV.

"All right," she said to the blank screen. "No promises."

Paula lay back in the chair, closed her eyes, and tried to ease away the pain.

PART TWO

7

CARLUCCI WAS DREAMING. He was on a train to Seattle, and had just realized something was terribly wrong, when a phone started ringing somewhere on the train. He couldn't see the phone, but it seemed to be getting closer, louder with each ring, and then he realized he was dreaming and the phone was his own, pulling and dragging him out of the dream.

The train shook and broke apart and Carlucci opened his eyes. The phone beside the bed rang again. The clock said 3:25 A.M. Fuck. He was still half back in the dream, only barely awake. When he was younger he came awake almost instantly. Another ring and he grabbed for the phone, picked it up, put it against his head. "Yeah?"

"Frank, this is Pete. Sorry to wake you up."

Oh, shit. "What is it, Pete?"

"You're going to want to see this one, Frank."

"Who's the victim?"

"I'd rather not say. Let me give you the address."

"All right, hold on a sec." Carlucci swung his legs over the side of the bed and sat up, turned on the tiny nightstand lamp, picked up the pen and pad beside it. "Fire away."

It was an address in Pacific Heights, but it wasn't familiar. Carlucci repeated the address back to LaPlace, then took down the phone number.

"Is Joseph there with you?"

"Yeah," LaPlace said. "He's going through the place right now with Porkpie."

"Good. Okay, I'll be right out. See you in a few minutes."

Carlucci hung up the phone and remained seated on the edge of the bed, still trying to wake up. He felt old.

"Who was that?" Andrea asked, her voice little more than a mumble.

"Pete." He looked over at her, but she was on her side, facing away from him. Usually she slept through his middle-of-the-night phone calls.

"Somebody dead?" she asked.

Carlucci almost laughed. "Yeah, of course." He expected her to ask who, but she didn't say anything. "I was dreaming," he said. Andrea mumbled something. "I was on a train to Seattle. I'd thought I could take the train to Seattle, do some business, then take the train back in time for dinner the same day. Once I was on the train, I realized I'd badly miscalculated, that it took twenty hours to get to Seattle. Then the phone rang and I woke up."

"You can't take a train from here to Seattle," Andrea said. "You have to go over to Oakland."

"I know that," Carlucci said. "It was a dream." He realized then that Andrea was still half asleep. "I've got to go," he said. He got up from the bed. "I'll be back when I can."

"Is somebody dead?" Andrea asked again.

"Yes," Carlucci said. "Somebody's dead."

Carlucci had to show his police ID to get through the security checkpoint and drive into the Rio Grande section of Pacific Heights, which turned his foul mood even blacker. Rio Grande, what a crock. The only running water in Pacific Heights was in the water mains and sewers. Carlucci hated the whole setup—the residents had put together a self-appointed council and talked and bribed the city into selling them the public roads in the Rio Grande section so they could put up their own checkpoints, hire their own security forces, and keep out the "undesirables." Two other parts of the city had done the same thing since, and several more were working on it.

Carlucci parked several houses down from the address LaPlace had given him and remained in the car a minute, looking over the street. It was still dark, without even a hint of the coming dawn. Two unmarked police cars, a black-and-white, the coroner's van, and a Rio Grande Security car were all congregated in front of a beautiful three-story Victorian house, its windows lit up. All the other homes on the street were dark, but Carlucci thought he could make out movement in some of the windows—morbid curiosity tugged at the wealthy, too.

He got out of the car and walked up to the brightly lit Victorian. A Rio Grande Security guard stopped him on the porch, then let him through after he again showed his ID. Carlucci was ready to chew someone's nose off.

Just inside the front door, bare feet swinging about eye level with the three cops standing around it, the blood-streaked body of a naked man hung from the stair railing above the entryway, neck impaled on a huge, sharp metal hook; a long, thin spike ran through his belly and emerged from his spine. Carlucci stared up at the dead man's face for a minute, but couldn't place it. It didn't even look familiar. It also didn't look happy—undamaged, but in agony, eyes and mouth both open and wide.

Hong was one of the cops. Mason, the coroner's assistant, was another. Both men were smoking. Carlucci didn't recognize the third, a woman uniform.

"Jesus," Carlucci said. He looked at Hong. "Who is he, Joseph?"

"Robert Butler."

Robert Butler? Then it hit him, and he realized why LaPlace had called him. Robert Butler was one of the names on the Prime Level Feed given to the slugs on the mayor's nephew's case. Business partner or something like that.

Carlucci stepped around Butler's body, toward the uniform, and put out his hand, gaze flicking back and forth between her and the body. Butler had been in good shape, maybe even handsome. Hard to tell with that look on his face. "Lieutenant Carlucci," he said.

The uniform shook his hand. "Officer Martha Tretorn," she said. "My partner and I were first-on-scene."

"Tretorn," Carlucci said, looking at her. "I've heard good things about your work."

She gave him just a touch of a smile, said, "Thank you, sir."

"Where's Pete?" he asked, looking at Hong.

"In the first-floor flat," he said, gesturing down the hall at a closed door. "Talking to the woman who found the body. Butler owned the building, lived on the upper two floors, and rented out the first. The woman found him. On her way out, or in—there seems to be some 'confusion' over that."

"She doesn't know whether she was coming home or going out when she found the body?" Carlucci said.

Hong nodded. "Let's just say the story is in a state of flux. I couldn't get much from her; she didn't seem to want to talk to me." Hong gave Carlucci a hard smile. "Wrong kind of eyes, I think. That's why Pete's with her now."

"Hey," Mason broke in. "Can we take him down now? Porkpie's got all the pictures. They wanted me to wait until you got here so you could see him." Mason grinned. "They probably wanted you to see the schlong this guy has. Pretty fucking amazing, isn't it?"

"Yeah," Carlucci said, not smiling. "Amazing." He shook his head, then nodded. "Sure, Mason, take him down. Where's Porkpie?"

"Upstairs, on another run-through of Butler's place."

"All right, Joseph, let's go up. You've been through it once?" Hong nodded, and Carlucci said, "You can give me a rundown, then." He turned to Tretorn. "Go ahead and help Mason get the body down," he said. "You'll love working with him. He's a lot of laughs."

Again, that touch of a smile from Tretorn. "I've noticed, sir. I'll be glad to help."

Carlucci and Hong climbed the wooden steps, followed by Mason and Tretorn, who would have to work on getting the body down from the top of the stairs. As Carlucci and Hong reached the open door, Tretorn said, "Lieutenant?"

"Yes?"

"My partner's inside with the crime-scene techs. Sinclair. Could you send her out to give us a hand?"

"Sure." Sinclair. He knew that name. What had he heard about her? But then, entering the hall and looking toward the kitchen, where Sinclair stood in the doorway, he remembered. Sinclair was a stunning woman about six foot four, with long blonde hair tied at the base of her neck and hanging halfway down her back.

"Sinclair?" Carlucci said. The tall blonde turned to him. "Tretorn needs a hand out there." Sinclair nodded and walked past them and out of the apartment.

Carlucci stuck his head into the kitchen. One of the crime-scene techs was on her hands and knees, picking up something with tweezers. Porkpie was sitting on a stool at the counter, smoking a cigarette. He shook his head at Carlucci, which meant he was working, thinking about something, and shouldn't be disturbed. Which was fine with Carlucci. Porkpie was the department's top crime-scene tech. Carlucci backed out of the kitchen and gestured for Hong to join him in a room off the hall, which turned out to be a library. All the walls were covered by bookcases; there was a large work desk and chair, and two reading chairs.

"Joseph, how did you and Pete get called in on this? Not just coincidence, is it?"

Hong smiled. "No. Pete and I got McCuller to let us put a tracer into the system, keyed to all the names, addresses, and phone numbers on the Prime Level Feed. Anything that would come up on any of those people, even a parking ticket, would trigger a call. When Butler's address came up on the 911 call, Minsky called us in. We weren't far behind Tretorn and Sinclair. We held off until we had a pretty firm ID on Butler, then Pete called you."

Carlucci nodded, said, "Good work, Joseph. Look, I haven't had a chance to go through all the Feed text yet; all I did Friday was take a run at the names. What's Butler's connection to the nephew? Something about business dealings, right?"

"Yes. They owned several companies together. An investment firm, another that does bio-implant research, a pharmaceutical distributor, and the largest recruiting company in the city."

"Recruiters? The vans?"

Hong nodded. "Yes, that kind of recruiting. Scumbuckets. The companies have been indicted several times."

"Ah," Carlucci said, interest rising. "What for?"

"Securities fraud. Attempted bribery. Data theft. Twice for false imprisonment."

"False imprisonment because of what the recruiters were doing?"

"Yep."

"Let me guess," Carlucci said. "No convictions."

"You got it."

Carlucci nodded. "Big fucking surprise." He glanced around the library, but didn't see anything that immediately caught his eye. "All right, let's go look around the place, show me what you and Porkpie found."

As they moved from room to room, and from the second floor to the third, Carlucci tried comparing this residence to the penthouse apartment of the mayor's nephew, and he was surprised at how different they were. Butler and the nephew may have been in business together, but as people they didn't seem to be anything alike.

All the expensive high-tech equipment and gadgetry was here, just as it was in the nephew's, from picture phones and A.V. environments to computer links and reality-sims to slotters and ion poles in every room. There was even a similar security system, which had apparently been just as ineffective, now completely dead. But here everything was made or covered with natural colors and fabrics and expertly integrated with real wood and cloth and leather furniture, plaster walls, wood trim, nature-tone carpeting, and hundreds of books; various other objects, such as glasses, pens and notepads, vases and planters and candles, made the place look lived in. The nephew's penthouse was cold, sterile, a metal-and-glass showcase. Robert Butler's house was warm and comfortable—a home.

They were on the third floor, and had just entered a room set up for entertainment. There was a small sofa, two large foam chairs, and a huge video-and-sound system built into one wall.

"See what Porkpie found in here," Hong said. He went to the video control panel, powered up the system, read from a piece of paper he'd taken out of his pocket, and punched a series of buttons. He tuned the monitor to a channel of static and video snow, then punched more buttons. The wall adjacent to the monitor gradually became transparent, revealing a huge wall safe surrounded by computer-driven access panels.

"Jesus Christ," Carlucci said. "How in hell did Porkpie find this?"

Hong smiled. "You know Porkpie. He said he's seen a few of these setups, and downstairs he found this taped to the bottom of the coffee maker." Hong held up the piece of paper. "Something just clicked in his head, he claims, and he started looking around for it. Fiddled with this until he figured what the numbers on the paper meant, and here we are."

"That guy." Carlucci shook his head, staring at the safe through the transparent section of wall. "I'd sure like to see what's inside that thing."

"Porkpie says getting into the safe is going to be a lot harder than finding it."

"Yeah, no shit. Who's that guy the department calls in, Collins?"

"Collier."

"Right, Collier. Wonder how he'll do with this."

Hong shrugged, but didn't say anything. They stood staring at the wall safe for a minute until LaPlace walked into the room and joined them.

"Brings tears, doesn't it?" LaPlace said, gesturing at the safe.

"Only if we don't get in," Carlucci said. He turned to LaPlace. "So what's with the woman?"

LaPlace shook his head. "Changing stories, that's what. First she told Joseph she found the body on her way *out*. Then she said no, she didn't mean that—she was shaken up, all that—she had been *coming home* when she found Butler. Where had she been? Real vague on that, who she was with, said it was her personal business, cha cha cha. I let it go for a while, but a little later on, she lets it slip again, that she was going *out* when she found him. I didn't say a thing, and she didn't realize she'd said it again. If I had to bet on it, I'd say she was on her way out when she found Butler."

"What's she worried about, if that's the way it happened?" Carlucci wondered aloud.

"Maybe she doesn't want to tell us where the fuck she was going at two o'clock in the morning," LaPlace said. "Or how, if she was up and awake, getting ready to go out, she didn't hear a thing while old Robert Butler was being gored and having a hook rammed through his neck. Couldn't have been all that quiet. Anyway, we finally reached a point where she wasn't going to say any more without her fucking lawyer. I told her she wasn't a suspect, but she jammed up anyway." He shook his head. "She'll be in Monday with her attorney to make an official statement." He shook his head again. "I didn't see any point in pushing it, she wasn't going to open up."

"Anything else?"

LaPlace sighed. "No. She rented the first floor from Butler, but didn't know anything about him. She paid her rent, he left her alone, he seemed like a nice guy, but she really didn't know him, cha cha cha. I don't believe any of it, but that's all she'd say. End of interview."

"All right," Carlucci said. "Christ, this is getting swampy on us. Think we can keep the connection between Butler and the mayor's nephew quiet? Out of the news?"

"I don't see why not," Hong said. "The three of us are the only ones who know about it."

"Good. Let's try and keep it that way." He shook his head. "All right, let's wrap things up here. Do a quick chop on the reports, then go home. We'll get together first thing Monday morning at Spades, see where we are."

The sun was up by the time Carlucci pulled into the driveway. He shut off the engine, but remained in the car for a minute, looking at their house. It was a good home, well over a hundred years old, a little ragged in spots, but in fine shape. A good neighborhood, too, a small, tightly knit community for the most part, several blocks of families that watched out for each other. An island of security in the city. It had been a good place to raise their two daughters, and he hoped it would remain a good place to retire. Hard to know.

Carlucci got out of the car and walked up the steps to the front porch. No Sunday paper yet; too early. He unlocked the front door and went inside.

The house was quiet, almost silent. He stopped by Christina's bedroom and looked in through the open door. The bed was a twisted, misshapen bundle of sheets, blanket, pillows, and his daughter. He could make out a shock of wavy hair up in one corner, and a bare ankle sticking out from the sheets at the foot of the bed. Another year or two and she would probably be moving out, just as her older sister had done. He didn't want Christina to leave. Knowing Caroline didn't have many years left, he wanted to hang on to Christina as long as he could, as though he might lose her too. Afraid to wake her, he mentally kissed her on the forehead and moved on down the hall.

Andrea was still asleep, lying on her side. Carlucci bent over, kissed her lightly on the lips, then her cheek. Andrea smiled, murmured, and dug her face deeper into the pillow, but her eyes didn't open. Carlucci quietly left and walked to the other end of the house and the kitchen.

He looked at the clock. Ten after six. Lots of time before he was due to meet Paula Asgard. He made himself a cup of coffee and took it out to the small backyard deck, where he sat in one of the plastic chairs. The air was warm and quiet, a little muggy, but not too bad, and the sky was orange and pink and blue, the colors not yet looking sick as they almost certainly would later in the day.

Things were getting more complicated with the mayor's nephew, and he would start getting deeper into another mess when he talked with Paula Asgard, but for now Carlucci put all those thoughts aside. He wanted to enjoy the two free hours he would have this morning.

A thumping sounded on the fence, and a furry gray face appeared over the top, golden eyes wide, followed by the rest of the stocky cat's body. It was Tuff, the next-door neighbor's manx. Tuff crouched atop the fence for a moment, then dropped into Carlucci's yard, padded through the flower beds, and hopped up onto the deck. As Tuff approached the chair, Carlucci reached down and scratched the old gray cat's ears and cheeks and chin. Tuff purred loudly and deeply, and closed his eyes.

The cat was missing most of one ear, and had a nasty scar across his nose, just missing his left eye. He'd been a hell of a scrapper, fighting all comers, until Harry and Frances next door finally decided it was time for Tuff's balls to go. Tuff still defended his turf when he had to, but now he was fat, and incredibly gentle with people.

Tuff ducked away from Carlucci's hand and came around to the front of the chair. Carlucci held his coffee out of the way in anticipation, and the cat jumped up onto his lap, claws digging through his pants to his skin. Tuff turned one complete circle, then settled down across Carlucci's thighs, the deep purr kicking in again.

I could do worse than this, Carlucci thought to himself as he laid his free hand on the old gray cat. A lot worse. He brought the cup to his mouth and drank, scratching Tuff's head with his other hand. Things were going to get swampy, the rot was going to go deeper, but for now Carlucci felt as he imagined the old cat felt: warm, relaxed, and content.

8

PAULA SPOOKED. SHE spotted Boniface across the street and up a few blocks, heading her way. She ducked into Mama Buruma's spice shop and stopped just inside the door, blinded by the shift from bright morning light to heavy shadow and dim orange flames. Paula didn't move for a minute, listening to the East Asian techno-folk, letting her eyes adjust to the darkness.

Mama Buruma's—a long, narrow store lit only by small flickering candles—was empty except for Mama Buruma herself, who sat on a massive cushion behind the counter. Mama Buruma was fat, maybe even heavier than Graumann. The shop smelled of burning tiki spice, fireweed, and sweat. Tins and baskets and gel bubbles filled the display cases running the length of the shop. Vines and lush plants hung from the ceiling, insects flying among them.

"Ms. Asgard," Mama said, shifting position on her cushion. She wore a huge, loose dress of bright floral patterns, and her flesh shook with every movement. "Can I help you with something?"

As Paula stepped farther into the shop, she could make out the ten or twelve multicolored dermal patches on Mama Buruma's neck. She imagined them pulsing as they fed the big woman a steady stream of head juice. "No thanks, Mama. Well, maybe yes. Some mondo perv was tracking me out on the street."

Mama Buruma grinned and the flesh tightened around her eyes. "You want something to spike him with?"

"No," Paula said. "I was thinking of a way out. Through your stockroom."

Mama Buruma sighed and the smile melted back into her face. "You're too nice, Paula." She sighed again and waved her arm, flesh and sleeve flapping. "Go ahead."

"Thanks, Mama." Paula squeezed around the display case, pushed through the hanging tapestry, then worked her way around the crates and tubes and foam-packs in the stockroom. She pushed open the heavy metal door, stepped out into the alley, and let the door slam shut.

Paula leaned against the brick wall and waited, trying to decide what to do. It was probably coincidence, seeing Boniface just now. She had no reason to think he was looking for her. She couldn't stand the guy, because he'd hit on her repeatedly over the years, refusing to get the message, but he'd never come around looking for her. Still, she had just given Carlucci his name half an hour ago.

Paula thought he was a fuckhead, but there wasn't anything all that special about Boniface. He was one of a dozen or so names she'd given Carlucci: the people Chick hung with or brought in on his scams, people Chick had seen in recent weeks. Boniface hired out part time as a games courier, and it was hard to imagine that he had anything to do with Chick's death. But how could she know?

You're getting paranoid, she told herself. It came from spending two hours with Carlucci, talking about what Chick did, and who he did it with, running all those names at one time, seeing their faces one after another in her mind. People on the edges, like Chick, any one of which was all right alone. But talking about *all* of them had made Paula skittish.

Paranoia, she told herself again. Yeah, but that doesn't mean they're not after you. Ha, ha. So what was she supposed to do? She looked at her watch. Already late getting to the theater. Besides, Boniface knew she worked at the Lumiere; if he was trying to find her he could just go there. Or her apartment. He knew where she lived. Yeah, terrific, they *all* knew where she lived.

She shook her head, pushed away from the wall. *Relax, girl.* Boniface wasn't looking for her. No one was. Chick had been dead two weeks now, and nobody had shown up in her face. *Relax.*

She walked down the alley, emerged onto the sidewalk. Her throat closed up and her heart slammed against her ribs, *bam bam bam.* Boniface was twenty feet away, walking toward her.

Paula couldn't move. Boniface came up to her and stopped. Up close, she could see that under his street clothes he was in full courier rig, armored from neck to toes—someone would have to blow or chop his head off to stop him, and they still wouldn't be able to get what he was carrying.

"Hey, Paula," Boniface said, laying a gloved hand gently on her shoulder. "Heard about Chick. I'm real sorry. He was all right with me, you know that."

He pulled his hand back just before Paula would have knocked it away. Adrenaline was making her twitchy. Relax, she told herself once more.

"Thanks, Bonny," she said; he hated being called that.

Boniface frowned, then glanced over her shoulder. "I can't stay and talk now," he said, looking back at her. "I'm on a run. But if you need anything, a few bucks . . ." The frown slid into that nasty smile he'd used every time he'd hit on her. "Or maybe just some comfort. You know where I am."

Yeah, I know where you are, asshole. But she managed some kind of smile, said, "Thanks, Bonny," again, and stepped aside, waving him down the street.

Boniface's smile turned into a frown again, but he nodded and walked away. Paula watched him walk down the block, cross the street, then go into Ah Minh's. He *was* on a run. It *had* been a coincidence. But he was just as scummy as ever.

Paula breathed deeply several times, tried to shake out the excess adrenaline. Then she jammed her hands into her jacket pockets and headed for the theater.

By mid-afternoon most of the jitters were gone, and by the six o'clock intermission after the showing of *Xerxes Agonistes,* Paula was feeling almost normal. They had close to a full house, so the lobby was crowded now, people lined up for food and drinks, lined up at the bathrooms, the smokers huddled together in the corner next to the ventilators. Paula wandered through the lobby, checking on things, but everything seemed under control; for a change, everyone had shown up for work today so she wasn't understaffed.

She was headed for the stairs up to the projectionist's booth when a man moved in front of her. He looked familiar, though she didn't think she'd ever met him before. An inch or two taller than she was, slender, with short hair and wire-rim glasses. Kind of good-looking, in an odd way. She couldn't really tell how old he was—he could be in his late thirties, or he might be a youngish forty, forty-five.

"Excuse me," he said when she stopped. "Paula Asgard?"

"Yeah. Do I know you?"

"My name's Tremaine. I don't think we've ever met."

So, that's why he was familiar. The guy tried to keep low-profile, but he couldn't keep his own face completely out of the media. A bit of irony there.

"I'm a freelance journalist," he said when she didn't respond.

"I know who you are," Paula said. "I've read your stuff."

Tremaine smiled. "Is that good or bad?"

"Good." The guy did real investigative reporting, not sensationalist cheap-shotting, and if he couldn't get the papers or magazines or television to run his stories, which was often, he sent them out over the nets. He'd made a lot of enemies, but probably not very much money. He found stories where there shouldn't have been any, stories no one else could find, stories no one else knew existed. The anti-cancer implant scam at the UCSF medical school. The firefly distribution ring run by two senior partners of Maxie and Fowler, the largest and most prestigious law firm in the city. Like that.

"I want to talk to you," he said.

"What about?" Paula asked, instantly wary.

"Chick Roberts."

Paula didn't say anything at first. The sounds and images of the people in the lobby became a smeared blur, highlighting Tremaine's face. His voice had been neutral, as if what he was asking had little real importance, and his expression was just as unconcerned. But hearing Chick's name made her feel sick, and the morning's jitters came back.

"What about Chick?" she managed to say.

"I'm trying to find out why he was killed."

"Why?"

Tremaine shrugged, but didn't answer, and it was obvious to Paula that he wasn't going to say any more about it right now. "I'd like to get together with you," he said. "An hour, maybe longer, somewhere private. Any time, any place you like."

Paula didn't know what to say to him. Carlucci had warned her against talking to anyone, and she didn't feel good about the idea, anyway, talking to a stranger about Chick. But why did Tremaine want to know what happened?

"I can't," she finally said. When he didn't respond, didn't ask her why, she repeated herself. "I can't. I don't know anything about it."

"I'd still like to talk to you about him." He handed her a small black plastic card with light gray printing—his name, and several com numbers. Paula put it in her back pocket. "Just let me know." He started to turn away, then looked back at her. "Let me buy you dinner."

"I don't want to talk about him," Paula said, shaking her head.

"Just dinner," Tremaine said. He gave her a disarming smile. "You get to know me a little better, I get to know you, maybe you'll change your mind."

Paula shook her head again, unable to keep from smiling back. There was something damn charming about the guy. "I can't take the time. In fact, I'm on my way upstairs to fight with the projectionist over the sandwiches we're sharing for dinner."

"I understand," Tremaine said, still smiling. "I'll be back for the ten o'clock show. If you feel any different . . ."

"You're coming back to see *City Dogs*?"

"Wouldn't miss it."

"I guess that might be your kind of film."

Tremaine nodded, then said, "Enjoy your sandwich."

"I will."

Tremaine turned, then worked his way through the crowded lobby to the front doors.

Why did he want to know about Chick? What story was he working on? Christ, she had a feeling she was going to end up talking to the bastard. Paula turned and climbed the stairs.

•   •   •

Mixer was waiting in the lobby when she came down from the projection-ist's booth as the last film was ending. Leah was opening the front doors, and the coffee bar was closed up, but Mixer had managed to get a cup for himself anyway; he was holding it with the exoskeleton.

"Hey," Paula said. "What are *you* doing here?"

"You saw Carlucci this morning, yeah?" When Paula nodded, he said, "I want to talk. I'm hitting a wham-wham tonight, and I want to hear about your Carlucci talk before I go."

People began to filter out of the theater as the closing credits ran, and Paula and Mixer moved out of the way, behind the coffee bar. "Leah can lock up for me," Paula said, "but let's hold off until we empty out here."

The crowd coming out into the lobby grew, moved past them before narrowing as it squeezed through the front doors and out onto the street, loud and noisy. People who knew Paula waved or nodded to her as they passed, and Paula nodded back. The crowd eventually thinned, and then there were only a few stragglers as the credits finished and the theater went silent.

Tremaine was one of the last people out, and he stopped in front of the coffee bar. He smiled, glanced at Mixer, nodded and said, "Good night, Paula Asgard."

"Good night."

Tremaine strolled out the doors, moved into the street traffic, and was immediately gone from sight.

"Who was that?"

Mixer's voice had a testy edge to it and Paula looked at him, but his face was almost expressionless. "What?"

"I'm just asking who that guy was."

"Tremaine. Why?"

"The reporter?"

"Yeah."

"You know him?"

"No. He wanted to talk to me about Chick."

"Chick?"

"Yeah, Chick. He said he's trying to find out why Chick was killed."

"Tremaine? Why the fuck is *he* digging into this?"

"I don't know, Mixer. He wouldn't tell me."

"You're not going to talk to him, are you?"

"Why shouldn't I?"

"Hell, I don't know. He worries me, that guy."

Paula sighed and nodded. "Yeah, well, he worries me, too." She smiled at Mixer. "No, I'm not going to talk to him."

Mixer shook his head, but didn't say any more. Paula checked the the-ater to make sure it was empty, then asked Leah to lock up after Pietro, the projectionist, left. She got her jacket from the locked cabinet under the coffee bar and left the theater with Mixer.

They walked down to the corner, then swung right and headed up Polk. Sunday night, the street was full but low-key, people thinking about actually getting some sleep or heading off into dreamland of one kind or another. Mixer stopped at the street window of Sasha's Bad Eats.

"Let's get some coffee," he said.

"You want to go inside?"

"Not a chance. I'm going to be cooped up for hours with the wham-wham, I'd better stock up on fresh air." He turned to the purple-eyed kid at the window. "Large coffee and"—he glanced back at Paula—"large decaf, right?"

Paula nodded at the kid, who was bobbing to music Paula couldn't hear. The kid drew the coffee, then handed the cups out through the window after taking Mixer's money. Mixer and Paula sat on one of the concrete benches built along the front of Sasha's.

"So what did you and Carlucci talk about?" Mixer asked.

"Not much, really." She sipped at the coffee, which was almost as good as it was hot—she burned her tongue and nearly enjoyed it. "I told him what I know about what Chick had been up to lately, which is damn little. You know Chick, he didn't tell me shit, which was always fine with me. I gave him some names of people Chick ran with, his 'business' contacts."

Mixer cocked his head at her. "You think that's wise?"

"Jesus, Mix, you're the one who told me to go to Carlucci, what a great guy and honest cop he was. What's the point if I don't tell him what I know?" She shook her head, blowing on her coffee, sipping it. "Carlucci's already told me the whole thing could be risky. I'm willing to chance it for now. It's either that or drop it."

"What did you tell him about me?"

Paula turned to look hard at him. "Oh, I see. That's what you're worried about. Well, he does want to talk to you, Mixer, that's clear. If you don't go to him soon, he'll come looking for you, count on it." She sighed. "What was I going to tell him, Mix? He knows you knew Chick."

"Does he know Chick and I . . . did business?"

"Yes. But I didn't tell him what kind of business. And I didn't tell him about you talking to me the other night like you might have some idea why Chick got himself killed."

"I didn't say that."

"Not right out, you didn't."

Mixer didn't respond to that. He drank from his coffee, looking away from her. Paula put her hand on his knee, and he tensed for a moment, staring down at it.

"What is it?" Paula asked.

"Nothing," he said, shaking his head. He laid his free hand across hers, wrapping his fingers around it.

Paula felt cold sweat from his hand, and she could have sworn she felt his heart pounding hard now through his leg and wrist. What was going on? *God, don't tell me Mixer's got it for me, too.* Jesus, what was it today, was she secreting some kind of pumped-up pheromones? First Boniface, and what, now Mixer?

Mixer sighed heavily, then let her hand go and drank more of his coffee. "So Carlucci wants to see me," he finally said.

"Of course, Mixer." Paula took her hand off his knee and stuck it in her jacket pocket. Maybe she was just imagining things. "You going to tell him what kind of business you and Chick did?"

Mixer shrugged. "I don't know. Probably. What's he going to do, arrest me? Arrest Chick?" He shrugged again. He finished off his coffee, crushed his cup, then looked at his watch. "Gotta go. Checking out my own lines tonight on Chick."

"In a wham-wham?"

Mixer nodded.

"Careful," Paula said.

Mixer looked at her, smiled. "Always." He leaned forward, kissed her warmly on the cheek, then stood. "I'll be in touch. And don't talk to Tremaine." Before she could say a word, he was off and walking away, his right hand still working at the crushed coffee cup.

Paula watched him stride up the street, slipping in and out of the crowds until he turned a corner and was gone. She looked down at her own coffee cup, which was still half full and steaming. Some days, she thought, life is just one fucking mess after another. She set the coffee on the ground beside her, got up, and headed for home.

9

WHAM-WHAM, ALL right. Mixer hadn't been stupid, he'd pumped himself full of neutralizers before coming in, but the air in here was so gassed he felt like he was swimming through it, and the neutralizers were barely holding their own. He kept getting these sharp, intense flashes of desire, but the desire never locked onto anything specific; the neutralizers were doing their job. Mixer wondered what the gases were targeted for: booze, fireweed, gambling, booth time, smoke, heavy tipping. Probably *all* of the above. Without the neutralizers he'd be broke, fucked up, and out on the street in less than an hour. Which was, of course, just what some of the people in here wanted.

The wham-wham was underground in a Tenderloin subbasement warren. Mixer worked his way through the crowd in a maze of ion poles, cubicles and booths, tables and minibars, music pounding through dim colored phosphor lights. Close to capacity. There was just enough room to move from one spot to another without having to touch someone if you didn't want to.

Mixer was looking for Chandler, or if not him, then his proxies, Karl and Skeez, the freakoid twins. One or more of them were supposed to be here tonight, but Mixer almost hoped that if Chandler himself wasn't around, he *wouldn't* find the freaks. Bad news, those two.

The music was a loud, heavy machine dub, maxed out on the bass, and Mixer felt like he had bone boomers strapped all over his body. He should have taken aspirin along with the neutralizers; he was going to have a hell of a headache before too long.

Mixer moved over to one of the minibars, bought a bottle of Beck's, then wandered through the crowd, watching faces, latching onto snatches of conversation.

". . . something burning inside his head . . ."

"Style, man, kicks and style . . ."

". . . and he was taking his clothes off, enough to make you lose your breakfast."

". . . blood rushing up his neck . . ."

"Yeah, give me your slots, I'll bang your head . . ."

". . . *rush* . . ."

". . . slide, baby, into that body-bag . . ."

". . . *rush* . . ."

"Give. Give me those kicks, you . . ."

". . . *RUSH* . . ."

Rush, all right. Mixer stopped listening, letting the words wash through him with the pounding of the dub. A slow, high guitar was cutting through the heavy bass now, fine, fine stuff; he could just grab a seat somewhere, drink his beer, and listen. But he needed to find Chandler.

Chick got himself offed, and Chandler disappeared at the same time. Could be coincidence, but Mixer didn't believe it. Not when Chick had been trying to set up a deal of some kind with Chandler—wouldn't say what, just that it was big. Mixer didn't think Chandler had killed Chick, but there had to be a connection.

He passed a booth with its door still open. Inside was a naked man wrapped in a body-bag—a full body neural net—twitching and shaking on a cot, mouth open and drooling as the net sparked and sputtered. Fuck me, Mixer thought, no one should have to see that. He pulled the curtain shut and moved on.

Next to the booth was a gambling alcove, all the spots occupied. One woman was winning big, but she looked sick—apparently she was here to lose, maybe even go broke; she sure wasn't happy winning. The others were a mix, some of them pleased, some as sick as the woman. All of them appeared to be losing. That was one of the things that made a wham-wham interesting to Mixer—you never knew who would want what, and watching them was always a discovery.

"Hey, spikehead!"

The voice came at him from out of the noise and crowd and lights, and Mixer wasn't sure he wanted to find the source. The voice was vaguely familiar.

"Spiiiiiiikehead!"

From his left. Mixer stepped around an ion pole, static raising his hair for a moment, and saw the two freaks in an open booth, drinking from tall, fluted glasses. Karl, who leaned back against the booth wall, was six and a half feet tall; when he'd lost his right arm, he'd replaced it with a batch of three-foot-long metal chains that hung from his shoulder. Like Hook's croc, you always knew when Karl was getting close—*clink, clink, clink*. Skeez was shorter and stockier, with one eye that was a bright green glow-globe. Lots of stories about how *that* happened. He was sitting forward, saluting Mixer with his glass.

"Hey, spikehead, have a seat," Skeez said.

Mixer tossed his half-beer into a trash barrel and moved forward to within a few feet of them, but remained standing. "I'm looking for Chandler," he said.

Skeez laughed, and Mixer swore the green globe in his eye got brighter.

"Chandler doesn't want to be found," Karl said. He shrugged his right shoulder and rattled his chains. "He's gone to ground, says you should have gotten the message."

"When?"

"At the Caterwaul. A ghost message."

Mixer shivered inside, remembering that freaky, invisible presence on the eleventh floor, the window being pulled shut after he jumped. Ghost messages. He wouldn't be surprised.

"Yeah," he said. "I got the message."

"But here you are looking for Chandler," Skeez said.

"I *got* the message. I just didn't know what it was. Now I do."

Skeez slowly shook his head. "Not good enough."

Mixer started to back away, but Karl was too fast, on his feet and rushing forward, dipping and swinging the chains up and around, across Mixer's shoulders, wrapping around his right arm. Which was the exo. The chains clanked on the exoskeleton and Mixer grabbed them in his augmented fingers, twisting out and away from Karl, unwinding himself, but hanging onto the chains. Then he jerked the chains with everything he had, which sent streaks of pain down his back, but also pulled Karl off his feet and sent him sprawling across the floor.

Mixer still had hold of the ends of Karl's chains, was getting ready to drag the guy into a wall, when he glanced at Skeez. Skeez had a cattle prod out, pointed at Mixer.

"Drop the chains," he said. Mixer did. "We're going to have to make *sure* you've got the message," Skeez said. "Chandler insists."

"I told you," Mixer said. "I've got the message."

Skeez shook his head again, smiling. "Chandler's given us free rein." Karl struggled to his feet, hand on the table, and rattled his chains a few times. "We can have all the fun we want," Skeez went on. "As long as there's no permanent damage, nothing that can't be surgically corrected."

Karl started toward Mixer again, grinning, then abruptly stopped. The grin vanished, along with Skeez's smile, and they were both looking past Mixer.

"He's mine," a voice said.

Mixer turned to see a tall, stunningly beautiful woman standing just a foot behind him. Her hair was a glistening auburn, and her clothes were a dark, deep blood-red. "You'll come with me," she said, looking at Mixer.

Mixer looked back at Karl and Skeez. Both looked pissed as hell, but they didn't object, they didn't say a word. Skeez even sheathed the cattle prod and laid it across his lap. Mixer turned back to the woman.

"I can go with you?" he said.

"You *will* go with me."

Mixer didn't like the sound of that, and he had no idea who this woman was, but going with her *had* to be better than having the shit pounded out of him by the two freaks.

"All right," he said. "Let's go."

The woman hooked her arm through his and led him away from the freaks. They worked their way through the wham-wham, and people moved to make way for them. Uh-oh, Mixer thought, what didn't he know about this woman?

"Who are you?" he asked.

"Saint Katherine," she replied.

"Oh, shit."

"Exactly," St. Katherine said, smiling.

Before Mixer could move, he felt the collar whip around his neck and lock up. A jolt went up into his head, white lights exploding behind his eyes. Oh, fuck me, Mixer thought. Then there was another jolt, harder, his vision blacked out . . . and then there was nothing.

10

LATE TUESDAY MORNING, the air conditioning kicked back on. Carlucci looked up from his desk and stared at the wall vent; he watched the bits of whirling dust, listened to the clicks and whirs and squeals of obsolete machinery trying desperately to come back to life. He sat without moving, waiting for a cool wash of air, some relief from the heat and stagnation, but all he really noticed was the stench of burning oil, a smell the air conditioning always seemed to have in this building. The relief would come eventually, he knew that, but for now all he got was the stink. Everything back to normal. He left the fan running.

Carlucci looked down at the crumpled sheet of yellow paper on the desk—the list of names Paula Asgard had given to him. He should be working on the other two murders, Butler and the mayor's nephew, the two "real" cases at the top of his list. But he couldn't get the Chick Roberts case out of his mind. Fuck it, he thought. He picked up the phone and punched up Diane's number.

"Info-Services, Diana Wanamaker." That wonderful, throaty voice.

"Diane, this is Frank."

"Frank. The man of my dreams."

"Right," Carlucci said. "There's never *been* a man in your dreams."

Diane laughed. "True enough. What can I do for you?"

"Let me buy you lunch."

"That I can do, man o' mine. I'm scheduled for twelve-thirty. That all right with you?"

"Sure," Carlucci said. "Want me to come by?"

"No, I won't put you through all that. I'll meet you out front. And Frank?"

"Yeah?"

"Take me somewhere nice."

"Of course."

"Ah, yes." She sighed. He could almost see her shaking her head. "I don't think you even *know* any nice places."

"Twelve-thirty, in front of the building."

"Okay. See you then."

Carlucci put the phone down and picked up the sheet of yellow paper. He read over the names again, waiting for one of them to emerge from the others, carrying with it some special meaning, setting off a flash of memory or insight. Nothing happened. He took a pen and added Chick Roberts and

Paula Asgard to the top of the list, then folded the sheet and put it in his wallet.

Carlucci sat on the concrete steps in front of the station, waiting for Diane. The sidewalks were swarming with the midday crowds, every bench and available seat occupied by men and women eating their lunches. The air was heavy with the heat and damp, the sun glaring through thin, mustard-colored clouds overhead. The city was still waiting for the first cool-down that was supposed to come with autumn; sometimes Carlucci wondered if one year the fall and winter wouldn't even arrive, and the stifling heat and humidity of summer would just continue on without relief, relentlessly baking them all until everyone in the city went mad.

Carlucci closed his eyes, and for a few, brief moments imagined himself at Pine Crest, on the shore of the lake high in the Sierras. He could feel the cool, clean air washing over him, could even smell the pungent aroma of pine needles and wood smoke. It had been years since he'd been there, far too many years since he and Andrea and the kids had stayed at Tony and Imogene's cabin. Too many years since he and Tony had gone out on the lake before sunrise, the boat purring through the deep, cold water, surrounded by the dark green of trees as they headed for one of their secret spots for a few hours of fishing.

A hand on his shoulder abruptly brought him back, and he opened his eyes to see Diane standing over him.

"You looked like you were in heaven, Frank."

Carlucci smiled and nodded. "I was." He got to his feet and tugged at his pants. "And you brought me back to earth. Thanks a lot."

"Sorry."

Diane was a beautiful woman in her forties with light brown curly hair; her large, round glasses were attractive on her, and her smile always cheered Carlucci. She was, probably, the happiest person he knew.

"You look terrific," he said.

"I always look terrific." Diane took his arm in hers and they walked down the steps to the sidewalk. "Where to?"

Carlucci led the way through the crowd and into a stream of people flowing north. "Not far," he said. "A few blocks."

"Have I been there before?"

"Yes."

"Oh, God. Then it's one of your holes." But she smiled at him and squeezed his arm.

Pine Crest. With the heat and humidity and the people and noise pressing in on him from all directions, he could almost believe that Pine Crest was nothing more than a fantasy, that it didn't really exist. How long had it been? He hadn't talked to Tony or Imogene in years, didn't know if they even owned the cabin anymore. Was the lake still there, as cold and blue and deep as it had always been, or had the interior drought killed it off as well? He had no idea.

Carlucci cut off the street and into a crowded, shop-lined alley. Two doors up they entered Pattaya Thai Cafe, one of his regular places. Inside was swirling air from half a dozen fans and a babble of voices even louder than the noise outside. One of the waiters looked at Carlucci, pointed at the ceiling, then held up three fingers. Carlucci nodded, then led Diane through the jammed maze of tables and toward the back.

They had to go through the kitchen to get to the back stairs. "I remember this place," Diane said, shouting over the hissing, sizzling, clanging noises of the cooks. "They must have a dozen health code violations in here."

Carlucci just shrugged and smiled and motioned her up the wooden steps. They climbed four cramped half-flights, and by the time they reached the top, Carlucci was breathing heavily and sweating.

"You're out of shape, old man," Diane said.

"Thanks a lot. It's this damn heat."

The third floor was much quieter than the first, but it was nearly full as well, and they couldn't get a table anywhere near the open windows. The circulation was better, though, and the air was almost comfortable. They sat at a table under a pair of carved shadow puppets mounted on the wall; Carlucci could not decide whether the puppets were preparing to fight or embrace.

They ordered pork satay, hot and sour soup, lard nar rice noodles with shrimp, and Thai iced tea. Diane would eat at least as much as he would, but it wouldn't go to her gut like it did to his. She was right, he was out of shape; he needed to exercise. Christ, there were times he felt like an old man.

"How's Lissa?" Carlucci asked.

Diane smiled. "Still making me happy. We're going to Alaska in a couple of weeks, ten days of camping in what's left of the Refuge." She shook her head. "Even after nearly four years together she worries about the age difference. But that'll be fine. Our relationship may go into the toilet someday, but it won't be because of the age difference."

The waiter came by with their iced tea. Diane picked up her glass, said, "Cheers," then drank deeply. She set down the glass and looked at him.

"So tell me, Frank. What do you need from me?"

"Information," Carlucci replied.

"Frank." There was irritation in her voice. "Just tell me."

"What I need, I need off-line, Diane. I can't have Vaughn or McCuller or *anyone* know what I'm looking into."

"No record of a download, no trace of the search itself, that's what you want? Serious stuff, Frank."

Carlucci nodded. "Have you got a demon who could do it?"

Diane smiled, shaking her head. "What you mean, is, someone who can do it, who would be willing to do it, and who can be trusted."

"Yeah. That's it."

"How important is it, Frank?"

"Pretty damn important, I think, or I wouldn't be asking."

"You *think*?"

Carlucci didn't respond. He took out his wallet and pulled the yellow sheet of paper from it. For a moment he hesitated; then he unfolded it and handed it to her.

"I need whatever you can get me on these people," he said. "Especially any connections to each other." He almost asked her to concentrate on Chick Roberts, but decided it was better if he didn't steer her one way or another.

Diane studied the list, a frown working into her expression. She glanced up at him, back down at the list, then looked up at him again.

"Frank, even doing an off-line demon run isn't going to get you any more than what you've already got on these people."

"I haven't got *anything*," Carlucci said.

She looked at the list, shaking her head. "Chick Roberts . . . Tory Mango . . . Boniface . . . Jenny Woo . . . I don't know, maybe not *all* the names, but a lot of them. You've got what's in the feeds. I can't get you any more than that, Frank, even with a demon."

"What are you talking about?"

"That's where you got these names, isn't it?"

"From *where*, for Christ's sake?" Carlucci was getting that bad feeling in his gut again, burning through him along with his confusion.

"The slug sublevel feeds," Diane said. "For the mayor's nephew's case."

Oh, shit. Carlucci leaned back in his chair, looking at her. He didn't want to hear this. He picked up his glass and drank deeply from the thick, sweet, creamy iced tea. The cold liquid felt like molten ice in his belly, solidifying. He set down the glass and shook his head.

"I didn't get the names from the feeds. I haven't had a chance to look at any of them except the Prime and first sub."

"Then where . . . ?"

"A different case," Carlucci said. "Something completely unconnected to the mayor's nephew. At least that's what I thought." He leaned forward. "Which names—?" he started, but the waiter came by with the satay, cutting him off. When the waiter was gone, Carlucci started again. "Which names on that list are in the sublevel feeds?"

"Hell, I can't tell you for sure, Frank. My memory's good, but not *that* good." She looked down at the list. "Not all of them, probably, but at least half. The ones I mentioned, plus, oh, Poppy Chandler, I think . . . Ahmed

Mrabet . . . maybe Rossom." She looked back at him. "I can take these back and check for you, Frank, but you can do it yourself. You've got all the feeds, right?"

Carlucci just nodded, staring at the sheet of yellow paper. He reached across the table and picked it up, stared at the names for a minute, then folded the sheet and put it back in his wallet.

"If you want," Diane said, "after you've checked those against the feeds, I can arrange a demon run for the names that *aren't* in the feeds."

Carlucci shook his head. "Thanks, but . . . I've got a feeling the ones I want *are* in the feeds."

"What's this mean, Frank? About what you're doing?"

"Shit, I don't know. Nothing good." He shook his head again, then gave her a half smile. "Let's eat."

Carlucci picked up one of the skewers, dipped the meat in hot mustard sauce, and bit into it. The satay was good, but he was no longer hungry, and eating was nothing more than something to keep his hands occupied. He chewed, swallowed, then dipped the meat again.

What *did* this mean? Carlucci tried to organize his thoughts and work it all through logically. It was possible, barely, that the overlap of names was just coincidence—strange coincidences were more common in this job than most people thought. But Carlucci didn't believe it. Not this time, not with so many names overlapping the two cases. There had to be a connection.

Pressure was coming down through Vaughn and McCuller on both cases. But the pressure was to solve the one case, and bury the other. That didn't make sense, did it? If there *was* a connection, solving the one was liable to blow open whatever was involved in the other. So what was going on?

A couple of possibilities, it seemed to him. One: the pressure was coming from two different sources, down through the same conduit of Vaughn and McCuller, unknown to each other and, presumably, for different reasons. Or: the pressure was coming from the same source, but whoever it was didn't realize the two cases were connected; they wanted the one case solved, for one reason, and the other buried, for a completely different reason, unaware that the one could screw up the other.

The soup and noodles arrived. Carlucci continued to eat mechanically, hardly noticing the food, hardly noticing Diane. She knew him; she would let him alone as he ate and thought, and she wouldn't take offense.

So, two possibilities, and Carlucci didn't like either one. And of course there might be a third, or even a fourth possibility that hadn't yet occurred to him. And there was always the fallback position, which he liked even less: that *nothing* was what it seemed.

Fuck. This whole thing was far messier than he'd ever imagined. Until he had a better idea of who was applying the pressure on the cases, and why, he'd be stumbling blind, and there were too many ways to sink into deep shit.

"The food's not that bad," Diane said.

Carlucci looked up at her. "Oh, you still here?" he said, smiling. Her plate was empty, the serving plates were empty, but his own plate was still half full. Only the soup was gone. Carlucci put down his chopsticks. "I'm not hungry anymore."

"How bad is it?" Diane asked.

"Bad," Carlucci said. "Bad enough I'd really like to walk away from it all."

"But you can't."

Carlucci shook his head. "I can't."

"There's something else, Frank. Might be unimportant, but it probably won't make you feel any better."

"Great. What is it?"

"Tremaine's been digging around in the nephew's case. He's requested interviews with you, which we've turned down, of course. And he's been asking about the Butler case, wanted to know who was in charge of *that* one."

Terrific. What the hell was Tremaine after?

"Is there anything I can do to help?" Diane asked.

"No. Well, yeah. Forget you saw that sheet of paper. Forget we talked about anything except Lissa and the damn weather."

The waiter came by, raised an eyebrow at Carlucci, and, when Carlucci nodded, picked up the plates and took them away. Carlucci finished off his tea and chewed on what little ice remained.

"You'll crack your teeth," Diane said.

"Nag." He crunched twice more on the ice, then swallowed the tiny pieces.

"Frank?"

"Yeah?"

"If there's anything I can do . . ."

There won't be, Carlucci thought. He wouldn't allow it, he wasn't going to get her mixed up in all this. He would get *himself* out of it if he could.

"Thanks," he said. "I'll let you know."

He looked up at the shadow puppets on the wall. Fighting or embracing? Making love or war? He could see it now. He knew: they were preparing to do both.

11

THE ONLY REASON Paula saw him come in was because the place was half empty. It was Dead Wednesday at The Final Transit and the Black Angels were playing the ten o'clock slot, filler until the hip-lit crowd arrived and the Deconstruction Poets took over the stage for another of their shouting fests—poetry reading as primal scream therapy. Or was it the other way around?

The Black Angels were halfway through "The Dead Drive Better Than You," Paula backfilling with her bass for Bonita's solo, when Tremaine came into the club. Paula nearly missed a beat when she saw him standing in the doorway, staring at her and smiling, but she kept it together and moved farther back from the spots on Bonita, wishing for a moment that she could disappear from the stage altogether. What was it about Tremaine that made her feel so weird? She watched him work his way to a table against the side wall, maybe thirty feet back from the stage.

Then it was her time, and she moved up to the microphone, hot red light glaring down on her, and began to sing:

> "*There you go again,*
>   *Driving the wrong side of the road,*
> *Forgetting all your Zen,*
>   *Flashing along in hit-and-run mode.*
>
> *There you go again,*
>   *Swerving and skidding and sliding,*
> *Scattering women and men,*
>   *You at the wheel, but no longer driving.*
>
> *So never make fun of that Haitian Voodoo,*
>   *'Cuz the walking dead drive better than you do.*"

As always when she sang those last two lines, Paula had to work hard to keep from laughing. Stupid lyrics. Worst of all, she'd written them herself.

She glanced over at Tremaine, who was shaking his head and smiling; he held up his glass and tipped it toward her, then drank. Christ, Paula thought, she'd hardly met the guy, and she had to admit she was attracted to him, somehow, despite the fact that he wanted to talk to her about Chick. It was all too weird. She looked away from him, backed off from the mike, and dug into her guitar as if she were trying to rip the strings from her heart.

When the set was over, Paula put her guitar in its case, set it by the drum kit, then asked Sheela and Bonita if they could get by without her, loading up all their equipment.

"Sure," Bonita said, shrugging. "Fergus and Dolph are here tonight."

Fergus and Dolph were Bonita's two inseparable, six-and-a-half-foot-tall boyfriends. Huge men. Paula got the shivers whenever she thought about the three of them in bed together. Fergus and Dolph could handle all the loading by themselves, and would enjoy it.

"What's up?" Sheela asked.

"A friend dropped by during the set."

"Oh, yeah? Who?" Sheela stood on her toes to look past Paula and Bonita, searching the tables.

"Just a friend." Paula turned to Bonita. "Take my bass home with you?"

Bonita nodded. Fergus and Dolph came out of the club's back door, stepped onto the stage, and started unplugging the sound equipment. Bonita turned away and joined them.

"Who is it?" Sheela asked again. "That guy by the wall?"

Paula turned to see who Sheela was looking at, sure that somehow Sheela had picked out the right guy. Yeah, she had. She was looking right at Tremaine, who was calmly returning her gaze.

"Yes," Paula said. "That's him."

"Jesus, Paula, Chick's hardly been dead a couple of weeks."

Paula grabbed Sheela's arm, jerked at it until Sheela turned to face her. "Hey, back off, Sheela. You don't know what the fuck you're talking about. He's just a friend. Besides, anything like that, I don't answer to anyone but myself and Chick. And, as you so delicately pointed out, Chick's dead. Got it?"

Sheela pulled her arm out of Paula's grasp and looked down at the floor. She nodded slowly and walked back to her drum kit. Dolph was breaking it down, but Sheela pushed him away and set to work on it herself.

Christ, Paula thought, what's going on around here? She grabbed her jacket, stepped down from the stage and made her way to Tremaine's table. She leaned on the back of the empty chair across from him, but didn't sit down.

"Hello, Paula Asgard."

"Hello, Tremaine. You're not going to tell me this is a coincidence, are you?"

Tremaine smiled. "Of course not. I came here looking for you." He gestured at the chair. "Please, have a seat. Let me buy you a drink."

Paula looked at her watch. "A short one," she said. She pulled out the chair, hung her jacket over it, and sat. "The poets are set to go on in twenty minutes, and I want to be out of here when they start."

"The poets?"

Paula shook her head. "Don't even ask. Take my word for it, you don't want to be here either, unless you can get into two hours of incoherent screaming."

"Sounds lovely," Tremaine said.

"Yeah." Paula flagged down a waiter and ordered a Beck's; Tremaine ordered another warm ale.

The club was filling up. The Black Angels audience was almost gone, but the hip-lit crowd was pouring in; *flowing* in, Paula thought, with their capes and longcoats, several men and women draped in window-silk, the shiny fabric projecting television shows in shimmering color.

The waiter came by with their drinks. "Maybe we can go somewhere else," Tremaine suggested. "Where it's quieter."

"Maybe," Paula said. "I'll think about it." She still wasn't sure what to do about Tremaine. She drank deeply from her beer. Damn, it was good; she hadn't realized how thirsty she was. "You caught about half our set," she said. "How'd you like it?"

Tremaine shrugged. "It was all right. Good energy. But I guess I like my music slower and quieter."

Paula laughed. "Most people do. Fast and loud is the whole point of slash-and-burn. Like a shot of speed to your heart and head."

"You like it, don't you?" Tremaine said.

"I *love* it. It keeps me alive." Paula turned the bottle around and around in the ring of moisture that had formed beneath it. "So tell me," she said, cocking her head at him. "What keeps *you* alive?"

Tremaine didn't say anything for a minute. "The stories I do," he finally said.

"I can't talk about Chick," she told him.

"Why not?"

"Look, I don't know why he was killed, and I don't *want* to know why."

"Yes you do," Tremaine said.

Paula drank from her beer. "All right, sure. I want to know who killed him. But the whole thing scares me a little."

"It should."

"Thanks. That's reassuring."

He gazed steadily at her without speaking for a minute, then said, "Okay, we won't talk about Chick. Let's go someplace quiet and just talk, have a drink. No business, just personal, the two of us."

Paula smiled. "Bullshit. I got a feeling that with you, *everything's* business."

Tremaine smiled back. "That's probably true. But that doesn't mean it can't be personal at the same time. I'd like to know you better."

Paula drank again from her beer. She still didn't know what to think about him. She wanted to get to know Tremaine better, too, but she didn't know how much he could be trusted. Still, she thought it might be worth finding out, and she was about to suggest they go to a nearby pub, when Amy Trinh walked up to the table.

Amy Trinh was half-Vietnamese, half-Cambodian, and beautiful. Tonight she was wearing black jeans tucked into knee-high black leather boots, and an open, worn leather jacket over an incredibly bright white T-shirt. On her face was heavy eye shadow and liner, dark red lipstick, and an expression Paula didn't like one bit.

"Aw shit, Amy, you don't look like you've got good news."

Amy Trinh shook her head. "I don't, my good friend." She glanced at Tremaine, then looked back at Paula. "It's Mixer. Word on the nets is he got picked up by Saint Katherine a few days ago."

Paula stared at her, unable to speak for a minute. Her breathing had stopped, and she wondered if her heart had, too. Then, "Jesus Christ. How the *hell* did that happen?"

"Don't know. Something about a wham-wham. No details. But . . . He's due to go through the trial tonight. At least that's the hard-core guess. Midnight, probably. But definitely tonight."

Paula felt something heavy and cold drop in her stomach, a dull vibration rippling out from it and through her body. Oh, Mixer.

"We'll never find him before the trial, will we?" Paula said.

Amy shook her head.

Word always went out about the trials, flexing along the nets, but unless you were a part of the Saints inner circle you'd never learn the actual location. "You free tonight?" Paula asked. "Got your scoot?"

"Yes, and yes," Amy said, nodding twice.

"We can try anyway, can't we?" The dull, sick vibration was still thrumming through Paula.

"Sure."

"If nothing else, maybe we find him after, when they let him go." An ache was sinking into Paula's bones. "Pull him off the streets before the scavengers rip out whatever's left of him."

"Sure," Amy said again. She almost smiled.

A slow, steady grinding worked through Paula, cut through now with a demanding surge of adrenaline. She turned to Tremaine. "Gotta go. Another time, maybe."

"Who is—?" Tremaine started, but he cut himself off with a shake of the head. "Like you said, another time." As Paula was getting up from the chair, he said, "You still have my card?" When she nodded, Tremaine smiled. "Do what you have to do. I hope things work out." He paused. "And I'd like to see you again."

"Could be." Paula picked up her jacket and punched her arms through the sleeves. A strange thought flashed through her mind: Sheela would be glad to see her bailing on Tremaine. She turned to Amy. "Let's go." With one final glance at Tremaine, she said, "Bye and thanks for the beer," then she and Amy headed for the street.

Amy's scoot was half a block up from the club, plugged into a charger, and a teenage boy was squatting beside it, yowling. He'd tried to take the scoot, or rip something off it, and got juiced. Amy chuckled, then yelled "Asshole!" at the kid. "Leave my bike the fuck alone!"

The kid scrambled away, still howling, while people around them laughed. Amy de-commed the defense system, unlocked the two helmets and handed one to Paula. Amy climbed on first, then Paula got on behind her. The scoot was small, just big enough for the two of them, but it was jazz. Amy put everything she had into it—time and money and sweat—and it had all the power and cool she could ever want. She punched the scoot to life, the engine humming so quietly Paula wasn't sure she even heard it; then Amy flicked it into gear and they shot out into traffic.

The scoot was smooth and quick, and Amy maneuvered it gracefully in and out of traffic, shooting narrow gaps between moving and parked vehicles, leapfrogging around cars and vans, even riding the curb once to get past a city bus. Paula hung on tight as they headed for the Tenderloin.

The Saints. God damn, Mixer, what the hell happened? Crazy women living in the Tenderloin who had taken on the names and characteristics of historical saints—St. Lucy, St. Apollonia, St. Christina the Astonishing. The worst of them was a woman who sounded completely insane to Paula, the "head" Saint: St. Katherine. The Saints held periodic "trials" of other men and women, the trials based on what their namesakes had been put through, and St. Katherine's trials were the worst. Paula didn't know exactly what was done to the victims, but they emerged from St. Katherine's trials as complete neurological wrecks, with their language capacities pretty much shot to hell. Those that lived. The survivors of St. Katherine's trials made the net zombies look functional. *Jesus Christ, Mixer, how the hell did you let yourself get taken by her?*

The Tenderloin rose before them, growing as Amy weaved through traffic, headed straight for it. Then, as they reached the edge of the district, Amy swung the scoot around and they moved along the perimeter, slower now. A nearly solid wall of buildings loomed ten and twelve stories above them, marking the border of the Tenderloin; the wall of buildings, broken only by hidden, narrow alleys, enclosed something like sixty square blocks of a city within the city. A city that ran full speed through the night, slowing only when the sun rose. Paula had lived here once.

Amy braked, jumped the curb, Paula grabbing her harder; then they crossed the sidewalk and plunged down a flight of concrete steps, the scoot bouncing and jerking its way to basement level. At the bottom of the steps was an opening into a weirdly lit, covered alley. Amy headed the scoot into the dim alley, even slower now, her boots out and brushing the concrete for balance. The alley walls and ceiling were covered with what appeared to be patternless stretches of phosphorescent molds, which gave the alley a shimmering look.

Ahead, a metal gate barred their way, and Amy rolled to a stop. A short, thin man, hardly more than a boy, emerged from a doorway in the alley wall and barked something at them in what Paula thought was Chinese. He held something that might have been a weapon under his arm, though it looked more like a console of some sort.

Amy shook her head. "Don't speak that shit to me, you little fucker!" Then she shifted into Vietnamese.

The boy answered, still in Chinese, anger in his face. Amy snapped back at him, and finally the boy answered in Vietnamese. The two spoke back and forth for several minutes, the only words intelligible to Paula being "Amy Trinh" and "Paula Asgard." Finally the boy did something with the console and the gate crackled, a pulsing glow flowing over the metal. Then the boy disappeared back into the doorway.

"Fucking young punks," Amy said to Paula. "No pride. The Chinks still have the most power inside, and a lot of the young kids coming up want to be just like them. No pride, and no sense of history." She shook her head.

"Where did he go?"

Amy turned to her, grin visible under her visor. "Kid thinks he's bad shit, but he's afraid of making a mistake, let the wrong person through. He doesn't know me, so he juiced the gate and went to get authorization."

The kid reappeared, followed by a tall, handsome man with a thin moustache. "Amy," the tall man said, nodding.

"Hello, General," Amy replied.

The tall man smiled and shook his head. "Are you in a hurry?"

"Yes."

"Then this is not the time to talk. Perhaps some other night."

"Sure, General."

Still smiling, the tall man switched to Vietnamese and spoke to Amy for a minute. She responded, after which the man turned to the boy and said a few words. The boy, stiff and silent, fiddled with the console; there was more crackling from the gate, the metal dulled, a click sounded, and the gate swung open. Amy gave the tall man a mock salute, flicked the scoot into gear, and they shot forward.

The alley beyond the gate was more of the same: enclosed, and lit by the pulsing swatches of green and blue. Near the end, as pale gray light began to appear ahead of them, another gate was already open, and they drove through, Paula glimpsing a shadowed form standing back in a wall opening.

Then the alley ramped upward, a rectangle of light appeared, and moments later Paula and Amy shot up and into the Tenderloin night.

They emerged in the Asian Quarter. The sky was filled with lights: message streamers swimming through the air in flashing red, three and four stories up; above that a shimmering green, red, and gold dragon undulated, sparks shooting from its eyes, smoke pouring from its nostrils, and advertisements flowing along its body; and high above the dragon, a network of bright white lights and tensor wires webbed across the street, connecting one building to another, pulsing rapidly against the night sky.

The streets and walks of the Asian Quarter were as full of people, vehicles, and movement as the sky was of lights. Amy maneuvered the scoot into the thronging street traffic, a mass of bikes and scoots and carts and riks and vans. They were in the heart of the Asian Quarter, and they had to get out. The Saints were definitely a Western thing; no trace of them would even be allowed here. Paula and Amy would have to make their way to the Euro Quarter.

Paula had lived in the Tenderloin for six years, right where the Asian and Euro Quarters merged together. She had loved the energy, the unrestrained *life* that flowed through the streets and the air. She had lived here and breathed all of it into her, giving just as much back in her own way—with her music. The days had been for sleeping, the nights for living. An endless cycle of energy. But as she'd grown older, it had become too much for her. When you lived in the Tenderloin, you couldn't ever get away from it. Paula had come to need times of peace and quiet, relaxation, things she could never get while she lived here. She still loved the Tenderloin, but now only as a visitor.

Their pace was agonizingly slow. Paula craned around Amy's neck, but didn't see anything that unusual, just a typical street jam. Then, as they crept forward, she saw it: a pedestrian spillover from the sidewalk, flooding the street. Paula finally spotted the source, Hong Kong Cinema disgorging a huge audience through three doors while a crowd waited to get in for the next showing. The marquee floated in the air directly above the street, rolling the titles in Chinese, English, Vietnamese, and French. Paula hooked onto the only one she could read: *Ghost Lover of Station 13.* Shit, Paula thought, no wonder.

They slowed even further as they got closer to the theater, now at a lurching crawl. Paula breathed slowly, deeply, trying not to think of what might be happening to Mixer. She let her gaze drift slowly from side to side and behind them. Familiar places, old haunts. Hong Kong Gardens, the cafe next to the theater. Shorty's Grill across the street, sandwiched between Tommy Wong's Tattoos and Ngan Dinh Body Electronics. Back half a block, a favorite hangout of Paula's—Misha's Donuts and Espresso.

And then, amid the familiar places, Paula spied a familiar face, a woman legging a pedalcart three vehicles behind them. Jenny Woo. Like Boniface, a name Paula had given to Carlucci just a few days earlier. Like Boniface, someone she couldn't stand.

Paula swung around to face forward again. Another coincidence, like seeing Boniface? After all, Jenny Woo *did* live here in the Asian Quarter. But still . . . Boniface was harmless. Jenny Woo wasn't. Jesus.

They were finally past the Hong Kong Cinema, traffic eased, and their speed picked up a bit. Amy found a break at the next intersection and turned hard left, giving the scoot a blast to shoot through and down the street. Now they were headed straight for the Euro Quarter, only three blocks away.

Paula turned around again, but didn't see Jenny Woo. There were riks and bikes and a pedalcart behind them, but no one familiar in any of them. Maybe it *was* another coincidence. Maybe it wasn't even Jenny she'd seen.

For the next three blocks, Paula kept looking behind them, but never saw Jenny Woo again. Then they were crossing into the Euro Quarter, and Paula turned her attention back to the street in front of her and the shops and sidewalks around them. She couldn't worry about Jenny Woo. Mixer was more than enough to worry about. And it was Mixer's face, more than any other, that she wanted to see again.

Amy and Paula gave up just after dawn. As they'd expected, they'd had no luck ferreting out the site of St. Katherine's trial, they just got further confirmation that it was to take place, or already had, and that Mixer was definitely the "defendant." So they had spent the last hours of darkness cruising the streets of the Euro Quarter, occasionally venturing a block or two into the other Quarters, searching for a staggering, catatonic wreck. They'd come across an astounding number of candidates, but none of them had been Mixer.

Amy dropped Paula off at her apartment building as the sun was rising, with a promise to return later that afternoon to pick her up for another run through the Tenderloin. They both needed sleep and food, and rest for their burning eyes. Unspoken was what they both knew—the fact that they hadn't found Mixer within an hour or two of the trial, whenever it had been held, was bad. Real bad. The two most likely possibilities? Scavengers had picked him clean before Paula and Amy could find him. Or he hadn't even survived the trial. Paula didn't try to decide which was better.

She climbed the stairs to the third floor, walked down to her apartment, and unlocked the door. She stood in the doorway for a minute, listening. The building was so quiet. This early, most people were either still in bed or just waking up. She stepped inside and closed the door behind her.

The apartment seemed terribly empty. Paula wandered through it, making several circuits of the two rooms until she finally sat on the edge of her bed and stopped. Yes, it was the same place, nothing had changed. Except . . .

Two weeks ago she'd lost Chick. Now it looked like she'd lost Mixer as well. It was just too much. Paula lay back on the bed, staring up at the ceiling. She was tired, so tired. She closed her eyes, and wondered if she would ever get up again.

12

THIS TIME WHEN Mixer came to, he was naked from the waist up and strapped to a large, flat, horizontal wheel, his arms and legs spread-eagled, bound at the elbows and wrists, thighs and ankles. He was on his back, sweating in the stifling heat, his blurred gaze trying to bring the ceiling overhead into focus.

The ceiling seemed very far away, and after several moments Mixer realized it *was*—twenty, twenty-five feet above him. He found he could move his head, and he raised it, turned it from side to side. The wheel was about three feet off the floor, supported by . . . what? He couldn't tell. Though the ceiling was high, the room was smaller than he'd expected, maybe twenty by thirty. At the moment it was empty. There was a door at the other end of the room, but no windows. The walls were covered with prints and paintings and photographs depicting saints and martyrs, some dispensing good works, others being tortured and killed.

How the *fuck* did I get into this? Mixer wondered. And why St. Katherine? Why not one of the others, like the one who pulled all your teeth out of your head without any anesthetic? Right now he'd take that over having his brain gouged and jittered by St. Katherine's Wheel.

He let his head fall back on the wheel. He flexed his hands and feet, his arms and legs. Not much give. But his right arm. . . . They'd left the exoskeleton in place. He wondered if there was enough power in the exo to tear out the straps.

Mixer turned his head to the right. His vision was sharp now, and he could see the straps over his right arm and wrist, wrapped tightly over the exo. He didn't much like what he saw. The straps were made of woven metal strands. What were the chances of ripping through that, even with the exo? Not good, not fucking good at all.

Mixer rolled his head back, facing the ceiling once again, then closed his eyes. His stomach was fluttering, knotting up on him. Man, oh, man, he was scared. Dying was one thing. This was another. He'd seen a survivor of St. Katherine's Wheel. The guy had been a mess, like he had perpetual epilepsy—a walking seizure, with two "pilgrims" caring and begging for him like he was a holy man. And that's where I'm headed, Mixer thought. His one hope was that he'd be so far gone when it was over that he'd have no idea how fucked up he was, and how much he'd lost.

What he could use right now were a few of the neutralizers he'd taken for the wham-wham. Or *some* kind of drug. Something to freeze him down. Of course, that was part of what got him into trouble at the wham-wham, the neutralizers fucking up his judgment.

Goddamn wham-wham. How long had it been? Hours, or days? Days he thought. The Saints had kept him doped, he knew that much. Good stuff, though, since he felt pretty clear-headed. He'd come to several times, and he thought he remembered being given food and water, being taken to the can, but it was all pretty vague. He remembered different faces. St. Katherine's, hers he knew best—long and sharp and, he had to admit, beautiful; if she wasn't so crazy, and if she wasn't going to scorch his brain, he could fall in love with a woman who looked like that. There was another woman, older, dressed all in black, with a hard, worn face. And then a third, a woman with the most incredibly beautiful eyes he'd ever seen. Electric blue. Couldn't have been real, those eyes. St. Lucy.

Mixer opened his own eyes again. How long was he going to be here? The "trial" was going to start soon, he was sure of that. Why else strap him to the wheel?

The straps. Why not try? Nothing, absolutely nothing to lose. Mixer breathed deeply twice, closed his right hand into a fist, then pulled, trying to rip his right arm free. There was no give, and he pulled harder, trying to use his elbow for leverage. He could hear the whine of the exo motors straining, getting nowhere. Sweat dripped down his face, his neck, slid off his arm.

Nothing.

He kept on, but pain started in his wrist and moved up along his arm to his shoulder, then around his neck and back. The pain jacked up; he felt like something in his bones was going to pop, and he finally quit. The straps hadn't loosened a bit. His arm throbbed, and he felt a sharp pain in his shoulder. Damn exo. What good *was* it?

Fuck me, he thought. He was stuck here, and he was going to die. No, worse than die.

The door opened. Mixer wanted to close his eyes, pretend to still be out, but instead he turned his head and watched St. Katherine walk toward him. She was alone, dressed as she had been at the wham-wham—deep, blood-red cloak over more layers of red.

When she reached the wheel she stopped and looked down at him, smiling. He was at waist level to her, and she reached out, placed her warm fingers on his cheek, lightly brushing his skin. God, she was beautiful.

What the fuck am I thinking? Mixer asked himself. She might be beautiful, but she's insane and she's going to scorch my brain.

"It's all right," St. Katherine said, moving her fingers to his forehead.

No, it's *not* all right, Mixer thought. But there was something quite calming about her touch, and he almost believed her.

"How are you feeling?" she asked.

Even her voice was beautiful, deep and smooth, washing over him. For a moment he wondered if the air in the room was gassed, but decided it wasn't. St. Katherine's impact on him, he was sure, was all her own.

"Cat got your tongue?" she said, smiling.

What the hell did that expression *mean*? he wondered. "I'm feeling just terrific," he finally said. "What do you think?"

"Your trial will begin soon," she said. "I'm here to prepare you."

"Prepare me?" Mixer almost laughed, but it came out as a choking sound. Why was he even talking to this woman?

"Don't you want to know why you're here? What the trial is for?" She ran her fingers lightly across his face, down his neck, like soft warm feathers, then down his chest, tingling his skin. "Why I've chosen *you*?"

She was gazing into his eyes, and he could not turn away from her as her fingers moved downward, over his belly, and finally across his pants and to his crotch, where they circled and brushed and pressed lightly at him until, astoundingly, he began to get hard. This is fucking insane, he told himself. *I'm* insane, I'm as crazy as she is! He closed his eyes and clenched both of his fists. Preparation for trial. What was she going to do, crawl up on the wheel and mount him?

The motion of St. Katherine's fingers stopped and she pulled her hand away.

"If you survive the trial," she said, "you will be my consort." Then, "Open your eyes, Minor Danzig. Look at me."

Mixer opened his eyes, stunned to hear his birth name. How could she know that?

"My name is Mixer," he said, looking at her. "I've seen survivors of your trials, and they didn't look like consorts to me. They hardly looked human."

St. Katherine slowly shook her head. "They only survived in the crudest sense of the word. In truth, they all failed their trials, failed miserably."

"Did you 'prepare' all of them, too?"

"Yes."

"You did a piss-poor job, then. And I'm fucked." He moved his head from side to side. "Let's get this over with."

St. Katherine smiled, leaned over, and kissed him on the mouth. Then she pressed something on the side of the wheel and stepped back.

The wheel began to move. Mixer tensed, disoriented at first. He had expected the wheel to spin, but it didn't.

Instead, it angled upward, his head and arms rising while the lower end of the wheel dipped toward the floor, moving smoothly, steadily, until he and the wheel were vertical. The straps held him in place, but he could feel the strain on his arms as gravity tried to pull him to the floor. He coughed, struggling a moment for breath. Fucking great, he thought, I'm being crucified.

He was at the head of the room, facing St. Katherine. Two more large, metal wheels emerged from the wall behind him, one on either side; another slid out above him, suspended directly over his head.

"Your own wheel will remain stationary," St. Katherine said. "The others will turn, producing and casting the energies for the trial."

Her explanation meant nothing. All Mixer could think was that at least he wouldn't get dizzy. But what did it matter? He stared at St. Katherine, waiting for further explanations of what would be done to him, but she didn't offer any more.

The door opened again, and women filed into the room. Four in simple gray robes entered first, followed by six in lush, layered outfits like St. Katherine's, but in different colors. The six were followed by a dozen more in gray. What? Full-fledged Saints and novitiates?

The six Saints—Mixer recognized St. Lucy among them—sat in a row on the floor just a few feet in front of him, silent, gazing steadily at him. The novitiates sat behind them in four rows, just as quiet.

St. Katherine reached into the layers of her clothing, withdrew her hand, and held up a bundled neural net. She shook out the net, held it spread in front of her, then turned and displayed it to the Saints and novitiates.

"The Neural Shroud," she said.

Oh, fuck me, Mixer thought. He expected her to keep talking, mouthing ritual words and phrases, but she said no more, only bowed her head once. All the Saints and novitiates bowed their heads in return, and then St. Katherine turned and faced Mixer, holding the neural net up between them. Her face was crosshatched by the fine wires and nodes, and her skin seemed to shine behind the net.

She stepped forward and draped the net over Mixer's head, face and shoulders, the nodes tinging against the metal of the exoskeleton. The net was surprisingly light, but the fine wire dug into his flesh, not quite breaking the skin. A panic attack a lot like he had in elevators kicked in, sending a jolt to his heart and a flush to his neck and face. He managed to keep from crying out by breathing slow and deep and reminding himself that a lot worse was still to come.

St. Katherine took a step back. "You are to be torn to pieces on the wheels," she said, "just as my namesake, Saint Catherine of Alexandria, was to be torn to pieces on the wheels. For you, however, the pain and destruction will be mental, not physical. The three wheels around you will turn and generate holy energies, then transmit them into your brain through the Neural Shroud. Your mind, not your body, will be torn to pieces.

"But do not despair, Minor Danzig. An angel came to Saint Catherine of Alexandria and broke the wheels and spared her. Perhaps an angel will come during your trial, in one form or another, and spare your mind from the ravages of the wheels. If so, you will have been shown worthy." She paused, breathing deeply. "Worthy to be my consort for life."

St. Katherine's face seemed to glow, and Mixer thought she looked even more beautiful than before. His heart was banging around inside his chest, but he could not take his eyes away from her face. My mind's already gone, he thought.

The Saint smiled at him, a smile filled with passion and hope. Or was it his own desperate hope he saw in her face?

St. Katherine stepped to the side wall, pressed a panel with her hand. The wheels beside and above him began to slowly, slowly spin. St. Katherine walked toward the front row of Saints and stood before them. She said nothing, just looked at each of them in turn, then swung around to face Mixer and the spinning wheels. She lowered herself to her knees, placing her hands on her thighs, her gaze and smile fixed on Mixer.

Mixer suddenly became very calm. All the panic left him. He thought of Sookie, and he wondered if she'd become calm and unafraid just before the Chain Killer had murdered her. He hoped so. Then he thought of Paula, and a wave of grief rolled over him. He was going to miss her. Or would he? Even if he lived through this, he probably wouldn't even know who she was.

The wheels were spinning more rapidly now, and tiny sparks of blue and white electricity danced around their rims, glittering at him. The sparks grew, joined one another, formed thin, flickering strings of electric fire leaping toward him. Mixer gazed at the blue and silver fire above and around him, transfixed.

Then he realized a chanting had begun, and he looked out at the Saints and the novitiates seated before him. Their eyes were wide open, and they were all staring directly at him, lips parted, a long and deep, wordless chant welling from their throats. The sound wavered, sliding back and forth around itself. Mixer was mesmerized by the chanting, transfixed by the dancing strings of electricity surrounding him.

No, he was paralyzed. That's what it was. Paralyzed.

A single flash of electric blue fire arced from the wheel above him and struck one of the net nodes, stinging him. Suddenly his calm vanished, and the panic returned.

Mixer lost his breath for a moment. More flashes arced from the wheels to the net. Mixer could feel them firing along the net wires, jolting into him at the nodes, like cold, sharp needles. He twisted, pulled at the arm and wrist straps, knowing it was hopeless. *Oh fuck me*, he thought, *fuck you all!*

The wheels spun even faster, and flares of energy scattered from them, arcing into the nodes. Mixer felt a shaking in his head, like his mind was being electrocuted.

Pain skittered along his face and neck, tiny lines of it burning his skin. He hadn't expected that. Everything was going jittery inside him, his thoughts, even his vision, jumping around, flickering in and out. But he was also aware that something strange was happening to his right arm. He managed to turn his head and look at it.

His right arm—the exoskeleton, really—was twisting and straining against the straps, almost of its own accord, like a metal-sheathed snake. Mixer could just hear the high whine of the exo's motors working, shifting back and forth. The strangest thing, though, was the electricity coming from the wheels: it seemed to be focusing on his right arm and hand, on the exoskeleton, most of it now guided and pulled away from his head, funneled to and spread out along the exo. The electricity swam along the metal surface, and as the wheels continued to spin faster and pour out more energy, more of it flowed to the exoskeleton.

The pain in Mixer's head seemed to ease, but his right arm was on fire. He could see just enough to realize that now almost all the energy from the three wheels was funneling into the exo, flashing and glowing, making the metal shine and burn. *Shine and burn, shimmer and shake*, Mixer thought. Where the hell had that come from?

There was a bright, silent explosion of sorts, three of them, actually, one from each of the three spinning wheels, and the energy gouted from them like fountains. Some of it washed over his head and face, tingling his thoughts and shimmering his vision, but most poured into the exo and his right arm. He didn't notice anything different for a few seconds; then the pain blossomed in his arm and he screamed.

His arm *was* on fire. He couldn't even see it anymore, hidden by the flames of blue and white energy that surrounded it, swirling and heaving like an electric beast. This was, he realized, the moment when his mind should have been torn to pieces. Instead, it was his arm and hand.

More explosions, this time loud and bright, and Mixer screamed again, the pain in his arm unbearable, tearing him apart. His face was starting to burn now, too, the net wires burning into his skin. White and blue crashed all around him; he couldn't see anything, just wild shadows in front of him, leaping and flying. The Saints, he thought, they're going crazy. Or they're burning up along with me. Good, man. Burn, you crazy fuckers!

Then even the dancing shadows were gone, and there was nothing but painful silver-white light all around him. *I'm dying*, he thought, *I'm fucking dying*. Orange and red flared up behind his eyes, and he thought he felt his arm burned and torn away from his body. Mixer screamed one final time; his vision burst, and then he was gone.

13

IT WAS TIME for Carlucci to talk to the slug, and it was the last thing he wanted to do. So he set up an appointment for that night, then left the station to play pool.

When he stepped out of the buildings, he was hit by a wall of damp and heat. The clouds were thick and heavy, a sick brown-orange overhead, and he could barely tell where the sun was behind them—a pale, slightly brighter disk shimmering high above the buildings. It was going to rain soon, he was sure of that, but he had his raincoat, and he decided to walk.

A few blocks to Market, another block south, then up a few more blocks to Bricky's. "X" marks the spot, Carlucci thought to himself. The only sign anywhere was a tattered piece of cardboard in the window with the word POOL handwritten in faded black ink. The windows were so grime-coated, all Carlucci could see through them were vague, shifting lights and shadows. He pulled the door open and stepped in.

Inside was cooler and quiet. A time warp. The place probably hadn't changed in seventy-five years. Maybe even a hundred, Carlucci thought. Fifteen tables, low overhead lights above each, no other lights in the room except for a few beer signs behind the bar and a small orange-shaded lamp on Bricky the Fifth's desk. Most of the tables were occupied, but there were a few open. Players looked at him, but no one nodded or waved or smiled. Those who knew him knew he was a cop; they accepted him, because Bricky did, but that didn't mean they'd be friendly.

Bricky the Fifth sat behind his desk smoking a cigarette, watching Carlucci. He was tall and gaunt, short hair almost hidden by the red 49ers hat he always wore. He was only about forty, but looked at least ten years older. A year ago his son, Bricky the Sixth, had been gutted with a linoleum knife in front of the pool hall, two days after his wedding. There would never be a Bricky the Seventh.

Carlucci walked over to the desk and asked Bricky for a rack. Bricky nodded without a word, pulled out a tray of balls from a shelf behind the desk, and pushed them toward Carlucci, then made a note in pencil in an old spiral notebook.

Carlucci took the balls to an open table near the front corner, went to the bar for a bottle of Budweiser, then returned to the table and racked up the balls. He spent a few minutes picking out a cue, took a long drink from the beer, then placed the cue ball on the table and stroked it into the balls.

Carlucci spent the next hour playing alone. No one stopped by the table, no one said a word to him. He wasn't very good, but he enjoyed it, and it relaxed him. When he couldn't play his horn, he liked to play pool. His session with the slug would be awful, and he needed to relax and skim out before going.

Though he was near a window, he couldn't see any more of the streets than he'd been able to see of the pool hall from outside. He could hear the rain start, though, about ten minutes after he arrived. Surprisingly, the rain got stronger as he played, and gave no signs of blowing over. There hadn't been a good long rainstorm in months. People coming in off the street dripped water, and Bricky gave them towels to dry off; he wasn't going to let his tables get wet.

Carlucci nursed his beer through the hour; it went from ice-cold to warm, but he didn't mind. As he played, bits and pieces of the cases flashed across his thoughts, but he pushed them all aside, tried not to think about Chick Roberts or anyone else. He focused all his attention on the colored balls clacking and moving smoothly across the green felt.

After an hour, Carlucci took a break from the table. He got another Budweiser, then sat on a stool by the table; he stared at the now motionless balls, listened to the rain still coming down outside, drank from the bottle, and thought about the last few days.

Three cases: Chick Roberts; the mayor's nephew, William Kashen; and Robert Butler. Or rather, three murders, and all one case. Not on the books, not in the files, not for anyone else, but all one case for Carlucci. The more time that passed after his lunch with Diane, the more convinced he became that they all *were* connected in some important way. Carlucci felt caught between them, pressed and torn in several directions at once, and what he was afraid of more than anything else was that he was going to get fucked over by the whole mess. His career would be shot, or his life would go to shit, or he'd end up dead. The chances of coming out of this clean, he thought, were pretty fucking close to zero.

Options.

He could walk back to the station, work up a letter of resignation, effective today, and walk away from it all. He had the years, he'd come away with full pension and benefits. He'd have to go through a review, but he'd be able to lie his way through it; the committee would want to believe his lies, and they'd approve his resignation; probably they'd even drop a citation or two on him.

Carlucci didn't like that option one bit. It stank, and he would stink along with it.

He could just push forward with the nephew's case, forget he knew anything about Chick Roberts, not let the connections lead him anywhere; *avoid* the Chick Roberts case; hold back and let Hong and LaPlace drive the investigation of the other two cases, just stay out of their way. With any luck, they'd eventually dead-end, gradually pull back, and finally quit without solving them. Or somehow solve the damn things without blowing anything open, no spillover into *anything* else.

He didn't like that option much better. Too much could go wrong. And what about Paula Asgard?

Third option? He could push forward as hard as he could with everything, eyes open, knowing the whole fucking mess could blow up in his face.

Carlucci smiled to himself, shaking his head, and finished the beer. He didn't like *any* of his options. And what the hell was Tremaine's interest in all this?

He got a third beer, picked up his cue, pushed away all those thoughts again, and went back to playing pool.

It was still raining when he left Bricky's. Carlucci stood in his raincoat with his back against the pool hall windows, trying to keep out of the downpour. He had three more hours until his session with the slug, and now it was time to go see Brendan. He scanned the street, searching for a phone. Nothing on this side, but he spotted one across the street, just outside a pawnshop.

When he saw a break in the traffic, he dashed out into the rain and across the street, horns blaring at him as he juked in and out of the cars. Up the curb, across the sidewalk; then he ducked under the hood of the phone. He shook off the worst of the water, ran his card through the box, then punched in his code and Brendan's number.

Brendan answered almost immediately. "Chez Prosthétique," he said, a joke almost no one but Carlucci would understand.

"Brendan. This is Frank."

Brendan coughed, then said, "Funny, I thought you'd be calling soon."

"Can I come over?"

"Now?"

"Now."

Brendan hesitated, muffled the phone, and said something to someone else in his apartment. He came back on. "Give me fifteen minutes."

"Is it all right?"

"It's fine, Frank."

"See you in a bit, then."

"Right." Brendan hung up.

Carlucci put the phone back in the slot and looked out at the rain. If he walked, it would take about fifteen minutes, just right, but he would be drenched. Or he could stand here under the hood for ten minutes, then hope to flag down a cab or bus. Fuck it, he decided. He stepped out into the downpour and started walking.

•   •   •

When he reached Brendan's apartment building, Carlucci wasn't as wet as he'd expected. His raincoat had kept off the worst, and the rain had lightened up, though it had never quite stopped. Biggest rainstorm in weeks, and the gutters were flooding. Carlucci took the few steps up to the building entrance and pushed Brendan's bell. He identified himself, and Brendan buzzed him into the building.

Brendan lived on the second floor, his apartment in the back with views of the neighboring brick buildings, thick bushes, and the airwell. Carlucci knocked on the door, and Brendan pulled it open. Brendan and a young woman were standing barefoot in the front room, both wearing jeans and both naked from the waist up. A strange sight. The woman, who was probably in her thirties, was a Screamer; her lips had been fused together, and Carlucci caught a glimpse of the nasal tube in one nostril. He also couldn't help thinking that she had damn nice breasts. And of course Brendan had only an eight-inch stub protruding from his left shoulder where an arm should be.

"Frank, this is Mia. Mia, Frank."

Carlucci nodded. Mia nodded in return, then pulled a sweatshirt on over her head. She sat on the edge of a chair and buckled sandals onto her feet.

"Something to drink?" Brendan asked.

"No thanks, I've had enough."

"I haven't." Brendan padded out of the room and into the kitchen.

Carlucci took off his raincoat, looked around for someplace to hang it, but Mia got up from the chair to take it from him. She carried it down the hall and into the bathroom; Carlucci watched her hang it from the shower. "Thanks," he said when she returned. She smiled at him and nodded. At least he thought it was a smile.

Brendan came out of the kitchen with a tall glass of vodka over ice in his hand, and a towel draped over his stub. "Dry yourself off," he said. Carlucci took the towel from him and started with his hair. Mia came up to Brendan, took a deep sniff of the vodka, brushed her fused mouth against Brendan's lips. Then she nodded one more time at Carlucci and walked out of the apartment.

"Sit down," Brendan said. He carried his drink to the recliner across the room and dropped into the chair, splashing the vodka without quite spilling any. Carlucci took the only other seat in the room, a worn, overstuffed chair beside a table stacked with books; on top of one of the stacks was an old telephone. The front room had the view of the building next door: cracked brick and crumbling cement and metal grilles and shaded, glowing windows. Dusk was falling early with the clouds and the rain.

"She's a Screamer," Carlucci finally said.

"What clued you in?"

"You don't have to be sarcastic."

"You don't have to state the obvious." Brendan paused, drank deeply from the vodka; it would be the cheapest he could find. "She doesn't talk much, she doesn't smoke, and she doesn't mind fucking a gimp," Brendan concluded.

Carlucci didn't say anything. He'd had this kind of conversation with Brendan too many times, and it never went anywhere. They had known each other for twenty years, and they were still good friends of a sort, but Brendan had never been the same after he'd lost his arm. He had lost it five years earlier because of a fuck-up by his partner, Rossi, who was drunk at the time. Brendan began drinking too much himself, afterwards, and it wasn't long before his wife left him. He hadn't seen her in two or three years, hardly saw his two sons. He could have had the best artificial arm available, but he refused any kind of prosthetic, taking a perverse pride in his stump. He'd stayed on the force a while, behind a desk, and soon became a liaison to the slugs, doing most of the main interviews himself. No one liked the job, but Brendan was good at it, which was why Carlucci was here. Even that, though, hadn't lasted, and two years ago Brendan had resigned. Between disability and pension payments, he had enough money to keep himself in his cheap apartment and a steady supply of even cheaper vodka. Carlucci saw him once or twice a month. Miserable evenings, every one, but Carlucci couldn't abandon him.

"You've got a session with a slug," Brendan said.

Carlucci nodded. "I want your advice," he said. "I haven't had a session with a slug in over ten years." He shook his head. "Only had a couple, back when we were first bringing them into the department. Disasters, both of them. Then we got the liaison position going, and I've managed to avoid them ever since."

"You had people like me to do the scut work," Brendan said with a faint smile.

Carlucci nodded.

"But you can't do it this time."

"No," Carlucci said. "I need a private session."

Brendan nodded. "The mayor's nephew." It wasn't a question.

"Sort of," Carlucci said. "You up on the case?"

Brendan finished off his drink. "I'm a drunk, not an illiterate," he said. "Yes, I'm up on the case. Or as much as I can be from the news, and we both know how that is." He reached down beside his chair and brought up a half-full vodka bottle, refilled his glass. "What does 'sort of' mean?"

"There's more involved than just the mayor's nephew."

Brendan shrugged. "Robert Butler, sure. That was an easy connection to make. Partners in sleaze. I'm surprised none of the reporters have seen it yet."

"A couple have," Carlucci said. "We've killed it." He didn't see any reason to mention Tremaine's interest. "But there's more to it than Robert Butler."

"What, then?"

Carlucci shook his head. "I can't, Brendan."

Brendan studied him, sipping thoughtfully at his vodka.

"I just want your advice for dealing with the slug," Carlucci said.

Brendan remained silent, watching him. Carlucci finally looked away and stared out the window. Shadows moved behind a window shade in the building next door, two large shadows that seemed to be dancing with each other.

"Don't do it," Brendan said. Carlucci turned to look back at him, and Brendan was shaking his head. "You're roguing it, aren't you? Chasing ghosts." He continued to shake his head. "It's not worth it, Frank. Anything goes wrong, they'll bury you, they'll fucking launch you into the sun."

"It's not that simple."

"Oh fuck, it never is."

"Just help me with the slug, Brendan."

Brendan drank again from his vodka, then set it beside him. "Shit, I know you. Frank Carlucci, bull moose, bull elephant, bull whatever. Bullshit. I can't talk you out of it, can I?"

"Nothing's decided yet," Carlucci told him.

Brendan smiled. "That's what you say. Hell, might even be what you think." He breathed deeply once, and the smile disappeared. "All right, Frank. I can't help you much, but what I can . . . Which slug you seeing?"

"Monk. He was the first slug put on the case."

Brendan nodded. "Good. He's one of the best."

"What do you mean?"

"Jesus, Frank, you too? Man, everyone thinks the slugs are all the same, a bunch of freaks who mainline all that brain juice and sit around all day doing nothing but think. I mean, yeah, that's what they are, but they're not interchangeable. Some are better than others. Monk is fucking acute. He makes intuitive leaps that are just incredible. Sometimes they're insane leaps that are dead wrong. Most times, though, he's razored right in on it, and you have no idea how the hell he got there." He paused. "When's the session?"

"Tonight." Carlucci was fascinated, listening to Brendan. He hadn't noticed so much excitement and life in the man in months. Years.

"All right," Brendan said. "First thing you want to do is cancel the session, reschedule it for tomorrow. Or better yet, if time isn't that critical, wait a few days."

"Why?"

"Monk'll be pushing to get everything he can and be ready for you with his best analysis. Cramming himself full of every bit of information he can scrounge up. An extra push for the scheduled session. Which is good. But if you cancel and reschedule, he'll have a day or two free of pressure to swim around in all that info, maybe pull in a little something extra from here or there. Time to allow other possibilities to emerge, different connections to make themselves known. A chance for Monk's real strengths to manifest. Trust me, it's the smartest thing you can do."

Carlucci nodded. "All right. That's why I'm here. What else?"

Brendan shrugged. "It's hard, Frank. When you actually get in there and start talking to him, there's no formula, you just have to go with your gut. But don't try to guide Monk. Let him take you where *he's* going. That's what he's there for. Don't be surprised if his questions and replies don't seem to track. They don't, at first, if ever, because he'll be jumping all over the place, and you won't have any idea how he's getting from one thing to another. Just go with it."

He paused, looking at his drink, but didn't pick it up. He turned to Carlucci. "One last thing, Frank. Don't expect any pat answers. You may get answers that don't seem to mean anything at all. He might give you some names, or places, or just a few phrases that don't make sense. It won't do you any good to ask Monk to explain them, because he won't know what they mean, either. The intuitive leaps I was talking about. He'll give you as much explanation as he can. You'll just have to follow up whatever he gives you, fucking run it down, and hope it pays off." He shrugged. "With Monk, it probably will. It may not be what you want, it may not go where you want to go, but it'll take you to the heart of things." One final shrug. "That's all the advice I can give you, Frank. It's not much, but there it is. You'll do fine."

Carlucci nodded, thinking Brendan should still be on the force, working with the slugs, doing *something* with his life besides drinking it away. "Thanks, Brendan. I appreciate it." He stood. "I should get going."

"Wait," Brendan said. His expression fell. "Don't go yet, Frank." He pointed at the telephone beside Carlucci. "Call the station and cancel the session. Then stick around, have a drink with me. Just a little while."

Carlucci stood looking at Brendan for a few moments. Another drink wasn't what either of them needed. Christ. He finally nodded. "All right, Brendan. For a little while." He sat down again and picked up the phone.

14

THREE NIGHTS, AND nothing. Paula was exhausted, but she couldn't stop. She'd canceled one gig with the Black Angels, and she'd left the theater early last night and tonight. She wasn't sure how much longer she could keep this up. Amy had helped her when she could, but most of the time Paula had been on her own, skimming the streets of the Tenderloin at night, searching for Mixer.

She was halfway through night four and doing no better; what little hope remained was fading rapidly. She had strayed a few blocks into the Asian Quarter for a break, and now stood in front of one of her old haunts, Misha's Donuts and Espresso. Amy was supposed to meet her here at two. Paula punched the door aside and walked in.

Misha's hadn't changed. Haunting metallic echoes and tones washed through the room from the sound system—"ambient industrial," Misha called it. Ion poles sparked among the tables; booths around the edges were on platforms about four feet above the floor. Plasma tubes provided the lighting, deep reds and oranges glowing and flowing through them.

The place was nearly full. Paula worked her way to the counter, picked out two sour-cream-filled donuts, got a large black coffee, and sat at a small empty table set between an ion pole and a metallic stick tree. Sparks from the ion pole jumped across the table to the tips of the tree branches. The ion pole activity was supposed to make her feel better. It didn't.

She had taken only two bites from the first donut and a sip from the coffee when Jenny Woo slid onto the chair across the table from her, banging her elbows onto the tabletop. Her long, straight black hair was woven through with silver metal strands, which caught some of the sparks from the ion pole.

"Hey, Asgard." Jenny Woo flashed a split-second smile, but her expression was hard.

"Hello, Jenny." They didn't like each other at all, and neither tried to hide it. Jenny and Chick had had a brief but intense affair about a year ago, which ended when Chick got hit by another of his periodic bouts of impotence. All of Chick's affairs ended in impotence. Karma. Paula almost smiled, thinking about it.

"Why is it," Jenny Woo asked, "that I keep seeing you lately? Three, four times the last few days. You following me, dinko?"

"Why would I be following you?" Paula had seen Jenny a couple of times herself, and had assumed Jenny was following *her*. She pushed the plate toward Jenny. "Have a donut."

Jenny Woo leaned back in her chair. "What I asked myself," she said. "I come up with only one answer, and I don't like it. Chick."

"Chick."

"Yeah." Another flashing smile. "You know. The *dead* guy."

"I see you're torn up about it," Paula said.

"He was a good fuck, until he couldn't. After that, he wasn't good for anything." She raised a single eyebrow at Paula. "Which is what got him killed, really."

Jenny leaned forward, and Paula could see she was about to say something else, when Amy came up to the table.

"Hey," Amy said. "Am I interrupting anything?"

"Yes," Jenny Woo said. "Come back in five minutes."

Amy glanced at Paula, then turned back to Jenny Woo. "I know you, don't I?"

"Not like you think you do," Jenny said.

"And I don't like you," Amy concluded.

"No, you don't." Jenny smiled again, this time holding it for several beats. "Now flash, and leave us alone for five minutes, like I said."

When Amy looked at her, Paula nodded. Amy shoved her hands into her jeans pockets, then walked away.

"She with you on this?" Jenny asked.

"There is no 'this,' " Paula said. "She's helping me look for someone. It's got nothing to do with you or Chick."

Jenny Woo leaned forward again. When she spoke, her voice was quiet but firm. "Chick was an ambitious little shit who thought he had a lot more shine than he did. He didn't know his limitations. He didn't understand how dark things were until someone put a few holes in his head. Too late, then." Jenny shook her head. "Don't make the same mistake, Asgard. Leave it. Chick's dead, you can't change that, and getting dead yourself won't help anyone." She stood up. "I don't want to see you again."

Paula pretty much felt the same, but she didn't say anything. Jenny Woo started to turn away, then quickly swung back to face Paula.

"You *are* looking for someone," Jenny said. "Mixer. The trial of Saint Katherine, that frigid bitch."

"You know something," Paula said, trying to keep the desperation out of her voice.

"Oh yes," Jenny Woo said. "I know something."

"What?"

Jenny Woo shook her head, this time with the first genuine smile Paula had seen on her face. A nasty smile. "I never give information away, sweetheart. There's always a price. And there's not a thing you've got that I want." She paused, still smiling. "I like it this way, knowing that you *don't* know."

Paula wanted to get up and strangle Jenny Woo, or smash a chair over her head. She remained seated, silent. Karma would get Jenny Woo one day, she told herself. Except Paula didn't really believe in Karma. How could she, in this goddamn world?

"Goodbye, Asgard." Jenny was still smiling. She turned and marched away, pushing out the door and onto the street.

Paula sat without moving, staring at her coffee and donuts. No fantasies of Jenny Woo coming back and telling her what she knew about Mixer, no fucking chance of that. Shit. Paula just didn't know what to do.

Amy reappeared in front of her. Paula had forgotten. Amy sat in the chair, frowning. "Jenny Woo, right?"

Paula nodded.

"You know what she does?" Amy asked. "What she bootlegs?"

Paula nodded again. "Yeah, I know. Body-bags. Chick was in on it, too." She paused. "So was Mixer, at the 'retail' end." She shook her head.

"Great," said Amy. "And you're killing yourself looking for him."

Paula shrugged. "What can I do? He's my friend." She sighed. "Jenny Woo said she knew something about Mixer, about the trial. She refused to say what."

"I've heard something, too."

"You have?" Paula felt a tightening inside her chest. "What?"

"Nothing too specific. A contact on the nets says something went wrong with the trial. He didn't know what happened, didn't know if Mixer was alive or dead or what. The Saints are trying to keep a lid on, but he got the impression there was going to be some kind of public announcement in a day or two. And they never, *never* go public about their trials."

"Jesus," Paula said. "Is that good or bad?"

"No idea," said Amy, shaking her head. "But it probably isn't any worse than what we've been looking at."

Amy was right. They'd been expecting to find Mixer dead or completely wrecked, and there wasn't much that could be worse than that. "Worth hitting the streets again," Paula said.

"Maybe so," Amy replied. "But you're on your own tonight. I've got other business. Only reason I came down here was to tell you what I'd heard."

"Thanks, Amy. You've been a wonder, really."

Amy smiled, then said, "You know, chances are still shit for finding him, even if something good's happened. You haven't heard from him, which probably means they've still got him wrapped up, even if he isn't dead. They just might be gearing up to run through the trial again. Or, hell, who knows what else? Don't expect too much."

"I know, Amy, but I've got to have a little hope. I was just about down to none, and I can't keep going without it."

"Yeah." Amy stood. "I've gotta go. Luck to you, Paula."

"Thanks."

Amy left, and Paula watched her walk out of Misha's. She felt better than she had in days. She pulled the donuts back and reached for the coffee. A good shot of caffeine and a couple solid hits of carbos and she'd be ready to go back out onto the streets.

By dawn, what little new hope had pumped through Paula was pretty much shot. Exhaustion, she told herself—too many days without enough sleep. She felt like shit again.

She dropped onto an old concrete bench across the street from a shock shop. If she let herself, she could fall asleep here, become ripe meat for the street scavs. People moved all around her, and she closed her eyes, tried to imagine herself being ripped apart. Then she sensed someone sit beside her on the bench.

"Hello, Paula."

Paula opened her eyes to see Tremaine sitting next to her. The rising sun reflected off the shock shop window across the street, then off the left lens of Tremaine's glasses, obscuring his eye.

"You've been following me," she said.

"No," Tremaine replied, shaking his head. The shimmer of reflection shifted from one lens to the other and back again. "Or rather, yes, but only the last few minutes. I was in the Asian Quarter, on the edge, and I saw you sort of drifting back and forth between the Asian and Euro. You seemed lost. Wiped." He paused. "You know, Paula, you look terrible."

"Thanks a lot."

"Well, you do."

"Yeah. I *feel* terrible. Lack of sleep and food will do that to you." She shrugged. "I've been looking for someone."

"Mixer?"

A shot of fear sliced through her. "How did you know?"

"I was there, remember? At The Final Transit when your friend came in and said something about Mixer and Saint Katherine."

Paula looked askance at him. "You have a damn good memory."

"It helps in my business."

"Yeah, you're right." She turned away and looked at the shock shop. An old woman in heavy, flowing robes was closing up. Jesus, Paula thought, she must be roasting in those robes. Things had cooled down some with yesterday's rainstorm, but it was still warm, even this early in the morning. "Yes," she finally said, still not looking at Tremaine, "I've been looking for Mixer."

"You haven't found him."

"No."

"A close friend?"

"Yes."

"How close?"

Paula heard something familiar in his voice, and she turned to look at him. "Not that kind of friend. But a *close* friend."

Tremaine nodded.

"Chick Roberts was the one who was that kind of friend."

"I know," Tremaine said. His expression seemed to convey real sympathy, which surprised her for some reason.

"Aren't you going to ask me again about him being killed?" Paula said. Tremaine shook his head.

They sat without speaking for two or three minutes, watching the sun come up orange and crimson between the buildings, its outline shimmering through the haze.

"Let me take you home," Tremaine finally said.

"What do you mean?"

"I've got a car outside the Tenderloin. Just a few blocks away, a short walk." He paused. "You look like you could do with some sleep."

Paula looked at him, still trying to decide what kind of person he was. She didn't know yet, she just didn't know. But she nodded anyway. "Sure," she said. "Take me home. Why the hell not?"

The old Plymouth ground to a stop in front of her apartment building.

"Thanks for the ride," Paula said.

"Sure," Tremaine said. He put his hand on her shoulder. "You *are* exhausted. Get some sleep." He took his hand away.

"I will." Paula had been half expecting Tremaine to invite himself up to her apartment, and she'd been dreading having to tell him to fuck off, but now it didn't look like he was going to do that.

"Let me buy you dinner tonight," Tremaine said. "You could probably use a good meal, too."

"Yeah, probably I could." She shook her head. "But I might sleep through the night as well." There was something about this guy, something she liked. She smiled at him. "Make it tomorrow?"

"Sure. Tomorrow it is."

"Call me," Paula said. "I'm sure you know my number."

Tremaine nodded, and Paula got out of the car. She closed the door and stood on the sidewalk, watching as Tremaine and the old Plymouth pulled away from the curb, surprisingly sorry to see him go.

15

CARLUCCI HAD ARRANGED to meet Paula at noon by the Civic Center pond, a large oval four feet deep at its center, the water covered by a thick layer of green and brown muck. She was waiting for him when he arrived, pacing at the water's edge; after the morning rain, the overflow channels were draining slowly toward the streets, and she stepped over them as she paced back and forth.

As he approached, she saw him and stopped pacing. The skin beneath her eyes was dark and puffy, and the rest of her face was pale. For the first time since he'd met her, she looked her age, maybe even a little older.

"Hello, Paula," he said, putting out his hand.

"Hello, Lieutenant." She shook his hand, her grip firm in spite of the way she looked.

"Come on," Carlucci said. "Call me Frank."

"Okay. Frank."

"You look terrible."

She half smiled. "People keep telling me that. Think there's something to it?"

"Want something to eat?" he asked, gesturing at a cart nearby selling sausages and giant pretzels.

"God, no." Paula shook her head. "Coffee, though, I could use."

Carlucci nodded. There were a couple of coffee carts on the other side of the pond. "I'll buy," he said. "How do you want it?"

"Black," said Paula. "As black as you can get it."

Carlucci walked along the edge of the pond, stepping across the overflow channels, rolling up his shirt sleeves as he went. The heat was stifling again, as if they were back in July or August. Where the hell was fall?

He bought two large coffees from the girl running one of the carts; she couldn't have been more than thirteen, and she was pregnant. Carlucci gave her a tip that was double the price of the coffee.

When he got back to Paula, he handed her one of the coffees and they stood together sipping at them, gazing out at the muck-covered pond. Something heaved under the muck, out near the middle, and Paula laughed.

"I wonder what lives in there," she said. "I think everyone's afraid to clean off the crap and find out."

"Fish, or snakes," Carlucci suggested. "Turtles, maybe."

"Mutant alligators," Paula said. She looked at him. "I'm glad you called. I wanted to talk to you, but I didn't think calling your office was a good idea."

"I didn't give you my home number?" When Paula shook her head, Carlucci frowned. "Sorry. I should have. I thought I had."

"Why *did* you call?" Paula asked.

"I need to tell you some things." Carlucci hesitated, staring down into his coffee. "It's an incredible mess. It's not just Chick's murder anymore. There's a lot more involved."

"Like what?"

Carlucci shook his head. "Christ, I don't know. I mean, I know some of it, but I don't know what I should be telling you. Too much firepower, too damn many things that could blow up in my face."

"Are you dropping it?" Paula asked.

"No. I half wish I was, but no." He looked out at the pond and drank from his coffee. "There's no more screwing around. What I've done up to now has been pretty much risk-free, checking into a few things here and there. I've found a lot, but none of it good." He shook his head again and looked back at Paula. "Nothing's going to be risk-free any longer. Not for me, not for you. You've got to know that."

"But you're not going to tell me what's involved."

"I don't know. I keep thinking it's better for both of us if I'm the only one who knows." Damage control, Carlucci thought, if everything goes to shit on me. But he didn't say it.

"Look, that's up to you," Paula said. "But I'm not sure I can help much if I don't know what the hell's going on."

"I know. I'll think about it." He paused. "What I really need now is to talk to Mixer."

Paula gave a choked laugh. "Good luck."

"What is it?"

She slowly shook her head. "I've been looking for him for days."

"Why?"

"You know who the Saints are?"

"I've heard of them," Carlucci said. "Some women in the Tenderloin, they take on the names of old Saints, right? Most of what I've heard sounds a little crazy."

Paula gave him something like a smile. "Then most of what you've heard is probably true." The smile faded. "They take people off the street and put them on trial. 'Trial' meaning some kind of torture like the historical saints were put through." She paused, breathing deeply. "About a week ago they picked up Mixer. Saint Katherine was to put him on trial a few days ago." She turned away from him. "The survivors of Saint Katherine's trials end up with scrambled eggs for brains. I look like shit because I've been spending nights in the Tenderloin looking for him, hoping I could find what's left of the bastard before the scavengers pick him clean."

"No sign of him?" Carlucci asked.

"No," Paula said. "A friend told me last night that she'd heard something went wrong with the trial, but nobody knows *what*. No one knows what happened—if he's dead, if he's still alive, if he's fucked up, nothing." She looked back at Carlucci. "I've got a little hope, but not much. I wouldn't count on him for anything, if I were you."

"You think there's any connection between Chick's death and the Saints picking up Mixer?"

"I doubt it. The Saints live in another world, and I don't think it's got much in common with ours. They don't do anything for anyone but themselves."

"Is there anything I can do?"

"What do *you* think?" Paula said. Then, "Sorry." She drank the rest of her coffee and walked over to a trash can on the sidewalk. The can was overflowing, and Carlucci watched her standing in front of it, crumpling the cup in her hand, squeezing it over and over. Finally she shoved the crushed cup into the other trash, wiped her hands on her jeans, and walked back.

"Something else I need to tell you," she said. "One of the names I gave you last week. Jenny Woo."

"Yes."

"Something there, I think. She's worth an extra look. She thought I was following her, and she warned me off. Told me getting dead like Chick wasn't going to do anyone any good." She paused for a moment, then went on. "She and Chick were bootlegging body-bags. Anyway, she gave me the impression she knew exactly why Chick had been killed."

"All right," Carlucci said. "Anything like that will help." He took a business card from his wallet, jotted down his home number, and handed the card to Paula. "Any time, day or night, you need to call me, do it, all right?"

Paula stuck the card in her back pocket and nodded. "One other thing," she said. "You know who Tremaine is?"

Carlucci nodded, his gut tightening.

"He's poking around in this. He came to see me, wanted to talk to me about Chick."

"What did you tell him?"

"Nothing. What *should* I tell him?"

Carlucci shrugged. "I don't know if it really matters. That guy, if he's got a story, and puts it all together, nothing will keep him from sending it out over the nets."

Neither of them said anything for a few moments. Then Paula sighed heavily. "I've gotta go," she said.

"Mixer . . ." Carlucci started, but he didn't finish. She knew better. "Let me know if you find him."

Paula nodded again, then turned and walked away without another word. Carlucci watched her cross the plaza, hands jammed into her pockets, head down. She turned a corner and was gone.

Tremaine. I should talk to him, Carlucci thought. He probably knows more about what's going on than anyone.

Carlucci looked into his coffee cup, which was still half full. His stomach rebelled at the thought of any more coffee right now. He stepped to the edge of the pond and poured out what was left in the cup. *Drink up*, he said silently to whatever was living beneath the muck. *Drink up*.

Carlucci stood at the mouth of an alley across from the outer edge of the Tenderloin. One more meeting before returning to the station. He checked his watch. Fifteen minutes before Sparks was supposed to be there. Just about right. Sparks would be early.

He hesitated before entering the narrow passageway. The sun had broken through the clouds and haze and glared down on him; sweat dripped down his neck, rolled down his sides under his shirt. Steam rose from the alley floor where the sun sliced in. Sometimes, like now, Carlucci wished he still carried a gun. At least it wasn't nighttime.

He started into the alley. His first few steps were through the rising steam, but he was soon past it and into shadow, his shoes splashing through shallow rain puddles. Above him hung fire escapes and huge sprays of flowering bromeliads; water dripped on him, almost like rain.

Halfway along the alley, on the right, were two concrete steps leading up to a metal door. Carlucci climbed the steps and pushed open the door, which swung inward with an echoing screech. He stepped inside and closed the door behind him.

He had expected darkness, but dappled light came in through broken windows and large cracks in the walls, strangely illuminating the huge, empty, high-ceilinged room. An old machine shop or storage facility, Carlucci guessed. Cooler than outside, a welcome relief. The floor was a mix of broken concrete and dirt, scattered with wood and metal debris. A dark, open doorway broke the solid interior wall across from him, and Carlucci stood in the cool shadows, listening and watching the doorway.

A minute or two later he heard a harsh coughing, and Sparks appeared in the doorway. Sparks stopped for a moment, blinking, then came into the room. He coughed again, shaking his head. Sparks was tall and gaunt, his eyes dark, his cheeks hollow; a slice of light from outside cut across his neck, revealing the jagged lines of needle marks. Dermal patches were everywhere on the streets, but some people still needed those needles, straight shots to the veins, the heart.

"Carlucci," Sparks said. "You're early."

"So are you."

Sparks smiled. "Have you got anything for me?"

Carlucci worked his way across the rubble until he was just a foot or two from Sparks. Sparks was younger than Carlucci, but looked much older. He'd been a hot-shot demon once, freelancing for the cops in addition to several big corporations, hacking his way through life and getting rich, until one night his nervous system had taken a huge hit from a defective black-market head juicer. His career as a demon was over. His life was over. His career as a junkie had just begun.

Carlucci took a small wad of bills from his pocket and handed it to Sparks. "More later, if you can get me some whisper."

Sparks pocketed the money, then broke into a long coughing fit, doubled over for a minute or two before it eased. He straightened, coughed a few more times, then sighed heavily. "I'm dying," he said.

"I know," Carlucci replied.

"Can you get me into a hospice?" Sparks asked.

"I don't know." Carlucci turned away, unable to maintain eye contact. "I'll try, Sparks." He turned back to face the old junkie. Not that old, really, but old for a needle freak. "I'll try."

Sparks nodded, then said, "What do you want?"

"Chick Roberts." Carlucci paused for a few seconds as Sparks closed his eyes, locking in the name, then opened them again. "Jenny Woo." Another pause, Sparks's eyes closing, opening. "William Kashen." One final pause. "Robert Butler." Carlucci stopped, trying to decide whether to throw in Mixer. He wasn't completely sure where Mixer fit in, and he was afraid of complicating things. Gut feeling said to leave it there, so he did. "How are they connected?" he finished up.

Sparks made a sound that might have been a laugh. "Three of them are dead." Another cough. "Yeah, I'll see what I can come up with. I'll be in touch." He started to turn, then shifted back around, looking at Carlucci with his head cocked. "There's something to do with New Hong Kong in all this," he said.

Without another word, Sparks turned and walked back through the doorway. Carlucci remained where he was, feeling that their conversation, their meeting, whatever it was, wasn't quite finished. But Sparks was gone, and there was nothing more to say.

Carlucci walked back across the room, opened the door, and stepped out into the alley. The heat struck him hard, and he was dizzy for a moment. The plants overhead dripped steadily on him. Fuck this city, Carlucci said to himself. He took the two steps to the alley floor, turned, and headed for the street.

Amy was sitting on the steps of Paula's apartment building, head back against the brick, eyes shaded by pixie-specs. Paula's stomach dropped and turned in on itself when she saw her. She walked up the steps, and Amy stood.

"Have you heard something?" Paula asked.

Amy nodded. "The Saints made an announcement on the local net." She took a piece of paper from her jeans pocket. "'A pilgrim who took the name Mixer was put to Saint Katherine's Trial,'" she read. "'The trial was a glorious event, producing holy immolation never before seen in the trials. Clearly, Mixer was a chosen, a prophet, whose dying cries provided profound revelations to the gathered Saints and witnesses. He passed the trial superbly, in spirit if not in flesh, and will be remembered as a glorious martyr in the family of Saints.'" She stopped, looking up at Paula. "That's it."

"He's dead." Paula looked down at the piece of paper in Amy's hand. "Mixer's dead."

Amy nodded, but didn't speak.

Paula could hardly move, could hardly breathe. She turned her head slowly, squinted against the glare of the sun that seemed so hot and huge in the sky. The street and buildings were bleached out all around her. She turned back to Amy.

"I'm tired," she said. "I'm going to lie down for a while."

Amy nodded. "I'm sorry."

Paula gestured at the piece of paper in Amy's hand. "Can I have that?"

"Yeah, sure."

Paula took the sheet from Amy, folded it carefully, and tucked it into her pocket, next to the gravity knife. "Thanks." She went to the building door, unlocked it, and stepped inside.

Several hours later, Paula climbed the stairs of her apartment building again, Tremaine just behind her. Her legs felt heavy, her breath was short and halting. Even her sense of hearing seemed to go in and out—one moment their footsteps were loud and echoing in the stairwell, Tremaine's breathing clear and close, and the next a swirling filled her ears and she could hear nothing at all.

Tremaine was coming up to her apartment, and she knew where it all was headed, and she was half certain it was a terrible idea. She had no one to blame but herself.

They'd eaten dinner at Mai's, good food and even better wine—an expensive bottle of Chardonnay bought by Tremaine. A long, relaxing meal, followed by coffee and mint ice cream, then a walk through the noise and energy of the Polk Corridor. The sexual tension was strong, almost suffocating, and it was crazy to try to deny it was there. She didn't tell him about Mixer. She wasn't sure why.

Tremaine had suggested going somewhere for a drink, and Paula had said, Why not my apartment? It was quiet, they could be alone, talk, have some peace. You sure? Tremaine had asked. She hadn't been, but she'd said yes anyway, her heart pounding against her ribs.

And now, here they were, at her door. Paula unlocked the dead bolt, stuck another key in the main lock, punched in her security code, then turned the key. The lock clicked and she pushed open the door. The only light on in the apartment was a small fluorescent over the kitchen sink. Paula brushed her hand along the wall and turned on the overheads, which lit up the large room that served as kitchen and entry. She held the door wide, and Tremaine followed her in.

The kitchen half of the front room looked normal, with table and chairs, stove and refrigerator, but the other half was a mess, stacks and piles of boxes and bags and crates, all the stuff she'd kept from Chick's apartment—tapes, discs, books, sound system, video sets and cameras, recording and mixing equipment, his guitars. Paula stood staring at it for a long time, hardly aware of Tremaine beside her, noticing it all for the first time in days. Ever since she'd moved it here in Nikky's van, she'd been able to ignore it. Now, having invited Tremaine into the apartment, knowing what was going to happen, she felt like Chick's things were everywhere, overwhelming the place.

"What's wrong?" Tremaine asked.

Paula shook her head. "All this." She waved at it, afraid it was going to move and grow. "Chick. All this stuff is his. I haven't been able to do anything with it." And there was Mixer, too, dead like Chick, but again she didn't mention him.

There was a long silence, and Paula continued to stare at the clutter, not moving. She didn't know what to do or say.

"Do you want me to leave?" Tremaine asked.

Paula turned to look at him. He would, she realized. If she asked him to, he would turn around and walk out. "No," she said. "No." Her heart was beating harder again; she could feel it in her throat. "Stay."

Tremaine nodded, reached out and lightly brushed her cheek.

Still unsure, feeling sick to her stomach, Paula led Tremaine into the dark bedroom.

Shadows and dim light, the smell of sawdust and sweat. Tremaine's weight above her, his body slick and heavy, dipping and thrusting. Paula wanted to push him away, wanted to scramble out of bed, wanted to cry. She could not stop thinking of Chick.

Tremaine was warm, gentle, caring with her, but it didn't matter. It was a mistake, Paula thought, a terrible mistake, and it was way too late.

She saw Chick sitting by the open bedroom window, smoking a cigarette, blowing the smoke out into the night. She saw him sitting at the kitchen table, barefoot, shirtless and wearing blue jeans, drinking coffee, smiling at her. She saw him onstage beside her, wailing away at his guitar, hair sticky with sweat. And she felt his mouth on hers, his lips and tongue and fingers on her skin and inside her.

Paula squeezed her eyes shut, fighting back the tears, and held onto Tremaine with everything she had.

Paula woke, feeling strangely groggy. It was still dark. She was alone in bed. Had Tremaine gone? She glanced at the tiny glowing clock face next to the bed. Three-thirty. Would he have left without saying anything?

The apartment was quiet, but not silent, and she thought she heard faint sounds—tinkling, a click, a slight scraping. She was too exhausted to get up, and she was only half awake. She turned over, the bed creaking, and faced the wall. Was she even half awake? Paula put her hand out and pressed it against the wall. What did that prove? Where was Tremaine?

Time seemed strange, stretching out and closing in, spotted with fragmented dream images. Chick was dead, and now Mixer was, too. Then she heard the toilet flush, and the present seemed to lock back into focus. A few moments later she felt Tremaine get back into bed, settle in.

"Are you awake?" he whispered.

"No," she answered. She felt his arm wrap slowly around her, holding her. She closed her eyes and drifted back into sleep, unsure whether things were somehow all right, or were terribly wrong.

PART THREE

16

CARLUCCI SAT WITH Andrea and Christina on the back deck in the fragmented shade of a tattered umbrella. Christina had cooked breakfast for them and they'd eaten outside, and now they were drinking coffee and talking. It was rare that all three of them had a free day together. Gazing out over the lush, overgrown garden, Carlucci thought of how he needed to get out there and do some weeding and pruning; and there was his appointment tonight with the slug. But for now he intended to do nothing but sit and talk and enjoy the company of his family.

There was a thump and scrabbling at the fence, and Tuff's face appeared, golden eyes wide. As he perched atop the fence, he seemed unsteady. Christina got up, hurried to the fence and picked him up, cradling him in her arms and bringing him back to the deck. "Poor guy," she said, sitting down and holding him on her lap.

"Why?" Carlucci asked. "What's wrong?"

"Didn't I tell you? I was talking to Harry, and he said Tuff was having kidney failure." She shrugged, holding Tuff closer. "He's just getting old." She pressed her face against the gray cat's face, and Tuff tried half-heartedly to squirm away.

Carlucci felt bad for the old guy, and he found himself almost unconsciously reaching out and taking Andrea's hand in his; he was thinking of Caroline again, who would never have the chance to grow old.

Andrea smiled at him and squeezed his hand. Then, their thoughts running on similar tracks, she said, "I forgot to tell you. Caroline called last night, and she's coming over for dinner next weekend."

Carlucci returned Andrea's squeeze, smiled, and said, "Good. I wish we could see her more." Meaning more than one thing. He turned and stared at Christina, a terrible ache going through him—grief for Caroline and fear for Christina, fear of something taking her away as well.

The side gate squealed, and a few moments later McCuller came around the corner of the house. Carlucci wanted to tell McCuller to get the fuck out of his yard. He didn't want the man in his house, his yard, even his neighborhood.

McCuller approached the deck, smiling and looking too damn comfortable in his expensive suit. "I tried the front door," he said, "but there was no answer." He shrugged. "On the off chance, I came around."

"Lucky us," Carlucci said.

McCuller's smile tightened briefly, but he turned to Andrea and softened it. "Good morning, Andrea, good to see you again. Sorry to intrude."

Andrea forced a smile. "Hello, Marcus."

"Christina," McCuller said, turning to the young woman.

Christina nodded, but didn't say anything, didn't attempt to smile. She just held Tuff closer to her, as if trying to protect him.

McCuller turned back to Carlucci, no longer smiling. "Be ready at seven o'clock this evening. A car will be here to take you to a meeting."

Carlucci shook his head. "I have a session scheduled with a slug tonight."

"Cancel it. Your meeting's with the mayor. His personal car and driver will pick you up and take you to his house." McCuller put his right hand in his pocket, fingers of his left hand flexing. "Quite a privilege."

"Sounds more like a commandment," Carlucci said.

"If you choose to look at it that way."

"Why are you here, Captain? Why not just call?"

"The mayor asked me to make sure you got the message personally. This meeting is important to him, and he didn't want any . . . miscommunications."

"All right," Carlucci said. "I've received the message. I'll be ready."

McCuller seemed ready to say something else. But he shook his head, as though whatever he had in mind was pointless. Then, "I'll see you, Frank. Andrea, Christina." Without waiting for a response from any of them, he turned and walked away, around the corner and out of sight, the side gate squealing once more, rattling shut.

Carlucci stared at the spot where McCuller had stood, trying to ease the tension in his neck and head.

"Frank?" Andrea said. "Frank, he's gone."

Yeah, he thought, but it was too late. The man had soured his day, and Carlucci knew that no matter how hard he tried, it would stay that way.

At seven that evening, Carlucci stood on the sidewalk in front of his house, waiting for the mayor's car. He waved to Harry and Frances, who were sitting on their front porch next door in the last of the sun, drinking iced drinks, Tuff at their feet. It was hot and muggy, and Carlucci was already uncomfortable in the suit and tie Andrea had insisted he wear.

Shit, he said to himself, seeing the large, dark gray limo come around the corner. He didn't need this. What the hell would Harry and Frances think? The limousine pulled in to the curb, and before the driver could get all the way out, Carlucci was at the rear door and opening it for himself. He got in and quickly closed the door. The driver got back behind the wheel, closed his own door, and pulled the limo out into the street without a word.

The air inside the limousine was uncomfortably cold and dry, and Carlucci tried to open the tinted windows, but none of the controls worked. He did not want to ask the mayor's driver for anything. The guy probably earned twice what Carlucci did.

The journey was silent, seemed almost motionless at times, and Carlucci felt cut off from the world. No wonder the mayor didn't have a clue, traveling through the city like this, and living up on Telegraph. Or maybe the man knew exactly what he was cutting himself off from. Carlucci wondered if the mayor ever looked out the windows of the limo and watched the city go past him.

Carlucci did. Crossing the Panhandle, he looked out on the mass of tents and shacks erected on what had once been open park land; smoke rose from open fires, and shadows of people moved across the dwellings, stretched and flickered on fabric, wood, metal. Further on, they passed the fenced-in enclave of the University of San Francisco; through the chain-link Carlucci could see the outlines of the bunkers.

They drove through the Japan Center, heading north, passing between shiny, brightly lit buildings and glass-covered walkways, colorfully dressed men and women walking in complete security. They continued northward, avoiding the Tenderloin, then finally cut through Russian Hill, headed toward Telegraph. Crossing Columbus, they had to work slowly past a series of police barricades surrounding a block of burning buildings. Something heavy and hard crashed against the side window, but the glass didn't break, didn't show even a hint of damage, and the driver kept on as if nothing had occurred.

At the base of Telegraph Hill, they passed through a heavily fortified checkpoint, then started up the steep, winding road. At the top, just below the ruins of Coit Tower, the driver turned into a long drive as a metal gate swung out of the way and quickly closed behind them. As soon as the limo came to a stop, Carlucci opened the rear door, but this time the driver didn't even try to get out of the car.

Mayor Terrance Kashen's house didn't stand out from those surrounding it, but then all the houses, condos, and apartments on Telegraph were worth small fortunes, especially those here at the summit, built on what used to be public park land. In the growing twilight, Carlucci could see the shimmering glow of a Kronenhauer Field surrounding the house and grounds. But he couldn't see much of the house itself from the drive—most of the structure extended out from the hillside, facing north and slightly west, with what he imagined must be stunning views. Maybe even of the sunset, which was now blazing the sky and clouds with bright crimson and orange streaks, though the sun itself was no longer visible.

The front door opened and Mayor Terrance Kashen appeared, wearing both a smile and a dark suit with apparent ease. Carlucci walked up the stone path and shook the mayor's outstretched hand.

"Thanks for coming, Frank." The mayor stepped back to let Carlucci into the house.

"I didn't have much choice, did I?"

Kashen's smile broadened, and he closed the door. They were in a glass-walled, glass-floored entry, a pale creamy light diffusing from the glass. "There's always a choice," the mayor said. "It's just a matter of consequences."

He led the way from the entry, passing through a shimmering curtain of metallic fabric, then over a footbridge covering a brook that flowed out of the right wall and into the left. Then they were in the main room: huge and jutting out over the hillside, three walls of glass, with the view every bit as spectacular as Carlucci had expected: Alcatraz, with its flame towers ablaze, directly in front of them; stretching away to the north, far on the left, the Golden Gate Bridge, spans alight, orange flickers in the deepening twilight. As they approached the windows, the city itself appeared below them, glittering silver and gold and red. More lights bobbed out on the bay—private security cutters circling two large luxury yachts. The last remnants of the sunset lit the western sky with wide slashes of deep purple and crimson.

Kashen gestured toward one of two small leather couches that faced one another, next to the main window. "Have a seat, Frank." Carlucci sat, just back from the window, with the full view of the city below and facing the Golden Gate. Kashen remained standing. "Can I get you something to drink?"

Carlucci shook his head. Drinking with the mayor didn't seem like a good idea. The mayor nodded once in return, then sat on the other sofa, facing Carlucci. He settled back, crossing his legs.

"I'm told you're a good cop," Kashen said. "One of the best we've got." He paused. "An honest cop."

"Is that good or bad?" Carlucci asked.

The mayor smiled. "I'm also told you're insubordinate. Would that be true, do you think?"

Carlucci shrugged. "I just try to balance out those who spend too much time on their knees."

Kashen hesitated a few moments, then said, "Like Captain McCuller?"

Carlucci didn't respond. He wasn't going to get drawn in that deep.

"Well," the mayor said. "There's something to be said for both kinds of people. The world needs both kinds."

"I don't think so," Carlucci said.

The mayor smiled again. "Okay, Frank. The *political* world needs both kinds."

Carlucci wasn't sure he agreed even with that, but didn't think it really mattered. He wondered how long it was going to take Kashen to get to the point of his meeting. Or would all of this be part of the point?

"How old are you, Frank?"

Not a question Carlucci had expected. "Fifty-two."

"Really? You're in good shape for fifty-two. Well, perhaps 'shape' is the wrong word. You do look good for your age, though. Younger. I would have guessed mid-forties, maybe late." He paused, as though waiting for Carlucci to say something. Like what? Carlucci thought. Thank you? The mayor went on. "Fifty-two," he repeated. "If you had a choice, Frank, living another thirty years or so, your body slowing down, gradually falling apart—or living another hundred, hundred and fifty years, without aging, or aging so slowly you hardly notice it, which would you choose?"

At first Carlucci didn't think the question was serious, but as he watched the mayor studying him intently, waiting for his response, he realized the question *was* serious. What the hell was all this about?

He thought about the choices for a minute, then asked, "Would my family be able to live longer as well, or would it just be me?"

Kashen seemed puzzled at first. "Would that really make a difference?" Then, "I can see that with you it would. You're an interesting man, Frank." He pressed something on the square table beside the couch, and a moving hologram came to life above a well in the table. Four figures moved about just above the table, playing badminton—the mayor, his beautiful younger wife, and a teenaged boy and girl, presumably the mayor's son and daughter. After watching the hologram for some time, Carlucci realized that it was no more than about fifteen seconds of movement, repeated over and over.

"My family," the mayor said. He turned back to Carlucci. "I understand your older daughter has Gould's Syndrome."

Carlucci nodded, wondering if the man was deliberately trying to cause him pain. "Yes, she does."

"It must be terribly hard on you, knowing you'll probably outlive your own daughter."

"Harder for her," Carlucci said, a sharp edge to his voice. What the fuck was it with this man?

Kashen nodded. "Yes, I imagine so." He pressed the table again and the hologram snapped off. He looked at Carlucci. "One of my own family members is already dead," he said. "My nephew."

All right, Carlucci thought. Here it is, finally.

"We've been coming down hard on you," the mayor said. "On you and LaPlace and Hong." He paused, nodding to himself, stretching his arms out along the back of the couch. "I want to apologize. It's been unfair. As I said earlier, you're a good cop, and I know you've been doing your best." He uncrossed his legs, recrossed them. "I reacted the way I did because William was my nephew. He was family. The way you feel about your family, I'm sure you understand."

Carlucci wanted to shake his head. He didn't think there was much similarity between the two families. But he sat motionless, listening.

"The pressure's coming off," the mayor said. "You'll be able to do your job just as you would with any other case. You won't have Captain Mc-Culler or Chief Vaughn or me coming down on you anymore. We won't be demanding you do anything you wouldn't normally do." He made a dismissive gesture with his hand. "No more crazy overtime, no more extraordinary measures or expenses. We'll even take most of the slugs off, no sense wasting them. Treat this just as you would any other case."

There was a long pause, but Carlucci didn't know what to say. He felt certain Kashen wasn't quite finished yet. Carlucci continued to sit and wait. He wasn't going to ask anything, he wasn't going to make it any easier for the bastard.

"Okay, look," Kashen said. "The truth is, my nephew was something of a scumbag, wasn't he? You're on the case, you've been looking into his history, you know what he was involved with. I'm not going to pretend I just recently discovered what the son of a bitch was up to. I've known. He'd been in one illegal or immoral scam after another, and he was probably chest-deep in one more, and that's what got him killed. He probably had it coming. He was a scumbag. A rich one, but a scumbag nevertheless, and probably got killed by other scumbags." He paused, glancing away for a moment before looking back at Carlucci. "What I'm getting at, is, you don't need to go out of your way to solve this damn thing. It's just not worth it."

Finally, finally, Carlucci thought. "You're not asking me to bury the case, are you?"

The mayor stared directly at Carlucci, his gaze steady and hard. "No," he said. "Of course not."

Bull*shit*. That's *exactly* what he was asking. Carlucci didn't say anything.

"Just don't kill yourself over it." Kashen waved his hand again, the same gesture. "Like the session you've got scheduled with the slug. Nobody likes them, nobody likes to go through those damn interviews." He shook his head, grimacing. "Just cancel. Don't put yourself through it."

Yes indeed, Carlucci thought. He knew just what the mayor wanted. "Too many people know about the session," he said. "This is the second time I've postponed it. If I cancel now, right after I've had this meeting with you, it's going to look bad. Like you *are* asking me to bury the case."

The mayor seemed to think about that, and he nodded. "You're absolutely right, Frank. Don't cancel." He paused. "It's a private session, isn't it? No one else present, no one else listening, no recordings?"

"Yes. They almost always are. The slugs prefer it that way."

"Then no one would know if you just went through the motions, showed up, asked the slug a few innocuous questions, then got the hell out."

"That's right. No one would know. Just me and the slug."

Kashen nodded, smiling slightly. "Well. You do what you think is best, Frank. I trust you."

"What about LaPlace and Hong?"

"Tell them just what I've told you. Take the pressure off."

Yeah, right, and dump on a different kind, a worse kind. "Is that all?" Carlucci asked. He wanted to get out of this man's house.

The mayor nodded and stood. Carlucci pushed himself up from the couch and followed him back through the main room, across the water, and into the glassed entry. Kashen opened the front door, let Carlucci out, then came out onto the porch with him. The limo was waiting in the drive, the driver standing beside the front door.

"Thanks for coming out to see me, Frank." The mayor put out his hand, and the two men shook. "I feel good about this meeting. I'm confident we understand one another."

Carlucci nodded. *More than you think.* "Yes," he said.

Carlucci started down the walk, when Kashen stopped him. "You never answered my question, Frank."

Carlucci turned back to him. There was something here he didn't understand. Almost like some kind of offer. But what? "You never answered mine," he replied.

"About your family? Whichever you would prefer. With or without."

"Then it's not really a choice, is it?"

The mayor smiled and shook his head. "You're right, Frank. It's not." A brief pause, then, "Good night, Frank."

Carlucci turned away from the mayor and continued down the stone walk toward the limo.

It was nearly midnight by the time they met at Hong's family flat in Chinatown. Carlucci arrived first, LaPlace less than five minutes later. All of Hong's family—wife, father, three kids, and his two widowed sisters—were still awake, talking and playing cards and drinking tea in the enormous kitchen. Kim, Joseph's wife, offered to cook for them, but they declined, and after a few minutes of obligatory visiting, Carlucci, Hong, and LaPlace left.

They walked two blocks through the heart of the Chinatown night, nearly as bright and colorful and loud as the Tenderloin after dark. The smells of cooking food and incense, cigarette smoke and spiced perfume filled the air as they passed restaurants and stores, groceries and herb shops, gambling clubs and bars. They entered Madame Chow's Mahjongg Parlor and climbed four flights of stairs in the back to a small room with a single window, a table and four chairs, and an overhead light. Carlucci could barely get his breath. An ancient uncle of Hong's served them tea, then left them in private. Carlucci, Hong, and LaPlace sat at the table, just a few feet from the window, which let in the flashing and blinking colors of the street.

"Bet we're not going to like this," LaPlace said, breaking the silence. Hong lit a cigarette and stared at Carlucci, but didn't say anything.

"You'd win the bet," Carlucci finally said. He stared out the window, watching the colors shift and flicker, reflecting off glass and metal across the way. He thought about opening the window, letting in fresh air, but decided against it. He looked back at Hong and LaPlace.

"McCuller came by my house this morning with a message. A car would show up to take me to the mayor's house for a meeting. It did, and I went, and we had the meeting. Just me and the mayor and his million-dollar view."

"Fuck," LaPlace said. "More pressure to solve his nephew's case. Just what we need."

Hong shook his head slowly, taking a deep drag on his cigarette. "No," he said, speaking through the smoke. "It's worse than that, isn't it? Something different."

Carlucci nodded. "Yes, it's worse than that." He paused, glancing from one to the other. "He wants us to bury it."

"What the fuck?" LaPlace took off his glasses as if he could hear better without them, and stared at Carlucci. "He said *what*?"

"Not directly. He's not about to stick his ass out like that. But he made it clear. He apologized for all the pressure that's come down from him and McCuller and Vaughn, said it would stop, that he knew we were all good cops doing our best, that he got carried away because it was his nephew, but he knows his nephew was a scumbag who probably got what he deserved."

"And he wants us to bury it?" LaPlace asked.

"He said we should treat it like any other case. No extra measures, no extra time, no more spending a fortune on expensive lab work, all that. He said we shouldn't kill ourselves over it."

"Oh, terrific," LaPlace said. "That's subtle."

"Yes. He even told me to cancel my session with the slug."

"That would be a little obvious, wouldn't it?" Hong said.

"I told him that. He agreed, suggested I go through the motions, ask a couple of pointless questions and burn out. Private session, no one would know."

No one spoke for a minute or two. Hong finished his cigarette and lit another.

"So if we catch the guy who whacked his nephew," LaPlace finally said, "it causes big problems for the mayor."

"Apparently," Carlucci agreed.

"So why the *fuck* did he come down so hard on us to solve the damn thing in the first place? Two weeks with this shit."

"He didn't know," Hong said.

"What?"

"That's my guess, too," Carlucci said. "The mayor didn't know that solving his nephew's murder could dump him in the shit. He was doing the political thing, for PR, his family and all that."

"But somebody's clued him in," LaPlace said, nodding. "So what the fuck is going on, and what the fuck are we going to do about it?"

They were all silent again for a while, drinking their tea and thinking. None of them had any immediate answers, and it wasn't going to be easy to come up with the right ones.

"So what the fuck has that goddamn mayor got into?" LaPlace said. Then he shook his head. "We're probably better off not knowing. But what happens if we tank this case, after all the screaming about it from the mayor himself, all over the papers and the tube? Demotions? Or we just look like fucking morons?"

Carlucci shook his head. "Probably the mayor will make some kind of statement; he's checked into it, we've done a superb job on an impossible case, praise for the department, praise for us, probably citations, he's disappointed but understanding. We'd be fine."

"All right. More important, what happens we catch the guy, and the mayor takes it in the balls because of it? They can't fire us for doing our jobs—so what happens, somebody cuts off our legs or kills us?"

Carlucci didn't answer. What the hell could he say? He didn't know what would happen. But he was damn sure the mayor wouldn't go down without taking as many people with him as he could, one way or another.

Hong started to light another cigarette—though his last one was only half gone—then stopped, looked at Carlucci. "There's something else, isn't there? Some other thing happening in the middle of all this that Pete and I don't know about. Something *you* know."

Carlucci nodded. They had a right to know. Maybe not *what* it was, but at least that it was out there waiting to blow up in their faces.

"There's another case," Carlucci said. "Someone killed about a week before the mayor's nephew. The case got buried but good. There didn't seem to be any connection to the nephew, but now it looks like there is."

LaPlace put his glasses back on and looked at Carlucci. "You buried a case, Frank?"

"No. Someone else did. It doesn't matter who, someone who had no choice. I only found out about it by accident."

"And you've been poking at it," Hong said.

Carlucci nodded. "This whole thing is a lot messier than it looks. I don't know who's involved, or *why* all this shit is happening, but it's turning into a fucking nightmare." He paused, then said, "One other joker in this deck. Tremaine's been digging around in all this. I have no idea why. Frankly, I don't know whether that's good or bad."

Again there was a fairly long silence, broken only by the clinking of tea cups on saucers and the muted sounds from the street outside.

"I've never tanked a case before," LaPlace said.

Hong said nothing, just stared at the window, smoking.

"I know," Carlucci said. "Probably the smartest thing for us to do is let the nephew's case slide, go through the motions, don't follow up shit, and let the case die from lack of oxygen. It wouldn't really be burying it."

"And what about that other case, the one you're poking at?" Hong asked.

"I'd have to let that go, too. They're too damn connected. Anything I did might blow open the nephew's case."

"Why *are* you poking at this other case?"

"Personal reasons."

"But you would drop it?"

"Yes." It was one thing to risk his own career, another thing to risk theirs as well unless they were with him on it.

"Fuck." LaPlace got up from the table and went to the window; the colored lights flickered across his face.

"If we *don't* tank the case," Hong began, "we'd need to make it look like we were. Nothing obvious, nothing anyone else would notice, but something for the mayor to see. He wouldn't want us to be obvious. Maybe back off a little, make a statement or two about the case bogging down, something like that. Frank has his session with the slug, says nothing came out of it, even if the slug gives him gold." He put out his cigarette, breathing deeply. "We need to look like we're still working on the case, so we do it for real, and we keep everything we come up with to ourselves."

LaPlace remained at the window, but now he was looking at Hong, listening to his partner. "And what about Frank's other case?" he said.

Hong turned to Carlucci. "You'd have to bring us in on that one, too, Frank. If they're connected, it's got to be both, or none."

Carlucci looked back and forth between the two men. He hadn't been sure which way they would go on this, and he wasn't completely sure he was happy with the way it appeared to be headed. But it made him feel good, somehow; these two men, no matter how this all worked out, pumped him with something like hope.

"You're saying you're willing to jack the mayor on this and go after the case? Both cases?"

Hong turned to look at LaPlace, who shrugged. "We're not stupid, Frank. If it gets too scorched, we can always back off and pull out, can't we? None of us wants to get killed."

"Maybe," Carlucci said. "That's what I keep telling myself with this other case. But we can make mistakes."

No one spoke for a while. There was a strange tension in the air, a feeling they were on the edge. If they went ahead with the two cases, they would remain on the edge, an edge that would get narrower, and sharper.

"Ruben," LaPlace said, breaking the silence. "He's the one who buried this other case, isn't he? He's looked like shit for almost a month."

Carlucci didn't answer. He didn't really need to.

"I don't want to tank anything," Hong said.

LaPlace breathed in deeply once, then slowly let it out and nodded. "I'm with Joseph."

Carlucci sat thinking. He didn't want to back away from any of this either, but he was afraid of what they were letting themselves in for. They still didn't know what was at stake here, so it was hard to guess how far the mayor and whoever else would be willing to go.

"All right," Carlucci said. "I'll bring you in on this other case. I'll tell you all about it, I'll let you know everything I find out, and I'll ask for your advice, your judgment. But I've got to keep digging into it on my own. Just me. With the mayor's nephew, all three of us are *supposed* to be working on it. This other case is supposed to be buried. *Nobody* should be looking at it. If all three of us start screwing around with it, somebody's going to notice something. I've got to stay solo on it."

Hong and LaPlace looked at each other, then both briefly nodded and turned back to Carlucci. "We're in," Hong said. He took out one more cigarette and lit it. "So tell us about this other murder."

"All right." Carlucci ran his hand through his hair. "Just some guy," he began, recalling Ruben Santos's words: "Some part-time rocker, petty thief, ex-junkie. His name was Chick Roberts."

17

MIXER'S ARM WAS on fire. He twisted his body, tried opening his eyes, but they seemed welded shut. Red and orange flares erupted behind his eyes—the flames consuming his arm? Mixer opened his mouth, tried to cry out, but no sound emerged.

Then he felt something cool and wet on his forehead, cool fingers brushing at his face, something pressed against his neck. A patch? Finally, a whisper in his ear.

"Sssssshhhh, ssssshhhhh. You're fine, Minor Danzig, you're just fine. Now sleep."

Mixer thought he could feel the sleep pulsing into him, into his neck, and he had no choice, and it was fine with him; he had no objections at all. . . .

The next time he woke, his arm was still on fire, but it wasn't so bad. There was other pain, though, in his face, his back, a tremendous pounding in his head. He still couldn't open his eyes. His mouth, too, was stuck closed, but he managed to pry his lips apart. A short, harsh, coughing sound, scratching at his throat. He tried swallowing, tried again, finally got it. Then, "Is . . . is anyone th-th—?" Another cough.

"Sssshhhh, Minor Danzig." The same voice as before.

Cool, dry lips were pressed to his forehead, his cheek, his lips. His right arm was aflame, impossible to move, but his left was free and he moved it, brought it up near his face. The lips pulled back, but his hand met hair, an ear, soft skin. Then other fingers locked with his.

"Soon, Minor Danzig." Was that St. Katherine's voice? "You are healing well."

"My . . . eyes," he whispered.

"Your eyes are fine. The lids were badly burned. They're healing now. Tomorrow the bandages come off." The fingers squeezed his, massaging, reassuring. "Tomorrow you will see."

"My arm," he said.

There was a long silence, another squeeze of fingers. "Your arm," the woman's voice said. "Tomorrow you will see."

He woke again. Everything seemed darker, quieter. Night? Strangely, he was almost completely without pain. Even stranger, he was afraid. The world seemed to have disappeared.

"Saint Katherine?" He barely managed a whisper. "Saint Katherine?" Louder this time. Then, one final time, straining. "Saint Katherine?" He reached out with his left hand, moved it from side to side, feeling nothing, panic ratcheting up inside him. "Where are you?"

Then he heard a rustling, felt fingers taking his hand again, *two* hands taking his.

"I'm here," she said, voice sleepy. "It's all right, I'm here."

Mixer sank back, relaxing, the panic sliding away.

He felt a patch being pressed against his neck. "I . . ." he started, then forgot what he wanted to say. He squeezed the fingers holding him. Everything was fine.

Awake once more. The pain back, but easier now. St. Katherine at his side—he was certain now that it was she. The bandages still covered his eyes, but he saw a bright flash of light through them. A few moments later he heard thunder crash and roll, shaking glass. Then he noticed the sound of rain, heavy and steady.

"Hot thunderstorm," St. Katherine said. "It's pouring outside." A slight pause. A sliding sound, the room growing dimmer still. "Now, keep your eyes closed, let me take off the bandage."

She raised his head with one hand, worked at the bandage with the other. Mixer fought the urge to open his eyes, kept them shut until he felt the last of the bandage come away, the air cool and soothing on his eyelids.

"Beautiful," St. Katherine said. "They've healed beautifully. Go ahead, Minor Danzig. Open your eyes."

Mixer did, blinking. The light in the room was dim, a heavily shaded lamp in the corner. Window blinds closed.

The room was small, sparsely furnished. His bed, medical equipment, two small tables, two chairs. Bare walls that hadn't been painted in years. The only person in the room was St. Katherine, standing on his left. She was just as beautiful as he remembered.

He looked at his right arm and hand. He expected them to be heavily bandaged, but he couldn't be sure—plain white cloth was tented over them. The arm felt heavy. He could just see a patch of metal around his shoulder. The exo?

Mixer turned to St. Katherine. "My arm," he said.

St. Katherine stood, came around the bed to the other side. "We did everything we could," she said. "We saved it. Remember that, Minor Danzig. We saved it." She lifted the tented cloth, revealing his arm.

Mixer's arm was a confused mash of metal and scarred flesh and a few small, still-healing sections of raw skin. He could not believe that it didn't hurt more than it did, and he wondered what they'd pumped into him to keep the pain bearable.

"The exoskeleton fused to the arm," St. Katherine said. "To the skin, the muscle, in some places even the bone. Impossible to remove it without taking too much of the arm with it. Maybe up in New Hong Kong or some rich hospital they could do something else, but not here."

Mixer tried to lift the arm, managed it a few inches. Tried flexing his fingers, strange digits of metal and flesh. They, too, moved slightly.

"We had a choice med-tech work on the arm, the exo. You'll have movement, fingers, wrist, elbow, but it will be restricted." She reached for his face, turned it gently toward her own and gazed into his eyes. "A stiff, awkward arm, Minor Danzig, but you still have it."

Mixer lowered the arm, his shoulder exhausted from the effort of holding it up, and smiled at St. Katherine. "Got no complaints about the arm," he said. "Looks pretty fucking rabid to me."

She cocked her head, not quite smiling. "Is that good?"

Mixer gave a short laugh and closed his eyes. "Yes, that's good."

"How long has it been?" Mixer asked later that day.

"More than a week," St. Katherine replied. She handed him a strawed glass of ice water. Mixer held it in his left hand, got the straw in his mouth, and sucked hard. He was so thirsty, constantly thirsty. A med tech had come in and taken out the IV's and catheter. Solid food was on its way, St. Katherine promised.

"We kept you completely sedated to aid the healing, and to let us work on the arm."

"Why did you save me?" Mixer asked. "Why didn't you just let me die?"

St. Katherine turned away, and didn't speak for a long time. When she turned back around, there were tears in her eyes. Real tears, Mixer realized. Which made him feel strange.

"Because you survived the trial," she finally said. "Because you broke the Wheel. And because I love you."

Mixer slept, woke, slept some more. During his waking periods he began moving about, working out the stiffness in his limbs, his neck, everything. He ate and drank, used the toilet across the hall from his room. He stood at the barred window and looked out at the Tenderloin, the alleys and streets six or seven floors below him; at night there were drum fires in the alley, flames casting shadows up the building walls. Off to the right, he could just see the edge of the Core, the four square blocks of hell in the center of the Tenderloin, which reminded him of Sookie again. She'd had metal fused to her own arms and legs by the Chain Killer before he'd murdered her. The pain came and went, and he asked St. Katherine to cut back on the meds. She did.

There was no mirror in the room, no mirror in the bathroom, and he finally asked for one. His vague reflection in the window looked wrong, somehow. When St. Katherine brought him into a larger bathroom one floor below, with a large mirror above the sink, he saw why.

The spikes were gone from his forehead, burned and melted away; scarred, nearly smooth flesh remained behind. His eyebrows were just now growing back, stiff and coarse. Beard and moustache, too, had begun. His hair was uneven, stuck out from his head.

"I like the look," he said. And he did. He looked like someone else, which matched the way he felt.

"That's good," St. Katherine said, standing beside him. "Better if you are not recognizable."

"Why?"

They looked at each other's images in the mirror, reflected gazes meeting.

"Because you're dead."

They sat at the table of a small kitchen on the same floor as the larger bathroom. St. Lucy served coffee and joined them.

"Saint Lucy is my primary adviser," St. Katherine said. "Also our medical expert."

Mixer stared into St. Lucy's eyes. A stunning, deep blue, unlike anything he had seen before. "Are your eyes real?" he asked.

St. Lucy smiled softly. "Yes, they're real. They're not the eyes I was born with, but they're real." Her smile faded. "They're New Hong Kong eyes."

There was something pained in her voice, in her expression, and Mixer knew better than to ask any more about it. He turned back to St. Katherine.

"So why am I supposed to be dead?"

"We made . . . an announcement. Over the nets. You died a martyr. Something like a Saint yourself." She looked away, apparently uncomfortable. "A great trial, providing us with profound revelations."

"Why?" Mixer asked again.

"For your protection," St. Lucy said.

"We did something terrible," St. Katherine said, still not looking at him. "*I* did something terrible."

"It was a joint decision," St. Lucy put in.

St. Katherine shook her head. "You advised against it. *My* responsibility." She finally looked back at Mixer. "I came looking for you, Minor Danzig. For the trial. I came looking for *you*." She laughed harshly. "I entered into a contract, a contract of the damned. For money and . . . other considerations, I agreed to find *you* for my next trial. You were expected to go the way of all the others. You were to die, or lose your mind." The tears reappeared, welling in her eyes. "You did neither, Minor Danzig."

Mixer didn't know what to say. He looked back and forth between the two women. "Why do you call me Minor Danzig?" Not the question he really wanted to ask. "It's the name I was born with," he said, looking into St. Lucy's incredible blue eyes. "But it's not my name any longer. My name is Mixer."

"You've been reborn," St. Lucy said, smiling again. "It's only right that you reclaim the name you were given at birth." Then she gave a brief, graceful shrug. "You will need a new name, when you go out into the world again."

St. Lucy glanced at St. Katherine, then got up from the chair and walked out of the kitchen, leaving the two of them alone.

"Who wanted me dead?" Mixer asked.

St. Katherine wiped tears from her eyes. "I'm confused," she said, shaking her head, not quite looking at him. "I sacrificed my principles . . . no, not sacrificed. Sold them, for money and other things." She now looked directly at him. "But doing that brought me *you*, one who has broken the Wheel and passed the trial. The first, the only one ever. The one man proven worthy to be my consort. Selling out my principles brought you to me, so perhaps it was meant for me to do, perhaps it was the right thing, perhaps I was guided."

Mixer just shook his head. He finished his coffee, got up, and refilled his cup from the glass carafe on the stove.

"Perhaps . . ." St. Katherine said.

"No," Mixer said. "It was wrong. I think *all* your goddamn 'trials' are wrong. Murder, is what they are. You believe it's your calling; well, that's for you to figure out. But doing what you did to me, for money, contracting out, even for you it was wrong. Doesn't matter how it all turned out. Blasphemy, babe."

He stood with his hip against the counter, watching her. He held the coffee in his left hand, though it was awkward. His right arm was too heavy, and still hurt. St. Katherine remained silent a long time, returning his gaze. Finally she nodded.

"You're right, Minor Danzig. It was blasphemy, and I'll have to atone for that."

"Who wanted me dead?" he asked again.

St. Katherine sat up straighter in the chair, more confident and self-assured. Back to normal, Mixer thought. Was that good? She gave him a half smile.

"A woman named Aster," she said. "But she's not important, she was just a courier. She was working for someone else."

"Who?"

"She wouldn't tell us. What we did may have been blasphemous, but we didn't do it stupidly. Lucy and I weren't about to take the risk without knowing who was buying us." She finished her own coffee and joined Mixer by the stove, refilling her cup and emptying the carafe. "Wasn't easy tracing her, but we have hot demon resources. Angelic demons, of course," she said, smiling. "Took us nearly three days, but we found it."

"*Who?*"

"The trace led back to two sources," St. Katherine said. "First, the mayor of this great city, the Honorable Terrance Kashen. And then, through him, we were fairly certain, to New Hong Kong."

Jesus Christ, Mixer thought. The mayor. The New Hong Kong connection didn't surprise him; there had been hints from Chick before he got himself killed. But the mayor. Fuck these people. What the hell was going on?

"Do you know why?" Mixer asked.

St. Katherine shook her head. "We never got even a hint."

Mixer sighed deeply. "So, you were paid to kill me, and when I didn't die, when my brains didn't get scorched, you covered your asses and put out the word that I was dead."

"No," St. Katherine said, firmly shaking her head. "We could have let you die, and then it would have been the truth. We saved your life. You would have died without medical help. Lucy said it. We did it for your protection. So the mayor or whoever else won't come after you again."

"And you announced it over the nets."

"Yes."

He thought about Paula and Carlucci, Tia and Miklos and Amy, other people he knew, some friends, some not. They all must now think he was dead.

"Who knows I'm still alive?"

"Saint Lucy and I. The doctor, who is my sister. And the techs, but they don't know who you are. The other Saints and all the novitiates think you're dead. You *looked* dead when we carried you away."

Mixer shook his head. "But I'm supposed to be your consort now, right? I survived the trial. So how does that happen if I'm dead?"

A wry smile crossed St. Katherine's face. "I haven't worked that out yet."

Mixer looked out the small kitchen window. They were still several floors above the street. The day was bright and hazy, the sun glaring down through the sick mustard sky. What the hell was he going to do?

"I love you," St. Katherine said.

Mixer turned back to her, remembering now that she'd said it once before. "You don't even know me."

She smiled. "It doesn't matter. Besides, I *do* know you. I've been at your side for days, nursing you, watching you, talking to you, even when you couldn't hear me. I know you, Minor Danzig. And I do love you."

Mixer studied her face, looked into her eyes, and realized it was true. In her own way, whatever that was, whatever that meant to her, St. Katherine loved him. He thought it should frighten him, or repulse him, but for some reason it didn't. Mostly he felt uneasy, a little confused. He remembered thinking as he was strapped to the wheel that he could fall in love with someone who looked like her. She was still stunningly beautiful, and there was something compelling about her, the way she was with him. But she had tried to kill him. She had saved him, but she had nearly killed him. Could he ever care for someone who had done that to him? Someone as crazy as St. Katherine? He didn't know, and that disturbed him as much as anything else.

"Am I a prisoner here?" he asked.

"Of course not," she replied. "But you're still healing, you don't have much strength." She paused. "And it's going to be dangerous for you. It would help if the beard were longer."

"People think I'm dead. My friends think I'm dead."

St. Katherine nodded. "And you had better be certain who your friends are, and careful who you see." She paused. "Stay a few more days, Minor Danzig. Rest, and be cautious."

Mixer nodded. "I'll stay. And don't worry, I'll be careful." He smiled. "I've already died once. I don't want to do it again any sooner than I have to."

18

PAULA WAS FEELING reckless. Chick was dead, Mixer was dead, why not go all-fire? She was still uncertain about Tremaine, and she wanted to get away from that as well. Fuck Jenny Woo and the Saints and whoever killed Chick, fuck 'em all. Jenny Woo had thought Paula was following her? Fine, she'd do it for real, see if she couldn't find out what the hell was going on.

She thought about calling Carlucci and letting him know what she was doing, but he'd just try to talk her out of it, and she didn't want to be talked out of anything right now. Instead, Paula left a message for Bonita, canceling another Black Angels gig that night, and headed for the Tenderloin.

Paula had her own ways into the Tenderloin, at least one into each of the Quarters. Two—into the Euro and Arab Quarters—were expensive and unpleasant, and she avoided them. Her two ways into the Asian Quarter would take her right into the heart of where she wanted to be, but would be a hell of a lot more likely to alert Jenny Woo. The Latin Quarter was too far away, so she decided on the Afram.

The sun was setting, streaking dark, heavy incoming clouds with deep orange and red, and the heat of the day still shimmered in the air, baking up from the street and off the dark brick and stone and concrete all around her. It was probably going to rain sometime tonight; Paula could feel it weighing down on her.

She walked to the farthest reach of the Polk Corridor, then crossed into the DMZ between the Polk and the Tenderloin. DMZ was a bad name for the strip. After dark it got crazy, and by midnight was more of a free-fire zone than anything else. Now it was marginal, lights coming on and going off in windows, street traffic noisy and snarled, sidewalks jammed. Paula felt probing hands and fingers when she was bumped, saw crazed eyes staring at her, smelled panic and desperation in the air. A Black Rhino thundered down the street, clearing traffic as it ground up the pavement in its path, smashing vehicles aside. Paula leaped into the empty street in its wake, just in front of a pack of trailing Tick-Birds, ran behind it for a block, then cut up toward the Tenderloin, only two blocks from the Nairobi Cafe, her way in. She hurried along the two blocks, nervous energy pushing her close to a run. She'd have to settle down or she'd drive herself crazy.

She stopped across the street from the Nairobi Cafe, looking at the windows filled with lush tropical trees and plants and birds. A huge boa constrictor was wrapped around one of the trees, two feet of tail end dangling from a branch; a large, pop-eyed green lizard sat below the boa, flicking its tongue, eyes shifting with jerky movements. Paula crossed the street and pushed through the front door, still walking way too fast.

She was more than halfway to the rear of the cafe when she realized something was wrong. People turned to stare at her, and the noise level dropped, though the place didn't actually go silent. As she walked among the tables, she realized she was the only white person in the place.

The Nairobi customers were always mostly black, but never exclusively, and though she'd never seen any Asians in the place, there were always whites, usually a few Latinos. Neither, right now. Blacks at every table, at the bar, a lot of them looking at her. Shit. Shockley's Raiders had re-formed recently, pounding around the city, making things jittery again. She'd bet they'd made some hit in the last day or two that she hadn't heard about. Shit.

Paula kept going. No one tried to stop her. Maybe it wasn't smart, but she was already closer to the back than the front. When she reached the end of the bar, she walked around it and into the short hall leading to the bathrooms. She passed the women's room, the men's room, then hesitated before the curtained doorway at the end of the hall. Fuck it. Paula pulled the curtain aside and walked through.

The room in back was small and dark. Orange lamps in the corners, a few chairs, a desk with a computer. A big-boned man sat at the desk, staring at her. A woman sat in one of the chairs, smoking a cigarette.

Paula walked up to the desk, laid down two twenties, and said, "Paula Asgard." Her voice sounded perfectly calm, which surprised her.

"Your money's no good here, white girl." The man behind the desk made no move toward the money or the keyboard. "*You* are no good here."

"Paula Asgard," she said again, pointing at the computer. "I'm in there."

The man behind the desk shook his head. "Nobody white is in there," he said. "You pick up that money now, and go back out the way you came in."

Paula still had too much nervous energy, pumped up now with adrenaline, and it made her stubborn. And maybe stupid, but she didn't care. Her heart was beating hard, but she didn't care about that, either.

"Samuel Eko is a friend of mine," she said. "You call him upstairs, tell him I'm here."

"He's not your friend anymore, sugar," the woman said.

Paula turned to her. "Yes, he is. Samuel will always be my friend." She swung back to the man behind the desk. "You call him."

There was a long silence, no one moving. Finally the man behind the desk stood. "Wait," was all he said; and then he went out through the curtain.

Paula remained standing in the middle of the room, hands in jacket pockets, right hand gripping the hilt of the gravity knife. She kept her gaze straight ahead, at the unoccupied desk.

The woman put out her cigarette, gave a short laugh, then lit another. "You've got balls, sugar. Too bad you're about to get them cut off."

Paula didn't respond. She thought of Samuel Eko, hoping he was upstairs, reachable. She had known Samuel even longer than she'd known Chick. His sister, Angie, had been the percussionist in Heatseeker, the first all-woman band Paula had joined. When Angie had been killed, Paula and Samuel had become close friends, sharing their grief.

The curtain was pulled aside and Paula turned to see the big-boned man come into the room with Samuel Eko right behind him. Samuel was a tall man, well over six feet, almost thin, and one of the darkest men Paula had ever known. He approached her, smiling, and put his long arms around her. Paula hugged him back.

"Let's go," Samuel said. With one arm over her shoulder, he led the way to the door in the back corner of the room. He opened the door, and stepped back to let Paula go first.

"So long, sugar," the woman said.

Paula entered the passage, which led to the Afram Quarter proper, and Samuel Eko followed, shutting the door behind them. The passage was long and narrow, with an occasional door on one side or the other, and lit by bare incandescents spaced every twenty feet.

"You're a crazy woman," Samuel Eko said.

"Probably," Paula replied. "What did I miss? Something with Shockley's Raiders?"

Samuel nodded. They walked side by side, little space between them; Samuel had to duck at each light.

"They burned down an apartment building on Fillmore this morning. Killed eleven people."

"*That's* what the smoke was." She'd seen it from her apartment when she got up; smelled it, even.

"Same old shit."

They reached the end of the passage and Samuel pushed the door open. They stepped out into the Tenderloin, the sky now dark above the buildings, no stars visible through the thick clouds.

"Where you headed?" Samuel asked. They stood on the sidewalk, and Paula was certain that people on the streets were staring at them.

"The Asian Quarter."

"Why didn't you just go in there?"

"I should have."

"I'd better go with you," Samuel said.

Paula laughed. "Yeah, you'd better." It was only a few blocks, but Paula didn't want to do it alone. The streets didn't look much different from the Nairobi; Paula saw only one other white, a man walking with two black men. A real different feel from what she was used to here. They started walking.

"Sometimes I think we're never, absolutely *never*, going to get along," he said.

"Who?"

"Whites and blacks. Asians and blacks. *Anyone* and blacks. Hell, anyone with anyone else. Every time things seem to get better for a while, something like this happens. Two years ago it was the crucifixions on the Marina Green. Before that, it was those black crazies burning down all those Cambodian houses and stores. Five years ago it was the Tundra riots and the Mission fires. It's always something."

They stopped at an intersection, waiting for a traffic knot to unsnarl. All-percussion music was coming from a bar just down the street; the strong smell of spiced coffee made Paula want to stop at Kit's, a sidewalk cafe next to the bar, and have coffee with Samuel, but she knew it was impossible. Traffic cleared, and they crossed the street.

"You know my father came from the Sudan," Samuel Eko said.

"Yes," Paula replied. "And he met and fell in love with a Namibian beauty who made him the happiest man alive, who became his wife and the mother of his three sons and two daughters."

Samuel shook his head. "And I'm the only child of his still alive. Sometimes I think I'd like to go back to the Sudan. A simpler life."

"Starvation's always a simpler life," Paula said. "That doesn't make it better."

Samuel shrugged. "I know. I know it's fantasy. But I tell you, Paula Asgard, sometimes I need a little fantasy just to get through the day."

"I understand, Samuel."

They approached the Asian-Afram boundary. Most of the Quarters merged gradually into one another, with transitional areas of a block or two. Not here, though. The demarcation was sharp and obvious, as if a line had been painted in the street. Paula half expected to see checkpoints, with armed border guards. Maybe someday.

They stopped at the boundary and Samuel hugged her again. "Take care, Paula. You're rooting around in something risky, I can tell."

"Yeah? You a psychic, now?"

Samuel smiled. "You've got the feel."

"I'll be careful, Samuel."

"And, Paula? Best if you don't come back to the Afram Quarter for a while. Maybe a long while."

Paula breathed deeply, and nodded. "Goodbye, Samuel." She turned and strode into the Asian Quarter night.

Paula was more at ease on the streets of the Asian Quarter, and within minutes of saying goodbye to Samuel Eko she felt almost normal again, though still keyed up. As always, the streets and sidewalks were crowded, the vehicles hardly moving faster than people on foot. It was so bright that only by looking up, through the message streamers and strings of light, up past the balconies and hanging plants and signs, only by staring up at the dark and heavy clouds overhead, could she convince herself that it was night and not midday.

It took her four hours to find Jenny Woo, and then Paula almost walked right into her. First, Paula had tried Jenny's apartment above Hiep Quan's Tattoo Heaven, then a couple of nearby clubs, then the Foil Arcade, followed by run-throughs at a dozen sleazy bars and pits, finishing up at Master Hawk's Orgone Parlor. No Jenny Woo. She went back to Hiep Quan's, and almost walked into Jenny as she came out the door next to the shop.

Paula spun around and walked quickly away and into the crowd moving along the sidewalk, not looking back, then swung around the corner and pressed herself against the building wall.

Paula worked her way back to the corner, came around it, and looked toward Hiep Quan's. Jenny Woo wasn't in sight. She must have gone the other way. Paula pushed out into the crowd and hurried through it, searching for Jenny.

A pocket of foil dealers surrounded her, scattered when she growled at them. Club barkers reached for her, gesturing into shifting lights and dark shadows. A rat pack streamed past, keeping to the gutter, the leader chanting. Paula squeezed between people, jostled others, sidestepped a quartet of gooners.

Half a block ahead, she saw Jenny Woo dart into the street, zigzagging through traffic, shoving her way through two pop-sellers to reach the opposite sidewalk. Paula hurried forward, but stayed on this side of the road. Another block, and Jenny turned the corner, forcing Paula to cross the street. But she caught a light, used the crosswalk, and almost immediately picked her up again.

Two more blocks, another turn, and they were edging the Core, which made Paula nervous. She had to stay further back, because the crowds had thinned, and now they were moving along an alley half a block from the Core itself. Twice, when she crossed another alley, she could see the ruins of the Core over the barriers: the quiet, collapsing buildings, the crumbling brick and twisted metal, the broken glass and the dark holes. She shivered despite the warmth of the night.

Ahead, Jenny Woo ducked through a doorway. Paula stopped for a minute, then slowly moved forward, past plated-over windows, bricked-in doorways, until she reached the spot where Jenny had disappeared. A deep alcove, and an unmarked, heavy wooden door. Paula was feeling reckless, but she didn't feel stupid. She didn't try the door. Instead, she backed away, and looked around the alley, searching for a place where she could hole up and watch the doorway.

There was none, so she had to retreat to the end of the alley and the street. She stationed herself at the corner of the building across the alley, which gave her a view not only of the doorway, but of the Core barrier and the upper reaches of the Core itself, half a block away. She kept her hands in her jacket pockets; the feel of the gravity knife didn't give her much comfort.

Paula knew she was safe, but part of her kept imagining some subhuman monster emerging from the Core, clearing the barrier and sweeping down on her, capturing her and hauling her back over the barrier and into the depths of the Core, where unimaginable things would be done to her. She'd never been in the Core, didn't know anyone who had, but the stories were always there, too damn many for all of them to be false.

The side of the building across the alley seemed to open up, a huge section of metal and brick and wood sliding to the side with a tremendous rumble and creaking. A van worked its way out of the opening, shifting back and forth twice before it could get into the narrow alley, pointed toward Paula. Once it was clear of the opening, the section of wall slid back into place. The van came slowly up the alley, with just enough side clearance to allow people to press up against the building walls on either side of it. Paula hung back and watched the unmarked van. As it neared, she recognized the driver—Jenny Woo. Paula pulled back farther, back into the crowd. The van inched out of the alley, then forced its way into the slow traffic and moved down the street, headed away from the Core. Paula followed.

Following the van was almost easier than following Jenny Woo on foot had been. Paula could stay farther back and still keep the van in sight, and in the crowded streets of the Asian Quarter the van didn't make any better time than Paula did. It was only two in the morning, so the sidewalks were still jammed, and sometimes she had to push her way through knots of people, but it wasn't much of a problem.

Just five blocks from the alley, near the fringes of the Asian Quarter and along the perimeter of the Tenderloin, the van pulled off the road and dipped down a concrete ramp leading to the basement level of a brick building. Paula ran forward, then cautiously leaned over a pipe railing to look down. A wide metal door rolled up into the wall, and when there was just enough room, the van shot forward and into shadowed darkness. The door immediately reversed direction, and seconds later clanged shut.

Paula had lost Jenny Woo. The van would emerge from the other side of the building, *outside* the Tenderloin, and there was no way Paula could get to one of the Tenderloin exits she knew and get out to catch the van as it appeared. Even if she could, outside the Tenderloin she'd never be able to follow on foot.

A hand gripped her shoulder. Paula spun around and pulled away in one motion, hand going into her jacket and pulling out the gravity knife, charging it with a squeeze.

It was Tremaine.

Her heart was pounding, and strange feelings swirled around in her stomach. She didn't know what the hell to think or feel.

"I wasn't following you," Tremaine said.

Paula wasn't sure whether or not she believed him.

"We're both following the same person," he added.

"Who?" she asked, still not sure.

"Jenny Woo."

"Then we've both lost the same person."

Tremaine shook his head. "Not if we move now. I know where she's coming out. Are you with me?"

A bang decision. Why not? She had nothing to lose, did she? "Sure," Paula said. She cut the knife's charge and tucked it back into her jacket pocket.

Tremaine had a way out of the Tenderloin in the building next door, through a bubble courier office and a travel agency. His battered Plymouth was parked at the curb just a few feet away. Half a block down, Paula could see the van coming up another ramp, then turning away from them and heading down the street. The night was much darker outside the Tenderloin, the streets nearly deserted.

Tremaine seemed to be in no hurry. "I'm pretty sure I know where she's headed," he said. He unlocked the passenger door for Paula, then got in the driver's side, started the engine, and pulled out into the street. Two blocks ahead, the taillights of the van turned a corner and were gone from sight.

"So where's she going?" Paula asked.

"Hunter's Point."

The spaceport. Which almost certainly meant New Hong Kong. "She going up herself?" Paula asked. "Or delivering?"

"Delivering."

"Delivering what?"

Tremaine gave Paula a half smile without looking at her. "I don't know everything."

They turned briefly onto Market, then swung onto Fourth. The Marriott was a blaze of colored lights, surrounded by security guards and the shimmer of portable Kronenhauer Fields. But just past it, long abandoned, was Moscone Center, a low, dark shadow on their left, broken windows reflecting jagged strips of light. Paula thought she could still see the taillights of the van ahead of them, but she wasn't sure.

"What *do* you know?" she asked.

Tremaine didn't answer immediately. Rain started falling, light at first. Tremaine raised the windows, leaving small gaps for fresh air. They drove under the freeway, barrel fires burning against the concrete supports. The roadway was cracked and potholed, and the Plymouth bounced and creaked across it. When they emerged from under the freeway, the rain was a torrent.

"Before we talk about that," Tremaine said, "I want to be clear about something. The other night, what I did, what *we* did, had nothing to do with this." He looked at her a moment, then returned his attention to the road. "That was personal, not business. That was between you and me, and nothing to do with my story, or Chick Roberts." He twisted his head and neck and Paula could hear bones cracking, like knuckles. "I'm not saying this very well, am I? I'm having a lot of trouble with this." He glanced at her again, then looked away. "I like you, Paula. I think I like you a lot, and I want to spend more time with you, so I don't want you to think that all that the other night was just trying to get to you about this story."

They were crossing Mission Creek now, and Paula could smell the stench of stagnant water through the narrow openings in the windows. She wanted to believe him. Of *course* she wanted to believe him. And, she guessed, she mostly did.

"Okay," she said. But she didn't know what else to say.

They drove along slowly, in silence. Dark warehouses, small, low buildings on either side, a few street lights, everything streaked with the heavy rain. More barrel fires under shelter. Paula hoped the Plymouth was in good shape; this wasn't a part of the city she wanted to break down in.

"Then tell me," she said to him. "What *is* all this about?"

Tremaine shook his head. "You won't like this, but I can't really say much about it. It's a story I'm working on. I don't talk about my stories, not until they're done. It's pretty much all one way. I ask a lot of questions, but I don't answer many. I want to ask you about Chick Roberts. You can talk to me about him or not. I can tell you a few things, but you won't think it's enough."

"Tell me what you can, then," Paula said.

"Will you talk to me about Chick?"

"I don't know." She was lying. She would tell Tremaine what little she knew, but she didn't want him to know that yet.

Tremaine nodded once. He slowed, swung around a huge pothole, then picked up speed. They crossed water again, Islais Creek Channel. Two enormous ships were docked nearby, and their lights reflected like flashing, multicolored scales off the water. Paula wondered what it would be like to board one of those freighters and head out onto the open sea.

Tremaine took a hard left, and Paula looked ahead. There were no taillights, no signs of the van. "Did we lose her?"

"No. I'm taking a different way in. Too easy to be spotted following her this time of night."

There were small houses on either side now, interspersed among warehouses and other commercial buildings. Almost everything was dark. Then suddenly, as they got closer to the spaceport, more lights appeared, on the street and in buildings, and people were out. Shops were open, and the sound of machinery grew louder. Trucks and vans and cars moved along the road.

At the gates to Hunter's Point proper, Tremaine showed the guards a pass, and they let the car through. Just ahead, moving slowly in and out of the bright cones of light from overhead lamps, was Jenny Woo's van. The rain stopped, like a dam closing, leaving a bright sheen on the ground and dripping from all the vehicles around them.

"There it is," Paula said.

Tremaine nodded. He didn't follow the van. He swung around the perimeter of the large parking lot, then drove along the high, shielded fence. Paula kept her gaze on the van, which approached another gate, this one in the shielded fence and leading out onto the tarmac.

"We'd never get through the gate," Tremaine said. He pulled the Plymouth right up to the fence so they were facing the tarmac, turned off the lights, and cut the engine.

Far out on the tarmac, a ship stood in its gantry, outlined by bright lights. Other than that, the tarmac was bare. Paula looked over at the gate. Jenny Woo's van pulled away and drove out across the open pavement. It came to a stop about two hundred feet from the ship.

The ground opened up beside the van, and four people in gray overalls, standing on a platform, rose up from the opening, the platform stopping at ground level. Jenny Woo got out of the van, went around to the back and opened the rear doors. The four people stepped off the platform and began unloading the van.

They unloaded a huge, long crate shaped almost like a coffin, all four of them lifting the crate at the same time, then carrying it to the loading platform. They returned to the van, unloaded a second crate, then two more. Jenny Woo closed the van doors, got back in, and headed back to the gate. The four people and four crates on the platform descended slowly back into the ground, which then closed over them.

"What the hell is in those crates?" Paula asked.

"I don't know," Tremaine said.

She looked at him. "But you have an idea, don't you?"

He nodded. "I think people are in those crates."

"People?"

Tremaine nodded again.

"Alive, or dead?"

"That's the question, isn't it?"

Jenny Woo's van reached the gate, quickly passed through, and headed out of Hunter's Point.

"Are we going to keep following her?" Paula asked.

"No. She'll take the van back to the Tenderloin, then go home." He shrugged. "I have someone here, just outside Hunter's Point, who'll be picking her up in case she doesn't. And someone back in the Tenderloin. But she's done for the night." He paused, staring out at the tarmac. "I need to see what's inside those crates. I've seen the manifests, but they're identified as hydroponic equipment." He looked at Paula, then reached under the seat and pulled out a thermos and a ceramic mug. "Can I buy you a cup of coffee?"

Paula smiled and nodded. "Sure."

Tremaine poured coffee into the mug and handed it to her. Apparently he was going to drink straight from the thermos. Paula sipped at the coffee, which was hot and surprisingly good, though stronger than she liked. She imagined it eating away at her stomach.

"Are we waiting for something?" she asked.

"No. I just want to talk." He drank from the thermos, looked out at the tarmac and the ship again. "There's something happening here, and it's got to do with the recruiting vans, some of them, anyway, and New Hong Kong, and medical research they're doing up there. And there's something to do with the mayor, and the mayor's nephew getting himself killed. And, I'm pretty sure, something to do with Chick."

"I don't know why he was killed," Paula said, shaking her head. "I really don't."

Tremaine nodded. "I thought maybe you didn't. But you might know something, what he was up to, who he was working with, anything like that."

Paula shook her head again. "He was bootlegging body-bags. With Jenny Woo, and Mixer. Some other people I didn't know. But he'd been doing that a long time. And it wasn't something to get killed over."

"Probably not. But something was."

"I don't know. Chick didn't tell me about his 'business dealings,' and I didn't ask. I didn't *want* to know, because I didn't like any of it. Last couple of weeks before he was killed, hell, he didn't seem any different. I hadn't seen too much of him because he had so much going, but Chick did that a lot." She paused, looking at Tremaine. "He'd been fucking Jenny Woo, but that was over, months ago." She sighed, looking out the windshield, sipping her coffee. "Christ, what else? He was always fucking up, and this time it got him shot in the head." She turned back to Tremaine. "Why do *you* think he was killed?"

Tremaine shrugged. "I think he stumbled across something, and whatever it was, I think he was trying to sell it. And someone killed him for it, either the people he was trying to sell it to, or the people he'd taken it from. That's my best guess. I was hoping you'd know more."

Paula leaned back against the seat and closed her eyes, the ache starting up in her chest again. Why had she loved the goddamn fuck-up all these years? Screwing other women until the guilts twisted him up. Periodic bouts of abusing one drug or another. The smoking and the filthy bathroom and kitchen, and the irresponsibility he'd never grown out of.

But Chick had saved all the letters she'd ever written to him. And when she and Chick were together and they were ramped and on, they were something out of this fucking world—on stage, in bed, or just sitting together listening to music with the rain pouring outside. The best times of her life had been spent with Chick.

Paula opened her eyes and sat up, staring out at the tarmac and the gantry. "Take me home," she said.

When the Plymouth pulled in to the curb in front of Paula's apartment building, Tremaine didn't ask to come up, and Paula didn't invite him. They sat for a while in silence, the engine idling.

"Tremaine," Paula said. "What is that, first or last name?"

"Neither," Tremaine said. "Well, that's not true. It *is* my last name, but it's the only name I use on my stories. It's the only name I use anywhere."

"Isn't there something else I can call you? I feel weird calling you Tremaine. If we're going to be spending more time together, there must be something. Like a first name?"

Tremaine smiled. "Yes, there's a first name."

"So what is it?"

"Ian."

Paula smiled back at him. "That's a name that'll do." She got out of the car, closed the door, then stuck her head in through the open window. "Goodbye, Ian. Call me. Or I'll call you."

He nodded. "Goodbye, Paula."

She backed away, and Tremaine put the car in gear and pulled out into the street. Paula was tired, and didn't want to move. She stood on the sidewalk, watching the Plymouth drive away.

A cough sounded behind her, and Paula turned. A figure emerged from the building shadows, left hand outstretched.

"Got a buck, lady?"

The man's voice was harsh and croaking. His hair was ragged, almost choppy, his beard scraggly, and his face was smeared with burn scars between the ragged clumps of hair. The man's right hand was heavily bandaged, and the arm hung awkwardly at his side. He was a wreck, but there was something familiar about him.

With her right hand in her jacket pocket, fingers gripping the gravity knife, Paula dug into her jeans with her other hand, pulled out a couple of bills. A five and a one. She took a couple of steps forward, held out the bills, then set them in the man's outstretched hand. The man's fingers curled around the money; then he nodded and said, "Thanks, lady," and turned away.

The eyes. That was what was so familiar, his eyes. Paula watched the man shuffle down the street. Mixer. They were like Mixer's eyes, she thought, and another ache drove through her chest. Chick and Mixer. Jesus. Paula turned away from the man and climbed the steps to the building's front door.

19

CARLUCCI SAT IN the basement dark, listening to Miles Davis. Soundtrack pieces from an old movie called *Siesta*. He'd watched the movie once, but it was too damn weird for him; the music, though, was great. He watched the pulsing colored lights of the sound system, the shimmer of the street light pooling in through the tiny, high basement window. His trumpet lay on the sofa beside him, untouched for the last hour. All he wanted to do was listen to Miles blow.

The basement door opened, light slashing down the stairs. Christina stood in the doorway, a shadow outlined by the hall light.

"Dad?"

"Yes?"

"Sorry to bother you, but there's someone at the door for you."

"That's all right." He sat forward, blinking. "Who is it?"

"I don't know, she wouldn't say. A woman."

"I'll be right up." He picked up the remote and shut down the system, then climbed the stairs.

On the front porch stood a woman in dark robes, beautiful blue eyes gazing at him. "Frank Carlucci?" she said. Her hair was damp, and Carlucci could see wet sidewalk and street behind her.

"Yes."

"I'm Saint Lucy."

Carlucci looked at her, at her robes, her soft leather boots, her long hair, those stunning blue eyes. She didn't look crazy. "Saint Lucy," he finally repeated.

"Yes," the woman said. "One of the Saints."

"And you want to talk to me."

St. Lucy nodded. "It's about Minor Danzig."

"Who?"

"Sorry. Mixer."

Mixer. Carlucci took a step back. "Come on in. We can talk inside."

St. Lucy shook her head. "No, just come with me, please. Mixer is alive, and he wants to talk to you. I'm to take you to him."

Mixer alive. Was it true? Or just a scam to lure him somewhere? Looking at St. Lucy, he couldn't quite believe she was lying. Which meant nothing, he knew. He also knew that she wouldn't be answering too many questions from him. It was either go with her now, or not.

"Will we be going into the Tenderloin?" he asked.

St. Lucy hesitated a moment, then nodded.

"All right," Carlucci said. "I'll go with you. You want to come inside and wait for a minute? I've got to get a couple things, let my family know I'm going."

"I'll wait here," St. Lucy said.

Carlucci left the front door open. Andrea and Christina, in the kitchen, looked up at him as he came in.

"I've got to go out for a while," he told them. "I have no idea how late I'll be."

"Where's the woman?" Andrea asked.

"Waiting on the porch. She wouldn't come inside." He glanced back through the doorway, but couldn't quite see St. Lucy.

Carlucci went into the bedroom, opened the closet, and took out his shoulder holster; he worked his arms into it, then reached up onto the top shelf for his 9mm Browning, tucked it into the holster. Finally, he put on his slick-skin raincoat.

He returned to the kitchen, kissed Andrea and Christina goodbye, then joined St. Lucy on the front porch, locking the door behind him.

"You want me to drive?" he asked.

"No," she said. "We'll take the streetcar."

Carlucci nodded, then he and St. Lucy stepped down from the porch and headed down the street.

Carlucci never felt quite comfortable in the Tenderloin. He wasn't afraid, he just thought he stood out, that everyone on the street looked at him and knew he was a cop, knew he didn't belong. He *didn't* belong. He'd known cops who did seem to fit into the Tenderloin—Tanner, Koto, Francie Miller— but he wasn't one of them. The last time he'd been inside the Tenderloin was three years ago, when they'd brought out the Chain Killer.

It was sensory overload for Carlucci. The lights, the flashing and sweeping signs, the message streamers swimming through the air, vehicles of all kinds jammed into the roadways, and the swarming mass of people. Most parts of the city were crowded, but there was nothing like this anywhere else.

Carlucci and St. Lucy were in the Euro Quarter, but close to the Asian so that he caught occasional glimpses of a Red Dragon in the air a few blocks away, smoke pouring from its nostrils. Directly above them here in the Euro, tensor wires were strung across the streets from building to building, at the fourth floor and higher. Carlucci watched the flashes of color shooting across them.

St. Lucy took his arm, guided him into a narrow alley that wasn't as crowded as the street. Half a dozen barrel fires were burning, several people clustered around each one. A dogboy crawled past them, barking, the metal

tail wagging through his pants. Parrots squawked from a mass of bromeliads on a landing three floors above. Two squealing girls on bicycles ca-
reened along the alley, bumping against people and the alley walls.

St. Lucy stopped before a wooden door, took a set of keys from inside
the folds of her robes, and unlocked the door. She opened it, stepped quickly
inside, and pressed her hand against a wall plate. She pulled Carlucci in after her, then shut the door and locked it.

They were in a bare entry. St. Lucy led the way down a hall, then up a
stairway. The plaster walls were cracked, covered with a mosaic of paint
and peeling wallpaper. Light came from dim, bare bulbs in ceramic wall
sockets up near the ceiling. On the third floor they left the stairwell, entered
another hall. St. Lucy stopped just outside an open doorway, and gestured
inside. Carlucci approached the doorway and looked in.

Sitting at a table in a small kitchen was a bearded wreck of a man, his
forehead and upper cheeks swirled with burn scars. He was holding a thick
ceramic mug with a hand that was a hideous and fascinating fusion of metal
and flesh. The man raised the mug to his mouth, the movement stiff and unsure, then returned it to the table.

"I'll leave you alone," St. Lucy said. She touched Carlucci's arm, then
walked away, along the hall, down the stairs.

"Hey, Carlucci," the man said.

"Mixer?" There *was* something familiar about the man's voice, something about his face despite the beard and scars.

"Yeah, it's me. Hell of a disguise, isn't it?" He raised his mug. "Want
some coffee?"

Carlucci shook his head. For some reason he was reluctant to enter the
room. "People think you're dead."

Mixer nodded. "Come in and sit down, for Christ's sake. It's not catching."

Carlucci entered the room, walked to the table, and sat across from
Mixer. Close up, he could see it *was* Mixer sitting in front of him; but close
up, Mixer looked even worse. Especially the hand, scarred flesh fused to
metal, both flesh and metal bent and distorted in places they shouldn't be.
Mixer was wearing a long-sleeved shirt, and Carlucci had the impression
the damage extended up along his arm.

"Does Paula know you're alive?"

Mixer shook his head. "Other than Saint Katherine and Saint Lucy, you're
the only one."

"Jesus, Mixer, what the fuck happened?"

Mixer made a sound that might have been some kind of laugh. "The
Saints happened. Saint Katherine, especially." He looked away and breathed
deeply once. "Saint Katherine's Trial. Total burn, man." He held up his right
hand and stared at it, the metal and flesh melted together like cooled lava.

"I was wearing an exoskeleton. It kind of got fused to me." He finally looked back at Carlucci. "But I survived. And I'm alive."

Carlucci nodded. "And you're not a spikehead anymore."

Mixer smiled. "Yeah, how 'bout that?" He got up from the table, took his mug to the stove, and poured himself more coffee. There was an amber bottle beside the stove, and he uncapped it, poured some into the coffee. He turned to Carlucci, holding up the bottle. "How 'bout a drink?"

"What is it?" Not that it mattered, really.

"Bad Scotch."

"Sure," Carlucci said. He noticed that Mixer's right arm now hung limply at his side, and that he had switched to doing everything with his left. Mixer brought his own mug to the table, got another from the cupboard, hooked the handle with his left thumb and grabbed the bottle with fingers and palm, brought mug and bottle to the table, and set them before Carlucci. He poured Scotch into Carlucci's mug, then sat down heavily.

"How bad's the arm?" Carlucci asked.

"Bad," Mixer said. "But it gets better every day. They're trying to replace or repair some of the exo motors so they can help out more." He held the arm up for a moment, then dropped it back to the table. "It's what saved my life apparently."

Mixer left it at that, and Carlucci sipped from the mug. Mixer was right, the Scotch was bad; it burned his lips and tongue. But it also burned going down his throat and into his stomach, and Carlucci thought maybe that was good.

"The Saints announced you were dead." When Mixer nodded, Carlucci said, "Why?"

"They were paid to kill me."

After a long silence, Carlucci again asked, "Why?", meaning something different this time. And then, "Who?"

Mixer gave out the choking laugh sound again. "Yeah, those two questions are tied together, aren't they?" He drank from his coffee, then reached across the table for the Scotch and added more to his mug. "The mayor paid them," he said. "Not directly, of course, but they found out who it was." Mixer shrugged. "Why? I don't know, but I've got an idea."

"Which is?"

Mixer shook his head and drank again before continuing. "I don't really know anything, you gotta understand that. Which is why I never thought I had this kind of trouble. I don't know what it's about. But I can put Chick and the mayor's nephew together. I had connections to both, Chick was a friend, and they're both dead." He shook his head again. "I think maybe somebody decided I know more than I do." Mixer winced, put his hand to his shoulder and rubbed, twisting head and neck.

"You all right?" Carlucci asked.

"Christ, I'm alive. No complaints."

"That's another question," Carlucci said. "Why *are* you still alive?"

Mixer breathed deeply twice. "I survived the trial," he said. "Never happened before. The trial always leaves the accused dead, or a mental washout. I survived."

"But the Saints announced you did die in the trial."

"Most of the Saints think I did. Apparently I looked dead when they hauled me away. Saint Katherine and Saint Lucy are the only ones who know I'm alive. They saved my life. They got a doctor for me, nursed me. Saint Katherine and Saint Lucy saved my life."

"It was Saint Katherine's trial?"

"Right."

"And who took the contract to kill you?"

"Saint Katherine and Saint Lucy," Mixer said, smiling.

"Then why the hell did they save your life?"

"It's complicated." After a long pause, Mixer shook his head. "No, I'm not going to try to explain it. It doesn't matter."

"But they announced that you had died."

Mixer nodded. "For my protection. And theirs. We're all better off if the mayor and his pals think I'm dead."

Carlucci sipped more of the bad Scotch. He needed it. "All right, then. What *do* you know about this?"

Mixer drank, shifted in the chair; he slid his right arm slowly back and forth across the table, making a harsh, scratching noise. "Body-bags, to start with. Chick and I boot-legged them. We were in it with Jenny Woo and Poppy Chandler. The mayor's nephew provided a lot of the big financing."

"Body-bags," Carlucci said, shaking his head. He pictured a man completely wrapped in neural nets, twitching and twitching, eyes rolled back, foam spattering from his mouth. "Nice business," he said.

Mixer looked away, seemed to gaze out the kitchen window. There was nothing outside to be seen except grate-covered windows and crumbling brick across the way. "Yeah," Mixer said, "it's a fucked business. It's what we did." He turned back to Carlucci. "But it's not something to get killed over."

"So what is?"

Mixer shrugged. "Chick had something going with Kashen, or had hooked something from Kashen, I could never be sure. The nephew, not the mayor. Chick didn't talk about it, except to say he'd finally gone nuclear, and was going to make enough money never to have to do a deal again. He was going to retire." Mixer shook his head. "Well, he retired all right."

"And you don't know what he had?"

"No. Something to do with New Hong Kong, something to do with the mayor. It was all messy. Kashen and his uncle, that was a wonky deal, too. Kashen couldn't stand his uncle, but they were connected, they were logged into each other. Kashen was doing something for him, something to do with

New Hong Kong. But the way Kashen talked, he was getting ready to screw over his uncle somehow." Mixer shrugged again. "I think Chick was mixed up in all that. And Chick . . . man, that guy never knew when he was in over his head, and he always was. He wasn't nearly as smart as he thought he was, and it finally got him killed." He raised a ragged eyebrow at Carlucci, a distorted gesture with all the scarring. "*That's* what I know," he said. "Which shouldn't be enough to get me killed, but it just about did." He drank again, then held the mug out toward Carlucci. "I plan to know a hell of a lot more." He lowered his mug, then raised his right arm, rotating it slightly and wincing. "I've already paid for it, and I'm going to know just what the fuck I've paid for."

"How are you going to do that?" Carlucci asked.

"I don't know yet. Saint Katherine and Saint Lucy will help me, and they have a lot of strange contacts. And there's something else. You know who Tremaine is?"

Tremaine again. Carlucci nodded.

"He's digging into this mess," Mixer said. "He's been asking Paula about Chick. I got a feeling he might know more about what's going on than any of us."

Wouldn't be the first time, Carlucci thought. "I think I want to talk to him," Carlucci said.

"Yeah, so do I. Might not be too hard. He's been seeing Paula, I think."

"What do you mean?"

"Like, personally. You know." Mixer gave a harsh laugh. "Like maybe they're slippin' 'n' slidin' between the sheets." He closed his eyes for a few moments, then opened them. "I don't know," he said, somber now. "I think it started, he was asking her about Chick, and something happened between them. Sparks or something."

Sparks. Carlucci hadn't heard from Sparks yet, and he should have by now. If Paula and Tremaine were spending time together, what did that mean? Anything?

"I need to talk to Tremaine," he said to Mixer.

"I'm going to see Paula soon, let her know I'm still alive. I'll let her know you want to talk to him. I'll let her know *I* want to talk to him." He brought the mug to his lips, then looked down into it. "Fuck the coffee." He set the mug down, poured Scotch into it. He looked at Carlucci. "More?"

Carlucci finished off the Scotch in his mug, then held the mug out to Mixer. Mixer poured. "Tell Paula not to mention to Tremaine that I'm looking into Chick's death. Just that it's to do with the mayor's nephew."

"Okay."

They drank a while in silence. Mixer was obviously in pain, but didn't say anything.

"Is there anything you need?" Carlucci eventually asked. "Something I can do for you?"

"No," Mixer said. "What I need you can't give me." He paused, shaking his head. "Shit, I feel like an old man. Not just physically." He raised his right arm and gestured at his head with metal and flesh, not quite touching it with his fingers. "In here, too. I feel older inside."

"Wiser?" Carlucci asked.

Mixer smiled. "No, just older."

Mixer had survived the trial, he was still alive, but Carlucci wondered if he would ever really recover. "Are you all right here?" he asked. "They're not holding you? Against your will?"

"No, I'm fine. I know it sounds weird, but Saint Katherine and Saint Lucy are doing everything they can for me."

It was hard to believe, but Carlucci didn't doubt Mixer. There was a lot more going on here than he understood. He knew that much. He also knew it was time to go.

"Is there anything else?" he asked Mixer.

Mixer shook his head. "This was just about Chick, at first," he said. "That's all. Paula and I wanted to find out who killed him, and why. But there's more now. I want to see this whole fucking thing blown open. I want to know what the fuck is going on, and I want to see people pay. Anything I find out, I'll let you know. I want you to do the same."

Carlucci stood up from the table, shaking his head. "I can't promise that, Mixer."

"I know. Do what you can, though. Yeah?"

Carlucci nodded. "I will." Then, "I've got to go."

"Downstairs, Saint Lucy's waiting. She'll make sure you get out okay."

"If I see Paula before you do . . ."

Mixer shook his head. "Don't tell her you've seen me. I need to do that thing myself."

"All right." Carlucci started to leave, then turned back to Mixer. "Take care of yourself."

Mixer smiled and nodded.

20

MIXER HAD PUT it off for days, but now he finally went by his apartment. It was only a couple of blocks from where he was staying with St. Katherine and St. Lucy, but it seemed much farther; he felt he was walking into the past. He still had his keys—the Saints had saved his things after the trial—and he used them and his code to get into the building. He passed on the elevator and climbed the three flights of stairs to the fourth floor.

He didn't need his keys to get into his apartment. The door was wide open. Christ, he thought, nobody had even bothered to shut the door, not even his neighbors. How long had it been like this? Days? A week?

Inside, nothing. The place had been picked clean. Bits of trash lay on the floor, in the corners, but nothing else. No furniture, no books, no music, no clothes. In the kitchen was some rotting food, but no plates, no pots or pans. Even the refrigerator and stove, which came with the apartment, were gone. He was half surprised no one had ripped the cupboards from the walls and hauled those away.

In the bathroom, too, everything was gone, medicine cabinet cleared out; even the toilet paper had been taken. Mixer sat on the closed lid of the toilet, staring out at the empty apartment. Everything he owned was gone. Vanished. He wondered if it had been the mayor's ferrets who'd cleaned out the place, or scavengers descending on it once word got out that he was dead. Maybe both. It didn't really matter.

New life, he said to himself. St. Lucy was right. No more Mixer. Minor Danzig reborn.

He sat, not moving, trying to imagine what it would be like.

Mixer followed Paula for hours. He wasn't sure why. Afraid to go up to her and tell her he was alive? Everything seemed different, changed; maybe he was afraid *she* had changed, too, changed so much she wouldn't, or couldn't, be his friend anymore. He'd wanted her to be more than a friend, though, after Chick died. Even before that. He'd never been able to tell her. That was all impossible now; he knew that. Probably always had been. Now there was Tremaine, and St. Katherine. Crazy, all of it. He didn't know what he wanted.

He'd picked her up late afternoon coming out of her apartment building and followed her to the Lumiere. He bought a cup of coffee from a window cafe, drank it, then sat down near the corner across from the Lumiere, where he had a view of the entrance. He set the empty cup in front of him and settled in.

Two hours later, when Paula came out of the theater, Mixer had collected several bucks in change. I must look bad, he thought. He pocketed the money, dumped the cup, and took off after Paula, staying half a block back. She went to her apartment, stayed inside for fifteen minutes, then came back out and headed into the heart of the Polk Corridor as the sun was setting.

Paula stopped in front of Christiano's and leaned against the building. Mixer had to hang back, crouched beside a phone box. Looked like she was waiting for someone.

Not for me, Mixer said to himself. Paula thought he was dead. But he wasn't, and he needed to tell her. There was way too much unfinished; there was still Chick between them, and Chick's death, if nothing else.

If nothing else. *Jesus, Mixer, what the hell are you thinking?* He hadn't spoken a word to her, and already he was assuming that everything between them was dead and gone. Maybe the goddamn trial did fry his brain.

Paula *was* waiting for someone. Tremaine, of course. Mixer saw him before Paula did, coming down the sidewalk, wire-rim specs flashing the lights of the night. Mixer rose to his feet to get a better view. If Paula was singing for Tremaine it wasn't because of his looks. That had always been part of it with Chick, Mixer was pretty sure of that. But not with Tremaine.

When Paula saw him, she smiled and pushed off the wall. Mixer hadn't seen her smile like that in years, and it made his chest ache. She and Tremaine spoke to each other, then went into Christiano's.

Mixer felt suddenly hungry, and for more than just food. But food was something he could take care of. He crossed the street, walked past a target alley, and bought a falafel from an old Arab woman cooking on basement steps. As he ate, he wandered up and down the Corridor, never getting too far from Christiano's.

The street seemed to be on downers tonight. The air was heavy with heat and humidity, but it was more than that. People moved like they were in slow motion. Even a string of bone dancers shifted aimlessly along, arms and legs flapping limply. Weed hawkers called out to him, but they weren't trying very hard. The stunner arcade was half empty. The stagnant energy in the Corridor was dragging Mixer down, and he was already more than low enough.

He was only half a block away when he saw Paula and Tremaine come out of Christiano's. They stood for a minute on the sidewalk, looking around, talking, then headed in Mixer's direction. He pulled back into the entryway of a bone-slotting club and turned his face from the street until they had passed him. Then he moved back out onto the sidewalk and followed.

Paula and Tremaine didn't hold hands, or put their arms around each other, or kiss, anything like that, but there was something intimate about the way they walked together—the way Paula leaned her head toward Tremaine to say something, the way Tremaine touched her shoulder, the way he looked and smiled at Paula, and the way she laughed. It all made Mixer feel strange and drifty.

They stopped and looked in the window of a dinkum store, both laughing at something Paula pointed to. Half a block later they stood and watched a kinetic oil painting in the window of an art gallery. When they finally went into a spice and espresso bar, Mixer had had enough. He didn't wait for them. Instead, he turned back and walked in the direction of Paula's apartment.

Three things could happen, he figured. They could both come back to Paula's place; or they could go to Tremaine's; or they could each go their own way. The odds were good Paula would be coming home, one way or another.

Mixer still had keys to her place, more useful now than the ones to his own apartment. He unlocked the main building door, stood in the lobby for a few moments, then climbed the stairs and walked down the hall to her apartment.

He stood in front of her apartment door for a minute, keys in hand. He pocketed the keys. It would be too much for her, he decided. To come home and find a stranger inside her apartment. It would be bad enough to find him sitting in the hall.

Mixer sat on the floor, his back against her door, and waited.

21

PAULA WAS JUST as nervous this time, climbing the stairs to her apartment with Tremaine just behind her, but it was a different kind of anxiety. There was more excitement in it, as well as a stronger, different kind of fear. And, as before, she could not completely stop thinking of Chick.

They reached the third floor, and had just started down the hall when Paula sensed something wrong. She slowed, stared ahead, and saw a shadow, a form in front of her door at the end of the hall.

"What is it?" Tremaine asked.

"I don't know." She continued forward, saw that it was the form of a man; then, as they drew closer, recognized the man who had scrounged money from her the other night. She stopped a few feet from him. "What the hell are you doing here?"

"Don't you recognize me?" the man said. His voice didn't seem as harsh as it had that night. His head was tilted forward and to the side so that she saw mostly hair and beard.

"Yeah, I recognize you. I gave you money the other night, outside. And that's where you should be. Outside."

The man leaned forward and pushed himself slowly to his feet. His right arm, which had been bandaged before, was now bare—metal and scarred flesh twisted and melted together, almost shiny in the hall light. He turned to face her. "You still don't recognize me, Paula?"

His voice. She knew the voice. Paula stared at him, and her heartbeat kicked up, pounding away inside her. And the eyes, she knew those eyes, too. But it couldn't be. He was . . .

"Mixer?"

The man smiled without saying anything.

"Mixer?" she said again. And then she knew it was him, and she ran forward and threw her arms around him, hugging him tightly to her. "Jesus, Mixer, you're alive!"

"Yeah, Paula, I'm alive. But you're killing my arm."

She let him go, looked into his face, feeling the tears pooling up in her eyes, then put her arms around his neck, pressing his bearded face against her skin. "Mixer, I can't fucking believe it." She let go again, wiping her cheeks with the back of her hand, staring into his wrecked face. "Jesus, look at you." She shook her head, looking down at his arm. "Is that the exo?"

Mixer nodded.

"What the hell happened?" Then, "The Saints announced you were dead."

"I am," he said.

Paula didn't know what to say. Then she remembered Tremaine, and she turned around, saw him standing a few feet away. "Ian, this is my friend Mixer. Mixer, this is Tremaine."

"I know who he is," Mixer said. He smiled. "Ian?"

"You can just call me Tremaine."

"I will," Mixer said.

"Come on," Paula said. "Let's go inside where we can sit down and talk."

"I think I should go," Tremaine said.

"Oh, no," Mixer replied, shaking his head. "I need to talk to Paula, but I need to talk to you, too. You're not going anywhere."

Tremaine smiled. "I'm not?"

"No."

"Jesus," Paula said. "What the hell is all this?"

Tremaine shrugged, still smiling. "It's fine. I'm happy to stay. I'd like to know what Mixer wants to talk to me about."

Paula sighed and looked back and forth at the two men, who seemed to be having a good old-fashioned stare-down. She unlocked the door and let them inside, half-tempted to pull the door shut behind the men and lock them in. But she was too damn happy to see Mixer alive, and so she followed them in, turning on the apartment lights.

They all stood silently just inside the door, the kitchen on their left, the piles of Chick's things on their right. Paula waved at the kitchen table. "Sit down, both of you," she said. "Anyone want anything, coffee, tea, something to eat? Mixer?"

Mixer walked over to the table and sat in one of the chairs, laying his injured hand and arm on the table. "I could really use a drink."

Tremaine sat across the table from Mixer, and the two men continued to stare at each other.

"Tremaine?" Paula asked.

"I'll have whatever Mixer's having."

How accommodating, Paula thought. She went to the refrigerator, opened the freezer, and pulled out a bottle of Stolichnaya vodka. She looked at the bottle, her gaze unfocused, the cold seeping into her hand, making it ache. It was the only booze she had in the place; it was what Chick had liked to drink more than anything else. She got two small tumblers from the cupboard, took them to the table with the bottle. "Help yourselves," she said. She went back to the refrigerator and poured herself a glass of orange juice, then joined the two men at the table. Mixer was already draining his glass; he poured another.

"What happened?" Paula asked. "Are you okay?"

"Yeah, yeah, I'm fine," Mixer said, nodding. He laughed. "What happened? I'll tell you." He took a drink, stared into the small glass. "Chick used to drink this stuff, didn't he?" He looked at Paula, who nodded. "Well. I'm sure it'll do the job." He set the glass down, glanced at Tremaine, then turned back to Paula.

"I went to a wham-wham, remember? I'd pumped myself full of neutralizers, and they kept me from caving in to whatever they'd gassed into the place, but they made me a little misted, too, I think. I don't know. I was looking for someone, and I got into a little trouble with two freaks, and someone bailed me out. A woman. I wasn't thinking straight, like why were the two freaks afraid of her? By the time I figured it out, it was too late. She'd collared me, and I was gone."

"Saint Katherine," Paula said.

Mixer nodded. "That was her. There was this and that, a few days, and then the trial." He polished off his vodka, coughed, and poured some more. "Let's just say I survived, and this is what it did to me." He held up his right arm, rotated it. "Still pretty fucking rabid, isn't it?"

"But the Saints announced over the nets that you had died."

Mixer dropped his arm to the table with a thump. "It's complicated. But if I want to stay alive, I'd better stay dead. You can't tell anyone you've seen me, you can't tell anyone you know I'm alive." He turned to Tremaine. "You too."

"I understand," Tremaine said.

"Do you?"

"Who knows you're alive, then?" Paula asked.

"Two of the Saints. The rest think I'm dead. You and Tremaine." He paused, staring at Tremaine. "And Carlucci."

"You've seen him?" Paula asked, wondering why he was looking so intently at Tremaine.

"Last night." Still staring at Tremaine.

"Frank Carlucci?" Tremaine asked.

Mixer nodded. "Yeah, that Carlucci. And he wants to talk to you."

Tremaine smiled. "Really? I've made several interview requests, but I've always been turned down. And now he wants to talk to me. What about?"

"Something about the mayor's nephew. Bill Kashen."

"He thinks I know something about the murder?"

"Apparently."

Paula watched the two men, feeling there was some kind of strange contest in progress, some cat-and-mousing. But what was it all about?

"How do you know Carlucci?" Tremaine asked, glancing back and forth between Paula and Mixer.

Paula didn't say anything, remembering Carlucci's warning. No one was supposed to know he was digging into Chick's murder.

"Remember the Chain Killer a few years ago?" Mixer said.

Tremaine nodded.

"I got mixed up in that whole mess. By accident. I got to know Carlucci through a friend of his."

"Louis Tanner."

Mixer nodded. "That's the guy. See, you always know more than anyone expects. That's why Carlucci wants to talk to you. He knows you've been digging into stuff with the mayor, the mayor's nephew."

There was a long silence, and Paula was still afraid to say anything, afraid to give anything away. She didn't think anything bad would happen if Tremaine knew everything, but she couldn't know for sure. And she had made promises to Carlucci.

"Does Carlucci . . .?" Tremaine paused, as if unsure he should say anything. The reporter, trying not to give away more than he had to. "Does Carlucci know there's a connection between the mayor's nephew's killing, and Chick Roberts's killing?"

"Is there?" Mixer asked.

"I think so."

Mixer shrugged. "He didn't say anything about it. You'll have to ask him."

There was another silence, and Paula felt extremely uncomfortable. She wanted them both to leave.

"I don't suppose," Mixer began, "that you'd be willing to tell me everything you know about all this."

Tremaine shook his head. "Not a chance."

"You wouldn't happen to know why the mayor would want me dead, do you?"

"What?" Paula asked. "What is this?"

"Do you?" Mixer said again.

"No," Tremaine said. "Are you sure he does?"

"Not anymore," Mixer said, smiling. "He thinks it's done." Then, "Would you tell me if you knew?"

Tremaine nodded. "Yes." He paused. "Maybe you and I should talk sometime. Maybe we can help each other."

"Maybe."

Tremaine stood. Paula noticed that he hadn't touched the vodka. "I think I'd better go."

This time Mixer didn't object. He just said, "Don't forget. Carlucci wants to talk to you."

"I won't." Tremaine turned to Paula. "I don't know what to say. This is going to be difficult for a while, I guess. I'll call you soon, all right?"

Paula nodded, relieved that Tremaine was leaving, and feeling guilty about it.

Tremaine walked to the apartment door, opened it, and left, closing the door behind him.

"Are you sleeping with him?" Mixer asked.

"It's none of your fucking business," Paula said, furious with him. "That's the first thing out of your mouth, now that we're alone? I've been thinking you were dead, all these days, and that's what you've got to say to me?"

Mixer looked down at his glass. "Sorry," he said. He poured himself another drink, sucked some of it down. He looked up at Paula. "I *am* sorry, for Christ's sake."

Paula put her head into her hands, rubbing at her eyes. "It's all right." She reached out, took his right hand gently in hers, feeling the metal, the alternately smooth and ridged, scarred flesh. "Are you really okay?"

Mixer nodded. "Yeah."

"What *happened*?" she asked, knowing he hadn't told her everything while Tremaine had been there.

"Saint Katherine was contracted to kill me through her trial," Mixer said. "By Mayor Kashen."

"That's why you asked Tremaine."

"Yeah. Do you believe him? That he doesn't know? That he'd tell me if he did?"

Paula hesitated, feeling awkward. "Yes," she finally said.

"Yeah, I do too." He took a sip of the vodka, twisting his face. "Maybe you get used to this," he said, refilling his glass. "The trial scorched my arm and face instead of my brain, and I'm alive, and most of the time my head's all there. Saint Katherine and Saint Lucy took me away, and I guess I looked dead, because all the other Saints think the trial killed me. Saint Katherine and Saint Lucy took care of me. They brought in a doctor, they stayed with me night and day, Saint Katherine in particular. They saved my life."

"But Saint Katherine was supposed to kill you."

Mixer nodded. "Yeah. But I survived, and she believes I've been chosen. Chosen to be her consort." He paused. "She says she loves me."

Paula looked at him, watched his eyes blinking at her, his chest moving with each breath. "Does she?"

Mixer smiled. "Yes. I know it sounds crazy, and hell, it probably *is* crazy, but the woman loves me."

"And how do you feel about her?" Paula asked.

Mixer's smile faded, and he shook his head. "I have no idea."

"What are you going to do now?" Paula asked.

"I don't know. Stay dead for a while, that's for sure. Try to find out why the mayor wanted me dead. It's all tied up with Chick, somehow. And Tremaine probably knows more about what's going on than anyone else right now. I'll try talking to him again."

They sat at the table a while longer without talking. Paula finished off her orange juice, and Mixer drank one more glass of the vodka. He slid the glass back and forth, then stood. "I've gotta use the head."

While Mixer was in the bathroom, Paula cleared off the table, leaving the vodka and Mixer's glass in case he wanted more. She drank Tremaine's vodka, slowly, steadily, savoring it going down her throat cold and hot at the same time, melting its way down into her stomach. Then she put the glass in the sink and stood with her hips against the counter, looking at nothing. She was exhausted, drained.

She should be feeling ecstatic, seeing Mixer alive when she'd thought he was dead, when she'd spent days grieving for him, combining it with her continuing grief for Chick. And she was happy, she *was*, but she was anxious, too, worried about what was still to come. Mixer being alive didn't end things. In a sense, it only added to her worry.

Mixer came out of the bathroom stretching and grimacing. He looked at the vodka and glass, shook his head. "I don't need any more," he said.

Paula put the glass in the sink with the others, put the bottle back in the freezer. There wasn't much left.

"Would it be all right if I stayed here tonight?" Mixer asked. "I can hardly walk, and I'm not up to going back to the Tenderloin right now. The booze cuts the pain, but puts me out. I can sleep on the floor, on some blankets."

"Of course you can stay. And you don't have to sleep on the floor, Mixer. There's plenty of room in the bed."

"Are you sure?"

Paula nodded, smiling. "I'm sure." She walked up to him and kissed him on the cheek. "Let's go."

She went into the bedroom, turned on the nightstand lamp, thinking about the night Tremaine had stayed. It had been a night too mixed up with other things and there was no way to judge it, no way to know if it meant anything. She turned to Mixer. "You need help getting undressed?"

"No."

"Good. I'll be back in a minute."

Paula went into the bathroom, peed, then washed up, filling her hands over and over with water, splashing it across her face, rubbing at her eyes. She stared at her reflection in the mirror, at the dark patches under her eyes, at the tiny crow's-feet that were just developing, at the narrow crease in her forehead, thinking about Mixer's ruined face. She shook her head to herself.

Back in the bedroom, Mixer was stripped down to his boxers, sitting on the edge of the bed. Paula undressed, put on a light nightshirt that hung to her knees, then sat in her overstuffed chair, facing Mixer.

"You look awful, Mixer. Your hair looks like shit, the beard's a disaster, and your arm, well, you know what the arm is like." She smiled at him. "And you look just wonderful, absolutely wonderful. I'm so happy to see you alive."

Mixer smiled back at her. "I do look pretty bad, don't I?"

Paula nodded. "And that Saint Katherine woman loves you, anyway. Amazing."

"Yeah. She doesn't call me Mixer, by the way. She calls me by my birth name."

"And what's that?"

"Minor Danzig."

"Minor Danzig. It's a good name. Fits you. But I gotta tell you, you'll always be Mixer to me."

"I hope so," he said.

Paula got up from the chair and approached the bed. "Let's get some sleep."

Mixer nodded. It took them a few minutes to work it out so Mixer would be comfortable. Paula was afraid of rolling onto his arm in the middle of the night, but Mixer said it would be fine. Finally they were both settled in, and Paula turned off the lamp.

Paula lay on her side, gazing into the darkness of the room, slashes of light coming in through the window blinds. She could hear Mixer breathing, could feel the warmth of his body even though they were not touching.

"I slept with him once," she said.

There was a long pause, and Paula wondered if Mixer had fallen asleep. But finally he said, "Tremaine?"

"Yeah."

"And you were going to sleep with him tonight?"

"Probably."

Another long pause. "Do you love him?"

Paula almost laughed, shaking her head. "It's way too early for that, Mixer."

"Yeah, I guess so."

"But I like him." She felt she should say something more, but she didn't know what it would be.

She felt Mixer's hand rest for a moment on her hip, squeeze gently. "I hope it works out," he said. Then the hand was gone.

"Thanks, Mixer." Paula suddenly felt like crying, and she had no idea why. "Good night," she whispered.

"Good night, Paula."

Paula closed her eyes, and squeezed them tight against the tears.

22

THE INDIVIDUAL SLUG quarters were all different from one another. Some had a solid barrier between the small interrogator's cubicle and the slug's main quarters, with microphones and speakers so the police interrogator would never actually see the slug. Others had a glass barrier with a removable screen, so the slug could be seen if it wished.

Monk's quarters, however, were entirely different: there was no barrier, no separation of any kind. When Carlucci stepped through the door and into the dim, large room atop police headquarters, his first impression was of a constantly shifting maze. Wide, shiny black panels hung from the ceiling throughout the room, the bottom of each panel no more than a foot above the carpeted floor. All the panels were slowly turning, not in unison, creating and closing off ever-changing pathways through them. Pieces of furniture were placed among the panels—a couch, several chairs, small tables. Carlucci only saw the furniture in glimpses as the panels turned, could only see portions of the huge picture windows with their view of the city, got only hints of the information center far in the back.

The second thing that struck him was the heat—warmer than anywhere else in the building, as warm as outdoors at midday, but far, far drier. Already there was a scratchy feeling with each breath, the air was so dry.

The panels stopped turning. "Have a seat," a voice said, seeming to come from all around him. The voice was deep, booming. The lights dimmed a step or two. Small table lamps came on beside the chairs, then two more came on beside the couch, which was further back in the room, the lamps providing pockets of green-tinted light and casting new, sharper shadows. Carlucci smiled to himself, and sat in the nearest chair, setting his notebook and pen on the table beside it. Did Monk really think he would be awed by this show?

"Something to drink?" the voice asked. A man's voice, Carlucci decided, now with an echo effect. What crap.

"Coffee," Carlucci said. "Black."

Almost immediately a short, thin, elderly Asian man in a black suit appeared, zigzagging his way through the panels, carrying a tray with a clear glass cup of dark, steaming coffee. The man stopped just in front of Carlucci and held the tray out before him. Carlucci took the coffee and said, "Thank you." The man did not respond, only retreated two steps, then turned and walked back the way he had come.

"Don't worry," Monk's voice said. "He'll be going to his own room directly. We will have our privacy."

"I'm not worried," Carlucci said.

"No, I don't imagine you are."

There was nothing for a while, and Carlucci sipped at the coffee, studying the room. Two of the panels to his right, near the windows, began turning again, alternately narrowing and widening his view, but he was too far from the windows to really see much anyway.

Then all the panels began turning again, some more slowly than others, and Carlucci glimpsed movement far in the back, in the information center, a form lurching toward him. He saw two canes, two black-coated limbs half stepping, half dragging between the canes. Glimpses of a bloated torso, shoulders and arms strangely both muscular and bloated, all coated in a glistening black, like some luminescent wetsuit. A bloated and goggled face, head encased in a gleaming, studded helmet. The slug. Monk.

The slug staggered to the small couch flanked by console tables, and dropped heavily into it. The panels slowed, then stopped. He was perhaps twenty feet away, almost completely blocked from Carlucci's view by the panels; all Carlucci could see as the slug settled in was a gloved hand gripping both canes, swinging them up and over to set them behind the couch.

There was only labored breathing for some time, which gradually eased. Then the slug said, "Good evening, Lieutenant Carlucci." No more echo effect.

"Monk."

"You have not done this often," Monk said. Even without the amplification, Monk's voice was deep, authoritative.

"Just twice," Carlucci replied.

"Your friend Brendan McConnel talked with us quite a lot, until he resigned. How is Mr. McConnel?"

"He's fine."

Monk laughed. "No he's not. He's a drunk, and he's fucking a mouthless Screamer. We know what kind of sex he's *not* getting." A pause. "He shouldn't have resigned, he should have stuck with it. He understood us, I believe. I liked talking with him."

Carlucci wanted to respond, wanted to defend Brendan, wanted to tell Monk that he didn't know Brendan at all, couldn't know him, and had no right to judge what Brendan did or didn't do. But Carlucci kept it in. He needed things from Monk.

"Ask your questions," Monk said. "That's what we are both here for."

Carlucci wasn't sure where to start. He opened his notebook and stared at the questions he'd jotted on the tan, lined pages, but somehow they didn't seem right anymore.

"Are you concerned about our privacy?" Monk asked. "You needn't be. I have more detection equipment in here . . . Well, be assured, there is absolutely no way anyone will ever know what is said in here. And we both know Mayor Kashen would very much like to be hearing every word."

Monk made a sound something like a laugh. "And they did try to infiltrate with listening devices. You do not need to worry."

All right, Carlucci thought, just ask a question. "You've seen all the feeds. A simple question. Who killed William Kashen, and why?"

"Two questions," Monk corrected, "and neither of them simple." He paused, the fingers of his finely sheathed hand waving like drowsy snakes. "The answer to 'who' is probably irrelevant. An uninvolved professional hired for the purpose, most likely. Apprehending and arresting the man or woman who killed William Kashen would, presumably, close the case, but would not provide you with justice. Would not be able to lead you back to whoever did the hiring. And that, of course, is whom you really want. Answering the 'why' would probably give you the answers you are looking for. But not, once again, justice. You might learn who is responsible, and why, but you probably would not be able to convict, or even bring them to court."

"I'm aware of all the flaws in our justice system," Carlucci said, cutting in at Monk's first pause. "I don't give a shit about them at the moment. I asked you a simple . . . no, change that. I asked you a direct question. Can you help me with that or not? Can you help me with anything concrete related to the case?"

Another laughing sound from Monk, then silence. His fingers, all Carlucci could see of him, had stopped moving.

"Robert Butler," Monk said. "An obvious connection. Too obvious. Did Collier ever get the safe open? I never saw a report."

"Yes. The safe was empty."

"And so is the Butler-Kashen connection. Butler was killed, I *believe*, simply to misdirect. A surmise on my part, understand, with nothing *concrete*, really, to substantiate it. William Kashen was attempting to jack Butler just as he was attempting to jack his uncle, the mayor of this beautiful city, His Honor Terrance Kashen."

"Kashen was trying to jack his uncle," Carlucci repeated, hoping for some clarification.

"Oh, yes. Something which the mayor has only recently learned for himself. Which is why he's now called you off the case."

"I haven't been called off the case."

"Not officially, no. But he's asked you to bury the case nonetheless, hasn't he?"

Carlucci didn't answer. He felt he was on shaky ground, unsure where to step next. Too many dynamics he still didn't understand. What was Monk's role in all this? He seemed more involved, somehow, than Carlucci would have expected.

More of that strangled laughter. "The mayor, His Honor, will get his in the end," Monk said. "You just watch. He's not as crucial to things as he believes, and he will be hung out to dry."

"Hung out to dry by who?" Carlucci asked.

"By *whom*," Monk corrected. "That's a good question. But I don't have an answer to it for you."

Carlucci was certain Monk was lying. But what the hell could he do about it? Nothing. Nothing but wait, dig around, ask more questions, and hope for some inadvertent clue.

"How was Kashen trying to screw over his uncle and Butler?"

"That's far less clear," Monk said. "He was trying to sell something. Information of some kind. Now. Either the buyer got what he wanted and then killed Kashen—perhaps to shut him up, perhaps to avoid a very high payment—or Kashen's source for the information discovered that Kashen had 'borrowed' it from them, and called in the loan. With Kashen's life as interest."

"Very clever," Carlucci said.

"Sarcasm is more effective if it's subtler," Monk said. "It doesn't sink in immediately, and then the subject is never quite sure about the intent. Much more disturbing that way."

"Anything else?" Carlucci asked.

"Much more. We have hardly begun."

There was another long silence. Carlucci tried to remember what Brendan had told him. Let Monk go, let him wander around. Try not to guide him. Shit, not much chance of that.

"Your daughter," Monk said.

"What?"

"Caroline. She has Gould's, yes?"

"What the fuck does that have to do with this?"

"Nothing," Monk admitted. "I'm just talking, trying to get to know you better. It will make the session more productive."

"More productive for who?"

There was a slight hesitation, then, "For both of us. Gould's, yes?"

Carlucci sank back in the chair, closed his eyes. Christ, he was tired. "Yes, she has Gould's Syndrome."

"A drastically shortened life," Monk said. "A terrible shame. A terrible waste." There was a pause. "Would it help, to compensate, if you could greatly extend the life spans of the rest of your family?"

Carlucci opened his eyes and sat up. "What is all this?" he asked. "Someone else asked me something like that a few days ago."

"Who?"

"I don't remember."

"I'll bet you don't. It doesn't matter, it's nothing. It's in the air. A universal fantasy, a twenty-first century Grail. That's all. It was just a question."

No, Carlucci thought, there's something more than that. But what? Monk wasn't going to tell him.

"The Tenderloin," Monk said. "Part of the answer is there. With the Saints."

"The Saints?"

"You know who they are?"

"A little."

"Insane women," Monk said. "They can't have any answers. I don't know why I said it." Monk's voice sounded genuinely puzzled. "Perhaps they do, somewhere. But you won't be able to talk to them, you can't reach those women."

"You're a lot of help," Carlucci said.

Panels moved, turned edge on so he had a full view of Monk. Monk shifted on the couch, and the glistening black coating seemed to undulate over him. His goggled, helmeted head rose, craned forward. Pale, fleshy lips moved. "You want some real help?"

It sounded like a challenge. Carlucci nodded. "Yes, I want some real help."

Monk seemed to weave slightly, as though he had difficulty remaining upright. The lips formed an unpleasant smile.

"Chick Roberts," Monk said. "How's that for real help?"

Carlucci hesitated a moment, then asked, "Who's Chick Roberts?"

"You called up the case," Monk said. "A case that bypassed you, but you called it up. Came across the roadblock, and let it go. You didn't pursue it. Not officially. Later that day, you contacted Sergeant Ruben Santos, the officer in charge of the case, arranged to meet him outside the department building."

"We talked about the mayor's nephew."

Monk laughed. "You talked about Chick Roberts. No, I could never prove it, but I know you talked about Chick Roberts. You later called Paula Asgard, told her you checked into the case, that it was dead-ended, and that she should forget about it."

"Yes," Carlucci said. "The case was a dead end."

"The case was being buried."

"That's your interpretation."

"Yours, too," Monk insisted. "You told the girlfriend to forget about it, but *you* didn't, did you? You've been investigating it on your own, haven't you?"

"No," Carlucci said, trying to remain calm and assured. "I let it go. It wasn't my case."

Monk shook his head. "No, no, no, Lieutenant Carlucci. You kept investigating, you discovered that the Chick Roberts case is connected to William Kashen's."

"It is?"

Monk sighed heavily. "This obstinance does not help the session," he said. "We make far better progress if we work together. If we are completely open and honest."

"What a crock," Carlucci said. "This is supposed to be *my* interrogation, *my* investigation."

"You think so?" Monk said, smiling.

"What the hell are you after?"

Monk slowly shook his head and lay back on the couch, the bloated limbs and body sliding and shifting. Carlucci wished he could see the thing's eyes, not just those damn goggles. Monk's fingers flicked across something on the console beside him and the panels turned back, once more obscuring him from view. The panels weren't in exactly the same position, though, and Carlucci could see a strip of his body, another of his neck and face. He wondered if it was intentional. He watched Monk's gloved fingers pull some of the coating away from his neck, the fingers of his other hand applying a series of dermal patches to the bare skin. Then the coating was worked back.

"I'm just trying to help you," Monk eventually said.

"Then tell me, what's the connection between the Chick Roberts and the William Kashen killings?"

"The mayor wants them both buried," Monk said. "That's a hell of a connection."

"I don't know that that's true."

"It's true. You know it's true."

Carlucci rubbed at his eyes, his temple. He felt like the entire interrogation had gotten away from him. He didn't know what questions to ask. "What else?" he finally said. "What's the *real* connection?" When Monk did not immediately reply, Carlucci said, "What the hell is all this about? Why are these people killing each other? What is at stake here?"

Nothing from Monk. Gloved fingers tapped at the console. What was he doing? His head shifted, goggles and helmet, staring at something.

"The spikehead might have known," Monk said. "But the spikehead is dead."

"Mixer," Carlucci said.

"Yes, Mixer. There's the connection to the Saints."

"I don't understand," Carlucci said, though he understood perfectly well. "Mixer's dead?"

"The Saints put him on trial. And he died. They killed him. Yes, Mixer's dead."

So the slug didn't know everything. Carlucci wanted to tell him, wanted to rub that freakish face in it, but he said nothing. "Why was Chick Roberts killed?" he asked.

"I don't have the answer to that, either," Monk said.

Again, Carlucci felt certain the slug was lying. He wanted to order all the feeds sent to one of the other slugs, and set up another session, see if one of the other slugs would be able to give him something else, but he knew it was impossible. That would be pushing the mayor too far. He wished he understood where Monk stood in all this. There was something crucial there, something Carlucci didn't know.

He picked up his coffee, started to drink it, but it was lukewarm. A bad temperature. What had Monk given him so far? Nothing. A couple of small things. Butler's murder as diversion. Something about this longer life stuff. Nothing particularly useful, not even in a cryptic way. The entire session had gone nothing like Brendan had led him to expect. Monk had been far more active, far more aggressive, than he would ever have guessed.

"Why did you decide to become a slug?" he asked Monk.

No answer. Panels moved, revealing Monk again, and he gave that twisted, thick-lipped smile. "To get laid," he said. The panels shifted, cut him completely from view.

"Do you have *any* answers?" Carlucci asked.

"You haven't asked the right questions. And don't ask me what the right questions are. If I knew, I wouldn't tell you."

Carlucci pushed the coffee cup away, picked up his notebook, and stared at the questions he'd written, stared at the blank spaces between them.

"You haven't given me anything I didn't already know, or had at least guessed at," Carlucci said. It was a small lie, mostly true. He felt certain Monk had given him a lot of lies, most of them quite big.

The panels shifted, revealing Monk's face and one arm.

"I'll clue you on something," Monk said. "A big secret." He paused, as though unsure whether or not to continue. "You think we're here for you, don't you? That we slugs are ensconced here in this building for you, pumping ourselves full of reason enhancers and metabolic juicers, deforming our bodies so we can help you solve difficult cases." Monk shook his head, smiling again. "*You* are here for *us*."

Monk pushed himself up, reached behind the couch, and pulled out his canes. "The session is over," he said. He punched something into the console and the panels all began turning again, shifting back and forth as Monk worked up to his feet. Then he lurched away from the couch and headed toward the back of the room. Carlucci kept waiting for him to stop and turn around to say one more thing, take one more shot, but he never did. Monk staggered through the information center, around a corner, and was gone from sight. Then all but two small lights went out, and the room was filled with shifting, leaping shadows.

Carlucci stood, picked up his notebook. He watched the whipping, slashing shadows for a minute, then turned and walked toward the door. As he reached for the handle, he heard an echoing whisper roll through the air. He couldn't be certain, but he thought the whisper said, "*Your life, Carlucci.*" Carlucci waited, but there was nothing else. He pulled the door open and left.

23

PAULA ALMOST MISSED it. Of course, she hadn't been looking for it. She hadn't been looking for anything.

It was close to midnight, and she'd just come home after closing up at the Lumiere. Once again, when she walked into her apartment and turned on the light, she stared at the stacks of Chick's things, thinking she had to do something with them. But not tonight. She was too damn tired.

She did open one of the boxes filled with Chick's home-studio discs, some of them just audio, some with video as well. Flipping through the cases, she took out one called *Aphasia Sciatica,* which she didn't recognize. She brought it into the bedroom, powered up system and monitor, put the disc into the player, and sat back in her overstuffed chair to watch.

The disc was filled with speeded-out images of what appeared to be neural surgery, both brain and spinal, backed by lots of atonal screeching industrial music. Twenty minutes into the disc Paula was starting to nod off, kind of bored by the whole thing, when there was a brief blip in the picture and sound. She kept watching for a few moments; then her head jerked and she sat up, realizing something odd had happened. She grabbed the remote and stopped the disc, freeze-framing on the image of a hunchbacked woman, spinal cord exposed, her head twisted around, mouth open, eyes wide and staring at metal strands emerging from her spine. Paula reversed the playback, saw the electrified metal strands whipping about, coiling and uncoiling from the woman's spine as she silently screamed. The blip came and went again. Stop, then play, slow motion now. The blip was longer this time, a clean break in the video. Back again, frame advance, then freeze on the blip.

On the screen was an incredibly complex, detailed drawing, something like the interior topography of a huge insect. At the top of the screen, above a line of ideographs, were the words PART THREE. On both sides of the drawing were columns of dense, tiny text, all ideographs. She guessed the ideographs were Chinese. Not because she knew Chinese, but because she suspected New Hong Kong. Paula dropped to her knees and crawled forward, studying the text, but there was no other English anywhere. Was this what Chick had died for?

Paula got back in the chair and let the disc play at normal speed again. She watched intently for another fifteen minutes, listening carefully to the soundtrack, but there were no other breaks in either the audio or the video on the rest of the disc.

When it ended, Paula stared at the empty blue screen, thinking. "Part Three" sure as hell implied at least two other parts. Where were they? On other discs, of course. They had to be. But which ones? Or were the others taken when Chick was killed? But if they were, how was this one missed?

She went back into the front room, took another of Chick's homemade discs from the box, brought it into the bedroom, and popped it on. She watched it carefully, but when it ended half an hour later, she'd found nothing.

She returned to the front room and stared at the boxes and crates. There were hundreds of discs and tapes in various formats, some commercial, others homemade by Chick or other people. If there were more parts to this, how could she possibly find them without spending weeks searching through everything? She tried to think like Chick, tried to put herself in his place and figure out how *he* would have decided which discs or tapes to put this stuff on, figure out a key, but she quickly realized it was absurd. There was no way to find the other pieces without going through everything, disc by disc, tape by tape. And she'd need help for that.

Then what? Even if she found all the parts to whatever this was, what then? What the *hell* would she do with it? Who could she take it to?

Carlucci? He was digging into Chick's death, he was a cop, a good cop. That made a kind of sense.

Tremaine? He was doing this story, he was trying to find answers, too. No, not Tremaine. She didn't know him well enough yet, didn't know what kind of trust she could put in him. And Carlucci, she wasn't sure about him either, for some reason. There were too many funny things with the cops and Chick.

Mixer.

She went into the bedroom, put the *Aphasia Sciatica* disc in its case. Mixer was the only person she trusted completely.

One in the morning. But Mixer was in the Tenderloin, and in there it was Prime Time. Paula put on her jacket, put the disc in one of the inner pockets, and left.

The Euro Quarter was chaos. A train of Caged Men crawled through the streets, completely jamming up traffic. Chicken-wire cages on wheels were pulled by women in crash suits, two cables over each shoulder, two women to a cage. Inside each cage was a squatting, naked man, fingers gripping the chicken-wire walls. There must have been thirty cages in the train. Thumping drum music pounded from speakers in each cage. The men yelped, they scratched their genitals, they grinned. The women pulling the cages were faceless, features hidden by masks of bone. Horns and sirens blared in futile frustration; if anyone actually tried to get the Caged Men off the street, the women would start shooting.

Movement on the sidewalks wasn't much better. Paula didn't fight the crowds; she moved along with them as they shifted around the Caged Men and the string of dancing foot-followers in their wake. Everyone seemed angry. Paula ducked into Mr. Pink's Bookstop, just to get out of the crush. She hated Mr. Pink's. Perv heaven. Porn never seemed to change much. Paula wandered among the shelves, ignoring the stares of the men, the snickers of other women. How did they know? The cover photos on books and magazines made her queasy; she tried not to look at them, but as she walked along they kept clutching at her gaze. Finally, deciding this was worse than the crush outside, she pushed her way out of the store.

Ten minutes later, the crush eased as the last of the Caged Men rolled past. Paula was sweating, still feeling a little sick from Mr. Pink's. She had to make way for a band of the Daughters of Zion. They were obviously on the prowl, probably hoping to run into a pack of Heydrich's Fists and have a bang-out. Blood and gore and smashed faces. Great.

Eventually Paula found the alley Mixer had directed her to. Not quite as crowded, but hardly empty. Three or four drum fires burned; several people clustered around one, roasting an unrecognizable animal on a spit. A family of Screamers lurched past, two adults and two children all bound together at the wrists and ankles with rope. Paula located the door, pressed the intercom. There was a burst of static, which immediately cleared. "Yes?" A neutral voice, could have been a man or a woman.

"Paula Asgard," she said. "I'm here to see . . ." She caught herself. "To see Minor Danzig."

A long pause, then, "Wait." Another burst of static, then dead air.

"Wait for what?"

No response.

Paula waited, staring at the door. Were they trying to check her out? There were no windows in the door, nothing that looked like a screener. She looked up the wall, but didn't see anyone looking down at her.

"Paula."

The voice came from behind her. She turned to see Mixer smiling.

"Just had to make sure," he said. "Paranoia's our survival strategy right now." He came forward, kissed her cheek, then banged twice on the door. The door swung open, and a tall, stunning woman in long, blood-red robes stepped aside to let them in. The woman closed the door behind them and secured it.

"Paula, this is Saint Katherine. Paula Asgard."

St. Katherine smiled, took Paula's hand. Her fingers were smooth and warm; Paula had expected them to be cold.

"Why are you here?" Mixer asked.

Paula looked at St. Katherine. She didn't know this woman at all. She didn't care if St. Katherine *had* saved Mixer's life. But she felt awkward saying anything. No, not just awkward. Almost afraid. This was the woman who had nearly killed Mixer, who had killed or wrecked others.

"What is it, Paula?" Mixer said.

Paula turned back to him. "Can I talk to you alone?" She paused. "It's about Chick."

There was a long silence, Mixer looking at her; almost smiling, Paula thought. She glanced at St. Katherine, who showed no signs of leaving, and no signs of discomfort. There was something here, Paula realized, something she didn't quite understand, something between Mixer and St. Katherine.

Finally Mixer shook his head. "Saint Katherine and I are together in all this," he said. "Chick, the mayor, the mayor's nephew, all of it."

"I don't know her," Paula said. She turned to St. Katherine. "I don't know you. And so I don't trust you."

St. Katherine smiled. "It's all right. I understand." But she still did not make a move to leave.

"Do you trust me?" Mixer asked.

"I came to you with this. Not Carlucci, not Tremaine," she said, half wishing now she *had* gone to Carlucci instead.

"Then trust Saint Katherine," Mixer said. "Whatever you tell me, if she wasn't here, I'd tell her later."

Yes, Paula thought, something more had happened between them, something since Mixer had come to see her, telling her he was alive. His doubts and fears about St. Katherine were gone.

Paula nodded. She trusted Mixer, more than anyone else. She would trust St. Katherine, too. She took the disc from inside her jacket, held it up. "I've got something to show you."

A basement room, dark except for the colored lights of electronic displays on computers, sound and video systems, communication consoles. Paula sat on a small, hard chair; Mixer and St. Katherine were seated on her right, St. Lucy on her left. They stared at the image on the large-screen monitor. The text was sharp and clear, the ideographs quite beautiful; the diagram was still incomprehensible to Paula.

"The text is Chinese," St. Lucy said.

Paula had met St. Lucy only a few minutes earlier, but already she liked the woman. St. Lucy seemed so normal, so intelligent and grounded; Paula wondered how she could ever have joined the Saints.

"You read Chinese?" Paula asked.

"No. Only a few words and phrases. But I recognize it."

"What about the drawing, diagram, whatever the fuck it is?" Mixer asked, leaning forward.

"It looks medical to me," St. Katherine said.

St. Lucy nodded. "To me also. But . . ." She left it there. Then, "We know someone who should look at the diagram, who might know what it is. And someone who reads Chinese. Unfortunately, not the same person." She turned to Paula and smiled, shrugging gently.

"We need to go through all of Chick's tapes and discs," Mixer said. "You still have them?" he asked Paula. "You didn't sell or give any of them away?"

"No. Other things, yeah, but I kept all the music and video. I wanted to go through it, decide what to keep. Which probably would have been most of it. But . . ." Here was one of the things that bothered her. "If this is what Chick was killed over, why is it still here? Why didn't they take everything of Chick's when they killed him?"

"I wonder, too," Mixer said, "but I can make some guesses. Chick had this stuff, which he was trying to sell. Diagrams and text, apparently. Something big. Maybe we'll find out what. He found it by accident, or stole it." Mixer grinned in the light of the displays. "We know which was more likely. Now, Chick's not too smart, but he's not completely stupid, either. So he makes an extra copy, splitting it up and scattering the pieces around in his discs. When somebody comes after him, he's still got the original to hand over, trying to save his ass. But they kill him anyway." Mixer sighed. "So what do they do? They've got what they came for. They don't know if there's another copy. Hauling everything out of that place would take a lot of time and be damn conspicuous, and remember, this is a murder that's being buried, *someone's* trying to keep it quiet. And probably the original was in some encrypted format that would be damn hard to copy into readable text like this," he said, pointing at the screen. "But you know Chick, he was a fucking wizard with that kind of stuff. Looking at him, though, you'd never have a clue." Mixer shrugged. "Hell, it's all a guess. But we've got to look through everything and see if there's more."

"There's a lot to go through," Paula said.

"Yeah, I know. But we can get the Saints working on it, some of the novitiates. No one will know what it is; hell, *we* don't. They'll just be looking for pieces. Everything will be ice."

"And we'll get someone to come in and translate the text," St. Katherine said. "And someone to check out the diagrams. They will be people we can trust, of course."

"And then what?" Paula asked. "If we find the rest of it and figure out what it is, then what do we do?"

No one answered her. No one had any idea.

Paula sat at her kitchen table, drinking the last of Chick's Stolichnaya and staring at what remained of Chick's things. Most of the boxes were gone now, hauled away in several trips on foot by Mixer, St. Katherine, and St. Lucy. His home-studio equipment was still there, alone with some books and a couple of boxes of miscellaneous crap, but the music was all gone. Paula was depressed.

She felt like she was losing Chick, losing her memories of him. She'd get everything back from Mixer, but still . . . Chick and his music had turned into something else—murder and money and cover-ups and something big and secret going on up in New Hong Kong. Chick was disappearing.

The hole in her heart seemed to be getting bigger, somehow, and the vodka wasn't filling it. She drank off the rest of the glass and picked up the bottle. Empty.

She got up and walked into her bedroom, dug around in her discs, found the one she'd played over and over since Chick had died, the music video with the footage of the two of them making love here in this room, on this bed. "Love at Ground Zero." She put it on, sank back in her chair, and watched it once again.

As it played, the bluesy music surrounding the slow-motion images of their lovemaking in orange and yellow light, Paula pulled her knees up and wrapped her arms around them, pulling them in tight against her chest, jamming her chin into them. And when the song ended, and she watched the close-up of Chick's face silently saying "I love you," the open pit in her heart expanded, engulfed her, and swallowed her whole.

24

MIXER AND ST. KATHERINE stood in the darkness of the basement room, surrounded by electronics and boxes of Chick's discs and tapes, lit by shafts of pulsing display lights. Faint ether music played on the sound system, whispering from the speakers scattered around the room.

"It's in here," Mixer said. "I know it."

St. Katherine nodded. Her face was ghostlike in the pale amber light. Mixer wanted to breathe his life into it, into her. He didn't know when the change had occurred, but it definitely had. He would do almost anything for her.

"What do we do with it when we find it?" St. Katherine asked. "When we learn what it is."

"What do you mean?"

She looked directly at him, and he thought she might be close to smiling. Or smirking.

"It must be worth a fortune," she said.

Mixer shook his head, trying to read her voice.

"We could give Paula a piece of it. A large piece."

Was she serious? She seemed even closer to a smile now, but he wasn't certain.

"We'll do whatever Paula wants," he told her. "Chick paid for this with his life. I nearly paid with mine. We'll do whatever's right." He paused, still trying to read her expression. "When we know what it is, we'll know what's right. Paula will know what's right."

Now St. Katherine finally did smile, touched his scarred right arm lightly with her fingers. "I'm sorry," she said. "I was only giving you a bad time."

Mixer nodded once. He *could* read her voice. He did know her, somehow, knew she was telling the truth. Knew he could trust her. When had this happened? He wasn't sure, but he was glad it had.

"You loved her," St. Katherine said. "Paula Asgard."

"I still do. She's probably the best friend I've ever had." Sookie might have become the same kind of friend, Mixer thought, but she'd been killed before she'd reached fourteen. She'd never had a chance.

"I mean more than that," St. Katherine said. "You loved her more than as a close friend."

Mixer nodded, feeling that ache in his chest again. But it was more bearable now, like he could almost take pleasure in it. He watched the volume meters shifting slowly back and forth on the display in front of him.

"Yes, I did. For years. But there was always Chick. He got killed, but there hadn't been enough time. Maybe there never would have been, I don't know. Probably not. Then there was my own 'death.' Now, apparently, there's Tremaine." He turned back to St. Katherine, her eyes open and gazing back at him. "And now there's you."

"Me."

Mixer nodded. "You."

"Are you sure?"

Mixer shook his head. "I don't think I'll ever be sure about anything again."

St. Katherine touched his arm again, his shoulder, his cheek.

"This can wait a couple of hours, can't it?"

Mixer nodded.

Naked, St. Katherine was just as beautiful, just as stunning. Naked, her age showed, which made her more real to Mixer, and even more attractive.

They lay together on St. Katherine's bed, lightly touching, brushing one another. Gray dawn light came in through the blinds, slicing them with shadow. Mixer's breath was ragged, and he could feel his heartbeat pounding up his neck. In the heat of the morning, he was sweating.

"It's been a long time," he said. Trying to explain his anxiety, his awkwardness. "Several years."

"For me, too," St. Katherine said. "Twelve years. Since becoming a Saint."
She smiled at him. "I've been waiting for you."

Twelve years. Mixer could hardly imagine that much time anymore. Yet
she seemed calm, self-assured. I'm glad one of us is, he thought.

She kissed his arm, nipped at his scarred flesh, and a faint scratch of
pleasure shot up his arm, down his body. She seemed to sense it, and nipped
him again, gently scraped her teeth along the ridged skin. Mixer closed his
eyes, let the pleasure shoot through him, and his nervousness seemed to disappear.

They pulled at each other, kissed and licked and bit and tugged; they
clung to one another in the growing heat of the day, their skin slick with
sweat. Her taste was bitter and sweet, her smell sharp and biting; she
grabbed his hair, pressed his face into her so he could hardly breathe. She
shuddered, quaked against him.

Mixer lost himself in her, in her wet, salty skin, her taste and smell and
her harsh gasping cries. Struggling for breath, he became dizzy. He was
wrapped around her, she was wrapped around him, and they generated heat
and sweat and maybe even love. He kissed her deeply, then stared into her
golden eyes until she pulled him tight against her once more. Yes, he
thought, maybe even love.

25

CARLUCCI FINALLY HEARD from Sparks. On his way into work,
on the sidewalk just outside the building, a teenage bubble courier came up
to him, stuck a bubble in his hand and popped it. The courier shot off as the
message formed in the remains spread across Carlucci's palm: "Home. S."
Then the bubble material disintegrated, turning to powder, and Carlucci
wiped it from his hand, scattering the particles to the ground.

Carlucci walked into the building, checked in at the front desk, then left
through the basement garage, on foot. House call to Sparks.

Home for Sparks was in the DMZ along the western edge of the Tenderloin.
Eight-thirty in the morning was way too early for people in the DMZ; the
street was quiet, the sidewalks nearly empty. The weather had finally cooled
down a bit. Not cool, exactly, but not as hot as it had been; for a change,
Carlucci wasn't sweating. The sky was clear, with no sign of rain.

Carlucci walked past a sidewalk cafe, half a dozen puffy-eyed troubadours sucking down coffee, trying to wake up. One of the three women reached out and plucked at Carlucci's arm. She was young, but missing some teeth. Coughing badly, breath foul. A moniker sewed to her jacket: Sister Ray.

"Want your ding-dong sucked?" she asked between coughs. "Twenty bucks. You can't get it any cheaper."

Carlucci shook his head. It was a horrifying thought. The woman's friends laughed. At him or her, he couldn't tell. He walked on.

He stepped through an open doorway between a cone counter and a music store. Brick walls, metal grating, and plaster high overhead, but plenty of light. Halfway along the corridor, on the left, was another doorway. Carlucci ducked through, then descended concrete steps to basement level and a maze of corridors, not so well lit. The smell, too, was worse. The brick and concrete walls were covered with layers of graffiti and artwork. Doors every twenty feet or so. So early in the morning, it was fairly quiet. Faint Indian music came from behind one door as he passed by; muted laughter came from behind another.

The door to Sparks's place was wood, painted solid black. No other decoration. Carlucci knocked. A minute later he knocked again. He stood a little ways back from the peephole, so Sparks could see him. No sound for a minute, then the clicks of locks and bolts. The door opened, and Sparks gestured him inside.

Inside was a single room, with a tiny, one-square-foot window up near the ceiling in the rear wall, too small for anything but a cat or a rat to come through. There was a mattress on the floor, piled with blankets; a hot plate plugged into a cracked wall socket. Two lamps, shaded dirty-white; two bag chairs, and a television; on the screen were two talking heads, but there was no sound. In a narrow alcove carved out of the concrete, a toilet and sink. No tub, no shower. Sparks probably wouldn't use one anyway.

Sparks coughed as he crossed the room toward the bed. He looked worse than ever. Carlucci knew it wasn't just the bad light. The man was dying.

"Have you found a slot in a hospice for me?" Sparks asked.

Carlucci shook his head, feeling guilty. He'd asked a few people, but he hadn't really looked that hard. "I've checked around," he said, "but I haven't found anything yet."

Sparks nodded, sat stiffly on the mattress, bones audibly creaking. A box of disposable syringes lay open next to the bed, inches away from the hot plate. "Take a seat."

Carlucci sat in the closest of the bag chairs, sinking awkwardly into it. Sparks picked up a bowl, cradled it in his lap. Inside the bowl was a spoon and dark brown goop. Sparks ate a few mouthfuls, then held the bowl and spoon out to Carlucci.

"Want some?"

Carlucci shook his head.

"It's chocolate pudding," Sparks said.

Carlucci shook his head again, and Sparks put the bowl back on the floor.

"The whisper you asked for," Sparks said. "Almost impossible to get."

"But you got it."

"I got something. It was a fuckin' bitch." He stared hard at Carlucci. "You'd better watch your ass. Mistakes could get you dead. Just ask Chick Roberts or the mayor's nephew or Rosa Weeks."

"Who's Rosa Weeks?" Carlucci asked. The name wasn't at all familiar.

"Better you don't know, then," Sparks said. "Too much *gnosis* is bad for you."

"Tell me who Rosa Weeks is."

Sparks shook his head, making something like a smile with his pale, thin lips. "You're a stubborn bastard."

"Yeah," Carlucci said. "*Testa dura.* What my father used to call me."

Sparks coughed, spat brown-green phlegm onto the floor. "Rosa Weeks was a doctor. She gave physicals."

"Yeah? And so?"

"It will become clear, I think. Patience, Lieutenant."

Patience. Patience was something Carlucci had always had plenty of. Sometimes too much. He nodded and waited for Sparks to tell it in his own way.

"Here's the key," Sparks said. "Mixer and Chick and Jenny Woo were bootlegging body-bags. You know that?" Carlucci nodded, and Sparks went on. "You knew Mixer, right?" Carlucci nodded again, and Sparks said, "Another guy who got himself dead. Okay. Body-bags. One out of every ten body-bags was rigged. When they were switched on, a paralytic agent was patched into the wearer's body, and a location beacon activated. Jenny Woo would lock onto the signal, and go pick up herself a live, but quite immobile body. Box it up, and take it home. Well, not home. But someplace private. There, Dr. Rosa Weeks did a complete physical and work-up, then crated them up."

"Crated them up for what?"

Sparks grinned. "A trip to New Hong Kong."

New Hong Kong again. Damn that place. Not much was illegal up there, and no one on Earth could touch them. But there was plenty that was illegal here on Earth, here in San Francisco, and he could do something about that. Maybe.

"Why were they being shipped to New Hong Kong?"

Sparks shook his head. "No idea. You'll have to find that on your own. Course, my advice is, leave it the fuck alone. Forget about it, Lieutenant."

"Did Mixer and Chick know the body-bags were rigged?"

"No. I don't think so. The body-bags were one thing. Jenny Woo had her own separate deal going. But I think Chick found out, through Jenny Woo. From there I think he found out a lot more. Enough to get himself dead. That's what I mean. Ignorance is a lot safer."

"And Rosa Weeks?"

"She's dead, too. Yesterday morning. Probably won't show up on-line for a couple days. It'll come up accidental OD." Sparks nodded to himself. "You just watch."

"Why is she dead?" Carlucci asked.

"Mouth too big, I think. She had a pet to feed that was costing her a fortune, and she tried buying it with something she knew."

More dead people, Carlucci thought. Which was why he couldn't take Sparks's advice and forget about it all. He had to try to figure out what was going on. And he felt he was closing in on it.

"Anything else?"

Sparks nodded. "Yeah. The Saints killed Mixer in one of their fucking trials. Sounds like nothing to do with this, but I got a feeling it ties in somehow. Also, a lot of people picked up in Kashen's recruiting vans end up in the same place as the body-baggers, getting prepped for a trip to New Hong Kong. Some of them, and some of the body-baggers, maybe go up to New Hong Kong in pieces." Sparks coughed, shaking his head. "Not so sure about that info, but it sounds real."

"But you're sure about the body-bags being rigged."

Sparks nodded.

"And you're sure Mixer didn't know."

"Pretty sure. You can't expect much more than that. I'd tell you to ask him yourself, but he's dead. You wouldn't get much of an answer."

I *will* ask him, Carlucci said to himself. He's not *that* dead.

"One more thing," Sparks said. He leaned forward, picked up a syringe from a tray. Carlucci could see that it was already loaded, ready to go. Sparks held the syringe in his right hand, then reached with his other hand for a piece of mirrored glass propped against the wall. "Hold this for me," he said.

Carlucci shifted in the bag chair, crouched forward, and took the mirror from Sparks.

"Hold it up," Sparks said. "So I can see myself, damn it."

Carlucci held the mirror up. Sparks stared into it, stretched his neck, then began tapping at his skin with his left hand. He squinted, pressed his neck, tapped some more. Carlucci kept glancing at the syringe in his other hand. Was he going to have to watch this? Christ.

More tapping, more squinting and grimacing, then suddenly Sparks brought his right hand up and plunged the needle into his neck. He switched his grip, eased back the plunger. Dark blood came back into the syringe and Carlucci turned away.

"Hold still, God damn you!"

Carlucci steadied his hands, the mirror, but didn't look back at Sparks. He was glad there were still some things that made him queasy.

Sparks broke into a coughing fit and Carlucci brought his gaze back around. The needle was out of his neck. Sparks was nodding, waving feebly at him.

"Okay, okay," he whispered. He tossed the empty syringe a few feet away, then took the mirror from Carlucci with slow, steady hands and placed it carefully against the wall. Then he lay back on the mattress, closing his eyes.

Carlucci worked himself out of the bag chair and stood, looking down at Sparks. He took the wad of cash from his pocket, set it on the blanket beside Sparks.

"Frank?" His voice was soft.

"Yes."

"Don't bother about the hospice." Sparks briefly opened one eye, then closed it. "It's too late."

Carlucci nodded, though Sparks couldn't see him. "I'm sorry," he said.

Sparks slowly rolled his head from side to side. "It's all right, Frank. It doesn't matter."

But it does, Carlucci thought. It does.

Later that day, near noon, Carlucci met Tremaine at the Civic Center muck pond, almost exactly where he'd met Paula two weeks earlier. They bought Polish sausages with sauerkraut from a vendor set up near the edge of the pond, and sat on a bench facing away from the scum-covered water. They'd met once or twice before, Carlucci couldn't remember exactly when. Some story Tremaine was working on, some case of Carlucci's.

The Polish sausage was hot, spicy, and greasy; Carlucci was glad he hadn't loaded up on the onions. They didn't talk much as they ate, just a word or two, about nothing, really: the cooling trend, the rat pack asleep in a pile across the plaza. When they were done, Carlucci took the scraps, wrappers, and napkins to a trash can, then returned to the bench. They sat several feet apart, not really looking at each other.

"I've been requesting an interview for two weeks," Tremaine said. "I wonder why you agree to one now."

"I haven't," Carlucci said. "You won't be asking the questions. You'll be answering mine."

"Will I?"

"Yes. This is a police investigation."

"An *official* investigation?"

Carlucci looked at him, but didn't say anything.

"I think I'll just wait for the subpoena," Tremaine said.

"That's a crappy attitude, Tremaine."

"It's a crappy business."

"What, murder? Or journalism?"

"Both. And being a cop," Tremaine said. "All of it."

Neither of them said anything for a while. The sky was still clear, and the sun was shining down on them, not quite hot. The break in the heat was a good change. It brought the crazies out into the open, though, and they were filling the plaza as they woke up, stumbling and wandering around.

"Want some coffee?" Carlucci asked.

Tremaine smiled. "Add some acid to the grease congealing in my stomach? Sure, sounds terrific."

They got up, walked back to the pond and bought coffee from the pregnant teenager. They circled the pond, and stopped near another bench, but didn't sit. Someone had puked all over it.

"Which murder are you investigating?" Tremaine asked.

"This is *all* off the record," Carlucci said. "Every fucking word. Got it?"

"Got it." Tremaine sipped at his coffee, grimaced. "So, which murder?"

"The mayor's nephew. William Kashen. What did you think?"

"Not Chick Roberts?"

"No. Should I be?"

"You know about Chick Roberts being killed, don't you?"

Carlucci shrugged. "Something. Wasn't my case. Some punk. A drug killing."

Tremaine shook his head. "You don't believe that."

"I don't?"

"No. He was Paula Asgard's boyfriend."

"I don't really know Paula Asgard. Only because she's a friend of Mixer's."

"Yes, Mixer. A dead guy who's still alive."

"Are you trying to tell me the two murders are connected?"

Tremaine shook his head. "No. You already know that. I *know* you do."

"The Chick Roberts case is closed."

"Buried, you mean."

Carlucci started to put his foot up on the bench, then remembered the vomit. He found a clean spot for his shoe and leaned forward, stretching his other leg.

"Why don't *you* tell me what the connection is between the two?" Carlucci said.

"Why don't we make a deal, an information trade?"

"It doesn't work that way," Carlucci said. "No deals. I'm a cop."

Tremaine laughed. "Cops are always making deals."

"What's the connection?" Carlucci asked again.

"You *do* know it's there, don't you?"

Carlucci nodded. He guessed he had to give Tremaine something. "I know it's there. I just don't know what it is."

Tremaine drank some more of his coffee, then dumped the rest of it in the trash can next to the bench, shuddering. "Awful stuff." He paused, then went on. "I can't be sure of any of this, you understand. Not completely. But I believe it."

A few feet away, a trio of trance walkers formed a circle, arms linked, and began humming. The plaza was filling with people on lunch break, but the crowds avoided the trance walkers, giving them plenty of space.

"Chick, Mixer, a woman named Jenny Woo, and the mayor's nephew were all spliced together. They had business. Body-bags. I don't think the body-bags had anything to do with this, that's just how they knew each other."

So he doesn't know everything, Carlucci thought. But then, none of us do.

"Something's going on up in New Hong Kong," Tremaine continued. "That's the real missing piece. And the mayor's tied up with it, the mayor's wrapped up tight inside whatever it is. He was doing something with his nephew, connected to all this somehow. But the nephew got hold of something he shouldn't have had, and was getting ready to sell it. He was getting ready to fuck over his uncle and New Hong Kong both. Now, what I believe happened is this. Chick Roberts got hold of the same thing, probably from the nephew. And Chick tried to cash in. Kashen wasn't stupid, and he'd managed to be discreet. No one knew what he had, except his potential customers. But Chick Roberts was not so smart, and he was not so discreet, and it wasn't long after he put out the word that he got himself three bullets in the head."

Tremaine paused, sighing heavily. "Here it gets more speculative. My sources are pretty weak and incomplete, but this is the picture I've put together, and it makes a kind of sense. I think the New Hong Kong people had Chick killed. As soon as they scented their property in the wrong hands and up for sale, they took care of the problem. The first problem. The second problem was finding out where Chick had gotten his stuff. They traced it back to the nephew, and then did him. But . . . they didn't tell the mayor, because they didn't know whether or not the mayor was in on it with the nephew. So you had the mayor putting on the squeeze to solve his nephew's murder. Politics, family loyalty, whatever.

"But New Hong Kong stays on this thing, tracing everything back. They've *got* to find the hole in their security and plug it up, and they have to be certain about it. I think they found it, and it wasn't the mayor. Probably someone up in New Hong Kong who is now a piece of space debris. When they were sure the mayor wasn't a part of it, they told him what had happened, and told him to take the pressure off the case. You *have* been asked to bury the nephew's case, haven't you?"

Carlucci didn't answer, and Tremaine nodded.

"Anything else?" Carlucci asked.

"Isn't that enough?"

"It's all speculation," Carlucci said. "I can't do a goddamn thing with it."

"I won't give you my sources," Tremaine said. "Even if I did, they'd never testify in court, they'd never even give you a statement."

"I'm not asking for your sources," Carlucci said in disgust. He pushed off the bench with his foot, walked over to the trash can, and shoved his empty coffee cup into it. "It does make a kind of sense," he said to Tremaine. "But I'm not going to get any names, am I? The name of the guy who put three bullets in Chick's head. The name of the guy who gutted the mayor's nephew. The names of any of the people who are responsible for this goddamn mess."

"I don't think so," Tremaine said.

"And what the hell is it you want from me?"

"Any information you have about these cases that I don't have."

"There *isn't* anything," Carlucci said. He was lying, but not much. "You know more than anyone. Christ."

"Confirmation that the Chick Roberts case was buried. Confirmation that the mayor has asked you to bury his nephew's case."

"You can't be serious."

"I've got to ask."

Carlucci had to laugh. "Christ, you're something else."

"Is that a 'no comment,' or a denial?" Tremaine asked.

"It's jack shit, is what it is. I told you, not a fucking word is on the record. There is no response to your questions."

"They weren't questions. They were statements. I'm just asking for confirmation."

Carlucci shook his head. "You've been a lot of fucking help," he told Tremaine. Actually, Tremaine *had* been a help, but he wasn't going to admit it. "We're done." He turned and started walking away. "See you."

"Wait. Lieutenant."

Carlucci just shook his head and kept on walking.

One last meeting, this one at night with Hong and LaPlace. Carlucci felt they were getting close, so close to the answers, but he was afraid they wouldn't be able to make it all the way. They sat at the table in the Hong family kitchen; Hong's entire family had gone to the cinema to see *Ghost Lover of Station 13* for the second time.

Carlucci told them everything he'd learned from Tremaine, from Sparks, the odd bits of information he'd gleaned from Monk. And he told them about Mixer.

Hong smiled. "So the spikehead's still alive, stirring up the shit."

"Yeah, except he's not a spikehead anymore. It all got burned away."

"Well, we have something, too," LaPlace said. "Monk may have been wrong about Butler."

"What do you mean?"

"Joseph and I found this guy. You know, a guy who knew a guy. Name's Little Johnny. Wanted to buy his way out of an intent-to-distribute bust. Kanter had him, called us in to see the guy. Little Johnny seemed to think Butler had killed the nephew. Didn't know why. Little Johnny doesn't know Butler himself. He knows a guy. The guy he knows is Totem the Pole."

"The porno star?" Carlucci asked.

"That's him. King of prong. Little Johnny says Totem the Pole told *him* that Butler had killed Kashen. According to Little Johnny, our man Totem the Pole, in contrast to his onscreen persona as the great humper of women, in real life, well, he likes men, too. Robert Butler, for one. Butler did something for Totem. Apparently Little Johnny did, too, which is why Totem got so confessional with him. Little Johnny tried to get specific about what they did for each other, but I didn't think we needed those kinds of details. The details we needed, though, he wasn't so good with. How did Totem know? Was Butler as confessional as Totem? Little Johnny doesn't know. Little Johnny says Totem heard something the night Butler got killed, that Totem was in the building when it happened, he was downstairs with the woman who lived under Butler. What he was doing with the woman, no one knows. Changing orientation again, maybe. But Totem seemed to think Butler was killed as his reward for killing Kashen. Yeah, to shut his mouth, permanently. We went around and around with Little Johnny, he said this, he said that, cha cha cha. It doesn't all make sense. But some, maybe. We kept Little Johnny in a holding cell, with a promise for release, and tried to track down Totem the Pole."

"You didn't find him, did you?"

LaPlace shook his head.

"We got to his agent," Hong put in. "She said Totem the Pole was shooting a new movie, he was on location."

"Let me guess," Carlucci said. "New Hong Kong."

Hong nodded. "New Hong Kong."

"I don't think we'll be seeing Totem or his Pole in San Francisco any time soon," LaPlace said.

"What about the woman who lived under Butler?"

"She's gone too," Hong said. "We can't find her."

"Shit," Carlucci said, his voice little more than a whisper. He leaned back in his chair and rubbed at his neck. "What do you think, Joseph?"

"Like Pete says, it makes a kind of sense, but we can't do much with it. Butler's dead, Totem's gone and probably wouldn't be much help anyway, and Little Johnny is useless. It just doesn't lead us anywhere."

LaPlace got up from the table, shaking his head and pacing. "This whole thing is going to shit on us," he said. "I mean, I'm not worried that we're in trouble, but everything goes nowhere. We know more, but where does it get us? We're never going to get anything to go to court with, are we?

Are we going to get the guy who put holes in the punk's face? We don't know for sure that Butler killed the nephew, but even if he did, he's dead, and are we going to get the guy who put a meat hook through his neck? And the mayor? We can't touch him, and we sure as hell aren't going to be able to get to anyone up in New Hong Kong, are we?" LaPlace shook his head. "Not fucking likely."

Carlucci couldn't disagree with LaPlace. He'd been thinking pretty much the same thing himself. The closer they got, the worse things looked.

"The one thing we *can* get out of this," Hong said, "is knowing what happened, and why. That's worth something. Sometimes it's worth a lot."

Carlucci nodded. "Yes, Joseph, that can be worth a lot. But we don't even have that yet, do we? We're close to knowing what happened, but we sure as hell don't know why." Carlucci shook his head. "What is it? What is worth killing all these people for?"

Carlucci looked back and forth between Hong and LaPlace, but neither man had an answer for him.

26

"ETERNAL LIFE," MIXER said. "That's what's getting people dead."

"Eternal life," Paula repeated. It didn't seem real. Maybe it wasn't.

They were sitting around the table in the kitchen of the Saints' place: Paula, Mixer, St. Katherine, and St. Lucy. Early evening, dark outside, two bright overheads lighting the kitchen. On the table in front of Mixer was a stack of eight or nine discs. Chick's discs.

"Not eternal life," St. Lucy said. "Life extension. It's not the same thing."

"Close enough," Mixer said. "People who will want it won't make the distinction. Or won't care. And who *won't* want it?"

"I've heard rumors about New Hong Kong all my adult life," Paula said. "Rumors about this, the New Hong Kong medicos finding the key to life extension. Nothing ever happened, and I stopped paying attention a long time ago. Now you're telling me it's for real?"

"Maybe," St. Lucy said. "Yes, it's for real, though it appears that they don't have all the answers yet. But they're probably very close." She pointed at the discs. "It's laid out here, what they're trying to do, the directions they're working in, how they're going about it. Not a complete picture, but enough."

"What do you mean by not complete?"

"We've got eleven images, eleven 'pages,' you could say. But there are at least twelve. We're missing Part Seven. We can't find it anywhere."

"It's possible Chick never even had it," Mixer put in.

"And there might be more than twelve," St. Lucy said. "But it probably doesn't matter. All the parts most likely would still provide only an incomplete picture. The key thing is, what's on these discs would be enough for some other group with sufficient resources to start up their own research program along the same lines. Atlantis Two, for example. Gottingen Gesellschaft, for another, or any of the other big biotechs. Any of those people would be willing to pay a fortune for what's on these discs."

"Okay," Paula said. "So tell me what's on the discs."

"We brought in someone to make the text translations first," St. Katherine said. "Someone we felt we could trust. But when he'd finished, and he'd given us the translation, we realized what this was worth, and we were no longer sure about him. This is one hell of a temptation."

"So what did you do, kill the translator?"

St. Katherine smiled. "No, of course not. But we do have him . . . in protective custody until we decide what to do next." St. Katherine shrugged. "He understands. It'll all work out."

"And what about the medical expert you were going to bring in?" Paula asked.

"We brought her in next, and she confirmed what we and the translator had guessed at. She's a doctor, the one who kept Minor Danzig alive after the trial. The texts are highly technical and advanced, and she didn't understand some of the details, had to make some guesses of her own, but it's pretty clear what they're after, and how they're going about it."

"Is she in protective custody, too?"

St. Katherine shook her head, smiling again. "No. She's my sister, and I've trusted her with my life more than once. I trust her with this. She also has serious reservations about their research methods, and their projected treatments."

"What kind of reservations?"

"Moral."

Paula was almost afraid to ask. "Why?"

St. Lucy sighed heavily. "They're doing all their primary experimentation on people, that much is clear. Testing and evaluation on human subjects. Teresa, Saint Katherine's sister, feels fairly certain that a lot of the evaluation has to be done through autopsies. Or vivisection. Neither option is a pleasant one."

"Jesus," Paula whispered. "Where are they getting . . . ?" She didn't finish the question, the most obvious answer leaping into her thoughts. "The recruiting vans."

"Probably," Mixer said. "Probably some other source as well, because a lot of the people the vans pull in aren't in such great health, and we're not sure how much use they'd be. Except as a source of raw materials."

"Raw materials?"

"My sister thinks the longevity treatments themselves involve live tissue, blood products, brain tissue."

"So we've got testing done on human subjects, followed by autopsies or vivisection, and treatments developed from materials harvested from other human beings."

St. Lucy nodded.

"And this is what Chick was selling," Paula said. "A blueprint for this fucking shit."

"I doubt he had a clue," Mixer said. "He didn't read Chinese. Probably all he knew was that it was about longer life, and he knew that was worth a fortune."

Paula looked again at the discs. This was what Chick died for. Fucking great. "Longer life," she said. "How much longer? Forty, fifty years?"

Mixer laughed.

St. Lucy shook her head. "They don't know for sure, of course; they won't until somebody actually does it, but the text in these things," she said, pointing at the discs, "talks about a lot more than that. A hundred and fifty, maybe even two hundred extra years. Bringing the aging process nearly to a complete halt."

"And they want it *now*," Mixer said. "There's not going to be any miracle of reversing the aging process, and who wants to live an extra hundred years as a decrepit old fuck with a body that's falling apart? No, you want to start this as young as possible."

"But you don't think they actually have it yet," Paula said.

"Teresa doesn't think so," St. Katherine said. "Another guess on her part, but it's probably a good guess. Two things, she says. One, that's the impression she gets from the text, the way they talk about promising avenues, dead ends. Two, if they thought they had it—and they'll never be sure, of course, until someone tries it and lives for an extra two hundred years—but if they thought they had the answer, they wouldn't be able to keep it secret. They'll want customers, for one thing. They probably won't care so much then. But for now, they're still experimenting. They can't afford to let this get out. They don't want the competition, and they don't want the bad PR."

"They've got to keep their stream of fresh bodies coming in," Mixer said.

"Jesus Christ," Paula said. She remembered sitting with Tremaine in his car at Hunter's Point, watching the huge crates being unloaded from Jenny Woo's van. Bodies, Tremaine had said. He'd been right.

No one said anything for a long time. Paula kept staring at the discs, as if they had some kind of answer for her. Hell, they had the answers for someone.

"What do we do with it?" she finally asked.

"We were hoping you would have an answer to that," Mixer said.

"Me?"

Mixer nodded. "Chick paid for this with his life." He put his hand on the stack of discs, then pushed it toward her. "They're yours now. You tell us what we should do."

Paula didn't know what to say. St. Katherine put her hand over Mixer's, looking at Paula.

"Minor said you would know what to do. He said you would know what's right."

Paula stared at the discs again. She would know what was right? Maybe they should just destroy the discs, pretend they'd never seen them. As soon as she thought about it, though, she realized it would be pointless. There had to be something else.

"I think we should give them to Carlucci," Paula eventually said. "We should give him the discs, and tell him what we know. He's stuck his neck out trying to find out what happened to Chick. And I trust him."

"Passing the buck?" Mixer said, smiling. "Let Carlucci decide?"

"No. He might not take them. But he probably knows more about this than we do. He might be able to do something, use them to stop this shit somehow." Mixer snorted, and Paula said, "You have a better idea?"

Mixer looked at St. Katherine, then at St. Lucy. They both nodded, and he turned back to Paula. "Okay," he said. "We give them to Carlucci."

Carlucci stood at the head of the alley, in a warm, steadily falling drizzle, and watched the flames of the barrel fires ahead of him. His raincoat kept his clothes dry, but he wore no hat, and his hair and face were wet. He felt certain the last of the answers were waiting for him down this alley. He didn't know if that was going to be good or bad.

He had been home from work for an hour, settling in to watch a movie with Andrea and Christina, when the call from Paula had come. Brief and simple.

"We've got something for you," Paula had said. "You'll want this." Then, before he'd had a chance to reply, "Do you remember where Saint Lucy brought you?"

"Yes."

"We'll be waiting for you."

He'd known, then. Something in Paula's voice. She had the answers. She knew.

So here he was, in a warm and strange, heavy mist that softened the sounds of the Tenderloin night. Carlucci entered the alley, approaching a barrel fire surrounded by several men and women and sizzling from the mist and a rack of fish grilling above the flames. A man held out a brown bottle, said, "Want a beer, paisan? We've got plenty." Carlucci shook his head, said, "No thanks," and continued along the alley.

He passed another barrel fire and slowed, searching the building wall, hoping to recognize the right door. A cloaked figure stepped out of an alcove and stood directly in front of him. St. Lucy. She smiled briefly, touched his arm, then turned back and opened the door for him.

Inside the building, they didn't speak. St. Lucy led the way upstairs to the same small kitchen where he'd first seen Mixer after his trial. This time the kitchen was full: Mixer and Paula Asgard, and a tall, beautiful woman who had to be St. Katherine; and now St. Lucy and himself. On the table was a stack of media discs in cases, maybe ten of them.

"Please, sit down," St. Lucy said.

Carlucci hung his coat on the chair, face and hair still dripping. St. Lucy got a towel for him, while Mixer got up and put coffee and tea and a bottle of Scotch in the middle of the table, white ceramic mugs all around.

"Thanks for coming," Paula said.

"Sure." Carlucci finished drying off, set the towel on the counter, and sat. He tried to read their expressions, tried to guess whether what he was about to hear was going to be good or bad. But he couldn't tell much from their faces, only that he was in for something serious, and he'd already known that. Then, everyone at the table watching him, it began.

Mixer and Paula, with occasional help from the two Saints, told Carlucci first where the discs had come from . . . and then everything they knew about what was on them—the translations and diagrams, the certainties and the probabilities and the guesses; what New Hong Kong was working on, and how they were doing it. Life extension and autopsies and vivisection and bodies harvested for longevity treatments. Everything.

Carlucci asked a few questions as they talked, but mostly he listened. He grew increasingly tired and depressed as all the final pieces now came together, shifting into place. It was as bad as he'd expected.

"You don't seem all that surprised," Paula said when they were done.

Carlucci managed a slight smile. "I'm not, really." He paused, thinking. "I didn't realize it at the time, but I've had two rather oblique offers of a couple hundred extra years of life if I would forget about all this and bury a couple of murder cases."

"Now you can take them up on it," Mixer said.

Carlucci gave a short laugh. "Yeah, sure. I doubt the offers are still good." He looked directly at Mixer. "I know why the mayor wanted you dead."

"Tell me."

Carlucci did. He told them about Jenny Woo and the rigged body-bags. "You were bootlegging the body-bags with her and Chick," Carlucci said. "The mayor knew you and Chick were friends. He assumed you knew what was going on."

"I didn't," Mixer said.

"I believe you."

Mixer turned to Paula. "You believe me, don't you?"

Paula nodded. "I've never trusted anyone more," she said. She reached out and took his hand of metal and flesh, squeezed it gently.

"There's more," Carlucci said.

"How much more?" Paula asked. "Something about Chick?"

Carlucci nodded. "Yes, about Chick." He told them some of what he had learned from Sparks and Tremaine, about Chick and the nephew and the mayor and New Hong Kong. He even told them a little—leaving out names and details—of what had been going on inside the police force, the orders to bury cases, the pressure from the mayor.

"So now what?" Carlucci asked when he was done.

"We were hoping you might know," Mixer said.

"Me."

"It was Paula's idea to come to you."

"You looked into this mess when no one else would," Paula said. "You've been working on it from the beginning, taking risks. We thought you might be able to do something with the discs. Or you'd know what we could do with them. Something, maybe, to stop all this."

Carlucci didn't say anything for a long time. He felt lost, unsure if he could find a way through this. The last of the answers had been here all right, but that didn't mean he knew what to do with them. He looked around the table, then reached for the Scotch and filled his cup. "Give me an hour alone to think, all right?"

Paula looked at the others and nodded. The four of them got up from the table, and left the room.

Paula and Mixer sat on the fire escape outside Mixer's room, drinking beer and watching the container fires in the alley below them. The rain had become little more than a light, falling mist, warm on Paula's skin. The alley was filled with shadows, figures moving in and out of the firelight, music pounding from a boomer across the way, bells ringing somewhere out on the street. Loud cracks, maybe gunshots, but they were far away, maybe not even in the Tenderloin. Paula could see white and red lights of vehicles moving along the streets at either end of the alley.

"What do you think Carlucci's going to say?" Mixer asked.

Paula shrugged. "I almost don't care anymore."

"Two hundred extra years," Mixer said. "Live into the twenty-third century."

"Christ, who would want to?" Paula drank from her beer and shook her head.

"I would," Mixer replied. "I almost died. Didn't like it. I like being alive, and I'd like the chance to keep on doing it as long as possible." He snorted. "I won't get the chance, though."

"No," Paula agreed. "Neither of us will. If they find the answer up in New Hong Kong, only the rich and the big sharks will get a shot at it. We won't get shit." She shook her head again. "Fuck 'em. Let them have it."

Mixer laughed. "Yeah, well . . . Not everyone's going to take that attitude."

Paula looked at him and smiled. "No, they won't. That'll at least make it a little rougher for those rich fucks."

In the building across the alley, one floor down and just to the left, Paula could see a man and a woman standing next to each other by the open window. Their shoulders were pressed together, and they were talking, smiling. She heard the woman laugh, then saw her pull back and playfully slap the man's shoulder. The man grinned, then put his arms around the woman, and they held each other, the woman digging her face into the man's neck.

"You love her, don't you?" Paula asked.

"Saint Katherine? Yeah, I guess I do."

"It won't be easy," Paula said.

"No," Mixer replied. "But maybe easier than you think. We've both got gashes scorched in our brains, and they seem to match in a way. It'll work out."

"I hope so."

"What about you and Tremaine?"

Paula shook her head. "Who knows? All this crap, we've never had much of a chance."

"This will all be over soon, one way or another."

"You think?"

Mixer nodded. "Yeah, whatever Carlucci decides, there's going to be some kind of explosion. He won't just let it go. Not tomorrow, maybe not for a week or two, but it'll happen." He stared down at the container fires. "And when it does, I've got something in mind for Mayor Terrance Kashen."

Paula looked at him. "What, Mixer?"

Mixer shook his head. "We'll never have to worry about him again. That fuck." He wouldn't say anything more.

Paula looked away from him, back to the couple across the alley. "Chick sure got himself into something this time, didn't he?"

"You still miss him," Mixer said.

"Yeah. Always will. I don't know why. He could be a real asshole, sometimes." She smiled, looking at Mixer. "I guess you know that, don't you?"

Mixer nodded. "Mostly, he just didn't think. He never really meant to be an asshole."

"No." Paula finished off her beer, resisted the temptation to throw it over the side of the fire escape. She set it beside her and pressed her face into the railing bars.

"I've got to start playing again," she said. "I've bailed out on so many gigs lately, Sheela and Bonita are about ready to get a new bass player. Besides, I really miss it. I need it."

Mixer put his hands on her neck, worked at the tightened muscles. "Then do it," he said. He continued to massage her neck and shoulders for several minutes, strong and hard with his left hand, noticeably weaker with the right. The pain felt good, loosened the knots, but she imagined it must be hard on his injured hand and arm. She put her hands over his and stopped them. "Thanks," she said.

"Everything'll be okay," Mixer said.

Paula laughed once and shook her head. "No it won't."

"No," Mixer agreed. "It won't."

Paula pressed her face harder into the bars and stared down at the flames below.

Carlucci sat at the kitchen table and drank bad Scotch, trying to think. The alcohol wasn't going to help him, but he drank anyway, relishing the burning warmth it sent out from his belly. He stared at the stack of discs. Two hundred extra years of life. It wouldn't matter if it was *five* hundred, it would never do Caroline any good. She would still die before she was thirty. The thought of himself and the rest of his family living to be over two hundred years old while Caroline never made it out of her twenties made him ill. He knew it wasn't logical, that they were all going to significantly outlive Caroline anyway, but it still seemed somehow obscene to him.

Carlucci sipped at the Scotch, tongue and lips burning. The building was quiet; he could hear faint sounds of movement above him, but not much else. There was flickering light outside, visible through the kitchen window, but the Tenderloin's night sounds were muted. He felt very much alone.

What to do. Paula and Mixer and the two Saints wanted *his* advice. Because he was a cop? Yeah, he was a cop, and he was supposed to find out who committed crimes, collect evidence, and then arrest those responsible. And if he did his job well enough, a lot of those criminals would be tried and convicted and pay the price this society had decided they would pay. More or less.

But there had been plenty of crimes committed in this business, probably a lot that he didn't even know about yet, and he couldn't make one fucking arrest that would ever stick. There was no way he could see to make those who were ultimately responsible pay. This time, he could not do his job.

It wasn't his fault, he knew that. It wasn't from lack of effort, or some inadequacy of his. But he still felt ineffectual. There was nothing, it seemed, that he could do.

He got up from the table and walked to the small window. Leaning against the counter, looking down and out through the grimy window, he could just see the alley below, dark figures moving in and out of the light of fires. Why did they have fires? The nights didn't get cold. But there was something comforting about the drum fires, and he almost felt like going downstairs and taking up that guy's offer of a beer. It was a better offer than the ones he'd had from the mayor and the slug. It was an offer he could live with.

Directly across from him, a large, heavy cat sat on the ledge of a lighted, open window, chewing at its claws. A bright light flared overhead, and red embers showered down into the alley, but the cat wasn't in the least distracted. Fat cats, he thought. The mayor, his buddies, everyone up in New Hong Kong.

No, he could not do his job. Which left him with only two options.

Try to bury it all and walk away; let the mayor and Jenny Woo and New Hong Kong all go on, undisturbed, shipping their bodies, doing their research.

Or somehow blow it wide open, and hope nobody else got killed.

Carlucci returned to the table, sat, poured himself some more Scotch, and waited for the others to return.

27

"GIVE IT TO Tremaine," Carlucci told them. "Give him everything."

Outside the Tenderloin, Carlucci and Paula skirted the DMZ and headed for the Polk Corridor on foot. He'd had too much to drink, and was glad he wasn't alone; he didn't trust his own judgment. The drizzle had stopped, but everything was wet. It was well after midnight, and the sidewalk was almost empty. The street wasn't much busier.

No one had argued with him. No one had offered any other ideas. They had agreed to turn over hard copies of the text and translation and diagrams to Tremaine—Paula had them with her now, tucked up inside her jacket. They would all, Carlucci included, tell Tremaine everything they knew. And Carlucci had taken the discs, promising to destroy them once Tremaine's story was out.

"Do *you* want the discs?" Carlucci now asked Paula. "For Chick's music, his videos? No one but me would know."

Paula shook her head. "No, but thanks. I was thinking of asking you for them, but it's not worth the risk. Like you said, anyone finds out somebody has them . . . whatever music's on the discs, it won't really matter that much if I don't have it."

"I've thought about scattering them around the city," Carlucci said. It was a crazy idea that had come to him. "Drop one on the sidewalk here, toss one onto a roof in the Asian Quarter, leave another in a coffee shop. All around the city. See what the street does with them."

Paula smiled at him. "That's not such a bad idea."

Carlucci shrugged.

"You're not going to do it, though, are you?"

"No."

They continued in silence until they reached the Polk Corridor. There was more traffic, now, more lights and noise, more people. The sidewalks were almost crowded.

"Home," Paula said.

They passed Christiano's, where they'd eaten and talked, where he had told her he would look into Chick's death. It seemed to Carlucci like a long time ago. Things had changed quite a lot since then.

Music banged out of a window across the way, and two women were dancing to it in the street, hopping in and out of traffic, smiling when cars honked at them. A man with a see-through prosthetic arm nodded at Paula, who nodded back. Two heavy women bundled in long coats staggered down the sidewalk, cigarettes in hand, both of them drooling. Other things didn't seem to change at all, Carlucci thought.

A few more blocks, then they cut down a street to Paula's building. Carlucci stopped on the bottom step of the porch.

"You want to come in?" Paula asked.

"No. I should get home. Andrea will be wondering what the hell has happened to me."

"I wish I'd met her."

"Maybe someday."

Paula nodded and sighed. "Who'd have thought?" she said. "When I first tracked you down and asked you to check out Chick's murder. It seemed so simple, then. And it turned into such a mess." She paused. "I'm sorry I got you into this."

"Don't be," Carlucci said. "You couldn't have known. And it was the right thing to do. Sometimes that's what's most important."

"Is that why you think we should give it all to Tremaine?"

Carlucci shook his head. "I have no idea if it's the right thing. I just don't know what else to do."

Paula nodded. It seemed to be enough for her. "I'm never going to find out who killed Chick, am I?"

"No."

"It's over," she said. "But it's not."

"No," Carlucci said. "Things like this are never completely over."

Neither of them said anything for a minute. Paula took out her keys. "How are you getting home?" she asked.

"I'm going to splurge, catch a cab." He paused, then said, "Be careful, Paula. Tremaine does his story, this place'll get hairy when it breaks."

"I know." She shrugged.

"Will you be seeing him soon?"

"I guess."

"Tell him I'll talk to him."

"I will." She gave him a tired smile. "Good night, Frank Carlucci."

"Good night, Paula Asgard."

The mayor's limo, long and dark and silent, was parked in front of Carlucci's house when he arrived. Carlucci paid the cab driver, then waited for the cab to pull away. He watched his house, wondering how long the mayor had been here. He started up the walkway to the porch, thinking about the discs in his coat.

The rear door of the limo opened, startling Carlucci, and the mayor stepped out. Carlucci stopped, halfway along the walk, and waited for the mayor to join him.

The mayor's expression was hard and ugly in the light from the porch. "If you fuck me, Frank, I'll take you down with me."

Too late, Carlucci thought, *I already have.* "What are you talking about?" he asked.

"I told you to bury my nephew's case," the mayor said.

"No. I asked you if that's what you wanted, and you said no."

"Don't give me that shit, Frank. You understood what I wanted. You knew exactly what I was asking for."

Carlucci nodded, sighing. "I understood."

"I've been hearing things. And I don't like it. And not just about my nephew. The Chick Roberts case wasn't even yours."

"Who's Chick Roberts?"

The mayor's mouth twisted into something that might have been a smile, and he slowly shook his head. "You fuck. I made you an offer, once. Not just your life, but a much longer life."

"I didn't realize at the time what you were offering."

"You do now, don't you?"

Carlucci nodded.

"The offer won't be good much longer," the mayor said. "And you won't like the alternative. Your friend Mixer didn't. Now you bury this shit, and bury it fast, before all hell breaks loose. You understand?"

"I understand."

The mayor glanced toward the lighted windows of Carlucci's house, then looked back at him. "Do you?"

Carlucci nodded. "I understand," he repeated.

The mayor stared at him a while longer, then turned away without another word. Carlucci watched him climb back into the limo, slam the door shut. The engine started, headlights came on; then the limo pulled smoothly away from the curb and drove down the street.

Andrea opened the front door as he came up the steps. "Are you okay, Frank?"

Carlucci nodded. He stepped inside and Andrea closed the door, locking it and throwing the bolts.

"He was parked out there all evening," Andrea said. "It was starting to worry me." Then she wrinkled her nose. "You've been drinking. A lot."

Carlucci nodded again. "Too much." He smiled. "It seemed like a good idea at the time."

"Why, Frank?"

"I'll tell you."

Carlucci took her hand in his and led the way into the kitchen. It was going to be a long, long talk.

Paula stood just inside her apartment, her back against the door, looking around the room. Her gaze stopped on the remaining boxes of Chick's things. She would have to remind Mixer and the Saints that she wanted the music back, all those tapes and discs. All that was left of Chick.

Chick.

She walked into the bedroom, unzipped her jacket, took out the manila envelope filled with the text and diagrams from the discs, and tossed it onto the bed. Then she sat next to it, picked up the phone, and dialed Tremaine's number.

It rang several times, finally was picked up. "Hello?" His voice was husky with sleep.

"Ian. It's Paula."

"What is it? Are you all right?" Voice clearer, now, alert.

"I'm fine," Paula said. "I have something for you."

"What?"

"Everything."

There was another pause, longer. "Should I come over now?" Tremaine asked.

"Yes," Paula replied. "I want you here, Ian."

"I'll be right over."

Paula hung up the phone. She took off her jacket, then got up and sat in her recliner, facing the blank monitor. The disc with "Love at Ground Zero" was still in the player, but she couldn't bring herself to watch it.

"I did what I could, Chick." Her voice was a whisper, she could barely hear herself. "I did what I could."

She leaned back in the chair, closed her eyes, and waited for Tremaine.

BODY-BAGS, RECRUITERS, AND MURDER:
New Hong Kong's Search for Eternal Life

by Tremaine

This story is not really about "Eternal Life." This story is about life extension. But life extension so great it has the sound and feel of eternal life. Immortality. Life extension of as much as two hundred years.

Imagine living to be two hundred and fifty years old. Good, or bad? More importantly, at what cost?

The answer to this kind of life extension is not here yet, but it probably will be soon. And it will be the medical researchers of New Hong Kong who find it, because they are searching for it now, and they are closing in. They do not care, however, at what cost they find the answer. They do not care what the answer is. And for now, they will do anything to keep what they are doing a secret.

People have been killed in recent weeks, killed to keep this a secret. A guitarist and low-end drug dealer named Chick Roberts has been murdered. William Kashen, the nephew of San Francisco's mayor, has been murdered. Robert Butler, William Kashen's business partner, has been murdered. Rosa Weeks, M.D., and Poppy Chandler: two more murders. Almost certainly there have been others I am not aware of. There might be more to come. There is no way to know how or when this will all end.

But there was a beginning, a time when . . .

Epilogue

TWO WEEKS LATER, near midnight, Carlucci stood on the sidewalk outside The Palms, listening to the muted crash of music. Inside, the Black Angels were playing. Inside, was Paula Asgard.

A lot had happened in the last two weeks. Tremaine's story had gone out over the nets, and for the next several days the city was in turmoil. Huge crowds of protesters had surrounded City Hall and kept city officials from leaving for a day and a half, until the police and National Guard had broken through. Someone launched two rockets into New Hong Kong's headquarters in the Financial District, killing over thirty people and injuring hundreds. Small localized riots erupted throughout the city, most followed by large-scale looting and burning of cars and buildings. New Hong Kong suspended flights from Hunter's Point.

The day Tremaine's story broke over the nets, the mayor disappeared. There was a wild scene out at Hunter's Point, crowds at the gates being fought off by security forces. The mayor, in his limousine, forced his way through the crowd and the first gates, wanting to board the last ship to New Hong Kong. But the main security team stopped him—apparently New Hong Kong had hung him out to dry, just as Monk had hinted at, and ordered their security forces to prevent him from boarding. The mayor then left Hunter's Point, and hadn't been seen since. Word on the streets was that the Saints had kidnapped him and put him on trial. Carlucci didn't know if it was true or not, but he hoped it was. He didn't want to ever worry about Kashen again.

The day his story broke, Tremaine disappeared as well. Paula had called Carlucci to tell him. Afraid that New Hong Kong would come after him— enough people had died already—Tremaine had left the city. Paula didn't know where he'd gone, or how long he'd be away. She'd sounded depressed, and Carlucci thought he understood—she'd lost someone else. First Chick; then Mixer, in a way; and now Tremaine.

Carlucci hadn't seen her since that night with the Saints. They had talked several times on the phone, but their conversations were short and awkward, filled more with silences than words. Now, though, he had to see her in person. He hoped it would make a difference. She wasn't expecting him, but he thought it would be a good surprise.

He finally opened the door, the music blasting him, and he stepped into the clouds of music and smoke, flashing colored lights and a loud, jamming crowd. A young guy just inside the door with foiled hair and two metal hands (real or fake?) put one of his hands up, stopping him. He leaned forward, shouted into Carlucci's ear.

"You sure you want in here, old man?"

Carlucci nodded, and the guy shrugged. "Ten bucks. For the band."

Carlucci dug a crumpled wad of money out of his pocket and picked out two fives, handing them to the guy. The guy nodded, slapped Carlucci on the shoulder, and said, "Have a good time, old man."

Old man. Yeah. To the guy, who wasn't much more than a kid, Carlucci *was* old.

He could barely see the band at the other end of the long, narrow room, his view obstructed by the smoke, people at the raised tables, other people walking around or dancing with their hands in the air, and the half dozen blackened wood ceiling supports. Some of the smoke was illegal, he could smell that. There, he caught a glimpse of Paula, pounding at her guitar, wearing a white T-shirt and black jeans, screaming into the microphone. He couldn't make out a single word.

There weren't any vacant seats at the bar, and all the tables were full, so he worked his way to the side wall, found a spot to lean against between a woman in a crash suit and a guy in silver-strips who must have been close to seven feet tall. The smells in the place made him feel good, reminded him of the clubs he'd played in with the Po-Leece Blues Band. A different crowd, different sound, definitely, but something the same—people pressed in together, drinking and smoking, having a good time: there for the music.

A waitress in a black T-shirt, cutoffs, and heavy leather boots stopped by, and he ordered a draft. She said something back, the name of the beer, probably, and he shrugged, nodded.

Carlucci had a good view of the band from where he stood, right between two of the wooden posts. Drummer, lead guitar, and Paula on bass and vocals. Loud and fast, a lot louder and faster than he liked, but the energy was fine; he could feel that, he liked that part of it. And the bass pounding through the floor and wall, into his bones.

The waitress came back with his beer, sooner than he had expected; the beer a lot bigger, too, jumbo pint glass. He paid her, and she left. Carlucci looked back at the stage, and saw that Paula had caught sight of him. She was back from the mike, a break in the vocals, and she stared at him, hand banging away at the strings. Then she smiled, nodding once, the smile getting broader, and he knew it was okay. He smiled back at her and put up his hand, feeling kind of stupid. Like an old man.

He saw Paula lean over to say something in the guitarist's ear, and the guitarist nodded. Carlucci drank from his beer and tried to relax, settle into the music. He was still a little nervous.

The Black Angels played one more song, then Paula announced they'd be taking a short break. The quiet was a relief to Carlucci. There was still music playing over the sound system and people talking all around him, but it was quiet to him, the volume turned way down. Paula stepped off the stage and worked her way through the tables and chairs until she stood right in front of him, smiling. Carlucci couldn't help smiling back. She looked terrific—healthy sweat, good color in her face.

"It's good to see you," Paula said. "A hell of a surprise, but a good one."

"I'm glad to see you, too."

She winced. "Phone conversations have been kind of crappy, haven't they?"

Carlucci nodded, shrugged. He held up his beer. "Want some?"

"Love some." She took the glass from him and drank half of what was left. "Man, that's good."

"How are you doing?" he asked.

"Better. Every day better, I guess. Playing again helps. Helps a lot."

"I can see that. You look great."

She smiled. "Yeah, it does that for me."

"How about other things?"

Paula shrugged, the smile fading. "Still lots of different kinds of pain. But it's okay. That's getting better, too. You?"

"All right. I thought for a while I might be forced to retire, but it's all working out." McCuller had taken 'voluntary' retirement—apparently New Hong Kong and Vaughn had been unhappy with the way he'd appeared in Tremaine's story. Vaughn was still Chief, but accommodation had been reached—there were no hypocritical citations, but Carlucci, Hong, LaPlace, even Santos and Weathers, were all in good shape. Everything was back to what passed for normal.

"Good," Paula said. She took another long drink from the beer. "That other stuff, though. Politicians making a lot of noise about New Hong Kong, but it doesn't look like much is really going to change, is it?"

Carlucci shook his head. "Not really. Closer inspections of shipments to New Hong Kong for a while, a lot of handwaving about medical ethics, but that's about it. More money will shift around, and the bodies will start shipping again. Alive *and* dead. Like you said, lots of noise, but after a while it'll be pretty much the same again."

"About right," Paula said. "The fucking politicians want to have a crack at eternal life themselves."

"Yes. And the reality is, there isn't a hell of a lot they can do about New Hong Kong, anyway. Unless they want to try to blow them right out of the sky."

Paula smiled. "It's an idea."

"Yeah, ideas everywhere."

"I guess I was hoping Tremaine's story might change things a little more."

"I don't think Tremaine thought much would change," Carlucci said. "He said as much, really, when I talked to him the last time. He said he just wanted the truth to be known. Anything more than that would be one hell of a bonus."

"That sounds about right."

She took one more drink of the beer, then handed it back to him. They didn't talk for a bit, Carlucci trying to gear up to ask her about Kashen.

"Is it true?" he finally asked. "That the Saints put the mayor on trial?"

Paula looked at him for a few moments without saying anything, then nodded. "Yes, it's true."

"What happened?"

"He survived. If you could call it that." She sighed heavily, then went on. "I've seen him. He's a wreck. He's being cared for by an old woman and a young boy who think he's a holy man." Paula shook her head. "He has no idea who he is."

"Was Mixer a part of it?" Carlucci asked.

"Of course. He's one of them, now."

"A Saint."

"Yeah, a Saint." Paula shrugged. "It might be good. For Mixer *and* for the Saints."

Now was the time, Carlucci thought. He'd been holding it back, like holding back a treat, except she had no idea it was coming.

"I've got something for you," he said. "The main reason I came here tonight. I didn't want to wait until tomorrow."

"What?" She didn't seem to know whether to be eager or afraid.

"A message. I thought you'd want it right away."

He reached into his back pocket and took out the small, folded piece of paper, handed it to her. She opened it carefully, then looked at it. A short message. She read it silently, but he knew what it said. He'd had to copy it out himself:

> *Paula,*
> *Settled in, everything's fine. Miss you.*
> *Wish you were here.*
>   *Love,*
>   *Ian*

Carlucci watched her expression change, soften, watched just the hint of a smile appear.

"Love?" he said.

Paula looked up at him, smile widening. "Could be. I may find out someday." She folded the paper and put it in her jeans pocket. "Thanks."

Someone called her name from the stage and Paula turned. The guitarist was waving at her.

"Break's over," Paula said. "You going to stick around for the next set?"

Carlucci shook his head, but smiled. "Not my kind of music. I just wanted to get that to you. I just wanted to see you."

"Thanks again." She stepped forward and gave him a quick hug. "I've gotta go. Stay in touch."

"I'll have to."

"Yeah." Grinning now. "Bye, Frank Carlucci."

"Goodbye, Paula Asgard."

She turned and walked back toward the stage. Carlucci finished the beer, then set the empty glass on the nearest table, which was already half-covered with empty bottles and glasses. He looked back once more at the stage, and Paula, bass strapped on, waved to him. Carlucci waved back, then headed for the door.

At the entrance, the guy with the foiled hair and metal hands grinned. "Too much for you, old man?"

"Yeah," Carlucci said, laughing. "Too much."

He pushed open the door, feeling better than he had in days, and stepped out into the night.

Carlucci's Heart

Isabel

HER KEEPERS HAD called her Isabel, but she had not heard that name in a long time. She missed the sound of it, the warmth she felt inside whenever Donya, one of her keepers, had said it. *Isabel.*

She rarely got close to people anymore, though she often saw men and women here, watched as they moved past her hiding places. Strangers, all of them. But it was even more rare that anyone saw her.

Isabel was a long-tailed macaque, and she now lived in the Core, deep in the heart of the Tenderloin, wandering along its dark, subterranean passageways, squeezing through old ventilation shafts and rusted, twisted metal ductwork, climbing shadowy stairways through ruined buildings. Her fur was a rich brown and gray that almost shined on the rare occasions she stood in full sunlight, the sun beaming down on her through some jagged opening in the brick, stone, metal, or concrete. Her eyes were rimmed with soft brows. Her right index finger had been cut off at the first knuckle, but she did not remember how that had happened. She ate insects, and food scraps stolen from the people who lived in these old and crumbling ruins, and she drank water from pools that formed after the rains. She thought she had seen other monkeys in here, but she could not be sure.

Life was different for her now. She did not really know where she was, but most of the time it was darker and damper than it had been where she had lived before. She also felt heavier, and it had taken a while for her muscles to adapt to the extra weight. Here, no one came to feed and water her, no one came to talk to her. But here there was no cage. Here she was free.

Isabel had been quite sick just before she'd been released into the Core, and she had almost died. She couldn't be sure, but she thought her keepers had done something to make her sick. And when she had recovered, they had done something else, this time to make her sleep, and when she had awakened, she had been here, in the Core. Alone, and free.

She was a quiet, careful monkey now.

Isabel dozed, warm and comfortable. Dream images flickered through her thoughts. She sat on a flat stone, bathed in the light from the sun shining down on her through an uneven opening in the brick wall.

Sounds alerted her—scrape and click.

Isabel's eyes opened, her head jerked, and she whirled around, blinking in the light. A shadow moved toward her, a man holding up some kind of netting.

Isabel didn't hesitate. She attacked.

She lunged at the man's face, sharp incisors bared, clawing at him with her hands.

The man cried out, threw his arms across his face. Isabel's teeth slashed skin and muscle of an arm, a shoulder, her fingers clawed at air, then found hair and clothing, dug into something. The man jerked back, Isabel continued slashing and biting. Then the man fell backward, twisted around, and landed on top of Isabel, crushing away her breath. He kept rolling, and she let go.

She lay with eyes wide, gasping for breath that wouldn't come. Sharp pain sliced her chest. The man, howling now, scrambled away from her.

Breath returned with more sharp pain, and she bounded to her feet, dizzy but prepared to defend herself. But the man was gone, leaving behind a pile of netting. She could hear his screams fading into the darkness.

Isabel tasted blood, and knew it wasn't hers.

P A R T   O N E

Exposure

1

CAROLINE ENTERED THE DMZ at dusk. Not a great time of day, but better than it would be in an hour or so when darkness fell. She didn't want to be here at all, but this was where Tito lived. Tito didn't want to be here either, but he was broke and dying and he had no real choice.

Walking the streets of the DMZ—the narrow strip that ran along the north and west outer walled edges of the Tenderloin—was all right during the day if you really watched yourself; but at night the place turned into a free fire zone. After dark, the Tenderloin itself was a lot safer; even the cops avoided the DMZ once night fell.

Street traffic was practically at a standstill, cars and trucks and pedalcarts and bikes and jits creeping forward in jerking fits and starts amid shouts and curses and blasting horns—the final rush while light remained. The sidewalks were just as crowded, and Caroline had to shove her way along, pressed in by bodies on all sides.

She wore blue jeans and an old gray sweatshirt. Her sidepurse was wrapped tight against her ribs under the sweatshirt. In her back pocket was a canister of Ass-Gass.

A man wearing a wire head-cage blocked her way and screamed something at her, but his handler banged a shock stick against the head-cage, sparks flying and shutting him up. Caroline pushed her way around the man, who was now whimpering and shaking his head and blinking spasmodically. A shiver of pity rolled through her. The handler, a short squat woman in boojee overalls, snarled at Caroline as if she had been responsible for the man's outburst, and Caroline hurried away.

She worked her way along the block, fighting her own edgy claustrophobia and generalized anxiety. Across the way, the outer walls of the Tenderloin rose above the street like dark, inanimate guardians, buildings attached to one another, all gaps, streets, and alleys filled in, barricaded to keep the DMZ from leaking into the Tenderloin. In the dimming light, street lamps cast vague, amorphous shadows cut through with the glare and flash of shop signs, the syncopated flicker of slithering neon. The air was heavy with the stench of sweat, bubbling grease, and a sweetish, drifty burnt odor.

Just past Turtle Joe's she ducked into an alcove unmarked except for a crude skull-and-crossbones spray-painted in red on the crumbling brick arch. The grille-covered door was unlocked, as always, and she pushed it open. When she closed the door behind her, she cut off the noise and stink of the street.

The dimly lit entry was small, with a close, musty smell. Stairs were on the left, and directly in front of her was the hallway leading to the ground-floor rooms. On the right wall was a bank of mailboxes, but it had been years since any mail had actually been delivered to this building. The place was quiet. The Sisters of the Forgotten had already been through, delivering meals and comfort. The death house was settling down for the night.

A pale, thin girl about nine or ten stepped out of the hall and stared at Caroline. The girl was dressed in ragged, faded red overalls and black tennis shoes, and the right side of her face and neck was streaked with welts. She opened her mouth wide, hacked once, then ran back into the hall. A man yelled from far down the hallway, and a door slammed. Caroline turned away and started up the concrete stairs.

The stairwell was lit by bare bulbs screwed into ceramic sockets set in the cracked plaster ceiling. The walls were smeared with green and blue paint, streaked with soot. Graffiti was surprisingly sparse, and she didn't bother to read what was there. She was already familiar with most of it, and all of it was depressing.

Everyone in the building was dying. Some would die soon; others would be able to stretch out the pain and misery for a year or two. A few would die of newer, exotic diseases such as Chingala Fever or Pilate's Chorea or Passion, but most were sick with more mundane terminal diseases. Like Tito, who had AIDS. Caroline was grateful for the knowledge that, no matter how bad she got in the next few years, she would never end up in a death house like this.

She stopped on the third-floor landing and leaned against the wall, trying to catch her breath. She tired easily, so far the only manifestation of the Gould's Syndrome that would almost certainly kill her within the next several years. But she no longer felt sorry for herself. She would probably die before she was thirty, but it would be with less pain and suffering than most of those who lived here; it would be a hell of a lot less than what Tito was going through right now.

Tito was being ravaged by spiking fevers and monstrous headaches and a severe, recurring ear infection; some sort of neuropathy made his hands ache constantly; and right now he had a good strong case of thrush going so he could hardly swallow a thing. But he'd called her this morning from Mama Chan's where he'd actually eaten some breakfast, and said he was feeling better, so maybe some of the meds were finally working and he was through the worst of this phase. They were going to watch a couple of movies, and then she'd spend the night on the sofa, keeping him company.

She pushed away from the wall and walked toward Tito's room. The hallway was carpeted with a thin, stained brown runner worn through in spots and dotted with dozens of cigarette burns. The air smelled of sickness—a thick, warm, cloying stench. Muted sounds of televisions and radios leaked through the walls, interrupted by the occasional fit of coughing or other, unidentifiable noises.

She knocked on Tito's door. She thought she heard movement from inside, but there was no answer. She knocked again. "Tito, it's me. Caroline." More scrabbling sounds.

She tried the door, found it unlocked. She pushed it open and looked inside.

Mouse crouched in the rear corner, stuffing Tito's coin box into an already overloaded duffel bag. He looked at her and grinned, metal teeth flashing. Mouse was just under five feet tall and skinny, with short, spiky blond hair he never combed, and a neuro-collar grafted onto his neck. He wore a Mutant Alligators T-shirt, faded green jeans, and black Stasi boots. The neuro-collar flashed a patterned series of red lights, and Caroline wondered what that meant.

"Where's Tito?" she asked.

"Gone," Mouse said. He finished stuffing the coin box into the duffel bag and squatted on the floor with his back against the wall, blinking at her. He had tiny pink mouse eyes, and she never trusted them.

"Gone where?"

Mouse shrugged. "Mens came and took him."

"Who?"

"Two mens."

Tito's room was about fifteen feet square, and sparsely furnished—a foam rubber mattress, an old sagging camel-back sofa, a small metal desk and chair, a couple of short, rickety bookcases; a half-size refrigerator and a double-burner hot plate on top of some cheap plywood cabinets. There was a toilet stuck back in a tiny alcove; no bath or shower. Tito didn't own much, but as Caroline looked around the room, all the surfaces and shelves were pretty much bare. She stared hard at Mouse, at the huge, bulging duffel bag at his feet. Only the TV remained, still on its stand by the window. Maybe Mouse was going to come back for it on his next trip. Some friend he was.

"What the hell are you doing?" she asked him.

Mouse grinned and snapped his metal teeth. "Tito's not coming back. He don't need this stuff."

"How do you know he's not coming back?"

Mouse just shook his head.

"How do you know, Mouse?"

"Those mens. They take you away, take you to the Core, you never comin' back. I know."

Caroline shut the door, leaned back against it. She was starting to get pissed. "When were they here?"

"Half hour ago."

"Where were *you*, Mouse?"

"Hiding?" Then he tipped his head back and hacked out a laugh.

"Mouse. What did they want with him?"

"Don't know," he answered, with another shrug. "Don't want to know."

"Didn't you hear anything? They must have said things to Tito, asked him questions."

"Try not to listen. Hear no evil." Grinning again.

"Mouse. You heard something, didn't you."

"Maybe."

"Maybe what?"

That damn shrug again. Then, with a heavy sigh he said, "Maybe something about Cancer Cell." Mouse closed his eyes for a moment, grimacing.

"Cancer Cell?" The name was only vaguely familiar. "What the hell's that?"

"Ask you daddy," Mouse said. "You daddy's cop man, yes?"

"My father's a cop, yes."

Mouse got to his feet, grabbed the duffel bag, and hefted it. The weight gave him a definite list.

"Leave that here," Caroline said. "Tito might be back."

"No," Mouse said. "He's not coming back. You don't coming back from the Core."

"Leave it, Mouse."

"No." He crouched, then with his free hand pulled a gravity knife from his boot, chunked the blade into place. A nasty blade, gleaming. "No." He flashed his metal teeth at her one more time. The neuro-collar was now blinking a deep blue.

All right, Caroline thought. Everything Mouse was taking could be replaced when Tito came back. *If* Tito came back. She didn't think Mouse would actually hurt her, but it was always a possibility. So she moved away from the door, gave him a clear, wide path to it.

"Go, then," she said. "Now."

Mouse nodded. He closed up the blade, tucked the knife back into his boot, then staggered to the door, half-carrying, half-dragging the duffel bag. "You keep the TV," he said, grinning at her one final time. "Piece of shit, anyway." Then he opened the door, lurched through it, and headed down the hall.

Caroline slammed the door shut and threw the two dead bolts. She was suddenly very afraid for Tito. What the hell was Cancer Cell? She'd heard the name before, but she couldn't remember anything about it. She couldn't imagine Tito involved in anything that could get him kidnapped or killed. Or had he gone with them voluntarily? She wasn't sure she could trust Mouse's version of what had happened. Maybe no one had come for Tito. Maybe he'd just gone out for a while, and Mouse had decided to ransack the place. Mouse and Tito had been something like friends, but that might not mean that much to Mouse.

She crossed the room to the sink and opened the cabinet above it. It looked like all of Tito's meds were still there, forty or fifty little plastic bottles. She picked one up, shook it. Maybe half full. Same thing with two others she checked. If Tito had gone somewhere on his own, he would have taken some of them with him. But why hadn't Mouse taken them? Probably because they were all half-ass meds, the only things Tito could get from the free clinics—cheap antibiotics, weak painkillers, ineffective antidepressants, and unproven immune system boosters. Mouse probably couldn't get shit for them on the street.

Caroline took a quick tour of the room, but except for what was missing nothing seemed out of place. No signs of struggle. She went to the window, pulled it open, and looked out into the air well between the buildings. Night was falling quickly, and she could barely see the weeds and garbage at the bottom of the air well. She wasn't sure she'd be able to see a body if one was lying there. Then she craned her neck around, looking up. Brick walls rose to a rectangle of darkening sky three more floors above her. Boarded windows, screened vents, cracks of light, the rusted remains of what had once been a fire escape.

She pulled her head back inside, but remained at the window, her gaze unfocused. She would wait for Tito. Yes. She would wait through the night and see if he came back; she was better off not going out into the DMZ now anyway. And if Tito wasn't back by morning? Maybe wait some more; she'd worry about it then. She turned away from the window, walked over to the hot plate, and put on water for tea.

Caroline woke in the middle of the night, sitting up abruptly. She listened intently, unable to see a thing. Something had awakened her, some sound. Street noise filtered in through the window, the DMZ night—some kind of irregular banging, a motor revving, muted popping sounds, someone screaming in a strange, deep monotone—but she was sure that wasn't it. Something else. Something inside the building.

Heartbeat loud and fast, she sat without moving, eyes gradually adjusting to the darkness. The room was empty, no strange shadows or movements, and she didn't hear anything unusual—faint snoring from the room next door; tinny, Spanish music from somewhere below her; a creaking floorboard above.

There. Something. A hum she felt more than heard.

She eased the blanket aside and stood, then padded barefoot across the room to the door and put her eye to the peephole. The hall lights were out, but there was a faint, shifting blue glow. Her view was distorted by the peephole, and the glow was dark and dim and shadowy, but she could make out hooded figures moving past the door, steps slow, bodies swaying in unison to a slow, unheard rhythm.

What was this? Who were they?

Phantoms. She could almost see through them; inside the hoods, where their faces should be, she saw only darker shadows and a deeper blue glow. She shivered, feeling and hearing the deep, penetrating hum, feeling suddenly cold. She wanted to back away from the door, retreat into a far corner of the room, but she remained where she was, transfixed, hardly breathing, hardly moving. The ghostlike figures moved past the door and progressed slowly along the hall, humming and swaying, the glow fading until it was out of the peephole's range, and only complete darkness remained.

She returned to the sofa and sat, knees pulled up to her chin, and wrapped herself in the blanket. Where are you, Tito? What happened to you?

She remained on the sofa, watching the dark and listening to the night. She did not sleep.

2

RYLAND CAGE CROUCHED on the Tenderloin rooftop just before dawn, gazing out across the street at the dark, crumbling ruins of the Core. The Core was four square blocks of Hell in the black heart of the Tenderloin. Or four square blocks of Chaos, if you were a different kind of believer. Maybe it was a little of both. Walled off by street barricades and crash nets from the rest of the Tenderloin, the Core was a bleak pocket of ruined buildings, unnatural darkness and eerie quiet, and rubble-strewn streets deserted except for the shadowy movement of animals or ghosts. Strange lights did break through the darkness on occasion: flickering candles or fires visible through windows or shattered walls, pulsing glows of shimmering blue, pale drifting clouds of phosphorescence. Some people thought there was something supernatural about the Core, that it was inhabited by spirits, demons, banshees. Cage suspected the truth was far more horrible—that only human beings lived inside the Core.

Cage wore faded denims, a charcoal gray long-sleeved shirt, and black leather boots. His dark brown hair was long and straight and, though he was only thirty-nine, heavily streaked with gray. He wasn't tall, just five-foot-nine, but he was strong and quick. Sometimes not quick enough, though. A long thin scar ran along his jaw—a souvenir from a reluctant patient whose life Cage had been trying to save. And there were other scars, too, that weren't visible.

A muted flapping sound came from somewhere within the Core, and Cage searched the shadowy ruins for its source. He didn't see anything at first, only heard a faint, high whistle added to the flapping. Then a dark, shivering form rose from one of the taller buildings near the center. A strange glow came to life within the thing, giving it shape. It appeared to be an enormous dove, frantically flapping its wings and craning its neck as it climbed in an ever-widening spiral. But the motion of its wings was wrong, stilted and far too regular, and Cage knew it wasn't alive. When its spiraling route brought it closer to him, he could see pale white jets of propellant streaming from it.

The mechanical dove rose high above the Core, circling and climbing, becoming smaller and dimmer. The flapping sounds faded, and only the dim glow of its internal light was visible, a pale and shrinking blotch against the sky.

Suddenly the dove exploded with a brilliant burst of light followed by faint popping sounds. Hundreds of glittering message streamers fell through the darkness, like skyrocket flares that didn't burn out. The streamers drifted and fell with the air currents, spreading out over the Core and the Tenderloin.

One of the streamers drifted near Cage, and he stepped to the edge of the roof, steadied himself, then reached out over nine stories of empty air. He caught the message streamer and stepped back from the edge. The streamer glowed and tingled in his fingers, like electrified tinsel. He stretched out the streamer and read its message:

**YOU ARE BECOMING.
NOTHING CAN STOP YOU NOW.**

Fortunes from the Core, but without the cookie. He smiled, wadded the streamer into a tiny ball, and tossed it over the edge of the roof.

He stood gazing at the Core for a long time. Almost certainly he was going to end up in that godforsaken place before this business was over. He didn't much like the idea, but it was going to happen. He knew it.

Gravel crunched behind him, and he turned to see Nikki cross the roof toward him. She was a couple of inches taller than he was, and probably just as strong. Dreadlocks, gold cheek inlays, and a smile to die for. Black shock suit that hid her weapons and med-kit better than it did her figure. Cage loved her.

Nikki stopped about a foot away from him and frowned.

"These people are bloody assholes," she said. "Haven't even met them, but just talking to them, I already know they're assholes."

"I know," Cage said. "But we need them for this."

Nikki closed her eyes for a moment and shrugged. "Angel says they've arrived."

"Good. Let's go."

"Afterward, you want to go dancing?"

Cage nodded. "Maybe." Then, "Sure, we'll go dancing." And he got just what he was hoping for—Nikki's smile. "But first, let's see what we can do with the assholes."

They were to meet Stinger and his jackals in Binky's Arcade down on the second floor of the building. *Stinger.* Everyone's got to have a fucking moniker, Cage thought. It was absurd.

He and Nikki walked into crashing waves of sound and shifting colored lights. The place was crowded, the music and voices loud. The front section of Binky's was a series of stunner booths, and Cage watched the jerking forms visible through the opaque glass, the jerking almost in sync with the thumping sounds coming from within the booths—he'd probably end up treating some of these people over the next few days.

He moved past the stunner booths and onto the dance floor, Nikki right behind him. They pushed their way through the gyrating dancers, bumping and shoving and fending off flailing limbs. The air was stifling, heavy with perfume and smoke and sweat. His eyes burned.

The rear section of Binky's was a restaurant and bar. Cage and Nikki stepped through the array of acoustic baffles, and the sound cut back by more than half. It was still fairly noisy, but now the music was relatively muted. Conversation was possible.

Cage stopped and looked out over the tables and booths. He spotted Angel at the bar, who cut his glance toward a booth near the back. A tall, thin man in the booth caught Cage's eye. The man was older and better dressed than Cage had expected—he wore a dark suit and tie, and his short, thick, styled hair was more than half gone to gray. Mid to late forties, maybe even a little older. Cage had expected a young techno-punk or street medico. Three people sat in the booth opposite the man, but Cage could only see the top of the back of their heads.

"That Stinger?" Nikki said.

"I think so." Cage turned to her and smiled. "Maybe it won't be so bad."

"Hah."

Cage and Nikki made their way through the tables, and as they approached the rear booth the thin man nodded to those seated across from him. The three jackals slid out of the booth, walked to the rear, and stood side by side against the back wall of the restaurant, keeping their attention on Cage. All three were heavily muscled and wore cheap black suits over black T-shirts; all three looked ramped up to their eyeballs.

Up close, Cage could see that the thin man's suit was probably silk, and the dark green tie was made from reptile skin. The man sat with both arms on the table, hands relaxed. His jacket and shirtsleeves were too short, exposing his wrists. Or maybe this was the current fashion.

"You Stinger?" Cage said.

The man nodded. "You must be Cage."

"Yeah, I must be." He slid into the booth, and Nikki slid in next to him.

"Who's the nigger bitch with you?" Stinger asked. His voice was calm, his tone matter-of-fact.

Cage hesitated a few moments, eyes going hard, then said, "That's not helpful."

Stinger smiled. The index finger of his right hand rubbed at the pitted surface of the table, but he made no other response.

Nikki's hand lashed out across the table and latched into Stinger's wrist with her barbed finger hooks. She smiled back at him.

"Just try pulling away," she said. "We'll see what I rip out from under your skin."

Stinger didn't move, just looked down at the blood leaking from the tiny holes in his skin. Cage kept an eye on the jackals, who were leaning forward, tense, eyes wide, but waiting for a signal from their master.

"The nigger bitch's name is Nikki," Cage said.

Stinger looked at her, tipped his head slightly. "My apologies, Nikki."

The barbs retracted with faint clicks, and Nikki released his hand. Stinger brought his wrist to his mouth, then gently licked and sucked at the blood until his skin was clean and white again. He laid his arm back on the table and sighed. "Business, then?" he said.

Cage nodded. "Business."

A waitress approached the booth, but a look from Stinger warded her off. Cage stared at the man, assessing him. Stinger was twisted up way too tight, despite his outward appearance of calm; too slick and hard and mean. But there was something else, something he couldn't quite identify. Something *wrong* with Stinger.

Without shifting his gaze, Cage took a folded piece of paper from his back pocket and slid it across the table. "That's a list of the drugs we need, and the quantities."

Stinger took the paper, unfolded it, and read. His mouth twitched into a slight smile. "Don't want much, do you?" His voice was overly sarcastic; there wasn't much subtle about Stinger.

"That's what we need," Cage replied. There was something about Stinger's eyes. They were red, but in a strange way—not bloodshot, exactly. Injected. And the way his lips and tongue worked at themselves . . .

"You used to be a doctor," Stinger said to him, shaking his head. "What a fucking waste."

"I'm still a doctor," Cage replied.

Stinger continued to shake his head. "Slaving your ass off in street clinics and death houses. You used to have a hell of a practice doing image enhancements, making a goddamn fortune. A lot safer, too. And you slammed it all to do this? What happen, you get a dose of brain fever from one of your patients?"

Now Cage caught a whiff of something masked by Stinger's Body-Scent— like sweat gone sour. And a foul stench to his breath. Christ, Cage thought, the man is sick. Not with the flu or a cold, nothing simple like that. Drug-induced? Maybe. Some other toxin? Something bacterial? Viral? Something. Something bad.

"Well? Why'd you give it all up?" Stinger asked. He frowned, apparently waiting for a response.

But Cage wasn't going to give him one. He wasn't going to talk to this stranger about his life, the decisions he'd made. The only person he talked to about things like that was Nikki, and not always with her.

Nikki. Cage glanced at her hand, the one that grabbed Stinger and finger-hooked him, drawing blood. His hand out of sight under the table, Cage reached into the med-kit belted around his waist and removed two disinfectant wipes, pressed them into Nikki's hand. He rubbed her fingers with them until she got the message and began to work them herself.

Stinger sighed heavily, finally giving up on an answer. He tapped at the list. "You can't afford to buy all this," he said.

"No," Cage replied, working hard to keep his concentration on the business. He glanced at Stinger's wrist, at the tiny fresh droplets of blood that had formed on the surfaces of the finger-hook punctures.

"But you're willing to trade your services."

"Up to a point, yes."

"One day a week of image enhancements at the clinics of our choosing. Or perhaps other surgeries or treatments, depending on our needs. For one year."

Cage hesitated, still having difficulty concentrating. He was worried about Nikki, though he knew there was probably no reason to be. But he'd seen too much weird shit in the past few years. "One day a *month*, for a year," he finally said. "*If* we get monthly shipments of that size." He gestured at the piece of paper still laid out on the table under Stinger's hand.

Stinger laughed. "Too much, Cage. You overvalue your services." He paused, shrugging. "One day a month, fine. But only four shipments, one every three months. Not negotiable."

It probably wasn't. Besides, Cage didn't have the stomach for hard-edged negotiating with this man right now. Stinger was ill, and Cage wanted to get away from him; the man probably didn't even know he was sick. Cage hoped whatever it was wasn't an airborne transmitter, or that his nose filters could do the job; or the I.S. boosters he'd taken last week.

"All right," Cage said. "One year, four shipments. First delivery before I make a single cut."

"Good enough, Cage. We'll be in touch with delivery place and time, and with your first assignment."

Stinger put out his hand, but Cage didn't move. He stared at Stinger's hand, then up into Stinger's red-rimmed eyes. He nudged Nikki, and she slid out of the booth.

"I want to see you at the delivery," Cage said.

Stinger smiled. "What, is this some kind of setup? Entrapment?"

Cage didn't answer. Stinger and his people knew him better than that. But he very much wanted to see Stinger again, see if the guy got any sicker, see if he could figure out what Stinger had.

"We'll see," Stinger said, still smiling.

Cage and Nikki stood on the sidewalk, the signs for Binky's Arcade pulsing directly above them. The air out here was cool and fresh, and Cage breathed deeply.

"What the hell was all that in aid of?" Nikki asked him. "With the wipes? What was that about?"

He shrugged. He didn't want to worry her about what was probably nothing. "Stinger's sick," he answered.

"With what?"

"No idea. Just didn't want to take any chances."

"Great." Nikki dug into her shock suit with her left hand, brought out a wipe, and gave her right hand another thorough scrub, including the finger hooks. She walked over to a burn canister and tossed in the wipe.

"So what do you think about these people?" she asked when she rejoined him.

"Just what you said," Cage replied. "Assholes. And Stinger, in spite of his silk suit, the biggest asshole of all. But we'll do business. These guys have pharmaceutical resources no one else has, and at costs that beat the hell out of the streets."

"So you're pretty sure he's linked up to Cancer Cell?"

"Oh yeah. No one else could provide this shit, outside of New Hong Kong."

Nikki didn't seem convinced, but she half-nodded. "Let's go dancing, then."

Cage nodded back, and smiled. "Sure, Nikki. Let's go dancing."

3

CARLUCCI FELT LIKE shit. He threw off the covers and sat up in bed, slightly dizzy. A sheen of sweat coated his skin; his throat hurt, and his eyes ached. He looked at the clock. Almost noon. Christ.

He pushed himself up and onto his feet and staggered into the bathroom, where he threw cold water on his face, then drank deeply, wincing with pain each time he swallowed. Then he raised the toilet seat and pissed, one hand on the tank to hold himself up. He flushed, lowered the seat and lid, and sat down, resting up before getting into the shower.

Goddamn spring vaccination; every time it hit him like this. The semi-annual vaccination cocktails—five or six vaccines mixed together—didn't bother Andrea much, and Caroline and Christina, his two daughters, hardly felt any effects at all from them, but Carlucci got sick every damn time. He'd be all right by the end of the day, or maybe the next morning, but right now he wanted to drop into a coma for a few hours.

He popped some aspirins, took a shower, and by the time he got dressed and moved around a bit, he was feeling better. Andrea had set up the coffee maker before going to work, so all he had to do was start it. He ate two pieces of toast while waiting for it to finish, then took his coffee out onto the deck in the backyard.

The temperature was mild, and the sky almost clear, the blurred sun shining down through a pinkish-brown haze. Early spring after another mild winter, and there had been no heat waves yet. A pleasant time of the year in San Francisco. In fact, it was Carlucci's favorite time of year—the weather was usually good, and the homicide rate almost always took a dip.

Frank Carlucci was half an inch over six feet, and half a dozen pounds short of two hundred—a bit stocky, and constantly struggling to keep from changing from stocky to fat. He was closing in on fifty-six, and he needed more exercise than he got, but right now he felt like he could hardly walk.

He sat in one of the cushioned chairs, set his coffee on the small square table beside him, and looked out over the garden. The garden was lush and colorful and overgrown and streaked with rot and burn. It needed a lot of work. Neither he nor Andrea had managed to put any time into it yet, no weeding or pruning or thinning; nothing, really, since the fall. The big camellia in the back corner had already bloomed and dropped, the crocuses had come and gone, and half of the other plants in the yard were already beginning to flower. But there was too much brown streaking the leaves—it looked like rust—and there would be other problems less visible, all consequences of the crap in the air and the rain. He and Andrea needed to get out and do the special fertilizing, get some clean soil, and give the plants more filtered water.

At times like this, Carlucci thought seriously about retiring. He could sure spend more time out here, sitting in the sun and drinking coffee, puttering around in the garden; and more time sitting down in the basement and playing his trumpet. He'd like to build a greenhouse and grow vegetables. He'd like to read more. He was only fifty-five, but there were times when he felt older, and he was sick of that. A lot of it, he knew, was the job.

He had spent more than half his career in Homicide, and maybe that was too long. Carlucci was very good at his job, and he took satisfaction from that, from the cases he was able to solve, from the stimulation and rush he sometimes got from the work, and from the conviction that he in fact did some good.

But since his promotion to lieutenant, which pretty much took him off the streets, he had become less and less satisfied. The position was primarily administrative, supervising teams of detectives, assigning cases, overseeing his part of the division, and he didn't care that much for the job. He felt too distanced from the cases, almost uninvolved. He tried to make the job work better for him by stretching things—with a few of the Homicide teams, like Hong and LaPlace, or Santos and Weathers, he would attach himself as a kind of informal extra detective, working directly but unofficially on an occasional homicide. He also tried to get out on the streets with some regularity, maintaining his contacts and informants, his leeches and weasels. His superiors knew what he was doing, but they let it go because he was good, and because he never got too far out of line, and because they knew he was never going any farther up the ladder in the department.

But there were limits to what he could do, and those limits were getting to him. He wasn't sure how much longer he could put up with the situation. Recently he had been thinking he might have to do something drastic—either resign the commission and go back to the streets (which almost nobody ever did voluntarily); or retire. Vaughn, the Chief of Police, might not let him do the former, while he would happily encourage Carlucci to do the latter.

He got up and went back inside for a fresh cup of coffee. The house was quiet and peaceful; yet it also felt empty to him. Caroline had moved out several years earlier, soon after the Gould's Syndrome had been diagnosed, but it had only been a month now since Christina had done the same and moved into an apartment with her best friend, Paula Ng. He felt he should appreciate the quiet, the time alone with Andrea, but without the presence of his daughters he brooded even more than usual. He wished he saw them more often; Caroline, especially.

When he returned to the deck, he left the main door open, closing the screen. Let some fresh air into the house. He sat again, and looked up to see Farley, the gray kitten from next door, standing atop the fence, big eyes staring at him. A year earlier Frances and Harry's old cat Tuff had died, and six months later they had come home with Farley, who was tiny and skinny, but almost exactly the same shade of gray as Tuff had been, with the same gold eyes. Harry said it almost made him believe in reincarnation.

Farley scrambled down the fence, jumping the last three feet, and dashed up onto the deck. He pranced toward Carlucci, made a sound in his throat that was pretty damn close to a growl, then flopped onto the deck, purring and playing with Carlucci's shoelaces.

Carlucci sipped his coffee and closed his eyes, leaning his head back against the top of the chair. He *was* feeling better now, with the aspirin, the shower, the coffee, and the warmth of the sun. Still exhausted, but no longer feeling awful, and that was worth a lot.

He thought he heard the front door close, which surprised him, and he opened his eyes. Why would Andrea be home so early? He sat up, the movement startling Farley; the gray kitten jumped a few feet away, golden eyes wide, his attention on the screen door. Carlucci turned, but didn't see anyone.

"Andrea," he called. "I'm out here."

A few moments later someone appeared behind the screen, then the door squealed open. But it wasn't Andrea. It was Caroline, and she looked awful. Christ, had the Gould's gone active already? He stood up, too quickly, and nearly lost his balance. He reached out, got a hand on the chair arm, and steadied himself as Caroline hurried to him.

"Papa," she said, putting her arm around him to hold him up.

"I'm okay," he said. And then he put his arms around her, hugging her tightly. "Caroline." He didn't want to let her go. Her face was drawn, and she smelled funny. He held her slightly away from him, gazing into her face. "What's wrong? Are you sick?"

"I'm fine, Papa." She gave him a tired smile. "Better than you, I think. You look terrible. Your spring cocktail, yeah?"

Carlucci nodded. He sat back down, still holding Caroline's hand, and she sat beside him. "Are you sure you're okay?"

"I'm sure," she answered. "I'm just beat, and I'm really worried about a friend of mine."

He released her hand. "You want some coffee? There's still some in the pot."

"No." She turned away from him, her gaze toward Farley, who had settled at the far end of the deck, watching them, but Carlucci was pretty sure she wasn't even seeing the gray kitten.

"So what is it?" he asked.

Caroline rubbed her eyes with her palms, made a heavy sighing sound, then finally turned back to him. "It's my friend Tito." She left it there for a moment, then went on. "He's got AIDS, and he's living in a death house in the DMZ. Two days ago I went to visit him. He'd called me in the morning, he'd been pretty sick, but he was feeling a little better, and I was going to go see him. We were going to watch some television, nothing much, and then I was going to sack out on the sofa, keep him company." She frowned. "He was expecting me," she said. "That's the thing.

"When I got there, he was gone. A guy we know, Mouse, was cleaning out the place. Stealing everything he could jam into this big duffel bag he had. Mouse said two men had come and taken Tito away, and that Tito was never coming back. He said the men had something to do with Cancer Cell, and they'd taken Tito to the Core. And he said no one ever comes back." She shook her head. "I think I may have heard of them before. Cancer Cell. But I don't know who they are. I don't know anything about them."

Carlucci did. Not much, really, and most of that was gossip and rumor, tasteless jokes and unreliable speculation by other cops. But none of it was good.

"I waited for him," Caroline went on. "All through the night, then all day yesterday, and again last night. He never showed up, he never called. I finally gave up this morning and called your office, but Morelli said you were at home recovering from the vaccinations. I didn't want to call, in case you were sleeping, so I just came by." Her mouth turned into a bitter smile. "What was I going to do? Go to the police and file a missing persons? For a gay Mexican dying of AIDS and living in a death house in the DMZ?"

She was right, he thought. It would have been a waste of time. The report would have been tanked before she got out of the building.

"I asked Mouse what Cancer Cell was, and he told me to ask you." She rubbed at her right temple, grimacing. "Is there anything you can do, Papa?"

Carlucci shrugged. "Something, maybe. I've heard of Cancer Cell, but I don't really know anything either. A real low-profile group of people. Unlike most wackos, they don't like publicity. So maybe they aren't wackos. I don't know what they've done, or what their cause is, if they have one. Something medical, but Christ, these days that could mean anything, good *or* bad." He paused, thinking. "I'll ask around some, do some checking on Tito. I go back into work tomorrow, but I can make a couple of phone calls today, get something started."

Caroline reached across the chairs and squeezed his hand. "Thanks, Papa."

"Anything else? You want some lunch or something?"

She shook her head. "No. But I could really use a shower. Haven't had one in two days. I didn't really want to use the communal at the death house."

She stood, leaned over and kissed him on the cheek, then turned and went into the house. He watched her closely, the way each step seemed slow and deliberate. Maybe it was just what she'd said, exhausted from too much worry and not enough sleep. It was crazy, he knew it, he knew he couldn't change anything, but he could not stop himself from intently observing her every time he saw her, watching her closely and searching for some sign that the Gould's had gone active; some sign that her death was approaching. It was tearing him apart.

He sat back in the sun, drinking his coffee, listening to the faint sounds of the shower, and thought about what he could do for her, and for Tito.

4

LATE THE NEXT morning, Carlucci sat at his desk, still feeling crappy, but with a lot of the backed-up scutwork done—the stuff he just could not put off another day. He figured he could give himself an hour or so to see what he could do for Caroline and her friend Tito.

He had called in the day before and asked Lacey to put in a system tracer on Tito. If anything came in on Tito Moraleja—arrest, detention, parking citation, credit chip violation, warrants search, *anything*—Carlucci would be notified immediately. He didn't hold out much hope for that, but it was something. Then he'd talked to Diane Wanamaker in Info-Services and asked for a complete records search, see if Tito's name would come up anywhere. He hadn't held out much hope for that either, which turned out to be an accurate assessment. Diane's report was waiting for him first thing this morning. There were blood and print records available from an emergency admission at S.F. General two years earlier; an ID chip had been implanted at the same time. And there was a routine vice pickup from several years earlier that had been dropped. No criminal record, no association hits, nothing that would give a clue to what had happened.

Which left only one thing—Cancer Cell.

Carlucci activated the phone, called up the directory, then punched in Martin Kelly's number. Kelly worked in Counter-Intelligence. Not the top guy in CID, but probably the best. If anyone knew something about Cancer Cell, it would be Martin Kelly.

"Kelly here."

"It's Frank Carlucci."

"Hey, Carlucci. *Come estai?*" Sometimes Kelly talked and acted like he wished he was Italian.

"*Bene. Grazie.*" Carlucci smiled to himself, shaking his head. "It's almost noon. Can I buy you lunch?"

"Christ, no. I'm swamped here. You need to talk to me about something?"

"Yeah."

"You can buy me coffee, then. I can get away for a few minutes."

"Okay. You want me to come up there?" Carlucci asked.

"No. I'll meet you in Narcotics. They've got better coffee."

And a couple of private interview rooms, Carlucci thought. "Meet you there in ten minutes?" he asked.

"Ten minutes."

Carlucci did have to buy their coffees. Narcotics brewed the best coffee in the building, and they sold it to their fellow officers at a buck a cup. The proceeds paid for their annual forty-eight-hour-long New Year's bash out on Alcatraz.

Kelly and Carlucci took the coffee into a free interview room, which was small but quiet. They sat across from each other at the table, and Carlucci glanced around the room, noting the video cameras that should be off line, thinking about the hidden cameras and mikes. Narcotics guaranteed their interview rooms to be secure, but Carlucci never completely trusted them.

Kelly was dressed, as always, in a flashy, expensive suit, dark blue with glowing silver pinstripes and a tie with a wave pattern that continually washed across the fabric. Carlucci had known him for more than ten years, but they had never become friends. They got on each other's nerves when they spent too much time together, but Carlucci thought there was always something like mutual respect between them.

"So what's up?" Kelly asked.

"What do you know about Cancer Cell?"

"Jesus Christ, Carlucci. That's about the last thing I expected you to ask me." He leaned back in his chair. "What the hell case have you got going, and why haven't I heard anything about it before?"

Carlucci shook his head. "There is no case. Not exactly. Someone my daughter knows has disappeared and I told her I'd look into it. There's a chance it has something to do with Cancer Cell. That's all."

Kelly didn't say anything. He moved the paper coffee cup around and around in small circles on the table, staring at him.

"What is it?" Carlucci asked.

"You trying to run something on me?"

"Of course not. It's just what I said. Why? What's going on?"

Kelly frowned. "I wish I knew." He continued to stare at Carlucci, as if trying to decide something. "I've never liked this Cancer Cell business," he eventually said. "It always bothers me when you hear about something, or somebody, but you can never find out anything about them. The name pops up, but no one knows anything. You dig and you dig, and then dig even deeper, and all you come up with is a lot of what you know is horseshit." He sipped at his coffee, started to put it down, then drank again. He stared into his cup for a minute, then finally set it down and resumed making circles with it. "Cancer Cell is like that. I've been digging around at it for, I don't know, four or five years now, and I don't know much more now than I did before."

He paused again, looked around the room, then back at Carlucci. "Then a few weeks ago, I get a query on Cancer Cell from one of the slugs." He left it there, giving Carlucci a twisted smile.

The slugs were technically still human beings, though they didn't look much like it anymore. They lived in individual quarters on the top floor of the building, surrounded by all the computers and information access networks they wanted, and they pumped themselves full of intelligence boosters and metabolic enhancers until they became bloated, barely mobile creatures encased in formfitting, shiny black environment suits. Their job was to help the police solve difficult cases, but Carlucci didn't know a single cop who wanted to have anything to do with the slugs. Even his old friend Brendan, who had worked a lot with the slugs, had eventually resigned and was now trying very hard to drink himself to death.

"I didn't think much of it," Kelly resumed. "I didn't have anything to give the fucker anyway. But then you show up and ask me about the same thing just a few weeks later. Makes me very suspicious."

"Which slug made the query?"

"Does it matter?"

Carlucci shrugged.

"Monk. You know him?"

Monk. That made *Carlucci* suspicious. "Yeah, I know him. I had a session with him a few years ago." He pictured Monk the slug, a goggled, bloated thing enclosed in slick black, hardly able to walk, hardly human.

"But I haven't had anything to do with him since." He shrugged again. "Didn't like the bastard much."

Neither of them spoke for a couple of minutes. Carlucci wanted to reassure Kelly and get some information out of him. At the same time, he was trying to imagine what Monk's interest in Cancer Cell was all about.

"Carlucci, tell me. No bullshit. What's this with your daughter's friend?"

Carlucci related everything Caroline had told him. It really *wasn't* much—a strange deal, but with the added factor of Cancer Cell.

"You're being straight with me?" Kelly asked.

"Absolutely," Carlucci replied. "So what's bothering you so much?"

"I don't know," Kelly answered, shaking his head. "I've just got a bad feeling."

"What *can* you tell me about Cancer Cell?"

"Ah, hell, I don't know. It's one of those things. I'll be working on something else, maybe trying to track down the pipeline for black market pharmaceuticals coming down from New Hong Kong, and I'll be going through files on different people, this case or that, and the name comes up. Maybe someone mentions Cancer Cell in a recorded conversation, or an arrest interview. A couple of years ago someone, I don't remember who now, referred to them as 'medico-terrorists.' But what the hell does that mean? Do they try to block medical research, or are they running around performing experimental operations on people who don't want them?" He shook his head again. "Everything I ran across went nowhere."

"That's it?" Carlucci said. "That's all you can tell me?"

Kelly hesitated a long time before answering. Carlucci had the feeling the CID man was still trying to make some decision about him.

"I'm not the one to talk to," Kelly finally said.

"Who, then?"

Kelly looked down into his coffee cup, then pushed it away and leaned back in his chair. "Maybe two, three months ago, I ran across someone who seems to know something about Cancer Cell. She wouldn't tell me anything, but it was clear she had some hard data. She told me that if the time came that I really needed to know more, an important case, something like that, then maybe she'd be willing to talk to me some more. But maybe not even then."

"And what about when Monk sent that query? You tell him about her?"

"No, I didn't give him shit. Fuck the slugs."

"Who is she?"

Kelly hesitated one final time, then frowned and took one of his cards and a pen from his coat, jotted something on the back of the card, then slid the card across the table. Carlucci picked up the card and put it inside his shirt pocket without looking at it.

"Thanks, Kelly."

"Keep me hip on this thing, will you?"

Carlucci had to smile at that word. What decade did Kelly live in? What *century*? "I will," he promised.

He left the building to make the phone call. He walked several blocks, then stopped at a phone booth and looked at the back of Martin Kelly's card. Scribbled on it was the name Naomi Katsuda, and under that, Mishima Investments. He knew that name from somewhere. A Financial District company, he was sure of that, but why else was it familiar?

He used his dead-account card to activate the phone, called up the city directory, then clicked and scrolled through it until he found the number. He selected it, and someone answered immediately.

"Mishima Investments." A disembodied, sexless voice.

"Naomi Katsuda, please."

"One moment, sir."

The line went silently dead, then came back alive with a gentle, muted ring.

"Naomi Katsuda's office." A real person's voice this time, definitely male.

"I'd like to speak to Naomi Katsuda, please." With a place like Mishima, it was best to be as polite as possible.

"And who is calling, please?"

"Frank Carlucci."

"Ms. Katsuda is occupied at the moment, Mr. Carlucci. If you could leave me your number and the nature of your business, Ms. Katsuda will get back to you when she can."

Carlucci looked at the phone. It wouldn't take incoming calls, but that didn't really matter. What was he going to do, hang out here all afternoon waiting for a call that might not come?

"Sorry, I won't be reachable. I'll try back later."

"As you wish, sir."

Carlucci hung up, then crossed the street and went into Bongo's Heaven. All the tables were occupied, but he found a stool at the counter. He was beat, still recovering from the damn vaccination, and wasn't too sure about stomaching a Bongo Burger. So he ordered a bowl of the split pea, which was always good, and iced tea.

As he ate, he thought about Caroline, and Tito Moraleja, and his conversation with Martin Kelly, and Mishima Investments. He tried to remember where he knew that company from. Something from years before, maybe. But what? Then it finally snapped into focus, and he knew. Mishima Investments was one of New Hong Kong's two official Earth-based financial arms. The other was China Moon Ltd., which was headquartered directly across the street from Mishima in the heart of the Financial District. One Japanese arm, and one Chinese.

New Hong Kong. Carlucci had pissed off the orbital three years earlier, and he was sure they hadn't forgotten. He had been partially responsible for the public revelation that the medical research teams up in New Hong Kong were working on serious long-term life extension and that their research involved, among other things, abductions of people from Earth, forced experimentation, vivisection, political bribery, corruption, and murder. In the long run, there had been no serious consequences for New Hong Kong, more annoyance for them than anything else, but he suspected they still didn't care much for him.

When he was done with lunch, Carlucci went back to the phone across the street and called Mishima Investments. He got the same man, and the same noise about Naomi Katsuda's unavailability.

"All right," Carlucci said. "When will Ms. Katsuda be available? It's important I talk to her."

"If you could leave a number . . ."

"I told you before, that's not possible. When should I call back?"

"I'm sorry, Mr. Carlucci." A slightly condescending tone had worked its way into the man's voice. "Ms. Katsuda says she does not know you. If you would leave a number *and* tell me the nature of your business with her, perhaps Ms. Katsuda would be willing to return your call. Otherwise we cannot help you."

"I am *Lieutenant* Frank Carlucci, with the San Francisco Police Department, and I would appreciate your cooperation. I will not be available at my office, and I need to talk to Ms. Katsuda. So if you could please give me a specific time when I can call back and talk to her . . ." He left it at that.

There was a long pause, then the man said, "If you would hold just a moment, Lieutenant Carlucci."

"Sure."

Dead air, then the man's voice returned. "I'm putting you through to Ms. Katsuda."

"Thanks." But the man was already gone.

"Lieutenant Carlucci. Naomi Katsuda here. What can I do for you?"

"I'd like to talk to you."

"Talk away, Lieutenant."

"In person, I think."

She laughed softly. "That's dramatic. What about?"

"Martin Kelly gave me your name."

There was a slight pause, then she said, "Martin Kelly."

"Yes."

There was a longer pause. "I'm not sure I can help you," she said.

"I'm not sure, either, but I'd like to find out."

"I don't think you understand me," Naomi Katsuda said. "I'm not sure I *want* to help you, even if I can."

"I understood you," Carlucci said.

He waited through a long silence, trying to hear her breathing, some sign of life.

"Would tomorrow afternoon be all right?" she finally asked.

"Sure. Whatever works."

"Call tomorrow morning, then, and Tim will tell you where and when."

"Your secretary?"

"My assistant. I'll see you tomorrow, Lieutenant."

The line went dead again. Permanently, this time. Carlucci hung up the receiver and stood there beside the phone for a while, gazing at the street around him.

He should just let this Cancer Cell stuff go. It felt like trouble. But he couldn't, not yet anyway. His daughter had asked for his help, and he couldn't refuse.

5

WEDNESDAY EVENING, WHEN Caroline arrived at home after work, her sister Tina was waiting for her. She was sitting on the porch steps of the apartment building, a large paper bag beside her; she was wearing a short, dark blue shimmer skirt over a white body stocking. No bra, but then she didn't really need one—small breasts ran in the family. Tina looked just great, Caroline thought, smiling to herself.

"Hey, sis," she said.

"Hi, Cari." Tina was the only one who called her that anymore. She stood up and they hugged each other.

"What's up?" Caroline asked.

Tina shrugged, smiling. "I just decided I wanted to see you. I thought maybe we could spend the evening together, sit around and talk and like that." She bent over, picked up the bag, then straightened, smile broadening into a grin. "I brought rum and Coke."

"Oh, no," Caroline said.

"Oh, yes. You're off work tomorrow, aren't you?"

"I'm afraid so." She could not keep from smiling at her younger sister.

"Then let's get shitfaced."

Caroline was fairly drunk, but was trying to pace herself. Tina wasn't trying to pace herself, and she'd also smoked half a joint; now she had the giggles. Caroline had made a pot of tea, which they drank between glasses of rum and Coke. They were both going to pay for this the next morning, but Caroline didn't really care; she was relaxed and content and she hadn't had a good time like this in a long while.

"Have you seen Mom and Dad recently?" Tina asked. She was sitting on Caroline's bed, leaning back into a pile of cushions and pillows propped against the wall, holding her rum and Coke in her lap with both hands. On the nightstand beside her was a mug filled with tea and an ashtray with the remaining half joint.

Caroline was settled into her old overstuffed chair, feet propped on a cushioned ottoman that leaked bits of foam on all sides. She felt incredibly comfortable, her muscles slack. She had no desire to move. She managed to sip at her drink and nod at her sister.

"Saw Papa a couple days ago. At the house. He looked like crap." She smiled. "He'd just had his spring vaccination cocktail."

Tina picked up the joint, stuck it in her mouth, but didn't light up. She spoke with her lips pressed together, the joint wiggling up and down. "He'd better not make a surprise visit," she said, "or he'll have to bust our asses for possession." She giggled and the joint spit out of her mouth, slid off her body stocking and onto the bedspread. She picked it up and put it back in the ashtray.

Caroline's apartment was a large, spacious studio—one large room with a small kitchen separated from it by a counter and ceiling cabinets. She really couldn't afford it here in the Noe Valley Corridor, but her parents kicked in some money each month so she could live in a relatively safe part of the city. It made them a little crazy that Tina lived on the fringes of the Mission.

There was a scratching at the back door, in the kitchen alcove. Caroline tried to ignore it, but when it sounded again, more insistent this time, Tina sat forward, looking toward the kitchen.

"What's that?" she asked.

"That's just Lucas," Caroline said. "Ignore him. He'll go away."

"Who's Lucas?"

"Stray cat. He was hanging out a lot on the back stairs, and I made the mistake of feeding him a few times." She shook her head. "He was so skinny, all beat up and scrawny. I felt sorry for him. Now he's in better shape, all fattened up, and he won't go away. I try to discourage him."

"Why?" Tina asked. "You like cats. You should take him in."

Caroline shook her head again. "No. I don't want anything to be dependent on me." She paused, then looked away from Tina. "I mean, what would happen to him when I die?"

The room got very quiet. She hadn't meant to be that direct with Tina. Or maybe she had. She turned back to her younger sister, who looked like she was about to cry. Caroline smiled and shrugged.

"Is that why you stopped seeing Bryan?" Tina eventually asked.

Caroline gave a short laugh. "No. I slammed Bryan because he was a jerk." Lucas scratched at the back door again and Caroline grinned. "He was just like that damn cat, always scratching to get in."

Tina laughed, rocking forward and almost spilling her drink. She took a long, deep swallow and giggled.

"I need another drink." A glance up at Caroline, a sloppy grin. "You?"

"Not yet." Pacing, Caroline thought. One of us has to stay conscious.

She'd been feeling lonely again lately, and tried not to think about it too much. She almost missed Bryan. But she knew it wasn't Bryan she missed; she missed the company, affection, having someone to talk to; she missed the presence of another person, someone she cared for, and who cared for her. She'd never really had that with Bryan, but she felt as if she'd sensed hints of what that would be like. At times it depressed her that she probably would never know what love truly was. Tina, at least, would have years to find it.

She finished off her rum and Coke, but wasn't sure about another one, and she set her glass on the coffee table. She was already feeling a little bit out of control, and now her left eye was acting up again. It felt as if a kind of film had formed over it, not quite blurring her vision. She blinked several times, trying to clear it.

"What's wrong with your eyes?" Tina asked.

"Nothing. Just a twitch." Caroline kept blinking, but couldn't get rid of the strange sensation.

"How come you didn't see Mom the other day?" Tina's eyes were almost completely closed now, and her head and shoulders were swaying, as if she were listening to some music that Caroline couldn't hear.

"She was at work," Caroline said. "It was Papa I wanted to see, anyway. I wanted to ask him for a favor."

Tina opened her eyes, interested. "What kind of favor?"

"I've got a friend who has AIDS, and he's living in a death house in the DMZ. He's disappeared, and it looks like someone may have kidnapped him. I was just asking Papa if he could check into it, maybe help find out what happened."

"Why would anyone want to kidnap someone who's dying?" Tina asked.

"I have no idea."

"Did Dad find out anything?"

"I haven't heard from him, so I guess not yet."

Tina made a face. "Are the death houses as bad as I hear?"

Caroline nodded. She hoped Tina wouldn't ask for details; she didn't want to talk about it.

Tina didn't say anything for a long time, just sipped steadily at her drink, staring at Caroline, her mouth beginning to tremble.

"What is it, Tina?"

"You're not going to end up in one of those places, are you?"

Caroline tried to brush it off, smiling and shaking her head. "Of course not."

Tina took another long drink from her glass, put it down on the night-stand, hiccupped, then covered her face with her hands and started crying.

Caroline shut down. She couldn't take this, and so she cut off all feeling. It was something she had learned to do during the past couple of years, a kind of emotional survival strategy. *Bang, bang, bang, bang* went the barriers, and she simply stopped feeling anything at all.

She stood and deliberately walked over to the bed. Her left eye still threatened to blur out on her. She stopped beside the bed for a minute, watching Tina cry, then sat beside her younger sister.

Tina twisted around and reached out for Caroline, hugged her, and cried even harder. "I don't want you to die," she managed to get out between sobs.

"I'm not even close to being dead," Caroline whispered. She brushed at Tina's hair with her fingers, over and over, sensing vaguely that she was try-ing to comfort her little sister, but not really feeling it. "I've got a few years at least," she said. It might even be true.

They sat together on the bed for a long time, holding each other, Tina crying and Caroline running her hand along Tina's hair. The smell of bitter incense wafted in through the open window, followed by someone's laugh-ter out on the street. Caroline wanted to go out on the street right now, walk up and down the corridor, the night sky above her, colored light all around. Move in and out of the crowds, look at people sitting inside cafés and bars or touring through entertainment arcades. She did not want to be in this room thinking about her own death.

"I'm sorry," Tina finally said. She'd pretty much stopped crying, though she still held tightly onto Caroline.

Jesus, Caroline thought, maybe I do need another drink. "You don't have to be sorry," she said. She eased her sister away so Tina would look at her. Caroline smiled. "Why don't you smoke the rest of that joint and I'll have another drink. All right? We're supposed to be having fun."

Tina nodded, trying to smile back. But her hands shook as she picked up the joint.

Caroline got up from the bed and started across the room. She'd only taken a few steps when the vision in her left eye darkened, like a hand cup-ping her eye. She froze, afraid to move, but a few moments later her vision cleared. Even the filmy sensation was gone. She continued forward, slowly now; she picked up her glass from the coffee table and headed for the kitchen counter.

Halfway to the kitchen, she lost control of her left leg. It buckled under her, and she stumbled, pitched forward, and sprawled across the floor. Somehow she managed to hang onto the glass, though the ice cubes scat-tered across the rug.

"Cari, are you okay?"

Caroline nodded quickly. "Yeah, I'm fine. I just tripped."

"Maybe you don't need another drink," Tina said, giggling.

"Yeah." But she knew it wasn't the alcohol. Elbows burning, she slowly, carefully got to her feet, using her right leg for support. Her left leg seemed okay now, and she took a tentative step forward on it. Fine. Then another. Still fine. She turned back, knelt on the floor, and scooped the ice cubes into her glass. Every motion was slow and deliberate. She stood, skirted the counter, dumped the ice cubes into the sink, and rinsed out the glass.

Back at the counter, she put fresh ice in her glass and mixed another drink. Heavy on the rum. She stood at the counter, hand around her drink, and watched Tina smoke the joint. Tina seemed to be relaxing again.

But Caroline wasn't. Her heart was beating hard and fast, and she tried to breathe slowly and deeply. She didn't want to be afraid. Her left eye felt funny again, that damn filmy sensation, but she could still see with it. And her leg seemed fine. She took a long swallow of her drink and almost coughed from the extra rum.

Everything's fine, she told herself. Just fine. But she didn't believe it.

She walked carefully over to her chair and sat, holding her drink with both hands. Tina dropped the last bit of the joint into the ashtray and lay back against the pillows, closing her eyes.

"That's better," Tina said.

But it wasn't, Caroline thought. It wasn't better at all.

6

EARLY THE NEXT morning, Carlucci went out to the DMZ death house with Binh Tran. Tran's partner, Mahmoud Jefferson, was home with some nasty flu that was running through the department, a flu the vaccination cocktails apparently weren't targeted for, so Tran was solo for the day. Carlucci did not really want to go into the DMZ on his own, so he took Tran with him.

They drove a department car, parked a few blocks from the DMZ, then walked in. Early morning was the quietest part of the day in the DMZ, just like in the Tenderloin. Street traffic was steady, but the sidewalks were practically empty except for a few Dead Princes wrapped in their metallic shrouds and crouched against a building, and the occasional scrounger half lying on the ground with plastic begging jugs held out.

Carlucci and Tran were only a block into the DMZ when the clouds came in and the rain began. The rain was warm and light, little more than a drizzle. Looking around the DMZ, Carlucci realized the rain would never be strong and heavy enough to wash all this away. Which was a shame.

Caroline had given him directions and the keys to Tito's room, and he had no trouble finding the entrance to the death house with its red skull-and-crossbones painted across the bricks. Before entering, he and Tran put on surgical gloves and masks. A woman across the street screamed at them, and a guy hanging out in front of the shock shop next door told them to get themselves fucked. Tran shrugged, opened the death house door, and they stepped inside.

An old man lay on the lobby floor, just a few feet inside. His eyes were open and he looked dead. Carlucci watched him closely, but saw no signs of movement, no rise or fall of the chest, not a twitch in the mouth or eyes. Tran knelt beside the old man and put a gloved finger against the man's neck. He kept it there for a minute or two, shifting it from one spot to another, then shook his head and stood.

"What do we do?" he asked. His eyes seemed calm. "Is there someone we should call?"

Carlucci shook his head. "They take care of their own in here." He breathed deeply once, the mask only partially blocking the stink of death. "Let's go."

He led the way up the stairs to the third floor, reading some of the graffiti on the way: WAITING FOR DEATH/WITH BAITED BREATH. GOD MUST BE ONE MEAN SON OF A BITCH. GET ME OUT OF HERE NOW!!! DON'T FUCKING BOTHER—WITH *ANYTHING*. The stairwell didn't smell much better than the lobby.

When they emerged from the stairwell on the third floor, someone was walking down the hall toward them—a bald, gaunt man in jeans, no shirt covering a hairless chest that starkly revealed each rib. When the man saw Carlucci and Tran, he abruptly turned around and headed back the way he'd come, almost hopping, like some gangling, storklike bird, slapping his thigh with each step. He grabbed a doorknob, threw the door open, then hopped inside, slamming the door shut behind him.

Carlucci walked down the hall to the door Caroline said was Tito's, Tran just behind him. Mounted on the door was a printed notice, a white sheet of plastic with bold black letters:

ALL CONTRACTS WILL BE ENFORCED

He looked at Tran, who shrugged and shook his head. Carlucci didn't have any idea what it meant, either, nor who it was intended for. He'd have to ask Caroline if the notice had been posted the last time she was here.

He used the keys to unlock the dead bolts, slowly pushed open the door,

but remained out in the hall. The door swung all the way open until the
knob cracked against the wall. The room was quiet and empty.

Carlucci took a step inside. Suddenly there was a screech and a flash of
movement and he dropped to a crouch, instinctively reaching under his arm
for a gun that wasn't there. He threw himself back through and around the
doorway and into the hall, hearing a click as Tran chambered a round into
his Beretta and dropped into a crouch, ready to fire. There was another
screech, and flapping sounds. Tran's head jerked, then he broke into a grin
barely visible under the mask, sagged slightly, and lowered the gun. The
flapping sounds continued for a few seconds, then stopped.

"What?" Carlucci asked.

"Parrot," Tran answered, still grinning. He straightened, gun in hand,
and leaned carefully through the doorway. He took two more steps inside,
then holstered the Beretta and looked back at Carlucci. "Just a parrot."

Carlucci followed Tran into the room. Sliding back and forth on the
edge of a two-burner hot plate was a large blue parrot with just a few traces
of yellow on its face. The parrot bobbed up and down, then cocked its head
and squawked out something like, "I bow to you, o master."

There was no way this parrot had been here when Caroline had locked
up the room. She would not have forgotten to mention it; more than that,
she would never have left the parrot in the first place; she would have taken
the bird with her, made sure it would be cared for.

Carlucci looked at the window. Closed. What other way could the parrot
have used to get in? No fireplace, no open vents. Nothing that he could see.
The parrot must have been deliberately placed in this room. But why? Then,
looking back at the window, he noticed a rectangular piece of cardboard
taped to the bottom of the glass. He crossed the room, inspected it more
closely. Handwritten in blue marker were the words *ALL* CONTRACTS.

"What's it say?" Tran asked.

" 'All Contracts.' 'All' is underlined."

"Somebody's sending a message. With the parrot, too."

Carlucci nodded, then said, "Any ideas?"

"This Cancer Cell?" Tran turned back to the parrot, observing it without getting close enough for the parrot to lean forward and take a bite. The
parrot weaved from side to side, never taking its eyes off Tran. "Maybe the
parrot has the message," Tran said. "Maybe the parrot says something."

" 'I bow to you, o master'?"

Tran made a sound that might have been a laugh. "No. Something
else." He straightened, took a few steps back from the parrot.

The two men spent ten or fifteen minutes going through the room,
searching the cabinets and shelves, under the sofa, the blankets and sheets,
the refrigerator. Carlucci opened a cabinet above the sink and saw dozens of
pill bottles. He picked up a few, but they all seemed to be empty. Other than
that, neither of them found anything of real interest.

Tran stood in front of the parrot again, watching it bob and weave, shifting back and forth with tiny clicks of its claws.

"What do we have?" Tran said. "No crime, right? Just a missing persons?"

"That's right."

"Give it to CID." He turned to Carlucci. "The room, the two notices, the parrot. Have them come in, do the room, take the parrot in. There's something funny here. That Cancer Cell business. They can put someone on the bird, or have recorders going, see if it says anything. If it does, they let you know."

It wasn't a bad idea. Normally CID would have to be talked into it, be convinced there was something of real interest and substance here, the work of some group or gang or organization they might have to deal with; under normal circumstances, they probably wouldn't go for it. But he could call Martin Kelly in on it, and because it might have something to do with Cancer Cell, he would want it. He'd want it bad.

The parrot took off from the hot plate, flew around the room twice, then landed on top of the television set by the window. It rocked from side to side, then screeched out, "Asshole! Asshole!"

Carlucci sat on the arm of the sofa, half watching the parrot and half gazing out the window at the bricks and boarded windows of the next building just a few feet away. His nose itched and he raised a gloved hand toward his face, stopped, then scratched his nose with the cuff of his jacket sleeve.

There was something more going on here than just a missing persons case. He could feel it, deep in his gut. He peeled off his surgical gloves, tossed them onto the sofa, then took his phone out of his jacket pocket. "Yes," he said. "We'll call in CID."

Six hours later, Carlucci was processing himself through one of the Financial District checkpoints, on his way to meeting Naomi Katsuda. Even though he was a cop, he had to put up with the processing since he wasn't chipped for the Financial District, and he had to submit to a body search before going through an array of detectors.

He hated the Financial District. Gleaming metal and smooth concrete and polished stone and glass, shining towers rising from more concrete and asphalt—the Financial District was like an island in time. It was just about the only part of San Francisco that looked as if it existed in the twenty-first century, that seemed to belong in its own time. Walled off from the rest of the city, surrounded by huge subterranean vehicle parks for the tens of thousands of daily commuters, its own streets were relatively traffic-free, served by frequent clean-shuttles, bicycles, and pedalcarts. All freight deliveries were made between midnight and 5:00 A.M., and all the cleaning crews, inside and out, worked the same shift.

Clean and sterile and morally dead—that was the only way Carlucci could see it anymore. Money and data producing only more money and data, while the rest of the city went to shit.

Once through the checkpoint, he looked back across the barriers to the buildings of the Chinatown Corridor, which ran smack up against the Financial District border. The buildings were older, darker, dirtier, but that was real life out there; in here was something else altogether.

He walked the several blocks to the Embarcadero Centers, thirty- and forty-story office buildings perched atop three floors of interconnected retail space—shops and restaurants that only those who worked inside the district could afford. The morning's rain had stopped several hours earlier, but dark clouds overhead threatened new showers. The air had a warm and damp and electric feel to it.

Carlucci had liked the Financial District when he was in his late teens, early twenties, more than thirty years ago. It hadn't been cordoned off from the rest of the city then, there had been no checkpoints, no body searches, no arrays of detectors to pass through before entering. It wasn't his favorite part of the city—the goals of the businesses and law firms weren't any more high-minded back then—but he had liked the sense of motion and purpose that filled the streets.

He would take a bus downtown from the Richmond and wander the streets, walking in and out of the shadows of buildings anywhere from five or six stories high to more than fifty. Normal people worked here, coming in by car, bus, and streetcar from all parts of the city. Men and women who stank of weeks-old body odor and stale booze sat on benches and barked incoherently at passersby, or hunkered against stone steps, sticking their hands or cups out toward men and women in business suits. It wasn't always pleasant, but it was real.

He would buy a Polish sausage from a cart vendor for a couple of bucks, including all the onions he could scoop onto the thing. Now there were no street vendors of any kind. And there certainly weren't any stinking men or women asleep on the benches—they'd all been moved out.

At Embarcadero 2, he took the escalator to the second level, then wandered about until he found the open-air café where he was supposed to meet Naomi Katsuda. He stood by a mortared stone planter near the outer ring and looked out over the tables, all of which were sheltered by white umbrellas in case it rained; he had no idea what she looked like, but he assumed she was Japanese, and he assumed she would be alone. Fewer than half the tables were occupied—it was well past lunchtime and well before the dinner hour—and most of them by two or more people.

His gaze stopped on an attractive, dark-haired woman in her thirties who looked only vaguely Asian. But she stared back at him, nodded once, then looked away and casually lit a cigarette.

Carlucci worked his way through the tables and stopped by the woman.

She looked up at him with dark brown eyes. She smoked with her left hand, and kept her other hand on her lap. Her fingernails were painted a pale pink and her lips were silver.

"Naomi Katsuda?"

She gave him another crisp nod, then put out her right hand. "Lieutenant."

He took her hand, which was warm and dry, like the smoothest sandpaper.

"Please, Lieutenant, have a seat." She took one more quick, deep drag on the cigarette, then delicately crushed it out in the crystal ashtray that held two other butts. She'd either been here a while, or she was quite a smoker. Or maybe just nervous. But she didn't appear to be nervous, not in the least.

He sat down in the lightly cushioned plastic chair, which was surprisingly comfortable. Naomi Katsuda leaned forward and pressed a button on the umbrella pole.

"It will be just a moment," she said, settling back in her chair.

She didn't say anything more, and it was clear she wasn't going to right away. Carlucci studied her, and changed his guess about her age, raising it by a decade—forties, yes, not thirties. She probably colored her hair, but it looked quite natural, long and dark and straight. She wore a white linen jacket over a light blue blouse; he could no longer see her skirt or legs, but he remembered the skirt being short, the legs long and slim, like her arms.

A woman rolled a cart up to the edge of the table, the cart loaded with steaming coffee, teas, and trays of pastries.

"Tea," Naomi Katsuda said. "Darjeeling. And . . ." She pointed at a long, thin pastry traced with delicate lines of chocolate.

The waitress poured hot water into a small ceramic pot, added a tea bag to it, then set it along with a cup and saucer in front of Naomi. Then she used tongs to move the pastry onto a small plate, and set that beside the cup and saucer. She looked at Carlucci, waiting.

"Just coffee," he said. All of the pastries looked far too rich, and he really had no idea what most of them would taste like. "Black," he added.

The woman poured coffee into a cup, set it in front of him on a saucer, then said, "Will there be anything else?"

Naomi Katsuda shook her head, a short, quick gesture. "We will not want to be disturbed."

The waitress nodded, and rolled the cart away.

A flicker of light flashed through the dark clouds above them, and several seconds later came a dull rumbling. The air felt even heavier now, but there was still no rain.

"I'm only half Japanese," Naomi Katsuda said. "You *were* wondering, weren't you?"

"Something."

She smiled, started to light another cigarette, then stopped and looked at Carlucci. "Do you mind?"

"No."

"Do you smoke? No? I thought all policemen smoked." She smiled in a way that seemed both self-amused and condescending at the same time.

He was going to tell her that he'd quit a few years earlier, but suddenly he realized he did not want to tell her even the smallest personal detail about himself. Already he didn't like her. "No," was all he eventually said. "I don't smoke."

Neither spoke for a couple of minutes. Carlucci sipped at his coffee, and when Naomi finished her cigarette, she poured herself a cup of tea. She took a sip, then looked at him and said, "All right."

"Cancer Cell," he said. "Martin Kelly says you know something about them."

"Why are you interested?"

"My daughter has a friend who's been abducted by two men. A witness seemed to think the two men were involved with Cancer Cell. I'm trying to find out what happened to my daughter's friend."

Naomi Katsuda smiled, and raised one eyebrow. "That's it? That's what all this is about?" As if she couldn't quite believe it.

"Yes."

She shook her head, laughing quietly. "I'm sorry, Lieutenant. I'm sorry about your daughter's friend. But I can't help you."

"You know something about Cancer Cell, though, don't you?"

Her smile shifted into a frown. "I would rather you didn't mention that name again," she said. "It's not a good idea."

"What the hell is all the goddamn mystery about these people?"

"If you knew anything about them, Lieutenant, you would not ask that question."

"That's just the point, isn't it? I don't know anything about them. That's why I'm here. I've known Martin Kelly a long time, and if he says you know something substantial, then I'm sure you do."

"I'm not denying anything, Lieutenant." She paused. "There's an old expression, I'm not sure I have it precisely, but it's something like, 'A little knowledge is a dangerous thing.' "

"I'm familiar with the expression," Carlucci said. "I'm a cop, my job involves dealing with both knowledge and danger. I've been doing it a long time."

Naomi shook her head. "I'm not concerned about you, Lieutenant. I'm concerned about my own safety. Revealing knowledge to others can be even more dangerous than just having it."

"Kelly said you told him that if he needed to know more, for a case, you would help him."

Her expression had grown hard and unyielding. "I made no promises to him. But I agreed to meet you. And when I asked you what this was all about, you told me it's about some unimportant abduction. I am not about to take any risks for that."

"What if it had been my daughter who had been abducted, and not her friend?"

"I would have expressed greater sympathy for your loss, but my answer would have been the same. I would tell you nothing."

"And if my daughter's friend turns up dead, and abduction becomes murder, will you help then?"

She sighed with exasperation, smiling faintly. "There's something fundamental about this you just don't understand, Lieutenant. One insignificant murder would change nothing."

"Then what the hell would it take to get you to talk to me about these people?"

"Much more, Lieutenant." All traces of the smile hardened away. "You can come back to me when people are dying. Maybe I'll talk to you then."

"What the hell is that supposed to mean?" Carlucci asked, angry now. "People are dying all the time. People are dying right now while we're sitting here talking about bullshit."

"You'll know what I mean when it happens, Lieutenant. You'll know exactly what I mean." She shifted her gaze away from him, brought her teacup to her mouth, and drank. "We're done talking, Lieutenant. You can go now." She glanced back at him, the corner of her silver-painted lips turning up into a kind of smile. "I'll cover the check. I doubt you can afford it."

Coffee, tea, a pastry, how much could that be? But she was probably right, in here it would cost a fortune. Everything here was out of reach, including Naomi Katsuda.

He got up from the table, started to thank her, then thought, screw it, why should he? "Good-bye, Ms. Katsuda." She didn't reply, and she didn't look at him. Fuck you, too, he thought. He pushed the chair back in against the table and walked away from her.

Isabel

THERE WAS BLOOD everywhere. Monkey blood.

Isabel watched from the shadows of an old heat duct high above the floor, the grating long gone, her view unobstructed. A woman was skinning a dead monkey, and making a terrible mess of it.

The room was small, with plaster walls and a wood floor partially covered by cracked, stained linoleum and scraps of thin carpeting. The windows were boarded and papered over, and the door was barred shut; light came from a lamp on a wooden crate. Isabel could smell the blood and the stench of fuel from the makeshift stove against the far wall, burners lit beneath an enormous pot filled with water.

The lamp cast jerking, distorted shadows across the floor as the woman moved, but it brightly illuminated the monkey's face, which was as yet untouched.

Henry. Isabel thought it was Henry, who had been in a cage across the aisle from her in her old home; she thought she recognized the odd tuft of gray above his right eyebrow. She had a vague memory of Henry being sick, too, at the same time she was; a memory of Henry lying on the floor of his cage and looking at her, eyes blinking slowly. Now his eyes weren't blinking at all.

Isabel closed her own eyes, feeling sick, down inside her belly. She wanted to stop the smells, the images. But she couldn't, and she opened her eyes again and stared at the scene beneath her.

The woman was awash in blood, and she was breathing hard, swearing as she worked at the dead monkey. Blood covered her hands, streaked her arms, soaked into her clothes; some had splashed across her face. She rested a moment, wiped her face with the back of her hand, and smeared more blood across her cheek and eye. She swore again, blinking crazily. Then she breathed in deeply, dropped the knife to the ground and picked up a larger one, gripped it tightly. Staring into the dead monkey's face, she began sawing at the neck, trying to cut off its head.

Henry, Isabel thought.

She couldn't look anymore. She was feeling sicker, her throat burning now, something coming up from her stomach.

Isabel closed her eyes, then inched her way slowly and silently back along the heat duct, getting away from the room, away from the images and smells, just getting away. . . .

PART TWO

Infection

7

NIKKI GUIDED THE pedalcart around the corner and into the alley; Cage sat beside her, pumping his foot pedals, providing half the power. The gray early morning light darkened as they moved deeper into the alley, blocked by the buildings rising high on either side, the fire escapes, and the shaky planked walkways that crisscrossed the alley several floors above them. Cage was exhausted, working on two hours of sleep and half a pot of coffee; Nikki didn't look much better.

There was a lot of activity in the alley—people loading and unloading merchandise into and from carts and pinky-vans and scat trucks, other people standing around talking and drinking coffee, or walking across the creaking, sagging wooden planks, people and vehicles squeezing past each other in both directions—but it all was relatively low-key this time of day, not like the amphetamine buzz of the Tenderloin at night. The smell of bacon and frying butter was strong, filling the alley, and Cage's stomach burned with acids of morning hunger and coffee. Maybe he'd take Nikki out for breakfast when they were done here.

They let the cart roll to a stop on the right-hand side of the alley, ten feet short of a wide blue metal door set in the brick wall. The first- and second-floor windows of the building were painted over in dark brown and covered by rusting spiked metal grilles.

"This it?" Nikki asked.

"I think so. I'll see."

Nikki set the wheel brakes and Cage climbed down from the cart. The ground was uneven beneath his feet, the asphalt cracked and fissured, scattered with loose gravel and rock. He approached the dark blue door, each step a crunching sound, and banged on it. Almost immediately the door cracked inward, an inch or two at first, then a few more. There was only darkness behind the door, and he couldn't see anything more than shadows and the faint reflection of light from someone's eyes.

"Cage," a voice said from the darkness. Recognition rather than a question. But it wasn't Stinger's voice.

The door swung open another foot, letting in more light and illuminating the man inside. He was dark, thin, and young, in his twenties, dressed in pale khakis, his right arm meshed in silver and wired for body jolts.

"Come on in," the man said, stepping back. "I'm Tiger."

Another fucking moniker. And not very imaginative at that. Cage looked back at Nikki, gestured for her to stay with the pedalcart, and when she nodded he stepped through the doorway. Tiger closed the door, complete darkness returning for a moment, then dim lights came up.

They were in a narrow, empty corridor running the length of the building. Tiger led the way past several interior doors, then stopped in front of the last one at the end of the corridor. He pulled the door open, nodded for Cage to go in. The door automatically swung shut behind them, hydraulics hissing.

The room was small, maybe fifteen feet square, with dark gray painted cinderblock walls. No windows, but there was another door in the back corner, and beside the door, sitting on an overturned plastic crate, with her back against the wall, was a large, beefy woman dressed in pale khakis like Tiger's. Her hair was short and stiff, and she wore a dead neutral expression on her face. She gazed steadily at Cage, almost unblinking, but didn't say a word.

In the middle of the room, open for inspection with their foam-pack lids stacked to the side, were ten or twelve cartons of pharmaceuticals. Cage glanced at them, then looked at Tiger.

"Where's Stinger?"

"He couldn't make it," Tiger answered.

"He was supposed to be here."

Tiger shrugged, glanced at the woman sitting on the crate, but didn't say anything.

"Why isn't he here?"

Tiger hesitated, then finally said, "He's sick."

"Sick with what?"

Tiger cut his glance at the woman again, and shrugged once more. He wouldn't look directly at Cage. "The flu or something." He sniffed once, then pulled sheets of paper from his back pocket and handed them to Cage. "Here's the inventory list, you can check it against the merch. When you're done, we seal up the cartons and load you up."

Cage looked over at the woman, but her expression hadn't changed. There was clearly something about Stinger that made Tiger nervous. More than nervous—Tiger was scared. But it was obvious he wasn't going to talk about it here, not with this woman around. Cage decided to let it go for now.

He didn't spend more than fifteen minutes checking the contents of the cartons against the inventory sheets; he was more concerned with Stinger's health right now than he was with the pharmaceuticals. Besides, he and Madelaine would do a more complete inspection back at the clinic, and he knew it would all check out; these people weren't going to try to rip him off yet, not before they got any work out of him.

When he was done, Tiger helped him put the foam-pack lids back on the cartons, sealing each one with strip tape. The woman didn't make a move to help.

"Let's go get Nikki," Cage said, "and we can load up and get out of your way."

Another glance at the woman from Tiger. Cage didn't have any doubts about who was in charge.

"I think I'd better wait here," Tiger said.

"Thanks a lot." Don't push it, Cage told himself. He left the room, walked down the corridor to the big metal door, but didn't open it. He returned to the room, pulled the door open, and stuck his head inside.

"Hey, Tiger. The door's locked."

Tiger seemed confused for a moment, then nodded once and said, "Okay, I'll get it."

Halfway along the corridor, when the door to the room had swung completely shut, Cage stopped and faced Tiger, bringing the young man to an abrupt halt.

"All right," Cage whispered. "What the hell is wrong with Stinger?"

"I told you," Tiger answered without conviction. "He's got the flu or something."

"Bullshit. I saw him two weeks ago, and he was starting to get sick then, and it wasn't the goddamn flu. So what the fuck is it?"

Tiger tried to step back, but Cage grabbed his left arm to keep him close. He didn't think Tiger would use the body jolts on him.

"I'm not supposed to say anything," Tiger tried, a whine sliding in his voice.

"I don't care. I spent half an hour sitting across a table from the bastard, and I want to know what the hell it is I've been exposed to. I want to know what the hell it is that's got you so scared."

Tiger didn't say anything for a minute, but he was starting to sweat, and the sweat stank of fear.

"What is it?" Cage asked once more, his voice slow and quiet and firm.

"I don't know," Tiger finally said. "He's real sick. I think he's dying. But *nobody* knows what's wrong with him."

"Or nobody's saying."

Tiger shook his head. "I don't think they know."

"All right." Cage let him go. "What are the symptoms? Tell me what's happening to him."

"I don't really know that much. They're keeping him isolated. But he was getting really bad headaches, and his eyes were completely bloodshot, almost solid red, and he had red patches all over his skin, and he was starting to act real crazy. But I haven't seen him for a couple three days."

"Are you sure he's still alive?"

"I guess. They'd tell us if he died."

Cage gave him a wry smile. "Would they." Then he sighed, and asked, "Who is this 'they' you keep talking about?"

"The people I work for."

"Who are they?"

Tiger shook his head. "You know I can't tell you that. Don't even ask."

"Maybe you should bring me to him," Cage said. "I'm a doctor, maybe I can help."

"We've got doctors," Tiger said.

"Yeah, I'll bet. Lots of doctors, don't you?" He was tempted to come right out and ask Tiger if it *was* Cancer Cell he worked for, but there was no point. Tiger might not actually know it was Cancer Cell, and Cage was pretty damn sure he knew the answer, anyway.

"So what's got you so scared, Tiger?"

Tiger breathed deeply once and licked his lips. "I was helping carry him to see the docs, and he had some kind of seizure, whacking out all over, and then he puked up blood all over the place . . . all over *me*." Tiger shuddered. "I got his blood all over me."

And Nikki had put her finger hooks into him. Nikki had drawn blood.

"How long ago was this, Tiger?"

Tiger blinked a couple of times, wiped sweat from his lip. "T-two days ago? Maybe three."

"And how are you feeling? Besides scared?"

"Okay. I think."

"I'm sure you'll be fine," Cage lied. He couldn't be sure at all. "You look fine." He nodded down the corridor. "Go on back to your baby sitter."

"What about the door?"

"Christ, Tiger. The door's not locked." Cage turned and headed down the corridor, leaving Tiger to figure it out for himself.

When Cage opened the door, he found that Nikki had backed the pedal-cart to the door, ready for him. She was sitting on the hold, smoking a cigarette. He hadn't seen her smoke in three or four weeks; she'd tried to quit several times in the past year, and this last time had gone the longest. But he didn't mention the cigarette. Nikki smoking was the least of his worries right now.

"We ready to go?" Nikki asked.

Cage nodded. Nikki slid off the end of the cart, dropped the cigarette butt, and ground it out with her boot. How long had it been since the meeting with Stinger? Cage worked it out. Fifteen days. Nikki didn't seem to be sick at all, and she hadn't complained about anything, not even a headache. She was tired, but so was he. Fifteen days. It didn't mean shit.

They propped open the door with two wooden wedges, then Cage led the way down the corridor to the room where Tiger and the woman waited.

Cage made the introductions. "Nikki. Tiger." Then, with a gesture at the woman still sitting on the crate, he said, "I have no idea who she is. She doesn't talk." He looked at Tiger, who seemed uncomfortable again. "You going to help us load up?"

Tiger shook his head. "I can't."

Cage smiled, looked back at the woman. "How about you?"

The woman didn't reply, didn't move except to blink and breathe.

"That's not her job," Tiger said.

Cage laughed. "I know, Tiger. I know what her job is." He and Nikki each picked up a carton, and he raised an eyebrow at Tiger. "Are you allowed to get the door?"

Tiger hurried to the door, pushed it open, and held it for them. Cage and Nikki carried the cartons through, along the corridor, then out into the alley. Nikki opened the hold of the pedal cart, and they carefully placed the cartons inside.

"I'll get the next one," Cage said. They couldn't leave the cart alone now, so they would alternate trips.

She nodded. "Fine. And I'll have another smoke." Almost daring him to say something. When he didn't, she said, "No Stinger?"

"Nope. Didn't show."

"Why not?"

Cage shrugged and shook his head.

"Why not, Cage?"

"Tiger said he was sick. The flu."

"The flu."

"That's what he said."

Nikki took a cigarette from the pack in her top shock suit pocket, lit it with a stone-lighter. Neither of them said anything for a minute.

"I wouldn't worry about it," Cage eventually said.

"Yeah." Nikki dragged in deep on the cigarette, held it, then blew a long, steady stream of smoke into Cage's face. "Go get another carton," she said.

Cage nodded and headed back inside.

As he was leaving the room, carton in his arms, Tiger out in the hall holding the door open, Cage paused, seeing that Tiger was out of the woman's line of sight. He leaned toward Tiger and whispered rapidly. "Listen, Tiger. You'll probably be fine. But if you start to get sick, get the hell out of wherever you are. Come find me at the RadioLand Street Clinic, we'll take care of you. Got that?"

Tiger's eyes were wide, scared again, but he nodded. "RadioLand."

"You'll be fine." Then Cage headed along the corridor.

Twenty minutes later, he and Nikki had all the cartons packed and the hold locked up; they closed the blue metal door and climbed up onto the cart. Cage worked his feet into the pedals, but Nikki remained motionless, her arms lying across the wheel and her gaze unfocused.

"How sick is he?" she asked.

"Stinger?"

She nodded.

Cage shrugged. "Tiger didn't know."

Nikki turned to stare hard at him. "How sick?"

"Tiger didn't know," Cage insisted. "Besides, what are the odds? You used the antiseptic wipes. This is all a lot of worry about nothing."

Nikki stared at him a few moments longer, then turned to face forward. She gripped the steering wheel, dug her feet into the pedals, and started pumping.

8

WET AND UNCOMFORTABLE, Carlucci stood at the edge of the cliff and gazed down through the sagging chain-link fence at the ruins of the old Sutro Baths sixty or seventy feet below him. The heavier morning rain had eased, but still came down as a warm, dense mist, graying out the ocean and almost completely obscuring Seal Rocks out on the water. The drizzle masked all sound, and the air was unnaturally quiet around him; it was thick with the smell of salt. He could just make out the moving figures in the ruins below, perhaps half a dozen at the moment—two uniformed cops and several detectives. Soon there would be more. The two uniforms were erecting a protective tarp, sheltering the others and, presumably, the body.

Carlucci disliked this place intensely. Being here made him feel awful— as if he'd just awakened from some profoundly disturbing dream he could not remember. Disoriented, vaguely afraid, and depressed. Melancholy and bad memories.

There was, to him, something incredibly sad about the ruins, which had been here for more than fifty years; maybe a lot longer than that. He wasn't sure of the dates. But what he did know was that the Sutro Baths had been built at the very end of the nineteenth century—the largest public bathhouse in the world. He had seen pictures of the huge, glass-enclosed natatorium at the edge of the sea, interior photos of the half dozen saltwater swimming pools heated by enormous furnaces, the promenades and spectator galleries, hundreds, even thousands of people swimming, diving, shooting down water slides, socializing. But sometime in the second half of the twentieth century the baths had burned to the ground. The ruins—broken sections of concrete walkways, roofless remnants of small concrete or cinder block buildings scattered around the perimeter, and the old foundations, which filled with water like outdoor versions of the old swimming pools—had remained ever since, untouched except by vandals and the elements.

Carlucci turned to his left and gazed at the ugly rectangular buildings of the modern Cliff House, the source of his bad memories. Eight or nine years ago, out here to investigate the drowning death of a twelve-year-old girl, he had seen Andrea coming out of the Cliff House restaurant, hand-in-hand with a man he had never seen before. He had watched them kiss, then part, the man to a car and Andrea across the street to the bus stop. He had stood, not far from where he was right now, and watched her waiting, saw her smile and wave at the man as he drove past her, and Carlucci had wondered why the hell the man didn't give Andrea a ride, why he made her take the bus back into town. He had remained there unmoving, numb and disoriented, until the bus arrived; Andrea climbed aboard, and then the bus pulled away.

That night, as they lay in bed with the lights off and bright moonlight streaming in through the window, he had come right out and asked her about the man. After a long silence, Andrea had told him she'd been having an affair with the man for nearly a year. She'd also told him that, now that he knew, she would bring it to an end; she didn't want it to threaten their marriage. He had expected her to tell him who the man was, something about him, how the affair had started, things like that. But she didn't. He had wanted to know *why*, but she wouldn't talk about that, either. She said it didn't matter, that it had nothing to do with him, or the family, or their marriage, that it was something to do with her alone. Although he couldn't believe that entirely, Carlucci had sensed that in some important ways it was true. They hadn't talked about it again. As far as he knew, there had been no other affairs, before or since. But the memories of that day still hurt, even after all these years.

"Lieutenant?"

Carlucci turned to see Jefferson and Tran walking downhill along the cracked sidewalk toward him. Jefferson looked like he was still sick with the flu that had kept him home for more than two weeks—he was gaunt, his eyes were heavy, and he seemed out of breath.

"You all right?" Carlucci asked him.

Jefferson shrugged. "Better. The old boneman says I shouldn't be contagious anymore, and that maybe it would be good to get out a little." He smiled. "Don't know that this was what he had in mind, checking out a murder in the rain, but what the fuck."

They stood in the mist, which was getting heavier, and looked down at the cops standing under the protective tarp down near the edge of the ruins.

"Who was first on scene?" Tran asked.

"Santos and Weathers," Carlucci answered. "They'll be in charge of the case."

Tran nodded, said, "Ruben and Toni, good. We can do that."

Jefferson coughed several times, shook himself, then said, "Let's get down there."

Carlucci frowned at him. "You want to stay up here? Have Binh fill you in later?"

Jefferson was looking down through the drizzle at the muddy slope, the makeshift trails that twisted down and through the rubble. He nodded. "Yeah, maybe I'd better."

"Go on back to the car," Carlucci told him. "Get out of the rain."

Jefferson nodded again, said, "Thanks, Lieutenant," and started back up the hill. Carlucci and Tran walked in the opposite direction, along the sidewalk to an opening that had been cut in the chain-link fence and flagged. The opening was at the head of what appeared to be the best path down to the ruins. The slope wasn't as steep here, almost terraced. They worked their way slowly down the hillside, past crumbling walls half buried, past the remains of floors and pipes and an occasional piece of roofing. They used chunks of concrete or rock or tufts of grass for footing whenever possible. The drizzle had become so heavy now that he could barely see the vague outlines of the Cliff House, could barely see the ocean.

"Anything on that parrot, yet?" Tran asked.

"No. It swears a lot, but they haven't picked up much more than that. The CID people are starting to think we're crazy. Maybe we are. Maybe it's all a goddamn waste of time." Carlucci smiled. "Kelly's growing fond of the parrot, though. Says he might take it home when they're done with it." He stopped, trying to find a way past a steep, slick streak of mud. "How *is* Jefferson?"

"He'll be fine," Tran said. Carlucci looked at him, and Tran repeated himself. "He'll be fine."

Carlucci backtracked a couple of steps, worked uphill, then out along a strip of crumbling brickwork, dropping a couple of feet to a thick patch of sea grass. Tran dropped down beside him.

"Do you know why we've got extra teams called in on this one?" Tran asked. "It's only one victim, isn't it?"

Carlucci shook his head. "Ruben just said it was a hot one, and to get two extra teams down here as soon as possible. He wouldn't say why. I think Hong and LaPlace are already here. Yeah, there's Hong." The tall, thin detective was apart from the others, crouched at the edge of the old foundation, gazing into the leaf-covered water. His glasses were misted over, and Carlucci wondered how he could see anything.

The ground leveled out as they neared the old foundations, covered by large patches of ocean grasses and succulents, and walking became easier. A narrow path had been marked out along the beds of ice plant and concrete slabs, a futile attempt to preserve the integrity of the crime scene. They stayed on the path and made their way to the group of cops huddled under the tarp. There were two uniforms, who kept back, only partly out of the rain, and three detectives—Santos, Weathers, and LaPlace. Several feet away, still crouched by the water, Hong looked up and nodded at Carlucci. At the feet of the cops was a covered form laid out along the edge of the concrete foundation.

"I'm sure as hell glad you're here," Santos said as Carlucci and Tran squeezed in under the tarp. "I was afraid you'd be too late."

"Too late for what?" Carlucci asked.

"Someone's going to try to take this case away from us." He stared hard at Carlucci. "I don't want that to happen. You might be able to hold on to it for us."

"Who's going to try to take it?"

Santos shrugged. "Someone." He shifted to the side and looked up the slope to the road and fence at the edge of the cliff. Carlucci followed his gaze, but didn't see anything. Tran lit a cigarette, and almost immediately Toni Weathers and one of the uniforms followed suit. The falling drizzle on all sides kept the smoke contained, and it built up under the tarp, hovered around them.

"Morgan," Santos finally said.

Morgan was homicide lieutenant for the Financial District, which had its own separate department within the force. But the ruins of the Sutro Baths weren't anywhere near the Financial District.

"Do we have an ID?" Carlucci asked. That had to be what had Santos spooked.

"Oh yeah," Santos said. "She was chipped, and we got an instant hit, complete with goddamn flares and alarms."

"Who is she?"

"It's not who she is. It's who her father is."

"Who is she, Ruben?"

Santos shrugged again. "Naomi Katsuda."

Carlucci didn't say anything, just looked down at the covered form at their feet.

"You know her?" LaPlace asked.

Carlucci stepped toward the head, the other cops making room for him. He knelt beside the body and pulled the dark nylon cloth away from the face. Her skin was gray and cold and lifeless, the lips a smeared silver now, the eyes closed and bruised, but he recognized her. The initials "CC" had been neatly carved into her forehead. He stared at her for a minute, feeling almost dizzy. Then he covered her face and stood. A cold tremor of fear rattled through him, settling in his stomach where it continued to tremble.

"I met her once," he finally said.

"Cancer Cell," said Tran. When the others looked at him, he pointed at the body. "The letters carved in her forehead. Cancer Cell."

Only Carlucci knew why it had occurred to Tran, but he didn't want to explain now. He turned to Santos. "Why all the flares and alarms? And why are you worried about Morgan?"

"Her father, Yoshi Katsuda, is the CEO of Mishima Investments. And Mishima Investments is New Hong Kong."

Carlucci nodded, trying to work things out. Martin Kelly had never mentioned Naomi's father. Didn't he know? She hadn't mentioned it either. But Santos was right. Morgan would try to suck this case in, take it for his own, into Financial District jurisdiction where it would be investigated in complete secrecy, investigated in whatever way Mishima Investments and Yoshi Katsuda, and maybe even New Hong Kong, wanted it investigated.

"I won't let him take this case," Carlucci said. He looked up the slope, understanding now why Santos had been looking up there earlier. When Santos and Weathers had locked onto the identity chip in Naomi Katsuda's shoulder, and her identity had been confirmed, a bolt would have been transmitted directly to Morgan. It was surprising he wasn't here yet.

"Coroner's crew and crime scene techs should be here any minute," said Weathers. She looked at her cigarette, which was almost gone, then flicked the butt away, toward the ocean. Tran did the same. It probably didn't matter much, Carlucci thought. With all this rain and mud the crime scene was a mess anyway.

"Any idea how she was killed?" Carlucci asked.

Santos and Weathers both shook their heads. "You could almost wonder if it was accidental, except for the letters carved into her forehead. I'm pretty sure the carving was postmortem."

"She wasn't in the water, was she?" What he'd seen of Naomi Katsuda's face hadn't looked like a floater, unless she'd been in the water a very short time.

Santos shook his head again. "We found her just where she is now."

Carlucci glanced at the two uniforms, but they both shook their heads as well. The older of the two, a woman in her forties, said, "We didn't touch her, Lieutenant. We were just a few blocks away when the call came through, we flashed over here and marked off the path, then waited for the detectives."

"Who called it in?"

"Manager of the Cliff House restaurant," Weathers said. "A customer spotted it." She smiled. "I guess it spoiled their lunch."

Hong joined them under the tarp, his hair soaked, water dripping down his face. He wiped his glasses with a handkerchief.

"You find something over there?" Carlucci asked.

"No. I was primarily thinking about the job the crime scene techs are going to have." His mouth worked into the faintest of smiles. "They're going to have to drag all that, aren't they? Can you imagine the crap they're going to find in there? And probably none of it will have any connection to this."

"Oh, fuck," LaPlace said. "They're here."

They all looked up at the road that curved its way along the edge of the cliff. Two cars were just coming to a stop, pulling up over the curb and onto the sidewalk—a gray BMW, which was probably Morgan's, and behind it a black, medium-sized limousine. Two men got out of the BMW, Blaise Morgan and Alex Warsinske, Morgan's flunky. They approached the chain-link fence and looked down through the misting rain at the group of men looking back up at them. They wore slickcoats over their suits, but no hats, and they didn't look too happy to be standing out in the rain.

No one emerged from the limousine.

"Is Morgan waiting for us to come up there after him?" Santos wondered aloud.

"You don't want him to get his shoes muddy, do you?" LaPlace said. "Fucking thousand-dollar Italian shoes."

"Watch it," Carlucci said. "Italians make the best shoes."

LaPlace snorted. "Yeah, but who can afford them? Where the fuck were *your* shoes made?"

"Probably Guatemala," Carlucci said, smiling. The other cops laughed.

"Fuck him," LaPlace said. "He wants this case, let him climb on down here."

"Yeah," Weathers added, "and maybe that ferret Warsinske will end up on his ass."

Two more vehicles pulled up behind the limousine—the coroner's van and an old department junker with crime scene techs. Men and women climbed out of the two vehicles and, loaded with equipment and cases and a jacked-up stretcher, headed toward the break in the fencing. Morgan and Warsinske remained where they were, looking down at the ruins.

Carlucci turned back to Santos and Weathers. "All right, Ruben, Toni. This is your case. You've got Hong and LaPlace, and Tran and Jefferson. You need more help, just ask. You get any flak from Morgan or anyone else, send them to me. I'll run interference." He glanced at Tran. "Binh might be right about Cancer Cell. I'll let him explain. I don't know what the hell is going on here, but there's more involved than just Naomi Katsuda's death. We're keeping this goddamn case."

"Here he comes." LaPlace pointed up the slope.

Carlucci turned around and saw Morgan and Warsinske taking the first cautious steps through the break in the fence. The coroner's assistants and the techs were about halfway down the slope. Carlucci breathed in deeply once, let it out. "All right."

He stepped out from the shelter of the tarp; the drizzle was even heavier now, though he still wouldn't call it rain, exactly, and it was still fairly warm. The salt smell had grown stronger. He worked his way along the marked pathway, eyes to the ground.

Just before he reached the foot of the slope, he met the crews coming down and stepped to the side to let them pass. Most of the men and women nodded to him as they went by, and he nodded in return. When they were by him, he took a few more steps, then sat on the remains of a cinderblock wall, his slickcoat protecting his ass from the wet, and waited for Morgan and Warsinske. They were still only halfway down the slope, struggling with their footing, slipping on the mud, and Carlucci could hear Morgan swearing.

He looked back at the raised tarp. The body was no longer even partially visible, surrounded now by close to a dozen people. It was going to be a long and miserable afternoon for everyone. Maybe he *didn't* want to go back onto the streets. Maybe it *was* time for him to get out.

Morgan and Warsinske finally reached the bottom of the slope and approached. Warsinske hung back, as though trying to hide behind his boss.

"I want this fucking case," Morgan said.

Blaise Morgan was a handsome man, an inch or two taller than Carlucci, but probably five or ten pounds lighter. Even with his dark hair soaked by the drizzle, he looked slick and polished—he was the perfect man to run Homicide in the Financial District. He was also a good cop, though Carlucci thought that politics held way too high a priority for him. He looked down at Morgan's shoes; they probably *were* expensive Italian leather, but it was hard to tell with all the mud smeared over them.

"What are you looking at, Frank?"

Carlucci looked up. "Your shoes."

Morgan made a snorting sound. "They're probably ruined." Then, voice hard, "I want this case, Frank."

Carlucci shook his head firmly. "It's not your jurisdiction, B.J. It's not even close."

"You know who the victim is?"

"Yes."

"Her father is head of Mishima Investments, for Christ's sake. She worked for them, too. Mishima is my jurisdiction."

"If she'd been killed in the Mishima building, I'd agree completely. But she wasn't. We're miles from the Financial District, B.J."

"Maybe she *was* killed in the district, and her body dumped here."

Carlucci just shook his head, not bothering to respond.

Morgan pointed back up the slope at the limousine parked above them. "You know who's in that limo?"

"Yoshi Katsuda, would be my guess."

"Damn fucking right, Frank. He's her father, and he wants me to run the investigation. He knows me, he knows the teams that work in the Financial District, he knows we'll be discreet."

"I don't care," Carlucci said. "And I won't even be insulted by that. It's not your jurisdiction."

"You afraid I'll ghost the case? Find out who did it and let Katsuda work his own family justice?"

"It's not yours to ghost, B.J., so I don't think anything."

"You want to tell that to Yoshi Katsuda? Tell him you're ignoring his wishes?"

"If I have to."

"He's a powerful man, Frank, you know that. He could make your job a misery."

"I just don't give a shit."

Morgan didn't say anything for a minute, staring hard at Carlucci. Warsinske had come out from behind Morgan, but still hung back, waiting to see how all this was going to play out.

"And what if I go to Vaughn?" Morgan asked.

"He might give you the case. And he might not. Either way I'll raise a big fucking stink about it, and what will Yoshi Katsuda think about that?"

Morgan went silent again. He looked away from Carlucci, gazed at the people clustered around the body, then slowly turned to look up the hill at the limousine. Still no one had emerged from the limo, and Carlucci wondered if Yoshi Katsuda was staring down at them right now through the smoked windows. Or was he sitting calmly in the rear seat, eyes straight ahead, not really seeing anything, just waiting for Morgan to come and talk to him? Carlucci almost felt sorry for Morgan.

"We can work out some kind of cooperative arrangement," Carlucci finally said. He could play some politics, too, when he had to. He was probably going to need Morgan's help with this.

Morgan turned back to him. "In what sense?"

"Santos and Weather have caught this one. They'll need to do interviews with people at Mishima, maybe other people in the Financial District. If you help slick the way for them, I'll keep you regularly informed of the progress on the case. And then if you want, you can keep Katsuda up to date."

Morgan hesitated for a few moments, then sighed. "Sure, that could work. And you won't hold anything back from me?"

"Of course I will," Carlucci replied. "If I think it's necessary. But I'll give you enough."

Morgan smiled, shaking his head. "You know, Frank, it's a fucking miracle they made you lieutenant. I wish I knew what you had on the bastards."

"It's not like that, B.J."

"Yeah, yeah, yeah." He sighed again. "Okay, I guess that's about as good as it's going to get, isn't it?"

"Yes." Carlucci tipped his head toward the limousine. "You want me to talk to Katsuda?"

"No. I'll explain our 'cooperative arrangement.' I'll be able to do a better job of selling it to him than you would." They shook hands. "I'll be in touch, Frank. You too, all right?"

"I will, B.J."

Morgan turned and started up the hill, Warsinske just a few steps behind, scrambling after his boss like a sycophant. Warsinske would get his one day, Carlucci thought. Karma would catch up to the little ferret and bury him.

Carlucci turned and headed back toward the body.

That night, after dinner, Andrea made a pot of decaf and poured cups for both of them. Carlucci took his to the stove, opened the upper cabinet, and took out a bottle of Irish whiskey. He poured a good slug into his coffee, trying not to look at Andrea, who was almost certainly watching him. He sipped at the coffee, savoring both kinds of heat as they slid down his throat and into his stomach, like soothing liquid fire. He took one more long swallow, and finally turned around. Andrea was already gone from the kitchen; he followed her into the front room.

She was sitting in her chair, table lamp on beside her, a book open in her lap, reading glasses perched on the end of her nose. Carlucci crossed the room to his ancient recliner, set his cup on the book stand beside the chair, and sat. The chair had been his father's, and the leather was as dark and worn as his father's face had been the last years of his life. Sitting in the chair always made him think of his father, and gave him a sense of comfort and security.

"Rough day?" Andrea was looking at him over the top of her glasses.

"Yeah. I'm beat." He took another sip of the coffee. "I was out at the Sutro Baths this afternoon. There was a dead woman down in the ruins." He paused, revisualizing the scene, the heavy drizzle and gray skies and the cops working around the body. Andrea didn't say anything; she'd been through this so many times, and years ago she had stopped saying things like, "How awful." Now she just listened and waited, let him talk about what he needed to get out. It was something he greatly appreciated.

"I've got a real bad feeling about this one," he continued. "I had just talked to the woman a couple of weeks ago." He decided not to mention Caroline's part in the story. "I had asked her about a group of people I was looking into for a small thing at work, a missing persons I was checking out for a friend. But she wouldn't tell me anything, though it was obvious she knew something about this group." He paused, thinking back to the conversation, trying to remember her words. "She told me to come back and talk to her when people started dying."

Andrea took off her glasses and laid them on her book. "What did she mean by that?"

"I have no idea. She said I'd know what she was talking about when it happened. But I don't think she meant this. I can't exactly talk to her again now, can I?"

Neither of them spoke for a while. He took another long drink, but the whiskey didn't really seem to be helping much.

"While I was out there," he resumed, "I was standing up on the road, and I looked over at the Cliff House, and I couldn't help thinking about that day."

Andrea didn't reply immediately. She seemed almost frozen, staring at him, not even blinking. She closed her eyes for a moment, then looked at him again. "Frank, that was nine years ago."

"I know. But do you think I'll ever forget?" She didn't answer, and he shook his head. "I'm sorry, I'm giving you the wrong idea. It was a bad day. I mean, today was a bad day, and I want you to know I'd have a harder time getting through days like this without you. I'm doing a lousy job of it, but what I'm trying to tell you is, I love you, Andrea, and I'm glad you're here with me."

She sighed and gave him a soft, warm smile. But she didn't say anything. She didn't need to. Neither of them did.

9

THIS NIGHT, CAROLINE entered the DMZ well after dark. Not a smart thing to do, but she didn't care. Let the street scavengers swoop down on her and pick her clean. What the hell did it matter?

Two days of rain had given way to a mild heat wave. The temperature climbed into the eighties during the day, and didn't cool off much at night. It was still spring, so the heat wasn't too bad, but right now it was probably still above seventy, and humidity was fairly high. She liked this kind of weather.

The street was a mindless swarm of people and vehicles, flashing colored lights and barking voices, competing blasts of alarms and pounding music, all infused with the stench of weed smoke, spilled alcohol, rotting plants, and burning oil. She heard glass break nearby, an explosion of some kind, a hammering sound, then a loud braying laugh. Someone pawed at her face, and she knocked the hand away.

She wanted a drink. She wanted several drinks, but she didn't want to sweat and fight in the bars, so she went without.

Traffic was stopped at the intersection ahead, and a crowd had formed in the middle of the street. Feeling reckless, she climbed on the back of a bus stop bench to see what was happening, using a power pole for support. There was a large open space in the middle of the crowd, roughly circular, and inside it were three men in wire head-cages, bare from the waist up and all three lightning-leashed to their handlers. Caroline thought she recognized the stocky woman handler on the far side of the circle, the one she'd run into two weeks ago on her way to see Tito. The handler was shouting through the head-cage at her charge, presumably giving him instructions.

The crowd around the three men and their handlers was growing, and people were climbing onto stalled and parked vehicles, sidewalk stands, balconies, anything that afforded a better view. Before long, Caroline's own view would be completely blocked. Just as well, she thought, she didn't really want to see this. She knew what was coming—she could already hear the betting begin.

The three men were roped together in a kind of circle, or rough triangle, less than ten feet of rope between each of them; each man remained leashed to his handler, and the collars around their necks shimmered with electricity.

A man in body armor went to each of the head-caged men and slapped dermal patches onto their necks, half a dozen to each—probably crashers, deadeners, and skyrockets. Within minutes, the three men in head-cages would be completely wired and crazed. Finally, a set of metal handclaws was strapped onto the right arm and hand of each man. They would tear each other apart.

That was enough for Caroline. She climbed down from the bench and pushed into the crowd, working her way toward the buildings until she could get past the intersection. A frenzied roar swelled from the crowd, and she knew it had begun.

Once past the intersection, the crowds thinned, but the sidewalk was still full and hectic. A man bleeding profusely from a head wound staggered toward her, hissing at her as he went by. Two teenaged tattoo-girls shuffled along a few feet in front of her, arms wrapped around one another, their ponytails laced together with wire webbing. A rat pack ten or twelve strong marched steadfastly along the sidewalk, forcing people to move out of its way. Caroline got jammed up against a pokey booth; the gooner inside grinned and breathed a foul, warm stench into her face, nauseating her. Finally the rat pack swept past, the pressure eased, and she pushed away from the booth.

She walked along in a kind of daze, hardly paying attention to her surroundings, almost unconsciously fending of the hasslers and pervs. She just didn't feel much of anything.

She had been in this numb and dazed state of mind almost constantly since the night Tina had come by. She couldn't shake it, and most of the time she didn't even *want* to shake it. Most of the time she just didn't care.

In the years since the Gould's Syndrome had been diagnosed, Caroline had thought she'd come to terms with the disease. She knew its activation was inevitable, she knew it was ultimately terminal, and she had thought she had come to terms with the fear and the dread, and the self-pity.

Clearly she hadn't.

She'd been fooled, it seemed, because in all these years, other than developing a tendency to tire easily, the Gould's had not gone active. The markers had been picked up in a routine screening, and she'd been informed of what they meant. She had been given all the details of the disease, including the possible and probable ways it would progress once it had gone active, and she'd been told what the ultimate prognosis was. She'd known she would have several years before it went fully active, before the myelin sheathing of her central nervous system would begin to degenerate in earnest, but she'd also known that it was unlikely she would live to see thirty, and that no one with Gould's had ever lived past thirty-two. And she'd known there was no treatment for it, no cure. She'd known all that.

But apparently, in some deep and real way, she hadn't.

When the vision in her eye had gone funny and she'd lost control of her leg and sprawled to the floor, *then* she had known.

She was scared now, and she didn't want to be scared. And she was afraid she would never be able to get away from that fear.

She had stopped walking, and now stood at the inner edge of the sidewalk, leaning against a building wall. How long had she been standing here, people moving past her? She looked up, saw the sign for Turtle Joe's just above her head, and nodded to herself; probably this was where she'd been headed all along.

She walked past Turtle Joe's and turned into the alcove entrance to the death house. Everything looked the same: the crude red skull-and-crossbones, the grille over the heavy wooden door, the cracked brick and crumbling mortar of the arch and walls, the chipped and cracked and stained marble flagstones under her feet. Caroline pushed the door open, stepped inside, and closed the door behind her.

Quiet and dim light. Familiar smell of damp and sickness, and something acrid, almost burning her nose. The lobby was empty.

She took the stairs slowly, one deliberate step at a time, keeping her attention on her feet. Since that night with Tina her vision had been fine, and she hadn't lost control of her leg again, but she knew it could happen at any time, and she spent much of her time *waiting* for it to happen again. She couldn't help herself.

When she reached the third-floor landing, she didn't need to rest; instead, she kept right on walking down the hall toward Tito's old room. The black door looked just the same. But everything was so quiet she imagined that if she unlocked the door and found Tito inside, it would only be if he were already dead, lying on the floor, eyes open, waiting for someone to come and take him away.

She unlocked the dead bolt, then put her key in the knob, turned it, and pushed the door inward. There were lights on inside the room, and she froze, the door only half open. She remained motionless, listening, but didn't hear anything. Her heart was beating fast and hard, and her mouth went dry.

"Tito?" she ventured. She slid the key out of the knob, gripped it tightly in her right hand.

There was a slight rustle, then a soft, timid voice. "Who is it?" A woman's voice.

Caroline stepped carefully around the door. Huddled against the far wall, on the mattress that had served as Tito's bed, were a woman and a young girl. The woman appeared to be in her thirties, and the girl about nine or ten. Both had straight, dirty blond hair and dark blue eyes, both were dressed in T-shirts and jeans. Both of them looked scared.

"It's all right," Caroline said. "I'm sorry, I didn't mean to . . ."

"Do you live here?" the woman asked. "We were told the room was empty."

"No. I had a friend who lived here. He's been gone for a while."

"Is he coming back?" The woman coughed, glanced at the girl, then turned back to Caroline. "We don't have anywhere else to go."

Caroline breathed in very deeply, held it for a few moments, then slowly let it out, shaking her head. "No." The truth of that sank into her completely for the first time. "No, he won't be back. You can stay here." Exhaustion washed over her, combining with the earlier numbness, and she wanted to lie down on Tito's old sofa, go to sleep, and not wake up for days. "I'm sorry I bothered you," she said to the woman and the girl. "I'll just go."

"Wait," the woman said. "Can we . . . can we have your key?" She pointed at the key in Caroline's hand. "We can lock the door when we're inside, but we can't lock it when we leave. No one had a key."

Caroline nodded. She crossed the room and handed the key to the woman, wondering if the woman was contagious, wondering why she cared. The woman thanked her. Then, feeling awkward, Caroline asked, "Why are you here?"

"We don't have anyplace else to go," the woman said. "We haven't got much money."

"No, I meant . . ." She shook her head. "I'm sorry, just . . ." She tried to wave it off. What was she thinking? What was wrong with her? Leave these poor people alone. She started to turn away, but the woman reached out and touched her arm.

"My daughter's dying," the woman said.

Caroline looked at the young girl. She didn't look sick. Tired, maybe, and hungry, but not sick. But then *I don't look sick either*, she thought.

"I'm sorry," she said again. "Do you have any money?" A stupid question, she realized as soon as she asked. If the woman had any money she wouldn't be here with her daughter in this godforsaken death house.

"A little," the woman said. Probably a lie.

"Food?"

"The Sisters bring us meals."

They had nothing. Caroline looked around the room, saw an open suitcase with a few clothes, a few children's books on the sofa, but nothing else that hadn't been left behind by Mouse.

"Is there something I can do to help?" Caroline asked.

The woman didn't answer. Caroline knew she was not doing this very well. She looked back and forth between the woman and the girl, feeling cold and afraid again. "I'm dying too," she finally said.

No one said anything for a long time. Eventually the girl said, "Can you help us?"

Caroline looked at the woman. "Something," she said. "If you want me to."

The girl nodded. Her mother just said, "There's some tea here. Would you like some?"

Tito's herb teas. Nobody thought they were worth stealing. "Sure," she said, smiling. "That would be nice."

The little girl smiled back.

10

"I FEEL LIKE shit," Nikki said.

She was sitting in a black plastic chair by an open window in her apartment, her head resting against the wooden frame, eyes closed. Cage stood just inside the front door, watching her. The air was warm and stuffy, and stank of burned food.

"Why aren't you in bed?" he asked.

She gave him a tired smile and opened one eye. "I'm not that sick. I just feel crappy." She closed her eye. "I was heating up some soup and nodded off. I burned it."

The apartment was a fairly large one-room studio, with a separate kitchen alcove, and a full bath off the back corner. There wasn't much furniture. Nikki slept in a sleeping bag on an old cot, and she ate on a sheet of plywood laid across stacks of plastic crates. There was a single stuffed chair beside a floor lamp, where she read at night, and several black plastic chairs she used when working at her tapestry looms. All three of the vertical looms were set up now, two with tapestries just begun, the other with one nearing completion. She'd been working on this last one for well over a year, and like most of her tapestries it incorporated both Native American and Native African motifs, heavily abstracted; hundreds of colored threads dangled from the back of the loom.

"Have you eaten anything today?" Cage asked.

Nikki shook her head, dreadlock beads clicking against the window frame with each movement.

"Want me to cook you something?"

"Soup?" Nikki said, smiling again.

"Sure. Soup."

He crossed the room to the kitchen alcove, glanced at the pot of burned soup soaking in the sink, then opened the cupboard under the counter and dug around for another pot.

"Soup's above the stove," she said.

The upper cupboard was pretty well stocked with canned goods, though about half of it was cat food. Nikki fed the neighborhood strays down in the alley. She was allergic to cat dander, so she couldn't keep any cats in the apartment for herself.

Cage took down a can of chicken soup with rice and vegetables. "Chicken soup," he said. "Best thing for you."

"Yeah, yeah."

He opened the can, poured the contents into the pot, then turned on the burner and set the flame low. He stirred the soup a few times, then left it and walked back across the room, sitting in one of the plastic chairs a few feet from Nikki.

"Do you have a fever?"

She nodded, the sun flashing off her cheek inlays. "Not bad, though. Just over a hundred."

"You take anything for it?"

"Of course."

"What else? Sore throat, muscle aches?"

"Sore throat and a nasty goddamn headache." She grimaced. "That's all."

"Bad cold," Cage said. "Maybe some kind of flu."

"Yeah, probably." She opened both eyes, raised her head a bit, and looked at him. "You hear anything about Stinger?"

Cage shook his head. He wished he could say something to make her forget about Stinger, but he knew it wasn't possible. He couldn't forget about it himself—he kept seeing those injected eyes and the blood on Nikki's finger hooks, kept smelling that awful breath. And he kept hearing the fear in Tiger's voice. At least Nikki hadn't heard Tiger's story.

He scooted the chair right up to her, reached out and raised her chin, then felt her neck with his fingers. "Lymph nodes a bit swollen, but not too bad."

"Of course they're swollen."

He tipped her head so the sunlight fell directly on her face. He looked into her eyes and felt relieved; they were bright and clear, with no signs of hemorrhage. "Open your mouth and try to work your tongue down." She did; he made a slight adjustment of the angle and got a fairly good look at her throat. A little red, but it looked okay. He nodded and let her go. "You look all right. You might feel lousy for a week or two, but you know what to do." He smiled. "And I'll stop by regularly to see how you're doing, give you a hand."

"Thanks, Mom."

Cage got up, went into the bathroom, and washed his hands thoroughly with cidal soap. She was going to be fine. He returned to the stove and checked on the soup; steam was rising from the pot.

"Soup's ready," he said. "Come on over to the table."

"I think I'll just eat here," Nikki said.

Cage poured soup into a bowl, got a spoon and napkin, took it over to her. He set the bowl on the windowsill, spoon and napkin beside it.

"Thanks," Nikki said.

"Anything else I can get you? Something to drink?"

"No, that's all right. I'll make tea later."

"You want me to bring you something from the clinic? I'm going there now."

"This is supposed to be your day off, Cage."

"Madelaine's shorthanded today."

"You're always shorthanded at the clinic. Seven days a week."

He shrugged. "I'm just going by to check in, see how things are. I won't stay long."

Nikki snorted. She spooned some soup into her mouth. "Thanks again. It's good."

"So. Anything from the clinic?"

"No, Cage. I'm not dying. I'll be fine."

"I'll see you later, then."

She nodded and waved her spoon at him. He turned and left.

The RadioLand Street Clinic was on the ground floor of an old brick apartment building, half a block from the Core and in the vague and blurred border between the Latin and Euro quarters of the Tenderloin. The clinic was flanked by a Nightgames arcade on one side, and a head juicer shop on the other. Above it were three floors of hooker suites, and above that six floors of overcrowded apartments. Cage's own apartment was on the fourth floor, with the hookers—he got free rent and irregular meals in exchange for providing the women with free medical care.

Madelaine and the crew were holding their own. She looked tired, but she smiled when she saw Cage come in through the clinic door, and shook her head.

"Get out of here," she told him. "This is your day off."

There were maybe fifteen people waiting, sitting on the chairs, benches, and old collapsing sofas scattered through the room. About half of them looked quite ill; all of them looked dead poor. Only five or six children, though. Often there were twice this many people waiting for medical attention, so this was a pretty quiet day.

Franzee, a short, chunky, and very pretty redhead, kept the clinic running, working as nurse, clerk, and office manager; she was kneeling in front of an old man, talking to him and making notes. Buck, the clinic errand boy, was moving a gurney down the left hallway. And Madelaine stood behind the main counter, one hand resting on a stack of folders, the other holding a ceramic cup with bright red letters on the side saying, "DOCTORS AREN'T GODS. NOT EVEN CLOSE." The cup would be full of god-awful herb tea that smelled nearly as bad as it tasted. Madelaine was tall and thin, closing in on fifty, her hair almost completely white. She'd been working street clinics for more than thirteen years, and it never seemed to get her down, which amazed Cage. The clinic work got *him* down all the time.

A young woman came out of one of the examination rooms and gazed hollowly at him. Her face was drawn, her eyes dark and sunken. A gauze bandage was taped to her inner arm, probably over an IV shunt. The young woman approached the counter, gaze shifting from Cage to Madelaine.

"Vashti, remember," Madelaine said, her voice soft but firm. "Try to drink a lot of fluids. Water, herb teas, soup, juices, whatever. But more important . . . we'll send Buck over later today with a case of IV fluids. Do a bag every hour, like I showed you, all right? And if you start to feel worse, come back in. Call us if you have to, okay? If you can't get here one of us will come see you."

Vashti nodded, then turned and walked slowly out of the clinic.

Madelaine sighed. "Third probable cholera case today," she told Cage. "We'll know for sure later this afternoon, but I wouldn't bet against it. We may be in for another epidemic this summer."

"Christ," Cage said. "Sometimes I think we're living in a goddamn Third World country."

Madelaine smiled. "Face it, Ry, most of the U.S. *is* a Third World country these days." She shook her head. "Come on, get out of here. Paul's coming by to help for a few hours, we'll be falling over each other."

"When's he coming in?"

"About an hour."

"Maybe I'll just stay until he gets here, help you get through these people." Franzee was leading the old man into the examination room from which Vashti had just emerged.

"Ry, we don't need you. It's a beautiful day, go somewhere and relax. Get the hell out of the Tenderloin, go have a good time."

Cage smiled and nodded, giving in. "Yeah, I guess I will. All right, I'll . . ." He stopped, seeing Madelaine's eyes widen and her face tense.

"What the hell . . . ?" Her voice trailed off.

Cage turned around. Just inside the clinic doors was a man who could barely stand. He was Hispanic, Cage guessed, but it was hard to know for sure with all the large, bright red patches blazing across his skin. The man groaned, staggered a few steps, his movements palsied and unsure, eyes blinking frantically.

Before Cage could move toward him, the man dropped to his knees, then lunged forward and vomited blood across the waiting-room floor. Someone screamed and people scattered, trying to get as far from the man as possible. Cage couldn't tell if any of them had been splashed. Then the man vomited again, pitched forward, and collapsed in his own blood.

Cage ran behind the counter, where Madelaine was already pulling out gloves, masks, and oversuits. They both suited up, pulled on gloves and masks and booties—they were going to have to walk through the blood just to get to the man.

"Franzee!" Madelaine shouted. "Get the KillSpray! Now!"

Cage and Madelaine hurried to the man and knelt beside him. They turned him over and checked his air passage; it seemed to be clear, and the man was breathing almost normally. They rolled him onto his side so he wouldn't choke to death if he vomited again, and Madelaine checked his eyes while Cage checked the pulse. The man's heartbeat was strong, but fast, maybe a little irregular; nothing too serious yet. He glanced up at the man's face as Madelaine was shining a penlight into the man's left eye. The eye was severely injected, the vessels gorged and broken. Like Stinger?

"He needs to be in a freaking hospital," Madelaine said. She was just talking. They both knew no hospital would take him now; most would have dragged him out onto the street even if he'd collapsed inside their emergency rooms. No hospital would take him in, and no ambulance would pick him up unless he had a wad of cash or a nice fat insurance chip on him, and Cage was pretty damn sure the man didn't have either; that meant "no" for any of the private clinics. Only the organ scavengers would be willing to take him.

"The iso rooms?" Cage asked.

"Both empty. Let's go."

They picked the man up between them, Cage under the man's arms, Madelaine under the knees. The man was out. Franzee had suited up and started spraying down the bloody floor with the KillSpray, filling the room with the smell of bleach and sour lemon. Buck was suited up right behind her, dragging in the cleaners. Half of the people who had been waiting were gone; those who remained huddled in one corner of the room, watching with fear or exhausted complacence.

Cage and Madelaine carried the man through the waiting room, along the right corridor, and into the first isolation room. They laid him out on the bed and pulled his shirt off. Cage slapped vitals strips across the man's chest and arm and connected them to the wall-mounted monitors, which would give them heart rate, O_2 and CO_2 levels, and a running blood pressure. He grabbed a b.p. cuff to get the man's pressure; Madelaine started on a temp and went to work with a stethoscope on the man's chest.

"One-oh-five over fifty-five," Cage said. "No problem there."

Madelaine frowned. "Pulse is okay, but his temp's a hundred and six. Shit." Then she squeezed the tip of his finger, and they watched. Cap fill time was almost five seconds. Frown deepening, she said, "Let's get him on oxygen. His blood volume's crap right now."

Cage reached around the bed rail and pulled out a non-rebreather mask, stretched the line, then worked the mask over the man's face and turned on the oxygen.

They stood back a moment and looked at the man. His skin was almost completely covered with red rashes, the kind that were bleeding into the skin, and was peeling off around the nails. Almost all the lymph nodes were noticeably swollen, even those by his elbows.

"I want to get some blood work done on him immediately," Madelaine said. "I know, we can't do shit here, but we have Patricia do what she can. CBC and diff, general tox screen, whatever. And I want to get a drip going, normal saline, and run some Chill and mycosatrine into it. And get some hemo going into him. Who knows how much blood he's lost." She looked at Cage. "What do you think?"

He nodded. "Sounds good. The mycosatrine can't hurt, but I wouldn't count on it helping any."

Madelaine nodded. "But it *could* be bacterial."

Cage shrugged. "It's *something* infectious. Something nasty." He shook his head. "Maybe viral."

"What? Some hemorrhagic fever?"

"Christ, I hope not. But I've heard about another similar case right here in the Tenderloin, a lot of the same symptoms. I don't know." He kept seeing Stinger's injected eyes, kept thinking about Tiger's story and his description of Stinger, the red patches all over his skin, vomiting blood. Stinger's symptoms seemed awfully close to those of the man lying on the bed in front of him, and they were only half a block from the Core. And Cage could not get Nikki out of his mind. A bad cold or flu, he told himself again.

"Okay, let's see if he's chipped." Madelaine pulled the scanner from the portable diagnostics, got on-line, then pressed the scanner to the man's shoulder and shifted it around. The scanner beeped, and Madelaine said, "I'll be damned." She turned to the monitor as the info came up on the screen. "Tito Moraleja," she read. "Mexican national, expired residency permit. Great. He's got AIDS. No known medical allergies."

Cage shook his head and waved at the rashed and fevered body in front of him. "It isn't the AIDS that's doing this to him."

"No," Madelaine said. "But it's not going to help him fight this, whatever the hell it is."

Cage stared down at the man, then looked up at Madelaine. "He's going to die."

Madelaine nodded without looking at him. "Okay, Ry. Let's draw some blood, get the drip going, the hemo. But don't use too much of anything that might be crucial to someone else." She sighed heavily. "Then let's get cleaned up and out of here. I've got other people to take care of."

An hour later, the clinic was almost back to normal. Paul Cardenas, the third regular clinic doctor, had arrived, and Patricia, the med tech, was in the tiny makeshift lab in back, running Tito Moraleja's blood work. The waiting room still smelled of bleach, but it was clean. Madelaine had tried to get Cage to leave, but he wanted to stick around and see if anything turned up with Tito's blood.

He was sitting in one of the waiting-room chairs, drinking coffee and listening to a middle-aged woman mumble incoherently at him, when the phone rang. Franzee answered it, talked to someone for a minute, looked up the corridors at the closed examination-room doors, then over at Cage.

"You want to talk to this guy?" she asked. "He's a cop. He wants to talk to someone who's in charge here."

"You talk to him, Franzee, you're always in charge. You run this place."

Franzee scowled. "Very funny, Dr. Cage." She held up the receiver. "Now, you want to talk to him, or you want me to go bust in on Dr. Samione or Dr. Cardenas?"

Cage got up from the chair; the woman didn't stop mumbling. "I'll talk to him." He put his coffee cup on the counter and took the phone from Franzee. "This is Dr. Cage."

"Dr. Cage, this is Lieutenant Carlucci, with the San Francisco Police Department."

"Yeah? Is there a problem?"

"About an hour ago you ran an ID scan on someone. Tito Moraleja."

"That's right."

"Was he a patient?"

Cage hesitated, wondering what this was about. He'd never been a big fan of cops. But he went ahead and answered. "Yes, a patient."

"I don't suppose there's any chance he's still there?" The man didn't sound hopeful.

Cage hesitated again, even considered lying. But he just didn't have the strength for it right now. "Yes, he's still here."

"He is?"

"That's what I said."

"Would you be able to keep him there for a while? Not by force . . . uh, you could tell him Caroline's looking for him, that her father . . ."

"He's not going anywhere, Lieutenant. He's critically ill, and we've got him in an isolation room."

"I'll be there as soon as I can."

"What's this all about?" Cage asked. But the lieutenant had already chopped the connection. Cage handed the receiver back to Franzee. "I guess he's coming here to see our mystery patient."

"Maybe he'll get the guy into a hospital," Franzee said.

Cage snorted. "Not fuckin' likely. Probably a jail cell."

A patient alarm went off behind the counter, a high-pitched squeal. Cage bent over the counter, but couldn't see the panel. "Who is it?" he shouted at Franzee, already knowing.

"The mystery man!"

"Goddamnit." And he was at it again, hurrying around the counter and grabbing the suit Franzee handed him, ignoring the booties, jamming hands into gloves as Franzee tied the mask behind his head. Then he was running to the isolation room and crashing through the door.

The mystery man, Tito Moraleja, was convulsing violently. Tonic clonic, rocking the bed. The IVs had been ripped out of the shunts, and his eyes were half open, eyeballs completely red now and rolled up under the lids. Cage moved to the man's side and grabbed his upper arms, holding him down so he wouldn't take a flier off the bed. Hold on and wait, he told himself.

Madelaine came through the door, hurried around to the other side of the bed. Franzee and Paul rushed in behind her.

"Let's get him intubated," Cage said. "We still got some paralytics?"

Franzee nodded. "Pavulon. I'll get it." She shook her head. "But we don't have anything else for a rapid sequence. Maybe a sedative." Then she was gone.

Cage grabbed Tito's left arm, got an IV back into the shunt, which had, amazingly, stayed in the guy's arm. Franzee came back, and Madelaine first gave Tito a sedative, then injected the Pavulon. Almost immediately he stopped moving, though Cage knew that the poor bastard's brain was probably still seizing like mad; now they just weren't seeing it.

They got Tito intubated, then tried Ativan to stop the seizure. But the guy's vitals were bad—the fever was spiking, blood pressure was dropping. Then *bam*, he went into cardiac arrest before they could do a damn thing.

They worked hard on him. CPR, several shocks with the paddles, epinephrine and atropine; they did everything but crack him open. Cage even considered doing that, for about five seconds; here, that was an absurdity. But nothing worked, and fifteen minutes later it was over. Tito Moraleja was dead.

Madelaine looked up from the body, glanced at Cage, then turned to Franzee. "Get a blood tray over here now. Let's get some more blood out of him while we can, see if we can't find out what the hell it was that killed him."

"What we really need," Cage said, "is an autopsy."

"I know," Madelaine replied. "You're not suggesting we do it ourselves, are you? Here?" She cocked her head at him. "You're not *that* whacked, are you?"

Cage shook his head. "No. I know we can't do it. I just wish we knew someone who could. Or at least somewhere we could store the body."

Franzee came in with the blood tray. Madelaine took the syringe, lined it up just under and to the left of Tito's sternum, then plunged it in and up at an angle and right into the left ventricle of the heart. She got eight vials of blood out before it started clotting.

After the blood came nose, throat, and rectal swabs, and finally a sample of the vitreous humor from the left eye for toxicology. Franzee and Paul left to label and store all the specimens.

Cage and Madelaine stood on either side of the bed, gazing down at the body.

"Any more ideas?" Madelaine asked.

Cage just shook his head. "Who do we know who can test for weird bugs and viruses?"

"Why the hell are you hung up on this thing?"

"Gut feeling. Some things I've seen recently. So, who do we know who could do it?"

"Unless Tito turns out to be someone rich and famous, no one. You still have connections to the CDC?"

"Yeah."

"Think you could get any of them to do something?"

"On the blood of a dead Mexican who had AIDS? Not a chance."

"That's what I thought."

Cage stepped back from the body. "But we keep the blood and the other stuff, even if we lose the body. I've got a bad feeling Tito isn't going to be the only one to die this way."

Franzee stuck her head into the room. "Dr. Cage? Lieutenant Carlucci is here to see you. And to see him." She pointed at Tito Moraleja's body.

Cage nodded. "Tell him I'll be right out."

Franzee let the door close. Cage looked at Madelaine. "Let's go tell the lieutenant the wonderful news."

11

THE RADIOLAND STREET Clinic smelled of bleach, sour lemon, unwashed bodies, and the faint, cutting aroma of incense. A weird mix, Carlucci thought, but strangely not unpleasant. He stood at the counter, sweating, waiting for the doctors, hip and elbow against the rough plastic. A dozen people sat around the stifling waiting room, and most of them looked pretty sick. None of them looked at him; they probably didn't like cops. He imagined they had good reason for the sentiment.

Carlucci was damn glad he didn't have to come to a place like this for his own health care. The Police Department had its own fully staffed, fully equipped clinic and hospital, which made being a cop a highly desirable job, despite the risks and the bad hours and the low pay. Most of these people, on the other hand, were probably happy to have *any* kind of place to come to.

A man and a woman emerged from a doorway along the right hall and proceeded to strip off gloves and suits, tossing them into a molded plastic container built into the wall. The woman was older, her hair almost completely white, and her thin face was striking—still quite handsome. The man was probably in his thirties, though his hair had some pretty good streaks of gray. Carlucci could buy the woman as a doctor, but this other guy, with his faded black denims and boots and color-slashed T-shirt and neck tattoo—even if the tattoo *was* a caduceus—couldn't be. A street medico, maybe. The two of them approached the counter, and the man put out his hand.

"Lieutenant? I'm Dr. Cage, I talked to you on the phone. This is Dr. Samione."

Dr. Cage. Carlucci shook hands with each of them. Then the man said, "Madelaine, I'll talk to him about all this."

The woman smiled and nodded. "He's all yours, Ry."

Dr. Cage turned to Carlucci and raised an eyebrow. "You want to see him?"

Carlucci nodded. "Sure."

"Follow me." The young man led the way back along the corridor, then stopped in front of a large glass observation window.

Carlucci looked inside the room. A figure lay on the bed, sheets and blankets thrown back and bunched across his legs, his upper body and face exposed. The man's eyes were closed, but his mouth was open, rigid in a silent scream; his dark skin was covered with enormous red patches and blistered welts, spotted with blood.

"Dead?"

"Dead," the young man replied.

"He had AIDS," Carlucci said.

"It wasn't AIDS that killed him."

Carlucci nodded, but didn't say anything. He had a feeling there was more to come, and that he wasn't going to like it.

"So, is that Tito Moraleja?"

Carlucci shrugged. "I suppose. I've never seen him before. He was a friend of my daughter's."

Dr. Cage breathed in deeply, then slowly and loudly let it back out. "So you weren't planning on throwing him into a cell."

"No."

"I think we need to talk about this."

"All right, Dr. Cage."

"Just call me Cage. And let's go on back to the staff lounge." Cage smiled to himself. He continued along the corridor, and Carlucci followed after taking one more long look at the body of Tito Moraleja.

The "staff lounge" was a small, cramped room with a table and chairs, cheap plywood cabinets, a countertop stove, three or four cots stacked on top of each other with pillows and blankets, and two large refrigerators. A couple of Vornado fans circulated the hot, stuffy air, providing at least the illusion of relief.

"Have a seat," Cage said. He went to the larger refrigerator, which was covered with black and white photos cut from newspapers, magazines, or books. All of the pictures showed people with the weirdest expressions on their faces, all of them with food or drink in their hands. "You want something to drink? A beer, Coke, or something?"

Carlucci sat in one of the hard, wooden chairs. "A beer would be great," he said.

Cage opened the refrigerator. Inside, the shelves were packed with labeled vials and jars and tubes and plastic bags, blood and fluids and drugs. On the bottom shelf were bottles of beer and soft drinks. Cage pulled out two bottles of Black Orbit, closed the refrigerator, and brought the beer to the table, handing a bottle to Carlucci. The cap was a twist-off; the beer was cold and very bitter.

"It's not that good," Cage said, grinning, "but it's cheap."

Carlucci sipped at the beer, watching the young man across the table from him. Dr. Cage. Cage. He wasn't sure why it surprised him. Appearances had never meant that much to him. Cage was probably a good doctor; his heart was in the right place if he worked here, and the people who came to this clinic were probably damn lucky to have him.

"Why did he die?" Carlucci finally asked.

Cage shrugged. "No idea. But I'd sure like to know. It worries me. I was hoping you knew him. I don't suppose you have any idea where he's been the past couple of weeks, do you?"

Carlucci shook his head. "I've been looking for him all that time."

"Why?"

"I told you. He was a friend of my daughter's. He was living in a death house in the DMZ. She went to see him one day, and he was gone. There were indications he'd been abducted."

Cage sat back in his chair, staring at him. "By whom?"

Carlucci hesitated, then said, "No one knows."

"So your daughter doesn't know where he's been, either."

"No."

Cage shook his head. "Shit," he said, so quietly Carlucci barely heard him. "I'd like to find out what killed him, and where the hell he picked it up."

"Can't you do tests?" Carlucci asked. "An autopsy."

Cage snorted. "Look at this place. We've got a half-assed lab in back where we can do simple blood work, and simple almost certainly isn't going to tell us what killed Tito. We could send the work out to a real lab, but we don't have the money for that, and even that might not do shit anyway—it's all a goddamn shot in the dark. We've got *no* facilities to do an autopsy, there's absolutely *no* way we could get anyone else to do it, and we've got no way to keep the body here. Unless we find some relative or friend willing to foot the bill in the next few hours, we'll have to haul him to one of the crematoriums." He took a long drink from his beer, shaking his head; as he swallowed, the tattooed snakes seemed to writhe around the staff. "We *will* keep the blood and other samples in case anyone else turns up dead like him, but that's all we can do for now."

Carlucci felt like he was being invited to ask the question, and so he did. "You think someone else will die like Tito?"

"Oh, sure, somewhere, someday. I've heard something about a similar case around here a while ago. But *I* probably won't see another one. It'll probably remain a mystery, like a lot of other deaths. People die all the time in this city from unknown causes, just like they die all the time from conditions or diseases we can prevent or easily treat. It's a disgrace, but that's the reality."

Carlucci nodded, more to himself than to Cage. There was something disingenuous about what Cage had just said, about the way he'd said it. And Carlucci thought about what he would tell Caroline. She would want to know more. She would want to know who had taken Tito, and why, and she would want to know what it was that had killed him.

He looked across the table at Cage. The man was a doctor working in a street clinic in the heart of the Tenderloin, close to the streets. No, a *part* of the streets, out on the edges. And Carlucci was certain Cage was holding something back from him. He wondered if this was a kind of game they were playing, sending out feelers, testing for responses. He hesitated, reluctant to take the next step, but wondered what the hell he had to lose.

"You ever hear of Cancer Cell?" he finally asked.

Cage didn't move, but Carlucci saw something in the man's eyes, a brief widening of the pupils, a slight tensing of muscles, and he felt a shiver of satisfaction, knowing he'd been right.

Cage's mouth worked into just a touch of a smile. "Now why the *hell* do you ask me that?"

"You have heard of them."

"Let's say I have. Why are you asking?"

Carlucci hesitated again, then almost laughed at himself, at the absurdity. "Caroline, my daughter, said there was someone who saw Tito's abduction, and this guy thought Cancer Cell had something to do with it. That's all I know. I've heard of Cancer Cell, but I don't really know anything about them."

This time it was Cage who seemed to be evaluating Carlucci, trying to make a judgment. He pushed back from the table, stood, and grabbed his bottle of Black Orbit, then walked over to the counter and leaned against it, looking at him. Carlucci returned the gaze, waiting for the man to speak. Suddenly his stomach churned, and he knew Cage was going to say something that would change how he saw Tito's death, something that would change the coming weeks of his life. He wanted to stand up right now and walk out of the room and leave all this behind him. But he stayed.

Cage brought the bottle to his mouth, tipped it back, and drained the rest of the beer. He set the bottle on the counter and wiped his mouth with the back of his hand.

"I saw a guy two and half weeks ago," he said. "He looked and smelled sick. I haven't seen him since, but I just talked to someone who said this guy was in real bad shape, probably dying. Symptoms sounded a lot like Tito here." He paused, almost smiling, though Carlucci was sure it wasn't from amusement. "Thing is this," Cage continued. "This guy who's dying, who's probably dead by now, this guy worked for Cancer Cell."

Neither of them spoke for a while. The connection was obvious, but what did it really mean? Anything? Even if Tito and this other guy died from the same thing, did Carlucci have any business pursuing it? Tito was dead, and Carlucci's search for him was over. There was no evidence of a crime other than the original abduction, and even that was pretty shaky. Besides, it was just a dead Mexican who'd been living in a death house and would have died of AIDS pretty soon anyway, right? Who gave a shit?

Carlucci gave a shit, that was who, and so did Caroline. And then there was Naomi Katsuda, who definitely *had* been murdered and had the initials "CC" carved into her forehead, who had been a potential source of information about Cancer Cell and had told him to come back to her when people started dying.

It was all too much to walk away from. Carlucci felt a great weariness wash over him, settling in his bones. Whatever this all was, it was going to be a long, long haul, and none of it was going to be easy.

It was Cage, though, who broke the silence.

"I watch for disease," he said. "We've got so much of it these days. I look for patterns and strange occurrences and the signs of something deadly about to break out into the population." He shrugged. "I'm a doctor. It's not such a great time being a doctor. Or maybe the best time of all, there's so much work to do, so many people sick and dying with so many things, and getting worse all the time. I've given up much hope for reasonable large-scale prevention in this city, this country—no one in power is willing to spend the money. The wealthy, of course, are okay, but they've always been good at taking care of themselves. But for the rest of us, prevention's becoming a lost cause, with water and air quality steadily deteriorating, increasing malnutrition, decreasing health care resources . . . shit, I could go on and on. Treatment's not a hell of a lot better anymore, with the same caveat for the rich. Though even if you're rich and you get Chingala Fever or X-TB or Lassa 3 or half a dozen others, you're just as dead as the poor. But the rich have a lot less exposure, and they're generally healthier to begin with, and . . . and *blah blah blah*." Cage laughed. "Yeah, I know, I'm getting dangerously close to making a speech here. The point is, I watch and worry about shit like this, about two people dying from the same awful disease I've never seen before, especially when there's a connection to an outfit that does medical experimentation. And I worry that two is going to turn into a much bigger number and it'll get out of control and there will be dead people everywhere."

You can come back to me when people are dying, Naomi Katsuda had said.

"It's happened before in other countries," Cage went on, "and it's come close to happening here a few times. It is going to happen in this country someday, and it will probably come out of an area like this, like the Tenderloin, or the DMZ, or the Mission, where there are so many poor people crammed together with lousy health and lousy sanitation. And so I worry when something like this happens. It'll probably be nothing this time, but . . ." He left it there with a shrug.

"All right," Carlucci said. "Then tell me about Cancer Cell. Who the hell they are and why they worry you."

Cage shook his head. "*They* don't worry me, not exactly. It's the connection to them that worries me, and that's not quite the same thing." He looked at the empty Black Orbit bottle, then at Carlucci. "You want another?"

Carlucci thought about it for a minute. It was stifling in here, and the fans didn't seem to be helping much anymore, and his day hadn't gone well at all. He could do with *several* beers. "Sure," he said, unbuttoning the top two buttons of his shirt and pulling the knot of his tie halfway down his chest.

Cage walked over to the refrigerator for two more bottles. Carlucci had already revised his opinion of Cage a couple of times since he'd first seen him, and wondered if he would have to revise it again. Probably. Cage handed him a bottle, but didn't sit down again. He returned to his previous spot, leaning against the counter.

"First," Cage began, "I've got to say I don't know that I'd call Cancer Cell good or bad. I don't know enough about them, and I don't think even if I did that I'd make that kind of judgment. They're probably some of both, like most of us. I try not to make too many judgments about anyone." Then Cage laughed. "Well, I *try*." He drank deeply from the bottle, then stared at the label as if he was trying to decipher something. Finally he looked back at Carlucci.

"We get a lot of high-grade black-market pharmaceuticals from Cancer Cell. For the clinic. Now, no one we deal with ever actually says the words 'Cancer Cell,' but we know that's where it's all coming from. It *has* to be. Typical street stuff is just shit, and getting lab quality out of the domestic companies is just about impossible—the profits on it are so good they've got the best inventory control around. You *can* get the same stuff black-marketed down from New Hong Kong itself, but that's a lot more expensive, more than we can handle."

Carlucci knew. A friend of his, Louis Tanner, an ex-cop, used to barter black-market pharmaceuticals from New Hong Kong a few years ago. Some of it he sold, and some of it he gave away to clinics like this one.

"Most of what I know about Cancer Cell is distillation of rumors," Cage continued. "Working the essence of probable truth out of a mass of stories, guesses, wild speculation, street gossip, and wish fulfillment. What I do know is this: They do cutting-edge medical research. That's their main purpose. Everything else is in aid of that. And they do their research without any restrictions imposed by laws or regulations."

"Or ethics," Carlucci put in.

Cage shrugged. "I wouldn't know."

"Like New Hong Kong."

Cage shrugged again. "I don't even know what their end purpose is. New Hong Kong's goal is profit, but I don't think that's true for Cancer Cell. I do know that if you have an incurable disease, or an irreversible, debilitating condition, you can volunteer for experimental treatments from them. It's a risk some people are more than willing to take."

"You make it sound like they have signs up somewhere. VOLUNTEERS NEEDED. EXPERIMENTAL SUBJECTS. INCURABLE DISEASE? CALL THIS NUMBER TO APPLY."

Cage laughed. "No, that's New Hong Kong's style, not Cancer Cell's. Cancer Cell is discreet. But you work street medicine long enough, you hear things, and the picture comes together. Besides, just like they're a source for us, we're a source for them."

"A source of experimental subjects, you mean."

"Something like that."

"Have you ever sent anyone to them?"

Cage sighed. "It's not that simple. I have mentioned them to some of my patients over the years. Not by name, more the idea. Let the patient know the option was available."

"Any of them exercise that option?"

"I don't know. Probably. If any did, I never heard from them."

Of course not, Carlucci thought, because they're dead. He drank from his beer, which was no longer very cold. In the peak of summer, this room must be a goddamn hotbox. He watched Cage, the hip young clinic doctor, medic of the streets. He felt certain Cage wasn't telling him everything he knew about Cancer Cell. But that was okay. He sure as hell wasn't going to tell Cage everything he knew about Naomi Katsuda and her New Hong Kong connections. But he was probably going to have to tell Cage *something*. Cage was the only solid potential source of information about Cancer Cell he had, and he was going to need Cage's help.

"So all this worries me," Cage said. "I wonder what Cancer Cell is doing. Some kind of viral or bacterial research that's gone out of control? Or something worse, like deliberately infecting people? No idea why they would do that, but then I don't know them very well, do I? Most of all I worry about how contagious this crap is." Cage rubbed at his nose, then pinched the bridge, as if he were trying to massage away a growing headache. "Probably it all ends right here," he finished up. "With Tito. Just a fluke, a couple of dead people, nothing further. Unsolved mystery." He smiled.

"Maybe not," Carlucci said with a heavy sigh.

"What do you mean by that?" Cage asked, suddenly wary.

Carlucci was still trying to decide how much to tell Cage. He'd spent his career developing a deep reluctance to divulge more information than was absolutely necessary, except with other cops, and even then he had to be careful. But you couldn't always hold back everything; keeping other people too much in the dark could sometimes have all kinds of unintended consequences, a lot of them bad.

"Another case I have," he finally replied. "A woman was killed a few days ago. She had the initials 'CC' carved into her head."

"Could stand for a lot of things," Cage said. "Christian Coalition. I hear they're back in business, ranting and raving and preaching and putting on mass self-flagellations. Or Canadian Club. Maybe whoever killed her had way too much to drink. Blamed the booze."

This was a game Carlucci didn't feel like playing. Not in this stifling room with two dead people to think about, one of them definitely murdered.

"I had talked with her about two weeks before she was killed," he said, leaning forward in his chair. "I was trying to find out something about Tito, and her name was given to me as a possible source of information about

Cancer Cell." He paused, staring at Cage, wanting to make damn sure the man was listening to him, paying close attention. "She wouldn't tell me anything. She told me Tito's abduction wasn't even close to being important enough for her to take any risks." One more pause, deliberately for effect. "She told me to come back and talk to her when people started dying."

Cage was silent for a few moments. Then, quietly, he said, "Shit."

Carlucci nodded. "Yeah, shit is right. I want your help, Cage."

"How?"

"I don't know yet. Not exactly. I'd like to talk to someone who's a part of Cancer Cell. Could you arrange that?"

Cage's mouth twisted into a kind of frown. "It *might* be possible. It would take time, and it would be risky. They don't like anyone weaseling around in their business. And a cop? Jesus. But maybe I can find out something."

"I'll arrange for Tito Moraleja to be taken to one of the police morgues, maybe even get an autopsy done. I'll call it a connection to this other case I have."

"You're willing to do that?"

"Sure. Can you make arrangements for Tito's body to get to the Tenderloin perimeter? If I give you the name of a business, an address?"

"Of course. Even if I have to rent a cart and haul him there myself. Then you can get him out of the Tenderloin?"

"Yes." Carlucci took one of his cards and wrote an address on the back. It was an import/export shop in one of the perimeter buildings, with ways both in and out of the Tenderloin. The police department had an arrangement with the owner, Nanos Spyrodakis. For a price, they could move almost anything or anyone into or out of the Tenderloin. A dead body? Carlucci sighed to himself. Getting Tito Moraleja's body out was going to be expensive.

He handed the card to Cage. "Can you have him there in two hours?"

"Yeah, no problem," Cage said, looking at the address. He turned the card over. "I guess I'll need this card if I want to get in touch with you."

"Yes. And be discreet over the phone."

"Sure thing, Lieutenant." He tucked the card into the back pocket of his jeans. "I'll let you know if I find out something."

Carlucci got up from the chair, finished off the warm Black Orbit. "Thanks for the beer." He set the empty bottle on the table.

The two men shook hands and Carlucci turned to go.

"Lieutenant?"

"Yeah?"

Cage was smiling, but it was a fearful smile. "Whoever does the autopsy on Tito? Tell them to be *damn* careful."

12

THE PLAYGROUND WAS enclosed by metal-sheet fencing topped by razor wire and rusted saw blades, the fencing broken only by two narrow gates. The gates were manned by street soldiers from the Polk Corridor in full battle colors: dark red ankle scarves wrapped tightly around black leather boots; khakis spattered with what appeared to be bloodstains; shining silver serpent belts loaded with hand ammo; arms wired with coils of jolt-tubing; shielded glasses and dark green bush hats.

Caroline slowed as she approached the east gate with Lily and Mink, the mother and daughter who were now living in Tito's old room in the death house, waiting for Mink to die. They had walked the several blocks from the DMZ, Caroline acting as escort and guide. In fact, she felt more like a bodyguard, watching out for Lily and Mink because they didn't have much street smarts yet, and they gave off an aura of being ripe for the street scavs.

A large sign in block letters hung beside the east gate: NO CHILDREN ALLOWED WITHOUT A SUPERVISING ADULT. Caroline, Lily, and Mink stepped one at a time through the two detectors, then were patted down by a woman street soldier who smiled and chattered aimlessly about the weather, Caroline's shirt, Mink's hair, and the stench of the garbage. Then the three of them stepped through the main entrance and into the playground.

When Caroline had been a child, her parents had brought her here to this playground several times over the years, when they'd been in the neighborhood visiting friends. Back then, the place had been overgrown with lush plants surrounding the swings and slides and jungle bars, stands of bamboo had lined the perimeter, and an island of trees, shrubs, blooming flowers, and thick grasses had stood in the middle of it all, the island surrounded by a shallow lake of water that the children waded through, splashed and played in. You could buy ice cream bars or Sno-Kones, hot dogs and soda pop and misty ices. You could have a picnic on the island.

Several years earlier, however, the playground had been the site of a major skirmish in the Summer Polk Riots. The place had been strafed with defoliants and cratered by mortars, the few remaining plants burned by kerosene fires. The playground had been rebuilt, the equipment repaired or replaced, a few benches installed, the metal-sheet fencing erected around the entire grounds, and the Polk Corridor street soldiers had taken it over. The playground existed, but it wasn't the same.

And yet, the dry, bleached-out prospect bothered the children a lot less than it did Caroline. The playground was full of running, shouting, jumping, swinging, and laughing children who were having a great time. Mink stayed close to her mom until they reached an empty bench facing the denuded island that had once been nearly overgrown. Now the island was covered in sand, with several swing sets, a couple of twisting slides, and a large, multilevel maze of wire-mesh cages; it was still surrounded by a shallow, water-filled moat. Lily and Caroline sat on the bench. Mink stood beside them for a minute or two, watching the kids on the island, and those walking barefoot through the moat; then she ventured away from the bench and walked toward the small footbridge that spanned the water. She crossed the bridge, and tentatively approached the swing sets.

"She won't play for too long," Lily said. "She gets tired pretty fast."

"What does she have?" Caroline asked. She'd avoided the topic before this because Mink had always been present.

"Leukemia."

Caroline was surprised. She'd expected something more exotic, one of the newly discovered or newly resurgent diseases, little understood and untreatable. She'd thought leukemia in children was fairly simple to treat these days, with a high rate of success. She said as much to Lily.

Lily shrugged. "She didn't respond well to chemotherapy. Two courses of treatment, and it came right back both times. Another round was out of the question, because the chemo itself was almost killing her. The doctor said her only real chance was a bone marrow transplant, or replacement with artificial marrow." She shook her head, traces of a sad smile tucking up the corners of her mouth. "Maybe if my own marrow was compatible . . . but it isn't. People don't donate marrow, they sell it. The artificial marrow's even more expensive. Not to mention the operation, the follow-ups, the drugs, all that stuff. No money, no insurance . . ." She turned to look at Caroline. "No transplant, no replacement. Mink's going to die."

Caroline didn't know what to say. She felt even more depressed. "Is there a father?" she asked.

Lily snorted. "Sure there's a father. *Had* to be, right? One way or another. But who knows where the hell he is, if he's even alive." She sighed heavily. "I haven't seen him or heard from him in six years."

Caroline looked back across the water at the island. One of the swings became available and Mink climbed onto the wide fabric strap, grabbing the thick chains. From a standstill, she pumped her legs and pulled back and forth on the chains, and quickly got herself going. The arcs got bigger and bigger, and she let go with one hand, waved at Lily and Caroline with a big smile. The women waved back.

"How long does she have?" Caroline asked.

"Two months. Maybe three." Lily shook her head again. "No one really knows."

It was all so unfair. But then there was nothing new about that, and nothing Caroline could do to change it. She put her hand over Lily's and squeezed. Lily squeezed back, and the two women remained there on the bench, holding hands, and watching Mink play.

Caroline met her father in the lobby of one of the city's holding morgues. He looked more tired than usual, drawn and distracted, but he smiled and hugged her when she walked in. The lobby was cooler and darker than outside, but she suspected it was going to get even colder.

"You sure you want to look at him?" her father said.

"You said you wanted to make sure it was Tito."

"Well, he was chipped. And I could show you pictures. He doesn't look good. He looks pretty bad."

She smiled to herself. He wasn't completely sure how to act around her in this situation; half father, half cop. A woman in uniform sat behind a desk in the back corner, watching them with a bored and sleepy expression; otherwise the room was empty of people and furniture. Even the walls were completely blank, a depressing industrial gray.

"I want to see him," Caroline finally said. It was one of those things that was partially true, and partially untrue.

Her father nodded to the woman at the desk, who fiddled with the console in front of her. The door beside her clicked, and she said, "Go ahead, Lieutenant."

He led the way through the door, along a narrow corridor, down a flight of steps, along another short corridor, then finally through a heavy, solid metal door and into a large room brightly lit by fluorescents. Two gurneys stood near the center of the room, one empty, the other with a covered body. There was an old metal utility sink attached to one wall, and two walls were racked with refrigerated lockers. Caroline wondered how many bodies were being stored here right now.

Her father went to the head of the occupied gurney and waited for her. He put on a pair of surgical gloves he'd taken from his jacket pocket, then took hold of the cloth covering by one corner, and looked at her. She nodded, and he carefully folded back the cloth, exposing the head.

She didn't look down at first. She kept her gaze on her father, the exposed face in the lower edges of her vision. A faint, unfamiliar smell rose, a chemical smell. Some kind of preservative, she imagined. Or would that have been used yet? Maybe something else. Maybe she was imagining the smell.

She tried to remember whether she had ever seen a dead person before, up close like this. There was her grandmother's funeral when she was quite young, seven or eight, but she could not remember if there had been an open casket; if there had been, would she have been allowed to see her dead grandmother? There were simply no images from that funeral in her mind.

She'd been older, fifteen, when her grandfather had died, but the casket had been closed, she remembered that distinctly; her grandfather had lost so much weight in the course of his illness that, according to her father, he was almost unrecognizable. He and his sister had decided that no one should remember their father that way.

Caroline finally looked down. It was Tito. Yes, it was Tito, but he almost didn't look real. His lips were purple, his skin was strangely pale, like brown ash, covered with raw, red, purplish patches, and his open eyes looked like glass marbles. She felt a chill emanating from him, but she didn't know if that was real or imagined.

"Is it Tito?"

She looked up at her father, looked back at Tito, and nodded. So many times in the past few months he had been so sick that she'd thought he would be better off if he died soon, ended his suffering, but looking down at him now, now that he *was* dead, she was no longer so sure. She only knew that she was already beginning to miss him, and the pain of that was growing—slowly, but steadily.

Her father gently pulled the cover back over Tito's face, adjusted the cloth so it hung smoothly across the skin.

"I expected it to be colder in here," she said. Even as she spoke, it seemed to her a strange thing to say, but it just came out. "So the bodies won't decompose."

"He won't be out here long," her father replied. "He'll go back into one of the lockers as soon as we leave."

She nodded and reached out, laid her hand over Tito's chest. The cold seeped through the cloth and into her skin, even her bones, but she left her hand there, certain that it was important for her to feel that cold, to know what it was like. As though some crucial understanding would come from it. *She* would be that cold one day, and that day might not be that far in the future.

"What do I do to make funeral arrangements?" she asked.

"Nothing, for now."

She looked up at him. "What do you mean?"

"It could be a while."

"What are you talking about?"

"We need to have an autopsy done." He seemed ill at ease, which was so unlike him. "But it's a low priority, so it could be a while."

"Why an autopsy? He had AIDS."

Her father shook his head. "Yes, but that's not why he died." He was reluctant to go on. "Something else killed him."

"What?"

"No idea. That's why the autopsy."

"What the hell is going on here?"

Her father looked increasingly uncomfortable. "I really don't know,

Caroline. It's complicated, especially because I really don't know much right now. But there might be a connection to another case I have right now."

"What kind of connection?"

This time her father hesitated a long time. But if he knew her at all, he would realize that she would not let this go. He would realize he had to tell her.

"Cancer Cell," he finally said.

"So Mouse was right."

"Maybe. And maybe about the Core, too. Tito died in a street clinic in the Tenderloin, half a block from the Core."

"What happened, Papa?"

Apparently he *did* know her well enough, because he eventually gave her the whole story. He started with putting out the department tracers, and getting a hit after the street clinic checked Tito's identity chip. He told her about going out to the RadioLand Street Clinic and finding that Tito had already died. And he told her about meeting Cage, and Cage's concern about an infectious disease with some kind of connection to Cancer Cell.

"And there's a connection between that and another case you have?"

Her father nodded. "A murder case," he said. "Cancer Cell has come up in that case as well. But it could be a coincidence."

"You don't think so, though."

He sighed. "I really don't know, Caroline. I've got a lot of nothing on that case right now, so I'm following up every possibility. And in the meantime, Cage wants me to have Tito autopsied, see if we can't get some idea of what killed him. Maybe it won't be anything."

Caroline pulled her frigid hand back from the cloth over Tito, and stared at it.

"It's all right," her father said. "The cloth is impermeable."

But her hand was so cold, and she continued to stare at it, searching for some sign that no contagion had rubbed off onto it.

"Are you okay?" her father asked her.

She hurried over to the sink, turned on the tap with her elbows, and scrubbed her hands with large quantities of dispenser soap, the water as hot as she could stand it. Her father removed the surgical gloves and disposed of them in the wall bin beside the sink. Caroline continued scrubbing until her hands were red and painfully raw. She dried them with paper towels, tossed the towels into the bin, then turned to her father.

"I want to go now," she said.

13

CAGE WAS DREAMING of a giant anteater. The anteater, which appeared to be six or seven feet high at the shoulder and close to fifteen feet long, wandered slowly along the deserted streets of San Francisco, snuffling through tall, tropical ferns and dripping wet broad-leafed plants that grew everywhere.

Cage was standing alone at the second-floor window of an abandoned building, watching the anteater amble through the city. A phone began ringing somewhere. The anteater stopped, tilted its head, and looked at Cage. The phone kept ringing, the dream shook apart and darkened, and Cage shakily came awake.

The phone continued to ring, quietly chirping beside him. He hated that sound. The room was dark, almost quiet except for the phone. He glanced at the pulsing blue clock beside the bed: 4:43. He hadn't been asleep much more than an hour.

He finally reached for the phone, rolled onto his back, and put the receiver to his head. It rang once more, right in his ear. Cage pressed the answer button.

"Hello."

"Cage? Sorry to wake you." It was Paul's voice, which wasn't really a voice he wanted to hear right now. Actually, he didn't want to hear anyone's voice. "I've got a problem here."

Here had to be the clinic, which of course was only three floors below him. Which was not always a good thing, being that close.

"You need me to come down there and help out?" He could hardly imagine getting out of bed right now, let alone treating patients. He was exhausted after working two double shifts at the clinic in the past three days while squeezing in a full day of image enhancements at the Pacific Heights Aesthetic Modeling Center.

"Yes," Paul answered. "But not what you think. You know a guy named Tiger?"

That helped get Cage alert and awake. He pushed himself up into a sitting position.

"Yeah, I know Tiger. Is he there?"

"He's here, all right. And he's hysterical, demanding to see you, demanding to be given some pills or a shot, says he's sick with some deadly disease. He's scared, Cage. Don't know what he's scared of, and he doesn't seem to actually be sick, but he said you would know."

Christ. He knew, all right. "Okay, I'll be right down. Try to calm him down. Tell him I said he's fine, and I'll be there in ten minutes."

"Calm him down," Paul said. "Sure thing. He wants a shot, I'll give him one. Sedate his ass."

"Just hang on, Paul, and I'll be right down."

"All right. But make it quick." Paul broke the connection.

Cage nodded to himself. Yeah, make it quick. He swung his legs out from under the sheet and over the side of the bed, and sat there for a few moments, trying to will himself awake. But his body and mind kept trying to shut down. If he lay back right now, he'd go out, he knew it.

He took a brief, cold shower and got dressed. He thought about making a quick cup of coffee, but decided he'd better get downstairs right away and see Tiger. Coffee probably wouldn't do him much good anyway; he was beyond the help of caffeine.

Outside it was still fairly dark, but already warm. The day was going to be hot, and he wondered if they were heading into their first big heat wave of the year. The first one was always a killer; people would be dropping in the streets.

The clinic entrance was just ten feet down from the apartment lobby. There were only three people in the waiting room—two older men sitting together, and a young pregnant woman. Mike Wilkerson looked up as Cage approached the desk and nodded toward the left hallway. "Cardenas is with someone in Exam Two," he said. "Your man Tiger is in Four."

"We got any fresh coffee?" Cage asked.

Mike nodded. "Just made a pot five minutes ago. Want me to get you some?"

Cage shook his head. "I'll get it myself. Exam Four, you said?"

"That's it."

He started back toward the staff room, but pulled up when someone began banging on one of the exam room doors and yelling. From the inside. He turned back to Mike.

"Is that my guy?"

Mike nodded, laughing. "Paul locked him in. He kept jumping out into the hall and shouting for help."

"Christ. I guess the coffee'll wait." He reversed direction, came around the counter, then headed up the left hallway and down toward Exam Four. Tiger was still pounding on the door when he reached it.

"Hey!" Cage shouted. "Jam it in there, will you?"

Silence for a moment. Then, "Dr. Cage?"

"Yeah." He took the chart and clipboard off the wall hook, glanced at it. Paul had started the chart, but hadn't written anything except: *Tiger. Diagnosis: MADMAN!* Cage unlocked the door and opened it. Tiger stepped back and let Cage inside.

Tiger immediately began pacing and talking at the same time. "Oh, man, you gotta help me. He's dead . . . goddamn, he's dead . . . and you gotta. . . ." Tiger was flushed and sweating, rubbing at his head with one hand while wiping the other hand up and down on his thigh. "I think I'm sick . . . I *must* be sick . . . he's fucking *dead*!"

"Tiger!" Cage barked it at him.

Tiger stopped pacing and blinked stupidly at Cage. "What?"

"Sit down, for Christ's sake. Just calm down a minute, and sit."

Tiger didn't move for a few moments, still staring at Cage as if he didn't know where the hell he was. Then he looked around and sat in the chair by the tiny window that opened out into the alley. Cage remained standing.

"Okay," Cage said. "Who's dead? Stinger?"

"Yeah, fucking Stinger. And he died a mess. He was vomiting blood everywhere and screaming and his skin was peeling off, and then he just died."

"You saw this?"

Tiger shook his head. "No, I told you. They were keeping him away from everyone, in some kind of isolation room, in some building somewhere, I don't know. But a woman I know, one of the people I was helping carry him that time, she's got better connections than I do. She knows someone who was there, who saw him die. She says everyone's really worried. She said Stinger's not the first one to die like that."

Great, Cage thought, that's fucking great. Just what he wanted to hear.

Tiger stood up, holding out his hands. "I got his blood all over me!" he wailed. "You gotta do something, I'm getting sick, and you have to give me a shot or some pills or something so I don't die like that. You *told* me to come here. You gotta *do* something you fucking boneman!"

"Okay, Tiger, okay. Sit back down, and I'll check you out. I'll give you a full workup, okay?"

Tiger sat down again and rubbed both hands through his short hair, face twisting into a grimace. He muttered to himself, eyes blinking spasmodically. Cage put on a pair of disposable gloves, and Tiger lost it again.

"I *am* sick!" he cried out, jumping to his feet and pointing at the gloves. "See? You don't even want to touch me!"

"Jesus, Tiger, calm down, will you? I put gloves on for everyone, for every exam I do. Standard precautions. It doesn't mean anything." Cage felt like he was trying to talk a potential suicide off a rooftop, except he didn't know what Tiger would do if he completely lost control. He didn't want to find out.

He spent the next fifteen minutes running Tiger through a general physical, talking to him all the while, trying to keep him settled. He talked about anything that came to his mind, as long as there was no connection to Stinger—random babble about the clinic, the possibility of a heat wave, the message streamers he'd seen the night before about some religious wack who was trying to recruit people for a pilgrimage to the North Pole. Tiger seemed to gradually loosen up a little. The tension eased out of his neck muscles, the flush left his skin, the sweating slowed, and the panicky jumping around of his gaze dwindled away.

Tiger seemed healthy enough. His heart rate was elevated, but Cage would have been surprised if it wasn't. Blood pressure, too, was elevated the first time he took it, but pretty much normal when he took it a second time as he was about to finish up. Temp was just over ninety-nine, but that wasn't much of a fever. Nothing else of much significance showed itself. All in all, Tiger seemed to be healthier than most of the people Cage saw at the clinic, and Cage told him as much.

"You sure?" Tiger asked. "I haven't been feeling any too good."

"Like what?"

"Feverish, for one thing. All hot, like I'm burning up."

"You don't have a fever, Tiger."

"I've been breaking out in rashes."

Cage's heart jumped a little at that, but he hadn't seen any during the exam. "I didn't find any signs of rash anywhere," he said to Tiger.

"They're gone now. But I've also been getting headaches, and I'm not sleeping so good, and sometimes I've been sweating a lot, and sometimes I feel like I can't catch my breath."

"Classic symptoms of anxiety attacks," Cage told him.

"What do you mean?"

"Stinger's dead, and you had that blood splashed on you, and you're so worried about getting the same thing that you're getting anxiety attacks about it."

"You mean I'm making myself sick?"

"Probably."

"*Probably.* But maybe not."

Cage sighed. "That's right, maybe not. I can't be sure. But I think you're fine."

"Can't you give me something to keep me from getting what Stinger had?"

Cage shook his head. "It's not that simple, Tiger. I don't know what Stinger had. Even if I did, I probably couldn't do anything. What he had might not even have been contagious." He was trying to convince himself as much as he was Tiger; he was still really worried about Nikki, and this sure as hell wasn't helping. The last time he'd talked to her she was still sick, maybe even feeling worse.

Tiger rolled his head from side to side, popping his neck. "Rashida's friends sure are worried that it's contagious. It's making them crazy."

Okay, Cage thought. Here was his chance to try to push things with Tiger. "Who's Rashida?" he asked.

Tiger continued rolling his head around, and the neck bones kept making loud popping sounds; it made Cage a little queasy. "She's a friend," Tiger said. "I told you. But she's got better connections to the big stoners."

"Tiger. Who do you work for?"

"I work for Stinger, and Rashida. And Birgitta." Tiger grinned. "You remember, the woman who wouldn't help us load up? That was Birgitta. She's
a scary one, isn't she? Imagine what she'd do to a guy in bed."

"But who are they?" Cage pressed him. "Is there a name?"

Tiger shrugged. "I don't know, and I don't really give a shit. I just work
for them. I do the work and they pay me. That's all that matters."

"Do you ever work in the Core?"

Tiger stopped rolling his neck and stared at Cage. "Are you out of your
suffocating mind? We get close to the Core, sometimes, sure, but hell, look
at where *this* place is. No, I don't work in that goddamn place. Shit, I'm not
a genius, but I'm not a fucking moron, either. The Core." He shook his head
and grinned at Cage.

Cage decided not to push it any farther. Tiger didn't know. It was quite
possible he'd never even heard of Cancer Cell.

"So you really think I'm okay?" Tiger asked.

Cage nodded.

"And I can keep on working?"

"Sure. It wouldn't hurt to take a few days off, rest up a little. Tell them
you *are* sick, even though you aren't."

"Shit, I don't know about that. I need the work. I need the money. And
I take too much time off, they might give the job to someone else."

"Okay. Whatever you want. But before you go, you want to give me
your number and address? So I can check in on you."

Tiger nodded. "Sure." He breathed in deeply once, then slowly let it out.
"Maybe you're right, about the anxiety. I'm feeling a lot better now."

I'm glad *you* are, Cage thought.

An hour later he stood outside Nikki's door, hesitating. It was still way too
early, only seven in the morning, and the chances of Nikki being awake were
slim, but after his encounter with Tiger, Cage needed to see her. He needed
reassurance. He'd been so busy he hadn't seen her in three days, just talked
briefly with her a few times. He was afraid of what he would find.

He knocked softly. Nothing at first, and he was about to knock again
when he thought he heard movement from inside. Then Nikki's muffled
voice came through the door.

"Who's there?"

"It's me, Nikki."

"Who's 'me'?" she asked as she opened the door. She looked tired, but
she was smiling. She was wearing green sweatpants and a gray T-shirt, and
she was barefoot. "Come on in. I was just going to make coffee. Want
some?"

"I'd kill for some," Cage said. He followed her into the apartment.

The windows were open, letting in the warm, fresh early-morning air—

as fresh as the city ever got, anyway. Nikki went to the stove, where water was heating, and added extra coffee to the filter cone set on her glass pot.

"How are you feeling?" he asked.

She turned to face him, smile broadening. "Wiped. But great. By great I mean the fever's broken, the headache's gone, no more sore throat, no more crunching bone aches. I'm bloody exhausted, but just great. On the mend."

Cage felt tremendous relief. He stepped toward her, put his hands on her shoulders, rose up on his toes, and kissed her forehead. "Believe me, I'm glad to hear it. I was starting to worry."

"Some bloody awful flu," Nikki said. "The worst I've ever had, I think. But . . . it . . . is . . . over."

The water began to boil, and she took the kettle off the burner and poured the steaming water into the cone. Cage crossed the room to one of the windows and looked outside. The air coming in was continuing to warm, and he realized that it was going to be a burner by midafternoon. Activity on the street below was still fairly sedate, though it was starting to pick up a bit. It would probably remain a slow day until things began to cool down as the sun dropped. No one would be quite used to the heat yet.

Nikki handed him a cup of coffee, and they sat together by the window. They spent a few minutes in silence, drinking their coffee.

"You've been busy," Nikki said. "You haven't been mother-henning me the past couple of days."

Cage nodded. "Double shifts at the clinic, and then I had to do a stint yesterday performing image enhancements."

"Oh, right, for that shipment we got. You must be as tired as I am."

"Probably." He shrugged. "You remember Tiger, the guy who met us with that shipment?"

"Sure."

"He showed up at the clinic today. A couple hours ago. Paul called me down."

"Was he sick?"

"No, just worried. He *thought* he was sick." He paused, almost wishing he hadn't brought it up. But she had a right to know. Besides, she was getting over the flu or whatever it was she'd had. She obviously hadn't picked up whatever it was that had killed Stinger. "Stinger's dead."

"Yeah?" It was all she said. But her gaze never left him.

"Yeah. He got pretty sick, and then he died."

"What from?"

Cage shook his head. "Tiger has no idea. He's not a part of the 'inner circle.' He wasn't around, he hadn't seen Stinger in days. He just heard from a friend of his that Stinger had died."

Nikki's expression didn't change. "So why did he go to the clinic?"

"He'd been working with Stinger. He's worried he's getting sick, that he's got whatever Stinger had. But he seems okay."

She nodded slowly and gave him a rueful smile. "That's why you showed up here at this ungodly hour. Afraid you were going to find me on my deathbed?"

Cage smiled back. "Maybe a little."

"Sorry to disappoint you."

He laughed, shaking his head. "You never disappoint me, Nikki."

Nikki stopped smiling. "Except in love. I always disappoint you in love."

What could he say to that? Nothing. The two of them returned to silence, gazing out the window, drinking their coffee, and watching the day arrive.

14

IN A WEEK and a half, no real progress had been made in the Naomi Katsuda case, and now the whole thing seemed to be going to shit on them. The strange thing was, Carlucci wasn't getting any extra pressure to solve the case, not from Vaughn, and not from Yoshi Katsuda, Naomi's father, and that bothered him. He would have expected pressure from both. Even Morgan seemed to have dropped out of the picture; Carlucci hadn't heard from him even once since the day Naomi Katsuda's body had been found in the Sutro Bath ruins. When Santos and Weathers asked for a meeting with him away from the office, he felt certain he wasn't going to get good news. And he was right.

The three of them met in China Basin at eight o'clock in the morning. When Carlucci arrived, Santos and Weathers were standing at a wooden railing, drinking coffee and watching a freighter being unloaded on the docks below them.

Ruben Santos and Toni Weathers had been partners for seven years. Ruben was Toni's first assignment when she transferred into Homicide, and most people in the department had predicted the partnership wouldn't last a year. Ruben was a small, wiry redheaded Latino, a short-tempered man whose emotions regularly got the better of him, while Toni was a tall, big-boned blonde, an even-mannered woman with a sharp, analytical mind. And they had fooled everyone. They complemented each other, were fiercely loyal to one another, and they had become one of the best Homicide teams in the entire city.

As Carlucci approached, he noticed there was an extra cup of coffee for him on the rail between them, steam rising through a tiny opening in its lid.

They turned away from the ship and looked at him. Santos handed him the coffee and said, "I hate this fucking case."

Weathers gave Carlucci the faintest touch of a smile and one quick nod—her way of agreeing.

"You want to give it to Morgan?" Carlucci asked. "He's wanted it from the beginning." He knew what the answer would be.

"Hah," Santos replied. "Not a fucking chance. Besides, I'm not so sure Morgan would want it anymore." Santos had his coffee in his left hand, cigarette in his right; he took a long drink from the paper cup and a deep drag from the cigarette. "I'm going to kill myself with this shit," he said. Then, shaking his head, "That goddamn Katsuda. Yoshi, the father."

"What's the problem, Ruben?"

"What's *not* the problem?" He gave an exaggerated sigh. "The arrogant bastard won't talk to us, that's the biggest problem. More than a week since his daughter was killed, and he still won't talk to us. First, it's the grief thing, he's too upset over the death of his daughter. Then there was the funeral, more grieving, family members from out of town, family and friends down from New Hong Kong. Then he's too busy at the office, making up for time lost and trying to find a replacement for his daughter. We never get to talk to him directly, of course, it's always through one of his assistants. And we get messages from him, about how much he appreciates our efforts, and he'll talk with us as soon as he can, but he doesn't know anything about his daughter's death, or he would have talked to us sooner. Blah, blah, blah." He paused, hit on the coffee and cigarette again.

"We're trying to keep it chilled, right? I'm not out of control, Toni's doing a good job of keeping me smoothed out. We know we have to be careful. He's a fucking big shot, we can't just barge into Mishima and demand that either he talks to us or we'll arrest him. We haven't tried to get a subpoena. We know we've got a little political problem with this guy, so we've backed off. We're not a bunch of fucking gorillas, even if Morgan thinks we are. But this is bullshit, and we're going nowhere."

"I thought Morgan was supposed to help us out, slick the way for interviews."

Santos just shook his head in disgust, but didn't say anything. Weathers again gave Carlucci that faint smile. "Oh, yeah," she said, "Morgan's been a lot of help." But then she shrugged. "To be fair, I think Morgan's been trying, in his own supposedly diplomatic and sophisticated way. And I think he's a little embarrassed about the stonewalling, embarrassed that he doesn't seem to have any influence at all with Katsuda. He *has* managed to get us in to interview other people at Mishima, people who worked with her."

"But we can't get to Yoshi Katsuda himself."

Santos made a kind of growling sound in his throat. "Yeah, well, maybe we can. Now he wants to talk to you."

"Morgan?"

"No. Katsuda. That's the latest message we got—he would be happy to speak with Lieutenant Frank Carlucci. He doesn't come out and *say* he won't talk to anyone else, but it's pretty fuckin' clear."

"Why does he want to talk to *me*?"

Santos shook his head. "No idea."

Carlucci sighed. "Christ, that's all we need."

The three of them stood side by side, leaning against the railing and watching the ship below. Cranes were raising and swinging enormous crates from the ship to the dock; the crates were all marked with Japanese ideograms. A couple of U.S. Customs inspectors were wandering along the dock, glancing at the crates and talking to the dock workers, but neither of them seemed to be doing much actual inspecting.

"Will you talk to Katsuda?" Santos asked.

"Of course. Not much choice, is there?"

"Sure there is," Santos said, grinning. "We could just haul his ass in. Do a full strip and body cavity search. The fucking works."

Carlucci had to smile. "You'd like that, wouldn't you?"

"I'd love it. I'd take pictures."

Weathers, too, was smiling. "Wouldn't mind it myself," she said.

"I thought you said we weren't gorillas," Carlucci said.

Santos wiggled one eyebrow. "I lied." His grin vanished, became a grimace. "I hate New Hong Kong," he said. "I hate anyone who has any connection to that goddamn place."

Carlucci nodded, understanding him completely. He glanced down at the coffee in his hands. He hadn't finished more than half of it, but he couldn't drink any more. His stomach was burning. He walked over to a trash can, dropped the coffee in, and walked back.

"All right, let's forget about Yoshi Katsuda for now. You've been able to talk to other people, right? Follow other lines of investigation? So what have we got so far? Since I haven't heard anything new from you, I assume it isn't much."

"You assume right," Santos said. "We've got shit." And with that he turned away and gazed down at the ship below; he didn't say any more.

Carlucci turned to Weathers, who shrugged and mouthed *He's okay.* She gestured with her head and walked toward the trash can. Carlucci followed her, and after she tossed away her empty coffee cup she lit a cigarette.

They remained by the trash can for a minute, but Santos made no move to join them. He continued to lean over the railing, staring down at the ship and docks. Carlucci and Weathers began walking away from him.

"So," Carlucci said. "What do we have?"

"Ruben's right. We really don't have much of anything. We haven't been able to talk to the father, there is no mother, and there doesn't seem to be any other close family."

"What do you mean, no mother?"

"No mother. Katsuda never married. There was a surrogate mother. Katsuda provided the sperm, and some unknown woman provided the ovum. Unknown to us. Apparently it's a big family secret. Maybe because the mother wasn't Japanese. Naomi was raised by her father and a household of servants, and she lived with her father until about two years ago."

"Now *that's* interesting. How old was she, around forty?"

Weathers nodded. "Forty-one. There's lots of 'interesting' stuff about the family, and the circumstances around her murder, but none of it leads anywhere, at least not yet.

"No one, naturally, has *any* idea why anyone would want to kill her. Everyone we talked to at Mishima who worked with her was very politely cooperative, but no one knew crap. And no one knew her very well. No one at Mishima would own up to actually being her friend, and no one knew of anyone who *was* her friend."

"No boyfriend? Nobody she went out with on a regular basis? Or even irregular basis?"

Weathers gave him the slight smile again. "Now there's another interesting bit that hasn't gone anywhere yet, but just might. Naomi lived in a very expensive condo on Telegraph Hill. Ruben and I have talked to her neighbors in the building. Most of them didn't know her very well, either, although everyone in the building seems to know everyone else on sight—so they recognize anyone who doesn't belong. But again, no friends. One guy, though, said he talked to Naomi a lot, though never about much that he'd consider personal or intimate. Actually he said he talked to her a fair amount about himself, but she never talked about her own private life. But he did say he'd seen her several times with a woman, leaving or coming in, and a couple of times sitting together on her balcony. Always the same woman. He said he couldn't be sure, of course, but he had the feeling they were lovers. Nothing very specific—he never saw them kissing or even holding hands. He said there was just something about the way they were together, he always assumed they were lovers."

"Even if they weren't . . ." Carlucci began.

"Right. We need to talk to her."

"No name?"

"No name. We've got his description, and I think the guy's got an appointment with one of the sketchers this afternoon. But if she hasn't come forward by now, it's not going to be easy to find her. We can't exactly take the sketcher's image and put it on the evening news, or stick it in the papers, or send it out over the nets."

Carlucci smiled. "Why not? We do it at the same time we haul Katsuda in for Ruben's body cavity search and photo session."

Weathers laughed. "Yeah, that'll keep this case low-profile." She took one last drag on her cigarette, dropped it to the ground, and crushed it.

"Another funny thing about this woman, though. When we asked some of the Mishima people about the woman and who she might be, we got a lot of insistence that there was no way this woman could be Naomi's lover. They were quite certain that Naomi 'wasn't that way,' as most of them put it. The same people who said they didn't know her very well, who couldn't name any friends that she had or men that she went out with, these same people were absolutely certain about her sexuality." Weathers shook her head. "There's some kind of hang-up at Mishima about that. Probably doesn't mean anything, but it's one more interesting aspect of this damn case."

Carlucci stopped and leaned against the railing, rubbing his eyes. *This damn case* was right. "What about the Cancer Cell line?" he asked.

"Makes what we've learned about Naomi Katsuda look encyclopedic. We bring up the name, and we either get genuine confusion or what Ruben calls the 'dead fish-face' look followed by claims of ignorance. You *know* they know something about it, but they're not talking. No one's talking." She turned and smiled at him. "There you have it. Like Ruben said, we've got shit. But I've got a feeling, Lieutenant, that this isn't going to last. We'll find that woman, or something else will break, somewhere. Tran and Jefferson and Hong and LaPlace are all busting their asses on this." She nodded once. "We're going to find something and blow this wide open."

"Great," Carlucci said. "That'll make Yoshi Katsuda happy."

Her smile broadened into a grin. "Fuck Yoshi Katsuda."

He smiled back at her. "Let's go get Ruben before he decides to take a header onto the docks."

15

CAROLINE STOPPED AND leaned against the back of a credit chip gazebo on the corner. The street barriers walling off the Core rose just a block away, warning lights blinking in the hot, damp Tenderloin night. She felt almost overwhelmed by the rush of light and movement all around her, the press of people, the constant noise and the constantly shifting smells, the dazzle of flashing electric color.

She had come in from the Chinatown side, through Li Peng's Imperial Imports. There was no way she could use any of the police "gates," but Louis Tanner, an old friend of her father's, had given her a way in. She'd made Louis promise not to tell her father about this excursion of hers. The cost of entrance was fifty dollars left in a charity jar on the counter of Li

Peng's, a large and quiet Chinese herbal pharmacy. Then she'd walked through a back door and up seven flights of stairs, which had exhausted her. Then it was down seven more flights through clouds of smoke and lights, down through restaurants and gambling parlors, a public intimacy club, and finally out onto the street, inside the Tenderloin.

She had made her way through several blocks of heavy sidewalk and street traffic. Some of the alleys were less crowded, but she was afraid to venture into them; they tended to be darker, filled with steam and cooking fires, wild cyclists, and louder and sharper shouts and banging noises. Message streamers swam frantically through the air above the streets, bright green and red, shimmering with work advertisements, commercial come-ons, recruiting messages, and personal and political announcements.

And now here she was, a block from the Core, and half a block from the RadioLand Street Clinic; a block from the place Tito had disappeared into, and half a block from the place where he'd died. She could see the clinic sign across the street, simple blue phosphor letters glowing steadily in the night. Caroline continued to lean against the gazebo, gazing at the sign and resting. The night air was hot and heavy with humidity.

She pushed away from the gazebo wall, stepped toward the curb, then threw herself into a surge of foot traffic that swelled out into the street. She let herself be carried along until she got to the opposite sidewalk; once across, she broke away and moved close to the buildings, where she could walk along at her own pace. She passed a spice bar, a donut shop, a couple of unmarked doors, and a head juicer shop before she finally reached the clinic entrance.

Unsure of why she had come, she hesitated outside, wondering what she hoped to get out of meeting the doctor who had been with Tito when he'd died. Her father had said this doctor knew something about Cancer Cell, but so what? What was any of that going to change? Tito was dead. But she felt otherwise so directionless with her life right now, without much purpose, and this seemed like the only meaningful thing she could do. In some strange way, she felt she owed it to Tito.

The door swung outward and a woman emerged holding a baby in one arm, her other hand wrapped around the fingers of a four-year-old boy. The woman stared at Caroline a moment, eyes almost completely without expression, then turned and headed down the street with the children. Caroline caught the door before it closed, pulled it wider, and stepped inside.

The clinic waiting room was hotter than outside, but several fans blew the air around, which helped some, though it couldn't dispel the heavy odor of sweat. Ten or twelve people sat slumped around the room, and there wasn't much talking or movement. Behind the front counter stood a heavy redheaded woman with a pleasant face. Caroline approached her.

"Can I help you with something?" the woman asked. She smiled at Caroline, very friendly, but looked puzzled, as if Caroline didn't belong here.

"I called earlier today, and asked when Dr. Cage would be in. He's supposed to be here now, and I want to talk to him if he has some time."

"Yes, he's here. He's with a patient right now. If you want to sit down and wait, I'll let him know you're here when he's free."

Caroline nodded. "Thanks, I will."

"Do you want any coffee or tea or something to drink?" the woman asked her.

"No, thanks." She hadn't seen anyone else in the waiting room with coffee or tea. Did she stick out that much?

"I'm Franzee," the woman said. "And you?"

"Caroline." She and Franzee briefly shook hands.

She found an empty chair next to an old blind man who smiled at her as she sat down; he had only three or four teeth, and his face was quite wrinkled, but his dark, black hair had very little gray, and it was obvious that it wasn't dyed. She smiled back at him, remembered he couldn't see her, then said, "Hello." The old man's smile broadened, which did not reveal any more teeth, and he nodded a few times, but he didn't say anything.

She was exhausted. She didn't know if it was the heat, the trek through the Tenderloin, or the Gould's. Maybe all three.

A baby began to cry, and the boy holding it rocked it gently back and forth, cooing to it, patting and rubbing. Caroline closed her eyes and tried to block out the baby's cries.

She sensed someone standing in front of her and opened her eyes. A man stood just a couple of feet away, smiling at her. He was a good-looking man, even with the silly tattoo of a snake and staff on his neck, and his smile gave her a slight shiver.

"You wanted to see me?" the man asked.

"Are you Dr. Cage?"

"I am. And your name is Caroline?"

"Yes. Caroline Carlucci."

An eyebrow went up, and he said, "Oh. The lieutenant's daughter."

She smiled and nodded. "Sounds like the title of a romance novel—*The Lieutenant's Daughter.*"

He nodded, still smiling. "Yeah, it does. Wonder if it would be any good." When she didn't reply, he again said, "You want to see me?"

"I want to talk to you about Tito, Dr. Cage. And I want to ask you about Cancer Cell."

The smile vanished from his face, and he opened his mouth as if to say something, but then shut it. When he did finally speak, all he said was, "Forget the 'Doctor.' Just call me Cage."

"Do you have some time?" she asked.

He looked around the waiting room. "Yeah, probably. Let's go somewhere else, all right?"

"Fine." She got up from the chair.

Cage turned toward the front counter. "Franzee, I'll be across the street at Mika's. If you need me, buzz me over."

"Sure thing, Dr. Cage."

Mika's was an unusual spice and espresso bar across the street from the clinic—it ran up all six floors of the building, but only extended maybe thirty feet in from the street on each level, with half the tables out on tiny, individual balconies that jutted out from the building and over the sidewalk. Cage put some money in the hand of the man who greeted them just inside the door on street level. The man, dressed in a spotless white collarless shirt and black slacks, nodded at a woman dressed in exactly the same clothes, who in turn led them up a flight of stairs and out onto a balcony table on the second floor.

"It's too damn hot to be inside," Cage said as they took seats at the table.

The woman handed them menu cards and immediately left without a word.

"She's not our waitress," Cage explained. "They have a complex hierarchy here." He laughed. "I still haven't completely figured it out yet, and I've been coming here for two years."

Even outside on the balcony it was hot and muggy, but he was right, it would have been sweltering inside, since there was no air conditioning. Blues emerged from speakers mounted in the floor of the balcony above them, the vocals sung beautifully by a woman; the words sounded Russian. Although there were people seated and talking at balcony tables on either side of them, as well as above, the voices were all indistinct, camouflaged by the Russian blues and the sounds of people on the sidewalks just below, the street traffic and the shouts of hawkers, the blasting whistles of a pack of Rebounders wheeling along in the gutters. It was a good place to come and talk if you didn't want to be overheard.

"Better take a quick look at the menu," Cage said. "Someone'll be here for our order in a minute, and if you're not ready they don't come back."

"They don't come back at all?"

"Nope. Someone *else* will, eventually, a lower-level waiter or waitress, but it won't be for a while, and even when they do come and take your order it'll be a long time before you get it, even if it's only a cup of coffee. It's all part of the hierarchy I was telling you about."

"Okay," she said, laughing. She glanced at the menu card, which was spare. Coffee and tea drinks, spice concoctions, and a few imported beers. No food except for deep-fried onion rings and egg rolls.

A man wearing an old, ragged tuxedo and tennis shoes approached their table and looked expectantly at Caroline. "Green iced tea with lemon," she said without hesitation. "Sugar milk." He nodded quickly once and turned to Cage.

"Just coffee," Cage said. "Black, dark roast."

The waiter nodded again and left.

"Very good," Cage said, smiling at her.

Before she had a chance to ask him about Tito, a girl of about fourteen in a dark green ankle-length dress arrived with their drinks. She set them on the table and quickly left.

"I just realized something," Caroline said, reaching for her iced tea. "No one has said a word to us."

Cage nodded. "That's right. None of them will, until we're done and on our way out. Then Marko, the guy who met us at the front door, he'll talk to us, as much as we want. He and I have become pretty good friends over the past year."

"And you still have to bribe him to get a balcony table?"

Cage grinned. "That's why we're still friends." He sipped at his coffee, and the grin faded, but his gaze never left Caroline's face. "You want to talk to me about Tito and Cancer Cell."

Caroline nodded. She tried her iced tea, which tasted quite good, just sweet enough and refreshing.

"Why?"

"He was my friend."

"All right, he was your friend. I guess you've talked to your father about all this, then."

"Some. Enough to get me here. I know Tito died in your clinic, and not from AIDS. And I know that you and my father think Cancer Cell is involved somehow."

"So your father sent you to me?"

"No. He doesn't know I'm here. He probably wouldn't be thrilled. I think he'd just like me to drop it and go on with my life. Put it all behind me."

"But you can't do that," Cage said. Not a question, as if he understood her.

"No, I can't."

"So what is it you want to know?"

"I want to know what killed him. I want to know if Cancer Cell is somehow responsible. I have no idea why they did it, but apparently they were the ones who kidnapped him in the first place, and I guess I want to know why they did that, too."

Cage sighed. "I don't have any answers for you," he said. "I don't know what killed him. Probably never will. Your father was going to try to arrange for an autopsy, but the last time I talked to him he hadn't managed it yet." He shook his head. "I doubt it'll give us an answer anyway. And without knowing what killed him, it's pretty much impossible to know if Cancer Cell had anything to do with it. Hell, even if we did know what killed Tito, my guess is we still wouldn't know anything about Cancer Cell's involvement. They don't exactly advertise what they're doing." He frowned. "What *do* you know about Cancer Cell?"

"Nothing. As good as nothing, anyway." It occurred to her that he had been very careful and precise about answering her, and that he hadn't referred at all to one thing. "You didn't say anything about my last question," she said to him. "About why Cancer Cell would have kidnapped him in the first place."

He smiled. "You don't miss much." He leaned one elbow on the table, slowly turning his coffee cup in circles with his other hand. "Of course I don't really have an answer to that, either, but it's something I can make a guess at."

"So make a guess." He was being very cautious about Cancer Cell. Maybe there were good reasons for that.

"All right," he said. He drank more coffee and gave a sort of shrug. "Tito had AIDS. He was dying. Okay. The word on the street is that Cancer Cell will sometimes put together a 'contract' of sorts with terminally ill people. They agree to provide high-quality medications—antibiotics, painkillers, anti-virals, immune system boosters, whatever might help make them comfortable, or relatively symptom-free—in return for which the person agrees to allow Cancer Cell to use them for clinical trials of experimental drugs or procedures during the final stages of their disease."

"But Tito didn't have any high-quality medications," she objected. "All he had was crap he got from free clinics."

"Like ours," Cage said, smiling.

She shrugged. "Whatever."

"Fair enough. But how do you know that's all he had?"

She didn't, actually. She'd always just assumed. "I don't, I guess. He complained about them, said nothing he had did much good."

"In the final stages, *nothing* does much good, high-quality or not."

"I suppose." She remembered sitting with Tito while he lay on the sofa watching TV, hardly aware of her presence, his hands and feet in pain, but his gaze way deep inside the television set, farther in than the flickering images, all the way through them. She would speak to him, and he wouldn't respond. Like he was already halfway into another world; finding his way into it, learning how to leave this one.

And she realized that right at this moment she was much the same way, staring into her iced tea, having forgotten for a minute where she was. She looked back up at Cage, who was gazing steadily at her. "So why would he have been abducted?" she asked.

"Because he didn't want to honor his part of the contract. I've heard of it happening. Cancer Cell will do whatever is necessary to enforce the contract."

Caroline shook her head, finding it all a little hard to believe. "He never said anything about Cancer Cell. Never even mentioned them."

"He probably wouldn't have, even if he'd known. And he may not have known who he was dealing with. Most of the time when you deal with Cancer Cell, the name never comes up. I know someone who works for them who doesn't even know."

"Mouse knew."

"Who?"

"Mouse. Strange creature. Person. When I went to Tito's and found him gone, Mouse was there, cleaning out the place. He's the one who said it might have something to do with Cancer Cell. He said the two men who came and took Tito away were taking him to the Core." And Mouse had known her father was a cop. Mouse seemed to have known quite a lot. What did that mean about the little bastard?

"That would fit," Cage said. "That's where Cancer Cell is, right in the Core of the Tenderloin."

"So they took him to the Core, experimented on him, gave him some god-awful disease, and he ended up dying a horrible death."

"As opposed to the peaceful and painless death he would have experienced with the AIDS."

Caroline glared at him. "That's not the point," she said.

"No, you're right," Cage admitted. "I'm sorry." He glanced away for a moment, then back at her. "But we don't know if that's what happened. We don't even know for sure that he was abducted by Cancer Cell. But even if we accept that as a given, what happened afterward . . ." He shook his head. "There's just no way to know."

"I want to find out," Caroline insisted, adamant.

He tipped his head to one side and gave her a faint smile. He had deep hazel eyes that glittered with the lights from the street. "How do you plan to do that?"

"I don't know." No, she didn't know yet, but an idea was beginning to form, vague at this point, but slowly coming into focus. She finished off her iced tea and leaned back in the chair, watching him. Yes, she had to admit to herself that she liked him, and was willing to forgive his insensitive remark about Tito. "You seem to know an awful lot about Cancer Cell," she finally said. "Nobody else seems to know anything about them."

Cage waved a hand in dismissal. "It's mostly guesses," he said. "I've been working here in this clinic, half a block from the Core, for two years. Street medicine. Cancer Cell seems to be their own kind of street medicine. You hear things, that's all."

"My father said someone else died from the same thing that killed Tito."

"No, that's not quite right. He *may* have. It's just a guess."

"Another one of your guesses," she said, smiling.

"Yes. Another guess. I didn't see this guy die. I just heard about it from someone else, and even that was secondhand. The symptoms were similar."

"But the man who died was a part of Cancer Cell."

"Probably. Yes."

"So *you'd* like to know what happened to Tito, too."

Cage nodded. "Yes, I would."

At that point, the girl who had brought them their drinks returned to the table and looked back and forth between them with a questioning expression.

"You want another?" Cage asked.

"Yes, if you have time."

"Sure. They'll buzz me if they really need me, and I don't think our conversation is quite finished, is it?"

She smiled at him and shook her head. "No, it isn't."

He turned to the girl and said, "Two more, the same. Thanks."

The girl nodded and backed away.

They didn't talk as they waited for their drinks. Caroline watched the sidewalk and the street below them, the steady, heavy traffic on both. She liked the feel of it all, the energy that rose from the streets and the people and seemed to flow into her, juicing her up a little. But she had to remind herself of something her father had once told her—that the Tenderloin out on the streets was quite different from what went on inside the buildings and up on the rooftops, behind locked doors and windows, in the hidden mazes of basements and subterranean passages, in the vast warrens of apartments and skin parlors and drug dens and flesh arcades. The streets were relatively safe, along with the visible shops and cafés and clubs, but beneath it all, like the submerged portions of icebergs, was the real Tenderloin, and you never knew when some of that would break out into the open, out of control. A dangerous place if you didn't know where you were or what you were doing.

The girl brought fresh iced tea and coffee and took away the old glasses. Caroline took a long drink, refreshed and cooled by it. She wiped the cold, condensed liquid on the outside of the glass and spread it across her forehead.

"I want you to put me in touch with Cancer Cell," she said to Cage.

He didn't react much, but she could tell it wasn't at all what he had expected to hear from her. He sipped at his coffee, scratched at his ear; she could see that he wanted to smile, to dismiss what she had said as a joke, but he managed to keep the smile in check.

"Why?" he finally asked.

"I said. I want to find out what happened to Tito. I want to help *you* find out what happened to him and to this other guy. Find out if there *is* something to worry about."

He sighed, turning his coffee cup in circles again. "First, I'm not sure I would be able to put you in touch with them. Second, even if I could, you couldn't just straight out ask about Tito. You did that, you'd be lucky if they just cut everything off right there and told you to go away. You'd be lucky if they didn't haul you into the Core and make *you* one of their experimental subjects."

She smiled at him. "That's exactly what I want them to do."

"What the hell are you talking about?" Cage said, exasperated.

She breathed in deeply, and her smile faded. "I have Gould's Syndrome," she told him.

He was clearly taken aback, though whether it was from her admission that she had Gould's, or from the realization of what she was proposing, was unclear. He shifted in his chair, plainly uncomfortable, but he didn't say anything for a long time. When he finally did speak, all he said was, "I'm sorry."

"Thank you." Then, getting right back to it, she said, "I want you to put me in touch with Cancer Cell, and then I'll work out my own contract with them."

Cage shook his head. "That's crazy."

"What's crazy about it?" she asked him. Now that the idea was fully formed, now that she had given it substance by actually suggesting it aloud to him, it seemed perfectly reasonable to her. "I've got a condition that's terminal—just what they'd be looking for. I make them a deal. I'll offer myself up for any experimental treatments they might have for Gould's. Then I'll be inside, and I'll see what I can find out about what happened to Tito. I have nothing to lose."

"I suspect you have a *lot* to lose," he said.

"What do you mean?"

"The Gould's hasn't gone active yet, has it? You don't look like you're suffering any of the effects from it."

Caroline looked away from him, reminded of the incident at her apartment the night Tina had come over. "It's just recently begun," she said, still not looking at him. Suddenly her sureness deserted her, and the dread threatened to return. She turned back to him. "Most of the time I'm fine, but it *has* begun to go active, and I know what that means."

"Then you know that you might have several good years ahead of you, several years where you are, in fact, fine most of the time, like now. That seems to me like a *lot* to lose."

"I think I'm a better judge of that than you are."

"Yes, I suppose you are." Something seemed to have gone out of him, and he appeared suddenly very tired. "But I still think it's a lousy idea."

"Why?"

Cage held up his hands, shaking his head. "I don't really know anything about Cancer Cell, I don't have any idea what they would do to you. They give you some kind of experimental treatment, it could be extremely painful and debilitating. Maybe they'd just do some other kind of experimentation. Once you were in the Core, you wouldn't have much choice. If you were in the terminal stages, if you were really sick, I'd say sure, go ahead. But you're not sick."

"But now's the time to find out about Tito and this other guy," she insisted. "Two or three or four years from now, when I am really sick, it will either be too late, or it won't matter." She paused, tilting her head. "You do have a way to put me in touch with them, don't you?"

"Maybe."

"Will you do it?"

He leaned back, shaking his head and running his hand through his hair. "I don't know," he said. "I don't like it."

Caroline didn't push it. She sensed that would be a mistake right now, that he'd dig in and flat-out refuse. Better to let him think about it for a while, get used to the idea. Let his worries about Cancer Cell and some disease breaking out of them nag at him.

His head jerked to the right, eyes widening, his attention caught by something in the street below. Caroline turned, scanned the street until she saw what it was. Half a block away, weaving back and forth in the street, was a pedalcart slowly moving toward them, bumping into parked vehicles and other traffic as it came. A woman was at the wheel, pedaling weakly, slumped forward with beaded dreadlocks covering her face, barely in control of the cart. As it got closer it veered off the street through a gap between a minicab and a jit, then jounced up the curb and onto the sidewalk, scattering people before it crashed lightly against the clinic building, just a few feet away from the entrance and almost directly across from Mika's. The woman remained in the cart, almost upright now but apparently dazed.

Cage leaped to his feet, grabbed the balcony rail, and leaned out over the street.

"Nikki!" he cried.

Caroline looked up into his face, saw stark terror. She turned back to the street.

"Nikki!" he cried out again.

The woman looked up and across the street, searching. "Cage?" Then her gaze seemed to find him and she nodded once. She staggered out of the pedalcart, took a couple of steps forward, and stepped into the gutter, almost losing her balance. She held up one bare arm. Even from across the street there were two visible red patches on her dark brown skin. "Cage, I'm in trouble."

Then she sat down on the sidewalk, her feet still in the gutter, and dropped her head into her arms.

16

NIKKI.

Cage almost jumped to the street from the balcony, but held back. A broken ankle wouldn't do anyone any good. *Nikki.* Jesus. With one last look at her, he turned, pushed off the rail, and ran inside.

He bumped into a table, rattling glasses, grabbed someone's shoulder, barked out an apology, and bounced away narrowly avoiding the guy in the tuxedo, then shot toward the stairs. He took them two and three at a time, barely in control, and hit the ground floor running. There wasn't a clear path and he crashed into a woman, almost fell, spun around while somehow staying on his feet, then squeezed between two people and he was free. He flew past Marko, who shouted something after him, and went through the front door.

Out on the sidewalk he crashed into more people, but shoved his way through. At the edge of the street he hesitated and took a good look at the traffic; he didn't want to get himself killed. Breathing hard, he anxiously waited for a break. One lane at a time. An opening appeared and he took off, darting through the wake of a junker truck and just in front of a pair of scooters. Then there was a brief hesitation to let a public jit go by, and he was off again, shifting quickly left, hand on the roof of a delivery van, stutter-stepping behind another small truck, then between two parked cars and he was across, no more than twenty feet from Nikki.

She was still sitting on the curb, her feet planted solidly in the gutter, her head in her hands.

"Nikki," he said, barely more than a whisper, and he hurried toward her.

She looked up at him with alarm and held out her hand, warding him off. "Don't, Cage. For Christ's sake, don't get too close!"

He stopped, just a few feet away, then started forward again.

"Don't touch me, Cage. I mean it."

He stopped again, close enough now to reach out and take hold of her, but he refrained. Instead, he squatted, bringing his face level with hers. She didn't look good. Her eyes were red, her nose was running, and her breathing seemed labored. Even her dreadlocks appeared unkempt and limp.

"How are you doing?" he asked, feeling kind of stupid.

But she managed a tired smile. "Shitty. I'm sick, Cage. I'm in deep shit. I thought I was getting better, I really did, but was I ever wrong." Her smile faded and she slowly shook her head from side to side. "That fucking Stinger. I'd kill him if he wasn't already dead."

"Hang in there for a minute," he told her. "I'll get something set up for you in the clinic, and then we'll get you inside."

"You'd better get gloves and a mask on," she said firmly, "or I won't let you near me. You try to touch me with your bare hands, I'll kick your bleedin' balls in."

Cage had to smile. "All right. I'll be right back."

He stood and looked around, and immediately realized he wasn't going to have to ask people to stay back. They'd heard her yelling at him, and they were all giving her a wide berth, even as they stared.

Franzee met him at the clinic door as he came through. "What's going on out there?"

"It's Nikki. She's in bad shape. What's the status on the iso rooms?"

Franzee shook her head. "Both occupied." Then, still shaking her head, "Don't ask. You don't want to know."

"Exam rooms?"

"Three and Five are empty right now, I think. I'll check for sure."

Cage nodded. "All right keep one of them open."

He jogged down the hall to the staff room, grabbed a cot, a couple of blankets, and a pillow, then hurried back into the front room with them. He set them in front of the counter.

"Five?" he asked.

Franzee nodded. "It's open."

"Can you get that stuff set up in there? And I'll bring her in."

Franzee nodded again and dragged the cot down the hall. Cage put on a pair of gloves and pulled a medico-mask over his head, tugging it all the way down so it hung around his neck. He breathed deeply several times, trying to calm himself. Then he went out to get her.

Nikki hadn't moved, and though a crowd had gathered around her, they still kept back. There was a lot of mumbling and muttering, jockeying to get a better view. He wanted to strangle them all.

As he got close to her, she glared at him and pointed. "Put the damn mask on," she said.

"All right, all right." He pulled the mask up over his mouth and nose, then knelt beside her. "Think you can walk?" he asked, knowing damn well what her answer would be.

"I'm not a cripple, for Christ's sake. Of course I can walk."

He took her arm with his gloved hands and helped her to her feet. She took a couple of steps, then stopped and doubled over, her free hand on her knees.

"Nikki?"

She shook her head, her eyes clamped shut. "It's . . . it's okay," she got out, her voice croaking. Her hand was gripping his fingers so tightly his knuckles hurt. Then her grip eased, her eyes opened, she breathed in, and slowly straightened. "Okay," she said.

They made their way the last few feet to the clinic entrance. Just as they approached, the door swung open, held wide by Franzee. Cage led Nikki through the doorway, the waiting room, then along the hall to Exam Five, which was the last room at the end of the corridor. There he guided her to the cot and had her sit on it. Then he pulled up a chair, sat in front of her, and gave her a thorough workup. Focused on the task, on the details.

Her temperature was high, well over a hundred and two. Lymph nodes in her neck and under her arms and down around her groin were all swollen. Blood pressure was okay, though, and her pulse was still strong. The red patch on her arm looked like a severe rash. There was another small patch on the back of her other arm, and a third on the side of her neck.

When he was done, he helped her get dressed. She seemed so tired and weak, and she said her muscles and joints ached.

"I'm really thirsty," she said.

Cage filled a plastic cup with water and gave it to her. She drained it at once, and he gave her another, and finally a third.

"Have you taken anything for the fever?"

Nikki shook her head. "Not for a long time. I haven't been thinking any too clearly."

So he gave her some ibuprofen and a couple of acetaminophen, which she took with another cup of water. She dropped the cup onto the floor and slowly laid back and out on the cot, closing her eyes.

"I'm sorry," she said quietly. "I shouldn't have come here. You can't do anything. I just panicked."

"No," Cage said. "You did right. I'll figure out something for you."

Nikki rolled her head from side to side. "There's nothing. We both know that. I should just go home."

"No," he insisted. "Not nothing."

She smiled, her eyes still closed. "What, then?"

"I don't know yet. Something."

Neither of them spoke for a while. Cage sat almost motionless and watched her, a terrible pain slowly eating at his gut. It was terror, he realized. He was terrified of losing her.

But her breathing had eased, and she seemed calmer. The tension had left her face.

She opened her eyes and looked at him. "I'm going to die."

Cage shook his head. "We're *all* going to die, Nikki."

Her eyes flashed and she glowered at him. "Don't talk that kind of shit to me, Cage. I won't have it."

"I'm sorry," he said. Then, "But you're not going to die."

"Stinger and that other guy died."

"They didn't have any medical care."

Nikki gave a brief, harsh laugh. "And what the hell kind of medical care am I going to get? You guys are all good doctors, but this isn't a hospital, it's not even close."

"I'll get you into a hospital, Nikki."

She shook her head. "Yeah? Which one?"

"I don't know yet. I'll work out something."

Her expression softened as she watched him. "You will, won't you?"

Cage just nodded. He didn't know how he was going to arrange it, but he would figure out something. He was going to get her out of this goddamn place and into one of the top-flight hospitals where they would be able to keep her alive until they figured out what she had, or until it ran its course.

"I love you, Nikki."

"I know you do, Cage. And I love you, too. I'm sorry it couldn't ever be the way you wanted."

"You don't need to apologize."

"Sure I do," she said, smiling. Then she rolled onto her side and closed her eyes, "I'm going to sleep for a while now."

"Okay. I'll come back and check on you in a little bit."

Out in the hall, he disposed of the gloves and mask, then wandered into the waiting room. He was surprised to see Caroline Carlucci looking up at him from one of the chairs. He'd completely forgotten about her. He crossed the room and sat next to her.

"Sorry about taking off like that."

Caroline shook her head in dismissal. "How is she? Is it Nikki?"

"Yes, Nikki. I don't know how she is. She's sleeping. I don't know." He rubbed at his eyes with his palms, forcing the flash of brightly colored lights across his vision. He wished he could go to sleep himself.

"Has she got the same thing Stinger and Tito had?"

Cage nodded. He didn't want to open his eyes, not for hours. But he finally did, and looked at her. "I can't be sure, but I think so." Then he explained what had happened with Stinger and the finger hooks.

"She got sick a couple of weeks later, but I thought it was just the flu, something like that. It had been a long time. I was a little worried, but then she started getting better. We both thought she was through the worst of it, we both thought . . ." He grimaced, grabbing the back of his neck with his hand and rubbing. "Christ, we both thought wrong."

"What can you do for her?"

"I don't know. Get her into a good hospital, somewhere. No one will want to take her, so I don't know how I'm going to manage that, but I've got to. She'll die if she stays here." Then he looked at her again, a thought occurring to him. "Wait . . . maybe." He dug around in his jeans until he found her father's card. "I'm going to call your father," he said. "We'll see what kind of pull he's got."

"Cage?"

"Yeah?"

"When you talk to him, don't tell him I'm here. Don't even tell him you've seen me."

For the first time since Nikki had appeared on the street, he remembered what he and Caroline had been talking about at Mika's. He gazed silently at her for a few moments, feeling like he completely understood her. "I won't."

It took him several minutes to get through to Carlucci as a dispatcher tried tracking him down, but Cage finally heard his voice.

"I still haven't managed to get an autopsy for Tito, yet," Carlucci said.

"No, that's not why I called. I've got a big favor to ask for. A *huge* favor."

"Great," Carlucci said. "That sounds hopeful."

"I've got another one here. At the clinic."

"Another dead person?"

"No. Just sick. But with the same thing." He paused, trying to figure the best way to put it. Shit, just go straight with it. "Her name is Nikki, and she's my closest friend. She got it from Stinger, the other dead guy, and she means the world to me. Understand?"

There was just the slightest pause. "I understand," Carlucci eventually said. "What can I do?"

"I need to get her into a real hospital, or she's going to die. We can't do shit for her here."

There was a long silence at the other end of the line. Cage glanced at Caroline, who was watching him.

"You there?" he asked.

"Yeah, Cage, I'm here. I'm just thinking. All right, let me talk to some people. I'll call you back."

"Okay. Thanks, Lieutenant."

"Sure thing, 'Doctor.' "

Cage smiled and hung up.

"Anything?" Caroline asked.

"Maybe. He's going to talk to some people, then call back." He breathed deeply once, feeling some sense of relief. He had the feeling that Carlucci would come through. But he wasn't going to leave the phone until he heard something definite.

"Your closest friend," Caroline said.

"What?" He was only half paying attention to her.

"Nikki. What you said to my father. That she means the world to you."

"Yeah." Nodding, and thinking about her lying on the cot back in the exam room. "I know this is going to sound ridiculous, but . . . she saved my life. Not in a metaphorical or symbolic sense. The real thing. She pulled my ass out of some deep, deep shit years ago, down in L.A. Maybe I'll tell you about it sometime." He shook his head and looked back along the hallway, half expecting Nikki to walk out of Exam Five, smiling, arms out, saying she was just fine. "The least I can do now," he said, "is return the favor."

He wanted to go back and check on her, but he was afraid to leave the phone. It was irrational, he knew Franzee would answer it and come back to get him, but he just could not leave. He looked back at Caroline, trying to take his mind off Nikki.

"What happened over at Mika's?" he asked. "After I hurricaned out of there."

She smiled. "I took care of everything. A little bit of confusion. I tried to pay the wrong person, the girl. She was quite shocked."

The phone rang and Cage answered it before the first ring had quite finished.

"Cage," he said.

"An ambulance is on the way," Carlucci said. "We have a couple of street access points into the Tenderloin for emergencies. It'll pick her up and take her to St. Anthony's—that's the police and fire departments' hospital."

"Jesus. How did you manage that?"

"Sold my soul to the Devil."

"Shit, he can have mine, too," Cage said.

"It actually wasn't that difficult," Carlucci told him. "I just had to lie about a few things."

"I owe you, Carlucci."

"You sure do, Cage. I'll cash in someday. Anything else?"

"Not a thing."

"Then I'll let you go. It shouldn't be long, maybe fifteen, twenty minutes. And we'll talk about all of this later."

Cage said good-bye and hung up the receiver. He looked at Caroline. "Your father pulled it off. Ambulance is on the way. He's arranged to have her admitted to St. Anthony's."

"That's great."

He nodded. Now he could go back and check on Nikki.

"Cage," Caroline said. "One more thing."

"What's that?"

"*Now* will you help me get in touch with Cancer Cell?"

He didn't have to think about it this time. He nodded slowly. "Oh, yeah. As soon as possible."

Isabel

THINGS WERE GETTING strange in the Core. People were dying.

Isabel sensed the changes, she could smell them—the people in here now smelled like fear.

One day, in the shadowy light below street level, she saw a man die violently, shaking and screaming while several other people watched him, afraid to get close. And when the man had died, the people left him. Only later did someone come back, pour liquid over him, and set him on fire. Isabel smelled the stench for days whenever she got near that passage.

Another time, she saw the woman who had been cutting up Henry, saw her die in much the same way as the man, only she was alone in a room, surrounded by paper lanterns and multicolored rocks. Isabel felt a certain satisfaction when the woman stopped moving at last, dead.

Two other times in her travels she saw dead people, bodies twisted, eyes open, teeth bared, lots of blood. And she knew something bad was happening here.

She began searching for a way out.

She wasn't sure she actually wanted to leave the Core—she had the sense that outside the Core would be many more people, passages and rooms would be more crowded, there would be fewer places to hide, fewer places to be alone—but she felt a need to be prepared. If the Core continued to get stranger, crazier, and more out of control, she needed to have a way out.

She had a fairly good sense of the Core's boundaries, and so she explored them, probing. Although she occasionally wandered up staircases into the building floors at street level and higher, she really spent no time there looking for a way out; there were many ways out onto the streets themselves, but she could see the high, brightly lit electrified barriers blocking the streets, could see all the doorways and windows of the buildings outside the Core itself completely blocked by brick and metal or firmly secured wooden planks. The only way out would be underground.

Isabel did see men and women leaving the Core through below-ground passages, concrete tunnels, but there were always locked doors or other barriers she would not be able to pass. She would have to find her own way out.

Dawn had arrived, gray and already hot. The Core was quiet, her regular passageways empty. Isabel moved carefully along the outer perimeter, one hand on the corridor wall, feeling her way, feeling for an opening. The wall was cool, almost smooth, though there were cracks and chips in it, and places where mosses grew. Colorful markings covered much of the concrete.

There was a break in the wall, a branching corridor, narrow, maybe three feet wide. Isabel entered it, took a few steps forward, but it ended abruptly. Mortared brick blocked the corridor, sealing it from floor to ceiling, wall to wall. There was no way through.

Isabel crouched in front of the brick and examined the walls on both sides. On her left, just above her head, was a small, square opening covered by a deteriorating mesh screen. She reached up, gripped the screen with both hands, and tugged. The screen came free, scattering bits of dirt and dust and broken bits of metal.

Isabel pulled herself up and into the opening. She scraped her hips on the rough edges of the opening, but worked herself all the way in. She was inside a metal duct of some kind, the walls cool and smooth. She couldn't see anything, but she smelled damp earth from somewhere.

For several moments she didn't move, listening, sniffing the air. Then she crawled forward. Progress was slow; she couldn't move her limbs much. But she inched her way along through the dark.

She came to a T, the duct widening as it branched in both directions. Isabel took the right branch, figuring the left headed back into the Core. In the larger duct, the going was easier. She hadn't gone far when the duct bent right, narrowing once again. After a slight hesitation, she squeezed into the narrow section and continued crawling forward.

The duct opened out into dark open space. Isabel remained at the opening for a minute or so, trying to make out the room. There was actually a little more light here, and eventually she could see a narrow corridor. To her right, just barely visible, was the same brick wall, she realized; the other side.

She worked her way out of the duct and dropped to the floor. At the other end of the corridor from the brick wall was a dim rectangle of light. Isabel padded along the passage, then up several steps to a door with a glass window covered by cobwebs. She brushed away the cobwebs, then pressed her face against the glass.

On the other side of the door was a large room filled with boxes and crates, drums and large glass bottles, and all kinds of other miscellaneous junk scattered everywhere. Two men were sitting on chairs, smoking cigarettes and drinking from green bottles.

Isabel turned from the window and headed back down the steps. She would go back into the Core for now, but this was just what she needed—a way out.

PART THREE

Epidemiology:
Tracking the Source

17

SOMETIMES CARLUCCI HATED this goddamn job. He sat at his
desk, sweating in the heat and staring at the sketch artist picture of the
woman who *might* have been Naomi Katsuda's lover, the woman nobody
could find. And after a week of negotiations with Yoshi Katsuda, who supposedly wanted to talk to him, an interview had finally been arranged, but
it was still four days away. The case was going nowhere fast, and it pissed
him off.

He tossed the picture onto his desk and leaned back in his chair. Santos
and Weathers were doing everything they could, he knew that. But there had
to be another way to go at this case. And the only other way he could think
of was through Tito's abduction and death. So far, though, not much happened there, either. Cage hadn't come up with anything; in fact, when they'd
talked yesterday, Cage had said he now doubted he would ever be able to
arrange for Carlucci to meet with anyone from Cancer Cell. Something
about them being too wary of cops. Carlucci had the feeling Cage was being evasive, but he couldn't do a damn thing about that.

So what else? He leaned forward, dug around through the stacks of files
and notes on his desk until he found his file on Tito Moraleja. Then he leaned
back again, opened the file, and leafed through it. There wasn't much. Tran's
official report of their visit to Tito's room. An addendum about the parrot,
and several transcripts that had been made of the parrot's useless utterances.
CID had given up on the parrot in disgust, but Kelly had taken a liking to it,
named it Horus, and brought it home with him. And finally there were his
notes on his talks with Caroline and Cage. He glanced through them.

Mouse. That familiar name again. He knew it from somewhere, someone's weasel, something like that. Wait a minute . . . wait . . . He looked back at the parrot transcripts and skimmed over them. Yes, there it was: "... *mouse ... asshole ... it's the mouse in the house.* ..." Well, let's see what he could do with it. He cleared the piles away from his desktop, exposing the keyboard. The screen blinked to life and he ran a restricted search on Mouse's name.

He went down the hall and got a couple of cans of cold lemonade while he waited. The air wasn't much cooler out in the hall than it was in his office. Every time the air recycling system was renovated in the building, the promise was made that *this* time it would all work perfectly. It never did. What they needed to do was tear down the building and start from scratch. But that was never going to happen either.

When he got back to his office, the search was complete, and he had a large batch of records to sift through, most of which he knew weren't going to be at all relevant. He settled in, opened the first can of lemonade, and went to work.

An hour and two cans of lemonade later, he thought he'd found what he was looking for—notes about a guy named Mouse in two different reports made by Sandrine Binoche, an undercover narcotics cop. He didn't know her. He checked in with the duty logs, found out she was off-duty today; but he put out a priority call, and fifteen minutes later he had a callback from her.

"Lieutenant? Sandrine Binoche here."

"Sorry to bother you on your day off," he said.

"That's all right. I'm taking care of my sister's three kids while she and her husband take a bike ride—give them some time to themselves. And I can use any damn excuse to get a break from the little monsters for a few minutes. So what can I do for you, Lieutenant?"

"A case I'm working on. I'm trying to find out something about a guy named Mouse, and you mention someone with that name on a couple of your recent reports. You know the guy?"

"Oh, yeah, I know the guy. He's a nasty prick."

"What's he look like?"

"Short, skinny little bastard, maybe five feet at the most. He's got pink eyes, but he's not exactly an albino. Had all his teeth pulled a few years ago and replaced with a set of shiny metal choppers. Very attractive."

Carlucci nodded to himself as he listened to her while rereading Caroline's description of him. "That's the guy," he said. "That's the same guy, all right. What can you tell me about him?"

"He does a little of everything, none of it good. Sells a lot of crap drugs, which sometimes gets him shit-kicked by his customers, but he doesn't seem to mind it that much. Runs wireheads once in a while. Used to middleman for people trying to find body-bags. Acts as a courier for Fat Buddha on occasion. You know Fat Buddha?"

"Yeah." Fat Buddha was an empire builder in the DMZ, fancied himself a kind of crime lord. The cops had pretty much quit trying to get at the guy once they realized he kept to the DMZ and wasn't trying to expand out of it and into any other part of the city. Besides, he was a strange sort of stabilizing influence in the DMZ. "So where can I find Mouse? In the DMZ?"

"Sometimes. But he also spends a lot of time in the Polk Corridor, and that's the part of the DMZ you'd be more likely to find him in, where it butts up against the Polk. You sure you *want* to find him?"

"Yeah, I'm sure. Anything else I should know?"

"Just watch your ass, Lieutenant. You being a cop won't make one bit of difference to him. And watch his hands—he likes knives, and he always keeps a few stashed on him."

"All right, Binoche. Thanks."

An hour later, Carlucci was walking along the lower end of the Polk Corridor, just a couple of blocks from where it met the DMZ and then the Tenderloin. Two o'clock in the afternoon, the heat from the sun overhead was cut by a breeze blowing in from the west; but the relief came with a price—a terrible stench of rotting food that only let up whenever the breeze did.

This was the crappy end of the Polk. A few blocks north it began to slowly go upscale, blending into a somewhat prosperous retail core with bookstores, theaters, clothing boutiques. Here at this end was a different story. The bars were seedy, darker, and more numerous, the retail stores sold cheap junk and used merchandise, restaurants and coffee shops were risky to your health. Instead of hair salons, scarification parlors. Rather than a body-electronics store, a series of shock shops. And where you might find a day spa in the upper Polk, here you would only find hump rooms renting by the half hour.

Carlucci walked slowly along, searching the sidewalks and street for Mouse, glancing into stores and alleys. He hadn't gone two blocks when a boy who couldn't have been more than twelve or thirteen offered him a cheap blow job. Maybe it was better that he looked more like a pedophile than a cop, although it surprised and depressed him. Half a block farther on, he shook his head at another approaching boy before the kid could say anything.

He bought a cup of coffee and a sweet, sticky pastry of some kind from a man selling out of a basement window, then sat next to a couple on a nearby bench. As he worked on the pastry and coffee, he scanned the street and sidewalks, searching for Mouse. Some of the people moving past him were lethargic, dragged by the heat, but a lot more were moving fast, either speeded out or running on natural chemical imbalances—it was impossible to tell the difference between the two. Plenty of freaks, but no Mouse.

Just as Carlucci ate the last of the pastry, the guy next to him grabbed the wrapper out of his hand, wadded it into a ball, then popped it into his mouth and began chewing on it. The woman with him leaned forward, smiled, and said, "Thank you."

"You're welcome," Carlucci said. Then he got up, the man still chewing like mad, the woman still smiling, and walked off. There were too damn many people like that on the streets.

Carlucci walked slowly along Polk, looking into stores and doorways, glancing up at apartment windows, checking out people sitting or lying in parked cars. If he'd been a vice or narcotics cop, he could have made a half dozen different arrests right there on the street; of course, if he *had* been a vice or narcotics cop, he wouldn't have bothered with any of them. They were all too trivial.

He stopped on a corner and scanned the street in all directions, and decided it was pretty much a pointless waste spending any more time in the Polk. He couldn't put it off any longer, so he walked down to the end of the Polk and into the DMZ. The sidewalks became more crowded, and the walled boundaries of the Tenderloin seemed to radiate the heat from the sun, and there was no breeze here for some reason—the temperature seemed to jump five or ten degrees just like that.

He stood on a corner, blinking against the heat and the reflections of the sun coming at him from strange angles, and tried to adjust to the DMZ. Besides the greater heat, the feel of the air around him had changed. The lower end of the Polk was seedy and a little bit wacked, but the atmosphere here in the DMZ felt distinctly dangerous and deranged. He'd have gone a little bit crazy if he'd known Caroline had been coming here to visit her friend Tito, so it was probably better that he *hadn't* known. He certainly couldn't have stopped her.

Again he tried to keep an eye out for Mouse as he walked along, but now it was harder. There was more movement all around him, more noise, everything strangely colored and frantic and slightly out of sync from normal expectations, which gave him a constant jittery sensation at the edges of his attention, made it difficult to focus. Even the smells were different, everything with a slightly acrid tinge—cooking food, tobacco and pot and fireweed smoke, spilled booze, burning rubber, piss and vomit. Even the occasional strong scent of flowers from lush, overgrown plants hanging above the street had a bitter edge.

Carlucci stopped in front of an urban taxidermist and looked into one of the windows. Several complete, small animal skeletons were mounted on pedestals with identification labels: CAT; PARROT; FERRET; CHIHUAHUA. A sign dangling above them claimed that all the skeletons were guaranteed to have been organically cleaned by maggots and that no chemicals were used. In the other window were several huge, stuffed rats. Over them was a sign that said: BIG FUCKIN' RATS!! YOUR CHOICE, $10.00.

A shouted curse and loud laughter caught his attention and he turned away from the display windows to see what was going on. Two people were struggling with a fat, bare-chested man, trying to load him into an organ scavenger van. But it was unclear if the man was actually dead; he seemed to be moving, breathing maybe, perhaps even struggling against the two scavengers. Carlucci started toward them, unsure if he would actually intervene—it might only get him killed here. But as he got closer, and they shifted their hold on the man, Carlucci saw that most of the back of the man's head was gone, bloody red and gray of brain tissue exposed to the heat and the sun.

The heat was starting to get to him, along with the stench and a crazy kind of sensory overload. Just ahead, past a rocket-bottle joint, was a bar with its front doors open wide and some kind of slash-and-burn music blaring out into the street.

Carlucci stepped into the bar, almost blinded by the change in light. Light from the street came in behind him, casting strange shadows that mixed with the interior gloom and a jittery kaleidoscope of colored lights coming from the tiny stage. There was no band on the stage, just a couple of tall speakers and silhouette cutouts of four musicians.

The front section of the bar was a thick maze of tables, most of them full, with hardly enough room to walk among them. Booths lined the front windows, the glass tinted so dark almost no light came through them from outside. In the back was a long bar, also full. The people were all shouting at each other over the music.

Carlucci wondered how badly he wanted a beer. Badly enough. He worked his way through the tables and managed to squeeze into a spot at the bar. He leaned sideways against the Formica counter and scanned the room as he waited for the bartender. No sign of Mouse, but then he hadn't expected to see him; he was just hoping for a shot of absurd luck.

The bartender, a big, fat, ugly guy close to six and a half feet tall with a ponytail, stopped in front of Carlucci and squinted at him.

"A beer," Carlucci said. "Whatever you've got on tap."

The bartender cocked his head, then leaned forward until his face was only inches from Carlucci's. "I don't want you in here," he whispered.

"Why not?"

The bartender didn't answer, just shook his head and pulled back.

"I just want a beer," Carlucci said.

"I know what you are," the bartender said. But he stepped to the tap and pulled a beer into a large pint glass, then came back and set it in front of Carlucci. "Let's make it on the house."

"Let's not."

The bartender shook his head again. "Five bucks," he said. He took the money from Carlucci, stuck it in his shirt pocket, and moved down the bar.

Carlucci took several deep swallows. The beer wasn't very cold, and it didn't have much flavor, but any liquid cooler than the stifling heat was welcome. He drank some more.

Instead of turning around, he tried to scan the crowd by looking into the mirror on the back wall. But there were too few open spots on the mirror, and the lighting was so inconsistent that it was impossible. So he shifted around, leaned his back against the bar, and he got his absurd bit of luck: Mouse.

Mouse was just coming out of the back corner hall by the bathrooms, moving to the rapid beat of the music. Around his neck was a neuro-collar blinking green, presumably in time to his heartbeat. He smiled at people as he moved through the crowd, metal teeth flashing, slapping hands and heads. Someone scowled and flipped him off, and Mouse just laughed. He stopped at a table not far from Carlucci, leaned over, and slipped something into the front of a woman's blouse. The woman kissed Mouse on the cheek and bit his ear, and he moved on.

When it became clear that Mouse was headed for the front doors, Carlucci drained his beer, belched long and loud, then set his glass on the bar. He left another five on the counter, smiling to himself as he wondered if it would stay there long enough for the bartender to see it, then pushed off and headed casually toward the front entrance.

He was almost there when Mouse finally pushed through and out onto the street. Mouse glanced in both directions, then turned left. Carlucci squeezed past the last table, stepped out through the doors, and turned automatically left. And there was Mouse, just half a block away. Carlucci followed.

Although Mouse was as distinctive as they came, he was so short it was surprisingly difficult to keep him in sight. Carlucci would lose him for a minute or two at a time, then catch a glimpse, and not always where he expected. Mouse crossed the street once, so he was moving right along the boundary of the Tenderloin, but Carlucci stayed on this side. Mouse probably wasn't going into the Tenderloin, and if he did there would be no way to follow him. Mouse talked to someone in a beer kiosk, there was an exchange of money and packets, then Mouse came back across the street, now only twenty feet away.

Carlucci stayed with him to the end of the block, across the intersection, and along another half block. Then Mouse veered sharply to the left and disappeared from view. When Carlucci reached the spot where Mouse had disappeared, he was at the entrance to a narrow, filthy alley strewn with trash and shattered crates, lit as much by a couple of drum fires as by the light coming in from the street. Two men dressed in thrift store suits and ties stood in front of one drum fire, cooking large hunks of meat impaled on metal rods. The drum fire farther in was unattended, but burned brightly, casting flickering shadows up the alley walls.

Carlucci saw movement just past the second drum fire and caught a glimpse of Mouse's blinking neuro-collar. Hesitating for a few moments, he stood gazing into the alley, then shook his head and entered it.

"Hey!" said one of the men at the drum fire. "Got any barbecue sauce?"

The other man wheezed out a laugh, and Carlucci didn't reply. He nodded at the two men as he passed them, and they both laughed. The stench of
the cooking meat nauseated him.

The ground was covered with gravel and broken glass and potholes
filled with water and oil. He had to pay as much attention to his footing as
to the flickering lights and shadows in front of him.

When he reached the second drum fire, he stopped and searched the
gloom ahead. The alley appeared to dead-end about fifty or sixty feet farther on, the brick wall of the building on his left angling across to meet the
one on his right. There was one door on the left, some boarded windows,
and then on the right, up near the dead end, a break in the wall—a doorway
or alcove, or perhaps even a covered passage through to another alley or the
street. There was no sign of Mouse.

No, he was not that stupid. This was as far as he went. He didn't need
Mouse that badly.

Something slammed hard into his left shoulder, spinning him around
and knocking him to the ground. He tried to push himself up to his knees,
but his left arm collapsed under him, suddenly shot through with a hot,
searing pain. Confused for a few moments, he rolled onto his back and
scooted toward the alley wall, gaze darting around in search of his attacker.
No one was anywhere near him, but as the pain in his shoulder increased,
he finally realized what had happened: He'd been shot.

Shit.

How bad? He stopped for a moment and tried feeling around his left
shoulder with his hand. More pain, and lots of wet. He pulled his hand back
and looked at it. Shit again. Too goddamn much blood.

With his one good hand and arm he dragged himself to the alley wall,
then worked his way up into a sitting position. He hadn't heard the shot. Silenced? What the hell did it matter?

Christ, he wasn't thinking straight. He grabbed for the com unit on his
belt, pulled it free, and switched it on, pressing the emergency signal and
beacon. There was a faint crackle, and only a few seconds' wait before a
man's voice came on.

"Emergency response," he said.

"Officer down," Carlucci said. He didn't need to say any more, didn't
need to identify himself—his signal would do that.

"Lieutenant Carlucci?"

"Yes. I'm in real trouble here."

"Can you give me your location?" The beacon would work as a homing
device, but it would take time to lock on to it. The closer you could direct
them, the faster they could get there.

"The DMZ," Carlucci said. His heart sank as he said those words.
Christ, he didn't want to die here. "Near Polk . . ." Christ, what street had
he been on? What had he last crossed? He couldn't remember, he could

hardly think. "I'm in an alley," he managed to get out. "Off Larkin I think . . . ? Sutter . . . ?"

"Officers and aid cars rolling, Lieutenant. Stay with me now, all right?"

Carlucci got out a strangled laugh. "Sure. Where the hell am I going to go?"

He was almost directly across the alley from the drum fire, and he stared at the orange and yellow flames, watched the glow of embers inside the drum through small, jagged holes that had burned and rusted through the metal. The dispatcher was still talking to him, but he no longer paid any attention. He couldn't stay focused on anything but the flames.

Then he remembered the other drum fire, and he turned his head toward the mouth of the alley. He could see the two forms by the other drum fire, outlined by the light coming from the street, and he thought they were looking at him. But they were making no move to leave their cooking and approach him, which was just as well. He didn't need the kind of help they would offer.

". . . still with me, Lieutenant? Lieutenant? Come *on*, Lieutenant, say something."

"I'm still here," he finally managed to say, and he tried to focus back in on the dispatcher. He closed his eyes, hoping that would help. For a moment it seemed to, but with his eyes closed he felt an overpowering urge to drop off to sleep.

Then he heard movement off to his left, sensed a shadow, and he opened his eyes. Mouse was standing over him, grinning down at him with flashing metal teeth.

"Hey, Mr. Cop Man. I don't think you'll be needing this." His hand darted out and snatched the com unit from Carlucci's grip. He stepped back, then swung his boot forward and kicked Carlucci hard in the ribs.

Jesus Christ. Carlucci closed his eyes against the pain, against the sight of that nasty little prick standing over him. Binoche was right. He opened his eyes, tried to lurch up and grab for the com unit, but Mouse was too quick and jerked it out of the way.

"This what happens when you fuck around with the Mouse. Hah!" Mouse snapped his teeth at him.

Carlucci heard sirens, but there was no way to know if they were for him or not. Even if they were, they sounded too far away, they would never get here in time. And if Mouse walked away right now, even without doing anything else, if he took the com unit . . . Carlucci didn't know if anyone would be able to find him. He'd lie in this damn alley and bleed to death. Here in the fucking DMZ, for Christ's sake.

Suddenly Mouse jerked upright, eyes bulging. He took a single staggering step, then seconds later his face and forehead exploded, blood and flesh and bone splattering everywhere. The neuro-collar went crazy, flashing all kinds of colors as Mouse fell forward and collapsed across Carlucci, the com unit still gripped in his hand. Blood poured from what remained of Mouse's head, pooling on the ground next to Carlucci and soaking into his pants and shirt.

He tried to roll Mouse off of him, but he didn't have the strength. He was fading in and out. Mouse's neuro-collar was dead now, no lights at all. Carlucci tried for the com unit in Mouse's hand, but he couldn't reach it. He tried again to move Mouse, but still couldn't manage it.

His shoulder was going cold, and he could no longer feel anything in his left arm, his left hand. Blood was everywhere, slick and slippery, and the stink of it filled his nostrils, mixing with the stench of the cooking meat.

Sirens were getting louder. Or were they? Suddenly he couldn't hear them at all, he couldn't hear anything.

Then the sirens returned, loud and piercing, only to fade away once again.

This fucking place, he did not want to die here. The flames of the barrel fire seemed to grow, leaping upward, then out at him, licking him with their heat.

He tried to turn his head toward the mouth of the alley to see if anyone was coming, but when he did a shower of silver glitter washed over his vision. He let his head fall back, the glitter faded, and the flames returned.

There was a voice from the com unit, but he couldn't make out the words.

Sirens again. But they were too late, and it was all for nothing.

He closed his eyes and tried to hang on.

18

CAROLINE HAD IMAGINED the meeting would take place in the dead of night, in some dark, hidden subterranean room reached by endless and confusing twists and turns through dimly lit passages and guarded doorways. Instead, they met Rashida at midday, in the open courtyard of a three-story building.

A warm and steady rain had been falling since early morning. Caroline and Cage were led across the courtyard by a short man wearing jeans and sandals and a serape. Rashida, slim and dark with long black hair and dark brown eyes, was sitting at a table protected from the rain by a second-floor balcony. In front of her was a package of cigarettes, a stone lighter, and a beautifully worked turquoise and copper ashtray. She was smoking a cigarette, and nodded in greeting, asked them to sit down, then asked them if they wanted anything to drink.

"I can offer you coffee or tea, or lemonade," Rashida said. Her voice carried just the trace of an accent that Caroline couldn't identify, but assumed was Middle Eastern of some sort. "There is no alcohol here, but if you want, I can send Adolfo to buy some beer for you."

"Lemonade will be fine for me," Caroline said.

"The same for me," Cage added.

Rashida nodded at Adolfo. "Bring a pitcher."

Caroline looked around the courtyard. Across the way, sheltered from the rain by a large palm, a man squatted in front of a small brazier, cooking something on a grill suspended above the coals; from the smells that wafted across the courtyard, she guessed it was fish. Occasionally someone would come into the courtyard from one of several alcoves in the building, hurry through the rain, then enter one of the other alcoves. Two old women sat on a third-floor balcony down in the far corner, a tarp stretched over them from the roof to keep the rain off. The two women were drinking something from a dark brown bottle, small glasses in front of each of them. Every so often one of them cackled. Except for the steady clatter of the rain, the courtyard was fairly quiet, much quieter than the streets outside. Caroline was surprised that it could be so quiet anywhere inside the Tenderloin.

Beside her, Cage seemed antsy, constantly shifting positions in his chair, gaze darting in all directions. She wanted to put a hand on his shoulder or thigh, silently tell him to relax, but she thought that might embarrass him.

Adolfo reappeared, now wearing a wide-brimmed straw hat and carrying a tray with a large glass pitcher of lemonade and three ice-filled glasses. He set the tray on the table, filled all three glasses, then left.

Rashida put out her cigarette, then glanced back and forth between them. "I don't like this," she said. She sipped at her lemonade, then fixed her gaze on Caroline. "Cage tells me you want to meet with me. So tell me what you want."

"I need to get in touch with Cancer Cell," Caroline said. "Cage says you're involved with them. That you are a part of them, a member, whatever."

"Is that what Cage says?" Rashida shook her head. "I have nothing to do with Cancer Cell. I don't know anything about them, and I don't plan to learn anything about them. If that's why we're here, then this is all a waste of everyone's time." She sipped at her lemonade again, still shaking her head.

Caroline didn't say anything. She didn't know how to respond. She had nothing but Cage's word about Rashida, nothing to back herself up with, and she felt as if she'd been hung out to dry on this.

But Cage wasn't going to leave her there. He leaned forward, staring at Rashida. "Don't give me that crap," he said. "I *know* you're Cancer Cell."

Rashida smiled. "And how do you know that?"

"Tiger."

"Tiger?" Now she laughed, shaking her head. "I doubt Tiger even knows what Cancer Cell is."

"I doubt it, too," Cage agreed. "He doesn't know who he works for. But he works for you and Stinger, and I know Stinger, and Stinger's Cancer Cell, too. Or he was until he died."

Rashida continued to smile, but Caroline could see her struggling with it, and her eyes had gone hard.

"Yeah, I know he died, and I know you watched him die," Cage said.

No one said anything for a long time. Caroline was afraid Cage was going to push it, push at the way Stinger died, raise the question of what had killed him, and she realized she was holding her breath, trying to will Cage to let it go. She felt almost certain that if he pursued Stinger's death, it would be the end of this meeting, the end of their only chance.

But Cage didn't say any more about it. He slowly leaned back in his chair and drank from his own glass, then looked away, his attention shifting to the man who was cooking the fish.

Rashida had stopped smiling, and she turned to Caroline. "Why do you want to get in touch with Cancer Cell?"

"I have Gould's Syndrome."

Rashida nodded once, hesitated a moment, then said, "Okay. I'll ask it again. Why do you want to get in touch with Cancer Cell?"

Caroline took a deep breath, then answered. "There's no cure for what I've got. No treatment except for some symptom relief, nothing that really changes anything. And it's terminal. I'll probably be dead by the time I'm thirty, and no one can do anything about it." She shrugged. "But maybe Cancer Cell can. I have heard that they are out on the cutting edge of medicine, flying with experimental treatments, drug therapies. I am willing to offer up myself as an experimental subject in return for whatever Gould's Syndrome treatments Cancer Cell wants to try."

Rashida didn't reply at first, looking back and forth between them. She shook her head a couple of times, almost but not quite smiling, then she looked away. No one quite seemed to know what to say.

The rain had grown heavier and clattered loudly on metal canopies, plastic, the palm fronds, and the walkways. There was a cracking roll of thunder, and a few minutes later the rain became a deluge, dumping out of the sky. But that lasted only a minute or so, and then it let up until it was little more than a drizzle.

"Cage."

He looked at Rashida and said, "Yeah."

"You will leave now."

"What are you talking about?"

"Just what I said. This is as far as you go. You have nothing to do with this anymore. I'll talk to Caroline alone."

"And then what?"

She shook her head. "Good-bye, Cage."

"No, I'm not leaving now, I'm not leaving her alone here with you. I'm not leaving without knowing what's going to happen to her."

Caroline reached out for his arm, squeezed it. "Just go, Cage." She held his gaze, and nodded once. "Go on. You got me here. That's enough."

"It's *not* enough," he said, shaking his head.

"It has to be, Cage. It's *my* life, *my* disease. My risk. And I'll be fine."

He looked like he wanted to protest further, to argue some more with both of them, but he just shook his head again. He stood up from the chair, gripped Caroline's shoulder. "You take care of yourself."

"I will."

"And you . . ." he said, turning to Rashida. But he didn't say any more, just sighed, turned away, and hurried across the courtyard the way they had entered.

When he was out of sight, Caroline turned back to Rashida. "All right," she said. "It's just the two of us."

"I should have sent you away, too," Rashida said.

"Why didn't you?"

Rashida shook her head. She looked across the courtyard at the man who was cooking his fish over the coals, waited until the man glanced toward her, then signaled to him, holding up two fingers. The man nodded, did some things with plates and bottles, took some fish off the grill, and put more on. Then he stood up and hurried through the rain with two plates in his hand, crouching over to shield them. He set one plate in front of Caroline, the other in front of Rashida, then added napkins and forks.

"Thanks, Hernando."

Hernando nodded, then hurried back to his fire.

"Please," Rashida said. "Dig in. Hernando makes a great grilled fish. It's the sauce he brushes on." She began eating.

With her fork, Caroline cut a piece of the fish, watched the steam rising from it, and blew on it before putting it in her mouth. It was whitefish of some kind, very flaky and tender, and coated with a dark, sweet sticky sauce. Rashida was right, it was delicious.

They ate without talking, Rashida refilling both of their glasses. The rain continued to fall, but the air grew even warmer. At first, Caroline tried to figure out what was going on, what Rashida was trying to accomplish by sending Cage away, and then having the fish brought over. But she decided it didn't really matter. It was actually quite pleasant sitting here in the damp heat, listening to the rain fall all around them. She relaxed and let herself enjoy it.

When they had finished eating, Rashida signaled to Hernando again, who came and took away the plates. She lit a fresh cigarette, took a couple of deep drags on it, then looked at Caroline.

"You don't look like you have Gould's," she said. "How can I know for certain that you do?"

"The same way it was diagnosed in the first place. I'll be glad to give you a blood sample."

"You'll do more than that. You'll submit to a complete physical and we'll do the blood work and tox screens and whatever other testing we think is necessary."

"So you *are* with Cancer Cell," Caroline said.

"Better you just don't mention that name again," Rashida replied, and looked away. That was probably as close to an answer as Caroline would ever get.

Rashida finally turned back to her. "Has the Gould's even gone active yet? You look like you're doing fine."

"Yes, the Gould's has gone active. Just recently. Only one minor attack so far, but it was definite."

"But you might have years ahead of you of relatively good health. And you have no idea what's in store for you here, if we go ahead. *I* have no idea."

Caroline smiled. "You're making all the same arguments Cage made. He tried to talk me out of it, too." She paused. "I'm not sure I can explain it very well. But I know what the progression of this is like, and I don't look forward to it. Maybe if Can . . . if your people have something experimental they want to try, maybe the chances of it working will be better if I'm in the earlier stages. I'm just trying to give myself the best chance I can."

Rashida took a deep drag on her cigarette, then put it out, even though it was only half gone. "I have to be honest with you. I've never dealt with anyone with Gould's Syndrome before. I don't know if anyone has been doing any research on it, or has any treatment ideas. It's possible no one has anything, and that we *can't* do anything for you."

That was something that hadn't occurred to Caroline. But there was no point worrying about that now. "I understand," she said.

"Fine then," Rashida said. "We've got an exam room set up in the building here. We'll take care of that today. And we'll want you to stay here until the test results are in and I've had a chance to talk to people. Then we'll go from there."

"Okay. Let's go do it."

Rashida shook her head. "Not quite yet, if you don't mind. There's no hurry." She smiled. "I don't get out much. I'd like to just sit here a while, drink lemonade, smoke cigarettes, watch the rain, maybe have some more of Hernando's fish. Join me?"

"Sure," Caroline said, smiling back. "I'll skip the cigarettes." She leaned back in her chair, holding the glass of lemonade. She thought she should be apprehensive, maybe even frightened about what was to come. But she wasn't. She was very comfortable with Rashida, and she was, for the moment, quite content.

19

THE FIRST TIME Carlucci fully came to, it was night. He was on his back, surrounded by darkness except for a rectangle of light off to his left. He had the vague recollection of coming around maybe two or three other times, but he'd never been fully conscious, never completely realized what he realized right now: He was alive.

He felt almost giddy, despite the growing awareness of pain in his left shoulder and arm. Alive. He was alive, and Mouse was dead.

Where was he?

The room was dark, but his eyes were slowly adjusting to the darkness, and objects were becoming visible. He turned his head to the left, toward the rectangle of light—a doorway. He saw white walls, linoleum floors; then, at the far edge of his vision, hanging above him and to the right of the bed—he turned his head back to bring it in focus—reflecting the light from the hall, was a clear fluid bag hanging from a metal hook, with clear tubing running down and looping into his right arm.

Of course. He was in the hospital. Where else would he have been? He'd been almost afraid to find out.

He closed his eyes for a minute, tired from just that tiny exertion of looking back and forth and trying to decide where he was. Sounds filtered into the room now, sounds he hadn't noticed before—quiet, indistinct conversation; a squeaking wheel; a regular tapping sound, from outside the room but nearby; a gentle hum.

He opened his eyes again, and turning back to the right once more he could see the broken amber rays from a street light slashing in through the window blinds. Then there was a rustling sound, also from the right. He raised his head, fighting the vertigo, and looked over the side of the bed.

Andrea was asleep on a futon beside him, wrapped in a light blanket, her face on the pillow illuminated by bands of amber light. Her mouth, as usual, was partially open, and her hair was slicked to her cheek.

She was beautiful.

Seeing her brought a strange pressure to his heart and the beginnings of tears to his eyes. He lay back, gazing up at the blank, dark ceiling, and blinked back the tears.

He was alive.

He woke again later that same night. Nothing had changed. The hospital remained relatively quiet, though he heard someone pacing up and down the hall. Andrea was still asleep. A persistent, dull ache throbbed in his shoulder, but somehow he didn't mind it that much; the pain helped keep his head clear, and right now, in this dark peace and quiet, he wanted to think.

He wanted to think about who had shot him. Not Mouse. At first, right after he'd been shot, as he was crawling across the ground, scraping and cutting himself on the gravel and broken glass, he *had* thought Mouse was responsible. But Mouse had been in front of him, and he was pretty sure he'd been shot from behind. That was something he'd have to ask the doctor about. And then, of course, Mouse had been shot himself—he'd had his whole head blown off.

Carlucci thought about that some more, replaying what he could remember of that whole grisly scene. Two shots to Mouse, he thought. The first one that seemed to catch Mouse by surprise, then a few seconds later, with Mouse still standing, teetering above him, the one to his head.

Something blocked the light coming in through the doorway. Without turning his head, keeping his eyes half closed, he shifted his gaze to the left. Mostly what he could see was silhouette, but he recognized the uniform. Someone had stationed a cop outside his door. Carlucci didn't move, and a few moments later the cop backed out and moved out of sight. Carlucci could hear the creaking of a chair.

He almost laughed. Protection. Whoever had shot him in the DMZ wasn't likely to come after him in the department hospital.

He returned his thoughts to the shooting and the circumstances surrounding it. It was possible, he supposed, that the real target of the shooting had been Mouse, and he just got in the way. Or that no one in particular was the target, that it was just a random shooting—someone who saw two people in an alley in the DMZ and decided to shoot them. It wasn't an outrageous notion, though he had a hard time giving it much credence. It went against his training and experience—whenever a cop was shot, the assumption was always that the officer was either the intended target or got in the way of the commission of another crime.

He closed his eyes, having a difficult time focusing on the problem. His instinct was to assume that he had himself been the target, but did that really make sense? Could someone really have followed him, waiting for the opportunity, and taken it when he'd gone into the alley after Mouse? Or had he been set up by Mouse? That didn't make any sense either, since Mouse ended up with his head blown off. Besides, no one knew he was going to be in the DMZ, no one knew he was looking for Mouse.

Carlucci sighed heavily. He was going nowhere with this, just like the rest of the Naomi Katsuda case. In his gut, with no hard evidence to back it up, he believed there was a connection between the case and this shooting. But he couldn't at all make out what the connection was, and he had to admit that the whole idea seemed absurd on the surface. He closed his eyes and drifted quickly into sleep.

•   •   •

And the third time he woke, the room was full of light. Morning, he thought. A quiet, steady *click-click . . . click-click . . . click-click* came from the right. When he turned that way, he saw that the futon had been folded up into a small sofa, and Andrea was sitting in it, knitting. Knitting was something she did to relax, to keep her hands occupied; she'd taken it up when the two of them had quit smoking years earlier.

"Knitting booties for someone's new baby?" he said.

She looked up at him, gave him a huge smile. "Just a sec," she said. She made a note on her pattern, set the needles and sweater beside her, then got up and came over to him. She gripped his hand, squeezed, then leaned forward and kissed him. When she pulled back from him, he could see the tears welling in her eyes. "Hey, stranger," she said. She squeezed his hand again. "How are you feeling?"

He smiled. "Like somebody shot me." Then he shook his head. "I feel okay, I guess. Thirsty."

She poured a cup of water, held it for him while he drank through a straw. He drank all of it, she refilled the cup, and he drank a little more. Then he let his head fall back on the pillow, feeling a bit woozy, the cold water settling hard in his gut. "Thanks," he said.

She found an open spot on the bed and scooted up onto it beside him, taking his hand in hers again. "Jesus, you had me worried for a while, Francesco."

"How close was it?"

She slowly shook her head from side to side. "Too damn close. You'd lost so much blood by the time they got to you . . ." She brushed a couple of tears from her cheek. "The first ten or fifteen years you were a policeman I used to worry, I used to think about it a lot. But after a while I stopped worrying, because nothing ever seemed to happen to you."

"Just as well," he said. "Worrying wouldn't have prevented this from happening."

"But it might have eased the shock. I was just stunned when I heard. It was so unexpected, Frank. I . . . I was paralyzed." Tears were starting up again.

A uniformed cop appeared in the doorway, a young, beefy guy, hardly more than a kid. He looked nervous, hesitant about actually entering the room.

"Lieutenant?" the cop said.

"Yes?"

"Are you feeling up to talking? I'm supposed to let the investigating officers know when you come around, so they can talk to you."

"Who are they?"

"Uh, Younger and Oko— Okokr—"

Carlucci smiled at the young man's struggle. "Okoronkwo," he said.

The cop nodded. "Yes. Sorry, sir."

"That's all right. Go ahead and put the call in, but ask them to give me a couple of hours. But before you do that, I want you to put a call through to Detectives Santos and Weathers, tell them I need to talk to them. I want to talk to them *first*."

"You got it, sir." He backed away and walked down the hall.

"Toni and Ruben came in a couple of times to see how you were doing," Andrea said. "You're working on a case with them that has something to do with you being shot?"

He shrugged, and winced with the pain. "I don't know. It's possible."

"The Naomi Katsuda case?"

"Yes."

Andrea shook her head. "Then leave it to Ruben and Toni. Stay out of it. It's nearly gotten you killed."

He cocked his head, tried to look puzzled. "I'm sorry, did you say something?"

Andrea just shook her head again. She gave his hand another squeeze. "I better go call Christina. She's spent a lot of time here, but she's home right now. I promised I'd call her as soon as you came around."

"Yeah, I'd like to see her. What about Caroline?"

"I don't know," she said, frowning. She hesitated. "I haven't been able to get hold of her. No answer at her place. I've left messages, but haven't heard back from her."

"How long *has* it been?"

"A couple of days."

Carlucci didn't know what to say. He could feel the fear and panic rising in his gut. He closed his eyes and tried to breathe slowly and deeply. Caroline. For years he had worried about her because of the Gould's. Every time anything out of the ordinary happened, he worried. He'd never been able to control it. It was something that drove everyone in the family crazy, *especially* Caroline. So maybe he was overreacting again now. But when he opened his eyes and looked into Andrea's face, he knew he wasn't.

"Call Bernie," he told her. Bernie Guilder was a captain in the department, and Carlucci had known him his entire career.

"I already did," Andrea said. "He's started working on it. I'd hoped something would have come up by the time you came around."

"All right, all right. I'm sure . . ." But he stopped, realizing how stupid it was. "Go call Christina."

She nodded, slid off the bed, and gave his hand one more squeeze. "I'll be right back."

Then she left, and Carlucci was alone with his fear.

20

CAGE HATED HOSPITALS. Strange thing for a doctor, but there it was. When he was actually working it wasn't so bad; he had too much to think about. But when he wasn't acting as a doctor, when he was visiting a friend or relative who was a patient, his skin itched all over, and he broke out in a sweat.

He felt that way now, standing at the top of the stairs and looking down the long, bright hallway toward Carlucci's room. What didn't help was not knowing why Carlucci had called him. There was also the desire to go down to the second floor immediately, where Nikki was—he desperately wanted to see her, talk to her doctor again, but he wanted to get this visit to the lieutenant out of the way first.

He took a deep breath and started walking. A third of the way along the hall a cop sat outside a door, and Cage headed directly for her, figuring that was Carlucci's room. Of course with the all the security checks people had to go through every time they entered the hospital, that cop was probably unnecessary.

The cop stood as he approached. She was a tall, stunningly beautiful woman who looked like she could tear him apart without breaking a sweat, and he resisted the urge to salute. But he did check the room number on the wall beside her. Yes, it was Carlucci's room. The door was open a few inches, but he couldn't really see inside.

"I'm here to see Lieutenant Carlucci," he said.

"And you are?"

"Dr. Cage."

The cop smiled. "Am I supposed to believe that?"

"Believe it, Tretorn." It was Carlucci's voice from inside the room. "Has he got a stupid-looking tattoo of a snake on his neck?"

"Yes, sir." She continued smiling, not at all flustered by Carlucci's response.

"That's him, then. Let him in."

The cop raised an eyebrow, still amused, and gestured with her head toward the door. "You heard the lieutenant. Go right in."

"You aren't going to escort me into the room?" Cage asked.

She shook her head. "I don't think so."

She settled back in the chair, watching him and still smiling. He walked past her, then pushed open the door and entered the room. Carlucci was sitting up in the bed, his left arm in a sling, his shoulder heavily bandaged. Sitting in a chair was a woman about fifty, whom Cage assumed was Carlucci's wife, and standing on the other side of the bed was a young woman, probably about twenty, who looked a lot like a younger version of Caroline. Another daughter.

"Cage. This is my wife, Andrea, and my daughter Christina. And this is Cage. Dr. Cage."

He shook Andrea's hand and nodded to Christina. "How are you doing?" he asked Carlucci.

"I'm getting the hell out of here tomorrow," he said. "My doctor would like me to stay put for another two or three days, but I'm going crazy in this place."

"That's good. Better to get out and moving around as soon as you can."

"You going to see Nikki?"

Cage nodded. "Yeah. As soon as I'm done here."

"How is she?"

"The same, I guess. Not so good."

Carlucci looked back and forth at his wife and daughter. "Christina, Andrea, could you both go out in the hall for a few minutes? I need to talk to Cage privately."

They gave Carlucci kisses and good-byes, saying they'd be right back, then left. Andrea was careful to completely close the door behind her.

Carlucci adjusted his position on the bed, scooting himself up straighter. "I'm worried about my other daughter," he finally said.

"Sorry?"

"Caroline. The one who was Tito Moraleja's friend."

"Oh, right."

"She's missing."

"Missing?" Cage felt a terrible twinge of guilt.

Carlucci nodded. "For several days now. We haven't been able to get in touch with her at all. We've left messages she's never answered. Andrea's been by her apartment, and there's no sign of her being there recently. I've got some people in the department checking things out, but nothing's turned up."

"So why am *I* here?"

"I'm worried, Cage. I want you to keep your ear to the ground. She was pretty upset by Tito's death, and an old friend of mine who used to be a cop told me that Caroline had recently asked him about a way into the Tenderloin. I'm afraid she may have gone in there with the crazy idea of trying to figure out what happened to Tito."

He dug through a pile of stuff on the little table beside him, found a photograph, and held it out to Cage. Cage stepped forward and took it from him. It was a picture of Caroline sitting in the sun, smiling, eyes squinting against the light.

"That's her," Carlucci said. "You're on the streets inside. Keep a look out for her. I know it's a lot, but maybe ask around some." He paused. "You said you owed me, remember?"

Cage nodded, the guilt ratcheting up a bit. But he couldn't say anything to Carlucci. He had promised.

"I'll do what I can," Cage said.

"Thanks, I really appreciate it." He paused. "Let me ask again. Just the two of us. How *is* Nikki?"

"I don't know. In bad shape, I guess." Cage really didn't want to talk about it. "Her chances aren't good."

"I'm sorry," Carlucci said.

Ten minutes later Cage stood outside Nikki's room, waiting for Dr. Verinder Sodhi to show, panic rising in his chest again. He could see her through the rectangular window cut into the large wooden door. Nothing had changed. She still appeared to be asleep, her eyes closed, bits of hair damp and slicked to her face.

"Doctor Cage?"

Cage stepped back from the door and turned toward the voice. A short, dark-skinned, dark-haired man approached him, hand out. Cage shook Dr. Sodhi's hand.

"How's she doing?"

Dr. Sodhi shrugged, then shook his head. "The same, I'm afraid. No improvement."

"And you still don't know what it is she's got?"

"No, I'm sorry, I'm afraid not. We've been doing the testing right here in our labs, and so far we have not made a positive hit. I have taken the liberty of sending some blood samples to the CDC, with a rush notice, but I would not put much hope in that. We will be lucky if they do any testing within a month."

"She'll be dead by then."

Dr. Sodhi pursed his lips and tilted his head. "Or she will have survived. That, too, is a possibility. Besides, we are continuing our own testing. We may yet have some luck."

"Sure. Of course, even if you identify the disease or condition, you still may not be able to do a damn thing."

"That is true, Dr. Cage. But it may tell us *exactly* what to do. And even if not, it may help us focus the treatment."

Dr. Sodhi seemed so calm about the whole thing. But then it wasn't someone *he* loved dying in that room. Cage blew out a deep breath and shook his head to himself. He knew he wasn't being fair. "What *is* the current treatment?" he asked.

"We have been dosing her heavily with broad-spectrum antibiotics, but they do not seem to have had any benefit as of yet. If we had time, of course, we could try a number of courses of more specific antibiotics."

"But we don't have that time."

"Probably not. And of course, if it is a *virus,* which is my own inclination at this point, no antibiotic will be any good at all. We have also tried anti-fungals, but again without success."

There was a sudden flurry of activity around them, several medical personnel hurrying past and into a room two doors down. Cage tried to ignore the commotion, which had not distracted Dr. Sodhi in the least.

"All right. Antibiotics aren't doing any good, and if it is a virus, well, the reality is most of the antivirals are shit, no matter what their makers claim. Do we agree on that?"

Dr. Sodhi nodded with a faint smile. "I would sooner trust in prayer."

"So what *is* being done for Nikki? Anything?"

"Yes. We are constantly chasing her electrolytes. Her body cannot seem to maintain the proper balance. Every three hours we recheck her chems, and we change her drips accordingly."

"So what's the real problem?"

Dr. Sodhi pursed his lips again and frowned with his eyes. "Most of her major organ function is deteriorating. Kidneys, liver, also the pancreas. Her heart seems to be holding up, but not much else. We have even been forced to resort to a round of dialysis."

"What the hell is going on?"

"We've done MRIs. Her organs are . . . disintegrating."

"Christ." He turned away from Dr. Sodhi and looked in through the window at Nikki. She didn't look as if she was dying, but he knew she was. "What's the prognosis?" he asked, still looking at her.

"She is hanging on, but I truly do not know how much longer she can go on this way." There was a long pause, then Dr. Sodhi said, "She is not the only one dying like this."

Cage froze for a moment, his heart suddenly banging away at the inside of his ribs. He kept his gaze on Nikki for a few moments longer, then slowly turned back to Dr. Sodhi.

"What do you mean?"

Dr. Sodhi looked distinctly unhappy. "It is difficult to know for sure, of course, since we do not know what this is, and so have no way to positively identify it. But I have been talking with some of my colleagues—sorry, *our* colleagues—and I have heard of several similar cases. Most have some direct connection to the Tenderloin."

"How the hell do you know that?"

"I asked. Ms. Hester got sick in the Tenderloin, and as far as we know contracted it there, yes? From a man who also lived there. So I just asked. But there are so few cases right now, and no one knows what it is. Still, the illness is bad enough that doctors are starting to ask questions."

Cage shook his head. "But no one's getting any answers."

Dr. Sodhi sighed. "No, no one is getting answers."

Cage turned back once more to the window. "I'd like to see her, if it would be all right. Talk to her, if I can."

"It's possible. Sometimes she is coherent, sometimes not. But please, wear a mask and gloves when you go in, and dispose of them properly when you leave. You must know how important that is." The small man suddenly looked quite sad.

Cage nodded. "Thanks, Dr. Sodhi."

He opened the door to Nikki's room and stepped inside, wearing gown, gloves, and mask as Dr. Sodhi had insisted. The panicky feeling returned, and he breathed very slowly and deeply, fighting it down. When he felt he was back in control, he took the last couple of steps to the bed, his knees brushing against the metal frame.

Nikki appeared flushed, her skin and hair damp. The head of the bed was packed with monitors blinking in various colors, and Cage had to concentrate to avoid checking each of them individually, to avoid running his own diagnostic exam on her. She was not his patient, and he did not really want to treat her as one. He was sure he could do no better than Dr. Sodhi, and he wanted to be with Nikki as a friend, not as her doctor.

"Cage." The voice was a whisper. Her eyelids fluttered, then opened slightly, and she managed a faint, barely discernible smile.

"Hey, Nikki."

"I'm still alive."

"Yes, you are."

"I feel like shit." She coughed, and the smile twisted into a grimace of pain. She closed her eyes; her entire face was tight with the pain.

He took her hand in his, and her fingers gave a weak squeeze. Several moments passed, then the pain seemed to ease, and her face muscles relaxed a bit. But she did not open her eyes.

"Nikki?"

She opened her eyes. "I'm still here."

There was a long silence. Cage did not know what to say, and Nikki probably didn't have the energy to speak much, even if she wanted to. There was a padded chair against the wall, and he let her hand go, then pulled the chair over next to the bed. He sat facing her and took her hand once again in his. He could feel the warmth of her skin through the thin glove.

With the door closed, the room was very quiet. There was pulsing light from the monitors, but mercifully the volume had been turned off. The temperature was surprisingly comfortable, cooler than outside, but not cold the way air-conditioned rooms and buildings so often felt. But the room felt terribly empty—there were no signs of visitors, family, or friends. No flowers, no cards, no books or magazines or bubble messages. As if Nikki had never been here, or had already gone.

"I told you that guy Stinger was an asshole," she said.

"You were right. But he's a dead asshole." And immediately regretted saying it.

"I will be, too," she replied. "Dead, not an asshole."

"No, you won't."

"Cage, please, don't."

"I'm not, Nikki. You saved my life. It's my turn to save yours."

She smiled, but closed her eyes and slowly moved her head from side to side. "Not in this life," she said. "Maybe in the next."

"Nikki . . ." But he didn't know what else to say. She was right, and he couldn't stand it.

"I *do* think there's some other kind of life after this one," she said. Her voice was quiet, but strong. She opened her eyes, but she didn't look at him, just gazed up toward the ceiling. "Maybe reincarnation of some sort." She paused. "No, actually, that's an idea I kind of like, but not one that really *feels* right."

"What feels right?" he asked her.

"Survival of the spirit. Our consciousness. Not heaven, no angels or God or anything, but our spirits continuing on in some way, aware, and still connected a little to this world."

"Like ghosts?"

She smiled. "A little. Just there, just barely there so people sense our presence without knowing what it is they're feeling. Like a shiver of memory."

She didn't say anything else for a long time, and Cage realized that she very much believed what she had just said, and that it gave her a certain amount of comfort. She was having an easier time facing the idea of death, her own death, than he was.

"I'll come back and haunt you," she said, finally turning to look at him. "In a good way. When you feel something, that shiver of memory, don't be afraid of it. It'll be me."

Cage didn't know what to say. He wanted to tell her she wasn't a ghost yet, but she would say she would be soon, and then he'd say no, and then she'd get pissed at him again for trying to deny what they both knew was the truth—that she was dying, and there was nothing anyone could do. And he did not want to face that.

She squeezed his hand. "Let it go, Cage. Let *me* go."

He slowly shook his head. "I can't, Nikki. I just can't."

21

CAROLINE STOOD AT the open window of the room they had given her on the fourth floor, and looked out on the courtyard below. The sun was shining down through a hazy sky, baking the building and the courtyard; late morning, and already it was hot, though there was a slight breeze that came in through the window. Across the way, in the shade of a palm, Hernando crouched over his brazier of coals, just as he had two days earlier. This time he was cooking long, thin strips of dark meat. Hernando had spent much of the past two days there at his grill, cooking meat and fish and sometimes vegetables. Periodically he would fill a plate or two and disappear into the building. Other times people came to him with their own plates, which he loaded with food. He drank beer steadily as he cooked, one bottle after another. He seemed quite content.

Caroline, too, felt content, despite having been kept in this room for two days, effectively a prisoner. Two days with little to do, nowhere to go, and no responsibilities. Two days to read and doze and think. And she'd begun to rethink what she wanted out of all this.

The room was small, maybe ten feet square, with a bed, a stuffed chair, a very old dresser with empty drawers that smelled of cedar. Rashida had sent someone to Caroline's apartment to pick up a few changes of clothes, toiletries, and half a dozen books. Caroline wasn't locked in the room, and she had free access to the bathroom and shower down the hall one way, and the kitchen down the hall in the other direction. But there was always someone with her, watching her door, joining her in the kitchen, standing outside the bathroom waiting for her to emerge. She really didn't mind.

Rashida came several times to visit, and they talked about a lot of things, but never about Cancer Cell or experimental treatments or any of that. Sometimes she stayed for an hour or two, and they would go to the kitchen and have tea, or a bite to eat, and sit at the table, talking. Caroline had the feeling Rashida was lonely, that she didn't get out in the real world much. She liked Rashida, and she thought Rashida liked her.

She saw Rashida enter the courtyard from the street gate. Rashida glanced up at the window, then walked over to Hernando. She spoke to him for a few minutes, then crossed the courtyard and disappeared into one of the alcoves. A couple of minutes later there was a quiet knock, the door opened, and Rashida stepped into the room.

She stood just inside the door for a moment, watching Caroline, then walked over to the chair and sat in it, crossing her legs. "Testing's completed," she said.

"And?"

"You have Gould's."

Caroline smiled. "Did you expect anything else?"

"No. But we had to be certain."

"So do I start on some experimental treatment program?"

"It's not that simple," Rashida said. "There's a lot we have to talk about first."

Caroline nodded. She went over to the bed and sat on it, her back propped by the pillow against the wall. "Then let's talk."

"Your father's a cop."

"Yes, he is. Does that make a difference?"

"It makes some people suspicious."

"He doesn't know I'm here. He doesn't know I approached you, and he wouldn't approve if he did know."

Rashida smiled. "I'm sure that would be convincing to those who are suspicious."

"It doesn't sound like *you're* suspicious."

"I'm not. Not about that, anyway. I believe you. But I am suspicious about plenty of other things. And I'm suspicious about you."

"Why?"

Rashida shook her head, still smiling. "I'm not sure."

"Then were do we go from here?"

"That's up to you. I talked to people while we were waiting for the testing to wrap up. No one's done anything specifically with Gould's. But there is someone who has been doing research on other neurological disorders, working on possible treatment approaches, and he's quite interested in seeing you. Working with you." She grinned. "He'd love to get his hands on you."

Caroline nodded to herself, thinking. She'd planned to wait until farther along to present her proposal, but maybe this was the best time.

"How much would he love to get his hands on me?"

"I'm not sure what you mean."

"I'd like something in return for giving myself over to you and this man who wants to turn me into a lab animal."

Rashida frowned, sitting forward. "What is this? I thought what you were getting was a chance at a cure."

"That's not really very likely though, is it? Realistically, the best that can be hoped for is that maybe someone will learn a little something new about Gould's. Maybe a new direction to look in, maybe eliminate a few approaches. The reality is, I am almost certainly still going to die in a few years." She paused, and when Rashida didn't respond, she said, "Isn't that the most likely outcome of all this?"

Rashida eventually nodded. "Yes, that's most likely what will happen. So what is it you want?"

"I have a friend. Two friends, actually, a mother and daughter. The daughter, who's eleven years old, has leukemia. Two courses of chemotherapy have been ineffective. The leukemia has come back each time. Her only hope is a bone marrow transplant, either from a compatible donor, or with artificial marrow. They have no insurance, no money, so no one will do it. They're living in a death house in the DMZ, and the girl is going to die in a few months."

"And you want us to give her a bone marrow transplant."

"Yes."

Rashida shook her head. "That's a hell of a lot to ask for. It's expensive, time-consuming, with all the follow-up necessary. I doubt they'll go for it."

"I'm giving a lot in return," Caroline argued. "Several years of being a human guinea pig."

"And how do we know that? How do we know that once we've done the bone marrow transplant you won't just pull out?"

"You won't let me. You people are very persistent about tracking down people who don't honor the contracts they've made with you, persistent about forcing them to honor those contracts."

Rashida shook her head again, frowning. "You know way too much about us. How is that?"

"From Cage. He never thought this was a good idea, and he wanted me to know as much as possible about what I might be getting into. That's all. He tried to convince me to drop this."

Rashida sighed heavily. "I'm still suspicious. I like you, Caroline, but I don't trust you." She paused. "It doesn't matter for right now. I can't make that kind of decision. I'll need to talk to people, and there will be a lot of discussion, and frankly there's no way of knowing which way it will come down."

"Can we proceed with the rest of it until then?" Caroline asked.

"We'd better. Arrangements have been made, and if you back off now, there's a good chance this would be the end of it. You'd never hear from us again."

"Then let's do it. I'm willing to take my chances."

"And if we don't agree to do the bone marrow transplant for your friend?"

"I still have my own life at stake. And maybe there will be another favor I can ask."

"I wouldn't ask too many, if I were you. We are not in the business of handing out favors."

Caroline nodded. This whole thing was getting a little absurd, she thought. She really had no fear, but she was seriously beginning to question the notion that she had much chance of learning anything about Tito's death. Even if she ended up in the Core, they weren't going to be giving her free access to their facilities, she wasn't going to have long conversations with these people during which they would reveal all the Cancer Cell secrets, including what had happened to Stinger and Tito. But she still believed there was at least a chance, and that was worth something.

"So what's next?" she asked.

"Are you ready? To make a commitment right now, with no promises made about your friend? There is no going back after this. As you said, we do whatever is necessary to enforce our contracts. And we don't have much sympathy for extenuating circumstances."

"I'm as certain as I will ever be. That'll have to be good enough."

"Okay." Rashida stood.

"I'd like to call my parents before we go, let them know I'm okay. They're probably worried, they probably think I've disappeared."

Rashida shook her head. "I can't let you do that."

Caroline wanted to ask her why not, but figured that was pointless. So she tried something else. "Can you at least get in touch with Cage, ask *him* to call my parents?"

"Maybe. I'll think about it. Ready?"

Caroline nodded and stood. "Ready."

"I hope you're not claustrophobic."

Two hours later, Caroline was being carefully packed into a long, wooden box that looked uncomfortably like a cross between a casket and a shipping crate for weapons. The sides were lightly padded with foam rubber, and it was a tight fit. Rashida assured her that there would be plenty of air—the box was not airtight—but they gave her a mask and a small oxygen cylinder, and showed her how to switch it on. Just in case.

Rashida waved good-bye to her, smiling, then they placed the top on and screwed it down.

Rashida was probably right. Caroline could see tiny cracks of light above and around her. The wood smell was strong, combined with the odor of oil and something musty. She wondered what this crate had last been used for. Transporting someone else like her? She closed her eyes and tried to sleep.

It was hopeless, of course. Nothing happened for a long time, then she felt herself being lifted, carried a short distance, then set down. Then she was moving again, on a wheeled cart of some kind. She felt every bump, ever crack in the ground.

At first she thought she should try to keep track of her movements, her changes in direction, her trips up or down staircases. But she almost laughed aloud at the absurdity of it. That was even more hopeless than trying to sleep.

After a while, the wheeled cart stopped, and she was lifted again and carried a short distance before being raised and then lowered. Then all the cracks went dark as she heard a loud thud.

There was only silence and darkness for a long while. She lost track of time, almost dozed off. Then she felt a vibration, an engine, maybe, and she moving again.

It went on for more than an hour, though it was difficult to judge the passage of time. Moving, stopping, rolling, lifted up and set down, bumping along, crashing into a wall. The padding helped a little at first, but as time went on she felt more sharply each bounce, each rattle, each accidental drop by her carriers.

Finally the movement stopped, and she could hear the squeal of the screws being undone above her. A few minutes later, the top came off. Rashida looked in.

"You okay?"

Caroline nodded. Rashida took her hand and helped pull her up out of the box. She was in a small, windowless room. The walls and ceiling were concrete block, the floor was concrete, and all of the surfaces were painted a bright soft white. In one corner was a sink and a toilet, in another was a small mattress with blankets and pillows. A wooden rocking chair and an empty wooden bookcase leaning against the wall were the only other furnishings in the room.

"Where am I?" Caroline asked.

Rashida just laughed. She pointed at a brown duffel bag on the floor next to the crate. "Your books and clothes and things are in there," she said. "It's not much. And the door will be locked. So try and make yourself comfortable. This will be your home for a while."

22

HIS LEFT ARM in a sling, his shoulder bandaged and taped, Carlucci entered the Mishima building just before midnight. He still felt weak, and he had only been out of the hospital for two days, but he wasn't going to let this interview with Yoshi Katsuda wait any longer.

One of the guards at the front security desk studied his ID card and badge while another ran portable detectors over his body. A third guard stood a few feet back, the blinking lights on his armor showing a full charge. The first guard ran the card and badge through a scanner, and the second made a thorough but gentle search of the sling and bandage. When they were satisfied, they gave him a special access card for the express elevator that ran to the top floor. The second guard escorted him to the far end of the elevator banks, then waited until Carlucci used the access card and stepped inside. The guard was still standing there as the doors closed.

The ride to the top was smooth and fast, acceleration and deceleration only barely noticeable. Once the elevator had stopped, Carlucci had to use the access card once again to activate the doors. They opened in near silence, and he stepped out.

The reception area was large, with pale carpeting, the walls and ceilings the color and texture of beach sand. There were low couches and chairs, and several planters with bonsais. Sitting at the reception desk across the room was a woman with a silver metal face. One ear was flesh, but the other, like the rest of the woman's face, was metal. It had to be real, because Mishima would never allow *Faux Prosthétique,* which had been quite the fashion rage a few years earlier, on any of its employees. The shining metal contoured to her skull had to be the woman's real face.

He approached the desk in a hush of quiet.

"Lieutenant Carlucci." The woman's voice, emerging through segmented metal lips, was cool and smooth. "Mr. Katsuda is waiting for you." Her tongue and teeth appeared to be real, as did the eyes looking out at him.

To her left, the wall swung open. When he hesitated, the woman said, "You may enter now."

He walked through the opening, and the wall swung closed behind him. Katsuda's office was enormous, on the building corner, and the two exterior walls were floor-to-ceiling glass. Katsuda stood at one of the glass walls, looking out onto the city. Against the wall to Carlucci's right was a long, dark wooden desk, the top surface shining in the light from two small, shaded lamps on either end. They were the only lights on in the room.

Yoshi Katsuda turned to him. "Lieutenant, have you ever been in this office before?"

"No."

Katsuda nodded. "Come and see the view then," he said. "It is, I have to say, quite spectacular."

Carlucci joined him at the wall of glass. Katsuda was thin and almost as tall as Carlucci. He wore a tailored, dark silk suit, a white shirt, and a simple black tie. Since he was Naomi Katsuda's father, he had to be in his sixties, or even older, but his skin was so smooth, and there was very little silver in his dark hair; he looked easily ten or fifteen years younger.

Carlucci looked out through the window. Katsuda was right about the view. The lights of the city below them were bright and shiny, flickering silver and blue and amber, with other red and silver lights of vehicles swirling everywhere. The city looked brilliant and alive in the night, the filth and poverty and decay effectively camouflaged by the darkness and the gleam of the lights. Out across the water, in the bay, Alcatraz was a blaze of flood-lights and swirling neon. The casinos out on the former island prison had re-opened a few months earlier, and the island docks were aswarm with luxury boats. To the left was the Golden Gate Bridge, beautiful as always, un-changed over the decades, a stunning lattice of amber and crimson lights spanning the entrance to the bay.

As if noticing the sling and bandages for the first time, Katsuda said, "I see you've been injured."

"Someone tried to kill me," Carlucci said.

"But I see they did not succeed. Are you recovering well from it?"

"Oh, sure. I'm doing just fine."

"I am pleased to hear it."

"Thanks for asking." Carlucci took a deep breath. "Mr. Katsuda, I want to talk to you about a murder attempt that was more successful."

"My daughter."

"Yes, your daughter."

"You met with my daughter a few weeks ago."

Carlucci was taken by surprise, and didn't immediately reply, wonder-ing how Katsuda had known. Had his daughter told him about the meeting? Unlikely. Naomi Katsuda had been so circumspect about everything.

"Yes, I did meet with her. How did you know?"

"I could say that she told me about the meeting," Katsuda said, "but that would not be the truth." He gestured with his hand toward the two chairs near the other glass wall. "I think we'll be more comfortable if we sit," he said. "We will still have the view."

They walked over to the chairs and sat. "Can I get you anything to drink?" Katsuda asked. "I am sure we can provide you with whatever you like."

Carlucci smiled. "Yeah, I'm sure you can. But I don't want anything."

Katsuda nodded. "I, too, will pass." Then, resuming their discussion, he said, "We are a very influential and powerful family, which makes us the targets for any number of people—radical groups, criminals, even business competitors. Our security personnel have a directive to know where any of us are at any time, so that protection can be provided if it becomes neces-sary."

"I see." Carlucci paused, feeling a tiny rush of tension. "Is the surveil-lance around the clock?"

Katsuda hesitated before answering. "Yes," he finally said. "Why do you ask?"

"Where were the security personnel when your daughter was killed?"

Katsuda closed his eyes for a moment, then opened them again. "Trying to find her. Naomi didn't like being followed, even if it was for her own protection. That was the main reason she moved out of our home. And she became quite good at losing the surveillance. That night, she had again been successful. And it cost her her life."

"I'm sorry for your loss," Carlucci said, trying very hard to sound sincere. He did not like Yoshi Katsuda, and he had trouble believing the man was grieving over the death of his daughter.

"Thank you, Lieutenant. Now, shall we proceed with the official interview?"

Carlucci shrugged. "This is *all* a part of the interview," he said. "But before we go any farther, I want to know something. Why have you refused to talk to the investigating officers?"

Katsuda waved his right hand, a gesture of dismissal. "It was inconvenient. I did not want to talk to them."

"But they were investigating the death of your daughter."

"I could not help them. There was no point."

"You can't know that, Mr. Katsuda."

"Yes, Lieutenant Carlucci, I can know that. My security personnel had lost her that night, and I did not know where she was. I have no idea why anyone would want to kill her. There is no way I could help in the murder investigation of my daughter. And as I said earlier, it was inconvenient. I did not want to speak with them, and so I didn't." He paused. "I will be frank with you, Lieutenant. I have no faith in this city's police department. I do not believe they will solve my daughter's murder. I do not believe they will even come close. I did not want to waste my time with them." He paused again. "Power and influence can be extremely useful, and I use both freely."

Well, at least there's no bullshit from Katsuda about that. But that didn't mean the man wasn't hiding something about the case.

"Why are you talking to me, then?" Carlucci asked.

"I have been advised that it was in my best interest to speak with someone about the case. I have been advised that unless I did, the constant and rather annoying requests for interviews would not cease. Eventually, I was told, I might even become the subject of a subpoena. You are the supervising officer of the case. You are a lieutenant, a superior officer in the department. I prefer to speak with you."

Too good to deal with the peons, Carlucci thought, wanting very much to come out and say it. But it wouldn't be helpful.

"Do you know why your daughter met with me?" he asked.

Katsuda shrugged. "You asked her to." Telling him that the Mishima phone lines, too, were under surveillance, although that didn't come as a surprise.

"Do you know what we talked about?"

"No, but I can guess. My daughter had an obsession with a group of medical terrorists called Cancer Cell. I can think of nothing else she was involved with that would be of any interest to the police."

"She was involved with Cancer Cell?"

Katsuda shook his head. "Poor choice of words. The earlier phrasing is more accurate. An obsession. She was fascinated by them, and did what she could to learn about them. I tried to discourage her in this, but she was quite stubborn."

"What do *you* know about Cancer Cell?"

Katsuda gave a sigh of exasperation. A warning, Carlucci guessed. "I don't know anything about them. They were my daughter's obsession, not mine. They seemed dangerous. I avoid danger whenever possible."

Carlucci didn't push it. He didn't think he was going to come away from this interview with much, but he wanted every chance he had, and he wanted it to go as far as possible. He took a copy of the sketch artist image from his coat pocket, awkwardly unfolded it with his right hand, then leaned forward and held it out to Katsuda. Katsuda took the picture and studied it for a few moments, then looked up.

"Do you recognize her?"

Katsuda handed the picture back to Carlucci. "She looks vaguely familiar. Who is she?"

"We think a friend of your daughter's. A close friend."

Katsuda stared at him for a minute, his gaze unblinking. "My daughter was not a lesbian."

"I didn't say she was." Toni Weathers was right. There was something odd about this.

"You certainly implied it, Lieutenant."

"It's a possibility, that's all."

"No." Katsuda crisply shook his head, his eyebrows furrowed. "It is not a possibility."

He held up the picture again, moved it closer to Katsuda. "You don't know her."

"No. As I said, the picture is familiar. If she was a friend of my daughter's, I may have met her, or seen her at some time. But I do not know her."

Carlucci refolded the picture and stuck it back in his jacket. "So you don't think we can solve your daughter's murder?"

"No."

"Is it just your daughter's murder, or do you think the police are generally incapable of solving crimes?"

"I believe they are generally ineffective." Katsuda smiled. "I am just being frank, Lieutenant. If a major crime is committed on camera, or in front of numerous witnesses, or you have a confession, the police do an adequate job of following through. But when something is difficult and motives are obscure, as in my daughter's case, you are hopelessly lost. You simply do not have the resources, financial and otherwise, and the world has become much too complex."

"Are you undertaking your own investigation?" Carlucci asked. "With your own resources, 'financial and otherwise'?"

"That is my business, Lieutenant, not yours."

"It is very much my business, Mr. Katsuda."

Katsuda shook his head. "Not if I say it isn't. You are forgetting who has the power here, Lieutenant. It is not you."

"You might be surprised."

Katsuda smiled, amused. "I don't think so." He stood up. "I would say our interview is at an end."

Carlucci remained seated for a few moments, angry with himself for responding that way. Katsuda was right about the power, on a surface level. But there were other kinds of power, and Katsuda didn't know everything. He finally got up and shook Katsuda's hand.

"Thanks for talking to me," he said.

"I doubt if I was much help."

"That's all right. I guess neither of us expected much." He started walking toward the wall he had come through, though at the moment there was no opening. He stopped a few feet from it and waited.

"Lieutenant."

"Yes."

"Why did someone try to kill you?"

Carlucci turned back to look at him. "I don't know."

"Were you chasing rats?" Katsuda asked, smiling slightly.

Carlucci's breath caught for a moment. His heart beat hard against his chest, somehow noticeable right now. He was surprised—by *what* Katsuda had just revealed, and by the fact that he had revealed it at all. It told him something important about the man.

"Yes," Carlucci said. "I was."

"A dangerous occupation."

"So it seems," he agreed.

"Perhaps you should give it up."

"The rat is dead."

"No great loss for the world, I imagine. But no great gain, either. Nothing changed." Katsuda touched his hair with his fingertips. "Good night, Lieutenant."

Carlucci started to turn, then stopped. "The woman out front, at the desk."

"My assistant. Yes?"

"What happened to her?"

"What happened? To her face, you mean?"

"Yes."

"Nothing. She did not like the face she was born with, so she changed it. I'm certain I can arrange the same thing for you, if you wish."

Carlucci shook his head. "I'll pass."

This time when he turned around, the wall was opening, and he walked through.

23

CAGE WANDERED THE streets of the Tenderloin in a kind of trance. Nikki was dying. He knew that, and he couldn't get away from it. He had been back to see her twice more, but each time she'd been worse; neither time had she been coherent enough to talk. Neither time had she known he was there. She was dying.

It was midafternoon and the heat was intense. The air was heavy and muggy, but he hardly noticed it. The heat kept the street and sidewalk traffic light, which was just fine with him.

He bought a beer from a young woman caged into a tiny kiosk out on the edge of the sidewalk. Money went into one slot, the beer emerged from another, cold and wet. Cage could barely make out her features behind the narrow, thin bars, back in the darkness. She must be baking in there.

He sat on the curb in the shadow of a delivery truck and drank his beer. There was a sense in the street of people waiting—waiting for darkness, waiting for the temperature to drop, waiting for energy to return. Waiting for Nikki to die.

Jesus. And how many other people were going to die? In the days since his talk with Dr. Sodhi, Cage had made a few calls to other doctors and street medicos both in and out of the Tenderloin. Nothing explosive was happening yet, but cases were cropping up everywhere, many of the people already dead. Most inside the Tenderloin, but a few *outside*. No one thought too much about it yet, because no one was seeing more than one or two, and some none at all. Just another mystery disease or toxin attack. But the symptoms were too damn close to what Tito, Stinger, and Nikki all had.

Cage knew. Something was happening out there. Something was about to break out.

And he had helped Caroline work her way into Cancer Cell and the Core, right into the middle of it.

The street got suddenly quiet. There was a long break in the traffic, and

Cage stood, stepped out from behind the truck, and looked out into the street. Nothing at first, and then he heard the first cries and moans, and he knew what was coming—a Plague Parade.

Christ, that's just what he needed now. He almost walked away, almost hurried in the opposite direction where he could try to find a bar or a café, anyplace inside where he could avoid seeing it. But he remained where he was, and waited for it to reach him.

Once a month or so the Plague Parade would appear on the streets of the Tenderloin. The name wasn't really accurate; none of the people in the parades were dying of diseases that were truly plagues—unless you considered life in the twenty-first century a plague. But that didn't stop them from using the name; it sounded better. Or worse.

The street was completely clear now. Groups of plague hierodules would have gone ahead and set up human barricades on the planned route—men and women in hooded robes and carrying censers, legless men on motorized wheeled platforms, Screamers with their mouths surgically sealed, humming through metal nose tubes. And here, people were clearing out from the sidewalks without any help, ducking into buildings and alleys, shops and cafés; those who remained waited for the parade with exhausted acceptance or morbid interest.

An extremely tall woman led the parade. She wore a black and white body-stocking skeleton costume, a grinning skull mask over her head. Arms and legs moving nimbly, the skeleton woman danced from side to side as she led the parade down the street. But her dancing and grinning mask were the last vestiges of gaiety in the Plague Parade.

Following the dancing skeleton came two rows of four-wheeled carts pulled by barefoot men naked except for tattered loincloths. Each row consisted of six carts, and sitting in each cart were two or three people. Hand-painted signs hung from the sides of the carts, announcing the diseases within: ANKYLOSING SPONDYLITIS; LUPUS; EPSTEIN-BARR; HE-PATITIS G; MALARIA; MULTIPLE SCLEROSIS; and so on. Cage picked up the pattern right away: They were all chronic illnesses.

Next in the parade, on foot or wheeled platform, came the physical birth deformities section. People hobbled along on clubfeet, or with one leg noticeably shorter than the other, some walked by with short, flippered arms or deformed heads, and a small group of legless men pulled themselves along on wheeled platforms, digging spiked knuckles into the pavement with each swing of their arms. Two women led by children walked with clouded white eyes gazing up at the sky, wearing signs that said "Blind from Birth."

Then came the strangest part of the parade, something Cage had never seen before. Two lines of hooded figures moved slowly past, bodies swaying in unison to a subtly shifting, deep, and penetrating hum. He could not tell if the hum came from the marchers, or if it was being generated by some electrical device. Stranger still, even though it was midday and the sun was shining directly onto the street, the hooded figures were surrounded by a pulsing, dark blue glow that obscured the figures and the air around them; as they walked past, even people standing on the opposite side of the street became distorted and weirdly shadowed. And most disturbing of all, when Cage looked at the heads of the hooded figures, he could see nothing within the hoods, only a darker blue glow and darker shifting shadows, as if there were no heads or faces within. A terrible, cold shudder went through him, and he wanted to turn away, but he was transfixed, and could not tear his gaze from them until they were completely past him and nearly half a block away.

Dizzy and buzzing inside, he finally turned his head and stared down at the ground, trying to regain his equilibrium. He couldn't shake the feeling that he had just witnessed something terrifying. The rest of the Plague Parade moved past him, but he hardly noticed any more of it, hardly saw the caged wagon of half-naked and completely insane people leaping and shouting and shaking the bars, or the pedalcarts loaded with people in the late stages of terminal diseases. He was barely aware of where he was.

But by the time the tail end of the parade approached, he was feeling almost normal. He watched the last of the stragglers limp and drag past him—a young man with no hair, no left hand, and no left eye, and half a dozen surgical scars across his chest and abdomen; and a woman and child, both blond, apparently mother and daughter, walking hand in hand. Around the girl's neck hung a cardboard sign lettered in black marker:

**LEUKEMIA
NO MONEY**

The girl was listless, her feet dragging. The mother was angry and defiant.

Half a block farther on was the rear guard of the hierodules, walking backward, facing the vehicle traffic that inched along in their wake, filling the street once again. Cage remained where he was until all signs of the parade were gone, and the streets and sidewalks were back to normal.

Back to normal. And what good was that? A hopeless, deteriorating state of affairs.

He looked down at the empty beer bottle in his hand. He wanted to throw it through a window, or smash it over someone's head, smash it over his own head. Instead, he tossed it into a trash bin, crossed the street, walked down to the end of the block, and entered a phone bank. Time to try calling Eric Ralston again.

The bank was a narrow, dark aisle lined with small, cramped private booths. Signs above each booth declared, in all seriousness, that the phone lines within were guaranteed to be cleared and clean. No one believed the signs.

He ran his phone card through the reader, and punched in the number for the CDC in Atlanta, which he'd now memorized after a half dozen calls in the past two days. Half a dozen calls to Ralston, half a dozen messages left, and no calls returned.

Cage had gone to medical school in San Francisco with Eric Ralston, and they had become friends, despite being headed in different directions afterward—Cage had gone to Southern California to do image enhancements and make money, while Ralston had joined the CDC. Cage's life and career had changed drastically since then, but Ralston had remained at the CDC, where he was now some kind of research director. They had stayed in touch over the years, talking by phone every few months, seeing each other maybe once or twice a year.

The call went through, a woman answered, and Cage asked for Ralston's office. When he got Eric's voice-mail system again, he defaulted out of it and back to the woman.

"Yes, can I help you?" the woman said.

"My name is Dr. Ryland Cage, in San Francisco, and I've been trying to reach Dr. Eric Ralston for two days," he said. "I've left several messages, but he hasn't called back. It's urgent that I speak with him, so I need to know if he's actually been in his office, or is he away?"

"Just a minute, Dr. Cage, let me check."

He crouched on the floor of the cubicle while he waited, the phone cord barely long enough. Quiet strains of chamber music played over the phone; at least there were no commercials or promotional announcements.

A couple of minutes later the woman came back on. "Dr. Cage?"

"Yes."

"Dr. Ralston *is* out of the office. He's in the field, and he has been for several days. It's an open-ended assignment, so there's no way to know when he will be back in the office."

"Goddamnit." Cage closed his eyes for a moment; he wasn't going to give up. "As I said, it's urgent that I speak to him. There must be a number I can call to reach him, wherever he is."

"I'm sorry, Dr. Cage, you should know that I can't give out that information."

"I *have* to speak with him as soon as possible."

"I'm sorry, Dr. Cage. If you want to leave a message, I will note that it's urgent, so if he calls in—"

"Goddamnit, I've already left messages, and—"

She hung up.

Cage remained in a crouch, holding the silent phone to his ear and staring stupidly at the cubicle door. He breathed deeply and slowly, stood, and then punched in the CDC number. The same woman answered.

"Please don't hang up on me," he said, working hard to keep his voice calm and reasoned, afraid of pissing her off again. "This is Dr. Cage, and I apologize for losing my temper with you."

There was a long silence, and he was afraid she had hung up on him again. But then she spoke.

"Apology accepted," she said. "And I'm sorry I so easily lost patience with you. It's been a little hectic around here lately."

"Why?" Cage asked. "Is something going on?"

"Oh, who knows? They don't tell the support staff anything. They have panic attacks around here all the time and most of them turn out to be for nothing. But we always pay for it with this insanity."

"Yeah, that figures. All right. I know you can't tell me where he is, or how to reach him. But could you get a message to him, telling him that I've called several times, and that it's urgent I speak with him, give him my phone and pager numbers?"

The woman sighed. "It won't be easy. When they're out in the field, it's an 'emergency only' status for contacting them."

"This *is* an emergency," Cage said. "It really is."

"Okay," she said, relenting. "I'll see what I can do."

"Thanks. I really appreciate it."

"Yeah, yeah, yeah."

He gave her two numbers, adding the clinic number; she read them back to him, and said she would get to it as soon as she could.

"Thanks again," he said. "Keep my numbers, and the next time you're in San Francisco give me a call. I'll buy you dinner."

"Call me when you're in Atlanta," she said. "You'll never see me on the West Coast."

"I will. What's your name?"

"Never mind. Just call here, and if you recognize my voice, we'll go from there."

Cage laughed. They said their good-byes, and he hung up the receiver.

Back out on the street, in the oppressive heat and sun, Cage's foul, despairing mood returned in full force. He wasn't going to hear from Eric, and even if he did it wouldn't do any good. Afraid to commit resources to something without convincing evidence, afraid to look foolish as they had so many times in the past thirty years or so, no one at the CDC would do anything until it was way too late.

He stood in front of the phone bank, the sun baking him, his head swimming, and his vision bleaching. Where was he? Thinking, figuring, he worked out that he was only five or six blocks from Hanna's Hophead Hovel. Cage hadn't been there in months. Hanna's was a hip spice bar, décor from eighteenth-century China, pictures on the walls of people smoking opium, fake opium pipe candleholders on the table, dark shaded lamps. But in the basement rooms below was the real thing—an opium and hash den, with rooms rented out by the hour and servants who would bring you your drug of choice and watch over you.

He closed his eyes, wanting desperately to go there right now, rent out a room for a day or two, and slide into oblivion. But that was just as useless as the Plague Parades, just as futile. And he had made a promise to himself to put an end to that.

Nikki.

24

CARLUCCI STOOD AT an open fifth-floor window and looked down on the Tenderloin as dusk fell. Activity was increasing, the streets and sidewalks filling despite the heat. Sweat rolled down his cheeks, dripped down his sides from under his arms, and formed a sticky, itching band around his waist. The weather service had been predicting a break in the heat wave for three days now, and each day it just got hotter.

Carlucci didn't give a damn. Right now he didn't give a damn about much, not even his job. Two weeks since he'd been shot, and still there was no sign of Caroline, no hint of what had happened to her or where she was, or even if she was still alive. A few days earlier a letter had arrived at the house, mailed from the Sunset Post Office, saying that Caroline was all right, she was just away for a while, she was not being held anywhere against her will, and everything was fine, so they shouldn't worry. The letter was worthless; if it was meant to reassure him and Andrea, it failed completely. And as time went on, he had become more convinced that she was here somewhere, in the Tenderloin, and that it had something to do with Cancer Cell. So now, because he had nothing else to do, he was about to go into the Tenderloin himself and look for her, despite what he knew to be the futility of his task. If nothing else, maybe he'd stir something up. What was the worst that could happen? Someone would take a shot at him?

He knew he wasn't thinking clearly, and that later he would probably regret this, but right now that didn't matter. So he stood at the window, looking down at the street lighting up as darkness fell, and waited to descend. He rotated his arm and shoulder, slowly but steadily to keep it from getting stiff. No more sling, and not much left in the way of bandages, but he had to be careful so he didn't rip the wound back open. The pain wasn't bad, just a constant, annoying reminder to him of what had happened.

"Lieutenant? You're cleared."

Carlucci turned around. The cop was young, hardly more than a rookie, and Carlucci wondered why he'd been assigned here, to one of the police department's "gates" into the Tenderloin. This was usually a post for more experienced officers, where strange things came up and there was often a need for improvising, where the rule book sometimes had to be distorted or ignored altogether. Either someone had a lot of faith in the young man and was already grooming him for quick advancement, or someone had it in for the guy and was setting him up for a shitcan. He seemed like a nice kid, and Carlucci silently wished him well.

"Thanks," he said to the kid. Then he walked past him, through the door, and into the stairwell, and started down the steps.

After three flights, the steps ended at a locked door. Carlucci waited, hearing a thumping bass through the walls. There was nowhere for him to go, except back up. He had to wait nearly five minutes until finally the door unlocked and swung quickly open. A short, skinny, old man grabbed his arm and pulled him through. "Chop chop!" the man said in a loud whisper. The man slammed the door shut, jammed home the locks, then pulled down a large tapestry that completely hid the door.

The music was louder here, a wild and swinging reggae. He was in a corridor now deserted except for himself and the old man, who pulled at his arm again, urging him down the corridor away from the music. "Go downstairs."

"I know," Carlucci said. "I've been through here before."

But the man just shook his head, pointing with one hand and now pushing with the other. "Go now, downstairs and out the back."

Carlucci gave up trying to convince the man he already knew where to go. "Okay," he said. "I'm going." He walked down to the end of the corridor, then through a screen door to the outside and zigzagging wooden steps that went down into an alley.

He hesitated at the top of the stairs, his heart suddenly beating hard and fast and his ears ringing, thinking about the last time he'd gone into an alley. This was different, he knew that, but he couldn't completely stop that clutching at his chest and gut. He scanned the alley, which was short, a dead end only ten feet to his left where metal and stone and wood barriers had been erected as a wall between buildings and forming a part of the Tenderloin perimeter—no way in or out. The rest of the alley, maybe fifty feet out to the street, was empty except for trash bins and the scattered remains of an old motorcycle.

What the hell was he doing here? He shook his head and went down the steps. Then he hurried along the alley, turned the corner of the building, and plunged into the Tenderloin crowds.

At ten o'clock he was in the back of a pachinko parlor in the Asian Quarter, massaging his temples, trying to ease the headache he had from the constant clatter of balls and ringing of bells, the flashing lights and the dense clouds of cigarette smoke. He was sitting on a stool with his back against the wall, and he'd been here for fifteen minutes, waiting for a woman called Amy

Otani. Amy Otani was a weasel for one of the department's undercover narcotics officers. Carlucci had spent most of the day calling in favors and
promising more of his own to get the names of weasels and leeches in the
Tenderloin, anyone he could contact and ask about Caroline or Cancer Cell.
So far he'd come up empty, and he didn't really expect to do any better the
rest of the night.

A short, round woman in a black skirt and flowered blouse came
toward him, expression stern. She stopped only a couple of feet away,
frowning.

"You Carlucci?"

"Yes. You're Amy Otani?"

She blew air between her lips and shook her head, frown deepening,
then nodded quickly once. "Yes, yes. Come with me, quickly." She turned
and walked away.

He scrambled off the stool and hurried after her. She barreled around a
corner and down a dark narrow corridor, then up a flight of steps and into
a small room on the second floor. There was a desk and a couple of chairs,
and the rest of the room was filled with wooden and plastic crates. When he
entered, she closed the door behind him, then pointed to a chair, her arm
and finger stiff and demanding. He sat on the chair, then she moved around
behind the desk and sat, still glowering at him.

"You're a crazy man," she said. "You don't even have to tell me why
you're here. I already know, because the word is out. You're trying to find
Cancer Cell."

"Yes."

She shook her head again. "Yes, you're a crazy man. Always dangerous
to ask about Cancer Cell, even when you're being careful. And when you're
not being careful . . ." She made a kind of growling sound in her throat.
"And you're not being careful, Lieutenant. Not at all. You were almost
killed once, now you're trying again, looks like. Trying to make a success
this time, yes."

"No."

She snorted. "Yes. Same thing, what you're doing."

"Can *you* help me contact Cancer Cell?"

"You don't understand, do you? Anyone who tries to help you find Cancer Cell now is as crazy as you." Now she was almost smiling, as if she
couldn't believe he was serious. "This is my help, to warn you. To tell you.
You make things too difficult now. Cancer Cell knows, unless they are blind
and deaf and stupid. And they are not blind and deaf and stupid. No, Lieutenant. No one will help you."

'I'm trying to find my daughter."

Her expression became sorrowful. "If she *is* with Cancer Cell, the best
thing for you is to stop right now. Go home, forget it."

"I can't," he said.

"Then no one can help you." She pointed to the door. "Go, Lieutenant. Don't make problems for me."

He nodded, then got up and left.

Three o'clock in the morning, exhausted and depressed, Carlucci stopped by the RadioLand Street Clinic a third time, hoping Cage had showed up. The first two times, Cage hadn't been there, and the doctors and staff didn't know when he would be. Apparently he'd become unreliable the past few days, not following the schedule they had worked out for the week, showing up at odd times, not showing up when he was supposed to. Dr. Samione, the woman Carlucci had met the day he'd come by looking for Tito, remembered him. She didn't seem upset by Cage's behavior; she said they had adjusted. It was a stretch for all of them, but they just didn't count on him, so when he did show up it was a bonus. He was going through a very difficult time, she said; it would pass. Nikki? Carlucci had asked her. She had nodded, but didn't say anything else.

Now he was back, and surprisingly Cage was here. But he didn't seem to be working. He was sitting in one of the waiting-room chairs, drinking a bottle of Black Orbit beer. Haggard and drawn, he hadn't shaved in several days. As Carlucci approached him, Cage looked up and saluted him with the bottle.

"Good morning, Lieutenant. I am told you've been looking for me."

"Hello, Cage." He wondered if Cage was drunk. "Are you all right?"

"No. But I'm not drunk, if that's what you're really asking. *Are* you looking for me?"

"Indirectly. I'm looking for my daughter. Caroline."

Cage nodded. "She's still missing?"

"Yes."

"I'm sorry." He sighed. "But why do you want *me*?"

Carlucci gave him a half smile. "I'm desperate."

Cage laughed. "You'd have to be. Look at me, I'm a fuckin' mess."

"Nikki?"

Cage nodded, then shook his head from side to side. He finished off his beer.

"No improvement?"

"She's dying, Lieutenant. Your daughter's still missing, and Nikki's still dying. I don't know how she's managed to stay alive as long as she has, but it won't be long now. A day or two, maybe." He ran his hand through his hair. "I don't know where your daughter is."

"I want you to help me find her."

Cage laughed again, then nodded. "Let's go talk somewhere. Get something cold to drink."

"Back in your 'staff lounge'?" Carlucci asked, smiling.

"Christ, no. Not unless you want your brains boiled. But let me go get a couple of beers."

"All right."

He waited while Cage went into the back room at the end of the hall. The waiting room was half full, and it was hard to tell whether the people waiting were sick or just wiped out by the heat. Everyone was listless and quiet, the loudest noise in the room coming from the fans.

Cage came out from the back with two bottles in each hand. "It's hot," he said, shrugging. He gave Carlucci two of the bottles.

They went outside, and Cage gestured toward a bench half a block away, unoccupied for the moment. They walked down to it and sat, the extra bottles between them. Carlucci twisted off the cap and drank deeply. A sharp pain from the cold drove up into his sinuses, but the beer tasted awfully good right now.

"How's the arm?" Cage asked.

"It's all right. It aches quite a bit right now, but that's because I've been wandering around in this godforsaken place since dusk."

"Looking for your daughter?"

"Yes."

"Christ, Carlucci. If she's been missing all this time, what the hell are the chances you're going to see her walking around in here?"

"Pretty much zero." He looked at Cage. "But what would you do? Stay at home and wait to hear something? I've done enough of that."

"I understand," Cage said. "But what the hell do you want from me? I haven't seen her."

Carlucci took a folded photo of Caroline from his pocket and handed it to Cage. "Just in case," he said. "Keep an eye out for her. Ask around."

"Here? In the Tenderloin? Walk around and show people this picture and ask them if they've seen her? Are you out of your mind?"

"No. I don't really expect you to do that. What I really want you to do is put me in touch with Cancer Cell."

"Jesus, you *are* out of your mind."

"No. The first time we talked, you said you might be able to do it."

"Yeah, I said I *might,* and it turned out I didn't know what the hell I was talking about. Besides, that was then, this is now, and they're not the same." He cocked his head. "Do you have any idea what's going on in this city right now, with this goddamn disease, whatever it is? The one that killed Stinger and Tito, the one that's killing Nikki?" Without waiting for Carlucci to answer, he went on. "Of course you don't. No one does. But this thing is spreading. It's starting to pop up all over, but no one knows what it is, no one knows where it's come from. No one knows there are other cases out there. But this thing has probably come from the Core, somehow, and Cancer Cell has to know that. And the last thing they're going to want to do is talk to anyone. I think they've pulled in tight and closed the hatch over themselves."

Carlucci thought about that for a while. Then he said, "And if Caroline did try to contact them, what would they have done?"

"Who knows? But she probably didn't. How would she know how to do that?"

Carlucci just shook his head. None of it made much sense, but he didn't know where else she could be. "Are you *sure* you can't get in touch with them?"

Cage shook his head in exasperation. "Christ, Carlucci, I've been trying. I've got a bad feeling about this disease. I've been trying to get in touch with them for days now, and it's been a goddamn stone wall. They might as well not exist."

Carlucci didn't know what else to say. He had felt as if Cage was his last chance. "What the hell am I going to do?" he said.

But Cage didn't have an answer for him.

25

CAROLINE HAD BEEN in this room for well over a week. She was surprisingly comfortable in it, despite the locked door and the lack of windows. Two or three times a day she was taken to some exam room or lab, where Dr. Mike asked her questions, examined her, and ran her through batteries of tests. Dr. Mike was tall and emaciated, with wire-rim glasses and short, unkempt hair. He probably wasn't much older than thirty, but he acted as if he'd been a doctor all his life. Other than the questions he asked, he didn't talk much; Caroline wasn't sure that he really thought of her as another person. He was in a world of his own.

Rashida confirmed her impressions of Dr. Mike. Caroline and Rashida had talked a lot in the past week, and Caroline thought they were becoming friends. Rashida came by at least once a day, and often twice. In the evenings she would sometimes stay for hours. They would drink tea, talk, and listen to music on Rashida's disc player.

She almost felt she could tell Rashida the real reason she was here. One way or another, though, she was going to have to do something soon. She was learning nothing, really, about Cancer Cell, about what they were doing, what their facilities were like, or anything else. She had to admit that she knew no more about Cancer Cell or the disease that had killed Tito than she had known before coming here.

One evening Caroline was sitting on her bed, reading an older novel by Alana Wysocki, when she heard the door being unlocked. She looked up to see Rashida walk into the room and close the door behind her, then lean back against the door, looking at Caroline with an almost dead expression.

"What is it?" Caroline said, setting down her book.

"I believed you," Rashida said, her tone even and neutral. "More than that, I thought we were becoming friends."

"We are," Caroline replied. What had happened? She thought she should be frightened, but she wasn't.

"I don't think so." She remained at the door, watching Caroline.

"What is it?" Caroline asked again.

"Why are you here?" Rashida shook her head, as if she didn't expect a truthful answer.

Caroline decided not to give her any answer at all. She wasn't afraid, but she felt she had to be careful. She had the distinct feeling she didn't quite know what this was about.

"You *do* have Gould's Syndrome, don't you? There's no way you could have faked that, is there?"

"Of course I have Gould's."

"But this sad story about your friend's daughter with the leukemia, all a crock to suck me in."

"No," Caroline said, shaking her head. "Mink really does have leukemia. She and Lily are living in a death house in the DMZ, and without a bone marrow transplant, Mink is going to die."

"If you're not lying, that's even worse. Using them like this, to get close to us."

"I just want to help them," Caroline insisted.

"I should have known when it turned out your father was a cop. But we thought, hell, a cop's daughter isn't immune to things like Gould's. And you *do* have Gould's. But that's not why you're here, is it?"

"I don't know what you're talking about."

Rashida leaned forward, getting angrier. "You're really starting to piss me off," she said. "We've found out."

"Found out what?"

Rashida shook her head, smiling unpleasantly. "The daughter of some New Hong Kong big shot has been murdered, and the murder is being blamed on us. Nothing official yet, but it's clear. Someone carved 'CC' into her forehead, and the cops have made the connection they're supposed to make. And guess what? Your father is in charge of the investigation. Not only that, but he's been digging around the Tenderloin, trying to get somebody to give us to him. I'm not sure why, though. He's got *you* in here. What more does he need?"

"I don't know anything about that," Caroline said.

Rashida stepped forward, fists clenched, eyes wide. "You expect me to believe that?"

"It's the truth."

"God almighty." Rashida turned away, then paced back and forth in front of the door, shaking her head and half laughing.

"It's the truth," Caroline repeated. But she knew it was futile.

"I'd search you for some kind of transmitter, but we already did that. What were you supposed to do, find out exactly where we were and how to get in and out of here, then escape and show the cops the way in?"

Caroline got up from the bed and walked halfway across the room, then stopped, gazing steadily at Rashida. "I don't know anything about my father's cases. That's not why I'm here."

"Why then?" Rashida said, sneering. "You think we're going to find you a cure?"

Caroline hesitated a moment, then slowly shook her head. "No."

"Okay. Charitable works, then, to get this poor little girl her bone marrow transplant." The sneer was still there in her voice.

"I would love to get Mink a transplant, give her a shot at living, but that would have just been an added benefit. No, that's not why I'm here."

For the first time, Rashida looked uncertain. She watched Caroline closely, and finally said, "All right, then. Why are you here?"

"Tito Moraleja was a good friend of mine."

Rashida's expression changed from uncertainty to confusion, but she didn't say anything right away.

"You know who Tito was, don't you?" Caroline asked.

Rashida slowly nodded. "Yes, I know who he was. But—"

"You abducted him," Caroline said.

"Yes," Rashida admitted. "We had a contract, and Tito was trying to renege. It was just business. But I still don't understand. Are you trying to take revenge because we abducted your friend?"

"No, nothing as simple as that. I'm trying to find out what killed him. And what killed Stinger."

Now Rashida looked surprised, and a little stunned. "Jesus," she said. Then, "This really has nothing to do with your father's investigation, nothing to do with the Katsudas and New Hong Kong?"

"Nothing," Caroline said. "I really don't know anything about that. My father has no idea I'm here, and believe me, he'd go nuts if he knew."

Rashida nodded. "This is starting to make a little more sense."

"Maybe to you."

She laughed. "Let me go make some tea for us, and I'll be right back. We've got a lot to talk about."

Ten minutes later, Rashida returned with two large mugs of green tea. Things were clearly better between them, but Rashida had still locked the door while she'd gone for the tea. Caroline was sitting on the bed again, Rashida on the chair.

"How did you know about Tito?" Rashida asked. She was tense again. Maybe not about the same thing, but something.

"Cage," Caroline answered.

"Cage? How the hell did *he* know?"

"Tito ended up at his street clinic, and died there. I guess it was obvious it wasn't the AIDS. I hear it was pretty awful."

"Yes, I imagine. He was your friend?"

"Yes."

"I'm sorry. And what about Stinger? How did you know about *him?*"

"Cage again. I'd gone to talk to him about Tito, and he told me about Stinger."

"And how did he know about Stinger?"

Caroline smiled. "Your friend Tiger."

Rashida closed her eyes and sighed. "I should never have said anything to him. Big mistake."

"Why did you?"

Rashida opened her eyes, but frowned, almost closing them again. "I panicked. I got scared, seeing Stinger die that way. Tiger, well, he's a sweet kid, and he knew Stinger was sick. He'd helped me bring Stinger into the Core when Stinger went into crisis. He was afraid, too. He'd gotten some of Stinger's blood on him, and he was afraid he would get whatever Stinger had." She sighed again. "I had to tell him that Stinger had died." After staring into her cup for a minute, she looked back up at Caroline.

"So, what was it? You and Cage knew about two people who had died the same way? It could have been anything."

"It had Cage worried. Both people with a connection to Cancer Cell, both dying pretty horribly." Caroline hesitated, wondering how much she should say. Everything, she decided. "There was something else. A woman named Nikki."

Rashida nodded. "Yeah, Cage's partner."

"She's got it, too. Apparently she got it from Stinger."

"What a mess," Rashida said.

"Yes," Caroline said. "It's a mess. So tell me. What is it?"

Rashida didn't say anything. She stared at Caroline for a while, thinking, then got up from the chair.

"Aren't you going to tell me?" Caroline asked.

"I don't know. I'll have to talk to my colleagues. It's not that simple."

"Nothing ever is."

Rashida smiled and shrugged. "Let me ask you something. Mike, he doesn't really have much to go on with you, for the Gould's. Anything he tries will be taking shots in the dark. And whatever he tries might make you sick, fuck you up but good. Now that all this is out, why you're really here, do you still want to put yourself at his mercy?"

"I'm willing to trade myself for a bone marrow transplant for Mink."

"Forget Mink. Forget the bone marrow transplant. It's not going to happen. Just you. No other deals. You get nothing else, just an extremely improbable chance at some kind of treatment or cure. Are you willing to submit yourself as an experimental subject?"

Caroline didn't have to think about it very long. It was never for herself, she'd never held out any hope for it. "No," she said.

Rashida nodded. "That's what I thought." She walked to the door and opened it. "We'll talk again." Then she went through, closed the door, and locked it.

Caroline didn't hear from Rashida until late the next day. She didn't even hear from Dr. Mike. A woman she'd never seen before brought breakfast and lunch to her, escorted her to the shower, but never said a word.

Sometime around what she guessed was midafternoon, the locks clicked, the door opened, and Rashida stepped in.

"Want to go on a tour?" she asked.

"Of what? The labs?"

Rashida shook her head. "The Core."

Rashida led the way down a short, narrow passage that ended at a security door with coded electronic locks. She popped open a wall cubicle, took out two flashlights and a couple of what appeared to be black handguns. She handed one of the flashlights to Caroline.

"You ever use a stunner?" Rashida asked.

Caroline shook her head.

"Better you don't carry one, then." She put one of the stunners back, then keyed in codes for the door locks. Just before activating them, she checked a security screen. "All clear," she said. She activated the locks and the door hissed open. "Let's go."

Caroline followed her past the door, which automatically hissed closed behind them. They were in a concrete-walled corridor, dimly lit by irregularly spaced overhead lights.

"So we *are* in the Core," Caroline said.

"Oh, yeah. Nowhere but. How much do you know about it?"

"Nothing," Caroline admitted. "Stories you hear about crazy people living in here. Crazier stories about ghosts and strange creatures wandering the buildings."

"Well, some of the people in here are a lot weirder than ghosts, if you ask me. But most of them are also much less dangerous than you might imagine. You just need to know how to treat them, how to talk and relate to them, and you do that in ways that are unlike relating to normal people. Mostly you get into trouble if you say the wrong thing, or say something in the wrong way. If you just pay attention, and listen carefully, the clues are usually there. And when it's time to leave, you leave. That's all."

"You sure make it sound simple."

"In a way it is. Hopefully we won't run into too many of the locals, but if we do, just follow my lead. And when in doubt, just ignore them."

"But you've got a stunner with you," Caroline said.

Rashida smiled. "Of course. These *are* crazy people. Sometimes no matter what you do or say, no matter how careful you are, things go to shit. But we don't want to kill anyone, so we use stunners." She held up her weapon for a moment, then stuck it into her belt. "Follow me."

The passage angled slightly downward, and as they continued it became cooler and more damp, with an occasional puddle of muddy water on the floor and water dripping from the ceiling or down the walls. Then they took a side branch, unlit but strangely both hot and dry for a hundred yards until they emerged into another cool and damp main passage. This time they only went about fifty feet before Rashida ducked into an alcove and cement steps leading upward.

They climbed three flights and came out in the hallway of what had once been an office building. A few rotting remnants of carpeting and padding remained on the concrete floor, and light came in through a tall window at the far end of the hall. There were doors on both sides.

Rashida stopped at the last office on the right. The glass window was painted over so they couldn't see inside. "The Fat Man lives here," she said, smiling.

"The Fat Man."

Rashida nodded. "The Fat Man himself." Still smiling.

Caroline wondered if she was supposed to know who the Fat Man was. She didn't have a clue.

"Who's the Fat Man?" she asked.

"A kind of low-rent slug. You'll see."

Rashida tapped on the painted glass. A few moments later, a high-pitched voice said, "Who's there?"

"Rashida. And a friend."

The door cracked open, and an eye appeared in the narrow opening. Rashida waved at the eye. The door opened wider, revealing a tiny, ancient black woman in a light brown robe and sandals. Rashida and Caroline stepped inside, and the old woman slammed the door shut. "Is all right," she said to a tall, beefy man in the corner behind the door; he was holding a pistol in each hand, the guns pointed at Rashida and Caroline. The man spun the pistols around like a cowboy in an old Western and planted them in the holsters on his belt. Then he squatted on the floor and closed his eyes.

"Hallo, Rashida." The old woman grinned and cackled. She had no teeth, or at least none that were visible.

"We're here to see the Fat Man."

"Yes, yes, yes, he's expecting you. And you," she said, staring at Caroline. Then she waved at them and led the way to the door on the other side of the room. She kicked the door three times, then opened it and flapped a hand at them. "Go in, go in."

The room on the other side of the door was large and lit by dozens of candles, and oppressively hot. The stench of body odor hung in the air, biting at the nose. In the far corner, suspended in a hammocklike webbed chair that hung from the ceiling, was a fat, grossly bloated man wearing only shorts. His skin was drenched in sweat and from the chest up was dotted with a couple dozen dermal patches; he was sucking at a long flexible tube connected to a several-gallon tank mounted on the wall.

The door slammed shut behind them; the Fat Man stopped sucking on the tube and grinned. "Rashida, my darling one. You have something for me?"

"Yes, Fat Man. I do." She unbuttoned her shirt pocket and removed several packets of dermal patches. Then she stepped forward and held them out to him.

The Fat Man took the packets, opened them, and studied the patches for a minute. He sighed heavily and nodded. "Very good, my darling one." Then he turned to Caroline. "Tell me, new one. Why have you come to the Core?"

Caroline turned to Rashida, who nodded. "Tell him the truth."

She looked back at the Fat Man. "I had a friend who had been abducted by Cancer Cell—"

"To fulfill a contract, no doubt," he said.

"Yes, apparently. He got quite sick, somehow found his way out of the Core and into a street clinic, where he died. I came here to try to find out what it was that killed him."

"And what killed Stinger," the Fat Man said.

"Yes. And what is killing a friend of mine."

"And what has killed others here in the Core." He shook his head, which caused the webbing to shiver along with the rolls of fat on his body. "It's a terrible thing." When everything had stopped shaking, he said, "And you know nothing about your father's investigation of Naomi Katsuda's murder?"

She glanced at Rashida, starting to realize what was going on here.

"Answer me," the Fat Man said.

Caroline turned back to him. "No. I don't know anything about it."

"You have no intention of trying to discover the way in to Cancer Cell, then escaping so you can tell the police how to find them."

"No," she answered sharply, angry at the interrogation.

The Fat Man licked his lips, his tongue swollen and dark, then reached for the flexible tube and sucked at it again. He let the tube go and belched loudly, grinning. "She's telling the truth," he said to Rashida.

Caroline whipped around and glared at her. "You trust this . . . this *thing's* judgment more than you trust me?"

"I don't really know you, do I? I've known the Fat Man for years, and he's quite reliable." She sighed. "I'm sorry, Caroline, but we have to be sure. There's too much at stake. You must understand that."

Caroline closed her eyes for a moment and nodded. She understood. It was just so bizarre, being in this room with this gross, bloated thing judging her.

"Yes, I'm disgusting," the Fat Man said. "I'm fat and I'm ugly and I stink, but I'm smarter than anyone in the Core, smarter than most anyone in this entire city, and I know almost everything that's going on in here. That may not mean much to you, but it means everything to me."

Caroline watched him, morbidly fascinated by the way his bloated lips and tongue moved as he spoke, and when he was finished, she said, "Okay, Fat Man. Smart Man. What's the story with this disease?"

The Fat Man looked at Rashida, who shrugged, then nodded. "Tell her," she said. "Tell her everything."

"Everything? That would take my entire life, and I still would not be finished."

Rashida looked at Caroline and shook her head. "He's smart, but he's also one huge smart-ass." She turned back to the Fat Man. "Everything about the disease."

"I know, my darling one, I know." He sucked a few more swallows from the tube, knocked the tube away, then shifted his position in the web chair, farting several times as he grunted and moved about. Finally he seemed to be comfortable, and he turned his gaze and smile on Caroline.

"This disease started inside the Core," the Fat Man began. "Not inside Cancer Cell, but out here in the Core. Now, how the agent of the disease got inside the Core is a mystery even to me, but considering the nature of this place, not so surprising that something like this happened. A number of the Core residents came down with it, became quite ill, and after two or three had died, the others started going to Cancer Cell."

Caroline looked at Rashida for an explanation.

"We provide medical care to people in here. Compensation, if you will, for our expansion throughout the Core. We started out quite small, and we've added labs and production facilities over the years, snaking all through the buildings here as well as belowground, closing off quite a bit of the Core in the process. In return, to keep down the hassles and attacks from the crazier ones, we give them medical care. When sick people started showing up, we took them in and tried to help."

"We exchange information constantly," the Fat Man said, "and as the seriousness of this disease became apparent, we've been working together to try to learn as much as we can about it. They give me the hard data, and I do interpretation and analysis. I look at the trends, and the changes in the trends." His disconcerting smile was gone, and his expression had become quite serious and grave. "It started quite a while ago, months ago. And although it began here, not only has it made it out into the Tenderloin, it's gone out into the main city, though no one out there seems to know it yet. And it has changed. So much of this is guesswork, because reporting standards aren't exactly very high here in the Core." The Fat Man smiled and scratched at his crotch. Caroline tried to ignore it, and suppressed a touch of nausea. "But my best analysis indicates that initially the incubation period was rather long, perhaps as long as two or three weeks. Which is probably why, despite its high mortality rate, it has managed to spread out into the city."

"How high *is* the mortality rate?" Caroline asked.

"Close to one hundred percent."

Caroline's heart sank for Nikki, for Cage. "How close to one hundred percent?"

The Fat Man shook his head. "No known survivors. But I would never claim a full one hundred percent. There will be survivors somewhere, sometime. There will be people who are exposed to it who don't contract it. There always are. But those are going to be exceptions, *rare* exceptions." He paused, seemed to think for a few moments, then went on. "The incubation period, however, seems to be declining. From the reports I've been getting, from Cancer Cell as well as from my other sources in the Core, and my sources outside, in the Tenderloin and in the city, I would say the incubation period is down under a week. It might go down to just a few days. I would guess that over the next several weeks, there will be a small explosion of cases appearing. More inside the Tenderloin, but many outside as well. At this point, I would be very surprised if it hasn't been carried outside the city, into other states, perhaps even other countries." The Fat Man paused, then gave Caroline a tight, disturbing smile. "There's a plague in the making."

After leaving the Fat Man, Rashida brought Caroline to a small, roofless room at the top of the tallest building in the Core with an incredible view of the surrounding buildings of the Tenderloin.

It took them half an hour to make their way along a maze of passages, up and down staircases, encountering several clumps of odd people who let them pass with hardly a word, through two floors of rubble, and up one final rickety ladder to a locked hatchway. Rashida used a magnetic key to unlock the hatch, then they climbed through and into the room. She locked the hatch after them.

They sat together on a makeshift bench of boxes and cracked wooden planks, looking out through windows that had almost no glass remaining in their frames, and large holes that had been punched or blown into the walls. It was late afternoon, the brown-orange sun hanging low in the sky, but it was still hot. From here, the Core did not seem quite so awful, though it was still just four square blocks of rubble and ruins, and Caroline said as much to Rashida.

Rashida laughed. "You've had a very atypical tour through the Core, though. We avoided all the trouble spots, the places the real crazies tend to haunt, and we got lucky besides. So don't get romantic about this place. It's a hellhole, believe me." She laughed again. "But it's home."

"You trust the Fat Man's assessment of this thing, this disease, whatever it is?"

"He's a monster, but I've never known him to be wrong about anything of importance."

"And a human lie detector."

Rashida shrugged. "If you can call him human. He's been a great help to us over the years. Not just for the information, but acting as a kind of emissary for us with various groups in the Core. We probably couldn't have made it in here without him."

Caroline finally decided to just ask the question she most wanted to ask. "What *is* the purpose of Cancer Cell?"

Rashida didn't answer at first. She gazed out the window and down at one of the street barriers blocking off the Core from the rest of the Tenderloin. "That's hard to say. There is no single purpose for everyone, and things have changed over the years. But if there's been anything like an overriding philosophy, I'd say it would be to increase access to the best drugs and medical treatments available. Entities like New Hong Kong, governments, and corporations have essentially complete control over health care in this country, and it's not even close to being fairly distributed." She turned to Caroline. "But I don't need to give you a lecture about that, do I?"

"No, you don't. I know what it's like. I've been lucky, because my father is a policeman. But people like Tito don't have anything."

"We try to manufacture high-grade pharmaceuticals and make them available on the street, at a much lower cost than the drug companies allow. And we try to do cutting-edge medical research that places like New Hong Kong or the major drug companies can't be bothered with because there might not be a profit in it. And we want people on the street to have access to new treatments and procedures at something like an affordable price." She paused. "I guess we're just trying to equalize things a little. Bring a little fairness." She smiled and shook her head.

"But you experiment on people, sometimes without their consent."

"We always get their consent to begin with," Rashida said. "Sometimes they change their minds."

"Like Tito?"

"Like Tito."

"And then you abduct them and experiment on them by force."

"We enforce the contracts they willingly signed. We always fulfill our part of the contract, and we expect them to fulfill theirs." Her expression hardened, and she waved at the view they had. "This is the real world we're living in, and working in. Your friend Tito did quite well by us. You thought he suffered a great deal in the last months of his life, and he did. But his suffering would have been much greater without the drugs we provided for pain, to fight infections, to battle his depressions. In return, we wanted to be able to try experimental procedures, treatments, and drugs on him, so that if nothing else we might be able to help others in the future." She shook her head. "I'm not going to apologize for what we do, or how we do it. We've made some decisions, and we've provided tremendous benefits to people who otherwise wouldn't have access to the kind of drugs and health care we give them." She looked away from Caroline. "And *that's* the purpose of Cancer Cell. You can do what you like with it."

Caroline didn't say anything. They remained in the room for a long time, not speaking, and watching the sun set on the city, and the light begin to fail.

26

CAGE WAS HALF drunk when the call came through from Eric Ralston. He had been half drunk pretty much all of his waking hours the past couple of days. It was a compromise. He stayed away from Hanna's, and he wouldn't let himself get completely smashed, in case something came up at the clinic, but he had also given up on getting through the days completely sober. Nikki was going to die any day now. She had become comatose, unresponsive, kept alive by artificial lungs and heart and blood. It was amazing that she had hung on this long, but it wasn't going to continue. She was going to die.

He wanted to be with her, sitting at her side, but the doctors wouldn't let him, not when they didn't know what was killing her. Standing outside her door and looking at her through a rectangle of glass was just impossible. So he'd given up, went by twice a day to stare at her for half an hour, and spent the rest of his time wandering around in a trance.

He was in his apartment, sitting at the window, dazed by the heat of the day and the alcohol, drinking one more beer and watching the street below him, hardly registering a thing. His skin was slick with sweat. He wasn't even sure what time it was—sometime in the afternoon, he thought, judging by the heat, but it could have been noon, or four. The shadows should have given him an idea, but he couldn't concentrate on them enough to work it out. He didn't give a shit.

The phone rang. He looked at it, thought about not answering. He would be useless at the clinic right now. But the phone kept on ringing, and finally he answered, just to stop it.

"Yeah?"

"Cage? Is that you?"

"Yeah, it's me, who else would it be? Who are you?" He didn't recognize the voice.

"Eric."

"Eric." Then it dawned on him who it was, and he sat up straighter in the chair, blinking crazily, as if it would help drive away the alcohol haze. "Eric, for Christ's sake."

"Cage, you son of a bitch. I just talked to Mandy, back in Atlanta, and she gave me your number. She said you've been calling for three or four days."

"Yeah, where the hell are you?"

There was a long hesitation, then Eric finally said, "Right here, pal. San Francisco."

Fear jumped inside his chest, and Cage got to his feet. He began pacing around the apartment, still trying to clear his head. "How long have you been here?"

Another slight hesitation. "Five days."

"And you didn't call me?"

This time there was the longest silence of all, and Cage knew he wasn't going to like where this conversation went. He picked up his beer from the windowsill, took it over to the sink, and poured the rest of it down the drain.

"I couldn't," Eric finally said.

"But you are now."

"Against my better judgment. I'd been wavering, and when Mandy called, hell, I just decided I'd better."

"Why are you here in San Francisco?"

"Cage, you've got to promise me everything I tell you is confidential. And I don't mean half-assed. This is the real goddamn thing, my man, and I'm hanging my ass out over the fire by talking to you."

"I promise," Cage said, the fear jerking up a notch. He had stopped his pacing, and stood at the window. There was no breeze, and the heat and stink of the street drifted in to him. "I've got a terrible feeling that the reason I was calling you is the reason you're here."

Eric didn't reply, and Cage didn't know what else to say. He sat down again in the chair and leaned his head against the window frame, closing his eyes. He wanted another beer. He wanted ten, one right after another, sinking him into oblivion.

"Okay," Eric said. "Let me run this by you. Something superficially a little like some of the hemorrhagic fevers. But different, really. Unique. Severe, red oozing skin rashes. Severe organ deterioration. Vomiting blood. Seizures. Death."

Cage didn't answer right away, wishing somehow that none of this was real. Maybe it wasn't as bad as he feared. He opened his eyes. "That's it," he said. "How come you guys know about it, but no one around here does?"

"Hell, Cage, it's what we're supposed to do. Be on top of this shit when it happens."

"How the hell do you guys know *anything?*"

"We're getting some help. We've got sources, the people who picked this up and first notified us."

"Who?"

"I can't tell you that."

"Have you got ideas for treatment? From your sources or whoever."

"No," Eric said. "Not a damn thing. Our sources are pretty sure it's a virus, but that's it. And near as we can tell, it's pretty close to a hundred percent fatal."

Cage nodded to himself. His flicker of hope was gone, just like that.

"Why?" Eric asked. "Have you got someone in your clinic with it?"

"No." He paused. "Do you remember Nikki?"

"With the cheeks of gold?"

"Yes."

"Beautiful woman. Of course I remember her." Then, "Not her."

"Yes."

"How long has she had it?"

"Four weeks, maybe longer."

"And she's still alive?"

"Barely."

"Where is she, Cage? Not in your damn clinic, I hope. No offense, but—"

"No, she's in St. Anthony's."

"Then maybe there's hope. We've been hearing two weeks maximum."

"No," Cage said. "She's dying. Another day or two at most."

"Don't give up yet. You're a doctor, you know as well as I do that strange things happen."

"Yeah, I'm a doctor. And I've seen her going steadily downhill, no matter what they've done. Her internal organs are shot. There's no recovering from where she is, Eric. None."

"I'm sorry," Eric said.

There was a long silence. Cage wanted to hang up, return to his grieving, his waiting. His drinking. But there was too much more to come, he knew that.

"Okay, Cage, now listen to me." Eric's tone had changed, become stronger. "You've got to get out of there. Now. Today, tonight, whatever. The sooner the better."

"Get out of where?"

"The Tenderloin."

"What the hell are you talking about?"

"Remember what I said earlier. You can't breathe a word of any of this, or I'll lose my job. In fact, they'll throw my sorry ass in jail."

"I promised you once, for Christ's sake. I promise again. What the hell is going on?"

"As of dawn tomorrow, we're putting the Tenderloin in quarantine."

Cage started to laugh, then choked it off. "You fucking can't be serious, Eric."

"I'm serious, Cage. This is bad shit, and that's the only way we're going to stop it from breaking out."

"That's a crock of shit. It's not confined to the Tenderloin, if it ever was."

"It started in there, we know that."

"Maybe. I'll grant that. But if it did, it's already broken out. I know half a dozen probables outside the Tenderloin, which means there are probably a hell of a lot more than that."

"No," Eric insisted. "We're certain that as of right now it is completely confined to the Tenderloin. Any cases outside are just coincidentally similar."

"Jesus Christ, Eric, that's bullshit and you know it."

"That's the official position, Cage. The decision's been made."

"I can't believe I'm hearing this from you."

"Cage, do you know where this thing started?"

"How the hell would I know that?"

"You're an intelligent man. You're there on the streets. I figure you have a pretty good idea."

"Do *you?*"

"Oh, yeah. The goddamn Core, that's where." He paused, probably for effect. "Cancer Cell."

"It's a possibility."

"No, it's a certainty. And we're going to take care of them."

"What do you mean?"

"At the same time we establish the quarantine around the Tenderloin, we'll establish an interior quarantine around the Core. We'll bring everyone in the Core out, transfer them to an isolation clinic we're setting up out on Treasure Island, and then we'll go in and sterilize."

Cage started pacing again, all the effects of the alcohol apparently banished. "You people are all out of your fucking minds," he told Eric. "You can't quarantine the Tenderloin. You won't even be able to quarantine the Core. You have any idea what that place is like? How many ways there are into the Core? The kinds of passages and routes in and out?"

"The military is getting prime intelligence. They'll be able to set up the quarantine."

"They're kidding themselves, Eric. They'll never find all the ways into that place."

"They will." Eric was adamant.

"They won't. But even if they could, you know who's in there? You know *what's* in there?"

"Cancer Cell."

"Yeah, but they're only a small part. The Core is the weirdest fucking collection of social misfits and freaks in this hemisphere. They won't all come out and go into your nice isolation clinic. They'll fight you every step of the way."

"The military will be prepared for that."

"What are they going to do? Kill everyone who resists?"

Eric didn't answer. Cage stopped pacing a minute, trying to slow his breathing. He was getting worked up, and it wasn't helping anything.

"I can't believe I'm having this conversation with you," he said.

"I'm just . . . trying . . . to help you, Cage. I'm putting my ass on the line here. I called to give you a chance to get out before the quarantine goes into effect. I didn't call to argue CDC and military policy."

Cage stood by the window, slowly shaking his head and gazing out at the streets and buildings that were about to become a prison. Something was wrong with this whole thing. "You people are absolutely insane," he said. "*If* this disease started in the Core, it's already broken out of the Tenderloin. A quarantine is useless. And a quarantine of the Tenderloin won't hold together anyway. The whole thing is insane."

He waited a long time for Eric to respond. When he finally did, his voice sounded weary. "You have a better idea, St. Cage?"

Cage sat down, feeling weary himself. "Use your resources to help identify the virus, work on the development of a vaccine or treatments, public education to prevent its spread."

Eric laughed. "That's a joke, and you know it."

"Something's fishy about this whole thing, Eric."

"Don't push it, Cage."

"This is going to be a disaster."

Eric sighed heavily. "Get the hell out, Cage. Now."

"I can't do that, Eric."

"You're a crazy son of a bitch."

"So are you. So's the whole fucking CDC."

"Cage. Just remember your promise. Not a fucking word."

"Don't worry." His anger and frustration were almost gone, overtaken by exhaustion. There *was* going to be a disaster. "I guess I should thank you for calling me."

"Yeah, well." There was a long pause. "Cage?"

"Yeah?"

"I'm sorry about Nikki."

"Thanks."

What the hell else was there to say, for either of them?

"I'll call you," Eric said.

"Do that."

"Good-bye, Cage."

"Good-bye, Eric."

He hung up the receiver. Dawn. Less than twenty-four hours away.

Caroline. Jesus. She was in the Core. He had to try to get her out.

Another impossible task. There was no time. His only way to contact Cancer Cell was through Tiger, and Tiger didn't even known who the hell they were. He'd have to contact Tiger, who'd have to contact Rashida, if that was possible, and then . . . and then, nothing. Shit.

The phone rang. Eric again? He picked it up and answered.

It wasn't Eric. It was Dr. Sodhi.

Nikki was dead.

27

OUT OF DESPERATION, Carlucci requested a crash session with Monk, one of the department slugs. He was surprised when he got word that Monk agreed. That Monk wanted the session to begin at four o'clock in the morning was also a surprise, but a much smaller one. The slugs were strange creatures, to say the least.

He stood outside the slug's quarters on the top floor, waiting for the entrance to unlock. The entrance panel chimed, then the door slid aside. Carlucci was hit by a wave of stunningly dry heat. He had forgotten about the heat, so dry he could feel a scratching at his throat with each breath. He stepped inside, and the door slid closed behind him.

The last time he had been here, the *only* time, Monk's quarters had been a maze of constantly rotating panels casting bands of shifting light and shadow, obscuring the room. This time, however, the main room was completely open, though dimly lit. He could see the kitchen in the back corner, with a table and chairs, and huge picture windows that formed most of the wall to his right. Padded armchairs were set in front of the windows. Another spectacular view, probably, like the one from Yoshi Katsuda's office.

Monk came through a door and into the kitchen, half walking, half dragging himself with two arm-brace canes. His thick, bloated body was completely covered by a slick black material, like a thin, shiny wet suit, and his head was enclosed in a goggled, form-fitting flexible helmet studded with blinking lights. His lips were the only flesh visible.

"Come on back, Lieutenant." Monk's voice was deep, but normal. The other time Carlucci had been here, Monk had spoken to him much of the time through overhead speakers, his voice amplified and with a slight echo effect. "Have a seat." Monk dropped heavily into one of the overly wide arm chairs at the kitchen table.

Carlucci walked through the main room, his footsteps nearly silent on the carpeting, then sounding quite loud on the vinyl floor of the kitchen. He pulled out a chair across the table from Monk and sat.

"Do you want something to drink?" Monk asked. "You'll have to get it yourself, my manservant doesn't come on until six. The refrigerator is well stocked."

Carlucci shook his head, remembering now—an aged, thin Asian man in a black suit who had served him coffee. "Why no *Wizard of Oz* effects this time?" he asked.

Monk made a hacking sound that Carlucci assumed was a laugh. "Not much point to it. It didn't impress you last time, did it?"

"No."

"No. I wasn't going to waste your time or mine." Monk laid his black-coated arms on the table, gloved fingers wriggling like short, fat snakes. "It's been a long time since that session."

Not long enough. He wondered what Monk's face looked like under that strange helmet, what his eyes looked like behind the tinted goggles.

"You're here about your daughter," Monk said. "Caroline."

Carlucci didn't reply, too stunned. He shouldn't have been. He tried to remind herself of what Brendan had said about the slugs, and Monk in particular, three years ago—that they would regularly surprise you with the intuitive leaps they made, that they processed so much information so quickly from so many different sources, and were always well prepared for their sessions. Monk would have spent the past several hours trying to figure out why Carlucci had called for this crash session. He would know that word had gone out throughout the department about Caroline, that she was missing, that people were searching for her.

"You're also here to ask me about what's going on in the Tenderloin, about the possibility of a disease outbreak. Or you should be."

Carlucci leaned back in the chair, a sharp headache beginning already. He should have known.

"Why don't I just sit back and listen, then?" he said. "I don't need to ask you any questions. I can just listen to your answers."

"This is not a sideshow," Monk said. "I'm not performing like some huckster, trying to impress the rubes. This is my job. This is what the city pays me for. This is why you're here."

"Of course it's a sideshow," Carlucci replied.

"Is this your way of trying to charm me so I'll help you find your daughter?"

Carlucci slowly shook his head, sighing. He was being stupid. But it was hard, trying to talk to this thing across the table from him that looked like some mutant freak from a bad late-night movie.

"I'm sorry," he said. "That was unfair. It's four-thirty in the morning, I haven't slept, and I'm worried about her."

Monk nodded. He adjusted his position, making a strange squishing and slithering sound.

"You know she's missing," Carlucci said.

"She's not missing," Monk replied. "I know where she is."

Carlucci could feel his heart start racing, but he tried to stay calm, tried not to get excited, afraid this was some bizarre joke from Monk.

"Where?" he asked.

"In the Tenderloin. In the Core. With Cancer Cell."

Carlucci didn't know what to say. Too many questions rose, all at once. "Are you sure?"

Monk made a gesture that might have been a shrug. "I'm fairly confident in my analysis, but of course I can't be sure."

"Why?"

Monk shook his head. "I don't know."

It was like the last time. Every time Monk had said "I don't know," Carlucci had been fairly certain that the slug *did* know, or at least could make a pretty good guess. He felt exactly that way right now, and the frustration ate at his stomach, because he knew there was nothing he could do to force Monk to come clean.

"How do you know?"

This time it was Monk who sighed. "You know I can't answer that kind of question."

"Can't, or won't?"

"Can't. I rarely know exactly what information leads me to what conclusions. I can only tell you with a fair degree of certainty that she has, somehow, contacted Cancer Cell, and that she is with them, in the Core."

"Alive?"

That shruglike gesture again. "Presumably. You will just have to wait to find out."

"Or go in and get her."

Monk threw his head back and laughed, a hacking bray that grated on

Carlucci. He wanted to strangle the freaky bastard. It *was* an absurd notion, going into the Core, he knew that, but what did Monk know? It wasn't *his* daughter who was missing.

"What do you know about Cancer Cell?" Carlucci asked, keeping his anger in check.

Monk shook his head. "Nothing. I even requested a session with Kelly in CID, hoping he might know something, but he didn't."

"Why did you do that?"

"Information is my blood. I don't like not knowing about something that may one day become important."

There was something wrong about all this, too, Carlucci could smell it.

"You said I was here to ask about Caroline, which was right. And that I was here to ask about this disease thing, or should be. Why didn't you say anything about the Naomi Katsuda murder investigation? That, too, is going nowhere. Shouldn't I be asking you about that as well?"

"Yes, of course. That, it seemed to me, was a given. It didn't seem worth mentioning. Besides, I have nothing to offer concerning that case." He paused, glancing down at the table, then back up at Carlucci. "Her death is a complete mystery to me."

A lie. Carlucci was certain. There was something, he believed, to be learned from Monk's lies and omissions as well as from what he actually offered. The difficulty lay in deciphering them.

"How did you know I was interested in this 'disease thing'?"

"Tito Moraleja's body in the temporary morgue." Monk snorted with a twisted grin. "There's no connection between Moraleja's death and Naomi Katsuda's murder—your official rationale for holding the body with an autopsy request. So your interest had to lie elsewhere."

"And?"

Monk's expression, what little of it Carlucci could see, appeared to take on real gravity.

"You are right to be concerned. There is a very deadly disease that is preparing to break out of the Tenderloin. Caused by a virus, contagious, and with a mortality rate nearing one hundred percent. A disease with no preventative vaccine and no treatment. How's that for a fucking nightmare, Lieutenant?"

Once again, Carlucci didn't know how to respond. Monk seemed both so certain and so sincere. No fooling around, no deception, no showmanship. As if he *knew.*

He knew.

"What the hell is going on?" Carlucci finally asked.

"There's even a name for the disease, now," Monk said. "Core Fever."

"Monk—"

"Let's go over by the windows, and you'll be able to see firsthand."

"See what?"

Monk's only response was to struggle upright with his canes. Breathing heavily, he dragged himself out of the kitchen, then across the carpet toward the large picture windows. Carlucci remained at the table, watching until he reached one of the armchairs and dropped into it. He laid the canes on the floor at his feet, then craned his neck around to look at him. "Come on, Lieutenant. The answer to your questions."

Carlucci got up and walked over to the windows, keeping away from Monk. He remained standing, and looked out.

They had a fairly good view of the Tenderloin from here. Lights were going crazy all around it, bright floods and flares, spinning colored lights on emergency vehicles, blinking barrier lights. Looking down between two buildings, to the perimeter of the Tenderloin itself, he could see what appeared to be the beginning of a military cordon.

"What the hell is going on?" he asked again.

Suddenly a whole fleet of helicopters appeared, headed into the heart of the Tenderloin. They moved in quickly, and began landing on rooftops deep inside, and then he realized they were landing on buildings that roughtly enclosed the Core. Where Caroline was.

He turned to look at Monk, who was actually grinning. He stared at the slug, waiting for an answer. Monk finally give it to him.

"Quarantine."

Isabel

IT HAD BEGUN.

Isabel didn't know what was happening, but she knew it was time to go. Things were even crazier now, people running and screaming, loud bangs, the smell of smoke. There would be nothing for a time, almost dead silence, and then it would start up again, different, but somehow feeling all the same. It was too crazy, and she was afraid. Anything could happen.

She worked her way toward the opening she had found earlier, moving quickly and quietly along the passages, sinking back into shadows and alcoves whenever someone appeared.

A small fire burned within a circle of stones at one intersection of corridors. Isabel hung back, watching closely, waiting, but no one seemed to be near, and she quickly skirted the flames. A terrible smell came from within them.

There was a body, a dead fat man lying belly up, his throat cut and his eyes open.

Farther on, a woman squatted in front of a small pit dug out of the dirt floor, rocking on her haunches and humming, flanked by burning candles. Water glistened in the pit, and there was movement in the water. There was no other way, so Isabel slowly crept past, on the side of the pit opposite the woman. As she passed, the woman looked up and gazed at Isabel; the woman smiled, but continued humming and rocking, and made no other move. Isabel pushed on.

Finally she reached the short dead-end passage and entered it. The grate was still on the ground, the opening clear. She checked the main corridor once more to make sure there was no one nearby, then returned to the opening and pulled herself up and into it.

She squirmed forward as quickly as she could manage, afraid of being exposed. Her way was a little easier this time, since she knew what to expect. When she entered the wider duct, she took the right branch again, then right once more at the next chance, and before long she was emerging into the dark passage on the other side.

Isabel dropped to the floor. She stood unmoving for a long time, listening. Faint sounds came to her through the opening, but nothing from the passage around her. She moved forward to the rectangle of light at the far end, the window in the door. At the bottom of the steps she hesitated for a moment, then climbed them and put her face to the glass.

The room on the other side was the same, except that this time there were no people inside. Careful as always, she remained at the window for quite a while, watching. No one entered the room. Feeling safe, she took hold of the doorknob and tried to turn it.

The doorknob wouldn't budge. She tightened her grip, and turned harder. Still nothing. The door was locked, or the knob rusted shut. Once more with both hands gripping the knob, but again it wouldn't turn.

She was trapped.

PART FOUR
Quarantine

28

RASHIDA CAME INTO Caroline's room, flushed and breathing hard. She was wearing a surgical mask and gloves, and carrying a flashlight and a small leather bag.

"Come on," she said. "We have to go. *You* have to go."

"Go where? What's going on?"

"Quarantine."

"Quarantine? Where?"

"The Tenderloin. The Core. There's not much time. Let's go." Then she shook her head. "Don't bring anything with you. I'll give you the only thing you'll take out of here."

"What are you talking about?"

"Later. Let's go."

She followed Rashida out of the room and down the corridor. Tension and a sense of urgency infected the air, extra bursts of it exploding whenever someone rushed by, or she saw frantic activity in one of the open rooms they passed. They stopped for a few moments when they ran into Dr. Mike, who passed a silent message to Rashida, his eyes saddened. Then Dr. Mike went one way, and they went another.

"What's happening?" Caroline asked again.

They turned into an empty, narrow corridor, which ended at one of the Core gates. Rashida checked the security panel, unlocked the door, and pushed Caroline through. She stumbled forward in the dim light, then Rashida came through after her and sealed the door, bringing complete darkness.

Caroline didn't move, waiting for Rashida. Rashida's hand gripped her arm; the gloved fingers felt cold on her skin.

"Don't lose me now," Rashida said, her voice just above a whisper.

"Don't lose *me*," Caroline answered.

Rashida quietly laughed. Then, before they went any farther, she said, "The CDC and the military have quarantined the Tenderloin. They've announced the impending outbreak of a fatal disease whose source is the experimental laboratories of a medical terrorist group called Cancer Cell."

"How can they say that?"

"Hell, they can say any damn thing they want to, can't they? They're calling it Core Fever. They've announced that Cancer Cell's labs are in the Core, and they've sent in special troops and equipment to establish a second quarantine around the Core itself."

"Is that possible?" Caroline asked.

"Not completely," Rashida answered. "But they've done extremely well, far better than I would ever have imagined they could do." She paused. "They have very good intelligence." There was something about the way she'd said that last thing that implied betrayal. "They're going to destroy us."

"What do you mean?"

"Just that. They've given us until noon to come out through one of their quarantine stations, and that means everyone in the Core. There are teams in isolation suits ready to process us, then they're going to transfer all of us to isolation wards somewhere until we either get sick or stay healthy long enough to convince them that we haven't been infected. And then after we're all out, they're going to come through and sterilize the entire Core. But of course we won't all come out, and it's going to be a fucking disaster."

"What do you mean by that?"

"Forget about Cancer Cell. All the other people here in the Core, the social misfits, the psychopaths, you think they're all going to surrender themselves in a nice quiet and orderly manner? You think they're going to surrender themselves in *any* kind of manner? Shit. A few of them will, probably, but most of them won't. A lot of them will actively resist, with any means they have. Hell, even some of my colleagues will probably resist." She sighed heavily. "There will be bloodshed. And there will be a lot of it."

"And Cancer Cell will be destroyed," Caroline added. Her eyes had adjusted to the darkness, and she could faintly make out Rashida's features, enough to see her nod in reply.

"Wiped out. They'll destroy the labs, they'll burn and sterilize everything, they'll wipe out all records, they'll destroy whatever they can get their hands on." There was another pause. "But they won't get their hands on everything. We're getting *you* out of here."

"Through the quarantine?"

"Yes. There's a way they won't know about. A way that won't be blocked."

"How can you be sure?" Caroline asked. "What about the source of all their good intelligence?"

"Only four of us know about it. The four remaining original founders."

She shrugged. "I can't be sure. If one of the four of us is a weasel, then none of it matters anyway."

"Why me? Why not you, or one of the others?"

Rashida didn't answer right away. "We trust you," she finally said. "And one or all of us may *need* to go into isolation wards."

So that's what the mask and gloves were all about. Caroline didn't know what to say. She wanted to ask for more details, but decided it was better to let it go.

"Here," Rashida said, handing her the small leather bag. "You take these with you. That's our price for getting you out."

"What is it?"

"Backup modules of all of our most important records, all of our research. We're trying to transmit the same data out of the Tenderloin, but the military's managed to cut off almost every single transmission cable. We've got one left, but we don't know if it's getting through. And they're flying jammers in the air above the Core, blocking all air transmissions. And you better believe they're not going to let any of us take a damn thing with us when we leave."

Caroline looked down at the bag, feeling a strong sense of responsibility. She looked back up at Rashida. "What do I do with it once I'm out?"

"Hang on to it. Someone will get in touch with you. I'm not sure who it will be. That depends on who survives all this crap without being blown. But, this is important. It will be a woman who gets in touch with you. If a man approaches you, claiming to be one of us and asks for these, don't turn them over. Claim ignorance, run, brain the bastard, whatever. Got that?"

"Got it."

"Okay. Any other questions? No? Good; let's go."

Rashida didn't use the flashlight. The light was dim, but got brighter in spots, and there was usually enough to see ten or fifteen feet ahead. She seemed to know exactly where she was going.

They made a lot of stops and starts, sometimes retreating whenever someone appeared. Several loud echoing cracks sounded together, gunshots perhaps. At one point a hand reached out from a hollow in the wall, grabbing at Caroline, but Rashida smashed the hand with her flashlight, bringing out a brief cry. A figure shot out of the hollow and scurried down the passage in the direction from which they had come.

More sounds came from overhead, sometimes muffled, sometimes sharp and clear if Caroline and Rashida were near one of the stairwells leading up to the buildings above—banging sounds, grunting, music, loud hisses, a steady *whap! whap! whap!*, whimpering and hushed conversations and cackling laughter.

At one point, Rashida led the way up a metal ladder, then into a small room at street level with a paneled window. They crouched in the darkness, then Rashida opened the panels, letting in light and sound from outside. An amplified voice was blaring through the streets.

"...BY TWELVE NOON TODAY, AT ONE OF THE LIGHTED BARRIER GATES AT STREET LEVEL, OR ONE OF THE UNDERGROUND PROCESSING STATIONS. YOU WILL BE EXAMINED AND PROCESSED AND TRANSPORTED TO ISOLATION WARDS FOR YOUR OWN HEALTH AND SAFETY, AND FOR THE HEALTH AND SAFETY OF THE CITIZENS OF SAN FRANCISCO. . . ."

Rashida chuckled. "Right, that will be effective, appeal to their better instincts."

"... WILL BE SHOT. AGAIN, ALL RESISTERS WILL BE SHOT. THE SITUATION IS TOO GRAVE . . ."

She closed up the panels, bringing back the darkness. They remained in the room for a minute to let their eyes adjust back to the dim light, then Rashida led the way back down.

It wasn't much farther. They passed two bodies in the corridor, one face up with its throat cut, the other face down across the first. A little farther on they passed a woman sitting in front of a small pool of water; candles bobbed in the water, and the air smelled of burned wax.

Finally Rashida directed her down a short, dead-end passage, and they stopped in front of the left wall. There was an opening around chest level, but it was impossible to see more than a few inches into it.

"The grate's gone," Rashida said. She was looking around on the floor. "There it is." She picked it up, studied it, then set it back down, leaning it against the wall. She turned to Caroline. "This is it. You crawl through that duct. It will be a very tight squeeze at first, but it opens out at a T-branch. When it does, you go right, then right again at your first opportunity. You'll come out on the other side of this brick wall." She pointed at the bricked-up barrier across the passage. "There's another short passage, then a few steps leading up to a door to a basement storage room. To the left of the door, there will be a tiny depression in the concrete wall, and inside will be a key." She paused. "You'll be out. You'll still be in the Tenderloin, still in quarantine, but you won't be in the Core any longer."

"And what about you?"

"What about me? Who knows where I'll be?"

"Will I see you again?"

"Doubtful." There was a long silence. "Go, Caroline."

She wanted to give Rashida a hug, but it wouldn't be a smart thing to do. "I hope I do see you again."

"Just take care of that bag."

Caroline nodded. She put the bag in the duct first, pushed the bag forward, then crawled in after it. Rashida was right, it was extremely tight. She squirmed more than crawled her way along, her arms extended in front of her, pushing the bag forward as she went. Even breathing was difficult. But it wasn't long before she reached the T-branch, and the ducting widened. From there it was almost easy.

Hanging on to the leather bag, she stuck her head out of the duct and into the passage on the other side of the wall. Dark here, too, with a rectangle of light off to her left—the door. Caroline lowered the bag to the ground, then let herself slide out, dropping and rolling. She got to her feet, found the bag, and picked it up.

A scraping sound behind her.

Caroline froze. She listened hard, and thought she heard breathing. Slowly, so slowly, she turned around.

In the shadows, crouched against the wall, eyes wide, was a large monkey.

"It's all right," she said, keeping her voice soft. "I won't hurt you." It was hard to tell exactly how big the monkey was, or what kind it was. "It's all right," she said again.

The monkey didn't move. Keeping every movement slow and deliberate, Caroline walked along the passage toward the door. She periodically looked back at the monkey, but it didn't follow her. When she reached the steps, she climbed them, then felt around in the wall next to the door until she found the key.

She looked through the window. As Rashida had said, it was a basement storeroom, filled with crates and sacks and drums. There was no one inside. Caroline unlocked the door, and opened it.

She stood in the doorway and looked back at the monkey. She couldn't stand the idea of it being trapped in here. How had it got here to begin with? The same way she had, maybe. It could go back, she supposed, but that wasn't a good idea right now.

"Come on," she said. She gestured at the monkey to join her, and said, "Come on," again. "You can come out with me."

It was probably a stupid idea. What the hell would the monkey do out in the Tenderloin? But she still felt sick at the thought of trapping it in here.

"I'll leave the door open for you," she said. "You can leave if you want."

The monkey hadn't moved except to turn its head toward her. She could just see its eyes in the gloom.

"So long," she said.

And she left the door open behind her.

A half hour later she reached the RadioLand Street Clinic. Cage wasn't there, but Franzee said he had been hoping she would show up, and she told Caroline how to get up to his apartment. Soon she was standing outside his door, knocking.

"It's open," Cage called from within.

She opened the door and stepped inside. Cage was sitting at one of the windows, gazing down the street in the direction of the Core. She closed the door, took another couple of steps, and then he finally turned.

He stared at her for a minute, then a faint smile worked its way onto his face. "I can't believe you're here. I can't believe you got out."

She smiled back. It was good to see him. "Rashida got me out."

"Through the quarantine?"

She nodded. "Yeah. Have I got a story to tell you." But there was something strange about him, something sad and defeated, and then she realized what it had to be. "Nikki?" she asked.

"Dead," Cage answered, the smile disappearing. He breathed deeply once. "Dead."

29

CARLUCCI RODE IN one of the department helicopters above the city, swinging a wide arc around the quarantine perimeter. He wanted to get a sense of the whole picture, but they couldn't get too close without risking being shot out of the sky. Allegedly there was close cooperation between the army and the San Francisco Police Department, but in reality the army and the CDC were calling all the shots, and they were not allowing any encroachment of the airspace above the quarantine zone, police or otherwise.

The quarantine perimeter was irregular, but seemed to be fairly solid and settled in, street barriers manned by squads of armed soldiers, reinforced by trucks and jeeps and mounted gun posts. But the quarantine perimeter was not exactly synonymous with the Tenderloin perimeter—they hadn't been able to manage that. In several sections of the DMZ, meeting armed resistance, the army had eventually given up and included those strips of the DMZ inside the quarantine, like weird bubbles on the Tenderloin boundaries. Those would be sticky areas, too, in the long run; the Tenderloin, being for all practical purposes a walled city, was already self-contained, though maintaining a quarantine around it for very long would be difficult. But the DMZ strips were zones of chaos. The quarantine around them couldn't be very secure.

Farther inside the Tenderloin, the quarantine around the Core was nearly impossible to make out, too far away and obscured by the intervening buildings. But Carlucci tried to see if anything was happening, thinking about Caroline. He assumed she would come out with the other people from the Core, be processed and transferred to the isolation wards out on Treasure Island, but until he knew she actually had, he would worry.

He asked the pilot to set down on the rooftop where an observation site

had been set up for the police, on a building a block away from the Tenderloin but tall enough to give them a decent line of sight. The pilot nodded,
banked around, and five minutes later dropped Carlucci off. He hurried
away from the copter, and it took off, giving him one final blast of wind
from the blades.

He didn't know most of the cops at the roof's edge, but he was surprised
to see Vaughn, the Chief of Police, standing there with the others and watching him approach. Vaughn was a tall, thin man, handsome and graying with
distinction, charming without being slick—the perfect political animal on
the police force, which was why he was Chief. Even now in the growing
heat of the day he looked cool and comfortable in a light sand-colored silk
suit, dark brown shoes, and tie. Vaughn and Carlucci had been something
like enemies for years.

"Hello, Frank," Vaughn said as Carlucci reached the group. "Good to
see you."

"Andrew." They shook hands. "I'm surprised to see you out here."

"Dramatic moments for the city. The Chief should at least make an appearance out on the front lines, right?" Smiling, like they were sharing a
joke. Then his look turned serious. "I'm sorry to hear about your daughter."

"You say that as if she was dead."

"Frank, come on, that's not what I meant. But she has been missing for
a long time. I can imagine how I would feel if one of my children had gone
missing like that." Vaughn had two sons, one a lieutenant in the navy, the
other a rising corporate lawyer in one of the city's biggest law firms. "My
sympathies were sincerely given."

Carlucci nodded. They probably were. "Sorry," he said. "And thanks."
He nodded toward the Tenderloin. "What's been happening?"

"Not much, yet." They walked to the edge of the roof, two cops moving aside to make room for them. Then, subtly but clearly, all of the cops
moved away to give them a small zone of privacy. "It's not quite noon, yet,"
Vaughn said. "But I don't expect much to happen immediately. They'll wait
an extra hour for stragglers before going in with force."

From the edge of the roof they had a pretty good view of about two
blocks of Tenderloin perimeter and the quarantine line. As Vaughn had said,
things looked pretty quiet at the moment. The real action, though, wasn't
going to take place here, not yet anyway—it would occur at the Core, and
they couldn't see any of that at all from here. Just as well.

"What do *you* know about Cancer Cell?" Carlucci asked.

Vaughn laughed and looked at him quizzically. "Who have *you* been
talking to? Kelly?" He shook his head. "That man is obsessed with Cancer
Cell. He's the only person in the department who seemed to give a rat's ass
about them before today."

"I'm surprised you know about Kelly's interest." He didn't see any point
in pretending he wasn't aware of it himself.

"You shouldn't be, Frank. I make a point of knowing things like that about the officers working for me."

"And what are my interests?" Carlucci asked.

Vaughn smiled again. "Your obsessions are more abstract than most. But they are what should be, in good police officers, the obvious ones. Truth. And a striving for *rightness*. But they aren't obvious anymore, and they aren't held by many. I admire you greatly for those obsessions, Frank."

"Do you?"

"Oh, yes. I know what you think of me—my corruptions. They are great, it's true. But I'm much more complex than you give me credit for. I will never let you get in my way, Frank, but I do admire you. Accept the compliment. It *is* sincere."

He studied Vaughn, wondering if he had underestimated the man all these years.

One of the other cops called out, and there was pointing toward the Core. Carlucci and Vaughn turned to look. Something was rising above the ruined buildings, a strange podlike structure propelled in a jerking flight upward by a ring of jets trailing white smoke, a bizarre arrangement of fins and wings around it presumably acting as a steering mechanism. Big enough to contain two or three people. The pod continued to rise until it was forty or fifty feet above the buildings, then it veered away from the center.

Tracers shot up from the ground, followed a few seconds later by the ratcheting cracks of gunfire; they quickly zeroed in on the pod, tiny flashes appeared beneath it. Then there were several crumping sounds, and suddenly the pod exploded.

Bits of flashing metal sprayed out and down, along with larger chunks of what might have been body or structural parts, some licked by flames. A small piece with one of the jets apparently still intact spun crazily through the air, sometimes rising, sometimes diving, white smoke spinning about until it suddenly arced away and down and disappeared behind a building. Then all that was left in the air above the Core was dissipating smoke.

"A valiant effort," Vaughn said. "Unfortunately, there will be others. On the ground or in the air, it won't matter, they will all end like that." His voice seemed to carry real regret. "It's going to be bad in there."

"They'll be able to do it," Carlucci said. "Clear out the Core."

"Oh, certainly. But they'll be dragging bodies out of there, and a lot of their own. They have no idea."

"You have a better grasp on the realities than I would have expected."

Vaughn laughed. "Maybe when this is all over you and I should sit down and have a long talk. We might learn a lot about each other. We might like each other more."

"Yeah, maybe." His phone beeped. He took it off his belt, flipped it open. "Carlucci."

"Papa?"

"Caroline?" He could hardly believe he was hearing her voice, and a shiver went through him.

"Yes, it's me, Papa."

"Hold on a second." Vaughn was looking at him, eyebrow raised. Carlucci walked away from him and the others. "Are you all right? Where are you?"

"I'm fine, Papa."

He was standing out in the middle of the roof, far enough from the others for privacy, but he could see Vaughn still watching him.

"Are you in the Core?"

There was a slight hesitation, then Caroline said, "How did you know I was there?"

"A long and ugly story," he said. "Are you out?" He'd caught the "was."

"Yes, I'm out. That's a long story, too. But I'm still in the Tenderloin. I guess I'm going to be here for a while."

"Have you talked to your mom?"

"Yes, I called home first."

"Where are you now? Where are you going to stay? Maybe I can get you out." But he knew even as he said it that it would be impossible. They would not be making any exceptions with the quarantine.

Caroline just laughed. "Forget it, Papa, you can't get me out. But I'll be fine. I'm with Cage, and he said I can stay in Nikki's apartment. He said you knew who she was."

Again that word. "Yeah. Is she still alive?"

"No."

He nodded to himself. "Tell Cage I'm sorry."

"I will, Papa."

And then he didn't know what to say. She was out of the Core, she was temporarily safe, but she was still in the Tenderloin, stuck there for the duration of the quarantine.

"It's so good to hear your voice," he finally said. "We were . . . well, you know."

"I'm fine, Papa. It'll be strange for a while, but I'll be okay here. You know how to reach Cage, yes?"

"Yes. Is he there with you?"

A few moments later, Cage came on the line.

"I'm sorry about Nikki," Carlucci said.

"Thanks."

"Listen, Cage. The Tenderloin is your home. Caroline doesn't know it for shit. Take care of her, will you?"

It sounded as if Cage was laughing. Then he said, "You're her father, all right. She probably doesn't need it much, but I'll take care of her, Carlucci. Don't worry about her."

Yeah, right. "Thanks, Cage."

"You bet. Here she is again."

There was another short pause, then Caroline was back. "I'll be okay, Papa."

"I know. I love you, Caroline."

"I love you too, Papa. And I'll talk to you soon."

"Good-bye."

"Bye, Papa."

Carlucci clipped the phone back to his belt, then looked back at the other cops. Vaughn was still watching him. He didn't want to go back and answer Vaughn's questions. Besides, he'd seen enough here. He turned away, and walked toward the rooftop stairwell.

30

CAGE AND CAROLINE stood at the edge of Nikki's apartment rooftop, crowded in on both sides, leaning over the metal pipe railing and gazing down into the Core. The roof edges of all the buildings facing the Core were lined with people, like spectators at a sporting event, except most everyone seemed to realize that only disaster was coming.

The heat was incredible, and the acrid smell of sweat was heavy in the air, almost cloying. Below them, on the outer streets of the Core, the soldiers must have been roasting. Cage was surprised at how many there were, armed and armored, masked and gloved, some patrolling the outer perimeter, others manning the checkpoint processing stations that had been set up at the street boundaries and in the ground floors of a few of the border buildings. In the streets just outside the barriers, military ambulances waited, surrounded by more soldiers. Periodically one would pull away, lights flashing, heading out of the Tenderloin. Medical personnel were nearly invisible. And it was impossible to know what was going on underground—probably just as much activity, if not more.

He wasn't sure why they were here, watching. No, that really wasn't true, he realized. He knew why Caroline was here—in the short time she'd been inside, she'd developed an affinity, or at least a concern, for Cancer Cell. Maybe even the other people inside the Core. She wanted to know what was going to happen to them; she wanted to *see* what was going to happen. And he just wanted to be with her. Her presence helped ease the pain of Nikki's death. Being alone made everything worse.

It was twelve-thirty, but not much had happened yet. The repeating message blaring out over the speakers had changed, now announcing that the army was granting an extra hour before they went in to remove all remaining people by force.

Movement below them slowed, almost ceased completely, and the soldiers turned to one of the buildings across the street. One of them gestured, and the message broadcast was cut off. Everything got quiet.

"Hey!" It was a voice from inside the building. "Hey, don't shoot, I'm coming out. No one's going to shoot, are they?"

"No one's going to shoot you," an officer said. "Just come on out and proceed to the checkpoint."

A few moments later, a tall, skinny man wearing only a tiny racing swimsuit and sunglasses emerged from the building. He stepped gingerly, his bare feet treading lightly across the debris scattered all over the ground. He was a strange-looking man, his face deeply tanned while the rest of his body, from the neck down, was incredibly pale, glistening with an oily substance.

The man walked carefully out into the middle of the street, then stopped. He looked up at all the people on the rooftops, then raised both hands high above his head, grinning. Then he bowed, looked back at the soldiers, and said, "Take me to your leader!"

The soldiers approached, but didn't get closer than about five feet from the man. They used their rifles to point the way, and escorted him to an open doorway in the building next to the one Cage and Caroline were on. Cage leaned out over the railing, saw the man stop near the door until the hands of people in isolation suits took his arms and pulled him inside.

Cage turned to Caroline and smiled. "Too bad it couldn't all be like that."

She didn't smile back. "I'm worried about them. Rashida and Dr. Mike and the others. I don't think they're going to come out. I think they're going to stay in there as long as possible, and then they'll fight. And if they do that, they'll be killed."

"Probably. But it's their choice," he reminded her. "They could come out right now, leave everything behind."

"Everything is right," she said, her voice going hard. "Their work, their *lives* are in there." She shook her head. "Rashida seemed to think that wiping out Cancer Cell was one of the goals of this whole thing." She looked at Cage. "Do you think she was paranoid?"

He shrugged. "Maybe not. But it doesn't matter, does it? They *are* going to wipe them out."

"Thanks," Caroline said. "You're a real comfort."

One o'clock approached without further incident, at least not within their sight. They did hear a few scattered gunshots, but they couldn't tell if they were coming from another part of the Core, or somewhere else altogether.

Then Cage felt a slight tremor. Brief, but noticeable. He looked at Caroline. "Did you feel that?"

She had just started to nod when there came a string of muffled explosions, shaking the building. Then another string, and suddenly, just inside of the street barrier at the end of the block, the road opened up and caved in, sucking in half a dozen or more soldiers. Smoke poured out of the crater, and a third string of explosions went off, these much louder, and more pavement collapsed, catching several more soldiers.

Shouts and gunfire erupted, aimless and pointless as far as Cage could tell. The Core street barrier was right on the edge of the crater, and he could see it shifting, the tall structure of concrete and metal and wood tilting forward. Then the ground beneath it collapsed and it crumbled with crashing sounds and clouds of dust and smoke.

It was getting difficult to tell what was happening, with smoke and dust billowing everywhere, and chaos among the troops, but it looked as if troops from outside the Core were forming across the street just behind where the barrier had been, determined to prevent anyone from escaping through the breach. But it was probably pointless; it was difficult to imagine that anyone could actually climb up out of the crater to make an escape, and that would be the only way to get to the breached barrier without going through the Core troops, who were already pulling together. A group of them surrounded the crater, rifles aimed at the dark and smoking interior. Cage wondered how long it would be before they went in after their comrades.

Several objects came flying out of one of the buildings, hurtling toward one group of soldiers. When the objects hit the ground they burst into streaming sheets of flame. Gunfire followed quickly, which was immediately returned by the soldiers. Two explosions tore out huge chunks of the building. Someone screamed, then two more rockets or mortars struck the building, blowing a hole in the second floor. The gunfire seemed to intensify.

There was a cry on the roof a few feet away from them, and somebody staggered back, arm bleeding. There was another cry on the building next to them, and a woman pitched over the edge, falling five floors to the pavement.

Cage grabbed Caroline by the arm, pulled her back from the railing and down to the ground. "Stay put," he said. "Don't try to run yet."

She nodded, and they lay on the roof together while most everyone panicked around them. Cage watched people stumbling over each other, trampling anyone who fell. When the worst of it was well past them, they crawled a few feet farther back from the edge of the roof and sat up, watching the mad rush. Eight or nine people were lying on the roof, writhing in pain, moaning. Christ.

"You mind helping me?" he asked her. "I'd better start checking them out."

"Sure, whatever I can do."

They could still hear gunfire and explosions from the Core, more sporadic now, but not exactly fading away.

"Did I give you the key to Nikki's?"

She shook her head. He dug around in his pocket for his keys, unhooked Nikki's from the ring, and handed it to her.

"I want you to go down to Nikki's apartment. Inside the closet by the front door, up on a shelf, are a couple of med-kits. Those will have to do for now."

She nodded again. "I'll get back as quickly as I can." She got to her feet, staying in a crouch for the first few steps, then standing upright once she was about twenty feet from the edge of the roof. She hurried to the stairwell hatch, and Cage crawled across the roof to the closest victim.

By the time night fell, the worst of the fighting seemed to be over, but the Core was in flames. Cage and Caroline were back on the roof again, watching the buildings burn; gunfire was infrequent and sporadic. It seemed safer now.

The army had announced that everything was under control, the quarantine and the Core secure; there was only a bit of mopping up to do. The CDC, too, had made an announcement, that all residents of the Core, and all those who, in the skirmishes, had risk of exposure to them, were safely tucked away in isolation wards on Treasure Island. Everything was fine.

But there had been no official casualty reports on the broadcast media; all that was reported was that there had been some injuries. There was no mention of fatalities. The street newshawkers, however, *were* reporting numbers, though they were calling them guesses or approximations. The number of dead soldiers and medical personnel was being given in the thirties and forties, with the number of injured going over a hundred. Unknown numbers of civilian dead and injured in the Core, and small numbers of dead and injured outside the Core from stray gunfire and explosions. The newshawkers had raw footage of bodies being pulled out of the craters, or loaded into ambulances; there was lots of blood.

Now, though, things were quieter. There were few people on the rooftops now. And with the coming of darkness, the army seemed content to maintain the quarantine perimeter, and had ceased their forays into the Core buildings. It was too risky now, anyway, with nearly all of them on fire. It was completely unclear as to how the various fires had begun, or by whom. Fire department trucks and crews surrounded the Core, and though they periodically hosed down the perimeter buildings, they did not do a thing to even slow the fires in the Core buildings.

"They're going to burn it to the ground," Caroline said.

"They won't all burn to the ground," Cage replied. "We'll have some good hollow hulks left behind. Scarred and gutted, but with walls intact."

"But no people."

"No," he agreed. "No people."

"And no more Cancer Cell."

And no more Cancer Cell. Cage wondered if anyone knew what the real repercussions of that would be. Cancer Cell had been a good source of black market pharmaceuticals, a cleaner and cheaper source than most others.

"Yeah. And all this for nothing," Cage said.

"What do you mean?"

He shook his head. "This whole quarantine has been a fiasco from the beginning. This disease, whatever it is, isn't confined to the Tenderloin, and it sure as hell hasn't been confined to the Core for a long time, if it ever was."

"Who said it was?" Caroline asked.

"Oh, yeah, that's right, you were inside when all this came down. The CDC said it was. They claimed that most cases were confined to the Core, with possibly a few outside but definitely in the Tenderloin. *Maybe* it started, somehow, in the Core, but none of this," he said, gesturing at the flames licking up at the night sky, "will do much good."

"Then why do it?" Caroline asked.

"I don't know. Maybe they're ignorant or stupid, or so afraid of the reality that they deny what's going on. Or public relations, maybe, for when all hell breaks loose. They'll claim they did what they could as soon as they could." He gazed steadily into Caroline's eyes. "And maybe they had other purposes. That's why I said that maybe Rashida *wasn't* being paranoid." He shook his head. "The whole thing stinks. And they won't be able to hold it together once word gets out that more and more cases of the disease are showing up outside the quarantine."

"You're pretty sure about that, aren't you? That there are cases outside the Tenderloin."

He nodded.

"But maybe the quarantine will confine the worst of it, make it easier to deal with the cases outside, keep it from spreading."

"It's too late for that."

"How do you know?"

He shrugged. How could he explain it? A gut feeling that was almost a certainty. He turned back to watch the burning buildings. "I wonder how many people are still in there."

31

THE HEAT WAVE finally broke. Cool ocean air rolled into the city along with dark and heavy clouds, and it rained for two days. Temperatures plummeted, daytime highs finally dropping below eighty.

But the improved weather didn't improve Carlucci's disposition. The only thing he could do was his job. And for right now that meant Naomi

Katsuda's murder. Besides, he still believed there were connections between her murder and Cancer Cell and this impending plague.

But the damn case was still a dead end. Santos and Weathers had pretty much stopped working on it, not because of disinterest or even despair, but by default. There was nowhere else to go. The only lead now unexplored was Naomi Katsuda's mysterious friend, who remained unfound. And that was something he could work on; there was one more way to go with it, and he was the only one who could. He hated to do it, but there was no other way.

And so, at eleven in the morning, with the temperature a pleasant seventy-four degrees, he walked to the stretch of Geary Street that ran between the Financial District and the Tenderloin. He stopped in front of a door inside a small alcove, narrow, carpeted stairs visible through the glass. On the glass, in gold leaf lettering, were two business names: LINDSEY TRAVEL SER-VICES and ALICE BASSO, PHILATELIC CONSULTANT. On the right, mounted in the brick, were two intercom buttons, and Carlucci pressed one.

"Yes?" Alice's distinctive voice, recognizable even through the crackling intercom.

"Hi, Alice. It's Frank. Carlucci."

"Frankie, my darling boy. Come on in."

The door buzzed, and he pushed it open. He climbed the worn, dark green carpeted stairs to the second floor, then walked down the short hall to Alice's office. The door was open, and she had a customer inside with her.

The walls of Alice's shop were lined with bookcases, and the bookcases were crammed with stamp albums, stock books and binders, and small file drawers. One bookcase was filled with catalogs and other reference books. There were also two long glass display cases, two tables, and several chairs. Alice's customer, a man in his fifties wearing a business suit, sat at one of the tables, studying a stamp under an illuminated magnifier. Alice was sitting across from him.

She was closing in on eighty, and needed a cane to get around, but she was still a handsome woman. Tall and big-boned, with a beautiful smile and beautiful teeth, and thick silvery hair, she had a strong presence; her face was wrinkled and lined, but it suggested character rather than decay.

"Frankie." She was the only person he knew who called him that, the only person who had done so since he was fifteen, when he had insisted on being called Frank.

Her customer glanced at him, then returned his attention to the stamps in front of him. Carlucci approached the table, leaned over, and kissed Alice on the cheek. "Hello, Alice." He walked over to the one armchair in the room and sank into it, waiting for Alice's customer to finish.

The man stayed another hour, then wrote out a check and left with a small envelope he tucked into a locking leather briefcase. Alice got up with the help of her cane, walked behind the glass cases, and put the check in her safe. Then she limped over to the padded wooden chair beside Carlucci and dropped into it. She never sat in the armchair because it was too hard for her to get up from it.

"I want you to tell me that this is a social visit," she said to him. "That you're taking me to lunch and a couple of stiff drinks." She shook her head, smiling. "But I can tell from your face that this is just business."

"I need to talk to Istvan," he said.

"Oh, Frankie," she said, sighing heavily. "Istvan doesn't want to talk to you. You know that."

"I need him, Alice."

"Not this time, Frankie. He made me promise not to tell you."

Carlucci hated all of this, but he felt like he had no choice. He got up from the chair, walked behind the glass cases, and opened her address and com number file drawer.

"Don't do it, you bastard!" Her voice was anguished, but she knew she couldn't stop him. Nothing would stop him now, not even guilt.

He thumbed through the cards with Alice's fine and delicate handwriting, all in green ink. They weren't in alphabetical order, which made things difficult; he had never figured out what her system was. Then he found it: Istvan Darnyi. He copied down the address. There was no other number; Istvan had done without a phone for years. Then he closed up the file drawer.

"I'm sorry," he said, turning back to her. But she wouldn't look at him. There were tears on her cheeks, working their way down through the wrinkles. He felt awful.

He walked over to her and tried to kiss her cheek again, but she pulled away, holding up her hand.

"I'm sorry," he said again. "Good-bye, Alice."

But she still would not look at him, and did not answer.

Istvan's address was an apartment in North Beach. Carlucci stood outside the building, looking up at the third floor. He thought about walking away without talking to Istvan, leaving the man in peace, but he couldn't do it.

Istvan Darnyi had been a policeman for twenty years, a detective first in Vice, then Narcotics, and finally Homicide as his talents became apparent. What Istvan Darnyi was great at was finding people. He didn't need much to work with, and in fact the less there was, the better he seemed to work. A name without any other information, or a photograph without a name, or no name, no picture, just some other miscellaneous bits of information, that was all he needed. Just something to start with.

Istvan never forgot anything, never forgot a picture or chart or table he had seen, and had an uncanny knack for putting disparate pieces of information together. But that memory was also his burden. The longer his career went on, the worse each job was. Because as he would start working on finding someone, working with little information, his digging inevitably led to associations with past cases, and once that began, he could not put aside any of the memories or images of those cases, which included crime scene photographs, autopsy photos, firsthand viewings of mutilated corpses, or the anguish of friends and relatives of the dead, all of it swirling around in his head, filling his dreams and turning them into nightmares, disturbing his sleep so badly that eventually he would hardly be able to sleep at all until the investigation was over. And even then it would take days for him to put everything out of his memory, since even the slightest reminder would trigger it all back full force.

It got to be too much. Divorce had been the first price he'd paid, but not the last. It was killing him. He applied for full disability, which was granted, and he resigned. He had always been a stamp collector, more a hobby than anything too serious, but when he retired he retreated completely into the philatelic world, trying to keep the rest of the real world out and away.

But Istvan and Carlucci had once been close friends, and twice before Carlucci had asked him for his help. He had known what it cost Istvan, but each time the case had seemed important enough. And after both times he had promised never to ask for Istvan's help again. The last time, not quite believing Carlucci, Istvan had told Carlucci he never wanted to see him again, and he had disappeared. Until now, Carlucci had never tried to find him.

But here he was, feeling guilty, and feeling sorrow for his old friend. He truly had never intended to bother him again. So he made a promise to himself, that this time *would* be the last.

Apartment 3C. The name on the security system was Stephen Darnell. Carlucci pressed the button. A minute passed, then a harsh crackling voice answered.

"Yes."

"Istvan. It's Frank Carlucci."

There was a long silence, no response at all. But the intercom sounded as if it was still open. The silence continued, Carlucci waited. Finally the door buzzed, and he pushed it open.

Istvan met him at his apartment door, holding it open.

"Hello, Istvan."

Istvan just nodded, and closed the door as Carlucci entered.

Istvan led the way among tables and shelves, through two small rooms filled with boxes and albums of stamps, to the kitchen in the back. The kitchen was tiny, but bright, full of windows that looked out onto the street.

"Sit down," he said. There was a square, wooden table with two chairs. In the middle of the table was a crystal vase with blue and yellow flowers. "I'll make coffee." He seemed sad and resigned, as though giving in to the inevitable.

When the coffee was done, they began. Carlucci told Istvan everything he thought might have any relevance, from the day Caroline asked him to help find Tito, to the quarantines imposed by the CDC. Istvan listened, asking an occasional question. They drank strong black coffee, and Istvan, after closing the kitchen door so the smoke would not get to the stamps, smoked one cigarette after another. For the first time in a year or two, Carlucci felt that strong craving again.

When he was finished, he handed the sketch artist picture to Istvan, who took it from him and studied it. They sat in silence for several minutes, Istvan continuing to smoke as he thought and studied the picture.

He nodded once, then looked at Carlucci, his expression still sad. "I'll find her for you," he said.

"Thank you, Istvan." He paused, wondering if he could be convincing. "This will be the last time. I mean it. The next time I come to see you, it will be just for a visit. Just two old friends, talking."

"Don't bother," Istvan replied. "We are not friends anymore." He shook another cigarette from his pack and lit it. "I'll call you."

32

IT WAS RAINING again, and the sound of it spattering against the windows was soothing. Caroline lay on top of the sleeping bag spread across the old wood and canvas cot, eyes closed, listening to the rain. She was sick, and she was afraid to tell Cage.

Fever made her head swim, and she felt sick to her stomach. Swallowing was difficult, and there was a sharp and throbbing pain at her temples. It had come on so quickly, she hadn't been prepared for it. All this time, struggling with her fear of the Gould's, and now she may have contracted a disease that would kill her in a matter of days, not years. Crazy.

She opened her eyes and sat up slowly, leaning back against the wall for support. Where was the telephone? She couldn't remember. Her eyes ached. Maybe it was just a bad flu. Yeah, and maybe she was going to live to be ninety years old.

She looked around the room, and finally saw the phone on top of the small bookcase near the window. She had to call Cage, if only to tell him to stay away. She had volunteered to help out at the street clinic, and when she didn't show up, he would come looking for her.

After resting for a minute or two, she got to her feet and walked over to the phone. She picked up the receiver, then sat in the chair by the window. She raised the window and stuck her empty hand out into the rain. Yes, it was cool. She cupped her hand, let it fill with rainwater, then brought it back in and splashed it across her face. It felt great. She did it twice more, then sat back in the chair and punched in the clinic number.

Cage came anyway, as she'd known he would.

"Don't touch me," she told him when he came into the apartment. "Stay away." And she was reminded of Nikki sitting at the curb outside the clinic after crashing the pedalcart, yelling at Cage to stay away from her.

But he didn't stay away. "You know how many times I've been exposed to this disease?" he said. "Between Nikki and Tito and the other people I've seen at the clinic in the past few weeks? Way too many times. I must have some kind of natural resistance or immunity to it."

"Lucky you."

"Besides, we don't know that that's what you have."

She glared at him. "Yes we do."

He shook his head. "The incubation period's too short. Even if you were exposed to it the very first day you were in the Core, it hasn't been nearly as long as the time between Nikki's exposure and when she came down with it."

"We don't know when I was exposed. Besides . . ." She frowned, thinking about Rashida. "The incubation period has been getting shorter."

"How the hell do you know that?"

She told him what Rashida and the Fat Man had said about the changes they'd noticed, their thoughts and speculations about the disease.

He didn't say anything after that, but he made her take something for the fever, then put her back to bed. After making some tea for both of them, he sat in a chair that he pulled up near the bed.

"You should go," she tried again. "You should just leave me alone."

Cage just shook his head. She lay back on the cot and closed her eyes. She was glad he was here.

33

CAGE FELT AS if his life were coming apart on him. He thought maybe the whole world was coming apart.

He sat in a chair by the open window of what had once been Nikki's apartment, listening to the night sounds of the Tenderloin and watching the lights and people on the street below. Caroline was sleeping on the cot just behind him, and he listened to her breathing, which at the moment was calm and even.

Core Fever. There wasn't much doubt now. She had it, and she had it bad.

He couldn't believe he was going to go through this all over again. He'd never had much of a chance to recover from Nikki, and he felt completely unprepared to watch Caroline die. But, like so much else these days, he didn't have a choice. Not one he could live with, anyway.

It had been just two days since she'd called him. He had brought one of the clinic cots and moved into the apartment; he'd also brought extra sheets and blankets for Caroline to sleep in instead of the sleeping bag, hoping to make her more comfortable. He still worked his shifts at the clinic—he *had* to; things were falling apart there, too—but he slept and ate here, and nursed Caroline, feeding her when she could eat, making broth and tea for her, providing her with a steady stream of cold damp cloths for her face. He helped her make her way to the bathroom, and helped her shower once or twice a day to stay clean and cool. She tried to get him to wear gloves whenever he touched her, but she had given up on that after the first day.

They were seeing probable new cases of Core Fever every day at the clinic, and there was nothing they could do for those people. They had no facilities to care for them, no rooms or beds or staff. All they could do was send them home, where they were more likely to expose family members and friends and neighbors.

As far as Cage was concerned, the quarantine around the Tenderloin had become completely unconscionable. Clearly a majority of cases were inside the Tenderloin, but more cases of Core Fever were appearing *outside* the Tenderloin every day. In fact, cases were being reported outside of San Francisco, even as far away as New York City—not in the traditional media, which was being uncharacteristically reticent about those cases, but among doctors and other health professionals.

But the CDC was still claiming that the cases outside the Tenderloin were *not* Core Fever, and so maintained the need to continue with the quarantine. With no real hospital facilities in the Tenderloin, and no effective ways to isolate those who came down with Core Fever, the quarantine was turning a bad situation in the Tenderloin into a nightmare—leaving people who were dying without even the benefits of comfort care, and severely exacerbating the transmission of the disease.

Eric Ralston had become unreachable. The number he'd given Cage had been disconnected, and calls to the CDC in Atlanta went nowhere. If nothing else, he wanted to try to shame or guilt Eric into arguing with his colleagues for a dismantling of the quarantine, but he couldn't do that if he couldn't even talk to him.

The only positive thing Cage had heard in recent days were a couple of unconfirmed reports of people surviving Core Fever. But with no way yet to make a certain diagnosis, no antibody test or anything like it, it was impossible to know for sure if the survivors had actually contracted Core Fever rather than some other serious illness.

Yes, he decided, the whole world *was* coming apart.

"Cage?" Caroline's voice was quiet.

He turned around and looked at her. She was lying on her side, eyes barely open.

"How are you feeling?"

"Terrible."

"Do you think you can eat anything?"

"No. But I'm thirsty."

The water pitcher beside the cot was nearly empty, and the water was tepid, so he fixed a fresh batch of ice water, filled a glass, and held it for her, putting the straw in her mouth so she could drink without raising her head.

When she finished, she turned onto her back and closed her eyes. "Thanks," she said.

"Sure. Anything else?"

"Not right now."

There was a long silence, and he thought she had gone back to sleep. He sat and watched her steady breathing, feeling an ache in his chest. He hadn't known her very long, but he'd come to like her quite a lot, and he couldn't believe he was going to lose her before he'd even had a chance to really know her.

"Cage?"

"Yes."

"Have you told my parents yet?"

"No." He hesitated. "I wanted to be sure. I was going to call them tomorrow."

"Don't." She opened her eyes and looked at him. "Don't tell them."

"Why not?"

"What's the point? So they can worry themselves sick waiting to hear that I've died? They can't come here to see me, I can't get out, so what's the point?" She closed her eyes again, breathing hard for a few moments.

"They're your parents. They'd want to know. They'd want to talk to you. You might want to talk to them."

"No," she said one final time, opening her eyes to look at him. "Wait until I'm dead."

34

CARLUCCI WAS DRIVING himself and Andrea crazy, wandering around the house unable to sit still, until Andrea told him to stay put somewhere or get the hell out of the house. So he finally retreated to the basement and his trumpet, hoping that music would relax him.

It didn't help.

He was waiting for too much, unable to do anything *except* wait—for the quarantine to end so Caroline wouldn't be trapped inside the Tenderloin; for Istvan to get back to him about the missing woman; for some other break to materialize from Ruben and Toni or one of the other teams; for some resolution to the Core Fever situation. It was all making him nuts, and he felt like he was on speed, frazzled and jittery and wanting to rip off his skin.

The basement door opened, and Andrea came down a couple of steps. Miles Davis was on the stereo, the sound track from *Siesta,* haunting and beautiful.

"Turn that off, please." Andrea had to raise her voice above the music, but her tone was strangely uneven, her expression fixed and lifeless.

Something was wrong.

He grabbed the remote and cut off the music. The sudden silence was disquieting. He set his trumpet beside him on the couch and sat forward.

"What is it?"

Andrea took another couple of steps down, then sat on the stairs.

"Cage called."

"Caroline?" He wanted to stand up, but he felt suddenly immobile.

She nodded. "She's got it. Core Fever. She's got it." She gazed helplessly at him. "She asked him not to call us. But he thought we would want to know." She slowly shook her head from side to side. "But I don't," she said, her voice getting quieter, harsher. "This is something I don't want to know at all." And then she put her face in her hands, elbows on knees, and began to cry.

Carlucci felt dizzy, a terrible ache in his chest. He struggled to his feet, knees weak. When he was sure he wouldn't lose his balance, he walked to the stairs, grabbed on to the railing, and pulled himself up, one difficult step at a time until he reached her. He sat beside his wife, put his arm around her, her shaking driving through him, and then he, too, began to cry.

Incredibly, the day got even worse. He would not have thought it possible.

Andrea was sitting out in the backyard, staring at the garden, or perhaps at nothing at all. She hadn't moved for more than an hour after asking to be left alone. He stood at the kitchen window, looking out at her, wishing he could do something to comfort her, wishing he could do something to comfort himself, and wishing more than anything else that there was something he could do for Caroline. But he had been wishing that for years, and he could no more do anything for her now than he ever could.

The phone rang, and when he answered it there was someone babbling hysterically at him.

"Wait a minute, wait . . . just a second and calm down. Who is this?"

The babbling finally broke, there was some sniffling and wheezing, then, "Mr. Carlucci?"

"Yes. Who is this?"

"Paula. Paula Ng." Christina's roommate.

"Paula, what is it?"

"Oh, Jesus, Mr. Carlucci. It's Tina, I think she's got it."

He thought his heart stopped. Certainly his breathing did, and a strange, very quiet rushing sound filled his ears, and something funny happened to his vision, as if it had become pocked with bits of glitter.

"You think she's got what?" he finally managed to say, wondering if his voice was loud enough for her to hear. He could imagine only one answer to his question, but he had to ask it anyway.

"Core Fever. Oh, God, Mr. Carlucci, I don't know, maybe it's not, but she's so sick, and she was getting those rashes across her chest, and we didn't know what else it could be, but no one out here's supposed to be able to get it, but what else, I don't know, Tina got so scared and I got scared and—"

"Where is she, Paula?"

"On her way to St. Anthony's. I called an ambulance, I gave them Tina's insurance chip, and they took her to St. Anthony's, and they left me here, and I don't know what to do. I wonder was I too close to her or did we drink out of the same glass or what, am I going to get it too—?"

He hung up on her. He knew it was rude, he knew it was an awful thing to do, but he couldn't take it anymore, he couldn't listen to one more word of it.

There was a deep, thrumming ache driving through him, and he was barely aware of anything else. He felt as if his heart had collapsed, and could hardly beat anymore. He didn't move for a long time, several minutes, maybe longer. When he did finally move, it was only to return to the kitchen window and look out at Andrea, wondering how the hell he was going to tell her.

They sat together in the tiny visitors' lounge at the end of the corridor, gratefully alone. Christina was in an isolation room, in a drugged sleep. When Carlucci and Andrea had arrived, Christina had been scared, and became hysterical when they had come into the room with gowns and gloves and masks on; the doctors would not let them enter the room otherwise. She would not calm down, and eventually Dr. Sodhi had sedated her.

Technically Christina was diagnosed as ill from an unidentified agent, probably viral or bacterial, but they all knew. Dr. Sodhi pointed out that the CDC was not currently recognizing any cases of Core Fever outside of the Tenderloin, though they were asking that all presumptive cases be reported to them. This was Dr. Sodhi's second patient with Core Fever. The other had been Cage's friend Nikki. Nikki had lived for two or three weeks. Christina probably wouldn't.

Carlucci held Andrea's hand, the two linked hands resting on his thigh. Neither of them had spoken for a long time.

"Both of them," she said. "We're going to lose both of them." She began to slowly shake her head from side to side, making a faint, high keening sound. Then everything stopped, she dropped her hands to her side and opened her eyes, and turned to look at him. "I feel a little bit insane. And I want to become hysterical." Something like a smile appeared. "I can't quite believe this is happening, because I don't see how I can actually stand it if it really is, I don't see how I can stand it *without* going insane." Then the strange smile disappeared. "You know that feeling of relief you get when you wake up from a particularly disturbing dream, that almost rushlike sensation when you realize that it was a dream, and that you won't actually have to face whatever it was that was happening?"

Carlucci nodded, knowing exactly what she meant.

"I want that feeling, Frank, I want it so badly I could scream, and I know, I *know* I am not going to get that feeling. And that makes me want to scream even more." She paused, staring hard at him.

He continued his silence, helpless and paralyzed by grief.

"For Christ's sake, Frank, talk to me!" She pulled her hand back, balled it into a fist, and swung, punching his arm. "Talk to me!"

She struck him twice more, but he still could not say anything. Then she stopped, threw her arms around him, and buried her face in his shoulder.

35

SHE AWAKENED, AND opened her eyes. But the light hurt, and she closed them again. She felt awful.

Was she alone? She listened, heard sounds from the street coming in through open windows, but nothing from the apartment.

"Cage?"

"Yes."

"Are you here?"

"Yes, I'm here."

She heard floorboards creaking, the sounds of Cage settling into the chair beside the cot, then felt his hand take hers. She tried opening her eyes again, just a crack this time, wanting to see his face. Yes, he was there, looking down at her. She hadn't been sure.

She thought about raising her head to look around, look down at her arms, see if the rashes were there yet, but she didn't even try. It was impossible.

"Can I get something for you?" he asked.

She closed her eyes once more. "What time is it?"

"Uh, three-thirty, four, something like that."

"In the afternoon?"

"Yes."

"Tell me how Nikki saved your life," she said.

"Now?"

"Now." And she tried smiling, though she wasn't sure she managed it.

There was nothing for a while, and she wondered if he was gone. But she couldn't open her eyes to look for him.

"I was living in L.A.," Cage began. "Young hotshot doctor doing image enhancements for the rich and famous. Well, mostly just rich. A few who were on their way up and later became moderately famous. And I made a lot of money. Lived in a high-security beachfront condo, drove around in an armored convertible, zoned myself out in nightlife."

"You?" Caroline said.

"Yeah, me. Then I was kidnapped, by a group called El Espíritu de la Gente—Spirit of the People. They took me into a housing project in East L.A., one of the newer ones built just after the turn of the century, where . . ."

The image of Cage driving along a coastal highway in a convertible filled her vision, pulsing as it repeatedly flashed from left to right, her eyes flickering as she followed it. His hair blew behind him, longer than she'd ever seen it on him, arm resting on the door, a cigarette between the fingers of his right hand, miniature, shiny sunglasses covering his eyes. She almost laughed.

". . . the clinic had no intention of paying any kind of ransom, either in cash or medicine, but these people didn't care that much, they figured to force me to provide medical care for the people in the project. . . ."

Was that Cage talking? Yes, but what the hell was he talking about? Kidnappers? Oh, that's right, she'd asked him to tell her about Nikki saving his life . . . she had to pay closer attention.

". . . so they gave me this nice tattoo on my neck. They thought it was funny, and I guess it was. I didn't think so at the time, but I can see the humor in it now. I've never had any desire to remove it. It's a good reminder to me of what . . ."

Tito had a tattoo on his arm, a diamond necklace wrapping around his elbow. She should have looked for the tattoo in the morgue when she'd gone with her father to identify the body, then she would have known for sure . . . but that was crazy, that had been Tito, there was no doubt . . . and so cold . . . but she was so hot right now, and she couldn't imagine that she would ever be as cold as Tito was that day.

". . . no longer useful to them. In fact, I was becoming a problem. I knew, deep down in my gut, that they were going to kill me—it was the easiest way to take care of the problem. And that's when Nikki made her . . ."

Cage. She wiggled her fingers. Yes, he was still holding her hand, and it felt good, keeping her from completely coming apart and dissipating into the air, and she didn't want him to ever let it go.

". . . Nikki half dragging me down the hall . . ."

Nikki? Was she here? No, Nikki was dead, dead from Core Fever, the same thing raging through her right now.

"Cage? Are you here?"

He squeezed her hand. "Yes, Caroline, I'm here."

"Cage. Tell me how Nikki saved your life. That day at Mika's, you said you would tell me someday."

There was a long pause, and she wondered if he was still there, but he squeezed her hand again.

"Sure," he said. "I'll tell you." And he began. "I was living down in L.A., hotshot young doctor, doing image enhancements, and making a lot of money. . . ."

It was dark and she was alone. She lay on the cot with her eyes open, flashing colored lights from outside providing a strange illumination, casting a few shadows on the ceiling above her.

"Cage?"

No answer.

"Cage?" Louder this time.

Still no answer. She *was* alone.

Suddenly she was afraid. She was sick and she was dying and she didn't want to be alone, she wanted Cage here with her, holding her hand or placing cold wet cloths on her forehead, talking to her, bringing her tea or water, just *being* here.

It was hot, and she could hardly breathe. Her arms itched and burned and her joints ached and she thought her head was going to burst, and she almost wished it would, to release all the pressure building inside. Then she realized there were other pressures, too, farther down. Her bladder. Oh, God, she didn't think she could get up, but she didn't want to wet the bed, not now, not when she was alone and she would have to lie in it. . . . She remembered the bedpan Cage had brought, it was under the cot, but she didn't want to use that, either. Besides, if she could manage that, she could manage getting herself to the bathroom, it wasn't that far away.

What was happening to her?

She closed her eyes for a few moments, breathing slowly and deeply, gearing herself up for it. Then she opened her eyes, pushed back the sheet, and turned onto her side. She reached over the side of the cot, stretching until she touched the floor, then half rolled, half fell out of the cot and onto the floor, hitting her side and going over until she was on her back and staring up at the ceiling again, her nightshirt twisted underneath her. A giggle squeaked out of her as she imagined herself rolling her way into the bathroom, over and over. But she breathed in deeply again, then rolled halfway over once more and pushed herself up to her hands and knees.

It seemed to take her a long time to get to the bathroom, and yet, strangely, as she began to crawl across the old pink tiles of the bathroom floor, she was surprised that she was already there. She lifted the toilet seat lid, then pulled herself up onto the seat, leaning back against the tank with great relief. After resting for a few moments, she pulled up her nightshirt, and peed.

As she sat there peeing, amazed at how full her bladder had been, she struggled to keep her head upright, but finally she just leaned forward, elbows on thighs, and held her head with her hands. The room was spinning around her, but closing her eyes only made it worse, so she kept them half open and tried focusing on a piece of cracked tile between her feet.

When she was done, she wiped herself, reached back with her right hand, and flushed the toilet. Then she discovered she couldn't move. She wanted to stand up and walk back to the cot, or at least get back on her hands and knees and crawl, but she could not move.

She thought it should be possible, but somehow she just couldn't. She had no energy, and no will to call up any energy.

I'm dying, she thought. She couldn't move, and she was going to die here, and Cage was going to come in and find her sitting on the toilet, dead.

I'm dying, she said to herself again, and this time it drove deep into her, and she knew, for the first time she really knew it was true.

She lifted her head from her hands and looked around the bathroom, through the door and into the apartment, half expecting something to look different. Nothing did. She knew she was dying and nothing was different, and somehow it was all okay.

She could move again. She slid off the toilet and onto the floor, then stretched out on the cool, pink tiles, facing the door so she could see the rest of the apartment. The tiles felt soothing on her skin.

It *was* all right. She only wished she could think more clearly about it all, keep focused on what was happening to her, focused on this new knowledge, this final realization. But it was there, she knew it was there, and finally everything was all right, even dying.

36

CRACKS HAD BEGUN to appear everywhere: in the Tenderloin quarantine; in the CDC's insistence that Core Fever was confined to the Tenderloin; and in Christina's few remaining immune system defenses. She was going downhill fairly quickly. She was dying. Caroline, too, was dying, if she wasn't already dead. Carlucci hadn't been able to get through to Cage for almost two days, now, and had no idea what was happening with his older daughter.

Carlucci had tried taking time off work, but it was far worse for him with nothing to do. Andrea's disposition was different, and she took leave from the law firm, spending most of her time at the hospital with Christina. But Carlucci couldn't do it, and so he went back to work during the days, returning to the hospital in the evenings.

It wasn't much better at work, and he felt numb and helpless, wandering zombielike around the department. The Katsuda case was still completed stalled, and he couldn't bring any interest to any of the others. He heard nothing from Istvan Darnyi. He canceled the autopsy request for Tito Moraleja—they knew now what he had died from, and it didn't matter anymore—and released the body for cremation. Everything was dead-ended, including Carlucci.

Word running through the department was that the quarantine was about ready to give. Desperate for something to do, Carlucci went out to the rooftop observation post set up closest to the Tenderloin. The young cop who had been working at the Tenderloin entrance a few weeks earlier was stationed at the edge of the roof, sitting on a stool and looking through binoculars mounted on a tripod, and Carlucci joined him.

"Hello, Lieutenant. Good to see you again."

They shook hands. "I didn't catch your name that day," Carlucci said.

"Prosser, sir. Adam Prosser."

"Anything happening yet?" he asked.

Prosser shrugged. "Lots of activity on both sides of the quarantine perimeter, but no real moves yet. It's only a matter of time, though. You should see the soldiers. Nervous as hell. They know. The whole thing is stupid."

Carlucci agreed. He couldn't understand why the CDC and the military were trying to maintain the quarantine anymore. Rumors had been ramping around for weeks now of Core Fever cases outside the Tenderloin, but in the past couple of days the mainstream broadcast media were finally starting to report the same thing.

"You want to take a look, sir?" Prosser got up from the stool and backed away from the mounted binoculars.

Carlucci sat on the stool and looked through the binoculars. They were clear and powerful lenses, directed at a section of the quarantine perimeter surrounding one of the DMZ bubbles, soldiers and barricades stretched across a street just a block from the Tenderloin. But pressing up against the barriers from the inside was a mob of hundreds, swelling and shifting around. Lots of fists were raised, but he could also see knives and shock sticks and clubs and guns and stun-pumpers.

Prosser was right about the soldiers. They *were* nervous, and rightfully so. The mob threatened to burst through the barriers and overwhelm them, and the only thing that might stop them was mass slaughter by the army. Carlucci suspected that prospect terrified most of the soldiers.

He adjusted the binoculars, then moved them from side to side, checking out the surrounding area. Something caught his eye, and he stopped. Gone. He moved them, and found it again. Emerging from an alley half a block from the quarantine perimeter was a group of figures wearing hooded robes. They swayed in unison as they slid along, maybe twelve or fourteen of them in pairs. For a moment Carlucci thought he heard them chanting or humming, until he realized he was actually too far away from them, and whatever he heard had to be coming from something else, machinery nearby, something like that. But who were these people? They were slightly blurry, so he tried adjusting the focus, but he couldn't sharpen the image. A pale blue glow seemed to surround them, like an electric mist. He followed them as they swayed across the street and then entered another alley, disappearing slowly by twos until they all were gone.

He cut the binoculars over to the next street, hoping to see them emerge, but though he waited for several minutes, they didn't appear. He looked back at the previous street, then along other streets in the area, but didn't see any sign of them.

And then, about a block from the barriers where the mob threatened, Carlucci saw Istvan Darnyi. He was standing in the doorway of a Middle Eastern deli, talking to a heavyset man with dark hair and wearing a white apron. Carlucci swung the binoculars back to the barriers, where the tension continued to build, then back again to Darnyi, who was still talking to the man.

"Shit."

"What is it, Lieutenant?"

Carlucci just shook his head. He straightened, stood, and stepped away from the binoculars, searching the streets on his own. There, Darnyi, about two blocks away. He turned and headed for the stairs.

By the time he reached the deli, Darnyi was gone, and the doors were locked up. Carlucci put his face to the glass door, but there was no one inside, and all the lights were off except a cool white glow in the counter display cases, illuminating sliced meats and cheeses.

"You looking for someone, Lieutenant?"

Carlucci stepped back from the deli, looked around the street. There was no one around, though he was sure he recognized Istvan's voice.

"I'm right here," Istvan said, stepping out of a deep alcove no more than thirty feet away.

"Yes, goddamn it, I'm looking for you." He walked toward Darnyi, shaking his head.

"Why?"

"I saw you from an observation post. All hell's about to break loose at the quarantine perimeter"—he pointed down the street—"and we're no more than a block away. I don't want you killed before you find that woman."

Darnyi smiled. "Then we better get out of here."

But they'd hardly turned away when an explosion rocked the air, rattling windows, and gunfire erupted. Shouts ripped through the afternoon, and the noise of more explosions. But it wasn't coming from behind them, it was coming from the right, maybe another block or two away.

"That way," Darnyi said, pointing to the left.

They crossed the street, and then the gunfire and screams exploded down at the barriers, as if in response to the other shots and screams. Just before they went around the corner, Carlucci glanced down the street and saw the barriers begin to collapse, and the soldiers beginning to panic.

"Let's get the hell out of here," Istvan said. They broke into a run.

They'd run along one short block, and had started down a second when a convoy of military vehicles came around the corner and filled the street in front of them. Some went past them as they pressed against the buildings, but others stopped and blocked off the street and sidewalks.

Carlucci and Darnyi backed off, then headed around to the left, away from the Tenderloin. But they could see more military barriers being set up two blocks away.

"This is insane," Darnyi said. "They're going to try to hold the quarantine, contain the breakout with a new perimeter." They stopped, taking stock. "What's the matter with these people?"

Behind them, they could see a frenzied mob spilling out of the barriers amid gunfire and crumpling bodies, soldiers going down, a troop carrier already on fire.

"Inside," Carlucci said.

Darnyi nodded. They searched both sides of the street. The block was mostly abandoned and condemned buildings, which was just as well. A door was open across the street, and they ran for it. There was barely enough room to push through, and they managed to get it shut behind them. Searching in the dim light though dust and dirt and rubble, they found some two-by-fours and wedged the door shut.

They were in an entryway with no exits except for a stairwell leading up through darkness. They climbed up a flight, but the door on that level was locked, and they couldn't budge it. So they went up one more. The door here was unlocked, and they went through, emerging into a room filled with broken furniture and empty crates and piles of loose paper everywhere.

They approached the windows, safe for the moment two floors above the street, and watched the chaos below. People swarmed the street and sidewalks, mostly men, but some young women too, a few of them armed. Gunfire was blasting away all around them, punctuated by deep, loud explosions and scattered screams.

"The quarantine's a goner," Istvan said. "This will go on for two days at least. Then it will run itself out of steam, finally." He shook his head. "This is a bad one."

Carlucci nodded, thinking about Caroline. Would he be able to get into the Tenderloin now and get her out, or would he have to wait until all this settled down? He shook his head to himself. Get her out for what? So she could die in a hospital instead of where she was?

His phone rang. He unclipped and answered it.

"Frank." It was Andrea.

"What is it?"

"You'd better get to the hospital as soon as you can." There was a slight pause. "I don't think Tina's going to last much longer."

He looked out the window. The street was still full of people, waves surging from side to side. There was a burst of gunfire, and someone screamed.

"Frank, is that gunfire?" Andrea asked.

"Yeah. I'm in the middle of a goddamn riot. The quarantine's coming apart. Shit. All right, I'll get there as soon as I can."

He hung up. "I've got to go," he told Istvan.

"It's not so good out there right now."

"I don't have any choice."

Istvan nodded, but didn't ask anything.

"Call me as soon as you find her."

"Of course."

"I've got to go," Carlucci said again. He breathed in deeply, and prepared himself to plunge into the chaos below.

Isabel

THE CORE WAS dead.

Silence everywhere, and strange smells. Sometimes the air burned her nose, or something wet burned her feet or hands when she touched them. No people alive or dead. All the bodies had been cleared away. And through it all the smell of old fires and something terrible, sickening, she could not get it out of her nose; and black soot everywhere, on walls and ceilings and floors.

There were new passages now, and some old ways were gone. Walls had disappeared, collapsed timbers and stone had formed new ones; new openings to the outside had become plentiful, letting in the light of the sun or the moon.

Isabel explored the new Core, the buildings above the street where she had rarely dared to go before. No people, no bodies anywhere, in any of the rooms, and no animals except for dead rats already stinking or being eaten by other rats.

She had spent two weeks living in the dead-end passage just outside the Core and in the storage room on the other side of the door. There had been some food in the room and she occasionally had emerged from it into the city to scrounge for more food and water, but there were so many people, so much light and noise and color and madness everywhere that she had stayed below as much as possible. She would have spent all her time in the dead end passage, but during the first few days after she escaped the Core, terrible burning smells drifted through the air vent, and she'd been forced to move into the storage room to avoid them. But she had broken the lights in the room, making it dark and easier for her to hide if someone came. Only once did someone come into the room, but when they could not make the lights work they left, and didn't come back until yesterday. Then finally someone had returned, fixed the lights, and people began to work in the room again. Isabel decided it was time to return.

She found laboratories like the ones she had been raised in, but everything in them was burned or smashed or broken, all destroyed. She wandered though them, hoping to find food, but there wasn't any.

Isabel liked the new silence in the Core, the new echoes of her movements. She felt safe. Food would be a problem, but she could always go back through the storage room if she needed to. And she had a feeling that it would not be long before strange people moved back.

PART FIVE

Plague

37

CARLUCCI WATCHED CHRISTINA while Andrea slept. Christina had not been conscious for two days now, and the doctors didn't think she ever would be again. So it was a great shock when she opened her eyes and looked at him. Her face was flushed, her arms and neck covered with rashes. There was terror in her eyes.

"Who . . . who are you?" she whispered.

"Your father, Tina."

But her eyes widened, and her head jerked spasmodically from side to side. "No. No. You're . . . who *are* you?" Terror in her voice as well as her eyes.

The doctors would be pissed if they knew, but he couldn't let his daughter die like this, and so he reached up and pulled down his mask, revealing his face.

"It's me, Tina. Your father." He pulled the chair up closer to the bed. She reached out tentatively toward him, lightly touched his cheek with one finger.

"Daddy?"

"Yes, Tina, sweetie, it's me." He gently took her hand. "I'm here."

The terror left her eyes for a few moments, then seemed to return.

"It was the shot that gave it to me," she said. "The special shot. I know it." She was trying to raise her head up from the pillow.

"What shot, Tina?"

"Don't let them give you the special shot, Daddy." Then she let her head fall back and her eyes closed. "Daddy."

"I'm here, Tina."

"I'm so hot, Daddy."

"I know, sweetie. I know."

He continued holding her hand, but she didn't say any more, and soon her breathing deepened.

"Tina? Tina, baby, are you awake?"

There was no answer.

When Andrea came in an hour later, Carlucci disposed of the suit and gloves and mask, then called Paula.

"Paula, this is Frank Carlucci."

"Hi, Mr. Carlucci. How's Tina?"

"The same. Listen, Paula, I've got to ask you something. Maybe she was just feverish, but Tina said something about getting a shot, a special shot. Does that make any sense to you?"

There was a short pause, then Paula said, "Yeah, actually. About three weeks ago, someone from St. Anthony's came to the apartment for Tina. He said they were out giving booster vaccinations, and he gave her one."

Carlucci felt sick, one more terrible thing crashing down on him, but he tried to hold himself together.

"What about you?" he asked.

"No, it was only people with police health coverage, through St. Anthony's."

"A man, you said?"

"Yeah, some guy."

"What did he look like?"

"You know, white outfit and funny white shoes. A medico. I don't really remember, I wasn't paying that much attention."

"Okay, Paula. Thanks."

"What is it, Mr. Carlucci? Did the shot make her sick or something?"

"No, I was just checking. Thanks again, Paula, and I'll talk to you later."

"Say hi to Tina for me, will you? And tell her they won't let me see her, or I would."

"I will."

He broke the connection and stood there in the hospital corridor, afraid to move, afraid that if he did move, he would completely fall apart.

The checking was a formality, but he needed to have it confirmed, and it was. There had been no special booster vaccinations given, and even if there had been, St. Anthony's would never have sent anyone out to do it, they would have notified everyone in the program and asked them to come into the clinic itself.

Carlucci stood outside his daughter's room, looking in through the glass window in the door. Andrea was sitting next to the bed; Christina lay unmoving, eyes closed. She hadn't opened her eyes again.

He didn't know what to do with the information he now had. Someone had shot her up with Core Fever virus. Why? Something to do with him, it had to be, there was no reason for anyone to want to harm her, to kill her this way. But what? No threats had been made, before or after.

Or was that true?

He remembered Yoshi Katsuda hinting that being shot had been a message of sorts, a warning. But what the hell was this? No one had ever said to him, hey, stop investigating or your daughter will die. Nothing like that had ever been implied, by anyone.

Dr. Sodhi came down the hall and waved a greeting. As he approached he said, "Lieutenant, I'm glad you are here. I wanted to talk to you."

"About Tina?"

Dr. Sodhi shook his head. "No, not exactly. The CDC has made an announcement."

Carlucci snorted. "What, that they're canceling the quarantine?"

Dr. Sodhi smiled. "No. They recognize that the quarantine is over. I believe they would be too embarrassed to actually announce the official end of it. Better to ignore it, is their philosophy, I would imagine. No, they have announced that with the help of the medical facilities of New Hong Kong, the virus that causes Core Fever has been identified, and an antibody test developed. More than that, because the virus is very similar to one that New Hong Kong has recently been studying, they have a preventative vaccine ready to put into production."

Carlucci tipped his head. "That sounds like a crock," he said. "Like one huge pile of horseshit."

Dr. Sodhi shrugged. "Perhaps. But that is the announcement that the CDC has made. With the breakdown of the quarantine, they will go into production of the vaccine immediately, and begin distribution of it as soon as possible here in the city."

Carlucci wanted to laugh. It was all becoming so absurd. "Preventative," he said. "Not a treatment, not a cure."

"No."

"Then what good is it?" He turned away from Dr. Sodhi and returned to Christina's room.

And then, less than an hour later, she died. Quickly, and far more easily than they had ever expected. He and Andrea were both in the room trying to decide what to do for the night, when Christina went into a brief convulsion, and her heart stopped.

Doctors and nurses came rushing in, but Carlucci and Andrea had already discussed this. They stood at Christina's side and told the doctors "No." No attempted resuscitation, no trying to jolt her heart back into beating. They wanted to let her die in peace.

There were no arguments. All of the medical staff except for Dr. Sodhi left. Dr. Sodhi stayed only long enough to confirm that her heart had, in fact, stopped beating. Then he, too, left, and they were alone with her.

They left the hospital together. It was nearly midnight, but the sounds of the rioting were still loud. Istvan had been right, it would take at least a couple of days to die down.

Two uniforms were waiting in front of the hospital with a squad car to take them home. Carlucci recognized them but he couldn't remember their names. Springer, he thought, was one of them. He couldn't bring himself to ask.

They got into the backseat of the squad car. The two cops didn't say anything, just got into the front seat and pulled away from the hospital. No one said a word the entire trip out to their house.

When they arrived, the two cops remained in the car. Carlucci thanked them for the ride, then he and Andrea got out and walked slowly up the walkway, climbed the steps to the front porch, then stopped at the door.

"I don't want to go in, Frank."

"I know."

The house seemed different. Caroline and Christina had both been out of the house for some time, but now neither of them would ever enter it again, even for a visit. It *was* a different house now.

Andrea turned away from the front door, walked back across the porch, and sat down on the top step. Carlucci sat beside her, waved at the cops, and watched the squad car pull away.

The neighborhood was quiet. They were far enough away from the Tenderloin and the downtown area, and the rioting hadn't reached them. Probably never would; too much a residential neighborhood, and the quarantine had been miles away.

The night air was warm, the skies almost clear except for the normal haze. The moon was nearly full, and well past its zenith. A cat yowled from somewhere nearby. If he listened carefully, he could hear the faint popping sounds of gunfire, the muted sounds of breaking glass or screeching metal.

"What are we going to do?" Andrea said. "About Caroline, I mean. I want to see her again before she dies."

He didn't want to have to answer her; he felt he didn't have the strength to speak. But he swallowed, his mouth dry, and he said, "Maybe tomorrow it will be better. If we can get an escort—"

"I don't care about an escort. Just get us in there, Frank."

He nodded. "All right, I will."

They remained there, watching the moon and the blurred stars, and neither of them said another word.

38

SOMETHING CHANGED DURING the night.

Cage noticed it in her breathing first. For days it had been labored, but during the night it became deep and easy. Then her fever broke, and by dawn her temperature had dropped to just under a hundred and one.

He was afraid to hope. Nikki, too, had rebounded before getting worse. But that had happened before the Core Fever had really taken hold of her; that was not the case with Caroline. Still, he was afraid. He wasn't sure how much he could take; if he let himself hope, he didn't know if he could handle it when she worsened and died.

The day was coming, bright gray light flowing in through the glass. Cage raised a window, letting in the morning air. The streets of the Tenderloin were relatively quiet. Although the rioting had begun in the Tenderloin and the DMZ, it had spread outward from the Tenderloin perimeter, through the quarantine barriers, and out into the city. Frustration and rage had been directed outward, leaving the Tenderloin itself relatively undamaged and unharmed. The announcement of the test and vaccine for Core Fever had done little to calm people—there was too much suspicion, all of it probably justified—and the rioting had continued out in the city, but the Tenderloin's own natural barriers kept it outside.

The cot creaked, and Cage turned around. Caroline had rolled onto her side, facing him. Her eyes remained closed, but she looked as if she might open them at any moment. He was still afraid to hope, but she looked so much better.

Several hours later, her temperature finally dropped below a hundred. Even her color looked better. Cage sat beside her, waiting. Now he was beginning to hope in earnest; it was impossible not to.

In the late afternoon, he discovered her bladder had let go. He took off her nightshirt, moved her onto the sleeping bag on the floor and washed her, then took her nightshirt and the sheets down to the laundry room in the building basement. Back in the apartment, he washed the plastic sheeting in the tub, replaced it on the cot along with clean sheets, then moved Caroline back to the bed. She half awakened as he moved her, her eyes fluttered open, and she mumbled a few words, but she was soon asleep again, and he was sure she would never remember being awake.

He called in to the clinic, told them he wouldn't be able to make it in at all for a day or two. He couldn't tell Franzee why he wasn't coming in; he was afraid to say it aloud, to put his hopes into words. He had not realized he could be so superstitious.

As evening wore on, and her temperature didn't climb, his hope grew, though he could hardly believe what was happening. He sat in a chair beside her through the night, dozing, periodically checking on her. As dawn approached, her temperature was down to ninety-nine, and he knew.

Around six or seven, there was a knock at the door. When he got up and opened the door, Carlucci and his wife were standing out in the hall. They looked exhausted.

"I was going to call you in a while," Cage said. "I can't believe you're here."

"We wanted to see her one last time," Andrea said. "Be with her."

Cage smiled. "I think you may have wasted a trip."

"What the hell are you talking about?" Carlucci asked. "Is she already—"

Cage shook his head, cutting him off. "No. I think she's going to live."

She woke, unsure of where she was, or what had happened to her. Her eyes were still closed, and they started to open automatically, but she kept them shut.

How long had she been asleep? It seemed like days. Maybe it was. She'd been sick. Yes, that's what . . . Core Fever. No, impossible. Was she still alive? Yes, and not so hot anymore. What was happening?

Caroline opened her eyes. No, that couldn't be right. She was seeing her parents sitting beside her, and they were looking at her.

"Caroline?" Her mother's mouth moving, and it was her voice, but that was impossible, wasn't it?

Caroline closed her eyes again. She still ached a bit, but she felt better. On the other hand, she was still hallucinating. She was in Nikki's place, and if anyone would have been here with her it would have been Cage. Maybe she should just sleep a while more.

"Caroline?" Her father's voice this time, quiet and tentative.

She tried opening her eyes again, and they were both still there.

"Caroline, are you awake?" Her mother.

"Is it you?" she asked. Still thinking it couldn't be. "Where am I?" She moved her hand to the side, feeling the canvas. Yes, she was on the cot.

"You're in the Tenderloin," her mother said.

"Nikki's?"

"Yes," her father answered. "Nikki's apartment."

"Cage."

"He's here."

"How . . . ? You're here," she said. "How? I told Cage not to tell you. I made him promise."

Her mother reached out and took her hand, a sad smile on her face. "He broke his promise," she said. "Thankfully."

Caroline tried to pull her hand away, but she was too weak. "Don't touch me," she said. "Please, don't, you'll catch it."

Her mother shook her head. "There's a vaccine," she said. "Besides, Cage doesn't think we could catch it now. He thinks you're almost certainly not contagious anymore."

"Not . . . ? How can that be?"

"He thinks you're going to live."

No, it was too much. She had to be hallucinating. She closed her eyes once more, but she could still feel her mother holding her hand. And then, somehow, she knew. Her parents *were* really there, her mother was holding her hand. And, most of all, she was going to live.

She was going to live.

She slept for a while, and when she woke again, her parents were still in the room—her mother in a chair beside the cot, her father doing something at the stove or sink. She worked herself up with her elbows and looked around the apartment, but she didn't see Cage anywhere.

"Where is he?"

"Cage?" her mother said.

Caroline nodded, then dropped back onto the cot.

"He'll be back in a while," her mother said. "He said you were going to be fine, and he thought we could use some time alone together."

Caroline wanted to see him. He had stayed with her through it all, taken care of her, done everything for her. Risking himself, he had kept her alive, and she wanted to see him. Cage.

"How did you get here?" she asked. "Through the quarantine?"

"The quarantine's gone," her mother said.

"Why? Is the disease gone? Core Fever?"

Her mother shook her head. "No. It's a long story. The quarantine collapsed. Core Fever is everywhere. People knew. The quarantine was a joke."

"Then why . . . ?" Then she shook her own head in reply. "Never mind," she said.

Her father approached, holding a steaming mug. "Chicken broth," he said. "Cage said it would be good for you. You want some?"

She nodded. When was the last time she'd eaten?

They helped her sit up, propping her against the wall with pillows. She was still incredibly weak, and she could barely hold the cup. But the broth tasted good, and she slowly sipped at it, relishing both the taste and the heat going down her throat and into her belly.

When she'd finished the broth, her father brought the cup to the sink, then returned to the cot and sat down beside her mother. The way they were looking at her gave her a sinking feeling in her gut.

"What is it?" she asked.

"It's Tina," her mother said. "She got it, too."

"What?" Unbelieving. "Core Fever?"

Her mother nodded, but didn't say anything more.

"How sick is she?"

But her mother just shook her head, unable to speak, the tears beginning, dripping down her left cheek.

"No," Caroline said, shaking her head from side to side. "No."

But another voice inside her answered *Yes,* and she knew her sister was dead.

39

ERIC RALSTON FINALLY got in touch again. Now that the quarantine was gone, and all the announcements had been made by the CDC about tests and a vaccine, Eric called.

"I've been trying to reach you for days," Cage said, hardly bothering to hide his anger. He was in the clinic, between patients. The waiting room was full. "You bastards with your fucking quarantines."

"We did what we thought was best," Eric replied.

"Best my ass."

"Cage, give me a fuckin' break here."

"Why the hell should I?"

"Look, you want me to just hang up? I don't have to put up with this crap."

"All right, all right. Hold on a second, will you? Let me get this on another phone." He transferred the call from the clinic line to his own phone, then walked down the hall to the staff room, closed the door, and sat at the table. "Why *did* you call, anyway?"

"I'm calling to help you out, you ungrateful son of a bitch."

"Yeah?" Cage said. "And how are you going to do that?"

"You want some Core Fever vaccine for that shitty little clinic of yours?"

Jesus. "Of course I want some vaccine. How soon can I get it?"

"A few days. Shipments are already starting to come down from New Hong Kong, and it shouldn't be too long before their people get production going in labs here on the ground."

"New Hong Kong, those fuckers. You've been in bed with them from the very beginning of this, haven't you?"

"Cage, come on."

"They were your source, weren't they, for all the info on Core Fever? The source you said you couldn't reveal."

There was a long pause, and then Eric finally spoke again. "Let's just say they helped us quite a bit. Look, what's the point in slamming them? They were the ones who identified the virus and made the antibody tests possible. They're the ones with the goddamn vaccine, for Christ's sake! You should be grateful."

"I am *not* grateful," Cage said. "What I am is suspicious as hell. Aren't you? I mean really, Eric, the odds that the Core Fever virus is so close to some virus that they're studying that they've got a bloody vaccine all ready to go for it? What the hell is really going on?"

Another long silence. When Eric spoke again, his tone was cold. "Look, Cage. You want some vaccine or not? I told you before I don't have to listen to this crap. I'm trying to do you a favor. You think the vaccine is going to be readily available? Not for a long time, not until production really gets up and running."

"But aren't they going to make it available here in the Tenderloin first? This is the source of the damn disease, remember? The highest concentration?"

Eric laughed. "Get real, Cage. Do you think anyone here or in New Hong Kong gives a shit about the Tenderloin? Over the next couple of weeks or so, the only people getting the vaccine will be those with pull or money, preferably both."

"You bastards," Cage said, shaking his head to himself. "You quarantine the Tenderloin and bottle up the worst of Core Fever inside it, and then you don't give us the vaccine."

"I'm *trying* to give *you* some of it, Cage."

Neither of them said anything for a while. Cage tried to calm himself down, not lose his temper. Any vaccine he could get would be a godsend; he couldn't afford to lose that.

"I'm sorry," he said. "I know you're trying to help me out here. Probably risking your job, right?"

"Maybe not this time. They *know* the first batches should go into the Tenderloin. But listen to me, Cage. I'm doing the best I can. Yeah, it's all a mess, and it's not fair, but I am trying to do right by you, by some of those poor people inside with you."

"Have you been vaccinated yet?" Cage asked.

This time there was only the slightest hesitation, then Eric said, "Yes. Am I supposed to be ashamed of that?"

"No," Cage replied grudgingly.

"Thank you." Then he said, "Okay, I'll call you as soon as I can get a batch of the vaccine to you."

"Thanks, Eric."

"You're welcome, you son of a bitch."

"Later, when the worst is over, maybe we can have a normal conversation again, yes?"

"Yeah, maybe. I'll call you."

Cage broke the connection and went back out front to take the next patient.

40

CARLUCCI FELT LIKE they were bringing Caroline home from the hospital. In a way, that's what they were doing. She was still weak, though walking around a bit now, and she'd agreed to stay at their house for several days rather than go back to her apartment. Andrea had extended her leave from the law firm, and even Carlucci was taking time off from work.

They were all four walking around in a dead woman's apartment—he could not forget that, though he had never actually met Nikki—and it felt awkward. Andrea was fussing over Caroline, trying to make sure they had everything together. Cage had arranged for a car to take them to one of the police gates; there, outside the Tenderloin, would be a police car to take them home.

Cage came up to him, glanced at the two women. "I'd like to talk to you in private for a minute."

Carlucci nodded. They went out into the hall, which was deserted, and Cage closed the apartment door.

"About this vaccine," Cage said. "I don't know whether the cops are going to get an early crack at it or not, but I'm going to be getting some in the next day or two. So, if it looks like it'll be a while, you and Andrea can come by the clinic and I can take care of it for you."

"How the hell are *you* getting vaccine?" he asked Cage.

Cage smiled. "Like everything else, it's who you know."

Carlucci shook his head. "I don't know what's going on. I'm sure I'll find out when I get back."

"Think about it, though," Cage said. "I'll even go out to your place if you want. Caroline was lucky. Your other daughter wasn't. Most people won't be."

Carlucci nodded. "I'll find out what's happening through the department, and then I'll talk to Andrea about it. Thanks. I appreciate the offer."

Cage shrugged and smiled. "I told you before, when you got Nikki into St. Anthony's, that I owed you."

"Not anymore," Carlucci told him. "You've more than paid back with Caroline."

"I didn't do anything. There wasn't anything I *could* do. It was her own immune system that did the work."

"No," Carlucci insisted. "It was more than that. You stayed with her, you took care of her. You kept her alive. If you hadn't been there, she would have died."

"Maybe."

Carlucci knew there was no "maybe" to it. Cage had saved his daughter's life. He stepped forward, put out his arms, and hugged him. Cage didn't seem completely comfortable with it, but he didn't pull away. Carlucci released him and stepped back, grinning.

"I'm Italian," he said.

Cage smiled, maybe a little sheepishly. Then his expression got serious again. "There's something else I wanted to talk to you about. Some things that have gotten lost in the past few weeks."

Carlucci nodded. "Go ahead."

"The first time we met, you were trying to find out about Cancer Cell, and I was trying to figure out if there was some disease about to break out. Well, we know about the disease, and Cancer Cell doesn't exist anymore. But there's still a lot of weird shit around, a lot of things that just plain stink. I don't know whether you're digging into anything anymore, but—"

"I'm not done with Cancer Cell," Carlucci told him. "What do you mean, they don't exist anymore?"

"Everything they had was in the Core. Everything got destroyed when the army went in. I'm not sure how many of them even survived. They didn't all come out voluntarily."

"How do you know all this?"

"Caroline. When she feels up to it, ask her about what happened when she was in there with them. Food for thought."

"I will."

"But there's more. I don't know if there's a connection, but all this crap about New Hong Kong identifying Core Fever and having a vaccine for it, Christ, that stinks too. It's too damn much of a coincidence. I thought at first that maybe they were just trying to capitalize on Core Fever, and this would be some cooked-up vaccine that they'd sell to the government but wouldn't do any good. But that can't be. If it turned out to be useless, there'd be hell to pay, and even New Hong Kong can't afford that much bad publicity. So it's got to be a real vaccine for Core Fever."

"Well, I'm not done with New Hong Kong, either. I've still got a murder case that's tied in somehow to all this." He paused, wondering how much he should tell Cage. But he felt as if he had to tell *someone,* and he couldn't tell

Andrea or Caroline. Not yet. "And another murder case," he finally said. "My daughter Tina."

"Your daughter?" Cage said, confused.

Carlucci nodded. "A few days before she came down with Core Fever, someone showed up at her apartment claiming to be with St. Anthony's and claiming that there was some kind of supplemental vaccination booster program going on. And this guy gave her an injection of something."

"Jesus Christ." Cage looked stunned. "There was no 'booster' program, was there?"

Carlucci shook his head.

"Why?"

"I don't know, yet. I'm going to do everything I can to find out." He felt suddenly very tired, and he sighed heavily. "But first I'm going to get Caroline back home, and then I've got a funeral to arrange."

"I'm sorry," Cage said.

Carlucci nodded. Cage understood; he'd lost someone too.

41

"I'VE FOUND HER."

It was Istvan. Carlucci was in his office, his second day at work, four days after Tina's funeral. "Where is she?"

"No," Istvan said. "Not on the receiver." He paused for a moment. "You remember the place, the last time we talked?"

In the middle of the rioting, the room on the third floor of the vacant building near the DMZ. "Yes," Carlucci said. "I remember."

"Meet me there. Tonight, ten o'clock."

"All right."

Then Istvan hung up. Carlucci put the receiver down, staring at it. Istvan was probably right to be cautious. Ten o'clock. It was going to be a long wait.

By nine Carlucci was so alone in a dark, secluded section of Golden Gate Park, near the Panhandle, that he couldn't see how anyone could be tailing him. From the cover of a small stand of bushes at the edge of the park he watched Fulton Street, looking west. When one of the electric buses appeared a few blocks away, he stepped out onto the sidewalk and walked to the bus stop just before the bus arrived. He boarded alone, then got off under the multilevel freeway ramps near Van Ness.

From there he made his way on foot along streets that had been torn up and half burned by the riots. Few street lights were working, so the streets were lit by lights from apartment and restaurant windows and dozens of barrel fires fueled by wood from buildings that had been abandoned long ago or damaged in the recent disturbances. He wasn't exactly comfortable walking the streets, but everyone was wary, so they all tended to avoid each other. Finally he reached the border of the Tenderloin, worked his way past the ruins of the old quarantine perimeter, then up a few blocks to the vacant building.

The entire block was deserted and dark, lit only by a couple of amber street lights. Carlucci remained outside the building for a few minutes, listening, watching. Then he ducked into the entrance and crawled through the opening he and Istvan had found before. Once inside, he felt his way to the stairs, then up to the third floor. Faint light came in through the windows, casting the vaguest of shadows, showing the ruined furniture. But there was no movement.

"I'm here," Istvan said, stepping out from the back corner. He was alone.

"I was hoping she would be with you."

Istvan shook his head. "She's scared, Lieutenant. She won't tell me why."

If she was scared, then she was probably the person he needed to talk to. "What's her name?"

Istvan shook his head again. "I promised her I wouldn't say. I promised I wouldn't bring you to her."

"Then what the hell am I doing here?"

"You're going to talk to me."

"Talk to you."

"Yes. You're going to tell me how to convince her that it's safe for her to meet with you."

"And how am I going to do that?"

"You're going to tell me exactly why you're looking for her, and what you'll expect from her, what you'll *do* to her. The truth. Then I'll talk to her again, and she'll decide. If she decides yes, I'll make arrangements for a meeting. If she decides no, our business is ended."

"I told you," Carlucci said. "I'm investigating the murder of her friend. She's the only lead we've got left. We just want to know if she knows anything about Naomi's murder. If she's so scared that she's gone to ground, I'd guess she does." He shrugged. "That's it. I just want to talk to her about it."

"And if she *does* know something? What will you expect of her? Testimony in court?"

"I don't know. You know that, Istvan. It depends on what she knows."

"And if she does know something crucial, and you want her to testify, and she doesn't want to, will you take her in with force?"

"No. I'll try to convince her, but I won't try to force her to do anything she doesn't agree to. You know my word is good."

"Is it? How many times have you promised not to ask for my help again?" Istvan looked out the window at the deserted street below, and then he shook his head. "Go," he said. "I'll call you when I know."

42

THEY WERE SITTING on several hundred doses of Core Fever vaccine, and they didn't know what to do with it. Cage, Paul, and Madelaine were at the table in the staff room, surrounded by beer and soda bottles and melting ice they'd removed from the refrigerators to make room for the vaccine. The fans were blowing, but they had the door closed and locked, and the room was hot. If word got out on the street that they had Core Fever vaccine, they'd be overrun.

"Okay," Madelaine said. "Here's an idea. We don't tell anyone about it. But every patient who comes in, we vaccinate. Whatever they come in for, whatever we do for them, we also give them a shot of the vaccine. If they're sick with something, it's easy, we tell them it's an antibiotic. Same thing if we're treating a wound of some kind. A broken arm, ah, let me see, I don't know . . . okay, we tell them it's a shot of some special hormone that promotes bone healing or something like that. We improvise. We have Franzee keep a running list up front so we don't vaccinate anyone twice. We get enough people coming through here we'll go through the vaccine pretty damn quickly anyway."

It actually sounded like a pretty good idea to Cage, and he said so. He looked at Paul. "What do you think?"

Paul sighed. "I suppose. If someone already has Core Fever, the vaccine isn't going to do them any more harm. It's a wasted dose for us, but that's a lot better than what would happen if we made an announcement. But this is all bullshit. The feds should be starting here, vaccinating as many people as they can as quickly as they can. They'd be able to provide the security to keep things under control."

"Of course it's bullshit," Cage said. "But we do what we can with what we've got. We should be glad we've got *anything* the way those bastards are."

Paul gave a twisted smile. "Friends in high places."

"Better than nothing."

Paul shrugged. "All right, let's do it that way."

"Good," Cage said. "And we'll start right now with the two of you, and then you can send Franzee and Buck back here and I'll vaccinate them. When Mike and the others come in on their next shifts, we'll take care of them, too."

"What about you?" Madelaine asked.

"I'm going to pass," Cage said. "If I haven't gotten it by now, with my exposure, I never will."

Madelaine shook her head. "That's stupid, Cage."

"No it's not. I really believe I don't need it. Someone else does."

After vaccinating all four of the others, Cage stayed for a while in the staff room, sitting alone at the table with another beer, one of the fans blowing on the back of his head.

He missed Caroline. He missed her a lot.

He missed Nikki, too, so much sometimes that he wanted to smash his head against a wall. But Nikki was dead, and he knew he would never see her again. Caroline was still alive, he knew she was out there, but he had not seen or talked to her since her parents had taken her back to their house.

He was confused about his feelings for her. They had not known each other that long, and most of the time they had spent together had been while she was deathly ill. So how well could he know her? There was guilt along with the confusion. Irrational, he knew that, but he felt it nonetheless. Guilt over Nikki, who had died not that long ago. They had been friends, deep and close friends, and he had loved her.

He shook his head and finished off the beer. There was too much going on even to think about getting involved with someone, especially someone who might not return the feelings. He didn't know what, if anything, Caroline thought about him. He had been her doctor, though he had never really thought of her as a patient. So, better *not* to call her, better not to pursue anything.

Christ. It was all excuses. He was hopeless. Cage thought about having another beer, then decided against it. He would work for a while in the clinic instead. Vaccinate some people against Core Fever. Save some lives. That was, after all, why he was a doctor, wasn't it?

43

THE DMZ WAS a mess. The disintegration of the quarantine and the rioting that followed had left chunks of brick and stone and shattered concrete littering the sidewalks and alleys, some of it swept into piles, some not. Most of the broken glass had been cleared away, and plywood was nailed over half the windows on the street level. Building walls were pocked with bullet holes, and rust-colored patches of dried blood were everywhere.

Caroline worked her way through the ruins, feeling safer than she ever had before. The DMZ residents were too busy trying to pull things back together and get their businesses going again to make trouble, and there was a rather strange sense of community on the street.

She stopped in at Mama Chan's. Incredibly, all but one of the main street windows were intact. Inside, about half the tables were occupied. The usual Chinese music played on the tiny speakers scattered throughout the restaurant. Standing behind the counter near the back was Mama, a short, thin woman about a hundred and seventy years old—at least that's what Tito used to say.

Mama Chan waved at Caroline and called her over to the counter. "Have some soup," Mama said. "War wonton or egg flower. I make you some Chow Fun noodles."

Caroline shook her head. "Maybe later. I'm in a hurry, I'm trying to find someone. I just wanted to see how you were doing."

Mama shrugged. "I'm alive, and I can cook. Everything's a mess. You need some soup."

Caroline gave in without more fight. She didn't have the energy to argue, and if Lily and Mink were still in the death house, they weren't going anywhere. "Okay," she said. "War wonton soup, a *small* bowl. No noodles."

Mama Chan nodded, then of course dished up a large bowl of soup and set it in front of Caroline. She brought over a pot of tea, then walked down the counter to harass one of the waitresses.

The soup was good, and Caroline discovered she was actually hungry. She ate every bit of it, and almost wished she hadn't said no to the noodles. When she was finished, she left money on the counter, called out a thanks to Mama, and left.

Two blocks away, the death house seemed unnaturally quiet. The front door was propped open, and the lobby stank of rotting fruit. Would rioters have pillaged a death house? It seemed unlikely.

She climbed the stairs to the third floor, then walked down the hall to

Tito's old room. She was tired and hot, and was a little bit afraid of what she would find inside. She knocked, but got no answer. When she tried the door, it was unlocked; she pushed it open and stepped inside.

Lily was sitting in a chair by one of the windows, staring out into the airwell, an elbow propped on the windowsill, chin resting in her hand.

"Lily?" Caroline said.

"Go away." Lily didn't turn around.

No one else was in the room. A suitcase was open on the sofa, and in it were a few piles of clothes. The bedsheets were thrown onto the floor. Dirty dishes and glasses were scattered across the countertop and piled in the sink.

"Where's Mink?" Caroline asked.

"Where do you think?" Lily still didn't look at her. "Hanging out at the Luxury Arcade with all her friends, playing electric Ten Pins and Super-Skeet. Having a great time."

She took a few more steps toward Lily, but stopped while she was still several feet away. "She died?"

Lily finally turned to look at her. Her face seemed almost dead, her eyes dulled, her skin slack. But she didn't say anything.

"When?" Caroline asked.

"A week ago." She closed her eyes. "I don't know." She kept her eyes closed and her head swayed gently from side to side. "I. Don't. Know."

Caroline wanted to walk up to Lily and put her arm around her, try to comfort her, but she had the feeling it was exactly the wrong thing to do.

"Is there anything I can do to help?" she asked.

"Yes. You can go away. You can leave me alone. Or, if you have a gun, you could put it to my head and put me out of my misery. That would be all right, too." She opened her eyes and stared lifelessly at Caroline. "One or the other."

"I'm sorry," Caroline said.

But Lily didn't respond at all, except to turn back to the window and stare outside. Caroline turned around and left.

She returned to the Tenderloin. Physically the Tenderloin seemed much less changed than did the rest of the city—there was less evidence of rioting or looting, and there were very few people wearing masks or gloves—but the feel of the place wasn't much better. There was less fear in the air than in the city outside, but there was more despair and resignation. Too many people were dying, too many people had died. Life went on, but it wasn't the same.

No, it wasn't the same at all. Tina was dead, Mink was dead, Tito was dead, Nikki was dead. Probably Rashida and Dr. Mike were both dead.

And she was alive. She'd contracted Core Fever, but she was alive.

She had entered the Tenderloin the only way she knew, through Li Peng's Imperial Imports again, and now she wandered aimlessly through the Asian

Quarter. Dusk was falling, but it was still warm and humid; another heat wave had begun. Why couldn't it just cook Core Fever right out of the city?

Lights were coming on, flashing bright colors all around her, but the miasma in the air made the lights seem oddly lifeless. Streethawkers were listless, calling out products and prices without enthusiasm; even the message streamers swimming through the air above her seemed languid and less than enticing. Only the smell of cooking food, strong and seductive, was unaffected, though she noticed that people eating at outdoor cafés sat in odd arrangements, putting as much space as possible between themselves and other customers.

After nearly an hour of wandering through the Asian Quarter, she finally headed for her real destination: the RadioLand Street Clinic. She went from the Asian Quarter to the Euro, and then to the edges of the Euro and the clinic. Down at the end of the street, the old barrier to the Core was in ruins, and anyone could easily go in or out. But there was no reason to anymore. The Core was sterile and lifeless now; even the old inhabitants were gone, taken away and put into isolation, or killed. And Cancer Cell was no more.

She walked into the clinic. The waiting room was full, the air hot and stifling. She didn't see Cage or any of the other doctors, so she went to the front desk, where Franzee was talking to an old woman. When Franzee was done, she looked at Caroline.

"You're looking for Cage," she said, smiling. It wasn't a question.

"Yes."

"He's with a patient. Can it wait?"

"Of course. There's no hurry."

"I'd ask you to take a seat, but there aren't any."

"That's all right. I'll be fine."

She stood with her back against the wall, looking at all the people waiting to get in to see a doctor, and thought about Cage. She had tried not to think about him ever since her parents had taken her home from Nikki's apartment, and for the most part she had succeeded. But he was always there, in the back of her thoughts, waiting.

One of the doors down the hall opened, and two men came out. One was Paul. They went to the front counter, where they talked for a while, then the other man left, and Paul came over to her.

"You waiting for Cage, or is there something I can do?"

"Cage," she said.

Paul was grinning, staring at her.

"What?" she said.

"It's just so amazing to see someone who survived. It gives us all a little hope. So I'm happy as hell to see you."

She smiled. "Thanks, Paul."

"I'll talk to you later." He nodded at the waiting room. "Got some work to do here."

"Yeah, I noticed. What's going on, is it the Core Fever?"

"Some. But we've also had a cholera outbreak building all spring, and there was some kind of toxic gas release yesterday, which we're still seeing the effects of. One goddamn thing after another." He shrugged. "I'll see you."

She nodded, and he left to go take another patient. Sometimes she forgot that even before Core Fever had appeared this had been a busy place.

Paul took a young girl into one of the exam rooms, and a couple minutes later another door opened. This time it was Cage who came out. He saw her and stopped in the hall, staring at her. Then he finally came forward.

"Hey," he said.

"Hey yourself."

"What brings you to this bit of paradise?"

"You," she said, feeling her chest tighten.

Cage didn't respond right away. She couldn't tell what he was thinking, whether it was good or bad. So she waited.

"Hang on a minute, can you?" he said. "I've got a patient waiting, and I've got an injection to give him."

"Sure, go ahead." She gestured at all the people waiting. "You look like you're going to be pretty busy for a while."

He nodded. "Yeah, we're a little bit swamped, but my shift is about over. I've been here twelve hours straight, and Madelaine's coming in soon."

"Why don't I just meet you later? When you're done."

"All right. Where?"

"Nikki's. I thought maybe I'd stay there again, for a few days, if that's okay."

"Nikki's." He nodded. "All right. I don't know when, for sure. Maybe an hour or two."

"Whenever. I'll be there."

"It's good to see you, Caroline."

"It's good to see you, Cage."

Nothing had been touched in the place since her parents had taken her away. There was a notice that had been slipped under the door saying rent was late, and had to be paid in two days or Nikki would be evicted. She would talk to Cage about that, see if he knew where she could pay the rent.

She spent the next two hours cleaning the apartment—washing dishes, throwing out old, rotting food, sweeping and mopping the floors. She hung the sleeping bag out of the window to air it out, and tossed the sheets and pillowcase into a pile in a corner of the room, sheets she'd sweated in while she'd been sick. Tomorrow she would go back to her apartment, get some clothes, a few books, and other things.

She had just finished moving Nikki's tapestries against one wall when there was a knock at the door.

"Come in," she called.

Cage opened the door and stepped inside, carrying a couple of brown paper bags. "Dinner," he said, holding up the bags. "Thai food from a little place around the corner. You hungry?"

She nodded, smiling. "Very. And there isn't much here."

He closed the door and looked around the place. "You've been cleaning up. You really going to stay here?"

"For a while, yes."

"Why?"

She shrugged. "I'm not really sure. It seems like the right thing to do at the moment." She wanted to tell him that he was one of those reasons, but she could not yet bring herself to do it. Later, perhaps. Instead, she smiled and said, "Let's eat."

44

HER NAME WAS Amira Choukri, and she looked very much like the picture that the sketch artist had made. She was dark, her hair black with only a dusting of gray, and quite beautiful. Early forties, Carlucci guessed, maybe five-foot-five, or -six. She was wearing boots and jeans and a blue work shirt. If she was scared, she didn't show it.

It was close to midnight, and they were in what appeared to be an abandoned machine shop in an industrial area south of Market. Orange-tinged moonlight beamed in through dozens of cracked and broken windowpanes, casting a riot of shadows into the far reaches of the room. Carlucci, Istvan, and Amira sat on crates around a large electrical cable spool turned on its side. Istvan, with a sense of ritual, had brought cups and a large container of hot tea, and had just finished pouring cups for all of them.

"There will be no recording of this conversation," Istvan said.

"I know," Carlucci replied, holding up a hand. "You told me, and I didn't bring anything to do that."

"I am just confirming the ground rules," he said. "You may take notes, but this is not a formal statement. She will not sign anything."

Carlucci nodded. They had been through all this before. Maybe it was for Amira's benefit.

Istvan set a pack of cigarettes in the center of the cable spool, took one and lit it, then waved at Carlucci to go ahead.

"Why are you hiding?" Carlucci asked.

Amira glanced at Istvan, then took one of his cigarettes. She lit it and took a deep drag, staring at Carlucci. "If you don't know, I'm sure as hell not going to tell you." She cocked her head. "If you don't know, why are we here?"

Was this going to be one of those interviews where the person he talked to constantly played games with their answers? He hoped she was just being cautious.

"You knew Naomi Katsuda," he said. "If you're hiding, I'd guess you know something about her murder. That's why we're here. That's why I've been searching for you."

She gazed at him for a minute, then nodded once. "Yes, I knew her. We were friends."

"Just friends?" he asked.

She smiled and shook her head. "Friends isn't enough?" She sighed deeply. "Yes, we were more than friends. Yes, we were . . . lovers. We had to be discreet. Her father knew, but he couldn't stand the idea that his daughter wasn't straight. Wasn't 'normal,' as he used to say all the time. So he knew, but as long as we weren't open and public about it, he tolerated it."

"What would he have done if you hadn't been discreet?"

"We didn't want to find out. And as it turned out, we were right to be afraid."

Clouds were passing across the moon, and the light faded in and out. There was some illumination from a street lamp nearby, but it was dimmer than the moonlight, and Amira's features threatened to wash away in the darkness.

"What happened to Naomi?"

She smoked silently for a minute or two, looking away from him. She closed her eyes, and the clouds cleared away from the moon long enough to light the moisture at their corners, moisture that wasn't quite tears. Then she opened her eyes again and looked at him.

"Her father killed her, and carved up her forehead. That's what happened to her."

Jesus. Carlucci was stunned, completely unprepared for what he'd just heard. She hadn't said Naomi's father had arranged for his daughter's murder. No, her meaning was clear. Yoshi Katsuda had done it himself.

"How do you know he did it?" he asked.

"I *saw* him do it."

Jesus, he said to himself again. "All right. Tell me what happened."

Her cigarette was almost gone, and she dropped it to the concrete floor and lit another. She smoked in silence for a while, and Istvan, too, smoked steadily; Carlucci had to fight the urge to reach out and take one for himself.

"I was at Naomi's condo all day," she began. "I had the day off work, and I'd spent most of the day cleaning up around the place and getting things ready for dinner whenever Naomi got home. She'd said she'd probably be working late." She paused. "You've been in the condo, right?"

Carlucci shook his head.

"What the hell kind of investigation *is* this?"

"I'm not one of the investigating officers," he explained. "They've been through the condo, but I haven't."

"Then what the hell is your involvement in all this?"

"I'm the supervising officer on the case. And I'm doing everything I can to solve this damn thing."

She appeared to accept his explanation, though grudgingly, and she went on. "It's on two floors. The second floor is more like a huge loft, open, just a bedroom, and a bathroom. I was up there, taking a shower, when Naomi came home. It was late, close to eight o'clock. She stuck her head into the bathroom, told me she was home, and then went downstairs to have a drink and start on dinner." She stopped, looking outside through the cracked and shattered windowpanes. "I was out of the shower, and I was getting dressed when I heard the front door open. At first I thought she was just going out for a minute, something, but then I heard voices. Naomi's first, sounding pissed, and then someone else's. I listened hard, and recognized her father's voice. Knowing the way he felt about me, I decided I should stay out of sight, but I was curious. I got down on my hands and knees and crawled across the loft, as close as I could to the edge of the stairs, where I could hear them."

She stopped again, and Carlucci could see a tightening in her face. "But I couldn't really make out anything he was saying, and so I crept forward a little and looked over the edge. Her father was there, in the front room, with two of his security jackals, all of them facing Naomi. Then he finally said something I could make out. He said, 'You will never tell anyone. But you are my daughter, and so I will do this myself.' And then he moved so quickly I could hardly believe it. Suddenly there was a long thin knife in his hand and he shot forward and drove it into her chest." Amira was having a hard time breathing now, blinking frequently, still not looking at him. "She cried out, but it was so brief, hardly a sound. And then she fell back, and he released the knife, letting it go with her. There was some jerking . . . and then nothing . . . and I knew she was dead." She was shaking her head now. "So fast, so fast, and she was gone."

She looked at her cigarette, took one final deep drag on it, then tossed it onto the floor near the others. But this time she did not light another.

"I couldn't move. I watched him kneel beside her, pull the knife from her heart, then carve something into her forehead. I couldn't do anything to help her. Nothing. She was dead. And if they found out I was there, I'd be dead, too. So I crawled backward, slowly, so slowly, praying no floorboards would creak, until I was at the bed, and then I crawled under it, and waited. But no one came upstairs, no one even looked. I heard more sounds, doors opening and closing, and then after a while just silence. But I was scared. I didn't move from under the bed for hours. When I finally did, and went downstairs, there were no signs of anything. Naomi was gone. There was no blood anywhere. Nothing out of place, nothing odd except a half-filled wineglass on the kitchen counter. Nothing."

"If they didn't know you were there," Carlucci said, "why have you been hiding?"

She finally looked at him, and there was a bitter smile on her face. "I would have been next. He didn't know I had seen him kill her, but he also didn't know whether she'd told me whatever it was he had killed her for. He would assume she had. He wouldn't take any chances. If it was important enough to kill his own daughter for, he wouldn't hesitate to kill me just in case."

There was a loud scraping sound outside the machine shop, and a shadow shifted across the windows. He looked at Istvan, who returned his look, nodded, then got to his feet. He moved quickly and almost silently across the machine shop's concrete floor, to the side entrance and into the shadows. Carlucci and Amira waited in silence, neither moving.

There was strength in her, he decided, watching her, watching how she waited. She wouldn't scare easily, or without reason. He liked her.

A few minutes later Istvan returned. "It was nothing," he said quietly. "A kid scrounging through trash." He lit a fresh cigarette for himself, and Amira joined him.

"Why did Yoshi Katsuda kill his daughter?" Carlucci asked.

Amira shrugged. "That's the question, but I don't have the answer. Naomi wouldn't tell me what she knew." Again that bitter smile. "She thought it would be safer for me if I *didn't* know."

"But you must have some idea," Carlucci said.

"Sure. Some idea. But it doesn't mean anything. It had something to do with Cancer Cell. No big surprise there, they were Naomi's obsession."

"Why was she so interested in them?"

"Because they seemed to be trying to subvert New Hong Kong's overwhelming dominance of medical research. That, indirectly, worked to subvert Mishima, and in turn her father."

"Did she consider that good or bad?" he asked. "She *did* work for her father. For Mishima and New Hong Kong."

Her smile changed, became more amused. "It intrigued her." Then the smile left. "But I think she found out something about what New Hong Kong or her father was doing in relation to Cancer Cell. That's what had been bothering her, and it had been bothering her for months. I think it took her a long time to piece it together, to be sure. And I think she was just about there when her father killed her."

"Why are you still here in the city?" Carlucci asked. "Why not get the hell out?"

"I've lived here all my life. I don't really know anyone anywhere else. I don't see how I could have gone anywhere without leaving a trace somewhere, credit or ID. But here in San Francisco, I have resources, people I can count on, ways to go on *without* leaving any traces."

He smiled wryly. "Except for someone like Istvan."

Amira nodded, but didn't smile.

"Where are you staying now?" he asked.

Amira shook her head. "No. Because Istvan says I can, I trust you enough to come here and talk to you. But I don't trust you that much."

"Why do you trust Istvan?"

"Because he found me, and I'm still alive."

Simple enough. But this wasn't quite over yet. "I want to arrest the bastard," he said. "I want to lock him up, and I want to have him tried and convicted for the murder of his daughter."

"And I want to have Naomi restored to life."

"I can't arrange that, but I *can* take care of Yoshi Katsuda, if you testify. Eyewitness testimony is worth a lot to a jury."

But she just shook her head. "You think I'd live long enough to testify?"

"We'd make sure you would."

"Yeah. I'm reassured."

"If you don't testify, he remains a free man."

"If I don't testify, I remain alive."

"But will you ever be able to come out of hiding?"

Amira nodded. "That's a point. Someday, though. Something will change. Events. Maybe he gets Core Fever and dies or goes to New Hong Kong, or moves to some other city. Or all of this blows over. Someday."

She didn't sound very convinced, and he pushed it. "But that could be years from now. Or he could find you, if he looks long enough."

"I'll take that chance."

Carlucci couldn't give up, he couldn't just let this go. Knowing what had happened was not enough. "Here's another option," he offered. "Sign a full statement, detailing what happened. That will be plenty for a probable cause hearing. With murder and a serious threat of flight, there's a good chance we can get him held without bail. Maybe we'll be able to plea-bargain, it won't go to trial, and you won't have to testify."

"Fat . . . fucking . . . chance. He'll have the best and sleaziest lawyers money can buy. He'll fight every bit of the way. It'll go to trial."

He shrugged. "Maybe. Probably. But you can decide *then*. You can stay where you are, not with police protection, but with your own. But Christ, give us a chance to bring . . ." He was about to say, "bring him to justice," but he didn't think that was right. "To bring the bastard down. He killed his own daughter. I do *not* want to let this go."

"I don't either," she replied. "But it won't bring Naomi back to life, and I don't want to die. And if I do make a statement, and you arrest the son of a bitch . . . he'll really come after me, then."

Carlucci nodded. "Yes, he will."

Amira shook her head. "I don't know."

I don't know, she'd said. Not *no.* There was a chance. But he knew he shouldn't push it. He would have to wait, give her time to think about it, time to think about what she could live with and what she couldn't.

He nodded, and stood. "Thanks for talking to me," he said.

"Sure thing."

"Think about it. And let me know. Or let Istvan know."

She nodded. "I will."

45

ONCE AGAIN, WHEN things started to go to shit, Eric Ralston became unreachable. He was still in San Francisco, still at the Hyatt Regency, but for two days Cage put calls in, and for two days there was no answer. He left ten or more messages, but never got a call back. It had become a pattern, and it confirmed to him that his new fears were well founded.

It was the first time he had brought Caroline up to his apartment above the clinic. As he walked in with her, he was conscious of how empty it looked and felt, like no one lived here, as if it were more cheap hotel room than someone's apartment. The bare minimum for furnishings; a handful of books, a few dishes on the counter. No paintings, no decorations of any kind. Nothing that made it look like a man named Ryland Cage lived here.

"It's not much," he said, feeling defensive.

"I remember," she said. "I was here for a few minutes once before, the day I got out of the Core."

That was right. He'd forgotten. "Can I fix you some tea or coffee or something?"

"Sure. Hot tea would be good." She wandered around the room, looking at the few pieces of furniture, the nearly empty shelves.

"Searching for signs of intelligent life?" he asked.

She just laughed. He went over to the kitchen, filled the teakettle, and put it on the stove.

"The rest of this floor is all prostitutes?" she asked. When he nodded, she said, "And you trade medical care for this apartment."

"Yes."

"I think they're getting the better deal."

He shrugged. "Maybe so. It's fine with me."

"Maybe some of the ladies have offered their services to help make up for it, hmmm?"

Cage could feel himself flushing, and he didn't respond. Some of them *had* offered their services free of charge. He'd even taken a couple of them up on their offers over the past two years, but he wasn't going to tell Caroline that.

"Are you blushing?" she asked.

He kept his face to the stove, but he could feel the heat in his ears, and they felt exposed.

"I'm only teasing you," she said. "I'm trying to get a laugh out of you. The past couple of days you've seemed real worried about something."

He wondered if he should tell her about what they'd been doing at the clinic. But why not? He could trust her. And she'd been through plenty already.

"I know someone with the CDC," he said. "You probably know the supply of Core Fever vaccine has been pretty limited up to now, there hasn't been much available on the streets."

"Not much? How about none? Same old crap, people with money are getting first crack at it."

"Yeah. Well, my friend at the CDC, he's gotten me a couple of large batches of the vaccine for the clinic."

"But that's great, Cage! Why does that worry you?"

The water started to boil, making a sick whistling sound in the kettle. He filled a small teapot with steaming water, and added a couple of tea bags. "I hope green tea is okay," he said. "That's all I've got."

He brought the teapot and two large ceramic mugs over to the small table by the window. They sat across from each other, and he looked inside the pot. "It needs to steep some more," he said.

"Cage. What is it?"

He looked at her, a sense of dread filling him. He had really come to care for her, but it seemed an impossible time for anything like a real relationship to develop.

He smiled. "I'm sorry, I'm just a mess." He pointed at his own head. "Inside. Bear with me." Then he stopped smiling. "We've had the vaccine for two weeks now."

"Two weeks? I haven't heard a thing about it."

"Paul, Madelaine, Franzee, and I are the only ones who know."

"You've been sitting on Core Fever vaccine for two weeks, and you're not giving it to anyone? There are people dying every day from it!"

Cage shook his head. "We're not sitting on it. We've been vaccinating just about every patient who's come in."

"I don't understand. I haven't heard a word at the clinic, or anywhere else for that matter. I would think the clinic would be swamped if people knew you had the vaccine."

Cage nodded. "Exactly. The clinic would be torn apart. We've been vaccinating people without their knowledge. Whatever they come in with, we've been giving them a vaccination, calling it an antibiotic, or immune system booster, cholera treatment, whatever it takes."

"Then why so upset? There isn't something wrong with the vaccine, is there?"

"Depends on what you mean by something wrong. It could be worse, I suppose, it could be contaminated and be killing people. No, what's happening is, some people who have been vaccinated are coming down with Core Fever."

Caroline didn't say anything at first, thinking. Cage poured tea for them both.

"Maybe they were exposed to Core Fever before they got the vaccine."

Cage nodded. "We thought that at first. And that could be it for a few of them. But if your friend Rashida and the CDC people are right, the incubation period is down to two or three days. In the past few days we've had five or six people come in with Core Fever more than a week after they were vaccinated here. *They* don't know that, of course, but we do."

"What does that mean?"

"Three possibilities. One, that everyone's wrong about the incubation period, but that's the least likely possibility. Two, that the vaccine isn't completely effective. Or three, that the vaccine itself is giving some people Core Fever."

"That's possible? That the vaccine could actually cause the disease that it's supposed to prevent?"

"It's possible. It's happened before. It happened in the last century with an early version of polio vaccine. Depends on the nature of the vaccine. I've been trying to get hold of my friend in the CDC for two days now, see if I can't find out something. But either way is a serious problem. And either way, there's nothing we can do about it, because there isn't much of an alternative." He shrugged and gave her a kind of sick smile. "And that's what's been worrying me lately."

Caroline didn't say anything. She sipped at her tea, and gazed absently out the window.

Cage watched her, feeling depressed about everything—Core Fever, Nikki, his life, and Caroline. I *am* a mess, he thought. And, worst of all, he had no idea what to do about it.

Two hours later, he was still at the table by his window, looking down at the half-empty street below. Caroline was gone, back to Nikki's old place. The telephone rang. He got up, went over to the bed and sat, then picked up the receiver and answered.

"Cage."

"Cage, it's Eric."

He laughed. "About fuckin' time."

"I know, I know. But I'm pretty sure I know why you've been calling, and I've been trying to get some hard information so I'd have something to tell you. We've *all* been trying to get some hard information around here."

"Okay," he said. "Tell me why I've been calling you."

"The vaccine."

"The vaccine," Cage repeated.

"You've had people come down with Core Fever who have been vaccinated."

"Brilliant, Eric. First shot, bull's-eye."

"It's nobody's fault. The vaccine just isn't working out as well as we'd hoped."

"No shit." Cage closed his eyes and lay back on the bed. "What is it?" he asked. "Is the vaccine making them sick?"

"We don't think so. We're pretty certain that it's safe. It's killed virus, and the screening is damn good. We've been testing hundreds of samples the past few days, and not one of them has contained any live virus particles." Eric sighed. "We think the vaccine just isn't a hundred percent effective."

"You want to give me an idea of *what* percent effective, if it isn't a hundred?"

"We're only guessing right now, of course. It's been too soon, and we don't know what exposure rates have been—"

"Just get to it, Eric."

"Maybe fifty or sixty percent effective."

Jesus Christ. And that was probably high, because they'd want to put the best face on it they could.

"It'll get better, though. We've got people working on modifications right now. There's been more mutation of the virus than anyone expected. And we're stepping up production, going into full gear—"

"Stepping up production for a vaccine that's only fifty percent effective that you're still trying to change."

"It's *something,* for Christ's sake! And once we've made changes, and have a new vaccine, we'll give people who have had the first one the new one as well. Look, Cage, this is a logistical nightmare, can't you realize that? We're talking about trying to set up a vaccination program for three hundred and fifty million people. We're doing the best we can. . . ."

He had heard that too many times from Eric. Cage hung up on him, got up from the bed, and sat down by the window again, looking outside. The people down there in the street had no idea what was happening to them right now, or what was very likely to come.

46

IT WAS RAINING, so there was no moonlight, and the light from the street lamps was dim, two distant amber glows obscured by sheets of warm rain. Carlucci approached the abandoned machine shop, pulling his slick-coat tighter—a wasted gesture; he was already soaked. He hurried around the corner of the building, into the alley, then ducked into the side doorway.

Sheltered from the rain, he stood there a minute before going in. He was afraid to hope, but he could think of no other reason Amira would want to meet him tonight—she was going to go through with it. She wouldn't need to meet him just to tell him she wouldn't do it.

He opened the door, stepped inside, and closed it. Darkness and silence. Without the moonlight he could hardly see a thing inside the machine shop, only vague shadows against darker shadows. He waited, listening. Nothing. Maybe they were late. After a couple of minutes, his eyes adjusted enough to make out the crates and cable spool where they'd sat before, but there was no one there.

He took a flashlight from the slick-coat pocket and thumbed it on, sending a narrow beam of white light across the concrete floor.

"Shut that damn thing off!" Istvan's voice, a harsh whisper from somewhere above him.

Carlucci complied. He remained where he was, unmoving. Several minutes passed. If Istvan and Amira were anywhere around him, he couldn't hear them.

Finally the narrow white beam of a flashlight appeared on the other side of the machine shop, up at the top of the stairs leading to an open, second-story work area. The light beam bobbed as someone carried it down the steps, and soon he could make out two forms behind it, moving toward the crates and spool. He joined them.

Istvan and Amira sat on the crates, and Amira set a plastic folder on the spool. Inside were several sheets of paper.

"Let's do this right," she said. "Istvan told me. No question of authenticity. I've written it out myself, and I'll sign each page here in your presence." She took the sheets out of the folder and handed them to Carlucci. "Maybe you want to read it first, see if there's something I left out."

He sat on one of the other crates, used his own flashlight for light, and read through the statement. Everything was there, just as she'd told it to him when they'd been here ten days ago. Everything.

"It's fine," he said. He handed the pages back to her, and she signed and dated each one, then put them back in the folder and handed the folder to him.

"Will you testify?" he asked.

"Tell them I will," she said.

"But *will* you?"

"I don't know. Just do everything you can to avoid a trial, and we won't have to worry about it.

He had to be careful now. One move at a time, no missteps, cover his ass. And so, before he told Santos and Weathers, he went to the DA; he had to make sure he was going to get the support to go all the way.

Angela Del Carlo had been the district attorney for three years. She'd had to be hard and brash and tough to get the job in the first place, and she'd had to be tough to keep it. And she called all the shots on any high-profile case. There was no point in going to any of the deputy DA's with this; nothing would go forward without Del Carlo's approval. So Carlucci insisted on meeting with *her*.

It was late afternoon by the time he got in to see her, and she was in a foul mood. She was sitting behind her large, mahogany desk, which was covered with piles of papers and disks and a couple of different computer screens. She was wearing a dark brown suit, her hair tied back, and she was looking through a folder, turning the pages one after another.

"Have a seat, Frank." She looked up at him. "What the hell ever happened to the paperless office? We've been waiting for it since the beginning of this century, and I'd guess we'll still be waiting for it at the end of the century." She smiled. "That'll be fine with me, actually. If I ever have to read very much off a screen, that'll be the day I quit."

"Maybe something else will make you quit," he said. He sat in one of the two chairs on the other side of her desk.

Del Carlo frowned. "I don't like the sound of that, Frank. Especially with all this mystery, you won't tell me over the phone why you want to see me. Okay. Let's have it."

He held out the plastic folder with Amira's statement. Del Carlo took it from him, then sat back in her chair to read it. As he expected, she read it slowly and carefully, not glancing at him, not asking a question. When she was finished, she set it down on the desk and looked at him.

"Holy shit, Frank. You trying to shorten my career?"

"Not intentionally."

"That makes me feel much better." She shook her head, glanced at the folder again, then back up at him. "This is the real thing? I see your signatures, but . . . you talked to her? This is really her statement?"

He just nodded.

"You believe her."

"Yes."

"And she'll testify to this in court."

"She'd rather not have to," he said carefully.

"Yeah, no shit. But she will if necessary?"

"If necessary, yes."

"I hope to shit you've got her under police protection."

Carlucci shrugged. "Not exactly."

"What the hell does that mean?"

"I don't think she has much faith in police protection. She's in hiding, and she won't tell me where. That's probably best."

Del Carlo nodded. "But you have a way to get in touch with her when you need to?"

"Yes."

She sighed and slowly shook her head. "Yoshi Katsuda. Shit."

"I need to know," he told her. "If we go ahead and get an arrest warrant, will you prosecute? Will you put everything we've got into it and not roll over and drop the charges at the first hint of pressure from Katsuda and his attorneys?"

Del Carlo laughed. "Jesus, you're a bastard, Frank."

"I'm sorry I have to ask, Angela, but I need to know. This will be a monster if we go through with it. We'll take some vicious heat, you know that. I'm not going to stick my ass out over the fire, and *hers*," he said, pointing at the folder, "if I can't be sure of every bit of support you can bring."

She nodded. "You're right to ask, Frank. Has Vaughn seen this? I assume not, or I would have had him screaming at me already."

"No one's seen it except you."

"So if I told you to forget this statement, and just drop the whole matter. . . . ?"

Carlucci shrugged. "No one else knows. You wouldn't have to worry about anyone making a stink about it."

"And this woman, Amira?"

"I don't think it would break her heart if we dropped the whole thing."

"But she came forward with her story. A little late, maybe, but she came forward."

"Not exactly."

"That phrase again," Del Carlo said. "What do you mean by it this time?"

"She didn't come forward. We've been searching for her for two months."

"Who is 'we'?"

"Santos and Weathers and I. Santos and Weathers are the investigating officers on the case."

She cocked her head. "But they don't know about her statement?"

"No. I found her, and I didn't tell them. We didn't know what, if anything, she'd be able to tell us if we found her."

Del Carlo didn't say anything more for a while. He knew she was trying to decide what to do. But he also knew she wouldn't take long, she wouldn't sit on it for days like some people. She would probably make the decision right now, in the next few minutes, and once she'd made the decision, she would never look back.

He was prepared for any decision she made. Certainly he wanted to go forward, he wanted to nail Yoshi Katsuda's ass to the floor, he wanted the man to pay, and not just for what he had done to his own daughter. Carlucci was beginning to suspect that Katsuda was responsible for a lot more—more pain and grief, and probably more deaths. Maybe his own wounds from that day he was following Mouse. Maybe even Christina's death.

But he was also ready to accept Angela Del Carlo's decision if she wanted to bury it right here and now. If they went forward, they would all be digging through shit and heat for weeks or months. He wouldn't miss that.

Del Carlo breathed in deeply once, then slowly let it out as she nodded. "All right, Frank. Let's do it."

That night he drank several shots of whiskey during the evening, knowing he wouldn't be able to sleep without it. Andrea didn't say a word—probably she assumed he was drinking because of Christina. There was that, too, but he tried not to think about her too much right now.

And then Cage called.

"I didn't wake you up, did I?"

Carlucci shook his head, then realized Cage couldn't see it. Christ, he was about half smashed. "No," he said. Then, "How's Caroline?"

"Caroline's fine. She's not why I'm calling."

"What is it then?" He wanted to just hang up and crawl into bed. He didn't want to have to think about anything else right now except Yoshi Katsuda.

"It's about the Core Fever vaccine. I thought you might want to hear this."

"Go ahead."

"I've talked to someone in the CDC. They haven't announced it publicly yet, and I'm not sure they ever will. But the vaccine is only about fifty percent effective."

That gave him a bit of a jolt, waking him up. "Fifty percent? What does that mean, exactly?"

"About half of all people who have been vaccinated, if they are exposed to Core Fever, will come down with it despite the vaccination."

"Christ. That's not good."

"No."

"So one hell of a lot of people who think they're safe from Core Fever are going to get it anyway, and die."

"That's right."

"Well, that's depressing news. But why are you telling me? I can't do anything about it."

"I just thought you would want to know. It's one more thing in all this mess, and it stinks of New Hong Kong. It *all* stinks of New Hong Kong, and I thought you had some case with those fuckers involved."

"I do," Carlucci said. "You think New Hong Kong deliberately came up with a half-assed vaccine?"

"No, it's not that. I can't explain it, it's just a gut feeling, but there's responsibility, somehow. They've been involved in this shit from the beginning, every step of the way, and I think there's something there that we don't know about. We may never know what it is. But I thought you'd want to know."

Carlucci nodded to himself, thinking. "Yeah," he said absently. "I *do* want to know. I think I know what you mean." He paused, trying to hang on to the thoughts that were jumping around in his head. "Thanks for letting me know." And then, before Cage could reply, Carlucci hung up.

There was something. Too many connections, but no real explanations yet. He punched up the department, then asked to be transferred over to Info Services. Marx answered the phone, which was perfect.

"Marx, this is Carlucci."

"Hey, Lieutenant. What can I do for you?"

"Put a trigger into the system for me," he said. "For Monk."

"The slug?"

"Yeah, the slug. I want to be notified immediately of anything that he does, any calls he makes or visitors or interview sessions, any calls that come in, *anything* to do with him. Can you do that?"

"Sure."

"Can you do it in such a way that he won't know about it?"

"Trickier," Marx said, and Carlucci could almost see him grinning. "But yeah, I can do it."

"Thanks."

"You got it, Lieutenant."

Carlucci hung up. He was tired. But tomorrow promised to be an interesting day.

When Santos and Weathers came into his office the next morning, he handed them each a copy of the arrest warrant. The two of them sat down and started reading, but Santos almost immediately leaped up from the chair. He kissed the warrant and held it high above his head.

"God bless the Virgin Mary!" he cried out. "We're going to nail the bastard!"

"Take it easy, Ruben," Carlucci said. "Sit down. It's not going to be that easy. We're going to have hell ahead of us over the next few weeks."

Santos sat down, grinning, holding tightly to the warrant. "Yeah, but we're going to arrest that arrogant prick. And if we do it late at night, he won't be able to get a bail hearing, and he'll have to spend at least one day in the clink."

"Just hold on there, Ruben. That's exactly why I don't want you to get out of control. We're going to have to be very careful with all this. We have to think out every move. And arresting him at night is *not* what we want to do."

"Why not?"

"Because with the powerful attorneys he'll have, they'll find a judge who will hold a bail hearing even at two o'clock in the morning. And a judge who would do that for him is not a judge we want to have—he'll be out. And we're going to try like hell to have him held without bail. We don't want him to take off to New Hong Kong. We'd never see him again."

"You sound like you've talked with someone already about this," Weathers said.

Carlucci looked at her and nodded. "I have. Angela Del Carlo. Before I applied for the warrant, I wanted to make sure we'd have the DA's office behind us."

"And if they hadn't been?"

He only hesitated a moment. They had to know. "I would have buried it. You'd never have seen a warrant. You'd never have heard a damn thing about it."

Weathers nodded. She understood. Santos understood as well, but he didn't like it, and he scowled at Carlucci.

"How the hell . . . ?" Santos began. "How did you find out it was Katsuda? What the hell have we got for a case?"

"The sketch artist image you two got from that guy in Naomi Katsuda's condo."

"You found the woman?"

"I found the woman."

"How?"

Carlucci shook his head. "Sorry, Ruben. I can't tell you." But he did tell them about Amira's story, and the statement she'd made.

"Jesus Christ," Santos said, and he got up from the chair again, pacing back and forth in the corner of the room. He couldn't sit still. "But we're going to arrest the bastard."

"Yes," Carlucci said.

"When? Who?"

"The three of us," he answered. He stood. "Now."

Yoshi Katsuda was expecting them—there was no way to get up to his office without letting him know—but Carlucci didn't think he knew why they were coming. Carlucci had said there were some aspects to Naomi Katsuda's murder that urgently needed to be discussed, and, after some back and forth, Katsuda had agreed to see him.

There had been some confusion at the security post on the ground floor of the Mishima building. Carlucci had neglected to tell Katsuda that he wouldn't be alone, that two other police officers would be with him. There had been a call up to Katsuda's office, more discussion and negotiation; Carlucci had been insistent, stressing that Santos and Weathers were the investigating officers, and suggesting that they would not leave without seeing him. Finally Katsuda had cleared all three of them, and they had taken the elevator together up to the top floor.

Now they stood in the reception area, waiting. Santos kept staring at the woman with the metal face until Weathers elbowed him a couple of times.

"You should have warned me about her," Santos whispered to Carlucci. Weathers elbowed him again, and he grinned.

"Mr. Katsuda will see you now," the woman said.

"Ask him to come out here," Carlucci said.

The woman hesitated, then said, "Sorry?"

"I said, ask him to come out here."

She hesitated again, then picked up the intercom and spoke. A few moments later, the wall opened up and Katsuda came through it. He was dressed much as he had been the last time Carlucci had been here, in a dark suit and tie. He glanced at Santos and Weathers, then turned his gaze to Carlucci.

"There's something odd about this visit," he said. "I suspect you haven't been completely forthcoming with me."

Carlucci shrugged.

"You are under arrest for the murder of Naomi Katsuda," Santos said. He paused, waiting for a response. But Katsuda didn't say anything, he didn't even glance at Santos; he kept his gaze on Carlucci. Santos went on. "I will be reading you a list of your rights," he said. He took a card from his pocket to read from. There weren't going to be any mistakes. "If you have any question about any of them, feel free to ask. First . . ."

Katsuda waved at Santos, a gesture of dismissal, though he continued to look at Carlucci. "I waive the reading of those rights," he said. "I know what my rights are."

"I'm sorry," Santos replied. "I can't do that. We must read them to you. First, you have the right to remain silent. Second . . ."

Carlucci and Katsuda stared at each other as Santos went through the Miranda/Washington procedure. Katsuda's face betrayed no emotion, no expression at all other than bored indifference. Was he that confident? Or just that much in control?

When Santos was finished, he asked, "Do you understand these rights as I have read them to you?"

Katsuda nodded. "Yes, I understand them all quite clearly." And then a faint smile appeared on his face. "I understand a lot more now than I did before. And I will be calling my attorney before we leave here." He paused for a moment. "I'm impressed, Lieutenant."

"Don't be," Carlucci said.

"But I am. This will be futile for you in the end, but I am quite impressed that you are here with a warrant for my arrest."

"Is that an admission to the charges?" Santos asked. Weathers, a step or two behind him, was just shaking her head.

Katsuda finally turned to Santos, and gave him a disparaging look. "Of course not, *Officer*. Lieutenant Carlucci knows what I mean."

"So what does he mean, Frank?"

Carlucci shook his head. "Nothing, Ruben. Nothing that will ever be admissible in court." Then, to Katsuda, "You might be surprised Mr. Katsuda. About the futility."

The smile broadened. "I don't think so, but that would be interesting, anyway."

"I hope you find a jail cell interesting, too."

"I don't believe I will be in one long enough to find it anything at all."

Carlucci finally allowed himself a brief, small smile. "You might be surprised about that as well."

Late that afternoon, Carlucci left the courthouse in good spirits. Because of the serious nature of the crime, and the perceived flight risk, and in no small part because of the passionate and persuasive arguments of Angela Del Carlo, Yoshi Katsuda was being held without bail.

47

NIGHT HAD FALLEN. The air was warm, but it was raining, too, and the sound of it reminded Caroline of the day she had realized she had Core Fever, the day she'd thought she would soon be dead. She and Cage had found a table at a junk store, so she'd retired the plastic crates and plywood Nikki had used, and put the table next to the largest window looking out on the street. She sat there now with the lights off, drinking tea and watching the colored lights flashing below her. The nights, though still the busiest time in the Tenderloin, still noisy and active, no longer had quite the same frenetic quality as the first time she'd come here. People seemed halfhearted as well as wary and resigned.

But she was beginning to like it here in the Tenderloin, in this apartment. It had been Nikki's, but she was finally beginning to feel like it was her own. Another week or two, when she felt more sure about it, she would move everything from her apartment in Noe Valley, make it permanent here. She smiled to herself, thinking of how her father would feel about that. Mom, oddly enough, would probably understand.

There was a knock on the door, and she called out, "Come in." Cage had said he would stop by after his shift at the clinic, so she was expecting him. The door opened, then closed.

"What if it hadn't been me?" Cage asked. "I could have been some maniac."

She turned away from the window and looked at his dark shadowy form coming toward her. "You *are* some kind of maniac," she said, smiling.

"Ha, ha." He sat across from her. "And why no lights?"

"So I can see better outside. I like this, watching the signs, the message streamers, the lights of the cars. That woman there, in the kiosk." She pointed toward the end of the block, where an old woman sat inside a tiny kiosk, selling cold beer. The old woman was smiling, talking to customers, drinking a beer herself. "I've been watching her every night," Caroline said. "She isn't letting all this get her down, the people dying. Core Fever, everything else."

Cage sighed. "Is that an admonition?"

"It's an observation. And here's another one. I don't think I've seen you smile in days."

He shook his head. "What's to smile about? Maybe that old woman manages to enjoy her life down there because she stays half drunk and she doesn't know what's really happening around her. Do *you* realize what's happening here? In this city, in this country?"

"Yes," Caroline said. "I do."

"I wonder. We have a full-blown epidemic going that very soon will become a pandemic. It's already breaking out in other countries. The damn disease is almost one hundred percent fatal, and the only vaccine we've got for it, which isn't even being widely distributed yet, is only fifty percent effective. People are getting sick in droves, and they are dying in droves, and there is not a whole hell of a lot we can do about it. Unless something changes very quickly, and the odds are not good for that, this thing is going to kill off a good chunk of the population in this country, maybe even the world. And it's going to kill off a bigger chunk here in San Francisco. This city is going to be unrecognizable a year from now. Probably the entire country is going to be unrecognizable."

"I know all that, Cage. My sister died from Core Fever, and I almost died from it. But I'm not dead, and neither are you. We don't just stop living because the world is going to shit around us. I'm not suggesting we try to ignore it, or pretend it's not happening, but we also don't curl up in a ball somewhere and stop living, and that's what you're doing. You might just as well put a gun to your head and blow your brains out."

"I've thought about it," he said.

"No you haven't. I know you, Cage."

He nodded. "You're right, I haven't. But sometimes I wish I *could* give it serious consideration."

"Look at that woman down there," she said. "There's something important to be learned from her."

He gave her a half smile. "Unless you've managed to romanticize the shit out of her, and she's really just a drunken psychotic who *doesn't* have a clue to what's going on."

"That's better," she said. "Not much of a smile, but it's something." She stood. "You want some tea or coffee?"

"Yeah," he said, nodding. "Coffee."

"I'll put the water on."

When she returned to the table, his back was to her and he was gazing out the window. She came up behind him and put her hands on his shoulders. He stiffened a bit, briefly, then relaxed. It wasn't much of a response. She wanted him to put his own hands over hers, but he didn't.

Her heart was beating a little faster and harder now, and her breathing was a little funny. Could she be wrong about his feelings for her? She didn't think so. He'd never said anything, but she was sure she could feel it from him every time they spent any time together.

"I'm going to have to take the initiative with this, aren't I?" she finally said.

"With what?" he asked, still not looking at her.

"You know what I mean."

He breathed in deeply once, then slowly let it out and nodded. He turned around then and looked up at her, and she leaned over, bringing her mouth to his. She kissed him, and this time he did respond, and her stomach and chest twisted around in a half-sick, half-ecstatic sensation she hadn't felt in a long, long time.

At midnight it was still raining. They lay naked on the open sleeping bag, which they had laid out on the floor. The room was dark, but there was the flashing and blinking of lights from the street, and she could see the reflection of sweat on his skin.

"You're smiling," Cage said.

"Shouldn't I be?"

"Well, I don't imagine that was the most exhilarating and profound sexual experience you've ever had."

Caroline laughed softly. "It was the first time you and I have ever made love. Of *course* it was a little awkward. We *both* were awkward. I imagine that's pretty normal with two people who don't know each other that way."

She laid her arm across his chest and kissed his shoulder. "It certainly wasn't unpleasant, and it'll get better." She sensed his insecurity, and thought how absurd it was.

They lay for a while without talking. She really did feel quite wonderful, being beside him, feeling his skin against hers, feeling his heartbeat against her hand. It helped to remind her that she was still alive, and that despite everything happening around them, being alive was a wonderful thing.

"I know this is just crazy," he said, "but I feel a little guilty." He was staring up at the ceiling.

"Nikki?"

"Nikki."

"Why? Because this was her place?"

"Partly. And because I loved her, and she hasn't been dead for very long."

"Oh, Cage," she said.

"I *know* it's irrational, but it's there." He turned his head toward her, and managed a smile. "But I promise not to let it get in the way."

"I wonder if there's something wrong with you," she said, smiling back at him.

"What do you mean?"

"First, you fall in love with someone who doesn't love you in return."

"Nikki loved me," Cage said.

"Yes, but not in the same way."

"No, not in the same way. She never loved anyone that way. I didn't know that at first. I didn't understand that for a long time."

"Then she died. You lost her. Twice in a way. And now you're beginning to care for someone who's also going to die soon, in a few years at most."

Cage didn't say anything for a long time. He was facing her, but his gaze was unfocused, or focused on something far away that wasn't even in the room with them.

"Yes," he finally said. "Maybe there is something wrong with me. But I don't notice you objecting."

"No, I'm not objecting. A few months ago, I would have. I even kept putting off a stray cat that tried to adopt me, because I didn't want it to become dependent on me. I was afraid of what would happen to it after I died."

"So why the change?"

"Almost dying." She turned onto her back and gazed up at the ceiling herself. "I've come to terms with the Gould's in some real ways. Not completely, of course. I don't think that's possible. I suspect I'll have an occasional 'lapse,' wake up in the middle of the night absolutely terrified of dying, terrified and furious that I survived this disease that so many other people are dying from, only to have to die from something else in a few years while I'm still so young."

"Sounds to me like you've already had one or two nights like that."

"Maybe," she said, smiling again. She turned to him. "But I promise not to let *that* get in the way, either."

He reached across her, took hold of her hand. Then he pulled her on top of him, and soon their slick bodies were moving together once again.

48

CARLUCCI WAS ASLEEP and dreaming about Istvan Darnyi's apartment. He was sitting inside piles of stamp albums and stock books, open shoe boxes overflowing with loose stamps. He was trying to find stamps from the Italian states—Modena, Sardinia, Tuscany—but he was certain he wouldn't recognize them even if he saw them, and he wasn't all that clear why he was searching for them in the first place. So when the phone started ringing, bringing him out of the dream, he felt a great sense of relief.

His sense of relief faded quickly, however, as he came fully awake. The bedroom was still dark, only the faintest touches of gray to indicate morning was coming. A phone call this time of day was almost never good news. He grabbed the receiver to stop the ringing, trying to focus on the clock at the same time: 5:52. Jesus.

"Carlucci," he said.

"Lieutenant, this is Marx. Sorry to wake you up, but I've got something for you."

"Hold on a second."

He scrambled out of bed, glancing over at Andrea, who still seemed to be deep asleep, then stumbled out of the bedroom, down the hall, and into the kitchen, where he half collapsed into one of the chairs.

"All right," he said. "Go ahead."

"I was just getting ready to go off shift when it came through," Marx said. "The Monk trigger."

"Monk. What is it?"

"He's leaving."

"What?"

"He's leaving his quarters. He's arranged to have an ambulance van come pick him up at department headquarters, then take him to Hunter's Point."

The spaceport. "He's going to New Hong Kong," Carlucci said.

"That's what I would guess."

"What time?"

"The ambulance is scheduled to arrive at nine o'clock. I checked with Hunter's Point Security, and they have a special flight taking off at noon."

"Goddamn, Marx, you've done a hell of a job."

"Thanks, Lieutenant. But there's more."

"What?"

"It's not related, but I figure you want to hear about this."

"What is it?"

"Word is that Katsuda's managed to get a new bail hearing for this morning."

Carlucci closed his eyes. He wanted to crawl back into bed and go back to dreaming about missing stamps. "I didn't really want to hear that," he said.

"Sorry, sir."

"That's okay."

"He'll get out on bail, won't he, Lieutenant?"

"It doesn't look good." He opened his eyes and twisted his head from side to side. He must have slept wrong; there was a terrible, biting kink in his neck. "Thanks for calling."

"Do you want me to monitor Monk for you, keep track of what he's doing until he gets to Hunter's Point?"

"I thought you were getting ready to go off shift."

"I am, but I can stick around."

"You don't mind?"

"No. Never seen one of the slugs leave before. They just seem to stay inside their caves until they die. It could be interesting."

"Sure. I'd appreciate it. Give me a call if anything unusual comes up."

"Will do, Lieutenant."

Carlucci hung up. He sat at the kitchen table, trying to decide what to do. He wasn't going to let Monk leave without talking to him first, that much he knew. But he felt there was something more he needed to do. He got up and made some coffee, hoping it would help him think things through.

An hour later he was showered and dressed, and he was still trying to put his thoughts together. There were things out there he thought he was close to understanding, those odd connections, but he wasn't there yet. And he had the feeling that if he didn't get the rest of the way today, he never would.

He sat at the kitchen table again, drinking one more cup of coffee, and picked up the phone to call Angela Del Carlo. He finally got through on the third number he tried.

"This is Del Carlo." There was traffic noise in the background, and the faint sound of jazz.

"Carlucci here," he said.

"Shit." A horn blared and brakes squealed in the background. "Goddamn it. All right, Frank. I know why you're calling, and it's true. I'm on my way to the courthouse right now."

"What's it look like?"

"Shit, that's what. McAdamas is the judge."

"That's not good," he said.

"She'd let her own killer go free if the money was right."

He blinked and shook his head, trying to figure out the logistics of that. "All right. Let me know what happens."

"Sure thing." The connection clicked off.

One more phone call, this time to Cage. Carlucci had one final big favor to ask.

It was a little after eight by the time he approached the RadioLand Street Clinic. The streets and sidewalks of the Tenderloin were half empty; it was early in the morning, the dead time of day in here, but even so he figured it was probably worse than usual. Just like everywhere else in the city.

Cage met him as he walked in through the clinic entrance, then led him back to the staff room at the end of the corridor. The fans were going, keeping the room tolerable, just as they had been the first time they'd met. A lot had happened since they'd talked that day.

Cage picked up a small, narrow case, not much bigger than a paperback, and handed it to him. It might just fit inside his jacket pocket. "That's it," Cage said. "Two." He looked at Carlucci. "What are you going to do with them?"

"I don't know."

"Am I really supposed to believe that?"

Carlucci just shrugged.

"What is it?" Cage asked. " Revenge?"

"No. Some kind of justice, maybe."

"Sounds like a euphemism for revenge to me."

"Maybe so," Carlucci said.

"One last bit of news," Cage said. "I talked to my friend in the CDC late last night. Later today, they're going to make the announcement."

"That the vaccine isn't as effective as they've claimed?"

Cage nodded. "Too many news reports of people getting Core Fever after being vaccinated. They can't keep it quiet anymore."

"Then what?"

He shook his head. "I don't know. No one does."

Carlucci wasn't surprised. It kind of fit with some of the things he was putting together. Made sense of the timing.

"All right," he said. "Show me what to do."

As he neared Hunter's Point, traffic jammed up, slowed by crowds of people in the streets. He thought about putting up his flasher and punching the siren, but decided it might make things worse. Marx had said he was ahead of Monk anyway, and Monk wasn't going to get through this any faster than he was.

The crowds were headed toward Hunter's Point, something he should have expected. But there was no organization, just a chaotic milling that slopped over into the roadway. Carlucci moved forward in stops and starts, never reaching more than five miles an hour. The people moved back and forth in front of the car, sometimes turning to look at him, faces shiny with sweat. Night hadn't brought much relief from the heat, and the day was already beginning to warm up.

The crowds thickened and slowed as he got within sight of the main Hunter's Point gate. Security forces lined the fences, with a large contingent at the gates holding the crowd back. The main parking lot was nearly empty; the guards weren't letting any vehicles through. Several guards were directing vehicles away before they even reached the gate.

He thought he could talk his way into the parking lot, but decided it wasn't worth it. Hell, he might never get out. He swung the car away from the gates, drove a block, then turned a corner and pulled over to the curb. He locked up the car, then pushed into the crowd, forcing his way toward the main gate.

It took him nearly ten minutes to go the one block and the extra hundred yards to the gate itself. People shouted all around him, mostly things he couldn't make out. There were signs, though, held up above the crowd that let him know what this was all about: VACCINE NOW!! CORE FEVER KILLERS. NO MORE PHONY VACCINE! FREE VACCINE FOR EVERYONE!! The smell of the crowd, too, was bad—sweat and anger and fear. When he finally reached one of the guards, still twenty feet from the gate, he showed his badge and ID plates.

"Sorry, Lieutenant," the guard said. "The launch grounds are closed to everyone except authorized parties, and those going up on the next ship."

"I don't want to go onto the launch grounds," Carlucci said, almost shouting to be heard above the crowd noise. "I just want onto the parking lot. I've got official business with one of the people you *will* be letting through."

The guard opened his mouth, closed it, and frowned. He seemed unsure. "You don't have jurisdiction in Hunter's Point," he finally said.

"I know," Carlucci replied. "Let's call this cooperation between agencies. I'm not going to cause you any problems. I just need to talk to someone for a few minutes before he goes." The guard still seemed unsure, so Carlucci went on, "I need to talk to Monk. Monk *is* approved access, isn't he?"

The guard nodded. "All right," he said. "Come on through. But check in with Captain Reynoso at the Security building, all right?"

Carlucci nodded. The guard gestured toward one of his colleagues, and the two men walked Carlucci to the gate, clearing a path through the crowd.

After a brief talk to the gatekeepers, several guards formed a shield of sorts against the crowd, the gate opened, and Carlucci squeezed through, the gate and shield closing behind him.

He stood in the nearly empty lot and gazed out through the second line of chain-link fence to the tarmac and the lighted gantry and ship in the distance. The gantry lights sparkled, isolated out on the black tarmac, like they had no connection to the noise and smell of the crowd behind him. He glanced back at the crowd, then walked to the Security building by the gates leading onto the launch grounds.

Captain Reynoso was big, an inch or two taller than Carlucci, and she looked to be in a lot better shape. He showed her his ID and explained why he was here.

"Lieutenant, do I have your word that you won't be causing any trouble? That you won't be trying to arrest anyone, or prevent anyone with authorization from boarding?"

"You have my word," he said. "I just want to talk to Monk."

Reynoso seemed satisfied. She offered him coffee. He'd already had too much, but he accepted anyway. Reynoso went into another room and came back with two cups, handed one to him. The coffee was better than what he'd made at home.

They stood by the main window, looking out at the parking lot, the outer gates, and the growing crowds.

"It could get ugly out there," Carlucci said.

Reynoso nodded, but didn't seem concerned. "They've been out there for days."

"Can you handle it all right?" he asked. "I can call in help from the city."

She shook her head. "We'll be fine. Once we get our parties through, we can pull everyone inside, lock up the gates, and activate the fences. Fry anyone who tries to force their way inside." She turned to look at him. "My job is security, nothing else. I plan to keep my job."

He nodded. "I understand."

He stayed by the window and watched, waiting for Monk to arrive.

49

FIFTEEN MINUTES LATER he saw a large van working its way through the crowd. The van's emergency lights flashed steadily, and the horn blared, barely audible over the noise of the crowd surrounding it.

"This will be what we're waiting for," Reynoso said.

The van finally reached the main gate. People pounded on it and rocked it from side to side, though they could have no idea who was inside, or what they were doing here. Then the gate swung open and the van drove through. The crowd surged forward behind it and the Security guards pushed in on them, forcing them slowly back, struggling for a couple of minutes before they were able to get the gate shut again. By then, the van had pulled up next to the Security building and stopped.

"Normally we'd bring them all inside," Reynoso said. "But we've got unusual circumstances."

"You've got a slug," Carlucci said.

Reynoso sighed. "Yes, we've got a slug. Let's go." She signaled to the processing crew at the other end of the building, then walked out the door and toward the van. Carlucci followed.

The driver got out of the van and handed Reynoso a packet of documents. She glanced at them, then looked at the driver. "You and the attendants will have to wait here," she said. "My people will drive the van, take the passenger out to the ship, then bring the van back."

The driver nodded. "That's what we were told."

"You can wait inside." She nodded toward the building. "There are chairs. Coffee, other things to drink."

Reynoso approached the open side door, leaned inside. "Mr. Monk?"

"It's just Monk," said a voice from inside the darkness of the van.

"Okay. Monk. There's someone here who wants to talk to you. Now, you are on Hunter's Point grounds, under our jurisdiction, so you don't have to talk to him. It's up to you."

"Who the hell is it?"

"Lieutenant Frank Carlucci of the San Francisco Police Department."

A deep rolling laugh sounded from inside the van. "Of course I'll talk to him. I was more than half expecting him. Send him in. There's plenty of room."

Reynoso stepped back. "Go ahead," she said to Carlucci. "But don't take too long. We've got to get him processed and loaded up. We've got a launch time to meet."

Carlucci nodded. He approached the van, ducked his head, and stepped up, standing bent over just inside the panel door. There wasn't much light inside the van. Monk was ensconced in something like a wheelchair surrounded by displays, fluid containers, and medical equipment. He looked just the same: a bloated, deformed body enveloped by shiny black rubber, head encased in a helmet, eyes hidden by goggles.

Monk smiled at him, the thick, distorted lips shiny with moisture. Carlucci stared at the slug, his mind blank, unable to remember what he'd wanted to ask.

"Well, Lieutenant?"

"You lied to me," Carlucci finally said.

"Of course," Monk replied. "Many times." He licked his lips, the tongue as thick and bloated as the rest of him. "Three years ago, at our first session, I offered you a chance at New Hong Kong. A chance at a very long life. Real life extension. A hundred and fifty years or more."

"You were so subtle about it, I didn't even know it was an offer at the time. I didn't figure it out until later."

"Yes, that was a problem. But you wouldn't have accepted the offer anyway."

"No."

"See, that's when so many of your difficulties began." He shook his head. "You were never very cooperative, and you've paid a high price for that."

"Tell me now, Monk. What is going on? What has been happening all this time?"

Monk laughed. "I *will* tell you, Lieutenant Francesco Carlucci, and you'll be sorry when I'm done."

Maybe so, Carlucci thought. He could feel the weight of the case against his ribs. But they would both be sorry. He looked around for a place to sit, his back already sore from standing bent over, and finally settled on a metal crate behind the driver's seat. He could just sit upright without hitting his head on the van ceiling.

"All right," he said to Monk. "Tell it."

Monk made a sound that might have been a chuckle. He made an adjustment to one of the control panels attached to the seat, and a panel began blinking green. Monk finally turned his goggled eyes directly toward him.

"Just confirming that you are not employing any recording devices," he said.

Carlucci just shook his head.

"Okay," Monk said, shifting his position. "I'll start with the main thing." He stared at Carlucci. "You ready for this?" And he paused again for effect. "New Hong Kong is responsible for Core Fever. Not Cancer Cell. Not *nature*. But New Hong Kong."

He paused, as though waiting to let it sink in, or waiting from some response from Carlucci, but Carlucci didn't say a thing. It was one of those statements that you immediately realize isn't at all surprising, that you half knew already because it fit with so many other things. New questions started swirling around in his mind, but for now he said nothing, just waited for Monk to go on.

And Monk did. "It all flows out of that," he said. "Once they were certain that it had fully taken hold in the Core and had begun to spread outward from it, presenting an undeniable health threat, they stepped forward to help. They were able to identify it as a virus—not difficult, since they had provided it—and they advised the CDC on containment measures."

"The quarantines."

"Yes, the quarantines. Particularly the quarantine of the Core. That was the real goal from the beginning. Sterilization of the Core. The Tenderloin quarantine was camouflage." He waved a hand toward Carlucci. "Once that was accomplished, and enough time had passed to lend things a certain credibility, New Hong Kong announced the development of a vaccine for Core Fever."

"A vaccine they'd had all along."

Monk shrugged his bloated shoulders and nodded. "Yes, a vaccine they'd had all along. They would never have released a virus like that one unless they had a vaccine for it."

"That's real fucking humane of them," Carlucci said, barely able to keep his anger in check, along with all of the other questions that still waited to be asked and answered. "But the vaccine is only fifty percent effective."

"Probably closer to forty," Monk said. He might have winced; with so little of his face exposed, it was difficult to tell. "That was a slight complication. It should have been close to one hundred percent effective. But somehow, probably through the use of the vector that introduced it into the Core, mutations occurred in the virus. There seem to be three major strains of Core Fever now, and the vaccine is only effective against one of them. Fortunately it is the dominant strain."

"You call forty percent dominant?"

"It's a little over forty percent of all cases, the other two each are responsible for less than thirty percent. And they're working on developing a combination vaccine. The numbers should get better."

"That's just terrific. It's insane, is what it is." Carlucci could hardly sit still; he wanted to stand up and pace, or just get up and smash something. He could hardly believe he was having this conversation.

"*Why?*" he finally asked. It was the question he had been dying to ask, the most important question of all, and it seemed unbelievable to him right now that Monk could give him anything resembling a reasonable answer.

"Several reasons, actually. It began with the need to eliminate Cancer Cell, and they came up with a way to do it that accomplished other desirable results as well."

"Cancer Cell?"

"Yes. It wasn't really sterilization of the Core that was the ultimate goal. It was the sterilization of Cancer Cell."

"Why?" Carlucci asked again.

"Business." Monk left it like that for a while, as if that answer explained everything.

"Business," Carlucci said.

Monk laughed. "Yes, of course. Cancer Cell was competition. It's that simple. Well, maybe it's not that simple, but that's the core of the matter." He laughed again.

"Competition," Carlucci said, prodding, trying to understand.

"Oh, yes, competition. One of New Hong Kong's most profitable businesses is the manufacture of high-grade, specialized, very expensive pharmaceuticals. They've got the patents all locked up here on Earth, in pretty much any country that could produce them."

"I know all about that," Carlucci said. "They ignore laws they don't like, and exploit those laws that are useful to them."

"They *are* a practical bunch," Monk said. "But Cancer Cell paid no attention to patent laws. Not only were they manufacturing many of these high-grade pharmaceuticals—not quite to the standard of New Hong Kong, of course, but close enough—they were selling them on the street at drastically reduced prices. Now, that didn't have *too* much effect on the legitimate sales, but New Hong Kong's profits on the black market, on the streets, are actually greater than those on the legitimate end. And Cancer Cell was cutting way into those. They were trying to make these otherwise expensive and difficult-to-obtain drugs moderately priced and readily accessible. And the people in Cancer Cell didn't have very high standards of living. That made it easy to keep prices artificially low." Monk shrugged. "A noble ambition, certainly, but one quite at odds with New Hong Kong's own philosophy, and one increasingly at odds with their business plans."

He paused and licked his lips several times. He reached up for a piece of flexible tubing hooked up to a fluid bag, put it in his mouth, twisted a valve, and sucked on it. He offered some to Carlucci, but he refused.

"There was one more thing, which clinched the deal for New Hong Kong. It appeared that Cancer Cell's researchers were making significant progress in the life extension area. New Hong Kong simply could not abide that. New Hong Kong is going to have absolute and complete control of any life extension treatments that are ultimately developed. In the coming years, control of that will be control of just about everything in life."

"All of this, Core Fever, the quarantines, all these people dead and dying, all this was to eliminate a business competitor?" Even as he said it, it sounded incredible.

"Essentially, yes," Monk answered. "As I said, it also was to have other positive benefits."

"Like what?"

"The people in New Hong Kong thought the population could do with a bit of culling, if properly directed. A fatal disease epidemic that began in the Core and spread to the Tenderloin would pretty much target the kinds of people New Hong Kong wanted. Especially when a vaccine soon became available, in limited quantities, to the right people. You probably noticed the vaccine still hasn't become widely available, although that will change fairly soon."

"I noticed," Carlucci replied. He shook his head, still having trouble believing what he was hearing. "Except the vaccine isn't as effective as it's supposed to be, so a lot of the 'right people' will end up getting Core Fever and dying."

Monk nodded. "I'm afraid so. As I said, that was a complication."

"That's not a complication," Carlucci said. "It's a major fuckup."

"That, too," Monk agreed, smiling. "One of the other benefits was *supposed* to be good public relations from a successful vaccine. New Hong Kong seen as the world's savior. Well, not now."

Carlucci continued to shake his head. He turned away from Monk and looked out the open door of the van. From this vantage point he could see part of the mob pressing against the outer perimeter fencing, and he could just hear a generalized noise from them. "This is incredible. And how many people are going to die before this is all over?"

"Over the next five years," Monk said, "about seventy million people in this country alone."

Carlucci swung back around and stared at him. He hadn't expected an answer, and he was stunned into silence.

"That's a worst-case scenario," Monk continued. "If the vaccine never gets any better. Approximately twenty percent of the population. There will be similar numbers in other countries, though it will vary greatly. In undeveloped countries, the percentages will end up much higher. In industrialized countries, probably lower, because they are already starting to take preventative measures." He paused. "But if they improve the vaccine, especially if they can get it close to one hundred percent effective, those numbers will greatly drop. Not soon enough for San Francisco, of course, or most of California. Or, to be honest, for a lot of the country."

"And they may not be able to improve the vaccine at all."

"That's a possibility, yes. But the researchers up in New Hong Kong are very good at what they do."

Carlucci hung his head in his hands and stared at the floor. He felt sick, and dizzy. And then, one final thing fell into place. He raised his head to look at Monk.

"What was Yoshi Katsuda's part in all this?"

"He was a liaison of sorts. All plans were made in New Hong Kong, and

Katsuda's task was implementation of those plans here on Earth. He was to make sure everything went smoothly, make sure everything was done."

"But his daughter found out about it."

"Apparently. That was another complication, and he made it worse by killing her himself. He should have kept himself completely apart from that. He should not have spent the past two weeks in jail. He should not have caused New Hong Kong to expend so much in the way of resources to get him out." Monk cocked his head. "You know he's out, don't you?"

Carlucci nodded. "So he took care of everything here in San Francisco," he said.

"Yes."

"Did that include my daughter?" he asked. "Christina."

Monk hesitated. "What about her?"

"She didn't catch Core Fever from anyone. Someone came by, took advantage of her innocence, and pumped her full of Core Fever virus."

Again Monk hesitated, then he nodded once. "I'm impressed, Lieutenant."

"*Fuck* impressed. They killed my daughter, didn't they? And you knew about it."

"I said earlier. You've paid a high price for causing New Hong Kong so much trouble. You were one more side benefit to all of this. Both of your daughters would get Core Fever and die. You were to lose both of your daughters, and eventually they would have let you know they were responsible. They sent someone for Christina. They didn't have to for Caroline. She took care of that herself, going into the Core and contracting it there. Unexpectedly, of course, she survived. If it is any consolation, the decision has been made to leave her alone. They believe her survival has earned her the right to a continued life. Of course, with the Gould's she has a damn short life expectancy anyway." He paused. "Whether they will leave *you* alone is another matter. I have no idea what they will decide for you."

"They may not have to decide. After all, I've been vaccinated for Core Fever. If I become exposed to it, I've only got a forty percent chance of being protected."

"Limit your chance of exposure," Monk said. "That's my advice."

"Is that what you're doing? By going to New Hong Kong? Limiting your exposure?"

"Not really," Monk said. "If I had stayed in my quarters in the department, I could easily have eliminated any chance of exposure."

"But you have been vaccinated?" Carlucci asked.

Monk laughed. "Sure. Before it even broke out. And before we knew it wasn't all that effective."

Okay, that made it easier. "Then why are you leaving?"

"It's time. This country is going to be greatly changed over the next few years. No way to know how, exactly, but it's probably going to be a nightmare. Way too risky to stick around. No, it's time."

"Yes," Carlucci said. "It's time."

He took the case out of his coat pocket, opened it, and took out one of the syringes.

"Lieutenant . . . what is that?"

He didn't answer. He closed the case and tucked it away, then popped off the plastic cap over the tip of the needle.

"What . . . ? Don't come near me!" Monk cried. "HELP!" he shouted, pressing back in his chair. "HELP!"

Carlucci moved forward, grabbed hold of Monk with his left arm and his body, holding him fairly still. Monk squirmed and struggled, and he kept shouting for help, but he didn't have much strength, and the chair helped keep him pinned down.

Carlucci managed to keep him still, exposing Monk's left shoulder. Then he took the syringe and drove the needle through the black rubber and deep into Monk's upper arm. Monk cried out again, and Carlucci slowly squeezed the plunger until it would go no further.

He pulled out the syringe, and released Monk, staggering backward. He managed to keep his balance, sat down heavily on the metal crate. Then he picked up the case, put the empty syringe inside, closed it up, and tucked it back into his coat.

"What did you do to me?" Monk's voice was hoarse with fear.

"You've got a forty percent chance," Carlucci said.

"What?"

"You're a slug," he said. "You're intelligent. You figure it out."

Captain Reynoso leaned in through the open side door and looked around the inside of the van.

"I thought I heard shouting," she said. "Is there a problem?"

"I don't think so," Carlucci replied.

"He—" Monk began.

But Carlucci cut him off. "You want to tell Captain Reynoso what I did, and why?"

Monk kept quiet. Reynoso stared at him a while, then turned to Carlucci. "I need to start getting him processed," she said. "With all his special equipment, it will take longer to get him aboard."

"I'm done here," Carlucci said.

Reynoso nodded and backed away from the van. Carlucci turned toward the door.

"Wait," Monk said.

Carlucci turned back. He was surprised to see Monk smiling, though it was a strange and twisted smile. "I'm waiting," he said.

"I didn't know you had the balls to do something like this," Monk said. "I would have bet against it."

Carlucci just shook his head. "It has nothing to do with balls."

He turned back to the door and pulled himself out of the van and onto the tarmac. He half expected Monk to call him back again, but the slug didn't speak. Reynoso was waiting about ten yards away.

The chopping sound of a helicopter came from the north, growing louder, and Carlucci looked up to see a dark blue private helicopter approaching Hunter's Point. He watched the copter come in, pass overhead, then slowly descend in the middle of the empty parking lot. No one emerged from the cabin until the blades had come to a complete stop and the helicopter was silent. Carlucci was not surprised to see Yoshi Katsuda step out onto the pavement.

Katsuda was accompanied by two large men who flanked him close on either side. Carlucci wondered if those were the same two men who had been with him when he had killed his daughter. Katsuda and the two men walked steadily toward him and the van, but stopped when they were still twenty or thirty feet away. Carlucci had the sinking feeling he was not going to be able to get close enough to him.

"Good morning, Lieutenant," Katsuda said, smiling. He was wearing one of his business suits, which meant they hadn't come directly from the courthouse.

"I see you took the time to change out of your prison clothes."

"They were not my style."

"What were the conditions of your release on bail?" Carlucci asked.

Katsuda shrugged, but didn't answer.

"Even McAdamas would not have released you without any conditions. You were certainly ordered not to leave the court's jurisdiction."

"That's true," Katsuda said, "but *you* have no jurisdiction here whatsoever."

"You're attempting to leave San Francisco illegally."

"I already have." He smiled again. "I am a fugitive from justice. But it doesn't matter. You can't do anything about it. My two assistants will not allow it, nor will Security here. I'm surprised they allowed you onto the grounds."

"It was a favor," Carlucci said. "Cooperation between security agencies. And I promised not to cause trouble." As he spoke, he tried to take a couple of casual steps closer, but he saw the two men tense. It was going to be impossible to get within reach of Katsuda.

"Then I assume you will honor your promise."

"The way you honor yours?"

"I am not an honorable man, Lieutenant. You are." And with that he started walking toward the Security building, the two other men sticking close and watching Carlucci.

"Will you be returning for your trial?" Carlucci asked.

Katsuda chuckled, and Carlucci watched as he walked the rest of the way to the building and then went inside.

"Lieutenant!" It was Monk's voice from inside the van.

"What?"

"Come here. I have a proposition for you."

He turned wearily toward the van, walked up to it, and put his head in through the side doorway. "What, Monk?"

"You've got another syringe in that case, yes? Loaded with active Core Fever virus? Meant for Yoshi Katsuda?"

"Yes," he answered. He saw no point in lying about it.

"You will never get close enough to him."

"I know that."

"But I will." Monk was grinning that twisted grin of his again.

"What are you saying?"

"Leave it with me. I can get it aboard with all the rest of my medical stuff. And I'll make sure Katsuda gets it. Maybe not right away, but sometime in the new few days, I'll have the opportunity. I will *make* the opportunity."

"Why would you do that?"

"I don't like the man," Monk said. "I never have." His face took on something like a grim expression. "I've never had a daughter," he went on. "And it is now physically impossible for me to have one. But I know this. A father does not kill his own daughter, not for any reason. You are a good father, Lieutenant, and you are one hell of a good cop. You've earned it." He paused. "I may be a dead man, and it may be at your hands, but you've earned it. That's why I would do it."

He didn't have to think about it long. As had happened every time they'd met, Monk once again surprised him. He took the case out of his coat pocket, crawled into the van and toward the back, and handed it to Monk. They looked at each other for a few moments, then Carlucci worked his way back to the side door and got out.

He stood by the side of the van for a minute, watching Katsuda inside the Security building, then started walking toward the gate and the mob pressing against the fence. Right now, he wanted nothing more than to go home.

50

HE STOOD WITH Caroline and Cage at the edge of the roof, six stories above the street, and looked out on the deserted ruins of the Core. It had been three days since his encounters with Monk and Katsuda out at Hunter's

Point. Not much had changed in the city. It was close to midnight, and a full moon shone brightly on the broken stone and concrete, flashing reflections from shattered glass and twisted metal. Nothing moved inside the Core.

"Whole neighborhoods of this city will look like this within a couple of years," Cage said. "Whole neighborhoods of other cities, too."

Carlucci shook his head. "You mean new ones. We've got a few areas like this right now, and L.A. already has entire neighborhoods that aren't any better. Not to mention New York, Chicago, Detroit, East St. Louis—"

"All right, all right," Cage said. "I take your point. New ones, more of them. Neighborhoods that right now seem alive and normal."

Normal. Carlucci wasn't sure that anything constituted a normal life anymore.

"Maybe they'll be able to improve the vaccine," Caroline said. There seemed to be real hope in her voice.

"It might take years," Cage replied. "It's foolish to hope too much."

"But sometimes that's all we've got," she said.

Carlucci looked at his daughter and smiled. He wasn't sure he could have held himself together if she had not lived through all this. He didn't know what he and Andrea would have done, how they would ever have managed to go on. They *would* have gone on, somehow, but he suspected it would have been awful, and that it would never have become any better over the years. As it was, they were still going to have some rough times ahead.

The city was unusually quiet. They could hear music playing somewhere nearby, Greek cantina, accompanied by drunken shouting and singing; a cat yowled, and a dog barked; a siren wailed in the distance, and then two cracking sounds—probably gunfire. Generalized traffic noise provided an almost soothing background to it all.

"Did anyone ever come to you for the disks the Cancer Cell woman gave you?" he asked.

Caroline shook her head. "No." Her disappointment was obvious. "But it hasn't been that long. Probably they're just being cautious after what happened. *I* would be." This time there wasn't much hope in her voice.

"Are you really going to move here, into the Tenderloin?"

"Yes," she said, nodding.

"Why?"

"That's not so easy to answer. Lots of reasons."

"Is Cage one of them?" he asked. He looked back and forth between them. "No one's said anything, but are you two . . . ?" He didn't know what words to use, what words wouldn't sound ridiculous.

Cage didn't say anything, but Carlucci thought the man was actually blushing. Caroline shrugged, half smiling.

"Yes," she said. "Something."

He let it go. They obviously felt awkward talking to him about it, though he wished they wouldn't. He very much hoped they could find some love and happiness with each other. There wasn't going to be a lot of either around this city for a long while."

"Look!" Caroline pointed at one of the buildings inside the Core. "Did you see that?"

"What?"

"Something moved. An animal, maybe. Or a person. Could somebody still be in there?"

"Not *still*," Cage said. "Nothing was left alive in there after the military sterilizers went through, not even the rats. Only the cockroaches and ants. But I wouldn't be surprised to see people moving back in already. When you think about it, it's not much worse now than it was before, and all kinds of people lived there then." He paused. "It's what we do, I guess. We just go on. The story of so-called civilization."

Carlucci thought about what Cage had said, and decided there was some truth to it. But he wasn't sure if it was good or bad.

"I feel tired and old." He wasn't sure why he said it; it just came out.

"You're not old, Papa."

"Maybe not, but I sure feel like it." He shook his head. "I've aged a lot these past few months."

"You just need a break from things," Cage said. "We could all use a break. Take a vacation, get out of this goddamn city for a few weeks. I'd bet you've got all kinds of vacation leave coming to you."

He nodded. "Maybe I'll take a permanent vacation."

"Retire, Papa?"

He nodded again. "I've been thinking about it."

"Mom says you'll never retire until they force you out."

"Maybe I'll surprise your mother." He smiled. "Surprise myself."

No one spoke for a long time. He scanned the ruined buildings, the empty rooms and broken walls. For the first time, he thought he understood a little why someone would want to live inside the Core.

"Papa?"

"Yes?"

"Papa . . ." She couldn't finish.

He looked at her. She seemed upset. "What is it, Caroline?"

"Papa, do you wish it had been Tina who had lived instead of me?"

Carlucci felt his heart collapsing inside him. "How can you ask that?"

"Because I have Gould's, and I'm going to die in a few years anyway. If Tina had lived instead of me, she would have had a long life ahead of her."

"Oh, Caroline." He turned and took her into his arms and pulled her tight, so tight against him. "We're so grateful you lived through it, you just can't understand what it's meant to us. We wish you both had lived, but never, never would we even think about the two of you that way." He held her even more tightly, trying to hold himself together. "Never."

He could feel her squeezing him in return, and he hoped desperately that it was okay, that he'd managed to say the right things—the true things. He looked at Cage, who was watching them uncomfortably.

"Take care of her," he said to Cage. He finally eased his hold of Caroline, and looked into her face, the tears smeared down her cheek. "And you," he said to Caroline. "You take care of Cage."

She nodded, trying to smile. "I will, Papa."

Then he pulled her to him and hugged her tightly again, afraid to let her go.

Isabel

ISABEL WATCHED THE three figures on the rooftop. She had come out into a patch of moonlight, had seen them outlined against the night sky, then had ducked back into the shadows, afraid she had been seen. Now she watched from darkness, through broken glass.

She was lonely. She had come to be very afraid of people, but now that they all were gone, and there were none of her own kind here, she missed them. Many had treated her badly, but a few had been kind.

The one called Donya, in her first home. Donya had taken such good care of them, would let them out of their cages when they weren't allowed, gave them special treats. And Donya had cried when Lisa got sick and was taken away and never returned.

And then, the one who had found her in the passage in the middle of all the craziness. She, too, had seemed kind, and had left the door open for her so she hadn't been trapped.

The rats weren't much company.

Isabel pulled back from the window and worked her way deeper into the building, staying in the shadows. Yes, she would welcome people back into the Core, and she was certain they would come.

But she would still be very, very careful.